LINDA HOWARD

says that whether she's reading them or writing them, books have long played a profound role in her life. She cut her teeth on Margaret Mitchell and from then on continued to read widely and eagerly. In recent years her interest has settled on romance fiction, because she's "easily bored by murder, mayhem and politics." After twenty-one years of penning stories for her own enjoyment, Ms. Howard finally worked up the courage to submit a novel for publication—and met with success! Happily, the Alabama author has been steadily publishing ever since, and has made multiple appearances on the *New York Times* bestseller list.

ELIZABETH LOWELL

New York Times bestselling author Elizabeth Lowell has won countless awards, including a Romance Writers of America Lifetime Achievement Award. She also writes mainstream fiction as Ann Maxwell and mysteries with her husband as A. E. Maxwell. She presently resides with her husband in Washington State.

KASEY MICHAELS

is the *New York Times* and *USA Today* bestselling author of more than sixty books. She has won the Romance Writers of America RITA Award and a *Romantic Times* Career Achievement Award for her historical romances set in the Regency era, and also writes contemporary romances for Silhouette and Harlequin Books.

FINDING HOME

LINDA HOWARD
ELIZABETH LOWELL
KASEY MICHAELS

Silhouette Books

Published by Silhouette Books

America's Publisher of Contemporary Romance

SILHOUETTE BOOKS

FINDING HOME

Copyright © 2002 by Harlequin Books S.A.

ISBN 0-373-48462-3

The publisher acknowledges the copyright holders of the individual works as follows:

DUNCAN'S BRIDE
Copyright © 1990 by Linda Howington

CHAIN LIGHTNING
Copyright © 1988 by Two of a Kind, Inc.

POPCORN AND KISSES
Copyright © 2001 by Kathie Seidick. Text revised for this edition
Copyright © 1988 by Kathie Seidick

This edition published by arrangement with Harlequin Books S.A.

® and TM are trademarks of Harlequin Books S.A., used under license. Trademarks indicated with ® are registered in the United States Patent and Trademark Office, the Canadian Trade Marks Office and in other countries.

Visit Silhouette at www.eHarlequin.com

Printed in U.S.A.

CONTENTS

DUNCAN'S BRIDE
Linda Howard   9

CHAIN LIGHTNING
Elizabeth Lowell   213

POPCORN AND KISSES
Kasey Michaels   453

DUNCAN'S BRIDE

Linda Howard

* * *

To Marilyn Elrod, my good friend,
who also taught me how to play
Shanghai and Spite & Malice

ACKNOWLEDGMENTS

I had several sources for the trivia
and obscure facts that I used in this book.
I would like to acknowledge *Myth Information*
by J. Allen Varasdi, Ballantine Books,
New York, c. 1989;
First for Women magazine, January 1990 issue;
and *Instant Facts* from the World Book
Desk Reference Set, Chicago, 1983 edition.

Dear Reader,

Home means many things to many people. To Madelyn, it represented something she longed for: a husband and family. She wanted those things so much she was willing to take a huge risk and answer the newspaper ad of a Montana rancher looking for a wife. Reese Duncan was lonely; he wanted a wife and family, but not an emotional attachment to said wife, and he worked too hard to find a wife by the more conventional means of dating and courtship. A newspaper ad was the most efficient way—and it brought Madelyn to him.

Madelyn was struck by a thunderbolt the moment she first saw Reese. Everything in her knew this was the man she had always known was out there, the one man for her. *Duncan's Bride* is the story of how Madelyn fought Reese's bitterness about his first marriage, his distrust of her in all matters concerning money, and of how she finally managed to make him see that "home" is many things, but the home represented by love and family is far more important than the home constructed of four walls.

I hope you enjoy reading their story.

Sincerely,

Linda Howard

Chapter 1

It was time he looked for a wife, but this time around he wasn't looking for "love" as part of the bargain. He was older and infinitely wiser, and he knew that "love" wasn't necessary, or even desirable.

Reese Duncan had made a fool of himself once and nearly lost everything. It wouldn't happen again. This time he'd choose a wife with his brain instead of the contents of his jeans, and he'd pick a woman who would be content to live on an isolated ranch, who was willing to work hard and be a good mother to their kids, one who cared more about family than fashion. He'd fallen for a pretty face once, but good looks wasn't on his list of requirements now. He was a normal man with a healthy sex drive; that would be enough to get the kids he wanted. He didn't want passion. Passion had led him into the worst mistake of his life. Now he wanted a reliable, common sense woman.

The problem was, he didn't have time to find her. He worked twelve to sixteen hours a day, trying to keep his head above water. It had taken him seven years, but it looked like

this year would put him in the black, finally. He had lost
half his land, a loss that ate at his soul every day of his life,
but there was no way in hell he would lose what remained.
He had lost most of his cattle; the huge herds were gone,
and he worked like a slave taking care of the remaining
heads of beef. The ranch hands were gone, too; he hadn't
been able to afford their wages. He hadn't bought a new pair
of jeans in three years. The barns and house hadn't been
painted in eight.

But April, his ex-wife, had her outstanding debts, incurred
before their marriage, paid. She had her lump-sum settlement. She had her Manhattan apartment, her expensive wardrobe. What did it matter to her that he'd had to beggar himself and sell his land, his herds, wipe out his bank accounts,
to give her the half of his assets to which she felt "entitled"?
After all, hadn't she been married to him for two whole
years? Hadn't she lived through two hellish Montana winters, entirely cut off from civilization? So what if the ranch
had been in his family for a hundred years; two years of
marriage "entitled" her to half of it, or its equivalent in cold,
hard cash. Of course, she had been more than happy to settle
for the cash. If he didn't have that much, he could sell a
little land. After all, he had oodles of it; he wouldn't miss a
few thousand acres. It helped that her father was a business
magnate who had a lot of connections in Montana as well
as the other western states, which explained why the judge
hadn't been swayed by Reese's arguments that the amount
April was demanding would bankrupt him.

That was another mistake he wouldn't make. The woman
he married this time would have to sign a prenuptial agreement that would protect the ranch in case of divorce. He
wouldn't risk so much as one square foot of the dirt of his
children's heritage, or the money it would take to run it. No
woman was going to take him to the cleaners again; she
might leave, but she wouldn't leave with anything of his.

Given the way he felt, he would have been just as happy
to remain single for the rest of his life if there hadn't been

the question of children. He wanted kids. He wanted to teach them to love the land as he had been taught, to leave that land to them, to pass on the legacy that had been passed on to him. More than that, he wanted the life that children would bring to the empty old ranch house, the laughter and tears and anger, the pain of childish fears and the shouts of joy. He wanted heirs of his bone and blood. To have those children, he needed a wife.

A wife would be convenient, too. There was a lot to be said for available sex, especially since he didn't have the time to waste trying to find it. All he needed was a solid, steady, undemanding woman in his bed every night, and his hormones would take care of the rest of it.

But unmarried, marriageable women were scarce in that part of the country; they were all packing up and moving to the cities. Ranch life was hard, and they wanted some excitement in their lives, some luxuries. Reese didn't have the time, money or inclination to go courting, anyway. There was a more efficient way to find a woman than that.

He'd read a magazine article about how many farmers in the Midwest were advertising for wives, and he'd also seen a television program about men in Alaska who were doing the same. Part of him didn't like the idea of advertising, because he was naturally a private man and had become even more so after his disastrous marriage. On the other hand, he wouldn't have to spend a lot of money just put a few ads in the personal sections of some newspapers, and money meant a lot to him these days. He wouldn't have to meet the women who didn't appeal to him, wouldn't have to waste time driving here and there, taking them out, getting to know them. He didn't particularly want to get to know them, not even the one he would eventually choose to be his wife. There was a hard layer of ice encasing him, and he liked it that way. Vision was much clearer when it was unclouded by emotion. The impersonality of an ad appealed to that part of him, even though the private part of him disliked the public nature of it.

But he'd decided that was the way to go, and Reese Duncan didn't waste time once he'd made a decision. He would put the ad in several of the larger newspapers in the West and Midwest. Drawing a pad of paper toward him to begin framing how he wanted the ad to read, he wrote in bold, slashing strokes: WANTED: A WIFE...

Madelyn Sanger Patterson sauntered back into the office after lunch. You never got the sense that Madelyn had hurried over anything, her friend Christine mused as Madelyn strolled toward her. Nor did you ever think that Madelyn sweated. It was ninety-five degrees outside, but no dampness or wrinkles marred her perfect oyster-white dress, set off by the periwinkle silk scarf draped artfully over one shoulder. Madelyn was a clotheshorse; everything looked good on her, but her own sense of style and color added a panache that stirred women to envy and men to lust.

"You're a disgusting person," Christine announced, leaning back in her chair to better appraise Madelyn's approach. "It's unhealthy not to sweat, unnatural not to wrinkle, and ungodly for your hair not to get mussed."

"I sweat," Madelyn said with idle amusement.

"When?"

"Every Tuesday and Thursday at 7:00 p.m."

"I don't believe it. You give your sweat glands an appointment?"

"No, I play racquetball."

Christine held up her fingers in the sign of the cross to ward off the mention of exercise, which in her opinion was the eighth deadly sin. "That doesn't count. Normal people sweat without exertion in weather like this. And do your clothes wrinkle? Does your hair ever hang in your face?"

"Of course."

"In front of witnesses?" Satisfied she had won that exchange, Christine looked pleased with herself.

Madelyn propped herself against the edge of Christine's desk and crossed her legs at the ankle. It was an angular, almost masculine pose that looked graceful when Madelyn did it. She tilted her head to study the newspaper Christine had been reading. "Anything interesting?"

Christine's mother always mailed her the Sunday edition of their newspaper from Omaha, so Christine could stay up-to-date on local news. "My best friend from high school is getting married. Her engagement announcement is here. A distant acquaintance has died, an old boyfriend has made his first million, the drought is driving feed prices sky-high. Usual stuff."

"Does she hold the old boyfriend against you?"

"Nah. She couldn't stand his guts when we were dating. He was a know-it-all."

"And it turns out he did know it all?"

"Evidently. It's disconcerting when things turn out to be exactly as they seemed."

"I know," Madelyn sympathized. "It's hard on your natural skepticism."

Christine folded the paper and handed it to Madelyn, who enjoyed newspapers from different cities. "There's a good article in here about relocating to a different part of the country for a job. I wish I'd read it before I left Omaha."

"You've been here two years. It's too late for culture shock."

"Homesickness is on a different timetable."

"But are you really? Or are you just in a blue mood because you broke up with the Wall Street Wonder last week and haven't found a replacement yet?"

Christine sighed dramatically. "I have a bad case of heart-bent."

"What's a dent to a Sherman tank?"

"Bent, not dent!"

"Then shouldn't it be 'heartbend'?"

"That sounds like something you get from diving too deep, too fast."

"Surfacing."

"Whatever."

They grinned, content with the exchange, and Madelyn returned to her own office with the newspaper in hand. She and Christine honed their wits on each other with mutual enjoyment while still maintaining a totally amicable relationship. Madelyn had learned early that not everyone enjoyed that kind of conversation. Several teenage boyfriends had been, in various degrees, insulted, angered, or intimidated, which had promptly ended her fledgling relationships with them. Boys were too caught up in their hormonal urges and too wildly protective of their newfound masculinity to tolerate what they saw as the faintest slight to that masculinity, and unfortunately, Madelyn's lazy wit often seemed to offend. She sighed, thinking about it, because somehow it didn't seem that things were much different now.

She stared at her desk. It was disgustingly and disgracefully clear. She could either stay at the office for the rest of the day or go home, and it wouldn't make a bit of difference either way. Odds were, no one would even know she had left, unless she stopped on the way out and made a point of telling someone. That was how often her phone rang.

There were advantages to being the stepsister of the owner. Boredom, however, wasn't one of them. Being idle was excruciating for her. The time was swiftly approaching when she would have to kiss Robert's cheek, thank him for the thought, but politely decline to continue with this "job."

Maybe she should even consider moving away. The West Coast, maybe. Or Fiji. Robert didn't have any business concerns in Fiji. Yet.

She unfolded the newspaper and leaned back in her chair with her feet propped on top of the desk and her ankles crossed. The decision would wait; she had been working on the problem for some time now, so it would still be there when she finished reading the paper.

She loved out-of-town newspapers, especially the smaller ones, the weekly editions that were more folksy gossip-columns than anything else. The Omaha newspaper was too large for that kind of coziness, but it still had a midwestern flavor to remind her that there was, indeed, a life outside New York City. The city was so large and complex that those who lived in it tended to be absorbed by it. She was constantly looking for windows on other ways of life, not because she disliked New York, but because she was so curious about everything.

She skipped over World Affairs—they were the same in Omaha as in New York—read Midwestern and local news, learning how the drought was affecting farmers and ranchers but creating a booming business for the slaughterhouses, and who had married or was intending to. She read the sale ads, compared the price of real estate in Omaha to that in New York, and was, as always, amazed at the difference. She was skipping around through the want ads when an ad in the personals caught her attention.

"Wanted: a wife for able-bodied rancher. Must be of steady character, want children, and be able to work on ranch. Age 25 to 35 preferable."

Those interested should contact said able-bodied rancher at a box number in Billings, Montana.

Madelyn was instantly diverted, her imagination caught by the ad, though she wasn't certain if she should be amused or outraged. The man was practically advertising for a combination brood mare and ranch hand! On the other hand, he had been brutally honest about his expectations, which was oddly refreshing after some of the personal ads she'd seen in the New York newspapers and magazines. There had been none of that slick "Sensitive Aquarian needs a New-Age Nineties woman to explore the meaning of the universe with him" hypersell that told one nothing except that the writer had no concept of clarity in the written word.

What could be learned about the rancher from that ad, other than his honesty? His age could be anywhere from fifty on down, but since he wanted children she thought he would be younger—probably in his thirties or early forties. Also, that bit about children probably meant one could take the able-bodied part literally. If he wanted a wife of steady character, he probably wasn't a party animal, either. He sounded like a sober, hardworking rancher who wanted a wife but didn't have the time to look for one.

She had read an article several months ago about mail-order brides, and though she'd found it interesting, she had been put off by the impersonality of it all. It was evidently a big business, matching Oriental women with men in Western nations, but it wasn't limited to that; farmers and ranchers in the less-populated states had started advertising, simply because there were so few women in their areas. There was even an entire magazine devoted to it.

Really, this ad was the same in intent as the slick ads: someone was looking for companionship. The need was the same the world over, though it was often couched in more amusing or romantic terms.

And answering the ad was doing nothing more than agreeing to meet someone, like a blind date. It was a way of making contact. All relationships began with a first date, blind or otherwise.

She folded the paper and wished she had something to do other than ponder the issue of social advertising.

She could go upstairs and pound on Robert's desk, but that wouldn't accomplish anything. Robert didn't respond well to force; he wouldn't disturb the smooth running of his offices just to give her something to do. He had offered her the job as a means of giving her a focus in life after losing both her mother and grandmother within a short length of time, but both of them knew that the job had outlived its purpose. Only an incurable optimism had kept her at it this long, hoping it would turn into something legitimate. If she pounded on Robert's desk, he would lean back in his chair and smile at her with his wickedly amused eyes, though his mouth seldom actually joined his eyes in celebration, and say, "The ball's in your court, babe. Serve it or go home."

Yes, it was time to go on to something new. The shock of grief had led to inertia, and inertia was even harder to handle, otherwise she would have left over two years ago.

Wanted: a wife.

She picked up the newspaper and read the ad again.

Naw. She wasn't that desperate. Was she? She needed a new job, a change of scenery, not a husband.

On the other hand, she was twenty-eight, old enough to know that the swinging life wasn't for her. Nor was city living, really, though she had lived in cities most of her life. As a child in Richmond, she had dearly loved the weekends when she had visited her grandmother in the country. Though it had been only a rural house, not an actual farm, she had still reveled in the peace and quiet, and longed for it when her mother had remarried and they had moved to New York.

No, she wasn't desperate at all, but she was curious by nature and badly needed a diversion while she decided what sort of job she should look for, and where. It was like a first date. If it clicked, then it clicked. She had nothing against Montana, and wouldn't that be a wild tale to tell her grandchildren, that she'd been a mail-order bride? If, as was far more likely, nothing came of it, then no harm had been done. She felt far safer answering an ad from a Montana rancher than she would one from a freestyle urbanite.

Feeling a bit exhilarated from the daring of it, she quickly rolled a sheet of paper into her top-of-the-line electronic typewriter, wrote a reply to the ad, addressed an envelope, put a stamp on it and dropped it down the mail chute. As soon as the silver metal flap swallowed the envelope, she felt a peculiar, hollow feeling in her stomach, as though she had done something incredibly stupid. On the other hand, she had had this same feeling the first time she'd gotten behind the wheel of a car. And when she'd ridden one of the super rollercoasters. *And* when she'd gone to college, flown for the first time, and gone on her first date. This same feeling had accompanied almost every first in her life, but it had never been a forerunner of disaster. Instead she had thoroughly enjoyed all those firsts. Maybe that was a good sign.

On the other hand…a mail-order bride? *Her?*

Then she shrugged. It was nothing to worry about. The odds were that she would never hear from this Montana rancher. After all, what could they have in common?

Reese Duncan frowned at the New York return address on the envelope as he slit it open and removed the single sheet of typewritten paper inside. What would anyone in New York know about life on a ranch? He was tempted to toss the letter into the trash; it would be a waste of his time to read it, just as this trip into Billings to pick up the mail had been a waste of time. Today there had been only this one response to his ad, and from New York, of all places.

But the overall response to the ad hadn't been exactly overwhelming, so he might as well read it. In fact, this was just the third answer he'd gotten. Guess there weren't too many women in the world anxious for life on a Montana ranch.

The letter was short, and remarkable in the information it *didn't* give. Her name was Madelyn S. Patterson. She was twenty-eight, had never been married, and was healthy, strong and willing to work. She hadn't sent a picture. She was the only one who hadn't.

She was younger than the other two women who had responded; they were both in their thirties. The schoolteacher was his age, and not bad to look at. The other woman was thirty-six, two years his senior, and had never worked at a paying job; she had remained at home to care for her invalid mother, who had recently died. She was plain, but not homely. Both of them would have far more realistic expectations of the vast, empty spaces and hard life on a ranch than this Madelyn S. Patterson.

On the other hand, she might be some small-town girl who had moved to the big city and found she didn't like it. She must have read his ad in a hometown newspaper that had been mailed to her, because he sure as hell hadn't wasted his money placing it in the *New York Times*. And he hadn't had so many responses that he could afford to ignore one. He would make the same arrangements with her that he'd made with the others, if she were still interested when he wrote to her.

He tapped the folded letter against his thigh as he left the post office and walked to his pickup truck. This was taking up more time than he could truly afford. He wanted to have everything settled by July, and it was already the middle of May. Six weeks. He wanted to find a wife within the next six weeks.

Madelyn almost dropped her mail when she saw the Montana address on the plain white envelope. Only nine days had passed since she had answered the ad, so he must have replied almost by return mail. In those nine days she had convinced herself that he wouldn't answer at all.

She sat down at her small dining table and ripped open the envelope. There was only one sheet inside.

Miss Patterson,
My name is Reese Duncan. I'm thirty-four years old, divorced, no children. I own a ranch in central Montana.
   If you're still interested, I can see you two weeks from Saturday. Let me know by return mail. I'll send you a bus ticket to Billings.

There was no closing salutation, only his signature, *G. R. Duncan*. What did the *G* stand for? His handwriting was heavy, angular and perfectly legible, and there were no misspellings.

Now she knew his name, age and that he was divorced. He hadn't been real before; he had been only an anonymous someone who had placed an ad for a wife. Now he was a person.

And a busy one, too, if he could only spare the time to see her on a Saturday over two weeks away! Maddelyn couldn't help smiling at the thought. He certainly didn't give the impression of being so desperate for a wife that he had been forced to advertise. Once again she had the distinct impression that he was simply too busy to look for one. He was divorced, the letter said, so perhaps he had lost his first wife precisely because he was so busy.

She tapped the letter with her fingernails, studying the handwriting. She was intrigued, and becoming more so. She wanted to meet this man.

Madelyn S. Patterson had answered promptly, which the other two hadn't; he had yet to hear from them. Reese opened her letter.

Mr. Duncan, I will arrive in Billings on the designated date. However, I can't allow you to pay for my travel expenses, as we are strangers and nothing may come of our meeting.

My flight arrives at 10:39 a.m. I trust that is convenient. Enclosed is a copy of my flight schedule. Please contact me if your plans change.

His eyebrows rose. Well, well. So she preferred to fly instead of taking the bus. A cynical smile twisted his mouth. Actually, so did he. He had even owned his own plane, but that had been B.A.: before April. His ex-wife had seen to it that it had been years since he'd been able to afford even an airline ticket, let alone his own plane.

Part of him appreciated the fact that Ms. Patterson was sparing him the expense, but his hard, proud core resented the fact that he wasn't able to afford to send her an airline ticket himself. Hell, come to that, even the bus ticket would have put him in a bind this week. Probably when she found out how broke he was, she'd leave so fast her feet would roll back the pavement. There was no way this woman would work out, but he might as well go through the motions to make certain. It wasn't as if applicants were beating down his door.

Madelyn invited Robert to dinner the Thursday before her Saturday flight to Montana, knowing that he would have a date on Friday night, and she wanted to talk to him alone.

He arrived promptly at eight and walked to her small liquor cabinet, where he poured himself a hefty Scotch and water. He lifted the glass to her, and as always his eyes smiled without his mouth joining in. Madelyn lifted her wineglass in return. "To an enigma," she said.

He arched his elegant dark brows. "Yourself?"

"Not me, I'm an open book."

"Written in an unknown language."

"And if your covers were *ever* opened, what language would be there?"

He shrugged, his eyes still smiling, but he couldn't refute the charge that he held himself off from people. Madelyn was closer to him than anyone; his father had married her mother when she was ten and he sixteen, which should have been too great an age difference for any real closeness, but Robert had unaccountably taken the time to make her feel welcome in her new home, to talk to her and listen in return. Together they had weathered first the death of his father, then, five years later, that of her mother; most stepsiblings probably would have drifted apart after that, but they hadn't, because they truly liked each other as friends as well as brother and sister.

Robert was a true enigma: elegant, handsome, almost frighteningly intelligent, but with a huge private core that no one was ever allowed to touch. Madelyn was unique in that she even knew that core existed. No one else had ever seen that much of him. In the years since he had inherited the Cannon Companies, he had reshaped the various enterprises and made them even larger and richer than before. An enormous amount of power rested in his lean hands, but not even the Cannon empire seemed to reach that private center of him. The inner man was a citadel, inviolate.

It was as if he kept himself leashed, his fires banked. Women flocked around him, of course, but he was particular in his bed partners and preferred monogamy to musical beds. When he chose a particular woman friend, they were usually together for at least a year, and he was entirely faithful to her for as long as the affair lasted. One of his ex-amours had gotten drunk and cried on Madelyn's shoulder at a party shortly after Robert had ended their affair, sobbing that she would never be able to love another man because how could anyone compare to Robert? The woman's drunken confession had, so far, been pathetically accurate; she had drifted into a couple of affairs, but both of them had been short-lived, and since then she had stopped dating entirely.

Now he was watching Madelyn with his amused eyes, and after a minute she answered her own question. "Your language would be an obscure one, dead, of course, and translated into a cipher of your own invention. To paraphrase Winston Churchill, you're an enigma inside a puzzle wrapped in a riddle, or some such complicated drivel."

He almost smiled; his lips twitched, and he dipped his head to acknowledge the accuracy of her assessment. He tasted the Scotch, savoring the smoky bite of it. "What's for dinner?"

"Conversation."

"A true case of eating our words."

"And spaghetti."

He gave the Scotch a pained look and set the glass down; he didn't think it would go well with pasta. Madelyn gave him an angelic look that deepened the amused expression in his eyes. "So what are we conversing about?"

"The fact that I'll be looking for a new job, at the very least," she said as she went into the kitchen. He followed her, and without hesitation began helping her carry the food to the table.

"So it's time, is it?" he asked shrewdly. "What made you decide?"

She shrugged. "Several things. Basically, as you said, it's time."

"You said, 'at the very least.' And at the most?"

Trust Robert to see the implication of every little word. She smiled as she poured wine into their glasses. "I'm flying to Montana this Saturday."

His eyes flickered just a little, signalling his intense interest. "What's in Montana?"

"Not what. Who."

"Who, then?"

"A man named Reese Duncan. There's a possibility of matrimony."

There were times when a look from Robert's pale green eyes could slice like a razor, and now was one of those times. "That sounds like a weather report," he said in an even tone. "Care to give me a percentage? Forty percent chance of matrimony? Fifty?"

"I don't know. I won't know until I meet the man."

He had been forking the pasta onto his plate, but now he carefully laid the utensils down and took a deep breath. Madelyn watched him with interest. It was one of the very few times when she could say she had seen Robert actually surprised.

He said, very carefully, "Do you mean you haven't met him yet?"

"No. We've corresponded, but we've never actually met. And we might not like each other in person. There's only a very small chance of matrimony, actually. In weather terms, no accumulation expected."

"But it's possible."

"Yes. I wanted you to know."

"How did you get to know him?"

"I don't know him. I know a little about him, but not much."

"So how did you start corresponding?"

"He advertised for a wife."

He looked stunned, really stunned. Madelyn took pity on him and ladled the thick, spicy sauce over his pasta before it grew cold, since it looked as if he had totally forgotten about it.

"You answered a personal ad?" he finally asked in a strained voice.

She nodded and turned her attention to her own plate. "Yes."

"Good God, do you know how risky that is?" he roared, half rising from his chair.

"Yes, I know." She reached over to pat his hand. "Please sit down and eat. You wouldn't panic if I'd told you I'd met someone at a singles bar in Manhattan, and that's a lot riskier than meeting a rancher from Montana."

"From a health viewpoint, yes, but there are other things to consider. What if this man is abusive? What if he has a criminal record, or is a con man? Just how much *do* you know about him?"

"He's your age, thirty-four. He owns a ranch in central Montana, and he's divorced, no children. I've been writing to a box number in Billings."

From the sharp look in Robert's eyes, Madelyn knew that he had made a mental note of everything she'd told him and wouldn't forget a single detail. She also knew that he would have Reese Duncan thoroughly investigated; she thought of protesting, but decided that it wouldn't make any difference. By the time Robert had his report, she would already have met Mr. Duncan and formed her own opinion. She could even see why Robert felt alarmed and protective, though she didn't agree that there was any need for it. Mr. Duncan's blunt correspondence had reassured her that this was a man who dealt in the unvarnished truth and didn't give a damn how it looked or sounded. It was relaxing not to have to gauge the sincerity of a come-on line.

"Can I talk you out of going?" Robert asked. "Or at least into delaying your meeting?"

"No." She smiled, her gray eyes aglow with anticipation. "I'm so curious I can hardly stand it."

He sighed. Madelyn was as curious as a cat, in her own lazy way. She didn't scurry around poking her nose into every new detail that came her way, but she would eventually get around to investigating any subject or situation that intrigued her. He could see where an ad for a wife would have been irresistible to her; once she had read it, it would have been a foregone conclusion that she had to meet the man for herself. If there was no way he could talk her out of going, he could make certain she wouldn't be in danger. Before she got on that plane, he would know if this Reese Duncan had any sort of criminal record, even so much as a parking ticket. If there was any indication that Madelyn wouldn't be perfectly safe, he would keep her off the flight if he had to sit on her.

As if she'd read his mind, she leaned forward. She had that angelic expression again, the one that made him wary. When Madelyn was angelic, she was either blisteringly angry or up to mischief, and he could never tell which until it was too late. "If you interfere in my social life, I'll assume that I have the same freedom with yours," she said sweetly. "In my opinion, you need a little help with your women."

She meant it. She never bluffed, never threatened unless she was prepared to carry through on her threats. Without a word, Robert tugged his white handkerchief out of his pocket and waved it in surrender.

Chapter 2

The flight was a bit early landing in Billings. Madelyn carefully scrutinized the small group of people waiting to greet those leaving the plane, but she didn't see any lone males who appeared to be looking for her. She took a deep breath, glad of the small reprieve. She was unexpectedly nervous.

She used the time to duck into the ladies' room; when she came out, she heard her name being called in a tinny voice. "Madelyn Patterson, please meet your party at the Information desk. Madelyn Patterson, please meet your party at the Information desk."

Her heart was beating a little fast, but not unpleasantly so. She liked the feeling of excitement. The moment was finally at hand. Anticipation and curiosity were killing her.

She walked with an easy stride that was more of a stroll than anything else, despite her excitement. Her eyes were bright with pleasure. The Billings airport, with its big fountain, was more attractive than the general run of airports, and she let the surroundings begin to soothe her. She was only a little nervous now, and even that small bit wasn't revealed.

That must be him, leaning against the Information desk. He was wearing a hat, so she couldn't see his face all that well, but he was trim and fit. A smile quirked her mouth. This was a truly impossible situation. A real wild goose chase. They would meet, be polite, spend a polite day together; then tomorrow she would shake his hand and tell him she had enjoyed the visit, and that would be the end of it. It would all be very civil and low-keyed, just the way she liked—

He straightened from his relaxed position against the desk and turned toward her. Madelyn felt his eyes focus on her and grow intent.

She knew the meaning of the word *poleaxed*, but this was the first time she had ever experienced the feeling. Her lazy walk faltered, then stopped altogether. She stood frozen in the middle of the airport, unable to take another step. This had never happened to her before, this total loss of composure, but she was helpless. She felt stunned, as if she'd been kicked in the chest. Her heart was racing now, pounding out a painful rhythm. Her breath came in short, shallow gasps; her carry-on bag slipped out of her fingers and landed on the floor with a soft thud. She felt like a fool, but didn't really care. She couldn't stop staring at him.

It was just old-fashioned lust, that was all. It couldn't be anything else, not at first sight. She felt panic at the very idea that it could be anything else. Just lust.

He wasn't the most handsome man she'd ever seen, because New York was full of gorgeous men, but it didn't matter. In all the ways that did matter, all the primitive, instinctual ways, call it chemistry or electricity or biology or whatever, he was devastating. The man oozed sex. Every move he made was imbued with the sort of sensuality and masculinity that made her think of sweaty skin and twisted sheets. Dear God, why on earth should this man ever have had to advertise for a wife?

He was at least six-three, and muscled with the iron, layered strength of a man who does hard physical labor every day of his life. He was very tanned, and his hair, what she could see of it under his hat, was dark brown, almost black. His jaw was strongly shaped, his chin square, his mouth clear-cut and bracketed by twin grooves. He hadn't dressed up to meet her, but was wearing a plain white shirt with the cuffs unbuttoned and rolled back, ancient jeans and scuffed boots. She found herself frantically concentrating on the details of his appearance while she tried to deal with the havoc he was wreaking on her senses, all without saying a word.

None of her excited imaginings had prepared her for this. What was a woman supposed to do when she finally met the man who turned her banked coals into a roaring inferno? Madelyn's first thought was to run for her life, but she couldn't move.

Reese's first thought was that he'd like to take her to bed, but there was no way he'd take her to wife.

She was everything he'd been afraid she would be: a chic, sophisticated city woman, who knew absolutely nothing about a ranch. It was obvious from the top of her silky blond head down to the tips of her expensive shoes.

She was wearing white, not the most practical color for travel, but she was immaculate, without even a wrinkle to mar her appearance. Her skirt was pencil-slim and stopped just above her knees, revealing knockout legs. Reese felt his guts tighten, just looking at her legs. He wrenched his gaze upward with an effort that almost hurt and was struck by her eyes.

Beneath the loose, matching jacket she was wearing a skimpy top in a rich blue color that should have made her eyes look blue, but didn't. Her eyes made him feel as if he were drowning. They were gray, very gray, without a tinge of blue. Soft-looking eyes, even now when they were large with…dismay? He wasn't certain of the expression, but belatedly he realized that she was very pale and still, and that she'd dropped her bag.

He stepped forward, seizing on the excuse to touch her. He curved his hand around her upper arm, which felt cool and slim under his warm palm. "Are you all right? Miss Patterson?"

Madelyn almost shuddered at his touch, her response to it was so strong. How could such a small thing produce such an upheaval? His closeness brought with it the animal heat of his body, the scent of him, and she wanted to simply turn into his arms and bury her face against his neck. Panic welled up in her. She had to get out of here, away from him. She hadn't bargained on this. But instead of running, she called on all her reserves of control and even managed to smile as she held out her hand. "Mr. Duncan."

Her voice had a small rasp to it that tugged at him. He shook her hand, noting the absence of jewelry except for the plain gold hoops in her ears. He didn't like to see a woman's hands weighted down with rings on every finger, especially when the hands were as slim as hers. He didn't release her as he repeated, "Are you all right?"

Madelyn blinked, a slow closing and opening of her eyelids that masked a deep shifting and settling inside. "Yes, thank you," she replied, not bothering to make an excuse for her behavior. What could she say? That she'd been stunned by a sudden surge of lust for him? It was the truth, but one that couldn't be voiced. She knew she should be charming to ease the awkwardness of this meeting, but somehow she couldn't summon up the superficial chatter to gloss things over. She could do nothing but stand there.

They faced each other like gunfighters on a dirt street, oblivious to the eddies of people stepping around their small, immobile island. He was watching her from beneath level brows, taking his time with his survey but keeping his thoughts hidden. Madelyn stood still, very aware of her femaleness as he looked her up and down with acutely masculine appraisal, though he revealed neither appreciation nor disapproval. His thoughts were very much his own, his face that of an intensely private man.

Even shadowed by his hat brim as they were, she could tell that his eyes were a dark green-blue-hazel color, shot

through with white striations that made them gleam. They
were wrinkled at the outer corners from what must have been
years of squinting into the sun, because he sure didn't look
as if he'd gotten those lines from laughing. His face was
stern and unyielding, making her long to see how he'd look
if he smiled, and wonder if he had ever been carefree. This
man wasn't a stranger to rough times or hard work.

"Let's go fetch your other luggage," he said, breaking
the silent confrontation. It was a long drive back to the ranch,
and he was impatient to be on the way. Chores had to be
done no matter how late he got back.

His voice was a baritone, a bit gravelly. Madelyn registered the rough texture of it even as she nodded toward the
carry-on bag. "That's it."

"All of it?"

"Yes."

If all her clothes were in that one small bag, she sure
hadn't made any big plans to impress him with her wardrobe,
he thought wryly. Of course, she would impress him most
without any wardrobe at all.

He bent down to lift the carry-on, still keeping his hand
on her arm. She was pure, walking provocation, totally unsuitable for ranch life, but every male hormone in him was
clanging alert signals. She was only going to be here for a
day; why shouldn't he enjoy being with her? It would be
sort of a last fling before settling down with someone better
prepared for the job, and job it would be. Ranching was hard
work, and Madelyn Patterson didn't look as if she had ever
been exposed to the concept.

Right now, though, he didn't mind, because she was so
damn enticing and he was dead tired of the relentless
months—years—of sixteen-hour days and backbreaking
work. He would take her out to eat tonight, after his chores
were done; maybe they'd go to Jasper's for some dancing,
and he'd hold her in his arms for a while, feel the softness
of her skin, smell her perfume. Who knew, maybe when they
went back to the ranch it wouldn't be to separate beds. He'd

have to be up front in telling her that she wasn't right for the job, so there wouldn't be any misunderstanding, but maybe it wouldn't make any difference to her. Maybe.

His hand naturally moved from her arm to her back as he led her out of the terminal. Deliberately he set about charming her, something he had once done with women as effortlessly as he had smiled. Those days were far in the past, but the touch remained. She chatted easily, thank God, asking questions about Montana, and he answered them just as easily, letting her relax and get comfortable with him, and all the while he studied her face and expressions.

Strictly speaking, she was merely pretty, but her face was lit by a liveliness that made her stunningly attractive. Her nose had a slight bump in it and was just a tiny bit crooked. A light dusting of freckles covered the bridge of it and scattered across her cheekbones, which were exquisitely chiseled. World-class cheekbones, just like her legs. Her lips weren't full, but her mouth was wide and mobile, as if she were forever on the verge of smiling. Her eyes were the grayest eyes he'd ever seen. They were calm, sleepy eyes that nevertheless revealed on closer inspection an alert and often amused intelligence, though he didn't see what she found so amusing.

If he'd met her before his rotten marriage and disastrous divorce, he would have gone after her like gangbusters, and gotten her, too, by God. Just the thought of those legs wrapped around his waist brought him to instant, uncomfortable arousal. No way, though, would he let his gonads lead him into another unsuitable marriage. He knew what he wanted in a wife, and Madelyn wasn't it. She didn't look as if she'd ever even seen a steer.

None of that decreased his physical response to her one whit. He'd been attracted to a lot of women at first sight, but not like this, not like a slam in the gut. This wasn't just attraction, a mild word to describe a mild interest; this was strong and wrenching, flooding his body with heat, making him grow hard even though he sure as hell didn't want to here in the middle of the airport. His hands actually hurt from wanting to touch her, to smooth over her breast and hip in a braille investigation of those sleek curves.

He felt a twinge of regret that she was so out of place, so totally unsuitable for his purposes. Walking beside her, he saw the sidelong glances that other men were giving her. Women like her just naturally attracted male speculation, and he wished he could afford to keep her, but she was too expensive for him. Reese was broke now, but at one time he had been accustomed to money; he knew how it looked and smelled and tasted, and how it fit. It fit Madelyn Patterson as perfectly as her silky skin did. She was slim and bright in her Paris-made suit, and the perfume sweetened by her warm flesh cost over two hundred dollars an ounce. He knew because it was one of his favorites. He couldn't even afford to keep her in perfume, much less clothes.

"What sort of work do you do?" he asked as they stepped into the bright sunshine. Those terse little letters she'd written hadn't revealed much.

She made a face, wrinkling her nose. "I work in an office without a window, doing nothing important, in my stepbrother's company. It's one of those jobs made for family." She didn't tell him that she'd turned in her notice, because he might assume she had done it thinking that she would be moving to Montana, and the one had nothing to do with the other. But her racing pulse told her that if he asked, she'd be packed and moved in with him so fast he'd think she owned her own moving company.

"Have you ever been on a ranch?" He asked it even though he already knew the answer.

"No." Madelyn looked up at him, something she still had to do despite her three-inch heels. "But I do know how to ride." She was actually a very good horsewoman, courtesy of her college roommate in Virginia, who had been horse mad.

He dismissed any riding she might have done. Recreational riding was a far cry from riding a workhorse, and that was what his horses were, trained and as valuable in their own way as a racehorse. It was just one more area where she didn't measure up.

They reached his truck, and he watched to see if she turned up her nose at it, as dusty and battered as it was. She didn't blink an eye, just stood to the side while he unlocked the door and placed her bag on the middle of the seat. Then he stepped back for her to get in.

Madelyn tried to seat herself and found that she couldn't. An astonished expression crossed her face; then she began to laugh as she realized her skirt was too tight. She couldn't lift her legs enough to climb up on the seat. "What women won't do for vanity," she said in a voice full of humor at her own expense and began tugging up the hem of the skirt. "I wore this because I wanted to look nice, but it would have been smarter to have worn slacks."

Reese's throat locked as he watched her pull up the skirt, exposing increasing amounts of her slim thighs. Heat exploded through him, making him feel as if his entire body were expanding. The thought flashed through his mind that he wouldn't be able to stand it if she pulled that skirt up one more inch, and in the next split second his hands shot out, catching her around the waist and lifting her onto the seat. She gave a startled little cry at his abrupt movement and grabbed his forearms to brace herself.

His mouth was dry, and sweat beaded on his forehead. "Don't pull up your skirt around me again, unless you want me to do something about it," he said in a guttural tone. His pulse was throbbing through him. She had the best legs he'd ever seen, long and strong, with sleek muscles. She'd be able to lock them around him and hang on, no matter how wild the ride.

Madelyn couldn't speak. Tension stretched between them, heavy and dark. Fierce, open lust burned in his narrowed eyes, and she couldn't look away, caught in the silent intensity. She was still gripping his forearms, and she felt the heat of his arms, the steely muscles bunched iron-hard under her fingers. Her heart lurched at the sharp realization that he felt some of the turmoil she had been feeling.

She began babbling an apology. "I'm sorry. I didn't intend—that is, I didn't realize—" She stopped, because she couldn't come right out and say that she hadn't meant to arouse him. No matter how she reacted to him, he was still essentially a stranger.

He looked down at her legs, with the skirt still halfway up them, and his hands involuntarily tightened on her waist before he forced himself to release her. "Yeah, I know. It's all right," he muttered. His voice was still hoarse. It wasn't all right. Every muscle in his body was tight. He stepped back before he could give in to the impulse to move forward instead, putting himself between her legs and opening them wider. All he would have to do would be to slide his hands under the skirt to push it up the rest of the way— He crushed the thought, because if he'd let himself finish it, his control would have shattered.

They had left Billings far behind before he spoke again. "Are you hungry? If you are, there's a café at the crossroads up ahead."

"No, thank you," Madelyn replied a bit dreamily as she stared at the wide vista of countryside around her. She was used to enormous buildings, but suddenly they seemed puny in comparison with this endless expanse of earth and sky. It made her feel both insignificant and fresh, as if her life were just starting now. "How far is it to your ranch?"

"About a hundred and twenty miles. It'll take us almost three hours to get there."

She blinked, astonished at the distance. She hadn't realized how much effort it was for him to come to Billings to meet her. "Do you go to Billings often?"

He glanced at her, wondering if she was trying to find out how much he isolated himself on the ranch. "No," he said briefly.

"So this is a special trip?"

"I did some business this morning, too." He'd stopped by the bank to give his loan officer the newest figures on the ranch's projected income for the coming year. Right now, it looked better than it had in a long time. He was still flat broke, but he could see daylight now. The banker had been pleased.

Madelyn looked at him with concern darkening her gray eyes. "So you've been on the road since about dawn."

"About that."

"You must be tired."

"You get used to early hours on a ranch. I'm up before dawn every day."

She looked around again. "I don't know why anyone would stay in bed and miss dawn out here. It must be wonderful."

Reese thought about it. He could remember how spectacular the dawns were, but it had been a long while since he'd had the time to notice one. "Like everything else, you get used to them. I know for a fact that there are dawns in New York, too."

She chuckled at his dry tone. "I seem to remember them, but my apartment faces to the west. I see sunsets, not dawns."

It was on the tip of his tongue to say that they would watch a lot of dawns together, but common sense stopped him. The only dawn they would have in common would be the next day. She wasn't the woman he would choose for a wife.

He reached into his shirt pocket and got out the pack of cigarettes that always resided there, shaking one free and drawing it the rest of the way out with his lips. As he dug in his jeans pocket for his lighter he heard her say incredulously, "You *smoke*?"

Swift irritation rose in him. From the tone of her voice you would have thought she had caught him kicking puppies, or something else equally repulsive. He lit the cigarette and blew smoke into the cab. "Yeah," he said. "Do you mind?"

He made it plain from *his* tone of voice that, since it was his truck, he was damn well going to smoke in it.

Madelyn faced forward again. "If you mean, does the smoke bother me, the answer is no. I just hate to see anyone smoking. It's like playing Russian roulette with your life."

"Exactly. It's my life."

She bit her lip at his curtness. Great going, she thought. That's a good way to get to know someone, attack his personal habits.

"I'm sorry," she apologized with sincerity. "It's none of my business, and I shouldn't have said anything. It just startled me."

"Why? People smoke. Or don't you associate with anyone who smokes?"

She thought a minute, treating his sarcastic remark seriously. "Not really. Some of our clients smoke, but none of my personal friends do. I spent a lot of time with my grandmother, and she was very old-fashioned about the vices. I was taught never to swear, smoke or drink spirits. I've never smoked," she said righteously.

Despite his irritation, he found himself trying not to laugh. "Does that mean you swear and drink spirits?"

"I've been known to be a bit aggressive in my language in moments of stress," she allowed. Her eyes twinkled at him. "And Grandma Lily thought it was perfectly suitable for a lady to take an occasional glass of wine, medicinally, of course. During my college days, I also swilled beer."

"Swilled?"

"There's no other word to describe a college student's drinking manners."

Remembering his own college days, he had to agree.

"But I don't enjoy spirits," she continued. "So I'd say at least half of Grandma Lily's teachings stuck. Not bad odds."

"Did she have any rules against gambling?"

Madelyn looked at him, her mouth both wry and tender, gray eyes full of a strange acceptance. "Grandma Lily believed that life is a gamble, and everyone has to take their chances. Sometimes you bust, sometimes you break the house.'' It was an outlook she had passed on to her granddaughter. Otherwise, Madelyn thought, why would she be sitting here in a pickup truck, in the process of falling in love with a stranger?

It had been a long time since Reese had seen his home through the eyes of a stranger, but as he stopped the truck next to the house, he was suddenly, bitterly ashamed. The paint on the house was badly chipped and peeling, and the outbuildings were even worse. Long ago he'd given up trying to keep the yard neat and had finally destroyed the flower beds that had once delineated the house, because they had been overrun with weeds. In the past seven years nothing new had been added, and nothing broken had been replaced, except for the absolute necessities. Parts for the truck and tractor had come before house paint. Taking care of the herd had been more important than cutting the grass or weeding the flower beds. Sheer survival hadn't left time for the niceties of life. He'd done what he'd had to do, but that didn't mean he had to like the shape his home was in. He hated for Madelyn to see it like this, when it had once been, if not a showplace, a house no woman would have been ashamed of.

Madelyn saw the peeling paint, but dismissed it; after all, it wasn't anything that a little effort and several gallons of paint wouldn't fix. What caught her attention was the shaded porch, complete with swing, that wrapped all the way around the two-story house. Grandma Lily had had a porch like that, and a swing where they had whiled away many a lazy summer day to the accompaniment of the slow creak of the chains as they gently swayed.

''It reminds me of Grandma Lily's house,'' she said, her eyes dreamy again.

He opened her door and put his hands on her waist, lifting

her out of the truck before she could slide to the ground. Startled all over again, she quickly looked up at him.

"I wasn't taking any chances with that skirt," he said, almost growling.

Her pulse began thudding again.

He reached inside the truck and hooked her carry-on bag with one hand, then took her arm with the other. They entered by the back door, which was unlocked. She was struck by the fact that he felt safe in not locking his door when he was going to be gone all day.

The back door opened into a combination mudroom and laundry. A washer and dryer lined the wall to the left, and the right wall bristled with pegs from which hung an assortment of hats, coats, ponchos and bright yellow rain slickers. A variety of boots, most of them muddy, were lined up on a rubber mat. Straight ahead and across a small hall was a full bathroom, which she realized would be convenient when he came in muddy from head to foot. He could take a bath without tracking mud or dripping water all through the house to the bathroom upstairs.

They turned left and were in the kitchen, a big, open, sunny room with a breakfast nook. Madelyn looked with interest at the enormous appliances, which didn't fit her image of what the kitchen of a small-scale, bachelor rancher should look like. She had expected something smaller and much more old-fashioned than this efficient room with its institutional-sized appliances.

"The house has ten rooms," he said. "Six downstairs, and four bedrooms upstairs."

"It's a big house for just one person," she commented, following him upstairs.

"That's why I want to get married." He made the comment as if explaining why he wanted a drink of water. "My parents built this house when I was a baby. I grew up here. I want to pass it on to my own children."

She felt a little breathless, and not just from climbing the stairs. The thought of having his children weakened her.

He opened a door directly across from the top of the stairs and ushered her into a large, pleasant bedroom with white curtains at the windows and a white bedspread on the four-poster bed. She made a soft sound of pleasure. An old rocking chair sat before one of the windows, and what was surely a handmade rug covered the smooth, hardwood plank flooring. The flooring itself was worth a small fortune. For all the charm of the room, there was a sense of bareness to it, no soft touches to personalize it in any way. But he lived here alone, she reminded herself; the personal touches would be in the rooms he used, not in the empty bedrooms waiting for his children to fill them.

He stepped past her and put her bag on the bed. "I can't take the whole day off," he said. "The chores have to be done, so I'll have to leave you to entertain yourself for a while. You can rest or do whatever you want. The bathroom is right down the hall if you want to freshen up. My bedroom has a private bath, so you don't have to worry about running into me."

In the space of a heartbeat she knew she didn't want to be left alone to twirl her fingers for the rest of the day. "Can't I go with you?"

"You'll be bored, and it's dirty work."

She shrugged. "I've been dirty before."

He looked at her for a long moment, his face unsmiling and expressionless. "All right," he finally said, wondering if she'd feel the same when her designer shoes were caked with the makings of compost.

Her smile crinkled her eyes. "I'll be changed in three minutes flat."

He doubted it. "I'll be in the barn. Come on out when you're ready."

As soon as he had closed the door behind him, Madelyn stripped out of her clothes, slithered into a pair of jeans and shoved her feet into her oldest pair of loafers, which she had brought along for this very purpose. After all, she couldn't very well explore a ranch in high heels. She pulled a white cotton camisole on over her head and sauntered out the door just as he was starting downstairs after changing shirts himself. He gave her a startled look; then his eyes took on a heavy-lidded expression as his gaze swept her throat and shoulders, left bare by the sleeveless camisole. Madelyn almost faltered as that very male look settled on her breasts, and her body felt suddenly warm and weighed down. She had seen men cast quick furtive glances at her breasts before, but Reese was making no effort to hide his speculation. She felt her nipples tingle and harden, rasping against the cotton covering them.

"I didn't think you'd make it," he said.

"I don't fuss about clothes."

She didn't have to, he thought. The body she put inside them was enough; anything else was superfluous. He was all but salivating just thinking of her breasts and those long, slender legs. The jeans covered them, but now he knew exactly how long and shapely they were, and, as she turned to close the bedroom door, how curved her buttocks were, like an inverted heart. He felt a lot hotter than the weather warranted.

She walked beside him out to the barn, her head swiveling from side to side as she took in all the aspects of the ranch. A three-door garage in the same style as the house stood behind it. She pointed to it. "How many other cars do you have?"

"None," he said curtly.

Three other buildings stood empty, their windows blank. "What are those?"

"Bunkhouses."

There was a well-built chicken coop, with fat white chickens pecking industriously around the yard. She said, "I see you grow your own eggs."

From the corner of her eye she saw his lips twitch as if he'd almost smiled. "I grow my own milk, too."

"Very efficient. I'm impressed. I haven't had fresh milk since I was about six."

"I didn't think that accent was New York City. Where are you from originally?"

"Virginia. We moved to New York when my mother re-married, but I went back to Virginia for college."

"Your parents were divorced?"

"No. My father died. Mom remarried three years later."

He opened the barn door. "My parents died within a year of each other. I don't think they could exist apart."

The rich, earthy smell of an occupied barn enveloped her, and she took a deep breath. The odors of animals, leather, manure, hay and feed all mixed into that one unmistakable scent. She found it much more pleasant than the smell of exhaust.

The barn was huge. She had noticed a stable beside it, also empty, as well as a machinery shed and a hay shed. Everything about the ranch shouted that this had once been a very prosperous holding, but Reese had evidently fallen on hard times. How that must grate on a man with his obvious pride. She wanted to put her hand in his and tell him that it didn't matter, but she had the feeling he would reject the gesture. The pride that kept him working this huge place alone wouldn't allow him to accept anything he could inter-pret as pity.

She didn't know what chores needed doing or how to do them, so she tried to stay out of his way and simply watch, noting the meticulous attention he paid to everything he did. He cleaned out stalls and put down fresh hay, his powerful arms and back flowing with muscles. He put feed in the troughs, checked and repaired tack, brought in fresh water. Three horses were in a corral between the barn and stable; he checked and cleaned their hooves, brought them in to feed and water them, then put them in their stalls for the night. He called a ridiculously docile cow to him and put her in a stall, where she munched contentedly while he milked her. With a bucket half full of hot, foaming milk, he went back to the house, and two cats appeared to meow imperiously at him as they scented the milk. "Scat," he said. "Go catch a mouse."

Madelyn knew what to do now. She got the sterilized jugs she had noticed on her first trip through the kitchen and found a straining cloth. He gave her a strange look as she held the straining cloth over the mouth of the jug for him to pour the milk through. "Grandma Lily used to do this," she said in a blissful tone. "I was never strong enough to hold the bucket and pour, but I knew I'd be an adult the day she let me pour out the milk."

"Did you ever get to pour it?"

"No. She sold the cow the summer before I started school. She just had the one cow, for fresh milk, but the area was already building up and becoming less rural, so she got rid of it."

He set the bucket down and took the straining cloth. "Then here's your chance for adulthood. Pour."

A whimsical smile touched her lips as she lifted the bucket and carefully poured the creamy white liquid through the cloth into the jug. The warm, sweet scent filled the kitchen. When the bucket was empty she set it aside and said, "Thank you. As a rite of passage, that beats the socks off of getting my driver's license."

This time it happened. Reese's eyes crinkled, and his lips moved in a little half grin. Madelyn felt more of that inner shifting and settling, and knew that she was lost.

Chapter 3

"There isn't much nightlife around, but there is a beer joint and café about twenty miles from here if you'd like to go dancing."

Madelyn hesitated. "Would you mind very much if we just stayed here? You must be tired, and I know I am. I'd rather put my feet up and relax."

Reese was silent. He hadn't expected her to refuse, and though he was tired, he'd been looking forward to holding her while they danced. Not only that, having people around them would dilute his focus on her, ease the strain of being alone with her. She wasn't right for him, damn it.

On the other hand, he'd been up since four that morning, and relaxing at home sounded like heaven. The hard part would be relaxing with her anywhere around.

"We could play Monopoly. I saw a game in the bookcase," she said. "Or cards. I know how to play poker, blackjack, spades, hearts, rummy, Shanghai, Spite and Malice, Old Maid and Go Fish."

He gave her a sharp glance at that improbable list. She

looked as innocent as an angel. "I lost my Old Maid cards, but we can play rummy."

"Jokers, two-eyed jacks, threes, fives, sevens and Rachel are wild," she said promptly.

"On the other hand, there's a baseball game on television tonight. What the hell is a rachel?"

"It's the queen of diamonds. They have names, you know."

"No, I didn't know. Are you making that up?"

"Nope. Rachel is the queen of diamonds, Palas is the queen of spades, Judith is the queen of hearts, and Argine is the queen of clubs."

"Do the kings and jacks have names?"

"I don't know. That little bit of information has never come my way."

He eyed her again, then leaned back on the couch and propped his boots on the coffee table. She saw a hint of green gleam in his eyes as he said, "The little plastic doo-hickey on the end of your shoelaces is called an aglet."

She mimicked his position, her lips quirking with suppressed laughter. "The dimple in the bottom of a champagne bottle is called a punt."

"The empty space between the bottle top and the liquid is called ullage."

"A newly formed embryo is called a zygote."

"Bird's nest soup is made from the nests of swiftlets, which make the nests by secreting a glutinous substance from under their tongues."

Madelyn's eyes rounded with fascination, but she rose to the challenge. "Pink flamingos are pink because they eat so many shrimp."

"It takes light from the sun eight minutes and twenty seconds to reach earth."

"The common housefly flies at the speed of five miles an hour."

"An ant can lift fifty times its own weight."

She paused and eyed him consideringly. "Were you lying about the bird nests?"

He shook his head. "Are you giving up?"

"Never use all your ammunition in the opening salvo."

There wouldn't be much opportunity for follow-up salvos, he thought. In about eighteen hours he'd be putting her on a plane back to New York and they would never meet again.

The silence that fell between them was a little awkward. Madelyn got up and smiled at him. "I'll leave you to your baseball game, if you don't mind. I want to sit on the porch swing and listen to the frogs and crickets."

Reese watched her as she left the room, her hips rolling in a lazy sway. After a minute he heard the squeak of the chains as she sat down in the swing; then the creaking as she began pushing it back and forth. He turned on the television and actually watched a little of the ball game, but his mind was on the rhythmic creaking. He turned the television off.

Madelyn had been swinging and dreaming, her eyes closed, but she opened them when she heard the screen door open and close, then his boots on the wooden porch. He stopped a few feet away and leaned his shoulder against one of the posts.

His lighter flared; then the end of the cigarette glowed as it began to burn. Madelyn stared at his dim figure, wishing she had the right to get up and go to him, to slide her arms around his waist and rest her head on his shoulder. When he didn't speak, she closed her eyes again and began drifting in the peaceful darkness. The late spring night was comfortable, and the night creatures were going about their business as usual. This was the type of life she wanted, a life close to the earth, where serenity could be drawn from nature.

"Why did you answer the ad?"

His rough-textured voice was quiet, not disturbing the night. A few seconds passed before Madelyn opened her eyes and answered.

"For much the same reason you placed it, I suppose.

Partly out of curiosity, I admit, but I also want to get married and have a family.''

"You don't have to come all the way out here to do that."

She said, "Maybe I do," and was completely serious.

"You don't have any boyfriends in New York?"

"I have friends, yes, but no one I'm serious about, no one I'd want to marry. And I don't think I want to live in New York. This place is wonderful."

"You've only seen it at its best. Winter is frozen hell. Every place has its drawbacks."

"And its advantages. If you didn't think the positives outweighed the negatives, you wouldn't be here."

"I grew up here. This is my home. The Eskimos are attached to their homes, too, but I wouldn't live there."

Madelyn turned her head and looked out into the night, sensing what was coming and wishing, praying, that he wouldn't say it. She could tell from the way he'd been throwing up those subtle obstacles and objections what he was going to say.

"Madelyn. You don't fit in out here."

Her right foot kept up the slow, steady rhythm of the swing. "So the visit has been a failure?"

"Yes."

"Even though you're attracted to me?" In the darkness she could be bolder than she would have been otherwise. If faint heart ne'er won fair lady, she was sure that the fair lady ne'er won with a faint heart, either.

"The spark goes both ways." He stubbed out the cigarette on his boot heel and flipped it out into the yard.

"Yes. So why am I unsuitable for your purposes?"

"You're real suitable for the purposes of bed," he said grimly. "I'd like to take you there right now. But out of bed—no. You won't do at all."

"Please explain. I like to understand my rejections."

Suddenly he moved away from the post and sat next to her on the swing, setting it to dipping and swaying with his weight. One firmly planted boot took control of the motion and began the gentle rocking movement again.

"I was married before, for two years. You're like my first wife in a lot of ways. She was a city person. She liked the entertainment and variety of a big city. She'd never been on a ranch before, and thought it was romantic, just like a movie—until she realized that most of a rancher's time is spent working, instead of having a good time. She was already restless before winter came, and that just put the frosting on the cake. Our second year was pure hell."

"Don't judge me by someone else, Reese Duncan. Just because one woman didn't like it, doesn't mean another won't."

"A man who doesn't learn from his mistakes is a damn fool. When I marry again, it'll be to a woman who knows what ranch life is like, who'll be able to work with me. I won't risk the ranch again."

"What do you mean?"

"This ranch was once one of the biggest and best. You can tell by looking around you that it used to be a lot more than what it is now. I had the two best breeding bulls in four states, a good insemination program going, over four thousand head of beef, and fifty people working for me. Then I got divorced." He lifted his arm and rested it along the back of the swing. She could see only his profile, but even in the darkness she could make out the bitter line of his mouth, hear his bitterness in his voice. "April's family had a lot of influence with the judge. He agreed that two years as my wife entitled her to half of my assets, but she sweetly decided that a lump sum settlement would do just fine, thank you. I nearly went bankrupt. I had to liquidate almost everything to buy her off. I sold land that had been in my family for over a hundred years. That was seven years ago. I've been working my ass off since then just trying to keep this place going, and this year it looks like I'll finally make a profit again. I want kids, someone to leave the ranch to, but this time I'll make a better choice of woman."

She was appalled at the cause of his circumstances, but still said tartly, "What about love? How does that fit into your plans?"

"It doesn't," he replied in a flat tone.

"What if your wife wants more?"

"I don't plan to spin her a pretty story. She'll know where I stand from the first. But I'll be a good husband. I don't stray, or mistreat women. All I ask from a wife is loyalty and competence and the same values I have."

"And to be ready to stand as a brood mare."

"That too," he agreed.

Disappointment so sharp that it felt like a knife stabbed into her midsection. He was going to marry someone else. She looked away from him and reached deep for the control she needed. "Then I wish you luck. I hope you have a happy marriage this time. Do you have any more applicants?"

"Two more. If either of them is interested in ranch life, I'll probably ask her to marry me."

He had it as cut-and-dried as any business deal, which was all it was to him, even though he would be sleeping with his business partner. Madelyn could have cried at such a waste of passion, but she held on to her control. All she could do now was cut her losses and try to forget him, so she wouldn't measure every man she met against him for the rest of her life.

The darkness hid the desolation in her eyes as she said, "A jackrabbit can run as fast as a racehorse—for a short distance, of course."

He didn't miss a beat. "A group of bears is called a sloth."

"The Pacific Ocean covers almost sixty-four-million square miles."

"The safety pin was invented in 1849."

"No! That long ago? Zippers were invented in 1893, and it's a good thing, because wouldn't you hate to get caught in a safety pin?"

* * *

She was quiet on the drive back to Billings the next morning. The evening had ended well, with the hilarity of their mutual store of odd facts, but the strain had told on her in the form of a sleepless night. She couldn't bear the thought of never seeing him again, but that was the way it was, and she was determined to keep her pain to herself. Nothing would be gained by weeping all over him, which was exactly what she felt like doing.

He looked tired, too, and it was no wonder when she considered how early he'd had to get up for the past two days, and how much driving he'd done. She said, "I'm sorry you're having to go to so much trouble to take me back."

He shot her a glance before returning his attention to the road. "You had a wasted trip, too."

So she was categorized under "Wasted Trip." She wondered wryly if her other dates had merely been flattering her all these years.

It was only about half an hour before her flight when they reached the airport. He'd timed it nicely, she thought. She wouldn't have to rush, but on the other hand, there wasn't time for a lengthy goodbye, and she was glad. She didn't know how much she could take. "You don't need to park," she said. "Just let me out."

He gave her another glance, but this one was strangely angry. He didn't speak, just parked and came around to open the door for her. Quickly she jumped out before he could catch her by the waist and lift her out again.

Reese's mouth had a grim set as he put his hand on the small of her back and walked with her into the terminal. At least the skirt she was wearing today was full enough that she could move freely, but the way it swung around her legs was just as maddening, in a different way, as that tight white skirt had been. He kept thinking that this one would be even easier to push up out of the way.

Her flight was just being called when they reached the gate. She turned with a smile that cost more than she could afford and held out her hand. "Goodbye, Reese. I wish you luck."

He took her hand, feeling the smooth texture of her fingers in contrast to his hardened, callused palm. She would be that smooth and silky all over, and that was why he was sending her away. He saw her wide, soft lips part as she started to say something else, and hunger rose up in him like a tidal wave, crashing over barriers and sweeping everything away.

"I have to taste you," he said in a low, harsh tone, carrying her hand upward to tuck it around his neck. "Just once." His other arm circled her waist and pulled her to him as he bent his head.

It wasn't a polite goodbye kiss. It was hard and deep. His mouth was hot and wild, with the taste of tobacco and himself. Madelyn put her other arm around his neck and hung on, because her legs had gone watery. The force of his mouth opened hers, and he took her with his tongue. He held her to him with painful pressure, crushing her breasts against him and cradling her pelvis against the hard, aching ridge of his manhood.

Vaguely she heard other people around them. It didn't matter. He was making love to her with his mouth, arousing her, satisfying her, consuming her. He increased the slant of his head, tucking her head more firmly into his shoulder, and kissed her with all the burning sensuality she had sensed in him on first sight.

Her heart lurched as pleasure overrode shock, swiftly escalating to an almost unbearable tension. She not only welcomed the intrusion of his tongue, she met it with her own, making love to him as surely as he was to her. He shuddered, and for a second his arms tightened so fiercely that she moaned into his mouth. Instantly they loosened, and he lifted his head.

Breathing swiftly, only inches apart, they stared at each other. His expression was hard and sensual, his eyes dilated with arousal, his lips still gleaming from the moisture of their kiss. He was bending back toward her when another call for her flight stopped him, and he slowly released her.

Her entire body ached for him. She waited, hoping he would say the words that would keep her there, but instead he said, "You'd better go. You'll miss your flight."

She couldn't speak. She nodded instead and walked away on shaky legs. She didn't look back. It was bad form for a grown woman to howl like an infant, and that was what she was very much afraid she would do if she gave in to the need to see him for even a split second.

She had gotten off the plane in Billings feeling confident and alive with anticipation. She left twenty-four hours later feeling shattered.

Robert met her plane in New York, which told Madelyn how worried he'd been. She gave him a parody of a smile and saw his pale eyes sharpen as he immediately read her distress. The smile wobbled and collapsed, and she walked into his arms. She didn't cry; she didn't let herself cry, but her chest heaved with convulsive breaths as she fought for control.

"I'll kill him," Robert said in a very soft, almost gentle tone.

Madelyn shook her head and took one more deep breath so she could talk. "He was a perfect gentleman. He's a hard-working, salt-of-the-earth type, and he said I wasn't suitable for the job."

He rocked her gently back and forth. "And that hurt your ego?"

She raised her head and managed a real smile this time, though it was just as wobbly as the first. "No, I think he managed to break my heart."

Robert gave her a searching look, reading the expression in her bottomless gray eyes. "You don't fall in love in one day."

"Sometimes you don't, sometimes you do. He didn't feel the same way, so it's something I have to live with."

"Maybe it's just as well." Keeping his arm around her shoulder, he guided her toward the entrance. "I investigated him—I know, you told me not to," he added warily as he saw the menacing look she gave him. "But he would be a tough man for any woman to live with. He's understandably bitter about the raw deal he got in his divorce—"

"I know," she said. "He told me about it."

"Then you know that any woman he marries will have a cold marriage. He's still carrying a lot of anger inside him."

"I saw the ranch. He has reason to be angry."

"His ex-wife and her family took him to the cleaners. I've dealt with them—cautiously. You have to be careful when you wade into a pool of barracudas."

"I'd like for you to ruin them financially, if you can, please," she said in the manner of a socialite idly asking for another glass of champagne.

"That won't give him back what he lost."

"No, but I'm vindictive enough that I want to see them get what they deserve."

"You don't have a vindictive bone in your body."

"Yes I do," she said in the same gentle tone he occasionally used, the one that made smart people back away.

He kissed her hair and hugged her closer. "So what are you going to do now?"

"Carry on, I suppose." She shrugged. "There's nothing else I can do."

Robert looked at her, wryly admiring her resilience. Madelyn was a trooper; she always carried on. Sometimes she needed a crutch for a while, but in the end she stood upright again and continued on her own. Reese Duncan had to be a lot of man to have gotten to her this way.

Two weeks later, Reese got back into his truck after seeing his latest visitor, Juliet Johnson, off on the bus. He cursed and slammed his fist against the steering wheel, then lit a cigarette and began smoking it with fast, furious puffs.

This had all been a damn waste of time and money. The

schoolteacher, Dale Quillan, had taken a good hard look at the isolation of the ranch and politely told him she wasn't interested. Miss Johnson, on the other hand, had been willing to take on the job, but he couldn't bring himself to make the offer. That was the sourest woman he'd ever met, humorless and disapproving of almost everything she saw. He'd imagined her as the family-oriented type, since she had sacrificed her life to care for her invalid mother, but now he figured she had been more of a cross than a blessing to the poor woman. She had informed him tartly that she would be willing to perform her duties by him once they were sanctified by marriage, but she hoped he didn't plan on a lot of foolish shenanigans because she didn't believe in such. Reese had told her just as sharply that he believed she could rest easy on that score.

Three applicants. One he wouldn't have, one wouldn't have him, and the other was all wrong for the job.

Madelyn. Long, beautiful legs. Silky blond hair and deep gray eyes. A soft mouth and a taste like honey. What would ranch life do to someone that elegant and unprepared?

But he'd spent two weeks turning his bed into a shambles every night because his frustrated body wouldn't let him sleep, and when he did manage to sleep he dreamed about her and woke up in even worse shape than when he'd dozed off. His loins ached, his temper was frayed, and he was smoking twice as much as normal. Damn her for being more than he wanted, or could afford.

She had clung to him and kissed him with such a fiery response that he hadn't been able to sleep at all that night, but she'd walked away from him without a backward glance. If she'd turned around just once, if she'd shown the least reluctance to go, he might have weakened and asked her to stay, but she hadn't. She'd even wished him good luck in finding a wife. It didn't sound as if his rejection had wounded her too badly.

He could have kept her. It drove him half-wild to know that she would have stayed if he'd asked her, that they could have been married by now. She would be lying under him every night, and the bed might get torn up, but it wouldn't be out of frustration.

No. She was too much like April. If he ever let her get her claws into him, she would rip him to shreds even worse than April had done, because even in the beginning he'd never been as hot to have April as he was to have Madelyn. She was used to city life, and though she'd appeared to like Montana and the ranch, the real test was living through a winter here. She'd never make it.

He ground out the cigarette and lit another, feeling the smoke burn his throat and lungs.

Fury and frustration boiled over. He got out of the truck and strode to a pay phone. A call to Information got her number. This was probably another waste of time; at this time of day she'd be at work, but he was driven by an urgency he bitterly resented and was still unable to resist.

He punched in her number, and an operator came on the line to tell him how much money to deposit. He dug in his pocket for change, swearing under his breath when he saw he didn't have enough.

"Sir, please deposit the correct amount."

"Just a minute." He got out his wallet and flipped through the papers until he found his telephone credit card and read off the account number to the operator. He hadn't used the card in seven years, so he hoped it was still good.

Evidently it was, because the operator said, "Thank you," and he heard the electronic beeps as the call went through.

It rang three times; then there was a click as the receiver was picked up and that warm, faintly raspy voice said, "Hello."

"Madelyn."

There was a pause; then she said, "Yes. Reese?"

"Yes." He stopped as a truck roared by, waiting until he could hear again. "You've been out here and seen what it's like. Are you willing to marry me?"

The pause this time was longer, and his fist tightened on

the receiver until he thought the plastic might crack under the pressure. Finally she said, "The other two didn't work out?"

"No. What's your answer?"

"Yes," she said calmly.

He closed his eyes as the almost unbearable tension eased. God, he might be making a mistake as bad as the one he'd made with April, but he had to have her. "You'll have to sign a prenuptial agreement giving up all rights to the property I own prior to marriage and waiving any right to alimony or a lump sum settlement in case of divorce."

"All right. That's a mutual agreement, isn't it? What's yours remains yours and what's mine remains mine?"

Irritation lashed at him. "Of course."

"Fine, then."

"I want a certification from a doctor that you're in good health."

"All right. I require a certification from *your* doctor, as well."

The irritation threatened to become rage, but he held it in control. She had as much right to be reassured about his health as he did to be reassured about hers. Sexually transmitted diseases didn't stop at the Montana border, and AIDS wasn't the only concern people should have.

"I want the wedding within two weeks. When can you get out here?"

"How long is the waiting period?"

"Five days, I think. I'll have to check. Can you get here next week?"

"I think so. Give me your number and I'll call you."

He recited his phone number; then silence crackled along the line. He said, "I'll see you next week."

Another pause. Then, "Yes. I'll see you then. 'Bye."

He said goodbye and hung up, then leaned against the booth for a minute, his eyes closed. He'd done it. He'd asked her to marry him against all common sense, but this time he would protect himself and the ranch. He'd have her, but he'd keep her at a distance, and all the legal documents would keep the ranch safe.

He lit another cigarette and coughed as the acrid smoke stung his raw throat. In his mind's eye he saw her incredulous face when she'd looked at him and said, "*You smoke?*" He took the cigarette out of his mouth and looked at it; he'd smoked for years, and usually enjoyed it, but he'd been smoking too much lately.

You smoke?

Swearing again, he put out the cigarette. As he strode angrily back to the truck he passed a trash barrel, and without giving himself time to think he tossed the cigarette pack into it. He was still swearing as he got into the truck and started it. For a few days he was going to be in the mood to wrestle grizzlies, and he didn't look forward to it.

Madelyn slowly replaced the receiver, numb with shock. She couldn't believe he'd called. She couldn't believe she'd said she would marry him. She couldn't believe anything about their conversation. It had to be the most unromantic, businesslike, *insulting* proposal on record. And she'd still said yes. Yes! A thousand times *yes*!

She had to be in Montana in a week. She had a million things to do: get packed, get the apartment closed up, say goodbye to all her friends—and have a physical, of course. But all she could do right now was sit, her thoughts whirling.

She had to be practical. It was obvious Reese wasn't giving the marriage much of a chance, even though he was going into it for his own reasons. She wondered why the other two hadn't worked out, because he'd been so adamant that she was wrong for the job. But he wanted her, she knew, remembering that kiss at the airport and the way he'd looked at her. She wanted him, more than she'd ever thought it was possible to want a man, both physically and emotionally, but was that enough to hold together a relationship when they were faced with the day-in, day-out routine that marriage entailed? Would she still love him when he had a cold and was grouchy, or yelled at her for something that wasn't her fault? Would he still want her after he'd seen her without makeup, stumbling around in the morning with uncombed hair, or when she was in a bad mood, too?

Looking at it clearly, she decided that she should ask the doctor about birth control pills while she was there. If everything worked out and they decided to have children, it would be easy to go off the Pill, but what a mess it would be if she got pregnant right away and then the marriage fell apart. It was something she would already have discussed with Reese if their situation had been a normal one, but nothing about this was normal.

She was making a complete change in her life, from urban to rural, from single to marriage, all without really knowing the man she was marrying. She didn't know his favorite foods or colors, his moods, how he would react to any given situation; all she really knew about him was that his store of miscellaneous knowledge rivaled hers, and that she responded more violently to him than anyone she'd ever met before. She was definitely following her heart here, and not her head.

Reese would want the marriage ceremony to be conducted with as little fuss as possible, before a magistrate or a justice of the peace. She didn't mind that, but she made up her mind that Robert would be there, and her friend Christine. They could be the witnesses, rather than two strangers.

Robert was less than thrilled with the news, as she had expected. "I know you fell for him, but shouldn't you give this more time? You've met him once. Or did you get to know him *really* well during that one meeting?"

"I told you, he was a perfect gentleman."

"Ah, but were you a perfect lady?"

"I'm good at whatever I do, but I've never claimed to be perfect."

His eyes twinkled, and he leaned over to pinch her cheek. "You're determined to have this man, aren't you?"

"He gave me this chance, and I'm taking it before he

changes his mind. Oh yes, we're getting married now if I have to kidnap him.''

"He may be in for a surprise," Robert mused. "Does he know about that bulldog stubbornness you hide behind that lazy walk and talk?''

"Of course not. Give me some credit. He'll learn about that in due time, after we're married." She smiled that sweet smile.

"So, when do I get to meet him?''

"The day of the wedding, probably. No matter what you have scheduled, I expect you to drop everything and fly out when I call you.''

"Wouldn't miss it.''

Christine was even less encouraging. "What do you know about ranch life?" she asked ominously. "Nothing. There are no movies, no neighbors, not even any television reception to speak of. No plays, no operas or concerts.''

"No pollution, no having to put six different locks on my door when I go out, no getting mugged when I go shopping.''

"You've never been mugged.''

"But there's always the possibility. I know people who've been mugged several times.''

"There's the *possibility* of a lot of things. It's *possible* I may even get married some day, but I'm not holding my breath waiting. That isn't the point. You really have no idea what life on a ranch is like. At least I have *some* idea. It's a hard, lonely way to live, and you're not the isolated type.''

"*Au contraire,* dear friend. I'm just as content by myself as I am surrounded by people. If I had to live in Outer Mongolia to be with him, I'd do it.''

Christine looked amazed. "Ye gods," she blurted. "You're in love!''

Madelyn nodded. "Of course. Why else would I marry him?''

"Well, that explains the sudden madness. Does he feel the same way?''

"Not yet. I'm going to do my best to convince him, though."

"Would it be wasting my breath to point out that that usually comes *before* the part where you say 'I do'? That courtship usually covers this phase?"

Pursing her lips, Madelyn considered it, then said, "No, I think it would come more under 'falling on deaf ears' than 'wasting your breath.' I'm getting married. I'd like you to be there."

"Of course I'll be there! Nothing could keep me away. I have to see this paragon of manly virtues."

"I never said he was virtuous."

In complete understanding, they looked at each other and smiled.

Chapter 4

They were married in Billings twelve days later. Madelyn was exhausted by the time of the wedding, which was performed in the judge's chambers. She had gotten only a few hours of sleep each night since Reese's phone call, because it had taken so much time to pack up a lifetime of belongings, sorting through and discarding what she wasn't taking, and packing what she couldn't bear to do without. She had also gotten the required physical and expressed the results to Reese, and hadn't been surprised when she had received his results by express mail the same day.

She had shipped numerous boxes containing books, albums, tapes, CDs, stereo equipment and winter clothes to the ranch, wondering what Reese would have to say about having his home taken over by the paraphernalia of a stranger. But when she'd spoken to him during two brief telephone calls he hadn't mentioned it. Before she knew it she was flying to Billings again, but this time she wasn't coming back.

Reese didn't kiss her when he met her at the airport, and

she was glad. She was tired and on edge, and the first self-doubts were creeping in. From the look on his face, when he started kissing her again he didn't intend to stop, and she wasn't ready for that. But her heart leaped at the sight of him, reassuring her that she was doing the right thing.

She planned to stay at a motel in Billings for the five days until their marriage; Reese scowled at her when she told him her plan.

"There's no point in paying for a motel when you can stay at the ranch."

"Yes, there is. For one thing, most of my New York clothes are useless and will just stay packed up. I have to have Montana clothing—jeans, boots and the like. There's no point in making an extra trip later on to buy it when I'm here already. Moreover, I'm not staying alone with you right now, and you know why."

He put his hands on her waist and pulled her up against him. His narrowed eyes were dark green. "Because I'd have you under me as soon as we got in the house."

She swallowed, her slender hands resting on his chest. She could feel the heavy beat of his heart under her palms, a powerful pumping that revealed the sexual tension he was holding under control. "Yes. I'm not ready to start that part of our relationship. I'm tired, and nervous, and we really don't know each other that well—"

"We're getting married in five days. We won't know each other much better by then, baby, but I don't plan on spending my wedding night alone."

"You won't," she whispered.

"So one of the conditions for getting you in bed is to put a ring on your finger first?" His voice was getting harsher.

He was angry, and she didn't want him to be; she just wanted him to understand. She said steadily, "That isn't it at all. If the wedding were two months away, or even just a month, I'm certain we'd…we'd make love before the ceremony, but it isn't. I'm just asking you for a little time to rest and recuperate first."

He studied her upturned face, seeing the translucent shadows under her eyes and the slight pale cast to her skin. She was resting against him, letting his body support hers, and despite his surging lust he realized that she really was tired. She had uprooted her entire life in just one week, and the emotional strain had to be as exhausting as the physical work.

"Then sleep," he said in a slow, deep voice. "Get a lot of sleep, baby, and rest up. You'll need it. I can wait five days—just barely."

She did get some sleep, but the emotional strain was still telling on her. She was getting married; it was natural to be nervous, she told herself.

The day they signed the prenuptial agreement at the lawyer's office was another day of stress. Reese was in a bad mood when he picked her up at the motel, growling and snapping at everything she said, so she lapsed into silence. She didn't think it was a very good omen for their marriage.

The prenuptial agreement was brief and easily understood. In case of divorce, they both kept the property and assets they had possessed prior to their marriage, and Madelyn gave up all rights to alimony in any form. She balked, however, at the condition that he retain custody of any children that should result from their union.

"No," she said flatly. "I'm not giving up my children."

Reese leaned back in the chair and gave her a look that would have seared metal. "You're not taking my children away from me."

"Calm down," the lawyer soothed. "This is all hypothetical. Both of you are talking as if a divorce is inevitable, and if that's the case, I would suggest that you *not* get married. Statistics say that half of new marriages end in divorce, but that means that half don't. You may well be married to each other for the rest of your lives, and there may not be any children anyway."

Madelyn ignored him. She looked only at Reese. "I don't intend to take our children away from you, but neither do I intend to give them up. I think we should share custody, because children need both parents. Don't try to make me pay for what April did," she warned.

"But you'd want them to live with you."

"Yes, I would, just as you'd want them to live with you. We aren't going to change that by negotiation. If we did divorce, I'd never try to turn our children against you, nor would I take them out of the area, but that's something you'll just have to take on trust, because I'm not signing any paper that says I'll give up my children."

There were times, he noted, when those sleepy gray eyes could become sharp and clear. She was all but baring her teeth at him. It seemed there were some things that mattered enough to rouse her from her habitual lazy amusement, and it was oddly reassuring that the subject of their children, hypothetical though they were, was one of them. If he and April had had a child, she would have wanted custody of it only as a way to get back at him, not because she really wanted the child itself. April hadn't wanted to have children at all, a fact for which he was now deeply grateful. Madelyn not only appeared to want children, she was ready to fight for them even before they existed.

"All right," he finally said, and nodded to the lawyer. "Strike that clause from the agreement. If there's ever a divorce, we'll hash that out then."

Madelyn felt drained when they left the lawyer's office. Until then, she hadn't realized the depth of Reese's bitterness. He was so determined not to let another woman get the upper hand on him that it might not be possible for her to reach him at all. The realization that she could be fighting a losing battle settled on her shoulders like a heavy weight.

"When do your stepbrother and best friend get here?" he asked curtly. He hadn't liked the idea of Robert and Christine being at their wedding, and now Madelyn knew why. Having friends and relatives there made it seem more like a real wedding than just a business agreement, and a business agreement, with bed privileges, was all Reese wanted, all he could accept.

"The day before the wedding. They won't be able to stay afterward, so we're going out to a restaurant the night before. You can be here, can't you?"

"No. There's no one at the ranch to put the animals up for the night and do the chores for me. Even if I left immediately afterward, it's almost a three hour drive, so there's no point in it."

She flushed. She should have thought of the long drive and how hard he had to work. It was a sign of how much she had to learn about ranching. "I'm sorry, I should have thought. I'll call Robert—"

He interrupted her. "There's no reason why you should cancel just because I can't be here. Go out with them and enjoy it. We won't have much chance to eat out after we're married."

If he'd expected her to react with horror at that news, he was disappointed. She'd already figured that out on her own, and she didn't care. She intended to be his partner in rebuilding the ranch; maybe when it was prosperous again he could let go of some of his bitterness. She would gladly forego restaurant meals to accomplish that.

"If you're certain..."

"I said so, didn't I?" he snapped.

She stopped and put her hands on her hips. "I'd like to know just what your problem is! I've seen men with prostate problems and women with terminal PMS who aren't as ill-tempered as you. Have you been eating gunpowder or something?"

"I'll tell you what's wrong!" he roared. "I'm trying to quit smoking!" Then he strode angrily to the truck, leaving her standing there.

She blinked her eyes, and slowly a smile stretched her lips. She strolled to the truck and got in. "So, are you homicidal or merely as irritable as a wounded water buffalo?"

"About halfway in between," he said through clenched teeth.

"Anything I can do to help?"

His eyes were narrow and intense. "It isn't just the cigarettes. Take off your panties and lock your legs around me, and I'll show you."

She didn't want to refuse him. She loved him, and he needed her, even if it was only in a sexual way. But she didn't want their first time to be a hasty coupling in a motel room, especially when she was still jittery from stress and he was irritable from lack of nicotine. She didn't know if it would be any better by their wedding day, but she hoped she would be calmer.

He saw the answer in her eyes and cursed as he ran his hand around the back of his neck. "It's just two damn days."

"For both of us." She looked out the window. "I admit, I'm trying to put it off. I'm nervous about it."

"Why? I don't abuse women. If I don't have the control I need the first time, I will the second. I won't hurt you, Maddie, and I'll make certain you enjoy it."

"I know," she said softly. "It's just that you're still basically a stranger."

"A lot of women crawl into bed with men they've just met in a bar."

"*I* don't."

"Evidently you don't crawl into bed with the man you're going to marry, either."

She rounded on him. "That's unfair and you know it, because we aren't getting married under the usual circumstances. If you're not going to do anything but snap at me and try to pressure me into bed, maybe we shouldn't see each other until the wedding."

His teeth came together with a snap. "That sounds like a damn fine idea to me."

So she spent the last two days before her wedding alone, at least until Robert and Christine arrived the afternoon before. She hadn't expected Reese to drive to Billings every day, and in fact he hadn't, except to meet her at the airport and to go to the lawyer's office, but it disturbed her that they had already quarreled. If their marriage survived, it looked like it would be a tempestuous one.

When she met Christine and Robert at the airport, Christine looked around impatiently. "Well, where is he?"

"At the ranch, working. He doesn't have anyone to look after the animals, so he isn't coming in tonight."

Christine frowned, but to Madelyn's surprise Robert took it in stride. It only took a moment's thought to realize that if there was anything Robert understood, it was work coming before everything else.

She hooked her arms through theirs and hugged both of them. "I'm so glad you're here. How was the flight?"

"Exciting," Christine said. "I've never traveled with the boss before. He gets red-carpet treatment, did you know?"

"Exasperating," Robert answered smoothly. "She makes smartmouth comments, just like you do. I kept hearing those sotto voce remarks in my ear every time a flight attendant came by."

"They didn't just come by," Christine explained. "They stopped, they lingered, they swooned."

Madelyn nodded. "Typical." She was pleased that Christine wasn't intimidated by Robert, as so many people were. Christine would never have been so familiar in the office, and in fact Madelyn doubted that the two had ever met before, but in this situation he was merely the bride's brother and she was the bride's best friend, and she had treated him as such. It also said something about Robert's urbanity that Christine did feel at ease with him; when he chose, her stepbrother could turn people to stone with his icy manner.

Now if only her two favorite people in the world would like the man she loved. She hoped he'd recovered from his nicotine fit by the morning, or it could be an interesting occasion.

They took a cab to the motel where she was staying, and Robert got a room, but Madelyn insisted that Christine stay in the room with her. On this last night as a single woman, her nerves were frayed, and she wanted someone to talk to, someone she could keep up all night if she couldn't sleep herself. After all, she reasoned, what were friends for if not to share misery?

They shared a pleasant meal and enjoyed themselves, though Madelyn wished Reese could have been there. By ten o'clock Christine was yawning openly and pointed out that it was midnight in New York. Robert signaled for the check; he looked as fresh as he had that morning, but he was used to working long hours and usually only slept four hours a night anyway.

"Will you sleep tonight?" he asked Madelyn when they got back to the motel, having noticed her shadowed eyes.

"Probably not, but I don't think a bride is supposed to sleep the night before she gets married."

"Honey, it's the night she gets married that she isn't supposed to sleep."

She wrinkled her nose at him. "Then either. I'm tired, but I'm too nervous and excited to sleep. It's been that way since he called."

"You aren't having second thoughts?"

"Second, third and fourth thoughts, but it always comes back to the fact that I can't let this chance pass."

"You could always postpone it."

She thought of how impatient Reese was and wryly shook her head. "No, I couldn't, not one more day."

He hugged her close, resting his cheek on her bright head. "Then give it all you've got, honey, and he'll never know what hit him. But if it doesn't work out, don't punish yourself. Come home."

"I've never heard such a bunch of doubting Thomases before," she chided. "But thanks for the concern. I love you, too."

By the time she went inside, Christine was already crawling into bed. Madelyn picked up the pillow and hit her with it. "You can't sleep tonight. You have to hold my hand and keep me calm."

Christine yawned. "Buy some beer, get wasted and go to sleep."

"I'd have a hangover on my wedding day. I need sympathy, not alcohol."

"The most I can offer you is two aspirin. I'm too tired to offer sympathy. Besides, why are you nervous? You want to marry him, don't you?"

"Very much. Just wait until you see him, then you'll know why."

One of Christine's eyes opened a crack. "Intimidating?"

"He's very…male."

"Ah."

"Eloquent comment."

"It covered a lot of ground. What did you expect at—" she stopped to peer at her watch "—one o'clock in the morning? Shakespearean sonnets?"

"It's only eleven o'clock here."

"My body may be here, but my spirit is on Eastern Daylight Time. Good night, or good morning, whichever the case may be."

Laughing, Madelyn let Christine crash in peace. She got ready for bed herself, then lay awake until almost dawn, both mind and body tense.

The dress she had bought for the wedding was old-fashioned in design, almost to her ankles, with eyelet lace around the hem and neckline. She pinned up her hair in a modified Gibson girl, and put on white lace hosiery and white shoes. Even though it was just going to be a civil ceremony, she was determined to look like a bride. Now that the day had actually arrived she felt calm, and her hands were steady as she applied her makeup. Maybe she had finally gotten too tired for nervousness.

"You look gorgeous," said Christine, who looked pretty

good herself in an ice-blue dress that did wonders for her olive complexion. "Cool and old-fashioned and fragile."

Fragile was a word Madelyn had never used to describe herself, and she turned to Christine in disbelief.

"I didn't say you *were* fragile, I said you *looked* fragile, which is just the way you're supposed to look on your wedding day."

"You have some interesting ideas. I know the something borrowed, something blue routine, but I always thought a bride was supposed to look radiant, not fragile."

"Pooh. Radiance is easy. Just a few whisks with a blusher brush. Fragile is much harder to achieve. I'll bet you stayed up nights perfecting it."

Madelyn sighed and looked at herself in the mirror again. "I didn't think it showed."

"Did you sleep any?"

"An hour or so."

"It shows."

When Reese knocked on the door, Madelyn froze. She knew it was Reese, and not Robert. Her heart began that slow, heavy beat as she crossed the room to open the door.

Reese looked down at her, his expression shadowed by his gray dress Stetson. With his boots on he stood over six-four, closer to six-five, and he filled the doorway. Behind her Madelyn heard Christine gasp, but Reese didn't even glance at her; he kept his eyes on Madelyn. "Are you ready?"

"Yes," she whispered. "I'm completely packed."

"I'll put your suitcases in the car."

He was wearing a charcoal pin-striped suit with a spotlessly white shirt. Madelyn recognized both the cut and fabric as being expensive, and knew this must be a suit he'd had before his divorce. He was breathtaking in it. She glanced at Christine, who still wasn't breathing.

"Christine, this is Reese Duncan. Reese, my best friend, Christine Rizzotto."

Reese gave Christine a half smile and touched his fingers to the brim of his hat. "I'm pleased to meet you, ma'am."

She was still ogling him, but she managed a weak, "And you, Mr. Duncan."

He picked up two of Madelyn's suitcases, nodded to Christine, and carried them out. Christine's breath escaped her with a whoosh. "That man is…is potent," she half gasped. "Now I understand."

Madelyn knew how she felt, and fingered the string of pearls around her neck. The nervousness was coming back.

Robert's pale eyes were cool when he was introduced to Reese, which bothered Reese not at all. They were polite to each other. Madelyn hadn't hoped for anything more. Their personalities were both too strong to allow for easy companionship.

It wasn't until everyone had checked out that she realized what he had said and turned to him in bewilderment. "You said you'd put the suitcases in the car. You don't have a car."

"I do now. You'll need something to drive when I have the truck out on the range. It isn't new, but it's dependable."

She was overwhelmed, and her throat tightened. It was a white Ford station wagon, a useful vehicle on a working ranch. She'd had a car while she'd been in college in Virginia, but that had been years ago, and she hadn't had any need for one in the city. With money so tight for Reese, this was a big gesture for him to make. If she had thought about it she would have bought her own car, but she hadn't.

The judge was waiting for them in his chambers. Madelyn opened her purse and got out the ring she'd bought for Reese, slipping it on her finger and closing her hand into a fist to keep it on. The judge saw her do it, and smiled. Christine took her purse from her, and after clearing his throat twice, the judge began.

Her hands were cold. Reese held her left one, folding his hard, warm fingers over hers to share his body heat with her, and when he felt her shaking he put his arm around her waist. He repeated the vows, his dark-textured voice steady. She learned that Gideon was his first name, something she hadn't known before and hadn't gotten around to asking. When it was her turn, she was surprised to hear her own vows repeated just as evenly. He slipped a plain gold band on her finger, and the judge smoothly continued, having seen Madelyn take out Reese's ring. Reese started with surprise when the judge did the ring ceremony again, and Madelyn slid a gold band over his knuckle. It was a plain band, like hers, but he hadn't expected a ring. He hadn't worn one before. The wedding band looked odd on his hand, a thin ring of gold signaling that he was now a married man.

Then he kissed her. It was just a light touch of the lips, lingering only a moment, because he didn't want to start kissing her now. He was under control, and he wanted it to stay that way. It was done. They were married.

Madelyn was quiet as they drove Robert and Christine back to the airport. Their flight was already being called, so they didn't have time to do more than hug her fiercely. Reese shook Robert's hand, and a very male look passed between the two men. Madelyn blinked back tears as both Christine and Robert turned back to wave just before they disappeared from view.

They were alone. Reese kept his arm clamped around her waist as they walked back to the car. "You look like you're about to collapse," he growled.

She felt light-headed. "I may. I've never been married before. It's a nerve-racking business."

He put her in the car. "Have you had anything to eat today?"

She shook her head.

He was cursing when he slid under the steering wheel. "No wonder you're so shaky. We'll stop and get something."

"Not just yet, please. We can stop closer to home. I'm still too nervous right now to eat anything."

In the end, they wound up driving straight to the ranch.

Reese carried her suitcases up to his bedroom. "There's a big walk-in closet," he said, opening the door to show her the enormous closet, as big as a small room. "But don't start unpacking now. You need to eat first."

She gestured to her clothes. "I'll have to change before I start cooking."

"I'll do the cooking," he said sharply.

There wasn't much cooking to it, just soup and sandwiches. Madelyn forced herself to eat half a sandwich and a bowl of soup. It all seemed so unreal. She was married. This was her home now.

Reese went upstairs and changed into his work clothes. Wedding day or no, the chores had to be done. Madelyn cleaned up the kitchen, then went upstairs and began hanging up her new clothes. His bedroom was much larger than the one she had slept in before, with a big private bath that included both bathtub and shower. The bed was king-size. She thought of lying in that bed with him and felt herself get dizzy. It was already late afternoon.

She was in the kitchen again, dressed more appropriately this time in jeans and a short-sleeved sweater, when he came in tired and dirty. "Are you hungry again?" she asked. "I can do something fast while you're showering."

"Just more sandwiches tonight," he said. "I'm not much interested in food right now." He was unbuttoning his shirt as he went up the stairs.

She made the sandwiches and sat at the table with him, drinking a glass of milk while he ate. She had never thought about how much a hard-working man needed to eat, but she could see she would have to cook twice the amount she had imagined.

"I have some paperwork to do," he said when he'd finished and carried his plate to the sink. "It won't take me long."

She understood. After she'd washed the few dishes, she went upstairs and took a bath. She had just left the bathroom, her skin flushed from the damp heat, when he entered the bedroom.

She stopped, biting her lip at the searing look he gave her from her tumbled hair down to her bare toes, as if he could see through her white cotton gown. He sat down on the bed and took off his boots, then stood and tugged his shirt free. His eyes never left her as he unbuttoned the shirt and took it off.

His chest was tanned and muscled and covered with curly black hair. The smooth skin of his shoulders gleamed as he unbuckled his belt and began unfastening his jeans.

Madelyn drew a deep breath and lifted her head. "There's something you need to know."

He paused, his eyes narrowing. She was standing ramrod straight, her pale hair swirling around her shoulders and down her back. That loose, sleeveless gown wasn't anything like the sheer silk confection April had worn, but Madelyn didn't need silk to be seductive. The shadow of her nipples pressing against the white cotton was seduction enough. What could she have to tell him that was keeping her strung as tight as fence wire?

He said softly, "Don't tell me you've decided to wait another couple of nights, because I'm not going for it. Why are you so nervous?"

She gestured at the bed. "I've never done this before."

He couldn't have heard right. Stunned, he released his zipper. "You've never had sex before?"

"No, and to be honest, I'm not really looking forward to it. I want you and I want to be intimate with you, but I don't expect to enjoy the first time." Her gaze was very direct.

An odd kind of anger shook him. "Damn it, Maddie, if you're a virgin why didn't you say so, instead of having that damn physical?"

She looked like a haughty queen. "For one thing, we weren't married before. Until you became my husband this morning it wasn't any of your business. For another, you wouldn't have believed me. You believe me now because there's no reason for me to lie when you'll find out the truth for yourself in a few minutes.'' She spoke with cool dignity, her head high.

"We were planning to get married."

"And it could have been called off."

Reese stared silently at her. Part of him was stunned and elated. No other man had ever had her; she was completely his. He was selfish enough, male enough, primitive enough, to be glad the penetration of her maidenhead would be his right. But part of him was disappointed, because this ruled out the night of hungry lovemaking he'd planned; he would have to be a total bastard to be that insensitive to her. She would be too sore and tender for extended loving.

Maybe this was for the best. He'd take her as gently as possible, but he wouldn't, couldn't, lose his control with her. He wouldn't let himself drown in her; he would simply consummate the marriage as swiftly and easily as he could and preserve the distance between them. He didn't want to give in completely to the fierce desire in him, he just wanted to ease himself and keep her in the slot he'd assigned to her. He wanted her too much; she was a threat to him in every way he'd sworn a woman would never be again. As long as he could keep his passion for her under control she wouldn't be able to breach his defenses, so he would allow himself only a simple mating. He wouldn't linger over her, feast on her, as he wanted to do.

Madelyn forced herself not to tremble when he walked over to her. It had been nothing less than the bald truth when she'd said she wasn't looking forward to this first time. Romantically, she wanted a night of rapture. Realistically, she expected much less. All they had shared was one kiss, and Reese was sexually frustrated, his control stretched to the limit. She was going to open her body to a stranger, and she couldn't help being apprehensive.

He saw the almost imperceptible way she braced herself as he came near, and he slid his hand into her hair. "You don't have to be afraid," he murmured. "I'm not going to jump on you like a bull.'' He tilted her head up so she had to look at him. His eyes were greener than she'd ever seen them before. ''I can make it good for you, baby.''

She swallowed. ''I'd rather you didn't try, I think, not this time. I'm too nervous, and it might not work, and then I'd be disappointed. Just do it and get it over with.''

A faint smile touched his lips. ''That's the last thing a woman should ever say to a man.'' It was also a measure of her fear. ''The slower I am, the better it will be for you.''

''Unless I have a nervous breakdown in the middle of it.''

She wasn't joking. He rubbed his thumb over her bottom lip, feeling the softness of it. It was beginning to make sense. A woman who reached the age of twenty-eight still a virgin had to have a strong sense of reserve about being intimate with a man. The way she'd kissed him had set him on fire, but this final step wasn't one she took easily. She preferred to gradually get used to this powerful new intimacy, rather than throw herself totally into the experience expecting stars and fireworks.

He picked her up and put her on the bed, then turned out all the lights except for one lamp. Madelyn would have preferred total darkness but didn't say anything. She couldn't stop staring when he stripped off his jeans and got into bed with her. She had seen male nudity before: babies and little boys, men in clinical magazines. She knew how the male body functioned. But she had never before seen a fully aroused man, and Reese was definitely that. She lost her hope for nothing worse than discomfort.

He was a big man. He leaned over her, and she felt totally dwarfed by the width of his chest and shoulders, the muscled power of his body. She could barely breathe, her lungs pumping desperately for quick, shallow gasps. By her own will and actions she had brought herself to this, placed herself in bed with a man she didn't know.

He slid his hand under her nightgown and up her thigh, his hard, warm palm shocking on her bare skin. The nightgown was pulled upward by his action, steadily baring more and more of her body until the gown was around her waist and she lay exposed to him. She closed her eyes tightly, wondering if she could go through with this.

He pulled the nightgown completely off. She shivered as she felt him against every inch of her bare body. "It won't be horrible," he murmured as he brushed her lips in a gentle kiss. "I'll make certain of it." Then she felt him close his mouth on her nipple, and the incredible heat and pressure made her moan. She kept her eyes closed as he stroked and fondled her body until gradually the tension eased and she was pliable under his hands.

Her senses couldn't reach fever pitch. She was too tired and nervous. He slid his hand between her legs and she jumped, her body tensing again even though she parted her thighs and allowed him the intimacy. His long fingers gently parted and stroked, probed to find both the degree of her readiness and the strength of her virginity. When his finger slid into her she flinched and turned her head against his shoulder.

"Shh, it's all right," he murmured soothingly. He stretched to reach the bedside table and opened the top drawer to retrieve the tube of lubricant he had put in there earlier. She flinched again at the cool slickness of it as his finger entered her once more and moved gently back and forth.

Her heart was slamming so hard against her ribs that she thought she might be sick. He mounted her, his muscled thighs spreading hers wide, and her eyes flew open in quick panic. She subdued the fear, forcing herself to relax as much as possible. "I'm sorry," she whispered. "I know you wanted it to be better than this."

He rubbed his lips over hers, and she clung to him, her nails digging into his shoulders as she felt his hips lift and his hardness begin to probe her. "I wish it were better for you," he said in a low, taut voice. "But I'm glad you're a virgin, that this first time is mine." Then he started entering her.

She couldn't prevent the tears that scalded her eyes and ran down her temples. He was as gentle as possible, but she didn't accept him easily. The stretching and penetration of her body was a burning pain, and the rhythmic motions of his body only added to it. The only thing that made it bearable for her was, perversely, the very intimacy of having her body so deeply invaded by the man she loved. She was shattered by how primitively natural it was to give herself to him and let him find pleasure within her. Beyond the pain was a growing warmth that promised much more.

Chapter 5

The alarm went off at four-thirty. She felt him stretch beside her and reach out to shut off the insistent buzzing. Then he sat up, yawning, and turned on the lamp. She blinked at the sudden bright light.

Unconcernedly naked, he went into the bathroom. Madelyn used the privacy to bound out of bed and scramble into her clothes. She was just stepping into her jeans when he came out to begin dressing. His eyes lingered on her legs as she pulled the jeans up and snapped them.

Surrounded by the early-morning quiet and darkness, with only the one lamp lighting the room, looking at his naked body seemed as intimate as the night before when he had entered her. Warmth surged in her as she realized that intimacy had many facets. It wasn't just sex, it was being at ease with each other, the daily routine of nakedness and dressing together.

As he dressed, he watched her drag a brush through her hair in several swift strokes, restoring it to casual order. Her slender body bent and swayed with a feminine grace that made it impossible for him to look away. He remembered the way it had felt to be inside her the night before, the tightness and heat, and against his will his loins responded. He couldn't take her now; she would be too tender. She had cried the night before, and every tear had burned him. He could wait.

She put the brush down and began plumping the pillows. He went over to help her make the bed, but when she threw the tumbled covers back to straighten the bottom sheet, she saw the red stains smeared on the linen and went still.

Reese looked at the stains, too, wondering if she had any pleasure to remember as he had, or if they reminded her only of the pain. He bent and tugged the sheet loose and began stripping the bed. "The next time will be better," he said, and she gave him such a solemn look that he wanted to hold her in his arms and rock her. If she had wanted it, he could have brought her to pleasure in other ways, but she had made it plain she wasn't ready for that. He wondered how he would be able to retain his control if she did give him the total freedom of her body. That one, restricted episode of lovemaking hadn't come close to satisfying the surging hunger he felt, and that was the danger of it.

He tossed the sheet to the floor. "I'll do the morning chores while you cook breakfast."

Madelyn nodded. As he went out the door she called, "Wait! Do you like pancakes?"

He paused and looked back. "Yes, and a lot of them."

She remembered from her earlier visit that he liked his coffee strong. She yawned as she went downstairs to the kitchen; then she stood in the middle of the room and looked around. It was difficult to know where to begin when you didn't know where anything was.

Coffee first. At least his coffee maker was an automatic drip. She found the filters and dipped in enough coffee to make the brew twice as strong as she would have made it for herself.

She had to guess at the amount of bacon and sausage to

fry. As hard as he worked, he would need an enormous amount of food to eat, since he would normally burn off four or five thousand calories a day. As the combined smells of brewing coffee and frying breakfast meats began to fill the kitchen, she realized for the first time what an ongoing chore just the cooking would be. She would have to become very familiar with some cookbooks, because her skills tended toward the most basic.

Thank God he had pancake mix. She stirred up the batter, searched out the syrup, then set the table. How long should she give him before she poured the pancakes on the griddle?

A heaping platter of bacon and sausage was browned and on the table before he came back from the barn, carrying a pail of fresh milk. As soon as the door opened, Madelyn poured four circles of batter on the griddle. He put the milk on the countertop and turned on the tap to wash his hands. "How much longer will it be until breakfast is ready?"

"Two minutes. Pancakes don't take long." She flipped them over. "The coffee's ready."

He poured himself a cup and leaned against the cabinet beside her, watching her stand guard over the pancakes. It was only a couple of minutes before she stacked them on a plate and handed it to him. "The butter's on the table. Start on these while I cook some more."

He carried the plate to the table and began eating. He was finished with the first round of pancakes by the time the second was ready. Madelyn poured four more circles on the griddle. This made an even dozen. How many would he eat?

He only ate ten. She got the remaining two from the last batch and slid onto a chair beside him. "What are you doing today?"

"I have to check fences in the west quarter so I can move the herd there for grazing."

"Will you be back for lunch, or should I pack some sandwiches?"

"Sandwiches."

And that, she thought half an hour later when he'd saddled

a horse and ridden out, was that. So much for conversation over breakfast. He hadn't even kissed her this morning. She knew he had a lot of work to do, but a pat on the head wouldn't have taken too much of his time.

Their first full day of marriage didn't appear to be starting out too well.

Then she wondered just what she had expected. She knew how Reese felt, knew he didn't want her to get too close to him. It would take time to break down those barriers. The best thing she could do was learn how to be a rancher's wife. She didn't have time to fret because he hadn't kissed her good morning.

She cleaned the kitchen, which became an entire morning's work. She mopped the floor, scrubbed the oven, cleaned out the big double refrigerator, and rearranged the pantry so she'd know where everything was. She inventoried the pantry and started a list of things she'd need. She did the laundry and remade the bed with fresh linens. She vacuumed and dusted both upstairs and down, cleaned the three bathrooms, sewed buttons on his shirts and repaired a myriad of small rips in his shirts and jeans. All in all, she felt very domestic.

Marriage was work, after all. It wasn't an endless round of parties and romantic picnics by a river.

Marriage was also night after night in bed with the same man, opening her arms and thighs to him, easing his passion within her. He'd said it would be better, and she sensed that it would, that she had just been too tired and tense the night before for it to have been pleasurable no matter what he'd done. The whole process had been a bit shocking. No matter how much she had technically known about sex, nothing had prepared her for the reality of penetration, of actually feeling his hardness inside her. Her heartbeat picked up speed as she thought of the coming night.

She started unpacking some of the boxes she had shipped, reassembling the stereo equipment and putting some of her books out. She was so busy that when she noted the time, it was almost dark. Reese would be coming in soon, and she hadn't even started dinner. She stopped what she was doing and raced to the kitchen. She hadn't even planned what they would have, but at least she knew what was in the pantry.

A quick check of the freezer produced some thick steaks and one pack of pork chops and very little else. She made mental additions to the grocery list as she unwrapped the chops and put them in the microwave to defrost. If he hadn't had a microwave she would have been in big trouble. She was peeling a small mountain of potatoes when the back door opened. She heard him scrape his boots, then sigh tiredly as he took them off.

He came into the kitchen and stopped, looking around at the bare table and stove. "Why isn't dinner ready?" he asked in a very quiet, ominous tone.

"I was busy and didn't notice the time—"

"It's your job to notice the time. I'm dead tired and hungry. I've worked twelve hours straight, the least you could do is take the time to cook."

His words stung, but she didn't pause in what she was doing. "I'm doing it as fast as I can. Go take a shower and relax for a few minutes."

He stomped up the stairs. She bit her lip as she cut up the potatoes and put them in a pan of hot water to stew. If he hadn't looked so exhausted she might have told him a few things, but he'd been slumping with weariness and filthy from head to foot. His day hadn't been an easy one.

She opened a big can of green beans and dumped it into a pan, then added seasonings. The chops were already baking. Bread. She needed bread. There were no canned biscuits in the refrigerator. She couldn't dredge the recipe for biscuits from her memory, no matter how many times she'd watched Grandma Lily make them. She found the cookbooks and began checking the indexes for biscuits.

Once she had the list of ingredients before her it all began to come back. She mixed the dough, then kneaded it and rolled it out as she'd done when she was a little girl. She couldn't find a biscuit cutter, so she used a water glass, pressing it down into the dough and coming up with a perfect circle. A few minutes later, a dozen biscuits were popped into the oven.

Dessert. She'd seen some small, individually wrapped devil's food cakes. She got those out, and a big can of peaches. It would have to do, because she didn't have time to bake. She opened the can of peaches and poured them into a bowl.

By the time she had the table set, Reese had come back downstairs, considerably cleaner but unimproved in mood. He looked pointedly at the empty table and stalked into the living room.

She checked the potatoes; they were tender. She mixed up a small amount of flour and milk and poured it into the potatoes; it instantly began thickening. She let them stew while she checked the chops and green beans.

The biscuits were golden brown, and had risen nicely. Now if only they were edible... Since she'd followed a recipe, they shouldn't be too bad, she hoped. She stacked them on a plate and crossed her fingers for luck.

The chops were done, finally. "Reese! Dinner's ready."

"It's about time."

She hurried to put the food on the table, realizing at the last minute that she had made neither coffee nor tea. Quickly she got two glasses from the cabinet and poured milk. She knew that he liked milk, so perhaps he sometimes drank it at dinner.

The chops weren't the tenderest she'd ever cooked, and the biscuits were a bit heavy, but he ate steadily, without comment. Heavy or not, the dozen biscuits disappeared in short order, and she ate only one. As his third helping of stewed potatoes was disappearing, she got up. "Do you want any dessert?"

His head came up. "Dessert?"

She couldn't help smiling. You could tell the man had lived alone for seven years. "It isn't much, because I didn't get around to baking." She put the small cakes in a bowl and dipped peaches and juice over them. Reese gave them a quizzical look as she set the bowl in front of him.

"Just try it," she said. "I know it's junk food, but it tastes good."

He did, and cleaned the bowl. Some of the fatigue was fading from his face. "The stereo in the living room looks like a good one."

"I've had it for several years. I hope it survived the shipping."

He'd sold his stereo system years ago, deciding that he needed the money more than he needed the music, and he'd never let himself think too much about it. When you were fighting for survival, you quickly learned how to get your priorities in order. But he'd missed music and was looking forward to playing some of his old classics again.

The house was full of signs of what she'd been doing all day, and he felt guilty about yelling at her because dinner hadn't been ready. The floors were cleaner than they'd been in years, and the dust was gone from every surface. The house smelled of household cleaner and furniture polish, and the bathroom had sparkled with cleanliness. The house was ten rooms and over four thousand square feet; his fancy city woman knew how to work.

He helped her clean the table and load the dishwasher. "What's that?" he asked, pointing to her list.

"The shopping list. The pantry has a limited selection."

He shrugged. "I was usually so tired I just ate sandwiches."

"How far is the nearest market? And don't tell me I'm going to have to go to Billings."

"There's a general store about twenty miles from here. It isn't a supermarket, but you can get the basics there. I'll take you there day after tomorrow. I can't do it tomorrow because I've got more fencing to repair before I can move the herd."

"Just give me directions. I don't think the food situation will wait until the day after tomorrow."

"I don't want you out wandering around," he said flatly.

"I won't be wandering. Just give me the directions."

"I'd rather you wait. I don't know how reliable the car is yet."

"Then I can take the truck."

"I said I'll take you day after tomorrow, and that's that."

Fuming, she went upstairs and took a shower. Why on earth was he so intractable? The way he'd acted, she might as well have said she was going to find a bar and spend the day in it. But then, that might have been what his first wife had done. Even if it were true, Madelyn was determined that she wasn't going to spend her life paying for April's sins.

She finished unpacking her clothes, hanging most of her New York clothes in the closet in another bedroom, since she wouldn't have much use for them now. It still made her feel strange to see her clothes in the same closet with a man's; she'd shared room, closet and clothes in college, but that was different. This was serious. This was a lifetime.

One thing about getting up at four-thirty: she was already sleepy, and it was only eight. Of course, she was still feeling the effects of not getting enough sleep for the past two weeks, as well as a very active day, but she could barely hold her eyes open.

She heard Reese come upstairs and go into their bedroom; then he called, "Maddie?" in a rougher voice than usual.

"In here," she called.

He appeared in the doorway, and his eyes sharpened as he took in the clothes piled on the bed. "What're you doing?" There was an oddly tense set to his shoulders.

"I'm hanging the clothes I won't use in here, so they won't clutter up our closet."

Maybe it was only her imagination, but he appeared to relax. "Are you ready to go to bed?"

"Yes, I can finish this tomorrow."

He stood aside to let her get past him, then turned out the light and followed her down the hall. Madelyn was barefoot and in another thin gown much like the one she'd worn the night before, and she got that dwarfed, suffocated feeling again, sensing him so close behind her. The top of her head would just reach his chin, and he had to weigh at least two hundred pounds, all of it muscle. It would be easy to let herself be intimidated by him, especially when she thought of lying beneath him on that big bed. She would be going to bed with him like this for the rest of her life. Maybe he had doubts about the longevity of their marriage, but she didn't.

It was easier this time. She lay in his muscular arms and felt the warmth grow under his stroking hands. But now that she was less nervous she sensed something wrong, as if he were keeping part of himself separate from their lovemaking. He touched her, but only under strict control, as if he were allowing himself only so much enjoyment and not a bit more. She didn't want those measured touches, she wanted his passion. She knew it was there, she sensed it, but he wasn't giving it to her.

It still hurt when he entered her, though not as much as before. He was gentle, but he wasn't loving. This was the way he would have treated either of those other two women he'd been willing to marry, she thought dimly, as a body he'd been given the use of, not as a warm, loving woman who needed more. This was only sex, not making love. He made her feel like a faceless stranger.

This was war. As she went to sleep afterward, she was planning her campaign.

"I want to go with you today," she said the next morning over breakfast.

He didn't look up from his eggs and biscuits. "You're not up to it."

"How do you know?" she retorted.

He looked annoyed. "Because a lot of *men* aren't up to it."

"You're repairing fencing today, right? I can help you with the wire and at least keep you company."

That was exactly what Reese didn't want. If he spent a lot of time in her company he'd end up making love to her, and that was something he wanted to limit. If he could hold himself to once a night, he'd be able to keep everything under control.

"It'll only take a couple of hours to finish repairing the fence, then I'll bring the truck home and go back out on horseback to move the herd."

"I told you, I can ride."

He shook his head impatiently. "How long has it been since you've been on a horse? What kind of riding did you do, tame trail riding on a rented hack? This is open country, and my horses are trained to work cattle."

"Granted, it's been almost a year since I've been on a horse, but I know all about liniment. I have to get used to it sometime."

"You'd just be in the way. Stay here and see if you can have dinner done on time tonight."

She narrowed her eyes and put her hands on her hips. "Reese Duncan, I'm going with you and that's final."

He got up from the table. "You'd better learn that this is my ranch, and what I say goes. That includes you. A few words by a judge doesn't give you any say-so in my work. I do the ranch work, you take care of the house. I want fried chicken for dinner, so you can get started on that."

"There isn't any chicken in the freezer," she retorted. "Since you don't want me to go shopping, I guess you'll have to change your request."

He pointed out to the yard. "There are plenty of chickens out there, city slicker. Meat doesn't always come shrink-wrapped."

Madelyn's temper was usually as languorous as her walk, but she'd had enough. "You want me to catch a chicken?" she asked, tight-lipped. "You don't think I can do it, do you? That's why you said it. You want to show me how much I don't know about ranch life. You'll have your damn chicken for dinner, if I have to ram it down your throat feathers and all!''

She turned and stormed up the stairs. Reese stood there, a little taken aback. He hadn't known Madelyn could move that fast.

She was back downstairs before he could get the truck loaded and leave. He heard the back door slam and turned. His eyes widened. She had strapped protective pads on her knees and elbows, with the kneepads over her jeans. She'd put on athletic shoes. She still looked furious, and she didn't even glance at him. Reese hooked his thumbs in his belt loops and leaned against the truck to watch.

She picked out a hen and eased up to it, scattering a few handfuls of feed to lure the birds. Reese lifted his eyebrows, impressed. But she made her move just a little too soon; the hen squawked and ran for her life with Madelyn in pursuit.

She dove for the bird, sliding along the ground on her belly and just missing the frantic bird. Reese winced and straightened away from the truck, horrified at the thought of what the dirt and rocks were doing to her soft skin, but she jumped up and took off after the hen. The bird ran in erratic circles around the yard, then darted under the truck. Madelyn swerved to head it off, and another headlong tackle fell an inch short.

''Look, just forget about the chick—'' he began, but she was already gone.

The bird managed to take flight enough to land in the lower branches of a tree, but it was still over Madelyn's head. She narrowed her eyes and bent to pick a few rocks up from the ground. She wound up and let fly. The rock went over the chicken's head. The hen pulled her head down, her bright little eyes glittering. The next rock hit the limb next to her and she squawked, shifting position. The third rock hit her on the leg, and she took flight again.

This time Madelyn judged her dive perfectly. She slid along the ground in a flurry of dust and pebbles, and her hand closed over one of the hen's legs. The bird immediately went wild, flapping her wings and trying to peck the imprisoning hand that held her. They grappled in the dust for a minute, but then Madelyn stood up with the hen upside down and firmly held by both feet, its wings spread. Her hands were dotted with blood where the furious hen had pecked her, breaking the skin. "Faster than a speeding pullet," she said with grim triumph.

Reese could only stare at her in silence as she stalked up to him. Her hair was a mess, tangled and hanging in her eyes. Her face was caked with dust, her shirt was filthy and torn, and her jeans were a mess. One kneepad had come loose and was drooping down her shin. The look in those gray eyes, however, kept him from laughing. He didn't dare even smile.

The chicken hit him in the chest, and he grabbed for it, just preventing the bird from making a break for freedom.

"There's your damn chicken," she said between her teeth. "I hope you're very happy together." She slammed back into the house.

Reese looked down at the bird and remembered the blood on Madelyn's hands. He wrung the hen's neck with one quick, competent twist. He'd never felt less like laughing.

He carried the dead bird inside and dropped it on the floor. Madelyn was standing at the sink, carefully soaping her hands. "Let me see," he said, coming up behind her and reaching around to take her hands in his, effectively pinning her in place. The hen had drawn blood in several places, painful little puncture wounds that were blue around the edges. He'd had a few of them himself and knew how easily they could become infected.

He reached for a towel to wrap around her hands. "Come upstairs to the bathroom and I'll put disinfectant on them."

She didn't move. "It's my hands, not my back. I can reach them just fine, thank you. I'll do it myself."

His muscled arms were iron bands around her; his hard hands held her easily. Her front was pressed against the sink, and his big body was against her back, hemming her in, holding her. She felt utterly surrounded by him and had the sudden violent thought that she should never have married someone who was almost a foot taller than she was. She was at a woeful disadvantage here.

He bent, hooked his right arm under her kness and lifted her with insulting ease. Madelyn grabbed for his shoulders to keep her balance. "The hen pecked my hands, not my feet," she said caustically.

He slanted a warning look at her as he started up the stairs. "Men who use force against women are lower than slugs."

His arms tightened, but he kept a tight rein on his temper. He carried her into the bathroom and put her on her feet. As he opened the medicine cabinet she headed out the door, and he grabbed her with one hand, hauling her back. She tugged violently, trying to free her arm. "I said I'd do it myself!" she said, furious with him.

He put the lid down on the toilet, sat down and pulled her onto his lap. "Be still and let me clean your hands. If you still want to fight after I'm finished, then I'll be glad to oblige you."

Fuming, Madelyn sat on his lap while he dabbed the small wounds with an antiseptic that stung sharply. Then he smoothed antibiotic cream on them and put Band-Aids over the two worst breaks. His arms were still around her; he was holding her as a parent would a child, to soothe it and tend its hurts. She didn't like the comparison, even if it was her own. She shifted restlessly, feeling his hard thighs under her bottom.

His face was very close to hers. She could see all the different colored specks in his eyes, green and blue dominating, but shot through with black and white and a few glittering flecks of gold. Though he had shaved the night before, his beard had already grown enough to roughen his cheeks and chin. The brackets on each side of his mouth framed the beautiful cut of his lips, and suddenly she remembered the way he had closed those lips over her nipple, sucking her tender flesh into his mouth. She quivered, and the rigidity went out of her body.

Reese closed the first-aid box and set it aside, then let his arm rest loosely across her thighs as he gave her a measuring look. "Your face is dirty."

"So let me up and I'll wash it."

He didn't. He washed it himself, slowly drawing a wet washcloth over her features, the fabric almost caressing her skin. He wiped her mouth with a touch so light she could barely feel it and watched the cloth tug slightly at her soft, enticing lower lip. Madelyn's head tilted back, and her eyelids drooped. He drew the cloth down her neck, wiped it across her exposed collarbone, then dipped his hand down inside the loose neck of her top.

She caught her breath at the damp coolness on her breasts. He drew the cloth back and forth, slowly rasping it across her nipples and bringing them to wet attention. Her breasts began to throb, and her back arched involuntarily, offering them for more. She could feel a hard ridge growing, pressing against her hip, and her blood moved heavily through her veins.

He tossed the washcloth into the basin and took his hat off, dropping it onto the floor. The arm behind her back tightened and drew her in to him as he bent his head, and his mouth closed over hers.

It was the same way he'd kissed her in the airport, the way he hadn't kissed her since. His mouth was hard and hot, urgent in his demands. His tongue pushed into her mouth, and she met it with her own, welcoming, enticing, wanting more.

She gave way beneath his onslaught, her head falling back against his shoulder. He pursued the advantage, taking her mouth again, putting his hand beneath her shirt and closing it over her breast. Gently he kneaded the firm mound, rubbing his rough palm over the nipple until she whimpered into his mouth from the exquisite pain of it. She turned toward him, lifting her arms around his neck. Excitement pounded in the pit of her stomach, tightening every muscle in her body and starting an aching tension between her legs.

With a rough sound of passion he bent her back over his arm and shoved her top up, exposing her breasts. His warm breath feathered across them as he bent to her; then he extended the tip of his tongue and circled one pink nipple, making it constrict into a tightly puckered nub and turn reddish. He shifted her body, bringing her other breast closer to his mouth, and gave that nipple identical treatment, watching with pleasure as it, too, tightened.

Madelyn clutched at him. "Reese," she begged in a low, shaking voice. She needed him.

This was the hot magic she had sensed about him from the beginning, the blatant sensuality. This was the warm promise she had felt lying beneath him at night, and she wanted more.

He drew her nipple into his mouth with a strong, sucking pressure, and she arched again, her thighs shifting. She felt like a dessert offered up to him, lying across his lap with her body lifted to his mouth, glorying in the way his lips and teeth and tongue worked at her breast.

"Reese," she said again. It was little more than a moan, heavy with desire. Everything that was male in him responded to that female cry of need, urging him to surge deep within her and ease the empty ache that made her twist in his arms and cry out for him. His loins were throbbing, his body radiating heat. If she needed to be filled, he needed to fill her. The two restrained matings he'd had with her hadn't been enough, would never satisfy the lust that intensified every time he looked at her.

But if he ever let himself go with her, he'd never be able to get that control back. April had taught him a bitter lesson, one that he relearned every day when he worked on his diminished acres, or saw the paint peeling on his house. Madelyn might never turn on him, but he couldn't take the chance and let his guard down.

With an effort that brought sweat to his brow, he lifted

his mouth from her maddeningly sweet flesh and shifted her to her feet. She swayed, her eyes dazed, her top twisted up under her arms and exposing those firm, round breasts. She didn't understand and reached for him, offering a drugging sensuality that he wouldn't let himself take.

He caught her wrists and held her arms to her sides while he stood up, an action that brought their bodies together. He heard her moan softly again, and she let her head fall forward against his chest, where she rubbed her cheek back and forth in a subtle caress that made him curse his shirt for covering his bare skin.

If he didn't get out of here now, he wouldn't go at all.

"I have work to do." His voice was hoarse with strain. She didn't move. She was melting against him, her slim hips starting a drumbeat roll that rocked into his loins and made him feel as if his pants would split under the pressure.

"Madelyn, stop it. I have to go."

"Yes," she whispered, rising on tiptoe to brush her lips against his throat.

His hands closed tightly on her hips, for one convulsive second pulling her into his pelvis as if he would grind himself into her; then he pushed her away. He picked up his hat and strode from the bathroom before she could recover and reach for him again, because he damn sure wouldn't have the strength to stop this time.

Madelyn stared after him, confused by his sudden departure and aching from the loss of contact. She swayed; then realization burst within her, and she gave a hoarse cry of mingled rage and pain, putting her hand out to catch the basin so she wouldn't fall to her knees.

Damn him, damn him, damn him! He'd brought her to fever pitch, then left her empty and aching. She knew he'd wanted her; she had felt his hardness, felt the tension in his corded muscles. He could have carried her to the bed or even had her right there in the bathroom, and she would have gloried in it, but instead he'd pushed her away.

He'd been too close to losing control. Like a flash she

knew what had happened, knew that at the last minute he'd had to prove to himself that he could still walk away from her, that he didn't want her so much that he couldn't master it. The sexuality of his nature was so strong that it kept burning through those walls he'd built around himself, but he was still fighting it, and so far he'd won.

Slowly she went downstairs, holding the banister because her knees felt like overcooked noodles. If she were to have any chance with him at all, she would have to find some way to shatter that iron control, but she didn't know if her nerves or self-esteem would hold out.

He was already gone, the truck nowhere in sight. She looked around blankly, unable to think what she should do, and her eyes lit on the dead chicken lying on the floor.

"I'll get back at you for this," she said with grim promise in her voice, and began the loathsome task of getting that blasted hen ready to cook.

Chapter 6

When Reese came in that evening, Madelyn didn't look up from the bowl of potatoes she was mashing. The force with which she wielded the potato masher went far beyond what was required and carried a hint of savagery. One look at her averted face told Reese she was probably imagining using that potato masher on him. He looked thoughtful. He'd expected her to be cool, maybe even a little hurt, but he hadn't expected her temper to still be at boiling point; it took a lot of energy to sustain a rage that many hours. Evidently it took her as long to cool off as it did to lose her temper to begin with.

He said, "It'll take me about fifteen minutes to get cleaned up."

She still didn't look up. "Dinner will be ready in ten."

From that he deduced that she wasn't going to wait for him. The thoughtful look deepened as he went upstairs.

He took one of the fastest showers of his life and thought about not shaving, but he didn't like the idea of scraping her soft skin with his beard, so he ran the risk of cutting his own throat due to the speed with which he dragged the razor across his skin. He was barefoot and still buttoning his shirt when he went back down the stairs.

She was just placing the glasses of iced tea on the table, and they sat down together. The platter of fried chicken was sitting right in front of his plate. He'd either have to eat the damn bird or wear it, he decided.

He piled his plate with chicken, mashed potatoes, biscuits and gravy, all the while eying the platter curiously. He continued to examine the contents while he took his first bite and controlled a grunt of pleasure. The chicken was tender, the crust crisp and spicy. Madelyn made a better cook than he'd expected. But the remaining pieces of chicken looked…strange.

"What piece is that?" he asked, pointing at a strangely configured section of chicken.

"I have no idea," she replied without looking at him. "I've never cleaned and butchered my food before."

He bit the inside of his cheek to keep from grinning. If he made the mistake of laughing she would probably dump the bowl of gravy over his head.

The meal was strained and mostly silent. If he made a comment, she replied, but other than that she made no effort to hold a conversation. She ate a small portion of each item, though minuscule was perhaps a better word. As soon as she was finished she carried her plate to the sink and brought back a clean saucer, as well as a cherry cobbler that was still bubbling.

Very little in life had ever interfered with Reese's appetite, and tonight was no exception. He worked too hard to pick at his food. By the time Madelyn had finished dabbling with a small helping of cobbler he had demolished most of the chicken, all the potatoes and gravy, and only two biscuits were left. He was feeling almost contented as Madelyn placed an enormous portion of cobbler onto a clean plate for him. A quick look at her icy face, however, told him that food hadn't worked the same miracle on her.

"How did you learn to cook like this?"

"There are cookbooks in the cabinet. I can read."

So much for that conversational gambit.

She went upstairs immediately after the kitchen was clean. Reese went into his office and took a stab at the paperwork that never ended, but his mind wasn't on it, and by eight o'clock he was glancing at his watch, wondering if Madelyn was ready to go to bed. He'd already heard the shower running, and the image of her standing nude under the steaming water had had him shifting restlessly in his chair. There were times when a man's sexual organs could make him damned uncomfortable, and this was one of them. He'd been hard most of the day, cursing himself for not having made love to her that morning, even though it would have been a huge mistake.

He tossed the pen onto his desk and closed the books, getting to his feet with restrained violence. Damn it, he needed her, and he couldn't wait any longer.

He turned out the lights as he went upstairs, his tread heavy and deliberate. His mind was on that searing, gut-wrenching moment when he first entered her, feeling the small resistance of her tight flesh, the giving, the enveloping, then the wet, clasping heat and his senses exploding. It was all he could do not to keep after her time and again, to try to remember that she was very new to lovemaking and still tender, to stay in control.

The bedroom door was open. He walked in and found her sitting on the bed painting her toenails, her long legs bare and curled in one of those positions that only females seemed able to achieve and males went crazy looking at. His whole body tightened, and he became fully, painfully erect. She was wearing a dark pink satin chemise that ended at the tops of her thighs and revealed matching petal pants. The satin molded to her breasts, revealing their round shape and soft nipples. Her blond hair was pulled to one side, tumbling over her shoulder, and her skin was still delicately flushed from her shower. Her expression was solemn and intent as she concentrated on the strokes of the tiny brush that turned her toenails the same deep pink as the chemise.

"Let's go to bed." His voice was guttural. He was already peeling off his shirt.

She hadn't even glanced at him. "I can't. My toenails are wet."

He didn't much care. He'd keep her legs raised long enough that the polish would be dry when he'd finished.

She capped the polish bottle and set it aside, then bent bonelessly over to blow on her toes. Reese unsnapped and unzipped his jeans. "Come to bed anyway."

She gave him an impatient look and got to her feet. "You go on. I'll go downstairs and read awhile."

He stretched his arm out in front of her when she would have passed, barring her way. His hand closed on her upper arm. "Forget reading," he muttered, pulling her toward him.

Madelyn wrenched away, staring at him in incredulous anger. "I don't believe this! You actually think I could want to make love *now*?"

His eyebrows lowered, and he hooked his thumbs in his belt loops. "Why not?" he asked very softly.

"For one very good reason. I'm angry! What you did stinks, and I'm not even close to forgiving you for it." Just the way he was standing there with his thumbs in his belt loops, his jeans open and his attitude one of incredible male arrogance, made her so angry she almost couldn't talk.

"The best way to make up is in bed."

"That's what men think," she said scornfully. "Let me tell you, no woman wants to make love with a man while she's still thinking how funny it would have been if he'd choked on a chicken bone!" She whirled and stalked barefoot from the bedroom.

Reese began swearing. Frustration boiled up in him, and for a moment he started after her. He reached the door and stopped, then slammed his fist into the door frame. Damn it all to hell!

* * *

The atmosphere was decidedly chilly between them the next morning when he drove her to the small town of Crook to buy groceries. Though she was no longer so furious, she was no less determined. He couldn't reject her one time and the next expect her to accommodate him without question. If that was his idea of what a marriage should be, they were both in for some rocky times.

To call Crook a town was to flatter it. There were a few residences sprawled out in a haphazard manner, a service station, a feed store, the general store, and a small café with the expected assortment of pickup trucks parked in front of it. Madelyn wondered just what sort of dangerous behavior Reese had expected her to get up to in Crook. Maybe he thought she'd run wild and drive on the sidewalks, which looked as if someone had already done so. They were actually wood, and were the only sidewalks she'd ever seen with skidmarks on them.

"Let's get a cup of coffee," Reese suggested as they got out of the station wagon, and Madelyn agreed. It would be nice to have a cup of coffee she didn't have to water down before she could drink it.

The café had five swivel stools, covered in split black imitation leather, in front of the counter. Three round tables were each surrounded by four chairs, and along the left side were three booths. Four of the stools were occupied, evidently by the owners of the four trucks outside. The men had different features but were identical in weathered skin, battered hats, and worn jeans and boots. Reese nodded to all of them, and they nodded back, then returned their attention to their coffee and pie.

He guided her to a booth, and they slid onto the plastic seats. The waitress behind the counter gave them a sour look. "You want something to eat, or just coffee?"

"Coffee," Reese said.

She came out from behind the counter and plunked two coffee cups down in front of them. Then she went back for the coffeepot and returned to pour the coffee, all without changing her expression, which bordered on a glare. "Coffee's fifty cents a cup," she said as if it were their fault, then marched back to her post behind the counter.

Madelyn sighed as she saw how black the coffee was. A tentative sip told her that this, too, was strong enough to strip paint.

One of the men eased down from the stool and went over to the corner jukebox. The waitress looked up. "I'll unplug that thing if you play one of them caterwauling love songs," she said, her voice just as sour as her looks.

"You'll owe me a quarter if you do."

"And don't play none of them god-awful rock songs, neither. I don't like music where the singers sound like they're being gelded."

Madelyn's eyes rounded, and she choked a little on the coffee. Fascinated, she stared at the waitress.

The cowboy was grumbling, "I don't know of nothing you *do* like, Floris, so just shut your ears and don't listen."

"I'll tell you what I like," she snapped. "I like peace and quiet."

"Then find some library to work in." He jammed his quarter into the slot and defiantly punched buttons.

A rollicking country song filled the café. Floris began clattering cups and saucers and silverware. Madelyn wondered what the breakage bill was every month if Floris began abusing the crockery every time someone played the jukebox. The cowboy glared, and Floris banged louder. He stomped back to the jukebox and fed it another quarter, but in the manner of vending machines everywhere, it took the coin but refused his selection. He scowled and beat it with his fist. The arm scratched across the record with a hair raising screech, then, having reached the end of the groove, lifted automatically as the record was returned to its slot, and silence reigned.

With a triumphant look Floris sailed through the swinging door into the kitchen.

"The waitress from hell," Madelyn breathed in awe, watching the door swing gently back and forth.

Reese choked and had to spit his coffee back into the cup. She didn't want to look at him, but the urge was irresistible. Without turning her head she glanced toward him and found him watching her, his face unnaturally stiff. She looked at him, and he looked at her, and they began snickering. He tried to control it and quickly gulped his coffee, but Madelyn was still giggling as he grabbed for his wallet. He threw a dollar and change on the table, grabbed her hand and pulled her toward the entrance. The door had barely closed behind them when he released her and bent forward, bracing his hands on his knees as a great roar of laughter burst from him. Madelyn collapsed over his back, seeing again the helpless, stunned look on the cowboy's face and the gleeful look on Floris's, and went off into helpless gales.

After her bad temper the laughter felt great. It was even more wonderful to hear Reese laughing, and a pang struck her as she realized that this was the first time she had heard him laugh. He rarely even smiled, but now he was hugging his ribs and wiping tears from his eyes, and still the deep sounds were booming up from his chest. She had an overwhelming urge to cry, but conquered it.

A lot of the tension between them dissolved as they bought groceries. Reese had been right; the general store did carry mostly basics, but Madelyn had carefully studied the cookbooks and knew what she could do with what was available. Thank God Reese wasn't a fussy eater.

A cheerful woman with a truly awesome bosom checked them out while carrying on a casual conversation with Reese. She eyed Madelyn questioningly, then looked down at the ring on her left hand. Reese saw the look and braced himself for the curiosity he knew would come. "Glenna, this is my wife, Madelyn."

Glenna looked startled, and her glance flew down to his own left hand. The gold ring on his tanned finger clearly astounded her. Reese carried on with the introduction, hop-

ing to bridge her reaction. "Maddie, this is Glenna Kinnaird.
We went to school together."

Recovering herself, Glenna beamed and held out her hand.
"I can't believe it! Congratulations! You got married, after
all this time. Why, just wait until I tell Boomer. We didn't
really go to school together," she said chattily to Madelyn.
"I'm ten years older than he is, so I graduated when he was
in third grade, but I've known him all his life. How on earth
did you catch him? I'd have sworn he'd never marry again—
Uh, that is…" Her voice trailed off uneasily as she glanced
at Reese.

Madelyn smiled. "It's okay. I know about April. As for
how I caught him…well, I didn't. He caught me."

Glenna's face regained its cheerful expression. "Took one
look and forgot about being a bachelor, huh?"

"Something like that," Reese said. He'd taken one look
and gotten hard, but the end result had been the same: the
leggy blonde with the lazy, seductive stroll was now his
wife.

As they left the store with Glenna waving at them, he
realized something that had him frowning thoughtfully as
they loaded the groceries into the station wagon: Glenna had
disliked April on sight, but had been perfectly comfortable
and friendly with Madelyn. Even though, in an indescribable
way, Madelyn dressed more fashionably than April, she had
an easy, friendly manner to which Glenna had responded.
Madelyn didn't dress as expensively as April, but what she
wore had a certain style to it, as if she had practiced for
hours to get her collar to stand up just so, or her sleeves to
roll up that precise amount. She would always draw eyes,
but she didn't inspire the sort of hostility from her own sex
that April had.

Style. He looked at his wife and thought of how she'd
looked the day before, with one kneepad slipping down her
shin and her hair hanging in her face. He hadn't dared laugh
then, but in retrospect he couldn't help himself and began to

chuckle. Even when chasing chickens, Madelyn did it with style.

Madelyn had been outside all morning, scraping the peeling paint off the house. Having brought the interior up to snuff, she was working on the exterior, and it was such a beautiful morning that she'd been enjoying herself despite the hard work. It was getting close to noon, though, and the temperature was rising uncomfortably. Sweat was making her clothes stick to her. Deciding that she'd done enough for the day, she climbed down from the ladder and went inside to take a shower.

When she came back downstairs, the first thing she saw was the bag containing Reese's lunch sitting on the cabinet. He was out repairing fencing again and wouldn't be back until dinnertime, but he'd forgotten his lunch and thermos of tea.

She checked the clock. He had to be starving by now. Quickly she emptied the thermos and filled it with fresh ice cubes and tea, then got the keys to the station wagon and hurried outside with his lunch. By chance she knew where he was working, because in the past two weeks he'd shown her around the ranch a little, and he'd mentioned this morning where he'd be. It was actually a safety precaution for someone to know where he was, and she frowned as she thought of the years he'd worked alone, with no one at the house to know where he'd gone or how long he'd been out. If he'd gotten hurt, he could have lain there and died without anyone ever knowing he'd been hurt until it was too late.

Her marriage wasn't even three weeks old yet, and already she could barely remember her previous life. She'd never before been as busy as she was now, though she had to admit she would gladly forego the housework to ride around the ranch with Reese, but he still refused to hear of it. She was certain that if anyone looked up the word ''stubborn'' in the dictionary, it would have Reese Duncan's picture beside it.

He'd decided where she would fit in his life, and he wouldn't let her get outside that boundary.

She could almost feel the hunger in him at night when he made love to her, but he never let himself go, never released the passion she sensed, and as a result she couldn't let herself go, either. Sex was no longer uncomfortable, and she desperately wanted more from their lovemaking, but the intensity she needed wasn't there. He held back, diminishing the pleasure they both could have had and thereby preserving that damned inner wall of his. She didn't know how much longer she would be able to bear it, how much longer it would be before she began making excuses and turn away from him in the night. The situation was dire, she knew, when she was actually looking forward to having her period!

She drove slowly, preoccupied with her thoughts and with watching for any sign of his truck out on the range somewhere. Like all ranchers, Reese paid no attention to roads; he simply drove across the land. The truck was a tool to him, not a prized and pampered status symbol. If it had been a Rolls he would have treated it the same, because it had no value beyond that of its worth as a working vehicle. So she knew the area where he was working, but that area covered a lot of ground and he could be anywhere in it. She didn't see him anywhere, but fresh tire tracks scored the ground, and she simply followed them, carefully steering around the rougher ground that Reese had driven over without concern, because the station wagon was much lower than the truck and couldn't negotiate such terrain.

It took her almost forty-five minutes to find him. He'd parked the truck under a tree, partially shielding it from view. It was the chance glint off a strand of wire as he pulled it tight that caught her eye, and she eased the car across the range to him.

He glanced up briefly as she approached but didn't pause in his work. Her throat tightened. He'd removed his shirt and hung it over the side of the truck bed, and his muscled torso glistened with sweat. She'd known he was strong, realized from the first that his body made her mouth go dry with almost painful appreciation, but this was the first time she had seen those powerful muscles bunching and flexing like that. He moved with a fluid grace that made his strength that much more noticeable. His biceps and triceps bulged as he hammered a staple into the post, securing the new strand of wire.

When he was finished he tossed the hammer onto the sack of staples and pulled his hat off, wiping the sweat from his face with his forearm. "What are you doing out here?" He didn't sound at all pleased to see her.

Madelyn got out of the car, carrying the thermos and sandwiches with her. "You forgot your lunch."

He walked toward her and took the thermos, twisting the top off and tilting it up to drink directly from the spout. His strong throat worked as he swallowed the cold liquid. He'd been working all morning without anything to drink, she realized. A drop of tea escaped his lips and ran down his throat. She watched it in painful fascination as it slid down his hot skin, and she envied it the path it was taking. So often she had wanted to trail kisses down his body but had held back because he didn't want that sort of intimacy. All he wanted was the release of sex, not the love expressed in slow, sensual feasting.

He set the thermos down on the lowered tailgate and reached for his shirt, using it to wipe the sweat from his face, shoulders, arms and chest. Tossing the garment back across the side, he eased one hip onto the tailgate and took the sandwiches from her. "The station wagon isn't meant for driving across the range," he said as he unwrapped a sandwich.

Madelyn's lips tightened. "I didn't want you to go all day without anything to eat or drink, and I was careful."

"How did you find me?"

"I followed your tire tracks."

He grunted and applied himself to the sandwich. It and another disappeared without another word being said between them. Madelyn lifted her hair off her neck, letting a slight breeze cool her heated skin. She usually braided her hair away from her face during the day, but she'd taken it down when she showered and hadn't put it back up again before she'd started searching for Reese.

Reese watched her graceful gesture, and his heartbeat speeded up. She was wearing a gathered white cotton skirt with one of her favorite white camisole tops, and a pair of sandals that were little more than thin soles with a few delicate straps. She looked cool and fragrant, while he was hot and sweaty, a result of the difference in the way they'd spent the day. Now that the house was clean and polished it probably didn't take much to keep it that way.

The breeze caught a strand of hair and blew it across her face. She shook it back, tilting her head to make all of her hair swing down her back.

Every movement she made was naturally seductive. He felt the response in his groin and in his veins, as his blood heated and began racing. It was becoming more and more difficult to keep his hands off her during the day, to keep from turning to her time and again during the night. He grew angry at himself for wanting her so much, and at her for doing everything she could to make it worse.

"Why did you really come out here?" he asked harshly. "I would've finished with this and gotten back to the house in another hour or so. I've gone without eating or drinking all day before, and I'll do it again. So why did you really come parading out here?"

Madelyn's eyes narrowed as she slowly turned her head to look at him. She didn't say anything, and the combined anger and sexual frustration built up even more pressure in him.

"Do you want me to stop work and play with you? Can't you go a whole day without a man's attention? Maybe you thought we'd have a sexy little picnic out here and you'd get your skirt tossed."

She turned to fully face him, her eyes locked with his.

Her words were slow and precise. "Why would I care? From what I can tell, sex isn't worth a walk across the yard, let alone chasing it down on the range. I've got better things to do with my time."

He took the verbal jab square on the ego, and suddenly it was too much. It was all too much, the wanting and not having, the needing and not taking. A red mist swam before his eyes, and his whole body seemed to expand as he blindly reached for her, catching her by the arm and swinging her up against him.

Madelyn was unprepared for the blurring speed with which he moved. She didn't even have time to take a step back. Suddenly he had her arm in a painful grip and with one motion brought her colliding with his hard body, almost knocking the breath from her. His mouth came down, hot and ravaging, not waiting for her compliance but taking it. His teeth raked across her bottom lip, and when she made a shaky sound of...response? protest? he used the opportunity to enter her mouth with his tongue.

Her heart lunged wildly in her chest as she realized he was out of control. His arms had tightened around her, lifting her off her feet, and his mouth took hers with bruising force. Elation swirled in her, and she wound her arms tightly around his neck as she kissed him back.

He hefted her onto the tailgate of the truck and reached for his shirt, tossing it down on the truck bed. With a motion so smooth it seemed like one movement he slid her backward and leaped to a crouching position on the tailgate; then he was pushing her down onto the shirt and lowering himself on top of her.

Dimly she realized that once you had unleashed a tiger, it wasn't so easy to get him back under control again. Of course, she wasn't sure she wanted to. The sunlight sifted down through the leaves, dappling his gleaming skin, and his eyes were fiercely primitive as he kneed her thighs apart. He looked wild and magnificent, and she made a soft whimpering sound of need as she reached for him.

He tore her clothes, and she didn't care. The seam of her chemise gave way beneath his twisting fingers, and the taut rise of her breasts thrust nakedly up at him. He sucked strongly at her while he shoved her skirt to her waist and hooked his fingers in the waistband of her underpants. She lifted her hips to aid him, but heard the rip of lace, and then he threw the shreds to one side. He transferred his lips to her other breast and sucked the nipple into his mouth while he worked at the fastening of his jeans. He grunted as the zipper parted, releasing his throbbing length, and he shoved both underwear and jeans downward with one movement.

His entry was hard and fast. Her body shuddered under the impact of it, and her hips lifted. He groaned aloud as the exquisite feminine sheath enveloped him, immediately changing his unbearable ache into unbearable pleasure.

Madelyn sank her nails into his back as she arched up, driven by an explosion of heat. Coiling tension tightened her body until she thought she would go mad, and she struggled with both him and the tension, crying out a little as her heaving body strained to throw him off even as her legs tightened around him to pull him deeper. If he was wild, so was she. He pounded into her, and she took him. Her hips hammered back at him and he rode her, wrapping his arms under her buttocks to pull her up tighter, to shove himself in deeper.

A great rolling surge exploded her senses without warning, and she gave a primal scream that sliced across the clear air. He kept thrusting heavily into her, and it happened again, the second time following the first so closely that she hadn't had time to regain her breath, and the second time was more powerful, tossing her even higher. She bit his shoulder, sobbing from the force of it, and suddenly she could feel him grow even harder and bigger inside her, and his entire body began shuddering and heaving. He threw back his head with a guttural cry that ripped up from his chest as his hips jerked in the spasms of completion.

The quiet afterward had a drifting, dreamy quality to it.

She could feel the sunlight filtering down on her skin, the heat of the metal truck bed beneath her, his shirt pillowing her head. A bird sang, and a breeze rustled the leaves and grass. She could hear the faint buzzing of a bee somewhere, and the slowing sound of his breathing.

They lay beside each other, his heavy arm across her stomach. She might have dozed. The breeze dried the sweat on her body with a gentle, cooling touch. After a long, long time that might have been only minutes, she turned into his arms and pressed her mouth to his.

He got his boots and jeans off this time. As rawly frenzied as the first time had been, this one wasn't much less. The force of his restrained hunger had built up until, like a flooding river overwhelming a dam, it had broken through and could no longer be controlled. He undid her skirt and stripped it down her legs; then she parted her thighs and reached for him again, and he couldn't wait a minute longer. The sight of those sleek legs opening for him was an image that had haunted his dreams. He'd intended to be easier with her this time, but as soon as he penetrated she made a wild sound in her throat and her hips rolled, and he went mad again.

This time when it was over he didn't withdraw, but lay on her in continued possession. "Reese," she whispered, her fingers sliding into his damp hair. He slid his thumbs under her chin and tilted her face up, slanting his head so he could drink from her in the long, deep kisses he'd been craving. He began to grow hard again, but he was still inside her and there was no urgency, only steadily increasing pleasure.

They were both drugged with it. He fondled her breasts, caressing them with both hands and mouth. Her slim hands moved over him like silk, sleeking over his broad shoulders and down the taut muscles of his back, finally cupping and kneading his buttocks. Lifting himself on his arms, he began a slow, steady thrusting. She surged upward, too, kissing his throat and chest and licking at his little nipples, half-hidden in the curls of hair on his chest. When her time was close, she writhed on the twisted bed of clothing, and he watched enthralled as her torso flushed and her nipples tightened. He caught her hips and lifted them, sliding her up and down on his impaling flesh, and the sight of her convulsive satisfaction brought him to the peak before she had finished.

The hot midday hours slipped away as they sated themselves on each other's bodies. Nothing else existed but sensual exploration and hot satisfaction. He kissed her from head to toe, tasting the sweetness of her flesh, delighting in the way she responded to his slightest touch. When her back became tender from rubbing on the hard bed he pulled her on top of him, watching her pleasure at the freedom it gave her to take him at her own pace.

He thought he had to be completely empty, yet he couldn't stop. He didn't know if he'd ever be able to stop. The peaks were no longer shattering, but were slow, strong swells that seemed to last forever.

Madelyn clung to him, not thinking, never wanting to think. This was the magic she had wanted, the burning sensuality she had sensed in him. No part of her body was untouched, unloved. Exhaustion crept in and entwined with pleasure, and at some point they went to sleep.

The sun was low when they woke, and the air was getting cooler. Reese pulled her into the heat of his body and smoothed her hair back from her face. "Are you all right?" he murmured, concerned when he remembered the violent intensity of their lovemaking.

She nuzzled her face against his throat, lifting one slender arm to curl it around his neck. "Umm," she said and closed her eyes again. She didn't feel like moving.

He sleeked his hand over her hip and up her side, then cupped her breast. "Wake up, honey."

"I am awake." The words were slow and muffled against his throat.

"It's almost sunset. We need to go."

"We can sleep here." She moved as if trying to sink into his skin, and her own hand strayed downward. He closed his eyes as her fingers closed gently around him. Her lips opened against his throat, then slid upward to his jaw. "Make love to me again, Reese. Please."

"Don't worry about that," he said beneath his breath. There was no way he could restrain himself now that he'd tasted her passion, no way she would let him, now that she knew. With a mixture of anger and despair he knew he'd never be able to keep his hands off her now. But the temperature was getting cooler by the second as the sun began dipping below the horizon; even though he was tempted to lie there with her, he didn't want her to get chilled.

He sat up and drew her with him. "Home," he said, his voice roughening. "My knees have had about all they can take. I want to be in bed the next time."

Her eyes were slumberous, her lips swollen from his kisses. "As long as it's soon," she whispered, and thought she would cry, she loved him so much.

Chapter 7

Her spirit was willing but her body went to sleep. She slept in his arms that night, her head on his shoulder and one leg thrown over his hip. Reese let her sleep, feeling the contentment of his own body as well as a certain wryness. If Madelyn had been seductive before, she was doubly so now. It was as if she had been holding back, too. That night, she hadn't walked past him without reaching out to touch him somewhere: a lingering hand sliding along his ribs, a gentle touch on his hand or arm, or a light ruffling of his hair, a tickle of his ear, a quick kiss on his chin, an appreciative pat on his butt, even a bold caress of his crotch. After denying himself for so long, he couldn't keep his hands off her, either. By the time he'd showered, eaten dinner and rested for an hour, the accumulated effect of all those caresses, both given and received, had had him hard and aching again. She had gone sweetly into his arms in bed, he'd made love to her, this time with lingering gentleness, and then she had gone to sleep before he'd withdrawn from her.

He'd stayed inside her for a long time, dozing himself and

luxuriating in the intimacy. When he tried to move she muttered a protest and turned with him, burrowing against him and retaining the connection. So he hooked his arm around her bottom and kept her locked to him all night, and he slept better than he had since the day he'd met her.

He was on his back and she was sprawled on top of him when the alarm went off the next morning. He stretched to shut it off while she wiggled sleepily on his chest like a cat. He rubbed his hand down her back. "Time to get up."

His early-morning voice was dark and rough. Madelyn settled her head in the hollow of his shoulder again. "Did you know," she said sleepily, "that more words in the English language start with S than with any other letter?"

"Ah, God, not now," he groaned. "Not before coffee."

"Chicken."

"I don't want to talk about any damn chickens, either." He struggled to wake up. "Canada is over two hundred thousand square miles larger than the United States."

"A pound of feathers weighs more than a pound of gold because of the different weighing systems used."

"Catgut comes from sheep guts, not cat guts."

She jerked upright, frowning at him, and he used the opportunity to turn on the lamp. "No gross stuff," she ordered, then settled back down on his chest. "A blue whale's heart beats just nine times a minute."

"Robert E. Lee's family home is now Arlington National Cemetery."

"*Mona Lisa* doesn't have any eyebrows, and the real name of the painting is *La Gioconda*."

"Quicksand is more buoyant that water. Contrary to Hollywood, you'd really have to work at it to go completely under in quicksand."

She yawned and was silent, listening to his heartbeat, a strong, steady drumming in her ear. As she listened it began beating faster, and she raised her head to look at him. His eyes were narrowed and intent. He locked his arms around her and rolled until she was beneath him, his legs between hers and spreading them wide. Madelyn clung to him and gave herself up to the now-familiar rise of ecstasy as he began making love to her.

"What are you doing today?" she asked over breakfast.

"Moving a portion of the herd to another section so they won't overgraze."

"I'm going with you."

He automatically started to refuse, and she gave him a hard look. "Don't say no," she warned. "I've already got steaks marinating in the refrigerator, and the baked potatoes are almost done, so they'll finish baking while the steaks are grilling. There's no reason for me to sit here every day when I can be with you."

"What I wonder," he muttered, "is if I'll get any work done at all. All right, I'll saddle a horse for you. But I'm warning you, Maddie, if you can't ride well enough to keep up, you won't go out with me again."

She showed up at the barn half an hour later wearing jeans, boots and one of his denim workshirts with the sleeves rolled up and the tails tied in a knot at her waist. Her hair was French-braided in one long braid down the center of her back, she wore a new pair of wrist-length gloves, and she looked as chic as if she were modeling clothes rather than heading out for a day of herding cattle. She carried a western straw hat and settled it on her head before she approached the horse Reese had saddled for her.

He watched as she gave the animal time to get acquainted with her, letting it snuffle at her arms, scratching it behind its ears. She wasn't afraid of horses, at least. April had never been around them, and as a result had been jumpy in their vicinity, which in turn made the horses skittish. Madelyn petted the horse and crooned to it, then untied the reins, put her boot in the stirrup and competently swung into the saddle. Reese eyed the stirrups and decided he had judged the length correctly, then mounted his own horse.

He watched her carefully as they cantered across a field.

She had a good seat and nice steady hands, though she lacked the easy posture he possessed, but he'd been riding since he was a toddler. The smile she gave him was so full of pleasure he felt guilty at not taking her with him before.

He set an easy pace, not wanting to push her too hard. When they reached the herd he explained how he worked. The herd was already divided into three smaller groups grazing different sections; the entire herd was too big for him to move by himself. He spent a lot of time moving them to fresh grazing and making certain they didn't destroy the plant cycle by overgrazing. He pointed out the bunch they would be moving and gave her a coiled section of rope. "Just wave it alongside the horse's shoulder in a shooing motion, and let the horse do the work if a cow decides to go in a different direction. All you have to do is sit deep in the saddle and hang on."

Sitting deep in the saddle was no problem; the big western rig felt like a cradle after the small eastern saddle she was familiar with. She took the coil of rope and practiced a few waves with it, just to be certain it didn't startle the horse. He treated it as commonplace, which, of course, to him it was.

She enjoyed the work. She liked being outside, and there was a sort of peace to riding alongside the cattle and waving a coil of rope at them occasionally, listening to the deep-throated bawls and learning the joy of riding a well-trained cutting horse. She liked watching Reese most of all. He had been born to do this, and it was obvious in every movement and sound he made. He rode as if he were a part of the horse, anticipating every change of direction, encouraging the cattle with whistles and calls that seemed to reassure them at the same time.

She felt almost dazed with pleasure, her senses overloaded. She had felt that way since the afternoon before, when his self-control had broken and he had taken her like a man possessed. Her body was sated, her emotions freed to reach out to him and shower him with the love that had been dammed up inside her. She had no illusions that the battle was won, but the first skirmish was hers; until yesterday, he would never have allowed her to pet him as she had been doing, nor would he have lingered in bed that morning to make love again. His face was still set in those stern, unsmiling lines, but he was subtly more relaxed. Judging from the past twenty-four hours, he must have had a difficult time controlling his sex drive. The thought made her smile.

They stopped for lunch and to let the cattle and horses drink from a small natural pond. When the horses had been seen to, Reese tethered them nearby and sat down next to her on the small rise she'd chosen for the site of their meal. He took off his hat and put it on the grass beside him. "How do you like it so far?"

"A lot." Her lips curved softly as she handed him a sandwich. "It's so peaceful out here, no cars, no telephones, no smog. You may have to help me out of bed in the morning, but it'll be worth it."

"I'll rub you down with liniment tonight." His eyes glinted at her. "Afterward."

That statement earned him a kiss. Then she straightened and unwrapped her own sandwich. "How am I doing? Have I done anything totally amateurish?"

"You're doing fine. The only problem is that I keep worrying you're going to get tossed and stepped on. You're the first female cowhand I've ever had."

He was very western in his attitude toward women, but she didn't mind him coddling her as long as he didn't also try to stop her from doing what she wanted. Since he was bound to do that, their lives together should never become too complacent.

He propped himself on one elbow and stretched his long legs out as he ate his second sandwich. She began to feel warm as she watched him; though he was simply dressed in brown jeans, a white shirt and those disreputably scuffed boots, he outshone male models she'd seen in tuxedos. His first wife had to be president of a Stupid Club somewhere, but the wretched woman shouldn't be allowed to get away with what she'd done to him. Madelyn had never before thought of herself as vindictive, but she felt that way about anyone who had ever harmed Reese. If she ever met April, she would snatch her bald-headed.

He found the cookies she'd packed and washed them down with the last of the tea. Feeding this man could be a full-time job, she thought fondly. If his children inherited his appetite, she'd never get out of the kitchen.

Thinking of having his children made her feel even warmer, but reminded her of something she'd meant to discuss with him. She turned to face him, sitting with her legs folded in front of her.

"There's something we have to talk about."

"What's that?" he asked, stretching out on his back and settling his hat over his eyes.

"Children."

One eye opened and peered at her; then he removed the hat and gave her his full attention. "Ye gods, are you already pregnant?"

"No, and even if I were, I wouldn't know yet, because it isn't time for my period. We didn't talk about it before we got married, so I didn't know if you wanted to wait before we had children or if you wanted to have them right away. When you called, it was almost time for my period, so when I went to the doctor for the physical I got a prescription for birth control pills."

He sat up, his face darkening. "You're on the Pill?"

"Yes. I've only taken it for this month. If you want to start trying to have children right away, I can stop."

"You should have discussed it with me before, or was that another one of those subjects, like your virginity, that you didn't think were any of my business?"

She gave him one of those sidelong glances. "Something like that. I didn't know you, and I didn't feel very comfortable with you."

He watched her for a minute, then reached out to take her

hand, rubbing his rough thumb over her soft palm. "How do you feel about getting pregnant right away?"

"I wouldn't mind. I want your children. If you want to wait, that's okay with me, too, but I don't want to wait more than a year. I'm twenty-eight. I don't want to be in my mid-thirties when we get started."

He thought about it while he studied the contrast of her delicate hand in his big, rough one. Now that he'd given in to the powerful physical attraction between them, he didn't want to give it up too soon. He wanted to fully enjoy her for a while before pregnancy put necessary limits on the wildness of their lovemaking. He carried her hand to his mouth and licked her palm. "Take the Pill for a few months," he said. "We'll talk about it again in the fall."

She shivered, a dazed expression coming into her eyes at the stroke of his tongue on her palm. As he pulled her down on the grass she asked, "Do you think you'll get your boots off this time?"

And he replied, "I doubt it."

He didn't, but she didn't care.

She went with him often after that. She helped him move cattle, inoculate them, and staple tags in their ears. After he'd cut and baled the hay, she drove the truck pulling the hay trailer around while he swung the heavy bales onto it. It was work that really required a third person, to stack the bales, but it was easier than when Reese had had to do it by himself. When she didn't go out with him, she continued with the project of scraping the house.

He finally noticed the difference in the house and investigated. The dusting of white paint chips on the ground told him all he needed to know.

He leaned against the kitchen cabinet and crossed his arms. "Are you scraping the house?"

"Yep."

"Don't pull the Gary Cooper routine on me. I want it stopped right now."

"The routine or the scraping?"

"Both."

"The house can't be painted until the old paint is scraped off," she said reasonably.

"I can't afford the paint, so it doesn't make any difference. And I don't want you climbing around on a fourteen-foot ladder. What if you fell while I'm out on the range?"

"What if you got hurt out on the range by yourself?" she retorted. "I'm careful, and I haven't had any trouble so far. It shouldn't take too much longer."

"No," he said, enunciating carefully. "I can't afford the paint, and even if I could I wouldn't let you do the scraping."

"*You* don't have time for it, so who else is going to do it?"

"For the third time," he yelled, "*I can't afford the paint!* What does it take to make you understand that?"

"That's something else we've never talked about. What makes you think *we* can't afford the paint? I supported myself before I married you, you know." She put her hands on her hips and faced off with him. "I have both a checking and a savings account, which I transferred to a bank in Billings. I also have a trust fund that I inherited from Grandma Lily. It isn't a fortune by any means, but we can certainly afford a few gallons of paint!"

Reese's face was like granite. "No. Remember our prenuptial agreement? What's yours is yours and what's mine is mine. If you spent your money on the ranch it would go a long way toward negating that agreement, giving you a claim to it on the basis of upkeep."

She poked him in the chest, her jaw jutting forward. "For one thing, G. Reese Duncan, *I'm* not planning on getting a divorce, so I don't give a flip what's in your precious agreement. For another, how much would it cost to paint the house? A hundred dollars? Two hundred?"

"Closer to two hundred, and no, by God, you're not buying the paint!"

"I'm not only going to buy it, I'm going to paint it! If you're so set on protecting the ranch from my scheming, then we'll draw up a contract where you agree to repay me for the paint—and my time, too, if you insist—and that will take care of any claim I could make against you. But I live here, too, you know, and I want the outside to look as nice as the inside. Next spring I'm planting flowers in the flower beds, so if you object to that we might as well fight it out now. The only choice you have right now is the color you want the house painted, and your choices are white and white." She was yelling by the time she finished, her face flushed.

He was more furious than she'd ever seen him before. "Do whatever the hell you want," he snapped and slammed out of the kitchen.

She did. The next time they went into town she bought the paint and brushes and paid for them with one of her own checks, glaring at him and daring him to start again. He carried the paint out to the truck with ill grace. The high point of that day was when they stopped at the café for coffee and listened to Floris berating her customers.

She had the house painted by the middle of August, and had developed a healthy respect for people who painted houses for a living. It was some of the hardest work she'd ever done, leaving her shoulders and arms aching by the end of the day. The most aggravating part was painting the hundreds of thin porch railings; the most nerve-racking was doing the second floor, because she had to anchor herself to something. But when it was finished and the house gleamed like a jewel, and the shutters wore a new coat of black all-weather enamel, she was prouder of her efforts than she had ever been before of anything she'd done.

Even Reese grudgingly admitted that the house looked nice and she'd done a good job, but he still resented the fact that she'd done it. Maybe it was only male pride, but he didn't want his wife paying for something when he couldn't afford it himself.

His wife. By the time they had been married two months, she had insinuated herself so completely into his life that there wasn't a portion of it she hadn't touched. She had even rearranged his underwear drawer. Sometimes he wondered how she managed to accomplish as much as she did when her pace seldom exceeded a stroll, but it was a fact that she got things done. In her own way she worked as hard as he did.

One hot morning at the end of August she discovered that she didn't have enough flour to do the day's cooking. Reese had already left for the day and wouldn't be coming back for lunch, so she ran upstairs and got ready. It was almost time they replenished their supplies anyway, so she carried the grocery list with her. It would save an extra trip if she did all the shopping while she was in town.

She loved listening to Floris, so she stopped by the café and had coffee and pie. After Floris had sent her only other customer stomping out in anger, she came over to Madelyn's booth and sat down.

"Where's that man of yours today?"

"Out on the range. I ran out of flour and came in to stock up."

Floris nodded approvingly, though her sour face never lightened. "That first wife of his never bought no groceries. Don't guess she knew nothing about cooking, though of course Reese had a cook hired back then. It's a shame what happened to that ranch. It used to be a fine operation."

"It will be again," Madelyn said with confidence. "Reese is working hard to build it back up."

"One thing about him, he's never been afraid of work. Not like some men around here." Floris glared at the door as if she could still see the cowboy who had just left.

After talking with Floris, Glenna's cheerfulness was almost culture shock. They chatted for a while; then Madelyn loaded the groceries into the station wagon and drove back to the ranch. It wasn't quite noon, so she would have plenty of time to cook the cake she'd planned.

To her surprise, Reese's truck was in the yard when she drove up. He was coming around from the back of the house carrying a bucket of water, but when he saw her, he changed direction and stalked over, his face dark with temper and his eyes shooting green sparks. "Where in hell have you been?" he roared.

She didn't like his manner, but she answered his question in a reasonable tone. "I didn't have enough flour to do the cooking today, so I drove to Crook and bought groceries."

"Damn it, don't you ever go off without telling me where you're going!"

She retained her reasonableness, but it was becoming a strain. "How could I tell you when you weren't here?"

"You could have left a note."

"Why would I leave a note when you weren't supposed to be back for lunch, and I'd be back long before you? Why *are* you back?"

"One of the hoses sprang a leak. I came back to put a new hose on." For whatever reason, he wasn't in a mood to let it go. "If I hadn't, I wouldn't have found out you've started running around the country on your own, would I? How long has this been going on?"

"Buying food? Several centuries, I'd say."

Very carefully he put the bucket down. As he straightened, Madelyn saw his eyes; he wasn't just angry or aggravated, he was in a rage. He hadn't been this angry before, even over painting the house. With his teeth clenched he said, "You dressed like that to buy groceries?"

She looked down at her clothes. She wore a slim pink skirt that ended just above her knees and a white silk blouse with the sleeves rolled up. Her legs were bare, and she had on sandals. "Yes, I dressed like this to buy groceries! It's hot, in case you haven't noticed. I didn't want to wear jeans, I wanted to wear a skirt, because it's cooler."

"Did you get a kick out of men looking at your legs?"

"As far as I noticed, no one looked at my legs. I told you once that I won't pay for April's sins, and I meant it. Now, if you don't mind, I need to get the groceries into the house."

He caught her arm as she turned away and whirled her back around to face him. "Don't walk away when I'm talking to you."

"Well excuse me, Your Majesty!"

He grabbed her other arm and held her in front of him. "If you want to go to town, I'll take you," he said in an iron-hard voice. "Otherwise, you keep your little butt here on the ranch, and don't you ever, *ever,* leave the house without letting me know where you are."

She went up on tiptoe, so angry she was shaking. "Let me tell you a few things, and you'd better listen. I'm your wife, not your prisoner of war. I won't ask your permission to buy groceries, and I won't be kept locked up here like some criminal. If you take the keys to the car or do something to it so it won't run, then I'll walk wherever I want to go, and you can bet the farm on that. I'm not April, do you understand? *I'm not April.*"

He released her arms, and they stood frozen, neither of them giving an inch. Very deliberately Madelyn bent down and lifted the bucket of water, then upended it over him. The water splashed on his head and shoulders and ran down his torso, to finally end up pooling around his boots.

"If that isn't enough to cool you off, I can get another one," she offered in an icily polite tone.

His movements were just as deliberate as hers as he removed his hat and slapped it against his leg to rid it of excess water, then dropped it to the ground. She saw his teeth clench; then he moved like a snake striking, his hands darting out to grasp her around the waist. With one swift movement he lifted her and plonked her down on the front fender of the car.

His hands were flexing on her waist; his forearms were trembling with the force it took to restrain his temper. His dark hair was plastered to his skull; water still dripped down his face, and his eyes were pure green fire.

His dilemma nearly tore him apart. He was trembling with rage, but there wasn't a damn thing he could do about it. His wife didn't back down from anyone, not even him, and he'd cut off his own hands before he would do anything to hurt her. All he could do was stand there and try to get his temper back under control.

They faced each other in silence for nearly a minute, with him still holding her on the fender of the car. She tilted her chin, her eyes daring him to start the fight again. He looked down at her legs, and a shudder ran through him. When he looked back up at her, it wasn't rage in his eyes.

Green eyes locked with gray. He hooked his fingers in the hem of her skirt and jerked it upward, at the same time spreading her legs and moving forward between them. She sank her hands into his wet hair and held his head while her mouth attacked his with a fierce kiss that held mingled anger and desire. He said, "Maddie," in a rough tone as he tore her underpants out of the way, then jerked at his belt and the fastening of his jeans.

It was just as it had been in the back of the truck. The rush of passion was hard and fast and overwhelming. With one hand he guided himself, while the other propelled her hips forward onto him. She moaned and wrapped her legs around him, then held his head so that their eyes met again. "I love you," she said fiercely. "I love you, damn it."

The words hit him like a thunderbolt, but her eyes were clear and direct, and he was losing himself in her depths. What had begun wild suddenly turned slow and hot and tender. He put his hand in her hair and tugged her head back to expose the graceful arch of her throat to his searching mouth. He began moving within her, probing deep and slow, and he said, "Maddie," again, this time in a voice that shook.

She was like fire, and she was all his. She burned for him and with him, her intense sensuality matching his. They clung together, savoring the hot rise of passion and the erotic strokes that fed it and would eventually extinguish it, but not now. Not right now.

He unbuttoned her blouse while she performed the same service for his shirt. When he had unclipped her bra he slowly brought their bare torsos together, turning her slightly from side to side so that her breasts rubbed his chest and his curly hair rasped against her nipples, making her arch in his arms.

"God, I can't get enough of you," he muttered.

"I don't want you to." Passion had glazed her eyes, making them heavy and slumberous. He took her mouth again, and he was still kissing her when she cried out and convulsed in a crest of pleasure. He held himself deep within her, feeling the hot, gentle tightening of her inner caresses around him. He would never find this kind of overwhelming passion with any other woman, he thought dimly. Only with Maddie.

Release left her weak, pliable. She lay back across the hood of the car, breathing hard, her eyes closed. Reese gripped her hips and began thrusting hard and fast, wanting that sweet weakness for himself. Her eyes slowly opened as he drove into her, and she closed her hands around his wrists. "I love you," she said again.

Until he heard the words once more he hadn't realized how badly he'd needed them, wanted them. She was his, and had been from the moment she'd walked through the airport toward him. He groaned, and his hips jerked; then the pleasure hit him, and he couldn't think for a long time. All he could do was feel, and sink forward onto her soft body and into her arms.

In bed that night, he gently traced his fingertips over the curve of her shoulder. "I'm sorry," he murmured. "I was out of line today, way out."

She kissed him drowsily on the jaw. "I think I understand more than before. Did April...?"

"Have other men? Yeah."

"The fool," she muttered, sliding her hand down to intimately caress him.

He tilted her head up. "I wasn't a saint, Maddie. I can be hard to live with."

She widened her eyes mockingly and made a disbelieving sound. He chuckled and then sighed, spreading his legs. What her hand was doing to him felt so good it was almost criminal. She was all woman, and this was going to end up only one way, but he wanted to put it off for a few minutes.

"You're right, I've been trying to keep you a prisoner on the ranch. It won't happen again."

"I'm not going to run off," she assured him in a whisper. "I've got what I want right here. And you were right about one thing."

"What?"

"Making love is one of the best ways to make up."

Chapter 8

Reese sold the beef herd for more than he had anticipated, or even hoped. With cholesterol-consciousness at such a high level he had been working to breed and raise cattle with leaner meat that still remained tender, and all his research was paying off. He made his mortgage payments with grim satisfaction, because he had enough left over to expand the herd come spring and bring in some new blood strains he'd been wanting to try. He'd be able to repair equipment when it needed it, instead of scraping and saving and doing without. He'd even be able to take Madelyn out to eat once in a while. It galled him that the limit of their outside entertainment was an occasional cup of coffee or slice of pie at Floris's café. He wanted to be able to take Madelyn places and spoil her, buy her new clothes and jewelry, all the things he had once taken for granted in his life. The ranch was a long way from being as rich as it had once been, but he was clawing his way back. He'd made a profit, by God! He was in the black.

Madelyn had gone into Billings with him when he con-

ferred with his banker. He'd expected her to want to go
shopping; though he realized more every day how different
Maddie was from April, he also wryly accepted that his wife
was a clotheshorse. The fact that she loved clothes was evident in the way she dressed even while working at the
ranch. It might be just jeans and a shirt, but the jeans would
fit her in a way guaranteed to send his blood pressure up,
and the shirt would look as stylish as if it had come straight
from Paris. What really got to him was the way she would
put on one of his white dress shirts, not button *any* of the
buttons, and knot the tails at her waist. She wouldn't have
a bra on under it, either. It was a style and a provocation
that he couldn't resist, and she knew it. First his hand would
be inside the shirt; then the shirt would be off; then they
would be making love wherever they happened to be.

She did shop, but again she surprised him. She bought
underwear and jeans for him; then she was ready to go home.
"I don't know how I ever stood a city as large as New
York," she said absently, looking around at the traffic. "This
is too noisy." He was astonished; Billings had less than seventy thousand inhabitants, and barroom brawls were far more
the norm than any gang- or drug-related violence. No,
Maddie wasn't like April, who had considered Billings nothing more than a backwater crossroads. To April, only cities
like New York, London, Paris, Los Angeles and Hong Kong
had been sophisticated enough for her enjoyment.

Madelyn was indeed glad to get back to the ranch. She
was happiest there, she realized. It was quiet, with the peace
that came only from being close to earth and nature. And it
was her home now.

It was the middle of the afternoon when they got back,
and Reese changed clothes to begin his chores. It was too
early to start dinner, so Madelyn went out on the porch and
sat in the swing. It was early autumn, and already the heat
was leaving the day. Reese said it wasn't unusual to have
snow in October, so the days when she would be able to sit
out on the porch were limited. Still, she was looking forward

to the winter, hard as it might be. The days would be short and the nights long, and she smiled as she thought of those long nights.

Reese came back downstairs from changing his clothes and found her there. The chores would wait a little while, he thought, and joined her on the swing. He put his arm around her and brought her closer, so that her head was nestled in the hollow of his shoulder.

"I was just thinking," she said, "It'll be winter soon."

"Sooner than you think."

"Christmas isn't that far away now. Could I invite Robert?"

"Of course. He's your family."

She smiled. "I know, but the warmth between you at our wedding wasn't exactly overwhelming."

"What did you expect, given the circumstances? Men are territorial. He didn't want to give you up, and I was determined to have you come hell or high water." He nudged her chin up with his thumb and gave her a slow kiss. "And I was a stranger who was going to be taking his sister to bed that night."

For a moment there was only the creaking of the swing. He kissed her again, then just held her. He hadn't known marriage could be like this, he thought with vague surprise. Both passion and contentment.

He said quietly, "Let's have a baby."

After a pause she said, "I'll stop taking the Pill." Then she reached for his hand and cradled it to her face.

The tenderness of the gesture was almost painful. He lifted her up and settled her astride his lap so he could see her expression. "Is that what you want?"

Her face looked as if it had been lit from within. "You know it is." She leaned forward and brushed his lips with hers, then suddenly laughed and threw her arms around his neck, fiercely hugging him. "Are there any twins in your family?"

"No!" he said explosively, then drew back and gave her a suspicious look. "Are there in yours?"

"Actually, yes. Grandma Lily was a twin."

Even the thought of twins was too much. He shook his head, denying the possibility. "Just one at a time, gal. No doubling up." He rubbed his hands up her thighs and under her skirt, then slid them inside her underpants to cup her bare buttocks. "You might be pregnant by Christmas."

"Umm, I'd like that."

His eyes glinted at her. "I'll do my best."

"But it'll probably take longer than that."

"Then I'll just have to try harder."

Her lips quirked. "I can't lose," she said in contentment.

The first snow did come in October, three inches of fine, dry powder. She learned that snow didn't stop a rancher's work, it only intensified it, though three inches was nothing to worry about. In the dead of winter Reese would have to carry hay to the cattle and break the ice in the stock ponds so they could drink. He'd have to find lost calves before they froze to death and move the herd to more sheltered areas during the worst weather.

For the first time, winter began to worry her. "What if there are blizzard conditions?" she asked him one night.

"Then I hope for the best," he said flatly. "I'll lose some calves during any bad snowstorm, but if it doesn't last too long the biggest part of the herd will weather it. The danger is if blizzard conditions or extreme cold last for several days. Then the cattle start freezing to death, and during a blizzard I can't get feed out to them. I have hooks attached to the barn and the house. When it looks like a bad storm, I run a static line between them and hook myself to it so I can get back and forth to the barn."

She stared at him, appalled at the years he'd coped by himself and the danger he'd been in. It was testimony to his strength and intelligence that he was still alive, and characteristic of his stubbornness that he'd even tried.

The preparations for winter were ongoing and not to be taken lightly. He moved the herd to the closer pastures where they would winter. Cords of firewood were stacked close to the back door, and the pantry was well stocked with candles and batteries, while he cleaned and tested two big kerosene heaters in case they were needed. The truck and car were both filled with new antifreeze and given new batteries, and he began parking them in the garage to keep them out of the wind. During October the temperature steadily slipped lower, until the only time it was above freezing was at high noon.

"Does it stay below freezing for six months?" she asked, and he laughed.

"No. We'll have cold spells and warm spells. It may be sixty degrees or higher in January, but if we get blizzard conditions or a deep freeze the temperatures can go way below zero. We prepare for a blizzard and hope for the sixty degrees."

As if to bear him out, the weather then showed a warming trend and inched the temperatures upward into the fifties during the day. Madelyn felt more confident, because he'd been making preparations as if they were going into six months of darkness. That was how he'd made it by himself for seven years, by being cautious and prepared for anything. Still, by his own admission the winters could be hell. She would just have to make certain he didn't take any chances with his own safety.

Robert flew in the day before Christmas and spent three days with them. When he first saw Madelyn he gave her a hard, searching look, but whatever he saw must have reassured him, because he relaxed then and was an affable guest. She was amused at the way Reese and Robert related to each other, since they were so much alike, both very private and strong men. Their conversation consisted of sentence fragments, as if they were just throwing out random comments, but they both seemed comfortable with it. She was amazed at how much alike they were in manner, too. Robert was smoothly cosmopolitan, yet Reese's mannerisms were much

like his, illustrating how prosperous the ranch had been before the divorce. They differed only in that she had never
seen Robert lose his temper, while Reese's temper was like
a volcano.

Robert was surprisingly interested in the working of the
ranch and rode out with Reese every day he was there. They
spent a lot of time talking about futures and stock options,
the ratio of feed to pound of beef, interest rates, inflation and
government subsidies. Robert looked thoughtful a lot, as if
he were weighing everything Reese said.

The day before he left, Robert approached Madelyn. She
was sprawled bonelessly across a big armchair, listening to
the stereo with her eyes closed and one foot keeping time to
the music. He said in amusement, "Never run if you can
walk, never walk if you can stand, never stand if you can
sit, and never sit if you can lie."

"Never talk if you can listen," Madelyn added without
opening her eyes.

"Then you listen, and I'll talk."

"This sounds serious. Are you going to tell me you're in
love with someone and are thinking of marriage?"

"Good God, no," he said, his amusement deepening.

"Is there a new woman on the horizon?"

"A bit closer than that."

"Why didn't you bring her? Is it anyone I know?"

"This is a family Christmas," he replied, telling her with
that one short sentence that his new lover hadn't touched
him any deeper than any of the others. "Her name is Natalie
VanWein."

"Nope. I don't know her."

"You're supposed to listen while I talk, not ask questions
about my love life." He drew up a hassock and sat down
on it, smiling a little as he noticed that she hadn't even
opened her eyes during their conversation.

"So talk."

"I've never met anyone with a clearer head for business

than Reese—excepting myself, of course," he said mockingly.

"Oh, of course."

"Listen, don't talk. He sees what has to be done and he does it, without regard to obstacles. He has the kind of determination that won't give up, no matter what the odds. He'll make a go of this ranch. He'll fight like hell until he has it the way it used to be."

Madelyn opened one eye. "And the point of this is?"

"I'm a businessman. He strikes me as a better risk than a lot of ventures I've bet on. He doesn't have to wait to build this place up. He could accept an investor and start right now."

"The investor, of course, being yurself."

He nodded. "I look for a profit. He'd make one. I want to invest in it personally, without involving Cannon Companies."

"Have you already talked to him about it?"

"I wanted to talk to you first. You're his wife, you know him better than I do. Would he go for it, or would I be wasting my time?"

"Well, I won't give you an opinion either way. You're on your own. Like you said, he knows the business, so let him make up his own mind without having to consider anything I might have said either pro or con."

"It's your home, too."

"I'm still learning to help, but I don't know enough about the business of ranching to even begin to make an educated decision. And when it comes down to it, my home is based on my marriage, not where we live. We could live anywhere and I'd be content."

He looked down at her, and a strangely tender look entered his pale eyes. "You're really in love with him, aren't you?"

"I have been from the beginning. I never would have married him otherwise."

He examined her face closely, in much the same way he'd

looked at her when he had first arrived, as if satisfying himself of the truth of her answer. Then he gave a brusque nod and got to his feet. "Then I'll put the proposition to Reese and see what he thinks."

Reese turned it down, as Madelyn had expected he would. The ranch was his; it might take longer and be a harder fight to do it on his own, but every tree and every speck of dirt on the ranch belonged to him, and he refused to risk even one square inch of it with an outside investor. Robert took the refusal in good humor, because business was business, and his emotions were never involved any more than they were with women.

Reese talked to her about it that night, lying in the darkness with her head pillowed on his shoulder. "Robert made me an offer today. If I took him as an investor, I could double the ranch's operation, hire enough hands to work it and probably get back most of the former acreage within five years."

"I know. He talked to me about it, too."

He stiffened. "What did you tell him?"

"To talk to you. It's your ranch, and you know more about running it than anyone else."

"Would you rather I took his offer?"

"Why should I care?"

"Money," he said succinctly.

"I'm not doing without anything." Her voice had a warm, amused tone to it.

"You could have a lot more."

"I could have a lot less, too. I'm happy, Reese. If you took the offer I'd still be happy, and I'll still be happy if you don't take it."

"He said you wouldn't take sides."

"That's right, I won't. It would be a no-win situation for me, and I don't waste my energy."

He lay awake long after she was sleeping quietly in his arms. It was a way to instant financial security, but it would require that he do something he'd sworn never to do: risk ownership of the ranch. He already had a mortgage, but he was managing to make the payments. If he took an investor he would be paying off the bank but taking on another debtor, at a price he might not be able to meet. The big lure of it was that, perversely, he wanted to give Madelyn all the luxuries he would have been able to provide before.

To take care of his wife as he wanted, he'd have to risk his ranch. He didn't miss the irony of it.

The day after Robert left, a big weather system swept in from Canada and it began snowing. At first it was just snow, but it didn't stop. The temperature began dropping like a rock, and the wind picked up. Reese watched the weather build into something nasty, and the weather reports said it would get worse. While he still could, he herded the cattle into the most sheltered area and put out as much hay as possible, but he wasn't certain he'd had enough time to get out as much as would be needed.

On the way back to the barn it started snowing so heavily that visibility dropped to about ten feet, and the wind began piling up drifts that masked the shape of the land. His own ranch became an alien landscape to him, without any familiar landmarks to guide him. All he could go on was his own sense of direction, and he had to fight to ignore the disorienting swirl of snow. His horse picked its way carefully, trying to avoid the snow-covered holes and indentations that could easily cause it to fall and perhaps break a leg. Icicles began to form on the horse's nose as the warm vapor of its breath froze. Reese put a gloved hand to his own face and found it coated with ice crystals.

A ride that normally took twenty minutes stretched into an hour. He began to wonder if he had missed the barn entirely when it materialized out of the blowing snow, and even then he would have missed it if the door hadn't been open revealing the gleam of yellow light. A brief frown creased his face; he knew he'd closed the door, and he certainly hadn't left a light on. But it had been too close a call for him to be anything but grateful; another half hour and he wouldn't have made it.

He ducked his head and rode straight into the barn. It wasn't until he caught movement out of the corner of his eye that he realized Madelyn had come out to the barn and was waiting for him, literally with a light in the window. She struggled against the wind to close the big doors, her slender body leaning into the teeth of the gale. The cow bawled restlessly, and the cats leaped for the loft. Reese slid out of the saddle and added his weight to Madelyn's, closing the doors and dropping the big two-by-eight bar into the brackets.

"What the hell are you doing out here?" he asked in a raspy voice as he grabbed her to him. "Damn it, Maddie, you can get lost going from the house to the barn in a blow like this!"

"I hooked up to the tension line," she said, clinging to him. Her voice was thin. "How did you get back? You can't see out there."

He felt the panic in her, because he'd begun feeling some of it himself. If he'd been five feet farther away, he wouldn't have seen the light. "Sheer blind luck," he said grimly.

She looked up at his ice-crusted face. "You have to get warm before frostbite starts."

"The horse first."

"I'll do it." She pointed toward the tack room, where he kept a small space heater. "I turned on the heater so it would be warm in there. Now, go on."

Actually, the barn felt warm to him after being outside; the animals gave off enough heat that the temperature inside the barn was above freezing, which was all that he required right now. Still, he went into the tack room and felt the heat envelop him almost unbearably. He didn't try to brush the ice from his face; he let it melt, so it wouldn't damage his skin. It had actually insulated his face from the wind, but too much longer would have resulted in frostbite. He'd had mild cases before, and it was painful enough that he'd rather not go through it again.

Madelyn unsaddled the horse and rubbed it down. The big animal sighed with pleasure in a way that was almost human. Then she threw a warm blanket over it and gave it feed and water, patting the muscled neck in appreciation. The animal had earned it.

She hurried to Reese and found him knocking chunks of snow off his heavy shearling coat. That shocking white layer of ice and snow was gone from his face; what was almost as shocking was that he already seemed to have recovered his strength, as if the ordeal had been nothing out of the ordinary. She had been in torment since the howling wind had started, pacing the house and trying not to weep uncontrollably, and finally fighting her way out to the barn so she would be there to help him if—no, *when*—he made it back. Her heart was still pounding. She didn't have to be told how easily he might not have made it back, even though she couldn't bear to let the thought form.

"It won't be easy getting back to the house," he said grimly. "The wind is probably gusting up to sixty miles an hour. We'll both hook on to the line, but I'm going to tie you to me as a safeguard."

He knotted a rope around his waist, then looped and knotted it around her, with no more than four feet of slack between them. "I want you within reach. I'm going to try to hold on to you, but I damn sure don't want you getting any farther away from me than this."

He put his coat back on and settled his hat firmly on his head. He eyed Madelyn sternly. "Don't you have a hat?"

She produced a thick woolen scarf from her pocket and draped it over her head, then wound the ends around her neck. They each got a length of nylon cord with heavy metal clips on each end and attached one end to their belts, leaving the other end free to clip to the line. They left the barn by the small side door; though the line was anchored right beside it, Reese had to grab Madelyn by the waist to keep the wind from tumbling her head over heels. Still holding her, he grabbed her line and hooked it overhead, then secured his own.

It was almost impossible to make headway. For every yard they progressed, stumbling and fighting, the wind would knock them back two feet. It tore her out of his grasp and knocked her feet out from under her, hanging her in the air from the line at her waist. Reese lunged for her, yelling something that she couldn't understand, and hauled her against him. It was obvious she wasn't going to be able to stay on her feet. He locked her against his side with a grip that compressed her ribs, almost shutting off her breath. She gasped for air, but couldn't manage more than a painful wheeze. She couldn't have yelled to make him understand, even if she'd had the breath, because the howling wind drowned out everything else. She dangled in his grip like a rag doll, her sight fading and her struggles becoming weaker.

Reese stumbled against the back steps, then up onto the porch. The house blocked some of the wind, and he managed to open the back door, then reach up and unhook both their lines. He staggered into the house and fell to the floor of the utility room with Madelyn still in his arms, but managed to turn so that he took most of the shock. "Are you all right?" He gasped the question, breathing hard from exertion. The wind had gotten worse just since he'd made it back to the barn.

She didn't answer, and sudden fear brought him up on his knees beside her. Her eyes were closed, her lips blue. He grabbed her shoulder, shouting at her. "Maddie! Madelyn, damn it, what's wrong? Are you hurt—wake up and answer me!"

She coughed, then moaned a little and tried to curl on her side, her arms coming up to hug herself. She coughed again, then went into a paroxysm of convulsive coughing and gagging, writhing from the force of it. Reese pulled her up into his arms and held her, his face white.

Finally she managed to wheeze, "Shut the door," and he

lashed out with his boot, kicking the door shut with a force that rattled it on its frame.

He unwound the scarf from her head and began opening her coat. The rope around their waists still tied them together and he hastily pulled the knots out. "Are you hurt?" he asked again, his face a grim mask.

Coughing had brought color to her face, but it was quickly fading, leaving her deathly pale. "I'm all right," she said, her voice so hoarse she could barely make a sound. "I just couldn't breathe."

Realization hit him like a kick by a mule. He'd almost smothered her with the force of his grip. His face grim, vicious curses coming from between his tightly clenched teeth, he laid her back on the floor as gently as possible and stretched out his leg so he could get his knife out of his pocket. Her eyes widened as he snapped the blade open and began slicing through the pullover sweater she wore under the coat. Beneath the sweater was a shirt, but it buttoned down the front and therefore escaped being cut off. When her torso was bare he bagan carefully feeling her ribs, his face intent as he searched for any sign of give, his eyes locked on her face to see the least hint of discomfort. She flinched several times, but the ribs felt all right. Her pale skin was already becoming discolored with bruises.

"I almost killed you," he said harshly as he lifted her in his arms and got to his feet.

"It wasn't that bad," she managed to say.

He gave her a violent look. "You were unconscious." He carried her up the stairs and to their bedroom, where he laid her on the bed. He shrugged out of his own coat and let it fall to the floor; then he very gently but implacably stripped her of every stitch and examined her from head to toe. Except for the bruising across her ribs, she was fine. He bent his head and brushed his lips across the dark band as if he would absorb the pain.

Madelyn put her hand on his hair, threading her fingers through the dark strands. "Reese, I'm okay, I promise."

He got to his feet. "I'll put a cold compress on it to stop the bruising from getting any worse."

She made a disbelieving sound. "Trust me, I can't just lie here and let you put an ice bag on my side! You know how ice down your shirt feels, and besides, I'm cold. I'd rather have a cup of hot chocolate, or coffee."

The strength of her tone reassured him, and another critical look told him that the color was coming back into her face. She sat up, rather gingerly holding her side but without any real pain, and gave him a wifely survey. "You're soaking wet from riding in that blizzard. You need to get out of those clothes, and then we'll both have something hot to drink."

She got dry clothes out for both Reese and herself and began dressing while he stripped and toweled off. She looked at her ruined sweater with disbelief, then tossed it into the trash. Reese saw her expression and smiled faintly. "I didn't want to move you any more than I had to until I knew what was wrong," he explained, rubbing a towel over his shoulders.

"Actually, I was a little relieved when the sweater was all you cut. For a split second I was afraid you were going to do a tracheotomy."

"You were talking and breathing, so I ruled that out. I've done one before, though."

"You've actually taken your pocketknife and cut someone's throat open?" she demanded incredulously, her voice rising.

"I had to. One of the hands got kicked in the throat, and he was choking to death. I slit his trachea and held it open with my finger until someone brought a drinking straw to insert for him to breathe through. We got him to a hospital, they put in a regular trach tube until the swelling went down enough for him to breathe again, and he did just fine."

"How did you know what to do?"

"Every rancher absorbs a lot of medical knowledge just in the ordinary workday. I've set broken bones, sewn up cuts, given injections. It's a rough life, sweetheart.'' His face darkened as he said it. It had almost been too rough for her. He could so easily have crushed her ribs.

He pulled on the dry underwear and jeans she had put out for him, watching as she brushed her hair and swung it back over her shoulder with a practiced toss of her head, every movement as graceful as a ballet. How could she still look elegant after what she'd been through? How could she be so casual about it? He was still shaking.

When she started past him on the way downstairs, he caught her and wrapped his arms around her, holding her to him for a long minute with his cheek resting on top of her pale hair. Madelyn circled his waist with her arms and let herself revel in his closeness; he was home, and he was all right. Nothing was said, because nothing needed saying. It was enough just to hold each other.

Reese paced the house that day like a restless cougar, periodically looking out the window to monitor the weather. He tried a radio station, but nothing came through the static. Around dusk the electricity went off, and he built a roaring fire in the fireplace, then put one of the kerosene heaters in the kitchen. Madelyn lit candles and lamps, and thanked the stars that the water heater and stove were gas-operated.

They ate soup and sandwiches by candlelight, then brought down quilts and blankets and pillows to sleep in front of the fireplace. They sat on their bed of quilts with their backs resting against the front of the couch and their legs stretched toward the fire. Madelyn's head was on his shoulder. He could almost hear her mind working as she stared at the fire, and he decided he might as well get it started before she did. ''A flag with a swallow-tail end is called a burgee.''

She gave him a quick look of delight. ''The small flag carried in front or to the right of marchers to guide them is called a guidon.''

''You want to do flags? Okay, we'll do flags. The study of flags is called vexillology.''

"The United States flag has seven red stripes and six white."

"That one's so easy it's cheating."

"A fact is a fact. Carry on."

"Bamboo is the fastest growing plant in the world."

"Cleopatra was Macedonian, not Egyptian."

They played the game for several more minutes, laughing at the more ridiculous items they pulled out. Then they got a deck of cards and played strip poker, which wasn't much of a challenge, since she was wearing only his shirt and a pair of socks, and he was wearing only jeans. Once she had him naked, she lost interest in playing cards and moved on to a more rewarding occupation. With flame-burnished skin they moved together and for a long while forgot about the swirling white storm that enveloped them.

The blizzard conditions had subsided by the next morning, though deep drifts had been piled up by the wind. The electricity came back on, and the weather report predicted slowly moderating temperatures. Reese checked on the herd and found that the cattle had withstood the storm in good condition; he lost only one calf, which had gotten lost from its mother. He found the little animal lying in a snowbank, while its mother bawled mournfully, calling it.

They had been lucky this time. He looked up at the gray sky, where patches of blue were just starting to show through. All he needed was a mild winter, or at least one where the bad spells didn't last long enough to endanger the herd.

He was pulling his way out of the morass of debt, but one year of profit was a long way from being home free. He needed the mortgage paid off, he needed an expanded herd and the money to hire cowhands to work that herd. When he could expand his capital into other areas so he wasn't entirely dependent on the weather and the market for beef, then he would feel more secure about their future.

The next few years wouldn't be easy. Madelyn wasn't pregnant yet, but as soon as she was they would have medical bills to consider, as well as the cost of providing for a growing baby. Maybe he should take Robert's offer despite his disinclination to allow anyone else any authority over the ranch. It would give him a financial cushion, the means of putting his plans into operation sooner, as well as taking care of Madelyn and their child, or children.

But he had been through too much, fought too hard and too long, to change his mind now. The ranch was his, as much a part of him as bone and blood.

He could easier lose his own life than the ranch. He loved every foot of it with the same fierce, independent possessiveness that had kept his ancestors there despite Indian attacks, weather and disease. Reese had grown up with the sun on his face and the scent of cattle in his nostrils, as much a part of this land as the purple-tinged mountains and enormous sky.

"I'll make it yet," he said aloud to the white, silent land. It wasn't in him to give up, but the land had required men like him from the beginning. It had broken weaker men, and the ones who had survived were tougher and stronger than most. The land had needed strong women, too, and if Madelyn wasn't quite what he'd planned on, he was too satisfied to care.

Chapter 9

At the end of January another big weather system began moving in from the Arctic, and this one looked bad. They had a couple of days' warning, and they worked together to do everything they could to safeguard the herd. The cold front moved in during the night, and they woke the next morning to steady snow and a temperature that was ten below zero, but at least the wind wasn't as bad as it had been before.

Reese made a couple of forays out to break the ice in the troughs and stock ponds so the cattle could drink, and Madelyn was terrified every time he went out. This kind of cold was the killing kind, and the weather reports said it would get worse.

It did. The temperature dropped all that day, and by nightfall it was twenty-three below zero.

When morning came it was forty-one degrees below zero, and the wind was blowing.

If Reese had been restless before, he was like a caged animal now. They wore layers of clothing even in the house, and he kept a fire in the fireplace even though the electricity was still on. They constantly drank hot coffee or chocolate to keep their temperatures up, and they moved down to the living room to sleep before the fire.

The third day he just sat, his eyes black with inner rage. His cattle were dying out there, and he was helpless to do a damn thing about it; the blowing snow kept him from getting to them. The killing temperatures would kill him even faster than they would the cattle. The wind chill was seventy below zero.

Lying before the fire that night, Madelyn put her hand on his chest and felt the tautness of his body. His eyes were open, and he was staring at the ceiling. She rose up on her elbow. "No matter what happens," she said quietly, "we'll make it."

His voice was harsh. "We can't make it without the cattle."

"Then you're just giving up?"

The look he gave her was violent. He didn't know how to give up; the words were obscene to him.

"We'll work harder," she said. "Last spring you didn't have me here to help you. We'll be able to do more."

His face softened, and he lifted her hand in his, holding it up in the firelight and studying it, slim and femininely graceful. She was willing to turn her hands to any job, no matter how rough or dirty, so he didn't have the heart to tell her that whenever she was with him, he was so concerned for her safety that he spent most of his time watching after her. She wouldn't understand it; they had been married for seven months, and she hadn't backed down from anything that had been thrown at her. She certainly hadn't backed down from him. Remembering some of their fights made him smile, and remembering others made him get hard. It hadn't been a dull seven months.

"You're right," he said, holding her hand to his face. "We'll just work harder."

It was the fourth day before they could get out. The wind

had died, and the sky was a clear blue bowl, making a mockery of the bitter cold. They had to wrap their faces to even
breathe, it was so cold, and it taxed their endurance just to
get to the barn to care for the animals there. The cow was
in abject misery, her udder so swollen and sore she kicked
every time Reese tried to milk her. It took over an hour of
starts and stops before she would stand still and let him finish
the job. Madelyn took care of the horses while he attended
to the milking, carrying water and feed, and then shoveling
out the stalls and putting down fresh straw.

The animals seemed nervous and glad to see them; tears
stung her eyes as she rubbed Reese's favorite mount on the
forehead. These animals had had the protection of the barn;
she couldn't bear to even think about the cattle.

Reese got the truck started and loaded it and a small trailer
with hay. Madelyn climbed into the cab and gave him a
steady look when he frowned at her. There was no way she
would let him go out on the range by himself in such bitter
cold; if anything happened to him, if he fell and couldn't get
back to the truck or lost consciousness, he would die in a
short while.

He drove carefully to the protected area where he had
herded the cattle and stopped, his face bleak. There was
nothing there, just a blank white landscape. The sun glittered
on the snow, and he reached for his sunglasses. Without a
word Madelyn followed suit.

He began driving, looking for any sign of the herd, if
indeed any of them had survived. That white blanket could
be covering their frozen carcasses.

Finally it was the pitiful bawling that led them to some of
the cattle. They had gone in search of food, or perhaps more
shelter, but they were in a stand of trees where the snow had
blown an enormous snowbank up against the tree trunks,
blocking some of the wind and perhaps saving them.

Reese's face was still shuttered as he got out to toss some
bales of hay down from the trailer, and Madelyn knew how
he felt. He was afraid to hope, afraid that only a few head

had survived. He cut the twine on the bales and loosened the hay, then took a shovel and dug an opening in the snow-bank. The anxious cattle crowded out of what had become a pen to them and headed for the hay. Reese counted them, and his face tightened. Madelyn could tell that this was only a fraction of the number there should have been.

He got back into the truck and sat with his gloved hands clenched on the steering wheel.

"If these survived, there could be more," Madelyn said. "We have to keep looking."

By a frozen pond they found more, but these were lying on their sides in pathetic, snow-covered humps. Reese counted again. Thirty-six were dead, and there could be calves too small to find under all the snow.

One cow had become trapped in a tangle of brush and wire, and her calf was lying on the snow beside her, watching with innocent brown eyes as its mother weakly struggled. Reese cut her free, and she scrambled to her feet, but then was too weak to do anything else. The calf got up too, stumbling on shaky legs to seek her milk. Reese put out hay for her to eat and continued the search for more.

They found seven survivors in a gully, and ten more carcasses not five hundred feet away. That was how it went for the rest of the day: as many as they found alive, they found that many dead. He put out hay, used an axe to chop holes in the ice-covered ponds, and kept a tally of both his losses and the ones that had survived. Half of the herd was dead, and more could die. The grimness of the situation weighed down on him. He'd been so close—and now this!

The next day they rounded up the strays, trying to get the herd together. Reese rode, and Madelyn drove the truck, pulling another trailer of hay. The temperature was moderating, if you could call ten below zero moderate, but it was too late.

One yearling objected to rejoining the herd and darted to the left, with the horse immediately following suit and getting in front of the impetuous young animal, herding it back the way it had come. The young bull stubbornly stopped, its head swinging back and forth, looking for all the world like a recalcitrant teenager. Then it made another break for freedom and bolted across a pond, but it was a pond where Reese had chopped holes in the ice near the bank, and it hadn't refrozen solid enough to hold the yearling's weight, which was already considerable. Its rear feet broke through, and it fell backward, great eyes rolling while it bawled in terror.

Cussing a blue streak, Reese got his rope and approached the bank. Madelyn pulled the truck up and got out. "Don't go out on the ice," she warned.

"Don't worry, I'm not as stupid as he is," he muttered, shaking loose a loop and twirling it a few times. He missed the first throw because the young bull was struggling frantically, and its struggles were breaking off more ice; it slipped backward and went completely under the icy water just as Reese made his throw. Still swearing, he quickly recoiled the rope as Madelyn joined him.

The second throw settled neatly around the tossing head, and Reese quickly wound the rope around the saddle horn. The horse began backing up under his quiet instructions and the pressure of his hand, dragging the yearling from the water.

As soon as the yearling was free of the water the horse stopped and Reese kept his hand on the rope as he worked to loosen the loop around the bull's neck. As soon as it was free, the animal gave a panicked bawl and bolted into Reese, its muscled shoulder knocking him sideways into the water.

Madelyn bit back a scream as she ran forward, waiting for him to surface. He did, only about ten feet out, but they were ten feet he couldn't negotiate. The numbing cold of the water was almost immediately paralyzing. All he could do was drape his arms over the edge of the broken ice and hang on.

She grabbed the rope and urged the horse forward, but she couldn't swing a loop and in any case wouldn't drag him out by his neck. "Can you catch the rope?" she called urgently, and one gloved hand moved in what she hoped was an affirmative answer. She slung the rope across the water toward him, and he made an effort to raise his arm and catch it, but his movement was slow and clumsy, and the rope fell into the water.

She had to get him out of there *now*. Two minutes from now might be too late. Her heart was slamming against her rib cage, and her face was paper-white. There was no help for him except herself, and no time for indecision. She pulled the rope back to her and ran to the pond, edging out on the ice herself.

He raised his head, his eyes filling with horror as he saw her inching toward him. "No!" he said hoarsely.

She went down on her belly and began snaking toward him, distributing her weight over as much of the ice as she could, but even so she felt it cracking beneath her. Ten feet. Just ten feet. It sounded so close in theory, and in practice it was forever.

The edge of the ice he'd been holding crumbled, and he went under. She scrambled forward, forsaking safety for speed. Just as he broke the surface again she grabbed the collar of his coat and pulled him upward; the combined pressure of their weight caused more ice to fracture and she almost fell in with him but she scrambled back just enough.

"I have the rope," she said, her teeth chattering in terror. "I'm going to slip it over your head and under your arms. Then the horse will drag you out. Okay?"

He nodded. His lips were blue, but he managed to raise one arm at a time so she could get the rope on him. She leaned forward to tighten the slip knot, and the ice beneath her gave with a sharp crack, dropping her straight downward.

Cold. She had never known such cold. It took her breath, and her limbs immediately went numb. Her eyes were open, and she saw her hair float in front of her face. She was under the water. Odd that it didn't matter. Up above she could see a white blanket with dark spots in it, and a strange disturbance. Reese…maybe it was Reese.

The thought of Reese was what focused her splintered thoughts. Somehow she managed to begin flailing her arms and legs, fighting her way to the surface, aiming for one of those dark spots that represented breaks in the ice.

Her face broke the surface just as the horse, working on its own, hauled Reese up on the bank. It was trained to pull when it felt weight on the end of the rope, so it had. She reached for the edge of the ice as Reese struggled to his hands and knees.

"Maddie!" His voice was a hoarse cry as he fought to free himself of the rope, his coordination almost gone.

Hold on. All she had to do was hold on. It was what she had been praying he would be able to do, and now it was what she had to do. She tried, but she didn't have his strength. Her weight began dragging her down, and she couldn't stop it. The water closed over her head again.

She had to fight upward, had to swim. Her thoughts were sluggish, but they directed her movements enough so that just when she thought her tortured lungs would give out and she would have to inhale, she broke through to the surface again.

"Grab the ice. Maddie, grab the ice!" He barked out the command in a tone of voice that made her reach outward in a blind motion, one that by chance laid her arm across the ice.

The wet rope was freezing, making it stiff. Reese fought the cold, fought his own clumsiness as he swung the loop. "Hold your other arm up so I can get the loop over it. Maddie, hold—your—other—arm—*up!*"

She couldn't. She had already been in the water too long. All she could do was lift the arm that had been holding on to the ice and hope that he could snare it before she went completely under.

He swung the loop out as her face disappeared under the water. It settled around her outstretched arm, and with a frantic jerk he tightened it, the loop shrinking to almost nothing as it closed around her slender wrist. "Back, back!" he yelled at the horse, which was already bracing itself against the weight it could feel.

She was dragged underwater toward the bank, and finally up on it. Reese fell to his knees beside her, screaming hell in his eyes until she began choking and retching. "We'll be all right," he said fiercely as he fumbled with the slip knot around her wrist, trying to free her. "All we have to do is get to the house and we'll be all right." He didn't even let himself think that they might not make it. Even though they weren't that far, it would take all his strength.

He was too cold to lift her, so he dragged her to the truck. Her eyes kept closing. "Don't go to sleep," he said harshly. "Open your eyes. Fight, damn it! Fight!"

Her gray eyes opened, but there was no real comprehension in them. To his astonishment, her fist doubled, and she tried to swing at him as she obeyed his rough command.

He got the truck door open and half boosted, half pushed her up onto the seat. She sprawled across it, dripping water.

The horse nudged him. If the animal hadn't been so close he would have left it behind, but a lifetime of taking care of his livestock prompted him to tie the reins to the rear bumper. He wouldn't be able to drive so fast that the horse couldn't easily keep pace, even though every instinct screamed that he had to get to the house and get both of them warm.

He pulled himself onto the seat behind the steering wheel and turned on the ignition, then struggled to slide the knob that turned the heater on high. Hot air poured out of the vents, but he was too numb to feel it.

They had to get out of their clothes. The icy wetness was just leaching more heat away from their bodies. He began fighting out of his coat as he barked orders at Madelyn to do the same.

She managed to sit up somehow, but she had almost no coordination. She had been in the water even longer than he had. He didn't have an easy time of it, but by the time he was naked she was weakly pushing her heavy shearling coat onto the floorboard. Ice crystals had already caked it.

He reached for her buttons. "Come on, sweetheart, we have to get you naked. The clothes will just make you that much colder. Can you talk to me? Say something, Maddie. Talk to me."

She slowly lifted one hand, with all the fingers folded down except the middle one. He looked at the obscene, or suggestive, gesture—it all depended on how he took it—and despite the gravity of the situation a rough laugh burst from his throat. "I'll take you up on that, sweetheart, just as soon as we get warm." A sparkle came into her eyes, giving him hope.

His teeth began chattering, and convulsive shudders racked him. Maddie wasn't shivering, and that was a bad sign. There were always a blanket and a thermos of coffee in the truck when he went out in the winter, and he pulled the blanket out from behind the seat. Even the simplest movement was a battle requiring all his strength, but he finally got it out and roughly dried them with it as best he could, then wrapped it around her.

With shaking hands he opened the thermos and poured a small amount of steaming coffee into the top, then held it to her lips. "Drink, baby. It's nice and hot."

She managed to swallow a little of it, and he drank the rest himself, then poured more into the cup. He could feel it burning down into his stomach. If he didn't get himself into shape to drive to the ranch, neither one of them would make it. He fought the shaking of his hands until he had downed the entire cup, then poured more and coaxed Madelyn into taking it. That was all he could do for now. He focused his attention and put the truck in gear.

It was slow going. He was shaking so hard that his body wouldn't obey. He was a little disoriented, sometimes unable to tell where they were. Beside him, Madelyn finally began shivering as the heat blasting from the vents combined with the coffee to revive her a little.

The house had never looked so good to him as it did when it finally came into view and he nursed the truck across the rough ground toward it. He parked as close to the back door as possible and walked naked around the truck to haul Madelyn out the passenger door. He couldn't feel the snow under his bare feet.

She could walk a little now, and that helped. With their arms around each other they half crawled up the steps to the porch, then into the utility room. The downstairs bathroom was directly across from the utility room; he dragged Madelyn into it and propped her against the wall while he turned on the water in the tub to let it get hot. When steam began rising he turned the cold water tap and hoped he adjusted it right, or they would be scalded. His hands were so cold he simply couldn't tell.

"Come on, into the tub."

She struggled to her knees, and Reese pulled her up the rest of the way, but in the end it was simpler for both of them to literally crawl over the edge of the tub into the rising water. She sat in front of him and between his legs, lying back against his chest. Tears ran down her face as the warm water lapped against her cold flesh, bringing it painfully back to life. Reese let his head tilt back until it rested on the wall, his teeth gritted. They had to endure it because it was necessary; they didn't have anyone else here to take care of them. This was the fastest way to get warm, but it wasn't pleasant.

Slowly the pain in their extremities eased. When the water was so high that it was lapping out the overflow drain, he turned off the tap and sank deeper until his shoulders were covered. Madelyn's hair floated on the surface like wet gold.

He tightened his arms around her, trying to absorb her shivering into him.

"Better?"

"Yes." Her voice was low and even huskier than usual. "That was close."

He turned her in his arms and hugged her to him with

barely controlled desperation. "I was planning to keep that bull for breeding," he said tightly, "but the sonofabitch is going to be a steer now—if he lives through this."

She managed a laugh, her lips moving against his throat. The water lapped her chin. "Don't ever get rid of that horse. He saved our bacon."

"I'll give him the biggest stall for the rest of his life."

They lay in the water until it began to cool; then he pulled the plug and urged her to her feet. She was still looking sleepy, so he held her to him while he closed the shower curtain and turned on the shower, letting the water beat down on their heads. She just stood in his arms with her head on his chest, the way she had stood so many times, but this time was infinitely precious. This time they had cheated death.

The water rained over them. He turned her face up and took her mouth, needing her taste, her touch, to reassure himself that they were really okay. He had come incredibly close to losing her, even closer than he had come to dying himself.

When the hot water began to go he snapped off the tap and reached for towels, wrapping one around her dripping hair and using another to dry her. Though her lips and nails had color now, she was still shivering a little, and he supported her as she stepped carefully from the tub. He took another towel and began rubbing his own head, all the while watching every move she made.

Madelyn felt warm, but incredibly lethargic. She had no more energy than if she had been recovering from a monster case of the flu. More than anything she wanted to lie down in front of the fire and sleep for a week, but she knew enough about hypothermia to be afraid to. She sat on the toilet seat and watched him towel dry, focusing on the magnificent strength made more evident by his nakedness. He gave her a reason to fight her lethargy now, just as he had when she had been on the bottom of the pond.

He cupped her face, making certain she was paying attention. "Don't go to sleep," he warned. "Stay in here where it's hot while I go upstairs to get your robe. Okay?"

She nodded. "Okay."

"I won't be but a minute."

She managed a smile, just to reassure him. "Bring my brush and comb, too."

It took several minutes, but he came back with her robe toasty warm from the clothes dryer, and she shuddered with pleasure as he wrapped it around her. He had taken the time to almost dress, too; he had on socks, unsnapped jeans and a flannel shirt left unbuttoned. He had brought socks for her, and he knelt to slip them on her feet.

He kept his arm around her waist as they went into the kitchen. He pulled out a chair and placed her in it. "Open your mouth," he said, and when she did he slid the thermometer, which he'd brought from the upstairs bathroom, under her tongue. "Now sit there and be still while I make a pot of coffee."

That wasn't hard to do. The only thing she wanted to do more than sit still was to lie down.

When the digital thermometer twittered its alarm, he pulled it out of her mouth and frowned at it. "Ninety six point four. I want it up at least another degree."

"What about you?"

"I'm more alert than you are. I'm bigger, and I wasn't in the water as long." He could still feel a deep inner chill, but nothing like the bone-numbing cold he had felt before. The first cup of coffee almost completely dispelled the rest of the coldness, as both the heat and the caffeine did their work. He made Madelyn drink three cups of coffee, even though she had revived enough to caustically point out that, as usual, he'd made it so strong she was likely to go into caffeine overdose. He watered it down for her, his mouth wry.

When he felt safer about leaving her, he deposited her on the quilts in front of the fire. "I have to go back out," he said, and he saw panic flare in her eyes. "Not to the range," he added quickly. "I have to put the horse back in the barn and take care of him. I'll be back as soon as I'm finished."

"I'm not going anywhere," she reassured him.

She was still afraid to lie down and go to sleep, even though so much caffeine was humming through her system that she wasn't certain she would be able to go to sleep that night. She pulled the towel off her head and began combing the tangles out of her hair.

By the time he got back, her hair was dry and she was brushing it into order. He stopped in the doorway, struck as always by the intensely female beauty of the ritual. Her sleeves dropped away from her arms as she lifted them, revealing pale, slender forearms. Her neck was gracefully bent, like a flower nodding in the breeze. His throat tightened, and blood rushed to his loins as he watched her; seven months of marriage and he was still reacting to her like a stallion scenting a mare.

"How are you feeling?" The words were raspy. He had to force them out.

She looked up, her slow smile heating his blood even more. "Better. Warm and awake. How are *you* after going back out into the cold?"

"I'm okay." More than okay. They were both alive, and there wasn't a cell in his body that was cold.

He insisted on taking her temperature again and waited impatiently until the thermometer twittered. "Ninety-seven point six. Good."

"My normal temperature isn't much more than that. It usually hovers in the low ninety-eights."

"Mine is usually around ninety-nine or a little higher."

"I'm not surprised. Sleeping with you is like sleeping with a furnace."

"Complaining?"

She shook her head. "Bragging." Her smile faded, and her gray eyes darkened to charcoal as she reached out to touch his face. "I almost lost you." He saw the flash of sheer terror in her eyes just before she closed them, and he grabbed her to him with almost desperate relief.

"Baby, I came a lot closer to losing you than you did to losing me," he said roughly, moving his lips against her hair.

Madelyn wound her arms around his neck. She didn't often cry; her moods were too even and generally upbeat. The two times she had cried since their marriage had both been the result of pain, once on their wedding night and again just an hour before when the warm water in the tub had begun bringing life back into her frozen skin. But suddenly the enormity and strain of what they had been through swept over her, and her chest tightened. She tried to fight it, tried to keep her composure, but it was a losing battle. With a wrenching sob she buried her face against his throat and clung to him while her body shook with the force of her weeping.

He was more than surprised by her sudden tears, he was astounded. His Maddie was a fighter, one who met his strength with her own and didn't flinch even from his worst tempers. But now she was sobbing as if she would never stop, and the depth of her distress punched him in the chest. He crooned to her and rubbed her back, whispering reassurances as he lowered her to the quilts.

It took a long time for her sobs to quiet. He didn't try to get her to stop, sensing that she needed the release, just as he had needed the release of savagely kicking a feed bucket the length of the barn after he had taken care of his horse. He just held her until the storm was over, then gave her his handkerchief for mopping up.

Her eyelids were swollen, and she looked exhausted, but there was no more tightly wound tension in her eyes as she lay quietly in the aftermath. Reese propped himself up on an elbow and tugged at the belt of her robe, pulling it loose and then spreading the lapels to expose her nude body.

He trailed his fingers across the hollow of her throat, then over to her slender collarbone. "Have I ever told you," he asked musingly, "that just looking at you gets me so hard it hurts?"

Her voice was husky. "No, but you've demonstrated it a few times."

"It does hurt. I feel like I'm going to explode. Then, when I get inside you, the hurt changes to pleasure." He stroked his hand down to her breast, covering it with the warmth of his palm and feeling her nipple softly pushing at him. Gently he caressed her, circling the nipple with his thumb until it stood upright and darkened in color; then he bent over her to kiss the enticing little nub. Her breathing had changed, getting deeper, and a delicate flush was warming her skin. When he looked up he saw how heavy-lidded her eyes had become, and he was flooded with fiercely masculine satisfaction that he could make her look like that.

Once he had tried to deny himself the sensual pleasure of feasting on her, but no longer. He let himself be absorbed as he stroked his hand down her body, savoring the silky texture of her skin, shaping his hand to the curves and indentations that flowed from one to the other, the swell of her breast to the flat of her stomach, the flare of her hips, the notch between her legs. He watched his tanned, powerful fingers slide through the little triangle of curls and then probe between her soft folds, fascinated by the contrast between his hand and her pale feminine body.

And the taste of her. There was the heated sweetness of her mouth; he sampled it, then tasted again more deeply, making love to her with his tongue. Then there was the warm, fragrant hollow of her throat, and the rose-and-milk taste of her breasts. He lingered there for a long time, until her hands were knotting and twisting in the quilt, and her hips were lifting against him.

Her belly was cool against his lips, and silky smooth. Her tight little navel invited exploration, and he circled it with his tongue. Her hands moved into his hair and tightly pressed against his skull as he moved downward, parting her thighs and draping them over his shoulders.

She was breathing hard, her body twisting and straining. He held her hips and loved her, not stopping until she heaved upward and cried out as the waves of completion overtook her.

She felt drained, more exhausted than before. She lay limply as he knelt between her legs and tore at his clothes, throwing them aside. She could barely open her eyes as he positioned himself and then invaded her with a slow, heavy thrust that carried him into her to the hilt. As always, she was faintly startled by the overwhelming sense of fullness as she adjusted to him.

His full weight was on her, crushing her downward. There was nothing gentlemanly about him now, only the need to enter her as deeply as possible, to carry the embrace to the fullest so that there was no part of her that didn't feel his possession. His lovemaking was often dominant, but she could usually meet it with her own strength. She couldn't now; there was a savagery in him that had to be appeased, a hunger that had to be fed. Even though he restrained himself so that he never hurt her, she was helpless to do anything but lie there and accept him, and feel her passion rising within her again with a beating rhythm.

He paused when his tension reached the critical level, not wanting it to end just yet. His green eyes glittered as he framed her face in his hands and measured the strength of her arousal.

He brushed his mouth against her ear. "Did you know that a man normally has..."

She listened to the words rustling in her ear, her hands tightening on his back as she struggled for control. Though she loved their trivia game, she wasn't in the mood for it now. Finally she gasped, "I wonder why there are so many, when one will do."

In his best big-bad-wolf voice, admittedly ragged, he said, "The better to get you pregnant, my dear," and he began moving again, hard and fast. And, sometime within the next hour, he did.

Chapter 10

Reese went over the figures again, but the totals didn't change. He got to his feet and looked out the window, his hands knotted into fists and his jaw set. All those years of work. All those *damn* years of work, for nothing.

He had done everything he could think of, cut down on every expense until there was nothing left that could be cut, and still those figures spelled it out in black and white: he had lost. The January blizzard that had killed half of his herd had pushed him so far under that the bank couldn't carry him any longer. He couldn't make the mortgage, and there would be no more extensions.

He had three options: one, he could let the bank foreclose, and they would lose everything; two, he could file chapter eleven bankruptcy and keep the ranch but ruin his credit; and three, he could accept Robert's offer to be an investor. He smiled grimly. Number three was an option only if Robert's offer was still open, considering that he had made it when the ranch was profitable and now it was going under fast.

He had been so close to making it. He thought that was what made the final defeat so bitter, that he had been close enough to see the end of debt. What April had started almost eight years before was finally coming to fruition: the destruction of his ranch. Who knew what her reasoning had been? Maybe she had done it because he had loved the ranch so much, more than he had ever even thought he loved her. It was his lifeblood, and he was losing it, unless Robert Cannon still wanted to invest. Reese went over the options again, but Robert was his only chance, and a slim one at that, because when Robert saw the figures he would have to be a hell of a gambler to go through with the deal. Reese didn't hold out much hope, but he would make the effort, because he couldn't do otherwise. He didn't have just himself to consider now; he had Madelyn, and he would do what he could to keep her home for her. She hadn't married him expecting bankruptcy or foreclosure.

It was March; snow was still on the ground, but the throbbing promise of spring was in the air. In another week or so buds would begin to swell on the trees and bushes; the land was alive, but the taste of ashes was in his mouth, because this might be the last spring he would ever see on his ranch.

He could hear Maddie in the kitchen, humming along with the radio as she gathered the ingredients for baking a cake. She'd gotten good at baking, so good that his mouth began watering every time those warm smells drifted his way. She was happy here. He hadn't married her expecting anything more than a work partner, but instead he'd gotten a warm, intelligent, amusing and sexy woman who loved him. She never seemed embarrassed about it, never tried to pressure him into giving her more than he could; she simply loved him and didn't try to hide it.

He didn't know how he would tell her, but she had a right to know.

She was licking cake batter from a wooden spoon when he walked in, and she gave him a wink as she held the spoon out. "Wanna lick?"

The batter was on her fingers, too. He started at her fingers and worked his way up the handle of the spoon, his tongue scooping up the sweet batter. When the spoon was clean he turned to her fingers to make certain he'd gotten it all. "Any more?"

She produced the bowl and swiped her finger around the edge, then popped it in her mouth laden with batter. "Your turn."

They cleaned the bowl like two children. That was probably Maddie's most endearing trait, the ease with which she found enjoyment in life, and she had taught him how to have fun again. It was just simple things, like their trivia game or licking a bowl, but he had lost the knack for having fun until she had entered his life and taken over.

He hated having to tell her that they might lose their home. A man was supposed to take care of his wife. Maybe that was old-fashioned and chauvinistic, but that was the way he felt. It ate at his pride like acid not to be able to provide for her.

He sighed and put his hands on her waist, his face grim. "We have to talk."

She eyed him cautiously. "I've never liked conversations that begin with that phrase."

"You won't like this one, either. It's serious."

She searched his face, her eyes becoming somber as she read his expression. "What is it?"

"When we lost half the herd, it put us under. I can't make the mortgage." That was it in a nutshell, as succinct and bald as he could make it.

"Can we get an extension—"

"No. If I had the full herd as collateral, then it would be possible, but I don't have enough beef on the hoof to cover the outstanding debt."

"Robert said you have the best head for business he's ever seen. What do we have to do, and what can we do?"

He outlined the three things that could happen, and she listened to him with an intent expression. When he had finished she asked, "Why don't you think Robert's offer would still stand?"

"Because the ranch is a losing proposition now."

"You're still here, and it was you he was willing to bet on, not X number of cows." Then she said, "There's another option you haven't mentioned."

"What's that?"

"I told you before, I have some money—"

He dropped his hands. "No. I've told *you* before."

"Why not?" she asked calmly.

"I've told you that before, too. It hasn't changed."

"Do you mean you'd actually give up the ranch before you would let me put my money in it?"

His eyes looked like flint. "Yes, that's exactly what I mean." Maddie had changed a lot of his attitudes, but that one was still intact and as strong as ever. A business partner was one thing, because rights were limited by contract. A marriage was something else, subject to the whims of a judge with little regard to fairness. April had proved that to him.

Madelyn turned away before her expression betrayed her. Not for anything would she let him see how that hurt her. With perfect control she said, "It's your ranch, your decision."

"Exactly, and it will stay my ranch, my decision, until the day I get thrown off."

Her mind was busy as she cooked dinner, and determination grew in her. If he thought she would stand by and see the ranch go under when she had the means to save it, he would learn differently. She didn't know how much the mortgage was, and she had told him the truth when she'd said that her trust fund was far from being a fortune, but surely it was enough to buy them some time until the ranch was on a firmer footing.

He'd never said he loved her. Maybe he didn't, but Madelyn thought he was at least fond of her. He certainly desired her, though it was true that a man could physically desire a woman without caring for her as a person. If he had lived with her for nine months and still thought she was capable of doing the sort of thing April had done, then perhaps he didn't care for her as much as she'd thought. She had been happy, but now her balloon was fast going flat.

Now wasn't the time to tell him she was pregnant. Or maybe it was. Maybe knowing about the baby would bring him to his senses, reassure him that she wasn't going anywhere, and that they had to use whatever means were at their disposal to save their child's inheritance.

But she didn't tell him. His mood varied from taciturn to biting sarcasm, the way it did when he was angry, and she didn't feel like prodding him into a full-scale blowup. Though she was only two months along, she was already beginning to feel the effects of pregnancy in lower energy levels and a slightly upset stomach—not the best time to battle with her husband.

He was still in a bad mood when he left the next morning, and he took a lunch with him, which meant he wouldn't be back until it was time for dinner. Madelyn hesitated for maybe five minutes.

She didn't like going behind his back, but if that was the way it had to be, then she would face the music later. It was a long drive to Billings; she might not make it back before he did, but that was another bridge she would cross when she came to it. While she was there she would also phone around for an obstetrician, because there wasn't any sort of doctor in Crook, and she didn't know of one any closer than Billings. It could get interesting around her delivery time, she thought, with her doctor a three-hour drive away.

She hastily dressed, got her checkbook and the necessary documents, and ran out to the car. It had snow tires on it if she needed them, but the highways were clear, so she hoped she would make good time.

She drove quickly but carefully, thankful that there wasn't much traffic to contend with, and reached the bank at eleven-thirty. She knew who Reese dealt with, having accompanied him before, and she only had to wait about fifteen minutes before the man could see her.

He was smiling the way bankers do, his hand outstretched. "Good morning, Mrs. Duncan. What can we do for you?"

"Good morning, Mr. VanRoden. I'd like to know the amount of our outstanding mortgage."

He stroked his upper lip as if he had a mustache, which he didn't, and looked thoughtful. "Well, I'm not certain I can tell you. You see, the mortgage is only in your husband's name."

She didn't bother trying to argue with bureaucracy or banking rules and went straight to the point. "If it's under two hundred thousand dollars, I want to pay it off."

There was nothing that got a banker's attention like money. He chewed his lip, studying her. She sat very calmly and let him try to pick up what clues he could from her appearance, though she had deliberately dressed that morning in one of her New York suits and twisted her hair up. If he could read anything in a charcoal suit with a pink silk blouse under it and an iridescent peacock pinned to the lapel, he was welcome to draw any conclusions he could.

He made up his mind with a minimum of dithering. "Let me check the file," he said. "I'll be right back."

She waited, certain of the outcome. No bank would refuse the repayment of a loan, regardless of who was doing the paying. She supposed a rank stranger could walk in off the street and pay off any loan he chose, as long as he had the means to do it.

VanRoden was back in less than five minutes with a sheaf of papers in his hand. "I believe we're ready to talk business, Mrs. Duncan. Mr. Duncan doesn't have enough in his checking account to cover the loan, so how were you proposing to pay it?"

"I have a trust fund, Mr. VanRoden. I transferred it from New York to another bank here in Billings. First, is the outstanding debt on the mortgage less than two hundred thousand?"

He coughed. "Yes, it is."

"Then I'll be back. I'm going to my bank now to have the trust fund transferred into my checking account. I've had full access to it since I was twenty-five, so there's no problem."

He pushed the telephone toward her. "Call them, so they'll let you in. They'll be closing for lunch shortly."

She smiled at him as she reached for the phone. "By the way, do you know a good obstetrician?"

A phone call later, it had been arranged for her to enter the other bank by a side door. An hour later she was back at the first bank, cashier's check in hand for the amount VanRoden had given her before she left.

She signed the necessary papers and walked out of the bank with the deed to the ranch and the papers that said the debt had been paid in full. She also had an appointment the following week with the obstetrician VanRoden's wife had used. She grinned as she got into the car. Contacts had their uses, even unlikely ones. Poor Mr. VanRoden had looked startled at being asked to recommend an obstetrician, then had offered his congratulations.

She had no illusions that everything was going to be fine now just because she had paid the mortgage. She hadn't done it lightly; she had done it with the full knowledge that Reese would be furious, but she was willing to fight for their future, their child's future. She had to deal with the scars left by Reese's first marriage, and this was far more serious than painting the house. As a matter of fact, he *had* drawn up a note stating that he would repay her for the cost of the paint and estimated labor, which she thought was ridiculous, but was a fair measure of how determined he was in the matter.

But knowing she had to tell him and knowing how to tell him were two different things. She couldn't just say, "I went into Billings today to make an appointment with an obstetrician because I'm pregnant, and by the way, while I was there I paid off the mortgage." On the other hand, that was certainly a good example of killing two birds with one stone.

She was still worrying it over in her mind when she got home at about four-thirty. There was no sign of Reese's truck, so perhaps she had made it without him even knowing she'd been gone. If he had come back to the house for any reason during the day, he'd ask questions as soon as he got back, and one thing she wouldn't do was lie to him. Delaying telling him about the mortgage was different from lying to him about it.

It was amazing how tired she was, and equally amazing how she could feel so exhausted but still feel well.

She would be having his baby sometime late in October or early in November, if she had figured correctly. The knowledge of it was like a great inner warmth, and she had never wanted anything more than to share it with him. Only the worry he had been enduring over the ranch had kept her from telling him, because she didn't want to give him something else to worry about. The stern lines in his face were deeper, and his eyes were habitually grim these days, as he faced losing everything he had worked so hard for, for so long. How could she burden him with the knowledge that now they had medical bills to consider, as well?

How could she *not* tell him?

As she changed clothes, her fatigue suddenly became overwhelming. She fought it, knowing that it was time to begin cooking dinner, but the thought of all that preparation made the fatigue even worse, and her stomach suddenly rolled. She broke out in a sweat and sank weakly onto the bed. What a great time for morning sickness to hit—late in the afternoon on a day when she needed all her wits about her. She sat there for a minute, and the nausea faded, but the fatigue was worse. There was no way she could summon the energy even to go downstairs; exhaustion pulled on her limbs and eyelids, dragging both down. With a sigh she stretched out on the bed, her eyes already closing. Just a short nap; that was all she needed.

Reese found her there. He had noticed that the kitchen light wasn't on when he got home, but he had taken care of the evening chores before going into the house. The kitchen was empty, with no sign of meal preparations in progress, and the house was strangely silent. "Maddie?" When there was no answer, a worried frown creased his forehead, and he searched the downstairs, then started up the stairs. "Maddie?"

He turned on the light in the bedroom, and there she was, curled on her side on the bed. She didn't stir even when the light came on. He'd never known her to nap during the day, and he was instantly alarmed. Was she sick? She had seemed okay that morning. He was dirty from the day's work, but he didn't care about that as he sat down on the side of the bed and turned her onto her back. She felt warm under his hands, but not unusually so. He shook her, and worry sharpened his tone. "Maddie, wake up!"

Slowly her lids drifted upward, and she sighed. "Reese," she murmured, but she couldn't keep her eyes open.

He shook her again. "Are you all right? Wake up."

Reluctantly she roused, lifting one hand to rub her eyes. "What time is it?" Then she looked at him again as realization sank in and said, "Oh my God, dinner!"

"Dinner can wait. Are you all right?"

Her heart lurched as she stared up at him. His face was lined and grayish with fatigue, but there was worry in his eyes, not irritation. Automatically she reached up to touch his cheek, stroking her fingers over the high ridge of his cheekbone. She loved everything about this man, even his stubborn temper. She took his hand and placed it on her belly. "I'm pregnant," she whispered. "We're having a baby."

His pupils dilated, and he looked down at his hand on her slender body. From the time she had stopped taking the birth control pills, every time he had made love to her he had been aware that he might impregnate her, but the reality of having her say she was pregnant was still almost a physical shock. His baby was growing under his hand, utterly protected in her flat little belly.

He slid off the bed onto his knees beside it, still dazed. "When?" he asked in a strained tone.

"The last week in October, or the first week in November."

He unsnapped her jeans and slid the zipper down, then spread the fly open so he could touch her skin. He pushed her sweatshirt up out of the way and slowly leaned forward, first pressing a light kiss to her belly, then resting his cheek against it. Madelyn stroked his hair and wondered if the baby would have dark coloring like him or her fairness. It was such a new, wonderful consideration, their child, created from the raw passion that still burned between them. Seven more months suddenly seemed too long to wait to hold it, to see Reese's powerful hands turn gentle as he cradled his child. "Do you want a boy or a girl?" she asked, still whispering, as if normal speech might spoil the sweetness of this moment.

"Does it matter?" He rubbed his rough cheek against her belly, his eyes closing as he luxuriated in the caress.

"Not to me."

"Or to me." Silence grew in the room as he fully absorbed the news; then finally he lifted his head. "Are you feeling sick?"

"I was a little nauseated, but mostly I was incredibly tired. I tried, but I just couldn't keep my eyes open," she said apologetically.

"Are you all right now?"

She thought about it, mentally taking stock of herself, then nodded. "All systems are go."

He moved back and let her get to her feet, then caught her to him and tilted her mouth up. The expression in his eyes was intense as he gave her a hard, brief kiss. "Are you certain?"

"I'm certain." She smiled and looped her arms around his neck, letting her weight swing from them. "You'll know if I'm feeling sick. I'll turn green and keel over."

He cupped her bottom and held her against him as he

kissed her again, and this time there was nothing brief about it. Madelyn held him tightly, her eyes closing as his familiar nearness sent warmth through her. She loved him so much it sometimes frightened her; she hoped he would remember that.

His lovemaking that night was achingly tender and incredibly prolonged. He couldn't seem to get enough of her, taking her again and again, staying inside her for a long time afterward. They finally went to sleep like that, with her leg thrown over his hip, and she thought it had never been more perfect than it was then, with Reese in her arms and his child in her womb.

A week later Reese walked back to the house from the barn with a defeated expression on his face. Madelyn watched him from the kitchen window and knew she couldn't put it off any longer. She simply couldn't let him worry any longer; better to enrage him than watch the lines settle deeper in his face every day. He would sit in his office for hours every night, going over and over the books, pacing and running his hands through his hair, then trying it again, only to come up with the same figures and no hope.

She heard him come in and take off his muddy boots; then he came into the kitchen in his sock feet. "The truck needs a new oil pump," he said tiredly.

She twisted the hand towel she was holding. "Then buy one." Tension was tightening her muscles, and she swallowed the faint rise of nausea.

His mouth was bitter. "Why bother? We won't be here another month anyway."

Slowly she hung up the towel then turned to face him, leaning back against the cabinet for support. "Yes, we will."

He thought he knew what she meant. He could call Robert—but Robert would have to be a fool to invest in the ranch now. He had put it off as long as he could, and now he didn't see anything else he could do. Madelyn was pregnant; she had her first doctor's appointment the next day, and money would be required up front. Then they were facing bills from the hospital, and he didn't have medical insurance. That had been one of the first things to go.

"I'll call Robert," he said gently. "But don't hope too much."

She put her shoulders back and took a deep breath. "Call Robert if you want, after I tell you what I have to tell you. You'll be in a different situation then and—" She stopped, looking at him helplessly, and began again. "I paid off the mortgage with my trust fund."

For a moment he didn't react at all, just watched her silently, and she started to hope. Then his eyes began to chill, and she braced herself.

"What?" he asked very softly.

"I paid off the mortgage. The papers are in my underwear drawer."

Without a word he turned and went upstairs. Madelyn followed, her heart pounding. She had faced his anger before without turning a hair, but this was different. This was striking at the very basis of his feelings.

He jerked her underwear drawer open just as she entered the bedroom. She hadn't stuffed the papers in the bottom; they were lying right there in plain sight. He picked them up and flipped through them, noting the amount and date on the documents.

He didn't look up. "How did you arrange it?"

"I went to Billings last week, the day you told me about the mortgage. Banks don't care who pays off loans so long as they get their money, and since I'm your wife they didn't question it."

"Did you think presenting me with a fait accompli would change my mind?"

She wished that he would stop using that soft voice. When Reese was angry he roared, and she could handle that, but this was something new.

His head came up, and she flinched. His eyes were like green ice. "Answer me."

She stood very still. "No, I didn't think anything would change your mind, and that's why I did it behind your back."

"You were right. Nothing would change my mind. I'll see you in hell before you get any part of this ranch."

"I don't want to take the ranch away from you. I've never wanted that."

"You've played your part well, Maddie, I'll give you that. You haven't complained, you've acted like a perfect wife. You even carried it so far as to pretend you love me."

"I do love you." She took a step toward him, her hands outstretched. "Listen—"

Suddenly the rage in him erupted, and he threw the sheaf of papers at her. They separated and swirled around her, then drifted to the floor. "That's what I think of your so-called 'love,'" he said with gritted teeth. "If you think doing something you knew I couldn't bear is an expression of 'love,' then you don't have any idea what the real thing is."

"I didn't want you to lose the ranch—"

"So you just took care of the mortgage. Any divorce court now would consider you a co-owner, wouldn't they? They'd figure I talked you into investing your inheritance and the prenuptial agreement wouldn't ·mean a damn. Hell, why should you get less than April? This· isn't the operation it once was, but the land is worth a hell of a lot."

"I don't want a divorce, I haven't even thought of divorce," she said desperately. "I wanted to keep the ranch for you. At least this way you have a chance to rebuild it, if you'll just take it!"

He said sarcastically, "Yeah, if it's worth more, you'll get more."

"For the last time, I don't want a divorce!"

He reached out and pinched her chin, the gesture savagely playful. "You just might get one anyway, dollface, because I sure as hell don't want a wife who'd knife me in the back like that. You weren't my first choice, and I should have listened to my instincts, but you had me as hot as a sixteen-year-old after my first piece in the back seat. April was a bitch, but you're worse, Maddie, because you played along and pretended this was just what you wanted. Then you slipped the blade between my ribs so slick I never even saw it coming."

"This *is* what I want." She was pale, her eyes darkening.

"Well, you're not what I want. You're hot between the sheets, but you don't have what it takes to be a ranch wife," he said cruelly.

"Reese Duncan, if you're trying to run me off, you're doing a good job of it," she warned shakily.

He raised his eyebrows. His tone was icily polite. "Where would you like to go? I'll give you a ride."

"If you'll climb down off that mountain of pride you'll see how wrong you are! I don't want to take the ranch away. I want to live here and raise our children here. You and I aren't the only ones involved in this. I'm carrying your baby, and it's his heritage, too!"

His eyes went black as he remembered the baby, and his gaze swept down her slender figure. "On second thought, you aren't going anywhere. You're staying right here until that baby's born. Then I don't care what the hell *you* do, but my kid is staying with me."

Coldness settled inside her, pushing away the hurt and anger that had been building with every word he said. Understanding could go only so far. Sympathy held out only so long. He didn't love her, and he didn't believe in her love for him, so exactly how much of a marriage did they have? One made of mirrors and moonshine, and held together by sex. She stared at him, her eyes going blank. Later there would be pain, but not now.

She said very carefully, "When you calm down you'll regret saying this."

"The only thing I regret is marrying you." He took her purse from the top of the dresser and opened it.

"What are you looking for?" She made no effort to grab

it from him. In any test of strength against him she would be humiliated.

He held up the car keys. "These." He dropped her purse and shoved the keys into his pocket. "Like I said, you're not going anywhere with my kid inside you. The only moving you're doing is out of my bed. There are three other bedrooms. Pick one, and keep your butt in it."

He stalked from the room, being very careful not to touch her. Madelyn sank down on the bed, her legs folding under her like spaghetti. She could barely breathe, and dark spots swam in front of her eyes. Cold chills made her shake.

She didn't know how long it was before her mind began to function again, but finally it did, slowly at first, then with gathering speed. She began to get angry, a calm, deep, slow-burning anger that grew until it had destroyed all the numbness.

She got up and began methodically moving her things out of Reese's bedroom and into the room where she had slept the night she had visited him. She didn't move a few token things in the hope that he would get over his temper, reconsider and tell her to stay put; she purged the bedroom of all signs of her presence. She left the mortgage papers lying where they were in the middle of the room. Let him walk over them if he didn't want to pick them up.

If he wanted war, she'd give him war.

Pride prompted her to stay in her bedroom and not speak to him; pregnancy insisted that she eat. She went downstairs and cooked a full meal in an effort to rub a little salt in his wounds. If he didn't want to eat what she had prepared, then he could either do it himself or do without.

But he came to the table when she called him and ate his usual hearty meal. As she was clearing the dishes away she said, "Don't forget the doctor's appointment in the morning."

He didn't look at her. "I'll drive you. You aren't getting the keys back."

"Fine."

Then she went upstairs, showered and went to bed.

The next morning they didn't speak a word all the way to Billings. When her name was called in the doctor's office, which was filled with women in various stages of pregnancy, she got up and walked past him to follow the nurse. He turned his head, watching the graceful sway of her retreating figure. In a few months she would lose her grace and the sway would become a waddle. His hand tightened into a fist, and it was all he could do to keep from swearing aloud. *How could she have done that to him?*

Madelyn was questioned, stuck, checked, probed and measured. When she had dressed she was directed into the doctor's office, and in a moment Reese joined her, followed shortly by the doctor.

"Well, everything looks normal," the doctor said, consulting his charts. "You're in good physical shape, Mrs. Duncan. Your uterus is enlarged more like thirteen or fourteen weeks than the nine or ten you think it should be, so you may be off on your conception date. We'll do an ultrasound when you're further along to get a better idea of the baby's maturity. It could just be a large baby, or twins. I see that your maternal grandmother was a twin, and multiple births usually follow the female line."

Reese sat up straight, his eyes sharpening. "Is there any danger in having twins?"

"Not much. They usually come a little early, and we have to be careful about that. At this stage of the game, I'm more worried about a large baby than I am twins. Your wife should be able to have twins without a problem, as their birth weight is usually lower than that of a single baby. The total is more, but the individual weights are less. How much did you weigh when you were born, Mr. Duncan?"

"Ten pounds, two ounces." His mouth was grim.

"I'll want to keep a very close eye on your wife if this baby approaches a birth weight of anything over eight pounds. She has a narrow pelvis, not drastically so, but a ten-pound baby would probably require a C-section."

That said, he began talking to Madelyn about her diet, vitamins and rest, and he gave her several booklets about prenatal care. When they left half an hour later, Madelyn was weighted down with prescriptions and reading material. Reese drove to a pharmacy, where he had the prescriptions filled, then headed home again. Madelyn sat straight and silent beside him. When they got home, he realized that she hadn't looked at him once all day.

Chapter 11

The next morning as he started to leave she asked coolly, "Can you hear the car horn blow from anywhere on the ranch?"

He looked startled. "Of course not." He eyed her questioningly, but she still wasn't looking at him.

"Then how am I supposed to find you or contact you?"

"Why would you want to?" he asked sarcastically.

"I'm pregnant. I could fall, or start to miscarry. Any number of things."

It was an argument he couldn't refute. He set his jaw, faced with the choice between giving her the means to leave or endangering both her life and that of his baby. When it came down to it, he didn't have a choice. He took the keys from his pocket and slammed them down on the cabinet, but he kept his hand on them.

"Do I have your word you won't run?"

She looked at him finally, but her eyes were cool and blank. "No. Why should I waste my breath making promises when you wouldn't believe me anyway?"

"Just what is it you want me to believe? That you haven't worked it so you have just as much claim to the ranch as I have? A woman made a fool of me once and walked away with half of everything I owned, but it won't happen again, even if I have to burn this house to the ground and sell the land for a loss, is that clear?" He was shouting by the time he finished, and he looked at her as if he hated the sight of her.

Madelyn didn't show any expression or move. "If that was all I'd wanted, I could have paid off the mortgage at any time."

Her point scored; she saw it in his eyes. She could have followed it up, but she held her peace. She had given him something to think about. She would give him a lot more to think about before this was over.

He banged out of the house, leaving the car keys on the cabinet. She picked them up, tossing them in her hand as she went upstairs to the bedroom, where she already had some clothes packed. In the two nights she had spent alone in this room, she had thought through what she was going to do and where she was going to go. Reese would expect her to go running back to New York now that she had a claim on the ranch, but she had never even considered that. To teach him the lesson he needed, she had to be close by.

It would be just like him to deliberately work close by in case she tried to leave, so she didn't, and felt fierce satisfaction when he came home for lunch after telling her that he would be out all day. Since she hadn't cooked anything, she made a plate of sandwiches and put it in front of him, then continued with what she had been doing before, which was cleaning the oven.

He asked, "Aren't you going to eat?"

"I've already eaten."

A few minutes later he asked, "Should you be doing work like that?"

"It isn't hard."

Her cool tone discouraged any more conversational overtures. She wasn't letting him off that easy. She had told him twice that she wasn't going to pay for April's sins, but it evidently hadn't sunk in; now she was going to show him.

When he left again she waited half an hour, then carried her suitcase out to the car. She didn't have far to go, and it wouldn't take him long to find her, a few days at the most. Then he could take the car back if he wanted, so she didn't feel guilty about it. Besides, she didn't need it. She fully expected to be back at the ranch before her next doctor's appointment, but if she wasn't, then she would inform Reese that he had to take her. Her plan had nothing to do with staying away from him.

There was a room above Floris's café that was always for rent, because there was never anyone in Crook who needed to rent it. It would do for her for as long as she needed it. She drove to Crook and parked the car in front of the café. The idea wasn't to hide from Reese; she wanted him to know exactly where she was.

She went into the café, but there wasn't anyone behind the counter. "Floris? Is anyone here?"

"Hold your water," came Floris's unmistakable sour voice from the kitchen. A few minutes later she came through the door. "You want coffee, or something to eat?"

"I want to rent the room upstairs."

Floris stopped and narrowed her eyes at Madelyn. "What do you want to do that for?"

"Because I need a place to stay."

"You've got a big house back on that ranch, and a big man to keep you warm at night, if that's all you need."

"What I have," Madelyn said very clearly, "is a pig-headed husband who needs to be taught a lesson."

"Hmmph. Never seen a man yet wasn't pigheaded."

"I'm pregnant, too."

"Does he know?"

"He does."

"He knows where you are?"

"He will soon. I'm not hiding from him. He'll probably

come through the door breathing fire and raising hell, but I'm not going back until he understands a few things.''

"Such as?"

"Such as I'm not his first wife. He got a dirty deal, but I'm not the one who gave it to him, and I'm tired of paying for someone else's dirt."

Floris looked her up and down, then nodded, and a pleased expression for once lit her sour face. "All right, the room's yours. I always did like to see a man get his comeuppance," she muttered as she turned to go back into the kitchen. Then she stopped and looked back at Madelyn. "You got any experience as a short-order cook?"

"No. Do you need one?"

"Wouldn't have asked if I didn't. I'm doing the cooking and waitressing, too. That sorry Lundy got mad because I told him his eggs were like rubber and quit on me last week."

Madelyn considered the situation and found she liked it. "I could wait on tables."

"You ever done that before?"

"No, but I've taken care of Reese for nine months."

Floris grunted. "I guess that qualifies you. He don't strike me as an easy man to satisfy. Well, you in good health? I don't want you on your feet if you're having trouble keeping that baby."

"Perfect health. I saw a doctor yesterday."

"Then the job's yours. I'll show you the room. It's nothing fancy, but it's warm during the winter."

The room was clean and snug, and that was about the limit of its virtues, but Madelyn didn't mind. There was a single bed, a couch, a card table with two chairs, a hot plate and a minuscule bathroom with cracking tile. Floris turned on the heat so it would get warm and returned to the kitchen while Madelyn carried her suitcases in. After hanging up her clothes in the small closet, she went downstairs to the café, tied an apron around her and took up her duties as waitress.

* * *

When Reese got home that night he was dead tired; he'd been kicked, stepped on and had a rope burn on his arm. The cows would begin dropping their spring calves any time, and that would be even more work, especially if a cold front moved in.

When he saw that the car was gone and the house was dark, it was like taking a kick in the chest, punching the air out of him. He stared at the dark windows, filled with a paralyzing mixture of pain and rage. He hadn't really thought she would leave. Deep down, he had expected her to stay and fight it out, toe-to-toe and chin to chin, the way she'd done so many times. Instead she'd left, and he closed his eyes at the piercing realization that she was exactly what he'd most feared: a grasping, shallow woman who wasn't able to take the hard times. She'd run back to the city and her cushy life-style, the stylish clothes.

And she'd taken his baby with her.

It was a betrayal ten times worse than anything April had done to him. He had begun to trust Maddie, begun to let himself think of their future in terms of years rather than just an unknown number of months. She had lain beneath him and willingly let him get her pregnant; for most of a year she had lived with him, cooked for him, washed his clothes, laughed and teased and worked alongside him, slept in his arms.

Then she had stabbed him in the back. It was a living nightmare, and he was living it for the second time.

He walked slowly into the house, his steps dragging. There were no warm, welcoming smells in the kitchen, no sound except for the hum of the refrigerator and the ticking of the clock. Despite everything, he had a desperate, useless hope that she'd had to go somewhere, that there was a note of explanation somewhere in the house. He searched all the rooms, but there was no note. He went into the bedroom where she had spent the past two nights and found the dresser drawers empty, the bathroom swept clean of the fragrant female paraphernalia. He was still trying to get used

to not seeing her clothes in the closet beside his; to find them
nowhere in the house was staggering.

It was like pouring salt into an open wound, but he went
into the other bedroom where she had stored her "New
York" clothes. It was as if he had to check every missing
sign of her inhabitance to verify her absence, a wounded and
bewildered animal sniffing around for his mate before he sat
down and howled his anger and loss at the world.

But when he opened the closet door he stared at the row
of silk blouses, hung on satin-padded hangers and protected
by plastic covers, the chic suits and lounging pajamas, the
high-heeled shoes in a dozen colors and styles. A faint hint
of her perfume wafted from the clothes, and he broke out in
a sweat, staring at them.

Swiftly he went downstairs. Her books were still here, and
her stereo system. She might be gone now, but she had left
a lot of her things here, and that meant she would be back.
She would probably come back during the day, when she
would expect him to be gone, so she could pack the rest and
leave without ever seeing him.

But if she were going back to New York, as she almost
certainly had been planning, why had she taken her ranch
clothes and left the city clothes?

Who knew why Madelyn did anything? he thought wearily. Why had she paid off the mortgage with her trust fund
when she knew that was the one thing, given his past, that
he would be unable to bear?

He'd never in his life been angrier, not even when he had
sat in a courtroom and heard a judge hand over half his ranch
to April. He hadn't expected anything better from April, who
had given him ample demonstration of just how vindictive
and callous she could be. But when Maddie had blindsided
him like that, she had really hit him hard and low, and he
was still reeling. Every time he tried to think about it, the
pain and anger were so great that they crowded out everything else.

Well, she was gone, so he'd have plenty of time to think

about it now. But she would have a hell of a time getting back in to get her things while he was gone, because the first chance he got he was going to change the locks on the house.

For now, however, he was going to do something he hadn't done even when April had done such a good job of wrecking his life. He was going to get the bottle of whiskey that had been in the cupboard for so many years and get dead drunk. Maybe then he would be able to sleep without Maddie beside him.

He felt like hell the next day, with a pounding head and a heaving stomach, but he dragged himself up and took care of the animals; it wasn't their fault he was a damn fool. By the time his headache began to fade and he began to feel halfway human again, it was too late to go to the general store to buy new locks.

The next day the cows began dropping their calves. It was the same every time: when the first one went into labor and drifted away to find a quiet place to calve, the others one by one followed suit. And they could pick some of the damnedest places to have their calves. It was an almost impossible task for one man to track down the cows in their hiding places, make certain the little newborns were all right, help the cows who were in difficulty and take care of the calves who were born dead or sickly. Instinct always went wrong with at least one cow, and she would refuse to have anything to do with her new baby, meaning Reese had to either get another cow to adopt it or take it to the barn for hand-feeding.

It was three days before he had a minute to rest, and when he did he dropped down on the couch in an exhausted stupor and slept for sixteen hours.

It was almost a week after Madelyn had left before he finally got time to drive to Crook. The pain and anger had become an empty, numb feeling in his chest.

The first thing he saw as he passed Floris's café was the white Ford station wagon parked out front.

His heart lurched wildly, and the bottom dropped out of his stomach. She was back, probably on her way to get the rest of her things. He parked next door in front of the general store and stared at the car, his fingers drumming on the steering wheel. The familiar anger exploded into the numb vacuum, and something became immediately, blindingly clear to him.

He wasn't going to let her go. If he had to fight her in every court in the country, he was going to keep his ranch intact and she was going to stay his wife. He'd been glad to see the last of April, but there was no way he was going to let Maddie just walk out. She was carrying his baby, a baby that was going to grow up in his house if he had to tie Maddie to the bed every day when he left.

He got out of the truck and strode toward the café, his boot heels thudding on the wooden sidewalk, his face set.

He pushed open the door and walked inside, standing in the middle of the room as he surveyed the booths and tables. There was no long-legged blonde with a lazy smile at any of them, though two lean and bandy-legged cowboys straddled stools at the counter.

Then the kitchen door opened and his long-legged blonde came through it, wrapped in an apron and carrying two plates covered with enormous hamburgers and mounds of steaming French fries. She flicked a glance at him and neither changed expression or missed a beat as she set the plates in front of the cowboys. "Here you go. Let me know if you want any pie. Floris baked an apple cobbler this morning that'll make you cry, it tastes so good."

Then she looked at him with those blank, cool eyes and said, "What can I get for you?"

The cowboys looked around, and one coughed when he saw who Madelyn was talking to; Reese pretty well knew everybody in a hundred-mile range, and they knew him, too, by sight if not personally. Everyone also knew Madelyn; a woman with her looks and style didn't go unnoticed, so it was damn certain those two cowboys realized it was her husband standing behind them looking like a thunderstorm about to spit lightning and hail all over them.

In a calm, deadly voice Reese said, "Bring me a cup of coffee," and went over to fold his long length into one of the booths.

She brought it immediately, sliding the coffee and a glass of water in front of him. Then she gave him an impersonal smile that didn't reach her eyes and said, "Anything else?" She was already turning to go as she said it.

He snapped his hand out, catching her wrist and pulling her to a halt. He felt the slenderness of her bones under his fingers and was suddenly, shockingly aware of how physically overmatched she was with him, yet she had never backed away from him. Even in bed, when he had held her slim hips in his hands and thrust heavily into her, she had wrapped those legs around him and taken everything he could give her. Maddie wasn't the type to run, unless leaving was something she had planned from the beginning. But if that were so, why was she here? Why hadn't she gone back to New York, out of his reach?

"Sit down," he said in a low, dangerous voice.

"I have work to do."

"I said to sit down." Using his grip on her wrist, he pulled her down into the booth. She was still watching him with those cool, distant eyes.

"What are you doing here?" he snapped, ignoring the looks the two cowboys were giving him.

"I work here."

"That's what I meant. What the *hell* are you doing working here?"

"Supporting myself. What did you expect me to do?"

"I expected you to keep your little butt on the ranch like I told you to."

"Why should I stay where I'm not wanted? By the way, if you can figure out a way to get the car home, feel free to take it. I don't need it."

With an effort he controlled the anger and impatience

building in him. It might be just what she wanted, for him to lose his temper in a public place.

"Where are you staying?" he asked in a voice that showed the strain he was under.

"Upstairs."

"Get your clothes. You're going home with me."

"No."

"What did you say?"

"I said no. N-O. It's a two-letter word signifying refusal."

He flattened his hands on the table to keep himself from grabbing her and giving her a good shaking, or from pulling her onto his lap and kissing her senseless. Right at the moment, he wasn't certain which it would be. "I'm not putting up with this, Maddie. Get upstairs and get your clothes." Despite himself, he couldn't keep his voice down, and the two cowboys were openly staring at him.

She slid out of the booth and was on her feet before he could grab her, and he was reminded that, when she chose, Maddie could move like the wind. "Give me one good reason why I should!" she fired back at him, the chill in her eyes beginning to heat now.

"Because you're carrying my baby!" he roared, surging to his own feet.

"You're the one who said, quote, that you didn't care what the hell I did and that you regret marrying me, unquote. I was carrying the baby then, too, so what's different now?"

"I changed my mind."

"Well, bully for you! You also told me that I'm not what you want and I don't have what it takes to be a ranch wife. That's another quote."

One of the cowboys cleared his throat. "You sure look like you've got what it takes to me, Miss Maddie."

Reese rounded on the cowboy with death in his eyes and his fist clenched. "Do you want to wear your teeth or carry them?" he asked in an almost soundless voice.

The cowboy still seemed to be having trouble with his

throat. He cleared it again, but it took him two tries before he managed to say, "Just making a comment."

"Then make it outside. This is between me and my wife."

In the West, a man broke his own horses and killed his own snakes, and everybody else kept their nose the hell out of his business. The cowboy fumbled in his pocket for a couple of bills and laid them on the counter. "Let's go," he said to his friend.

"You go on." The other cowboy forked up a fry covered in ketchup. "I'm not through eating." *Or watching the show, either.*

Floris came through the kitchen door, her sour expression intact and a spatula in her hand. "Who's making all the noise out here?" she demanded; then her gaze fell on Reese. "Oh, it's you." She made it sound as if he were about as welcome as the plague.

"I've come to take Maddie home," he said.

"Don't see why she'd want to go, you being so sweet-tempered and all."

"She's my wife."

"She can wait on men here and get paid for it." She shook the spatula at him. "What have you got to offer her besides that log in your pants?"

Reese's jaw was like granite. He could toss Madelyn over his shoulder and carry her home, but even though he was willing to bully her, he didn't want to physically force her. For one thing, she was pregnant, but more importantly, he wanted her to go home with him because she wanted to. One look at her face told him that she wasn't going to willingly take a step toward the ranch.

Well, he knew where she was now. She hadn't gone back to New York. She was within reach, and he wasn't giving up. With one last violent look at her, he threw his money on the table and stomped out.

Madelyn slowly let out the breath she'd been holding. That had been close. He was evidently as determined to take her back to the ranch as he was to believe she was a clone of his first wife. And if she knew one thing about Reese Duncan, it was that he was as stubborn as any mule, and he didn't give up. He'd be back.

She picked up his untouched coffee and carried it back to the counter. Floris looked at the door that was still quivering from the force with which Reese had slammed it, then turned to Madelyn with the most incredible expression on her face. It was like watching the desert floor crack as her leathered skin moved and rearranged itself, and a look of unholy glee came into her eyes. The two cowboys watched in shock as Floris actually smiled.

The older woman held out her hand, palm up and fingers stiffly extended. Madelyn slapped her own hand down on it in victory, then reversed the position for Floris's slap as they gave each other a congratulatory low five.

"Wife one, husband zero," Floris said with immense satisfaction.

He was back the next day, sliding into a booth and watching her with hooded eyes as she took care of the customers. The little café was unusually busy today, and he wondered with a sourness that would have done credit to Floris if it was because word of their confrontation the day before had spread. There was nothing like a free floor show to draw people in.

She looked tired today, and he wondered if she'd been sick. She'd had a few bouts of nausea before she'd left, but her morning sickness hadn't been full-blown. From the way she looked now, it was getting there. It made him even angrier, because if she'd been at home where she belonged she would have been able to lie down and rest.

Without asking, she brought a cup of coffee to him and turned to go. Like a replay of the day before, his hand shot out and caught her. He could almost feel everyone's attention fastening on them like magnets. "Have you been sick?" he asked roughly.

"This morning. It passed when Floris fed me some dry toast. Excuse me, I have other customers."

He let her go because he didn't want another scene like yesterday's. He sipped the coffee and watched her as she moved among the customers, dispensing a smile here and a teasing word there, drawing laughter and making faces light up. That was a talent of hers, finding amusement in little things and inviting others to share it with her, almost enticing them. She had done the same thing to him, he realized. The nine months she'd spent with him had been the most contented of his life, emotionally and physically.

He wanted her back. He wanted to watch the lazy way she strolled around the house and accomplished miracles without seeming to put forth much effort at all. He wanted her teasing him, waking him up with some outlandish bit of trivia and expecting him to match it. He wanted to pull her beneath him, spread her legs and penetrate her body with his, make her admit that she still loved him and would rather be with him than anywhere else.

He didn't understand why she wasn't in New York, why she had only come as far as Crook and stopped, knowing he would soon find her. Hell, running to Crook wasn't running away at all, it was simply moving a little piece down the road.

The only answer was that she had never intended to go back to New York. She hadn't wanted the big city; she had just wanted to get away from him.

The memory of all he'd said to her played in his mind, and he almost flinched. She remembered every word of it, too; she had even quoted some of them back to him. She'd told him at the time that he would regret saying them, but he'd been too enraged, feeling too betrayed, to pay any attention to her. He should have remembered that Maddie gave as good as she got.

She could so easily have gone to New York; she had the money in her checking account to do whatever she wanted, and Robert would welcome her back without question. So if she had stayed it had to be because she liked living in Montana. Even the question of revenge could just as easily have been played out from New York as from Crook, because it was her absence from his house that was punishing him. The emptiness of it was driving him crazy.

Eventually she came back by with the coffeepot to refill his cup and ask, "Do you want some pie with that? It's fresh coconut today."

"Sure." It would give him an excuse to stay longer.

The café eventually had to clear out some. The customers had other things they had to do, and Reese hadn't done anything interesting enough to make them stay. When Madelyn coasted by to pick up his empty dessert saucer and refill his cup she asked, "Don't you have any work to do?"

"Plenty. The cows dropped their spring calves."

Just for a second her eyes lit; then she shrugged and turned away. He said, "Wait. Sit down a minute and rest. You haven't been off your feet since I got here and that's been—" he stopped to check his watch "—two hours ago."

"It's been busy this morning. You don't stop working a herd just because you want to rest, do you?"

Despite himself, he couldn't help grinning at her comparison between a herd of cattle and her customers. "Sit down anyway. I'm not going to yell at you."

"Well, that's a change," she muttered, but she sat down across from him and propped her feet on the seat beside him, stretching her legs out. He lifted her feet and placed them on his knee, rubbing the calves of her legs under the table and holding her firmly in place when she automatically tried to pull away.

"Just relax," he said quietly. "Should you be on your feet this much?"

"I'd be on my feet if I were still at the ranch. I didn't cook sitting down, you know. I feel fine. I'm just pregnant, not incapacitated." But she closed her eyes as his kneading fingers worked at her tired muscles; he had a good touch, one learned from years of working with animals.

He had a good touch in bed, too. Every woman should have a lover like Reese, wild and hungry, as generous with his own body as he was demanding of hers. The memories pooled in her stomach like lava, raising her temperature, and her eyes popped open. If she let herself think about it too much, she would be in his lap before she knew what she was doing.

Reese said, "I want you to come home with me."

If he had been angrily demanding she could have met him with her own anger, but his quiet tone invited instead of demanded. She sighed and leaned her elbows on the table. "My answer is still the same. Give me one good reason why I should."

"And my answer is still the same. You're carrying my baby. It deserves to have its heritage, to grow up on the ranch. You even told me that was one of the reasons you paid the mortgage, to preserve the ranch for our children."

"I haven't taken the baby away from Montana," she pointed out. "I haven't even gone far from the ranch. The baby will have you and the ranch, but I don't have to live there for that to be possible."

"Miss Maddie, you got any more of that coffee?" a customer called, and she pulled her feet down from his lap without another word, going about her business with a smile.

Reese finally gave up and went home, but he tossed in the big bed all night, thinking of her breasts and the way she tasted, the way it felt to slide into her and feel her tight inner clinging, hear the soft sounds she made as he brought her to pleasure.

He had to mend fences the next day, and he worked automatically, his mind still on Maddie, trying to figure out how to get her back.

She'd made a telling point when she had asked him why she hadn't paid the mortgage before, if all she'd wanted had been a legal interest in the ranch that would override any prenuptial agreement, and now he had to ask himself the same thing. If that was all she'd wanted, why had she waited nine months? Why had she chased chickens and cows, fought blizzards and risked her own life to save his if she'd been planning on getting out? Even more telling, why had she gone off her birth control pills and let him get her pregnant? That baby she carried was a planned baby, one they had talked about and agreed to have. A woman didn't deliberately get pregnant if she'd been planning to spend only a few months and then get out. The land was worth a fortune; if money had been all she wanted, paying off the mortgage had entitled her to a great deal without the added, admittedly powerful, asset of a pregnancy. No, she had gotten pregnant only because she'd wanted this baby, and she had paid off the mortgage for one reason: to save the ranch for him, Reese Duncan. She might say she was saving her child's heritage, but the baby was still an abstract, an unknown person, however powerful her budding maternal instincts were. She had saved the ranch for her husband, not her child.

Beyond that, Maddie didn't need money. With Robert Cannon for a stepbrother, she could have anything she wanted just by asking. Robert Cannon had money that made April's family look like two-bit pikers.

It all kept coming back to the same thing, the same question. Why had she paid the mortgage, knowing how dead set he was against it, if she hadn't been planning to file for divorce? The answer was always the same, and she had given it to him. She had never tried to hide it. She loved him.

The realization staggered him anew, and he had to stop to wipe the sweat from his face, even though the temperature was only in the thirties. Maddie loved him. She had tried to tell him when he'd been yelling all those insults at her, and he hadn't listened.

Savagely he jerked the wire tight and hammered in the staple to hold it. Crow had a bitter taste to it, but he was going to have to eat a lot of it if he wanted Maddie to come back to him. He'd gone off the deep end and acted as if she were just like April, even though he knew better. April had never enjoyed living in Montana, while Maddie had wallowed in it like a delighted child. This was the life she wanted.

She loved him enough to take the chance on paying off the mortgage, knowing how angry he would be but doing it anyway because it would save the ranch for him. She had put him before herself, and that was the true measure of love, but he'd been too much of a blind, stubborn ass to admit it.

His temper had gotten him into a hell of a mess, and he didn't have anyone to blame but himself. He had to stop letting April's greed blight his life; he had to stop seeing other people through April-embittered eyes. That was the worst thing she had done to him, not ruining him financially, but ruining the way he had seen other people. He'd even admitted it to himself the day he had met Maddie; if he had run across her before marrying April, he would have been after her with every means at his disposal, and he would have gotten her, too. He would have chased her across every state in the country if necessary, and put her in his bed before she could get away. As it was, he hadn't been able to resist her for long. Even if the schoolteacher—he couldn't even remember her name—had said yes, he would have found some way of getting out of it. Maddie had been the only one he'd wanted wearing his name from the minute he'd seen her.

Damn. If only foresight were as clear as hindsight, he could have saved himself a big helping of crow.

Chapter 12

He walked into the café and immediately every eye turned toward him. He was beginning to feel like a damn outcast, the way everyone stopped talking and stared at him whenever he showed his face in town. Floris had come out of the kitchen and was arguing with one of the customers, who had ordered something she thought was stupid, from what he could hear, but she stopped yammering and stared at him, too. Then she abruptly turned and went back into the kitchen, probably to get her spatula.

Madelyn didn't acknowledge him, but no more than a minute had passed before a cup of hot coffee was steaming in front of him. She looked so good it was all he could do to keep from grabbing her. Her hair was in a loose French braid down her back, she wore those loose, chic, pleated jeans and a pair of deck shoes, and an oversize khaki shirt with the shirttails knotted at her waist, the collar turned up and the sleeves rolled, an outfit that looked impossibly stylish even under the apron she wore. He took a closer look at the shirt and scowled. It was *his* shirt! Damn it, when she'd left him she'd taken some of his clothes!

No doubt about it. He had to get that woman back, if only for the sake of his wardrobe.

A few minutes later she put a slice of chocolate pie on the table, and he picked up his fork with a hidden smile. They might be separated, but she was still trying to feed him. He'd always been a little startled by the way she had fussed over him and seen to his comfort, as if she had to protect him. Since he was a great deal bigger than she, it had always seemed incongruous to him. His own protective instincts worked overtime where she was concerned, too, so he supposed it evened out.

Finally he caught her eye and indicated the seat across from him with a jerk of his chin. Her eyebrows lifted at the arrogant summons, and she ignored him. He sighed. Well, what had he expected? He should have learned by now that Maddie didn't respond well to orders—unless she wanted to, for her own reasons.

There was evidently a rush hour in Crook now, at least judging by the number of customers who found it necessary to stop by the café. He wondered dourly if there was an alert system to signal everyone in the county when his truck was parked out front. It was over an hour before the place began to empty, but he waited patiently. The next time she came over with a refill of coffee he said, "Talk to me, Maddie. Please."

Perhaps it was the "please" that got to her, because she gave him a startled look and sat down. Floris came out of the kitchen and surveyed Reese with her hands on her hips, as if wondering why he was still there. He winked at her, the first time he'd ever done anything that playful, and her face filled with outrage just before she whirled to go back to the kitchen.

Maddie laughed softly, having seen the byplay. "You're in her bad books now, listed under 'Sorry Low-Down Husbands Who Play Around.'"

He grunted. "What was I listed under before, 'Sorry Low-Down Husbands Who Don't Play Around'?"

" 'Yet,' " she added. "Floris doesn't have a high opinion of men."

"I've noticed." He looked her over closely, examining her face. "How do you feel today?"

"Fine. That's the first thing everyone asks me every day. Being pregnant is a fairly common occurrence, you know, but you'd think no other woman in this county had ever had a baby."

"No one's ever had *my* baby before, so I'm entitled to be interested." He reached across the table and took her hand, gently folding her fingers over his. She was still wearing her wedding ring. For that matter, he was still wearing his. It was the only jewelry he'd ever worn in his life, but he'd liked the looks of that thin gold band on his hand almost as much as he had liked the way his ring looked on Maddie. He played with the ring, twisting it on her finger, reminding her of its presence. "Come home with me, Maddie."

Same tune, same lyrics. She smiled sadly as she repeated her line. "Give me one good reason why I should."

"Because you love me." He said it gently, his fingers tightening on hers. That was the most powerful argument he could think of, the one she couldn't deny.

"I've always loved you. That isn't new. I loved you when I packed my clothes and walked out the door. If it wasn't reason enough to stay, why should it be reason enough to go back?"

Her gray, gray eyes were calm as she looked at him. His chest tightened as he realized it wasn't going to work. She wasn't going to come back to him no matter what argument he used. He'd been on a rollercoaster of hope since the day he had seen the station wagon parked out front, but suddenly he was plunging down a deep drop that didn't have an end. Dear God, had he ruined the best thing that had ever happened to him because he hadn't been able to accept it?

There was a thick knot in his throat; he had to swallow

before he could speak again. "Do you...do you mind if I check up on you every day or so? Just to make sure you're feeling okay. And I'd like to go with you when you have a doctor's appointment, if you don't mind."

Now Maddie had to swallow at her sudden impulse to cry. She had never seen Reese diffident before, and she didn't like it. He was bold and arrogant and quick-tempered, and that was just the way she wanted him, as long as he realized a few important facts about their marriage. "This is your baby, too, Reese. I'd never try to cut you out."

He sighed, still playing with her fingers. "I was wrong, sweetheart. I have a phobia about the ranch after what April did to me—I know, you're not April, and I shouldn't take it out on you for what she did eight years ago. You told me, but I didn't listen. So tell me now what I can do to make it up to you."

"Oh, Reese, it isn't a matter of making anything up to me," she cried softly. "I don't have a scorecard with points on it, and after you tally up so many I'll move back to the ranch. It's about us, our relationship, and whether we have any future together."

"Then tell me what you're still worried about. Baby, I can't fix it if I don't know what it is."

"If you don't know what it is, then nothing *can* fix it."

"Are we down to riddles now? I'm not any good at mind reading," he warned. "Whatever you want, just say it right out. I can deal with reality, but guessing games aren't my strong suit."

"I'm not jerking you around. I'm not happy with this situation, either, but I'm not going back until I know for certain we have a future. That's the way it is, and I won't change my mind."

Slowly he stood up and pulled some bills out of his pocket. Maddie held up her hand dismissively. "Never mind, this one's on me. I get good tips," she said with a crooked smile.

He looked down at her with a surge of hunger that almost

took him apart, and he didn't try to resist it. He leaned down and covered her mouth with his, tilting her head back so he could slant his lips more firmly over hers, his tongue sliding between her automatically parted lips. They had made love too often, their senses were too attuned to each other, for it to be anything but overwhelmingly right. She made one of her soft little sounds, and her tongue played with his, her mouth responding. If they had been alone the kiss would have ended in lovemaking; it was that simple, that powerful. No other woman in his life had ever gotten to him the way Maddie did.

The café was totally silent as the few customers still there watched with bated breath. The situation between Reese Duncan and his spirited wife was the best entertainment the county had seen in years.

"Harrummph!"

Reese lifted his head, his lips still shiny from the kiss. The loud interruption had come from Floris, who had left the sanctuary of the kitchen to protect her waitress. At least that was what Reese thought, since she had bypassed the spatula in favor of a butcher knife.

"I don't hold with none of that carrying-on in my place," she said, scowling at him.

He straightened and said softly but very clearly, "Floris, what you need is a good man to give you some loving and cure that sour disposition."

The smile she gave him was truly evil in intent. She gestured with the butcher knife. "The last fool that tried drew back a nub."

It always happened. Some people just didn't know when to keep out of something. The cowboy who had gotten in the argument with her the first time Reese had brought Maddie in just had to stick his oar in now. "Yeah, when was that, Floris?" he asked. "Before or after the Civil War?"

She turned on him like a she-bear on fresh meat. "Hell,

boy, it was your daddy, and you're the best he could do with what he had left!''

It was the end of April. Spring was coming on fast, but Reese couldn't take the pleasure in the rebirth of the land that he usually did. He rattled around in the house, more acutely aware of its emptiness now than he had ever been before. He was busy, but he wasn't content. Maddie still wasn't home.

She had given him financial security with her legacy from her grandmother. Without the remaining payments of the huge mortgage hanging over him, he could use the money from the sale of last year's beef to expand, just as he had originally planned. For that matter, he could take out another loan with the ranch as collateral and start large-scale ranching again, with enough cowhands to help him do it right. Because of Maddie, he could now put the ranch back on a par with what it used to be, even with the reduced acreage. She had never seen it as it had been, probably couldn't imagine the bustle and life in a large, profitable cattle ranch.

He needed to make some sort of decision and make it soon. If he were going to expand, he needed to get working on it right now.

But his heart wasn't in it. As much as he had always loved ranching, as deeply as his soul was planted in this majestically beautiful range, he didn't have the enthusiasm for it that he'd always had before. Without Maddie, he didn't much care.

But she was right; it was their baby's heritage. For that reason he had to take care of it to the best of his ability.

Life was always a fluid series of options. The circumstances and options might change from day to day, but there was always a set of choices to be made, and now he had to make a very important one.

If he expanded on his own it would take all his capital and leave him without anything in reserve if another killing blizzard nearly wiped him out. If he went to the bank for another loan, using the ranch as collateral, he would be putting himself back in the same position Maddie had just gotten him out of. He had no doubt he could make it, given that he would be able to reinvest all of the money in the ranch instead of paying it out to a grasping ex-wife, but he'd had enough of bank loans.

That left an investor. Robert Cannon was brilliant; he'd make one hell of a partner. And Reese did have a very clear business mind, so he could see all the advantages of a partnership. Not only would it broaden his financial base, he would be able to diversify, so the survival of the ranch wouldn't come down to a matter of how severe the winter was. The land was his own legacy to his child.

He picked up the telephone and punched the numbers on the card Robert had given him at Christmas.

When he put the receiver down half an hour later, it was all over except the paperwork. He and Robert dealt very well together, two astute men who were able to hammer out a satisfactory deal with a minimum of words. He felt strange, a little light-headed, and it took him a while to realize what had happened. He had voluntarily put his trust in someone else, surrendering his totalitarian control of the ranch; moreover, his new partner was a member of his wife's family, something he never could have imagined a year before. It was as if he had finally pulled free of the morass of hatred and resentment that had been dragging on him for years. April, finally, was in the past. He had made a mistake in his first choice of a wife; smart people learned from their mistakes and went on with their lives. He had learned, all right, but he hadn't gotten on with living until Maddie had taught him how. Even then he had clung to his bitter preconceptions until he had ruined his marriage.

God, he'd crawl on his hands and knees if it would convince her to come back.

As the days passed he slowly became desperate enough to do just that, but before the need inside him became uncontrollable, he received a phone call that knocked the wind out of him. The call was from April's sister, Erica. April was dead, and he was the main beneficiary in her will; would he please come?

Erica met him at JFK. She was a tall, lean, reserved woman, only two years older than April, but she had always seemed more like an aunt than a sister. Already there was a startling streak of gray in the dark hair waving back from her forehead, one she made no attempt to hide. She held out her hand to him in a cool, distant manner. "Thank you for coming, Reese. Given the circumstances, it's more than I expected and certainly more than we deserve."

He shrugged as he shook her hand. "A year ago I would have agreed with you."

"What's happened in the past year?" Her gaze was direct.

"I remarried. I got back on my feet financially."

Her eyes darkened. She had gray eyes, too, he noticed, though not that soft, slumberous dove gray of Maddie's eyes. "I'm sorry about what happened in the divorce. April was, too, after it was over, but there didn't seem to be any way to make amends. And I'm glad you remarried. I hope you're very happy with your wife."

He would be, he thought, if he could only get her to live with him, but he didn't say that to Erica. "Thank you. We're expecting a baby around the end of October."

"Congratulations." Her severe face lightened for a moment, and she actually smiled, but when the smile faded he saw the tiredness of her soul. She was grieving for her sister, and it couldn't have been easy for her to call him.

"What happened to April?" he asked. "Was she ill?"

"No, not unless you want to call it an illness of the spirit. She remarried, too, you know, less than a year after your divorce, but she was never happy and divorced him a couple of years ago."

It was on the tip of his tongue to ask if she'd taken Number Two to the cleaners, too, but he bit it back. It would be petty of him in the face of Erica's grief. Once he would have said it, once he had been bitter enough that he wouldn't have cared who he wounded. Maddie had changed that.

"She had started drinking heavily," Erica continued. "We tried to convince her to get therapy, to control it, and for a while she tried to stop on her own. But she was sad, Reese, so sad. You could see it in her eyes. She was tired of living."

He drew in a sharp breath. "Suicide?"

"Not technically. Not intentionally. At least, I don't think so. I can't let myself think it was. But she couldn't stop drinking, because it was the only solace she had. The night she died, she'd been drinking heavily and was driving back from Cape Cod. She went to sleep, or at least they think that's what happened, and she became one more statistic on drunk driving." Erica's voice was calm and unemotional, but the pain was in her eyes. She reached out and awkwardly touched his arm, a woman who found it as difficult to receive comfort as she did to give it.

On the taxi ride into the city he asked, "Why did she make me her main beneficiary?"

"Guilt, I think. Maybe love. She was so wild about you in the beginning, and so bitter after the divorce. She was jealous of the ranch, you know. After the divorce, she told me she would rather you'd had a mistress than own that ranch, because she could fight another woman, but that chunk of ground had a hold on you that no woman could equal. That's why she went after the ranch in the divorce, to punish you." She gave him a wry smile. "God, how vindictive people can be. She couldn't see that she simply wasn't the type of wife you needed. You didn't like the same things, didn't want the same things out of life. When you didn't love her as much as you loved the ranch, she thought it was a flaw in her rather than accepting it as the difference between two very different people."

Reese had never thought of April in that light, never seen their marriage and subsequent divorce through her eyes. The only thing he had seen in her had been the bitterness, and that was what he had allowed to color his life. It was a blow to learn the color had been false, as if he had been wearing tinted lenses that had distorted everything.

He spent the night in a hotel, the sort of hotel he had once taken for granted. It felt strange to be back on firm financial ground again, and he wondered if he had ever truly missed the trappings of wealth. It was nice to be able to afford the posh minisuite, but he wouldn't have minded a plain motel. The years without money had rearranged his priorities.

The reading of the will the next day didn't take much time. April's family, too caught up in their grief to be hostile, was subdued. So was her father. April had thoroughly thought out the disposal of her possessions, as if she had anticipated her death. She divided her jewelry and personal possessions among family members, likewise the small fortune in stocks and bonds she had owned. It was her bequest to him that left him stunned.

"To Gideon Reese Duncan, my former husband, I leave the amount of his divorce settlement to me. Should he precede me in death, the same amount shall be given to his heirs in a gesture of fairness too long delayed."

The lawyer droned on, but Reese didn't hear any of it. He couldn't take it in. He was in shock. He leaned forward and braced his elbows on his knees, staring at the Oriental rug under his feet. She had given it all back, and in doing so had shown him the stark futility of the years of hatred.

The most ironic thing was that he had already let go of it. The inner darkness hadn't been able to withstand Maddie's determination. Even if he had never been able to rebuild the ranch to its former size, he would have been happy as long as he had Maddie. He had laughed with her and made love with her, and somewhere along the way his obsession had changed into a love so powerful that now he couldn't live without her, he could only exist.

His heart suddenly squeezed so painfully that he almost grabbed his chest. Hell! How could he have been so stupid? *Come home with me.*

Give me one good reason why I should.

That was all she'd asked for, one good reason, but he hadn't given it to her. He'd thrown out reasons, all right, but not the one she'd been asking for, the one she needed. She'd all but told him what it was, but he'd been so caught up in what he needed that he hadn't paid any attention to what *she* needed. How simple it was, and now he knew what to say.

Give me one good reason why I should.

Because I love you.

He strode through the door of Floris's café and stood in the middle of the room. The increase in customers was still going strong, maybe because Floris was safely isolated in the kitchen and Maddie was out on the floor charming everyone with her lazy drawl and sexy walk.

As usual, silence fell when he entered and everyone turned to look at him. Maddie was behind the counter, wiping up a coffee spill while she exchanged some good-natured quips with Glenna Kinnaird. She looked up, saw him and went still, her eyes locked on him.

He hooked his thumbs in his belt and winked at her. "Riddle me this, sweetheart. What has two legs, a hard head and acts like a jackass?"

"That's easy," she scoffed. "Reese Duncan."

There was a muffled explosion of suppressed snickers all around them. He could see the amusement in her eyes and had to grin. "How are you feeling?" he asked, his voice dropping to a low, intimate tone that excluded everyone else in the café and made several women draw in their breath.

Her mouth quirked in that self-amusement that made him want to grab her to him. "This isn't one of my good days. The only thing holding me together is static cling."

"Come home with me, and I'll take care of you."

She looked him in the eye and said quietly, "Give me one good reason why I should."

Right there in front of God and most of Crook, Montana, he drew in a deep breath and took the gamble of a lifetime, his words plain and heard by all, because no one was making even the pretense of not listening.

"Because I love you."

Maddie blinked, and to his surprise he saw her eyes glitter with tears. Before he could start forward, however, her smile broke through like sunshine through a cloud bank. She didn't take the time to go around the counter; she climbed on top of it and slid off on the other side. "It's about time," she said as she went into his arms.

The customers broke into applause, and Floris came out of the kitchen. She sniffed and looked displeased when she saw Madelyn hanging in Reese's arms with her feet off the floor. "I suppose this means I've got to get another waitress," she muttered.

Someone muttered back, "Hell, Floris, if you'll just stay in the kitchen we'll find you another waitress."

"It's a deal," she said, and startled everyone in the café by actually smiling.

He didn't wait to get back to the house before he made love to her; as soon as they were on Duncan land he stopped the truck and pulled her astride him. Madelyn thought her heart would burst as she listened to his roughly muttered words of love and lust and need. She couldn't get enough of touching him; she wanted to sink into his skin, and she tried to.

When they finally got to the house he carried her inside and up the stairs to their bedroom, where he placed her on the big bed and began stripping her. She laughed, a drugged, wanton sound, as she stretched languidly. "Again?"

"I want to see you," he said, his voice strained. When she was naked he was silent, struck dumb and enchanted by the changes in her body. They were still slight, but obvious to him because he knew every inch of her. There was just beginning to be a faint curve to her belly, and her breasts were a little rounder, even firmer than before, her nipples darkened to a lush reddish brown. He leaned forward and circled one with his tongue, and her entire body quivered. "God, I love you," he said, and laid his head on her belly, his arms locked around her hips.

Madelyn slid her fingers into his hair. "It took you long enough," she said gently.

"What I lack in quickness, I make up in staying power."

"Meaning?"

"That I'll still be telling you that fifty years from now." He paused and turned his head to kiss her stomach. "I have something else to tell you."

"Is it good?"

"I think so. Things are going to be changing around here pretty soon."

"How?" She looked suspicious. "I'm not sure I want things to change."

"I have a new partner. I called Robert a week or so ago, and he bought in. We'll be expanding in a big way as soon as I can get started on it. This is now the Duncan and Cannon ranch."

Madelyn burst into laughter, startling him into lifting his head from her stomach. "Whatever you do," she said, "don't call it the D and C. I don't think I could live on a ranch named after a surgical procedure!"

He grinned, feeling everything in him come alive under the magic spell of her laughter. "It'll keep the same name," he said.

"Good." Slowly her laughter faded, and she gave him a somber look. "Why did you call him?"

"Because I trust you," he said simply. "Through you, I can trust him. Because it was a good business decision. Because I wanted to show you how a really good ranch operates. Because we're having a baby. Because, damn it, I'm too damn proud to be satisfied with a second-rate operation. Is that enough reasons?"

"The first one was good enough." She put her hands on his face and stared at him, her heart in his eyes. It rattled him, even while it made him feel as if he could conquer the world, to see how much Maddie loved him. He started to lean down to kiss her when she said seriously, "Did you know that a ten-gallon hat will really only hold about three quarts?"

On the third of November, Madelyn lay in a labor room in Billings, holding Reese's hand and trying to concentrate on her breathing. She had been there over twenty-four hours and she was exhausted, but the nurses kept telling her everything was fine. Reese was unshaven and had dark circles under his eyes. Robert was somewhere outside, wearing a rut in the tile of the hall.

"Give me another one," she said. Reese was looking desperate, but she needed something to get her mind off herself.

"India ink really comes from China."

"You're really scraping the bottom of the barrel, aren't you? Let's see." A contraction interrupted her, and she squeezed his hand as it surged and peaked, then fell off. When she could speak again she said, "The sounds of stomach growling are called borborygmus." She gave him a triumphant look.

He cradled her hand against his cheek. "You've been reading the dictionary again, and that's cheating. I've got a good one. The San Diego Chargers got their name because the original owner also owned the Carte Blanche credit card company. 'Charge' is what he wanted the cardholders to say."

She laughed, but the sound was abruptly cut off as another contraction seized her. This one was a little different in intensity, and in the way it made her feel. She panted her way through it, staring at the monitor with blurring eyes so she could see the mechanical confirmation of what she felt. She lay back against his arm and said weakly, "I don't think it's going to be much longer."

"Thank God." He didn't know if he could hold out much longer. Watching her in pain was the hardest thing he had ever done, and he was seriously considering limiting the number of their children to one. He kissed her sweaty temple. "I love you, sweetheart."

That earned him one of her slow smiles. "I love you, too." Another contraction.

The nurse checked her and smiled. "You're right, Mrs. Duncan, it won't be much longer. We'd better get you into delivery."

He was with her during delivery. The doctor had kept careful watch on the growing baby and didn't think she'd have any trouble delivering it. Reese wondered violently if the doctor's idea of trouble differed from his. It was thirty-six hours since her labor had begun. Less than half an hour after he'd told her about the San Diego Chargers, Reese was holding his red, squalling son in his hands.

Madelyn watched him through tear-blurred eyes, smiling giddily. The expression on Reese's face was so intense and tender and possessive that she could barely stand it. "Eight pounds, two ounces," he murmured to the infant. "You just barely made it under the wire."

Madelyn laughed and reached for both husband and son. Reese settled the baby in her arms and cradled her in his, unable to take his eyes from the both of them. He'd never seen anything so beautiful in his life, even if her hair was matted with sweat and coming loose from her braid. God, he felt good! Exhausted but good.

She yawned and rested her head against his shoulder. "I think we did a good job," she announced, examining the baby's tiny fingers and damp dark hair. "I also think I'm going to sleep for a week."

When she was in her room, just before she did go to sleep, she heard Reese say it again. "I love you, sweetheart." She was too sleepy to answer, but she reached out and felt him take her hand. Those were three words she never got tired of hearing, though she'd heard them often during the past months.

Reese sat and watched her as she slept, a smile in his eyes.

Slowly his eyelids drooped as he succumbed to his weariness, but not once during his sleep did he turn loose of her hand.

* * * * *

CHAIN LIGHTNING

Elizabeth Lowell

* * *

For the people of Australia fair dinkum!

Dear Reader,

Sometimes you have to go a long way to find yourself.

Come with me to Australia, a special place where two very stubborn, wounded people flee for a vacation, only to find there is no place to hide from each other, themselves and love.

E. Lowell

Chapter 1

"What you need is a lover."

Mandy's head snapped up from the papers scattered across her desk. The movement was so sudden that it sent her silky, chin-length black hair flying, but a single glance told her that it was too late to deflect Anthea. The tiny dynamo who stood next to Mandy was already in overdrive; Anthea had that special gleam in her eyes, the one that came only when she had found a new "project." Mandy stifled both a sigh and a smile, pulled her scattering thoughts together and put away the masculine image that had sprung into her mind at the mention of a lover.

A thatch of unruly, sun-cured blond hair, strong, lean hands, jade-green eyes that never smiled.

"That's a wonderful idea," Mandy said cheerfully. "I'll stick up a bank and take my pick of the bachelors at the OCC auction tomorrow night." In neat, slanting printing she wrote on her calendar for the following day: Rob bank. Buy lover. Soonest. "Anything else? Have you found a replacement for Susie yet? Should I rob another bank and double the next receptionist's salary?''

''I have two excellent candidates.''

Mandy was careful not to inquire whether Anthea's candidates were for the position of OCC receptionist or that of lover for one Samantha Blythe. Mandy prayed that it was the former. She didn't want to be the focus of her boss's unpredictable charitable impulses, especially on the subject of men. The last thing Mandy wanted was another waltz around a marriage ring with the kind of easy-smiling, honey-voiced liar her husband had been.

''Both of them are presentable and skilled,'' Anthea continued, numbering attributes on small, immaculately kept hands. ''One of them was recently widowed and the other isn't married.''

A neutral sound from Mandy was more than enough encouragement for Anthea to continue her summary of the candidates. Nothing in her voice or demeanor gave a clue as to which position the candidates were slated to fill—office worker or bedroom athlete.

''Both of them had very clean, neatly kept hands, which is essential,'' the older woman said crisply. ''They both look strong and healthy, but it's hard to tell without trying them out. On the whole, I don't think either one will require on-the-job training. They seemed to be self-starters.''

Mandy made a strangled sound.

Anthea continued without a pause, not noticing the look on her executive secretary's face. ''Education and a sense of humor would be nice but aren't necessary. After all, no one expects anyone in that position to do more than take directions and follow through with a one hundred percent effort and no shilly-shallying. In the final analysis, all the job really requires is cleanliness, a generous portion of stamina and a willingness to take direction without sulking.''

''Stamina?'' Mandy asked faintly, banishing the images in her mind and wondering if Anthea was taking her usual bluntness to new highs. Or lows.

"But of course. Stamina is vital if the job is to be adequately filled."

"It is?"

Anthea gave Mandy an exasperated look. "Dear girl, do you have any idea how many receptionists I've lost because they had delicate constitutions? Too many. Now I look for someone sturdy. When you applied for the job I almost didn't hire you. You looked frail. Too thin. Too nervous," Anthea said with typical bluntness. "If it hadn't been for that determined chin and those haunting gold eyes of yours, I would have turned you down without a tryout."

Mandy started to speak, then realized it was futile. Anthea was in full sail.

"I was wrong," Anthea continued without a pause. "You've been with Our Children's Children for eighteen months and never taken a sick day, even after I doubled your work load by making you into my girl Friday." The older woman blinked and focused suddenly on Mandy. "You've never taken a vacation, either, come to think of it. No wonder you've looked so wan lately."

"You haven't taken a vacation, either," Mandy pointed out, sidestepping the implicit question as to why she had looked so washed-out for the past week or so. If her middle-of-September memories showed on the outside, she'd have to wear more makeup. Nobody in her new life knew what had happened almost two years ago. Mandy preferred it that way. Pity was her least-favorite emotional flavor. "If you're feeling guilty about being a slave driver, may I point out that it has been four years since Sutter has had more than five days off in a row—and those days were spent traveling to some other desperate spot on the globe."

For a moment Anthea looked startled. "No. It can't have been that long!"

"Four years, two months, ten days and—" she glanced at the clock "—fifteen hours and thirty-two minutes, to be precise. The latter is by his reckoning, but I certainly wouldn't care to argue the matter with him."

Anthea's faded green eyes narrowed suddenly. "Did he call while I was out?"

"Twice. Once from the airport and once from his condo. He said, and I quote, 'If Aunt Ant has signed me up for any more expert testimony on Capitol Hill, I'll box up the entire Senate and send it C.O.D. to hell.'"

Anthea sighed. "Poor boy. He does hate cities and committees. But he's so very impressive...."

Mandy barely caught herself before she muttered, "Amen." D. M. Sutter was very impressive indeed, whether it was as a land reclamation specialist, as a futurist or simply as a man. In the eighteen months she had worked for Our Children's Children, Mandy had seen Sutter only occasionally, always unexpectedly, and each time she had been unnerved by his sheer presence.

It was more than simply a matter of size. Mandy had known many men taller than Sutter's six feet one inch, or more heavily built than Sutter, with his lean muscularity, but none of the bigger men could have commanded attention in a crowded room just by standing quietly. Sutter could, and did. He had a rapier intelligence and unflinching pragmatism that showed in his jade-green eyes and in his face, tanned by foreign suns and drawn into harsh lines by having seen more human greed, suffering, fear and stupidity than any man should have to see.

"I got the feeling that Sutter wanted to go someplace... clean," Mandy said softly.

Shrewd, pale eyes measured Mandy. Few people except Anthea ever saw beyond Mandy's quick smile and sassy one-liners to the very private, intelligent and vulnerable woman beneath.

"You sound as though you would like to go there, too," Anthea said speculatively. "Somewhere clean."

For an instant the luminous amber of Mandy's eyes was darkened by shadows. There was no place on earth like that for her because wherever she went, her memories also went. But that wasn't Anthea's problem. So Mandy smiled and shook her head, denying the shadows in her eyes and making her shiny black hair fly.

"Not me. I've got three reports to run through my magic machine," Mandy said lightly, gesturing toward her word processor. As she did, she saw a familiar figure from the corner of her eye. "And a stack of letters as big as Steve's ego to—"

"Hey, I heard that!" Steve interrupted, calling from the doorway.

"—and a new picture to add to your finished projects' gallery," Mandy finished blithely, as though she had neither seen Steve nor heard his outraged yelp.

"A finished project?" Anthea asked. "Was Susie accepted by an agency?"

"Susie?" Steve asked simultaneously, forgetting about his wounded ego. "Did she call?"

Mandy's smile became compassionate rather than teasing as she turned toward Steve. The young lawyer was a walking cliché—tall, dark, handsome—but the cliché failed to cover his unguarded ego. He had fallen for Anthea's former receptionist and most recent "project." Unfortunately for Steve, Susie had seen only the dreams in her own eyes, not those in his. Though only eighteen, Susie had the face, body and discipline to become an international cover girl. What she had lacked was contacts and the thousands of dollars required to pay for a portfolio of highly professional photos to leave with agencies. Anthea had supplied the contacts, the cash and the plane ticket to Manhattan.

"Susie just signed on with an international modeling agency," Mandy said. "They're sending her to Paris on Tuesday."

Steve's mouth tightened, then curved into a sad smile. "That's what she wanted. I'm happy for her, I guess."

"Be happy for yourself," Anthea said crisply. "Susie was too young to settle down. Better that she find out what she's made of in New York than make herself and some decent young man such as you utterly miserable by getting married in California.''

''Is that the collection of international precedents on the use of rivers that flow through more than one country?'' Mandy asked quickly, changing the subject and gesturing toward the thick, dark folders gathered under Steve's arm.

He grabbed the new topic like the lifeline it was. Anthea had many fine points, but finesse wasn't one of them. Sutter was the same, impatient with people who lacked the common sense to avoid life's more obvious mine fields. Mandy, who had stumbled into one of those fields when she was Steve's age, had a great deal of sympathy for the young man's unhappiness. He was lucky to have escaped a bad marriage, but he was too young and too inexperienced to appreciate that fact. Mandy wasn't.

''Here's every precedent I could find,'' Steve said, flopping the bulging folders on Mandy's desk. Papers went flying in all directions. ''Oops. Sorry about that.''

''You'll be even sorrier when I tell you that the very papers you're carpeting the ceiling with are your entire presentation to the Senate Committee on Foreign—''

''Then don't tell me,'' Steve interrupted quickly. ''What I don't know won't hurt me, right?''

Wrong, thought Mandy. *Ignorance can not only hurt, it can kill.* But she hadn't known that at his age, so she could hardly blame him now.

''When you're finished picking up the mess,'' Anthea said to Steve, ''come into my office. The delegate from Belize has raised some ridiculous tribal legal precedent to prevent us from building that fish farm.''

Steve swore. ''Have you hinted that ten percent of all profits will go to him?''

''He wants half.''

''Sutter would raise hell,'' Steve said.

''Sutter would like to feed the old bandit to the fish,'' Anthea said calmly. ''However, if we waited for perfect leaders and perfect solutions, nothing would ever get done.''

The phone rang. Mandy reached for it immediately.

"If that's Mr. Axton," Anthea said quickly, "I'm out."

"For how long?"

"Until he arises from his dead posterior and writes OCC a check that will make me smile."

Mandy mentally added another zero to the figure she had been prepared to give Mr. Axton. Though most of the Sutter wealth was tied up in OCC's charitable trusts, enough remained to make Anthea a wealthy woman. Her childhood friends were even more wealthy. Mr. Axton was one of them. He had been trying without success to persuade Anthea to have dinner with him.

"You should auction yourself off at the fund-raiser tomorrow night," Mandy said. "I have a pair of silk harem pants that would raise more than Mr. Axton's posterior."

Anthea looked thoughtful for a few moments, then smiled widely. "The auction. Of course. Why didn't I think of that?"

"You did, remember? No one else would have had the sheer brass to ask men like that to auction themselves off for charity and eager divorcées." Mandy grabbed the phone on the fourth ring. "OCC, may I help you?" Pause. "I'm terribly sorry, Mr. Axton. Miss Sutter just stepped out." Pause. "Four zeros should do nicely, not including the two to the right of the decimal point." Pause. "Of course it's exorbitant, but I'm afraid Miss Sutter has a weakness for grand gestures—she makes so many of them, as you know."

Steve snickered. Anthea merely arched her silver eyebrows.

"That's very generous of you, sir. I'm sure she'll appreciate it."

Anthea waited impatiently until Mandy hung up the phone. "Well?"

"Thirty thousand," Mandy said succinctly.

"Lovely," purred Anthea. "The man is a scholar and a gentleman. I look forward to dinner with him. Make that two dinners."

"Two?"

"Oh, yes. He has wonderful hands." Pale green eyes focused sharply on Mandy. "You can always tell a man by his hands, dear. If you don't believe me, look at Sutter's someday. My brother might not have had the sense and grit that God gave a goose, but no one can say the same of his son. Pity the boy hasn't found a woman. I hate to see good genes go to waste."

"I thought you didn't approve of marriage," Steve said as he stacked a handful of the flyaway papers on Mandy's desk.

"Marriage?" Anthea smiled. "My dear boy, it will come as a great surprise to the men and women of this benighted world that marriage is a necessary precursor to conception." She turned to Mandy. "Do you have Susie's picture or did you put it on my desk?"

Mandy retrieved a folder from the out basket. "Right here."

"Good. Help me hang it while Steve chases paper. That makes two completed projects this week, you know." Anthea's lean, lined face settled into satisfied lines. "Lovely, just lovely. It couldn't have happened at a better time...."

Mandy followed her boss, torn between the desire to upbraid Anthea for her abrupt treatment of the lovelorn Steve and an impulse to hug the tiny dynamo for caring enough about the various people who crossed her path to take a hand in their personal destinies. An unintentionally imperious hand, to be sure, but very helpful all the same.

The south wall of Anthea's office was given over to photos of all sizes and settings. Their only similarity was that each featured a person who had been helped by a timely application of Anthea's money. There was a young man who had worked his way through journalism school and applied for the position of reporter at various papers in California, only to discover that having a car was a requirement for the job; without a job, he couldn't afford a car. Anthea had supplied the latter, the *Los Angeles Times* had supplied the former, and the young man had begun his career.

There was a picture of a young divorcée who had worked her way through school waiting tables while caring for her young child. All that had stood between her and a Ph.D. in psychology had been enough time off to write her dissertation. Anthea had supported the young woman until the dissertation was finished and accepted.

Susie's picture went next to the most recent of Anthea's successfully concluded "projects," a man and wife who had saved money all their lives in order to open a small restaurant, only to see their savings vanish when their accountant stepped on a plane to Rio with his mistress on one arm and a satchel full of money on the other. Anthea had replaced their stolen savings to the penny.

"Do you think their restaurant will be a success?" Mandy asked.

Anthea made a dismissive gesture with one hand. "Whether it is or isn't, the important thing is that they had the gumption to go after what they wanted. Most people don't. They're either too lazy or too frightened to reach for their dreams."

Carefully looking only at the picture, Mandy bit her lip and prayed that the heat rising in her face wouldn't show. She knew that Anthea's words hadn't been meant for her, but Mandy also knew that she was among the people who were too frightened to reach for their dreams.

Water still terrified her. She was better about water than she had been since the accident. Two months ago, for instance, she had managed to take a bath rather than a shower for the first time in nearly two years. Granted, the water had been only inches deep and it had taken her so long to screw up her courage and get into the tub that the water had been cold, but it had been progress all the same. Now she could step into a tub that had four inches of water in it without having to wrestle with fear while the bathwater went cold. She had tried six and then eight and then ten inches of water in the tub, only to panic at the feel of water climbing above her waist. It had taken her until last week to work back up to five inches of bathwater.

Some progress, she told herself derisively. *At this rate you'll be seventy before you ever get your face in water again.*

The thought of having her face covered by a cold, clutching, killing liquid made white replace Mandy's bright flush. She was more afraid of water than she was ashamed of being afraid. The source of her fear was as real as death. If she spent the rest of her life taking shallow baths or showers, so be it. She was alive, she had found a way to make a living that didn't involve water in any way, and she was able to sleep through the night without seeing the ocean surge up to claim the small plane—water rising slowly, slowly over the fuselage windows while she struggled to free herself and her husband, and then the endless black slide down into ocean's depths that had once fascinated and now repelled her.

Mandy blinked and realized that Anthea was looking at her as though expecting an answer to a question that had been asked.

"Are you all right?" Anthea repeated. "You look as though you've seen a ghost."

"Really?" asked Mandy, rallying. "Quick, give me a mirror. I've always wanted to see what kind of ditsy broad went around looking for ghosts."

Anthea's eyes narrowed. She started to say something, paused and finally turned back toward her gallery without a word. Seeing the faces of the individuals she had helped always made her feel as though life were more than an unremitting battle against poverty, greed and indifference. Somewhere out there, scattered across the face of the earth, were people who smiled more often because Anthea had smoothed one of the razor edges off their lives. She smiled more often, as well, taking pleasure from the pleasure she had brought.

Feeling anticipation of her next projects fizz softly in her blood, Anthea looked affectionately from picture to picture. With luck and a little arm-twisting in the right places, Mandy soon would be up there with the others, smiling. Unfortunately, Sutter wouldn't be among the glad of heart. But then, Sutter rarely was glad about anything.

Even knowing her nephew as well as Anthea did, however, she was a bit taken aback at just how much he *dis*liked the plan when she bearded her tawny tiger in his own quarters a few hours later.

"You did what?" Sutter demanded.

With an equanimity that few people could have mustered, Anthea faced the man looming over her. D. M. Sutter was always impressive, but with a brassy beard stubble, stone-green eyes, and eyebrows sun-bleached to a metallic gold—and teeth bared in what only an optimist would call a smile—Sutter looked frankly dangerous. The fact that he was wearing jungle-stained khaki shorts and no shirt at all did nothing to make him appear less malevolent. The lean, hard-muscled length of the man wasn't precisely soothing, either. It tended to remind people that the deceptively graceful tiger routinely dined upon the much bulkier, more obviously muscled water buffalo.

"I entered you in the OCC charity auction tomorrow night," Anthea said with outward calm. "Actually, you'll be the centerpiece. A surprise offering, as it were. A piece de resistance."

It sounded more like a coup de grace to Sutter. He muttered in fragments of languages Anthea was quite happy not to understand. He glared down at her. She was standing in front of him with her customary regal poise, serene in the rightness of what she was doing.

"Aunt Ant, you are my favorite person, living or dead, and—"

"Butter won't get it done, my boy," she interrupted with relish, stealing one of his favorite phrases. "You have been nominated and elected by acclamation and that, as they say, is that!"

"Anthea," Sutter said softly, knowing that yelling at the little tyrant wouldn't budge her, "what in God's name gives you the idea that I will stand around with my thumb in my, er, *ear*, while a pack of overwealthy, overwrought divorcées bid on what they hope will be my…services?"

"Three weeks of vacation."

He blinked. "Say what?"

"Three weeks at the location of your choice, during which time you do absolutely nothing you don't want to do. By definition, a vacation."

"Are you serious?"

"Very."

Sutter's cool green eyes assessed the woman in front of him. Although his aunt wore four-inch heels, she was still nineteen inches shorter than he was and weighed less than half what he did. He knew that the disparity in their sizes no more worried her than a wolverine worried about taking on a grizzly over a choice morsel of meat. Anthea knew, and Sutter had learned, that in most situations temperament counts for more than muscle. Sutter might be a nasty piece of business for the rest of the world to confront, but for the woman who had taken in a surly, near-violent teenager and had taught him the meaning of constructive discipline, intelligent dreams and clear-eyed affection, for this woman Sutter had only love.

And frequent bouts of exasperation.

This particular bout was right up against the precipice of true anger, however. Anthea had never interfered in Sutter's private life before. It had been an unwritten law between them; she didn't choose his women and he didn't choose her men. He could hardly believe that she had casually chosen to rearrange their mutual relationship at this late date.

"Anthea."

The word was hard-edged, the tone whiplike. He was tired, hungry, jet-lagged and as close to losing his temper as he had been since a wealthy Brazilian had offered to rent him a pair of eight-year-old twin girls for a night of casual recreation. Sutter had purchased the girls in thin-lipped silence, taken them to a Catholic convent, and then he had returned for a very brief, no-holds-barred chat with the man.

Closing his eyes, Sutter took in and released a long breath. What Anthea had done was aggravating, exasperating, irritating, maddening and presumptuous; but it wasn't evil. She didn't deserve the razor edge of a tongue honed in some of the world's most brutal places. Slowly he counted to ten in a language that had no numeral system. As an abstract intellectual exercise in controlling unruly emotions, it had few peers.

"Someday you'll push me too far," Sutter said finally, softly. "I don't know who will be sorrier when that happens—you or me."

Anthea let out a hidden breath and smiled very gently at the man who had become the son she had never borne. "I hope I'll never truly anger you, Damon. You're the center of my heart, you know."

Sutter's long, callused fingers touched her cheek lightly. "Without you, I wouldn't have had a heart." He grimaced. "All right, Ant. I'll be your damned sacrificial goat for the Our Children's Children bachelor auction. Once. Please don't ask me to do it again."

"I won't. That's a promise, Damon."

He smiled crookedly at the nickname she rarely used, just as he rarely called her Ant anymore. He bent and brushed his lips over both of her soft, faintly powdered cheeks.

"I'll make the travel arrangements tonight," Sutter said, straightening and stretching at the same time. "I hope whoever buys me doesn't expect a romantic tour of jet-set ports of call. What I have in mind for my holiday is less cloying."

"Let me make all the arrangements, dear. You look as though you would welcome a few hours of sleep."

Sutter's lips shifted into a hard curve. "I'll sleep better if *I* make the arrangements. If you know where I'm going, you'll have a full schedule of work set out for me when I arrive. That's not my idea of time off."

Anthea managed to look hurt and amused at the same time. "Not this time. It will be a true vacation for you."

"I know. But you don't. That's why it will be a true vacation."

Anthea's pale green eyes shifted focus for a moment as she considered ways of overcoming her nephew's stubbornness. None came immediately to mind, so she gave in gracefully. After all, there were many routes to any goal.

"Whatever you say, dear. Do get some sleep. You look grim rather than dashing. Any rational woman would think twice about bidding for you."

Sutter's eyes narrowed while he watched Anthea exit his condominium as unexpectedly as she had arrived. He didn't know what had lit a fire under her thin, aristocratic rear, but he sensed that she wasn't finished with him quite yet.

Chapter 2

Mandy looked quickly around the crowd, seeking Anthea. The movement made the thousands of tiny black bugle beads on her dress shimmer. Bias-cut, long-sleeved, high-necked, utterly backless and slit to the thigh, the dress nonetheless managed to look sensuously elegant rather than sexually provocative. But then, at the price the designer was asking for it, the dress had to do something more than just glitter. Mandy frowned as she remembered the cost. For the tenth time that evening she wondered how she had allowed Anthea to talk her into modeling Sharai's exclusive, costly creation.

Simple, Mandy told herself dryly. *You took one look at the dress and fell in love. The fact that Sharai is one of Anthea's former projects simply made the offer more impossible to refuse.*

A subtle flash of blue caught Mandy's eye. That would be Alice, one of the two receptionist candidates. Sharai had decreed that Alice wear a slinky cerulean dress that made her look like a blue candle flame burning in the crowd. The other candidate—Jessica—was breathtaking in red silk pants and a beaded strapless top. Apparently Anthea hadn't been able to decide which of the two women to employ, so she had hired both. Jessi was working as receptionist while Alice was learning the basics of Mandy's job. When Mandy had pointed out that soon she would have nothing to do, Anthea had laughed and said that the more quickly Alice could take over routine office duties, the more quickly Mandy would be freed to work with Anthea on her various personal and OCC projects.

Suddenly Mandy stopped scanning the crowd. Her abrupt stillness wasn't the result of a conscious choice to stop looking for Anthea; it was simply that Sutter was impossible to catalog and pass over in a single glance, even though he was seated in the shadows of the orchestra pit a few rows away. He wore a black suit coat, a dress shirt of a linen so fine that its surface was smoother than summer silk, and a rich black tie. The midnight color of his suit served to intensify the blondness of his thick, sun-cured hair, which in turn made his tanned skin seem very dark by contrast. Instead of making him appear civilized, the expensive clothes served only to heighten the aura of primal, barely leashed masculinity Mandy had sensed in Sutter the first time she had seen his picture on Anthea's desk.

OCC left Sutter out in that Brazilian jungle too long. I wonder if those cold green eyes can see in the dark.

Mandy forced herself to continue scanning the crowd, then sat down as swiftly as she could, feeling as though Sutter had been staring at her and at the same time telling herself that she was being foolish. Sutter was hardly likely to stare at her. She had spoken perhaps twenty words to him since he had returned, those words consisting of "yes, sir," "yes, sir," and "yes, sir," repeat as necessary.

A flurry of anticipation rippled through the crowd as the lights dimmed and the auctioneer stepped onto the stage to introduce the first of the bachelors who had volunteered to be auctioned off in the name of Our Children's Children. As though pulled by invisible strings, the crowd leaned forward for a better view of the stage. Jewels flashed and glittered in the low light, plush foldout chairs creaked, and conversations died throughout the large auditorium. The auctioneer was wearing another of Sharai's creations. Every movement of the auctioneer's body sent exotic tongues of luminescence licking through rich green fabric, defining the curves beneath without actually revealing their precise proportions. As a bit of seductive witchery, it was stunning.

"Good evening, ladies and gentlemen," the auctioneer said. "I have a mirror at home, so I know those gasps of admiration aren't for me. The gown I'm wearing is by Sharai. As some of you may know, Sharai gives ten percent of her profits each year to OCC. In return, OCC does its best to send clients her way. Several of the OCC staff are also wearing Sharai's creations tonight, compliments of the designer."

That was the cue for Mandy and five other women throughout the crowd to stand up and pirouette slowly in the prearranged spotlights. The dresses displayed the range of Sharai's elegant evening creations while the auctioneer gave a few facts as to price and availability of each costume. Silently Mandy kept telling herself that she needn't be shy— the audience certainly would be looking at the flashier dresses worn by the other women rather than at the relatively demure black dress she herself had chosen to wear.

Mandy repeated the comforting thought to herself for half of the required pirouette, then shivered involuntarily to a stop when she saw Sutter watching her from the shadows of the orchestra pit. Suddenly she felt naked, stripped of defenses, clothed only in a transparent shaft of light. The feeling was so unnerving that she swayed like a dark orchid in a sultry breeze. The movements sent networks of black lightning over the dress with each shivering breath she took. There was a flurry of appreciative applause from people who thought that the seductive swaying had been planned rather than involuntary. Mandy forced a stiff smile to her lips and prayed for the spotlight to black out before she did.

The spotlights snapped off, leaving only the auctioneer visible. There was a round of applause for the dresses. Mandy was so relieved to be invisible again that it was all she could do not to fall. She sat down in a rush, her face flaming and her heart beating far too fast.

"Gowns by Sharai!" the auctioneer said enthusiastically, leading a final round of applause. When silence came again, the auctioneer began speaking in a clear, trained contralto that carried easily to every corner of the music hall. "I'm sure you'll be as generous in your bidding as you were in your applause, so let's lead the first lamb to the altar."

There was scattered laughter.

"As you know," the auctioneer continued, "OCC, Our Children's Children, is a nonprofit foundation dedicated to promoting rational national policies of resource use, policies that will result in decent lives for our children and for our children's children. OCC was founded and funded by Jason Charles Sutter and Alicia Jean Sutter, the parents of Anthea Jean Sutter, who is the present administrator of OCC's diverse global projects. Foremost among those projects is what the press calls a 'think tank' located amid the redwoods in northern California. At present, the OCC retreat houses thirty-one academic, political, artistic and business leaders whose sole task is to…think. If that sounds easy, you're welcome to apply for the next opening. At last count there were more than one hundred applicants for each vacancy."

Mandy felt her heartbeat slow and the trembling in her body subside as the auctioneer's voice and the blessed darkness concealed her from Sutter's view. The man unnerved her. There was no explanation for it and no way to get around it. Even looking at his picture made her uneasy. He was precisely the kind of man that her husband Andrew had been—powerful, impatient, both scholar and man of action—only Andrew had worked for a university rather than for a charity. He had been an oceanographer renowned for his incisive intelligence and lofty academic principles.

What a pity Andrew's principles didn't preclude adultery.

Maybe then I wouldn't have spent a night of horror adrift on a cold sea. Maybe then I would have had a child to laugh with rather than the company of nightmares.

Maybe.

And maybe it all would have happened anyway. Maybe it wasn't a lack of principles that sent Andrew on the prowl. Maybe it was the simple fact that his student-bride didn't know how to please a man. Maybe if I'd been better in bed none of this would have happened.

Maybe. Oh, God, maybe....

Mandy shuddered violently but didn't try to suppress or deny the churning of her thoughts. She had learned the hard way that whatever she suppressed during the day returned to haunt her in the darkness of her dreams. Once she had understood that, she had begun to grapple more successfully with her emotions. All that remained now was for her to accept the fact that there was more than enough blame to go around in life and much too little joy. Andrew had failed her and she had probably failed Andrew and she had certainly failed their unborn child. Having acknowledged that, she had nothing left to do but live the rest of her life as best she could.

A wave of laughter called Mandy from her bleak thoughts. Her head snapped up as the auctioneer waved her index finger from side to side at the audience, imitating a parent chastising a child.

"Naughty, naughty," the woman murmured. "What I meant to say is that a good man is hard to find, rather than vice versa. The first of our hard—that is, *good*—men is Dr. Anthony Streano. He is Tony to his friends and has been known to respond to other names on rather more intimate occasions. I leave it to the lucky last bidder to discover what names and which occasions!"

The crowd laughed again while a man of middle age and height walked onto the stage. He smiled briefly before he took a seat at center stage in a pool of white light. Silence descended again while the auctioneer recited his "vital statistics'' in a sultry contralto that found double meanings in the most innocent phrases. As the last of the appreciative laughter died down, she described the ''date'' Dr. Streano had donated—a star-studded gala film opening in Hollywood.

''Remember,'' concluded the auctioneer, ''the money you bid goes directly to OCC. Each bachelor pays all costs for his proposed outing, just as he would on a more traditional date. There is no limit to the number of dates you may acquire, so bid often, and bid high! Your children's children will thank you.''

The auditorium's lights came up again so that the bidders could be spotted. The auction opened at one hundred dollars and rose quickly to one thousand. Finally a blushing, beaming woman not quite old enough to be the good doctor's mother walked up onstage to claim him. The doctor smiled, introduced himself and murmured something that made the woman glow. Grinning, laughing and attempting to ignore the occasional risqué comment from the audience, the pair exited the stage.

For the next half hour the bidding went briskly, as everything from a VIP tour of Disneyland to a Malibu barbecue to a ski weekend at Vail was auctioned. The men took the auctioneer's spicy teasing in good humor, plainly both gratified and chagrined to be in the position of seller rather than buyer in the dating game. The women, for their part, enthusiastically exploited the opportunity to see men on the sexual auction block for a change.

Mandy watched man after man walk onstage, sit down and smile while his attributes were numbered and his ''favors'' were auctioned off like a glorified box lunch. Some of the men were four-year veterans of the auction, but most had never before participated. Fully one-third of the purchased dates resulted in long-lasting relationships, a fact that tended to seriously deplete the pool of available bachelors OCC could call upon.

''Our final bachelor before we break for a champagne intermission is Jeremy Stanhope, owner of Stanhope Electronics and patent holder of a nifty little process that allows our computers to work ten times as fast as they used to. Jeremy is a newcomer to our auction, so let's make him very welcome.''

A tall, thin, obviously shy man walked slowly onstage while the audience applauded. He looked uncomfortable in his black tie and shifted restlessly from side to side while the auctioneer read his vital statistics. He was offering a week-long cruise on one of the ''Loveboats'' that plied the waters between Washington and Alaska. As the ''date'' was described, an appreciative murmur went through the crowd, followed by an enthusiastic hand. Because the costs of the excursion would be borne by the bachelor rather than by OCC, and the bids tended to reflect the cost of the date itself, the electronics tycoon's cruise amounted to a generous, if indirect, donation to OCC's coffers.

The bidding began at six hundred dollars and went rapidly higher. As had been the case with the previous auctions, the women who were too shy to bid outright had conned friends and family into bidding for them. Mothers bid for their daughters' birthday gifts and vice versa. The OCC auction was only in its fourth year, but already it was the most popular and lucrative of the many events on OCC's fund-raising calendar. The fact that the event had been preceded by a free champagne and caviar reception increased both the attendance and the generosity of the ultimate bids.

After the intermission, during which more champagne and canapés were consumed, the bidding intensified. In the second half of the auction, the ''dates'' offered were uniformly expensive vacations that often were unusual and always hotly contested among the bidders. As the bidding became more spirited, so did the innuendos. The comments from the audience went from flirtatious to nearly salacious. Good taste was skirted but never breached, and the men took the sexy teasing with comic-opera leers that brought laughter from the audience.

When the auctioneer introduced the last bachelor listed on the program, a former tight end for the Rams, by saying that this was one man who matched his job description, the audience shouted with laughter. Variations on the sporting theme—holding penalties, game-winning touchdowns, incomplete passes, hands-on scrimmages and punting for distance—were all explored by the auctioneer and the audience. The man himself was both huge and beautifully proportioned. He was offering a ten-day surfing safari to Hawaii. The bidding was a machine-gun blur of numbers that finally resolved into a three-cornered war among a trim matron, a blond society girl and Sharai.

Ten minutes later the bidding was over. Five thousand dollars poorer, Sharai walked onstage in a dress that looked like water flowing over her, giving the impression that with the next step, or the next, some of the feminine secrets lying beneath the cloth would be revealed. They never were, but the dress kept every man hoping. The former jock took one look at Sharai's near six feet of height and generously proportioned body, joined the wild applause and then casually scooped up the designer and carried her offstage in his arms. The look of surprise and then pleasure on Sharai's face made it clear that she believed her money well spent.

As soon as the thunder of applause diminished, the auctioneer spoke again. Her voice had lost its bantering, teasing tone.

"This brings us to the end of our scheduled program, but not to the end of our bachelor auction. We are truly privileged to have with us tonight a man who has dedicated his life to working for Our Children's Children. Whenever politics or war or natural disasters threaten OCC's overseas projects, this is the man who is sent to clean up the mess and put things back into working order again. Unfortunately, not all governments have been appreciative of his efforts on behalf of the earth's children—he has been harassed, shot, beaten and jailed. He has also received more awards, citations and jeweled medals than one man can wear. He told me earlier tonight that of the two—being harassed or being applauded—he would take the former. Nonetheless, he has volunteered himself and a truly spectacular Australian mystery vacation to some lucky and generous woman. Ladies and gentlemen, I give you Damon McCarey Sutter, internationally renowned futurist and director of Our Children's Children's overseas projects.''

As one, the audience came to its feet in a storm of applause. Mandy was among the first to stand. Sutter might unnerve her but she, better than anyone in the audience, understood what he had done for the success of OCC's projects in countries that most people didn't even know existed. The three months he had just finished in Brazil had been brutal. There were few places on earth where the gap between the rich and the poor was so wide, deep and final.

Sutter walked across the stage with the same lithe stride that had served him so well in jungles, deserts and mountains. He had made too many speeches in front of too many wealthy and powerful people to be bothered by stage fright. Yet, despite his best efforts to be charitable, he knew that there was a razor edge to his smile. He knew because the auctioneer was giving him the sideways, wary glances that people usually reserve for large, fanged animals that have been carelessly left unchained.

It's all for a good cause, he reminded himself for the twentieth time as he sat down, hoping to end the unwanted applause. He worked for OCC because he believed in it, not because he wanted to be known as a benefactor of worthy causes.

Suddenly Sutter spotted a svelte redhead sauntering down the aisle and taking a front-row, center seat. The body was by the best personal fitness instructors. The jewels were by Tiffany. The dress was by Sharai, purchased outright rather than merely modeled for the evening. The woman was stunningly turned out, unbelievably self-centered and had been pursuing Sutter with equal parts of energy and shamelessness for more than three years.

The redhead was not noted for her charitable nature. Sutter had little doubt that she had come tonight for the sole purpose of acquiring him for a few uninterrupted weeks of intense pursuit. As his name hadn't been on the program, there was only one way she could have discovered that he was auctioning himself off to the most generous bidder.

Damn Anthea, anyway! If that redheaded barracuda has the last bid, my so-called vacation will be undiluted hell!

Furious, Sutter reached up with outward casualness and tugged on his left ear. It was a signal of long standing between himself and his aunt. Whoever used it was calling for help in being extricated from an impossible social situation.

"Go see what the dear boy wants."

Anthea's unexpected purr of satisfaction at Mandy's elbow slid easily through the crowd's noise, making her jump. She hadn't even seen Anthea come down from the side aisle to stand beside her.

"But—" Mandy began.

"Quickly!" interrupted Anthea crisply. "The auction is about to begin and then it will be too late."

Bewildered, Mandy stepped out into the aisle, only to stop as a small, surprisingly strong hand gripped her forearm.

"Tell him if he wants me to make the last bid, he must also let me make the travel arrangements for his mysterious Australian holiday."

Mandy gave her boss a blank look, then responded to a less-than-delicate push by hurrying down the aisle toward the stage while the audience continued its enthusiastic standing ovation for D. M. Sutter. Just as people were beginning to sit down again, Mandy walked up the stage steps in a subtle glitter of black beads and discreetly touched the auctioneer's arm.

"Message for Sutter," Mandy said quietly. "Urgent."

"It can't wait?"

"You know how it is with hard men," Mandy retorted. "You take 'em where you find them."

The microphone picked up her words and relayed them

all over the auditorium, much to the audience's amusement. Mandy wanted to go through the floor but the boards were much too tightly fitted for that. Given no other choice, she brazened it out when Sutter hooked his index finger in an imperious, sexy gesture for her to come to him.

"It's not that he's rude," Mandy said clearly, knowing the microphone would do the rest. "It's just that none of the five languages he speaks is English."

Laughter echoed and reechoed through the auditorium. Sutter slanted Mandy a smile that was frankly dangerous as he crooked his finger again. Mandy knew better than to tease the tiger twice. She walked across the stage toward him, drawing on every bit of her insouciance to hide her underlying nervousness. Though the bodice of her dress was demure enough for a matron twice her age, the front slit showed glimpses of long, well-formed legs and inviting hints of thighs clad in the sheerest of black silk stockings. The rear view of Mandy was frankly breathtaking. Her back was shapely, smooth and defined by a faint shadow along her erect spine. The shadow deepened enticingly just before the fabric began again, clinging to her hips in a dark glitter of beads.

Mandy was grateful not to be presenting Sutter with the costume's back view. Even seated and wearing evening clothes, Sutter radiated the kind of raw physical presence that sent up warning flares telling her to beware of getting close. Yet there was no help for it. She had to get quite close to Sutter or run the risk of broadcasting every word of their conversation over the auditorium's sensitive sound system.

"You beckoned?" she murmured, bending down until her mouth all but brushed Sutter's ear. With each breath she took, the clean, male scent of him spread through her body, making her knees oddly weak. She swayed.

Sutter's hands snaked out with shocking speed, holding Mandy by the waist. His grip was powerful and his fingers were so long that they met in the small of her back. Male fingertips found smooth, naked skin, drawing a gasp from

Mandy. The low cut of Mandy's dress seemed to bother Sutter not one bit. There was strength in his grip but no sensuality. He moved his head sharply, seeking Mandy's ear beneath the silken curtain of her chin-length hair. His breath was as warm as his words were cold.

"Tell my sainted aunt that if Sissy buys me she finally will have succeeded in making me lose my temper."

Mandy had no trouble deciding that the "she" referred to was Anthea, not the mysterious Sissy. The icy tone of Sutter's voice and the steel quality of his grip on her convinced Mandy that the time for teasing the tiger was long past. There was only one way she was going to get beyond the reach of his powerful, unnerving presence, and that was to gather her scattering wits and tell the man what he wanted to hear.

"I think Anthea already knows," Mandy murmured. "She said, quote, 'Tell him if he wants me to make the last bid, he must also let me make the travel arrangements for his mysterious Australian holiday,' unquote."

What Sutter whispered next into Mandy's ear didn't bear translating, much less quoting to his maiden aunt.

"Is that yes or no?" Mandy asked with a coolness that was sheer bravado.

Sutter jerked his head back from her scented, swirling hair. For the benefit of the audience he smiled, but Mandy was close enough to see his eyes. She shivered and wondered how a man whose hands were so warm could have eyes like green ice.

"Yes," he hissed.

Mandy nodded her understanding because she knew she would stammer if she tried to speak. She turned and walked away, but with each step she felt Sutter's icy eyes boring into her naked back. Silently pitying whoever bought Sutter's vacation—and his unnerving, short-tempered company—Mandy hurried across the stage.

"Is the Australian vacation still on?" the auctioneer asked, covering the microphone before she spoke.

"You bet. The sooner the better. If I had the money, I'd buy the ticket myself and launch him with a bottle of champagne over his thick prow."

The auctioneer smiled as she looked from Sutter's hard, handsome face to Mandy's flushed cheeks. "Honey, didn't you know? The best ones always bite, and they bite in all the best places."

Mandy looked first shocked, then intrigued despite herself. The thought of Sutter's mouth closing on her flesh in sensual teasing made sudden heat expand deep inside her, flushing her from breast to thighs.

"Bon appétit!" Mandy muttered, and hurried from the stage, her cheeks burning.

Laughing, the woman turned back to the audience. "Relax, ladies, the Australian outing is still up for bid. Better move fast, though. The next phone call could change things and take this elusive hunk of steamy jungle beyond your reach forever. Before the bidding begins, Mr. Sutter requested that I warn you—the three weeks will be spent in one of the most little-known resorts in the world, a place where only a severely limited number of people are permitted to stay each year. The accommodations won't be luxurious. Leave your diamonds and designer clothes at home. You will be sleeping in a tent. You will be permitted to carry no more luggage than fits into a backpack, and that includes your purse. If these restrictions don't discourage you, then you are just the lady to accompany D. M. Sutter on his Australian mystery vacation."

If the women in the audience were discouraged, it didn't show. The bidding was opened by the stunning redhead. Her bid was equally stunning.

"Five thousand dollars."

The auctioneer picked up the bid without missing a beat and began skillfully working the audience. The next bid wasn't long in coming, nor in being topped.

"Six thousand," called the redhead.

"Is that Sissy by any chance?" Mandy asked Anthea.

Anthea's low purr of satisfaction was the only answer.

"I gather Sutter doesn't want to spend three weeks with her," Mandy said.

Anthea laughed. "The woman is a two-legged barracuda who loves nothing but her own reflection in the mirror. But even reflections have their uses."

Mandy hesitated but knew she should warn her boss that this wasn't the best way to fill OCC's coffers. "Anthea, Sutter is furious. Not hot furious. Icy furious. Why did he volunteer himself if he dislikes being auctioned off so much?"

The older woman winced. "He didn't volunteer himself. I did."

"My God," Mandy said faintly, looking at her boss in disbelief. "Do you have a death wish?"

"So long as Sissy doesn't have the last bid, everything will be fine," Anthea said with more determination than real self-assurance.

"The cost of keeping everything fine is seven thousand dollars," Mandy muttered, "and climbing fast. The women in this place must be blinded by the spotlights. Anyone with two eyes could see that going on vacation with Sutter would be like inviting a hungry tiger to take the first bite of your hamburger."

Then Mandy thought of what the auctioneer had said and winced.

Anthea laughed and patted Mandy on the arm. "You needn't worry. I suspect Sutter has arranged a vacation that will keep him at arm's length from his 'date' while still showing her a piece of the world that few people ever get to see. In fact I suspect he—" Anthea broke off abruptly. "That's it. No one is going above Sissy's eight thousand." Anthea's fingers tightened on Mandy's arm. "Bid ten."

"What?"

"I can hardly bid on my own nephew, can I? Do it!"

"T-ten," Mandy said.

"Louder!"

"Ten thousand dollars!"

There was a long pause while the audience swiveled to see the new bidder. At Anthea's prod, Mandy held up a trembling hand.

"Eleven," Sissy said coolly.

Anthea's elbow dug into Mandy's ribs.

"Eleven five," Mandy said.

"Twelve."

"Twelve five."

"Thirteen."

"Fifteen thousand dollars," shot back Mandy, not waiting for Anthea's response.

The audience murmured. There was scattered applause.

Mandy didn't even notice. She was looking across the footlights at Sutter's calm face and burning green eyes. The idea of the shallow, glittering Sissy buying Sutter as though he were a designer dress irritated Mandy unreasonably. The man might be impossible in a social setting, but he was undeniably brilliant and of proven physical courage. She doubted that Sissy was interested in those particular qualities, however. No doubt the only thing Sissy burned to know was whether Sutter's stamina extended to areas other than chopping through jungles for weeks on end.

And then Mandy heard the echo of her last bid rippling across the audience. She turned to Anthea with a stricken look. The older woman smiled and squeezed Mandy's hand in silent reassurance.

Sissy hesitated for a dramatic moment, looked over at Mandy and the tiny woman standing next to her, then turned back to the auctioneer.

"Fifteen thousand dollars," the auctioneer said. "Do I hear fifteen thousand five hundred? Fifteen five, anyone?"

Sissy sat down.

"Sold for fifteen thousand dollars to Samantha Blythe!" There was a burst of applause.

"Well, go on," Anthea said, prodding Mandy. "Go up there and claim your prize."

Wide, cognac-colored eyes fixed on Anthea. "What?"

"Sutter," Anthea said. "You're supposed to walk off-stage with him."

"But I didn't—"

"Of course you did," interrupted Anthea. "Everyone here heard you. Now get up there before you embarrass him."

"Embarrass? *Sutter?*"

The thought was so ridiculous and at the same time so delicious that Mandy laughed aloud. She was still smiling widely when she walked onstage, followed every inch of the way by the spotlight, her long legs gleaming in their black silk sheaths. In a glittering, slithering cloud of black fabric, she came to a halt a few feet away from Sutter.

And crooked her finger at him.

Chapter 3

Even two weeks later, the memory of that moment was enough to make Mandy shiver. Sutter's sudden, dangerous smile was burned indelibly into her memory, as was the feel of his hand on the naked small of her back as he escorted her offstage; but it was his eyes that haunted her. Gem hard, dismissive, saying as plainly as the words he had whispered in her ear that he thought she was silly and inconsequential.

That's your free one, little girl. You pull a stunt like that again and you'll feel like grass after an elephant stampede.

She had looked down his tuxedoed length to his polished calfskin shoes and then back up, all the way up to those cold eyes. *You needn't be so sensitive about the size of your feet. If they weren't elephantine, they wouldn't fit so neatly in your mouth.*

The memory of her retort made Mandy groan silently. She put her hands over her face, shutting out the sight of her empty desk. She had always had a quick mind and even quicker tongue, but never had she regretted the result quite so much. Sutter unnerved her. Half the time she wanted to hide when she saw him.

And half the time she couldn't resist the urge to needle him into noticing her. Thank God he had gotten a head start on his three-week vacation by leaving four days ago.

"Why did I crook my finger at him in front of all those people?" Mandy asked herself for the thousandth time. "What on earth made me think I could embarrass him? How do you embarrass a rock!"

Even the memory of Sutter's granite self-assurance irritated Mandy. Instead of becoming angry at her mocking gesture, he had simply stood, slid his hand up beneath her hair to the nape of her neck and smiled while he had found and casually stroked the sensitive, vulnerable knot of nerves, sending visible goose bumps marching over her arms. One golden eyebrow had lifted at her response, his glance had moved over her as though stripping away the dress, and then he had turned aside with an utter lack of interest. She could still hear his passionless, cutting words.

You didn't buy a lover, baby, though God knows you're hungry enough to have robbed a bank for it. Maybe you could buy a piece of Sharai's jock. Two on one looks about his style.

Heat flushed Mandy's face now as it had that night when she had realized that Sutter had read the flip note on her calendar: Rob bank. Buy lover. Soonest.

Mandy had to give Sutter full marks for good manners, though. He had hustled her offstage before he walked away from her, leaving her to field teasing, prying questions from the women who had surged up from the audience to congratulate her.

She had started to explain that she had purchased Sutter for his aunt, not for herself, but Anthea had arrived and shaken her head slightly. With a rather grim smile and hot cheeks, Mandy had endured the twittering congratulations in silence.

"Mandy? Yo, Mandy. Anyone home behind those two-hundred-proof eyes?"

"Alcohol isn't stable at anything much higher than a hundred and eighty proof," she said automatically to Steve, her mind elsewhere. "It sucks water out of the air, diluting the mixture until—"

"Lady, you know some really weird things," Steve interrupted, flopping some folders down on her desk. "Here are the precedents Anthea has been jumping up and down to get."

Mandy blinked and focused on the present, shutting out the disturbing, unnerving memory of Sutter's wickedly male smile and utterly cold eyes. "She has?"

"Steve," Jessi called from Anthea's office, "where are those precedents? Anthea has the premier's personal secretary on the phone!"

Steve snatched up the folders before Mandy could touch them. "Coming right up!"

With a stifled sigh, Mandy watched Steve disappear. No wonder she had been brooding over Sutter lately. She had no work piled up on her desk, nothing to think about except the anniversary of the day two years before when her life had come apart.

Anything was better than dwelling on that. Even Sutter.

The phone rang. Welcoming the distraction, Mandy reached for it. As she held it to her ear she heard Alice's voice saying, "OCC, may I help you?"

Mandy replaced the receiver with a gentleness that was at odds with her mood. She could take anything but inactivity. Since Alice and Jessi had come to OCC, Mandy's own work had been divided up and handed out to them. Despite repeated assurances and hints of better things to come, Anthea had given Mandy nothing new to do. As a result, Mandy had had far too much time with her own thoughts.

Two years ago today, minus a few hours.

Stop it! It's over and done, dead and buried. It happened and nothing can be done to change it.

Yes. And it happened two years ago today.

The pen Mandy had been holding slipped from her fingers to roll across the desk and off the edge onto the floor. With unfocused eyes she watched the pen bounce softly on the carpet. Memories turned uneasily, unquiet ghosts rippling through her mind. Her skin went pale and her heart beat too quickly. Automatically she forced herself to breathe more deeply, more easily, bringing color back into her face, telling herself that there was nothing to be upset about.

It's just a day like any other. Just a day. If there were a grave to visit you'd go and stand and think about it all over again. But there isn't a grave, so you'll sit at home and think about it over and over until you're numb and then you'll sleep and get up and it will be another day like any other day, one more day, another day farther from yesterday. And someday it will be far enough.

But not today. Today it's too close.

Abruptly Mandy stood up and began pacing around the large office, touching desks and chairs at random, wanting…

Out.

She stood utterly still, surprised by the fierceness of her desire to be outside, in the open, free. It had been a long time since she had felt so trapped.

Same day, different year. I shouldn't have tried a deep bath this morning. Too deep. The water triggered too many memories.

A shudder ripped through Mandy's body. Suddenly she looked around, knowing that she had to have something to do or she would go crazy. She strode into Anthea's office to demand work. Anthea, Jessi and Steve were bent over the folders, which had been spread across a large library table. Apparently the premier's secretary had had his question answered, for Anthea was no longer holding a phone.

Anthea glanced at her utilitarian watch. "You're a few minutes early, but I suppose it's best. Airport traffic can be so unpredictable."

"What?" Mandy asked.

"Airport traffic," Anthea said briskly.

"Why do you care about—"

"The flight leaves in two hours."

"The flight?"

"To Sydney."

"Where?"

"Australia."

"What?" Mandy demanded, knowing how Alice had felt during the free-fall down the rabbit hole.

"Isn't this where I got on?" Anthea smiled serenely. "Get your purse, Mandy. This is where you get off."

"Anthea, what are you talking about?"

"The flight," said Steve, barely suppressing a wide smile.

"The flight?" Jessi said instantly, laughing.

"To Sydney," Steve said.

"Where?" Jessi asked, deadpan.

"Australia," Steve said.

"What?" Jessi asked, right on cue.

Mandy smiled despite herself. "I sounded that bad, huh?"

"Nothing that my vacation won't cure," Anthea said, crossing the room.

Just as Mandy opened her mouth to ask, *"What?"* she caught herself, disappointing Steve and Jessi. Anthea pulled a brilliant pink-and-black-striped backpack from her executive closet and plopped the bag softly on the desk. Mandy eyed the backpack dubiously.

"I didn't know zebras came in pink," Mandy murmured.

"They don't," Anthea said calmly. "This is a tiger stripe."

"Oh. Well, that explains it."

Anthea smiled and patted Mandy's hand. "That's what I like about you, dear. You understand me."

"I do?"

"You certainly do."

"That's frightening. When did you say your flight left?"

"I didn't, so we'd better hurry."

Mandy snapped her mouth shut, knowing she was in a

losing battle. When Anthea was in high spirits, even Mandy's quick tongue had to take a back seat.

"Okay. Purse. Airport. Plane. Sydney," Mandy said. "I'll carry the tiger."

"Hold my calls," Anthea said over her shoulder.

For three weeks?

But the thought went no further than Mandy's smiling lips as she followed Anthea. She didn't want to puncture Anthea's high-flying mood; the prospect of a three-week vacation in Australia would be enough to make anyone slightly giddy. If it weren't for Sutter's presence at the other end—and the plane flight itself—Mandy would have envied her boss. Even with the flight and Sutter's uncertain company waiting at the other end, the thought of Australia was still enough to make Mandy dream. It had been so long since her horizons had been bounded by anything but office and apartment walls, memories and fear.

"This way, dear. We'll take my car," Anthea said.

A few minutes later Mandy tossed the backpack in the trunk of Anthea's sleek two-seat Mercedes.

"Are you sure you don't need more luggage?" Mandy asked. "For you, surely Sutter would bend his rules."

"It's all right. I guarantee I won't be inconvenienced by Sutter's rules in the least."

Anthea's sweeping assurance left no room for questions. Mandy closed the trunk and slid into the driver's seat.

"How about your passport?" Mandy asked. "Did you ever get that problem with it straightened out?"

That was why Sutter had left early; he hadn't had the patience to wait while his aunt untangled red tape.

"I finally called Senator Martin Thurgood. He took care of everything."

"What was the problem exactly? You never said."

"No, I didn't, did I?"

Mandy waited.

Anthea rummaged in her purse for the car keys. "There

you are. Better hurry, dear. Sometimes these international flights are overbooked.''

Mandy took the keys automatically. ''Mr. Axton guaranteed you a seat, didn't he?''

''The seat is guaranteed,'' Anthea agreed.

''Since he owns a huge chunk of the airline, I don't think you need to worry about getting bumped. The way Mr. Axton feels about you, he'd probably throw out the captain first,'' Mandy said dryly.

Anthea simply smiled.

The drive to the airport took only twenty minutes. Mandy let Anthea off at the curb, then zipped across five lanes of traffic to find a space in the one-hour parking lot. She grabbed the vivid backpack out of the trunk, slammed down the lid and raced on foot back across five lanes of traffic. The first-class window was closed, telling Mandy that Anthea had already been checked in. She followed the directions to the gate, expecting to catch up with Anthea. She wasn't at the security checkpoint, however.

''Did a tiny silver-haired lady come through here?''

''Yes, ma'am,'' said the guard, smothering a smile. ''Captain took her through himself on a cart. She had the wrong flight time. They're holding the plane.''

''But I've got her luggage!''

Mandy tossed the backpack and her purse on the conveyor belt to be X-rayed. She hurried through the arch, didn't set off any alarms, grabbed the backpack and purse and set off at a run despite her high heels. At first she thought there was no one at the designated gate. Then she spotted a glint of silver hair at the end of the tunnel leading to a huge Boeing 747.

''Anthea!''

''Hurry up, dear. They're waiting for you.''

Mandy ran down the slanted tunnel and held the backpack out to Anthea. She ignored it, taking Mandy's purse instead. She stuffed a fat business envelope into the purse and gave it back to Mandy.

"Everything you need is inside. Now hurry along."

"What?"

"Don't worry about a thing," Anthea continued, rolling over Mandy's objections as she guided her employee toward the plane's entrance. "I'm having your mail and newspaper held, Jessi will water your plants, Steve is taking your car in to be serviced and Alice will pick up your dry cleaning. Was there anything else needing your attention in the next few weeks?"

Openmouthed, unable to say anything, Mandy simply shook her head.

"Ms. Blythe?" called the stewardess from the opening. "I have to close the door in one minute."

"Run along," Anthea said. "Four hundred people are waiting for you." Suddenly she stood on tiptoe and gave Mandy a hug. "Enjoy your vacation. You've more than earned it."

"But I—"

"Shoo," Anthea interrupted firmly. "Steve and Jessi are waiting to help me hang another picture on my wall. Your picture."

Purse in one hand, pink-and-black tiger-striped backpack in the other, Anthea's latest project moved toward the waiting plane in a daze.

"And, Mandy," called Anthea clearly over her shoulder, "don't forget what I said about finding a lover. Australian men are marvelous!"

"Is your name D. M. Sutter?"

"Would it do any good to deny it?"

The man laughed. "Sorry, mate. Afraid not. I saw your picture on the telly last night."

Cursing under his breath, Sutter descended the last step leading away from the airplane, careful not to touch the metal handrail. Late September was spring in Bundaberg, but in the northeast corner of the Australian continent, spring was a relative term. The tropical intensity of the sun brought everything it touched up to a burning heat—including hand-rails.

"You a reporter?" Sutter asked, eyeing the tall, muscular, heavily tanned young man in front of him with little favor. Australian reporters made their American counterparts look like well-mannered choirboys.

"No worries, mate. My name's Ray. I'm a dive instructor over on Lady. I picked up a message for you along with your diving gear."

At the words "dive instructor" the grim look vanished from Sutter's face. He smiled and held out a tanned, callused hand. "Thanks for picking up my tanks for me. We had to dodge some early monsoon storms on the way from Kununurra. Took twice as long as it should have. Is the plane ready?"

"Just one more passenger and we can leave. Let's weigh you in."

Sutter followed Ray into the small air-conditioned passenger terminal. At a gesture from Ray, Sutter stepped onto a scale with his backpack in his arms. Ray's eyebrows went up. He gave Sutter's deceptively lithe length a reassessing look.

"You're a diver, right enough," Ray said.

Sutter's eyebrow lifted in a silent question.

"All muscle," Ray explained. "You weigh fifteen kilos more than you look."

"Is that a problem?" Sutter asked, remembering the strict weight restrictions for the flight to the island.

Shaking his head, Ray added Sutter's weight onto the running total he was keeping for the plane. "No worries, mate. We've got seventy kilos left on this run. Unless your wife is built like you, we'll do fine despite the heat."

"I don't have a wife."

"Right. Your Sheila."

"I don't have a Sheila."

"Then you've got worries, mate," Ray said, putting away his clipboard. "She's the one we're waiting for."

"Bloody hell."

Trying not to smile, Ray handed a folded piece of paper to Sutter. He eyed the note suspiciously, wondering what his aunt was up to now. The "early start" on his vacation had turned out to be two days of flying, followed by three solid days and most nights of slogging through some of Australia's choicer slices of tropical hell while discussing rain patterns and animal migrations with the most enigmatic natives Sutter had ever met anywhere on earth. He had a week's growth of itchy beard and hadn't washed himself in the same time—unless he counted periodic drenchings from Australia's early monsoon rains—and now he was standing around on a blistering cement apron in one hundred degrees Fahrenheit and ninety-five percent humidity, waiting for…just what the hell was he waiting for?

Muttering, Sutter unfolded the paper and read silently: *I'm sending my latest project. She needs a vacation as much as you do.*

The handwriting was both elegant and subtly imperious. The latter element was underlined by the sweeping signature. *Anthea.*

Sutter looked at the horizon and silently counted to one hundred and thirty in the language that had no numbers. Ray watched from beneath his battered bush hat with the same deeply wary look the auctioneer had used.

And two goats is twenty. I don't need this. A near moon and a rising sun is twenty-one. I need a bath, a night's sleep, a good meal and a drink. Plus two goats is twenty-three. I need peace and quiet. And a pregnant goat is twenty-five. I need to be left alone. I need a vacation, not one of Anthea's damned projects! And a full moon is twenty-eight….

It was several minutes before Sutter's eyes focused on the sugarcane fields that surrounded the small airport. The cane was in all stages of production from bare red earth furrows to saw-toothed plants taller than the tallest man. Beneath a heat-shimmering sky of towering clouds, varying stages of the cane's growth glowed in different shades of green, beginning with a pale chartreuse and progressing through a green so dark it was just short of black. With each movement of the hot, humid wind, the deceptively slender cane leaves shivered and swayed.

The wind shifted, bringing with it the rich aroma of Bundaberg's only claim to fame—a rum distillery.

"You wouldn't happen to have any of the local product on hand, would you?" Sutter asked at last, focusing on Ray.

"Huh?"

"Rum," Sutter said succinctly.

The diver's wariness vanished in a compassionate male smile. "Right. Got it in my kit bag. Follow me, mate. It will be too late to dive by the time we reach the island anyway."

For the thirtieth time in as many hours, Mandy refused an airline attendant's polite offer of food and drink. In the eternity since Anthea had blithely launched her latest project, said project had watched two in-flight movies, listened to everything from elevator music to Bach on the earphones and told herself repeatedly that she was sitting in a theater, not in an absurd piece of metal suspended by unknowable forces forty thousand feet over water so deep that it was almost entirely unknown to man.

On the whole, Mandy had been quite pleased with her handling of the trans-Pacific flight. She had managed to convince herself for several hours at a time that she was safe, if not quite sane. The flight on the 747 had been so long it had finally put her in an odd kind of trance, too tired to be actively frightened while the huge plane had chased midnight across half the world, never catching it, falling slowly farther and farther behind until an iridescent orange dawn had caught the airliner over the South Pacific.

Other people had looked out the window and murmured grateful appreciation of the glorious light sliding over the ocean. Mandy had closed her window shade and had kept it that way until the plane landed in Sydney. Every instant of the trip she had reminded herself that once the ocean went by, she was going to enjoy herself. Australia was the perfect destination for someone afraid of water—it was the driest continent on earth. After the landing she had walked off the plane with a soaring sense of pride and accomplishment that had lasted all through Customs and Immigration.

Then she had been directed to her connecting flight. Sydney wasn't her ultimate destination. A place with the unlikely name of Bundaberg was. Her flight was to leave in twenty-eight minutes. The plane was not a 747. It wasn't even half of one. It held less than one hundred people. If she hadn't been nearly dead from jet lag and a lack of food and sleep, she never would have allowed the too-helpful crew to lead her aboard, tuck her into a front seat and hand her a magazine. She hadn't exactly read the magazine during takeoff—she had tried to crawl between its pages.

After the first half hour of tightly clenched fear, her mind had slowly regained control of her body. She hadn't exactly relaxed, but she had been able to force her fingers to turn magazine pages rather than to dig uselessly into the armrests. Food was still impossible to consider, much less to eat; fear-induced adrenaline had killed her appetite beyond hope of easy resurrection. Even water nauseated her, so she had simply endured the dryness in her mouth. The light-headedness that had finally set in after thirty hours of absolute fasting was rather welcome. It took her mind off the size of the plane.

Mandy blinked, trying to remember what she had been attempting to read. Slowly her eyes focused on the creased, twisted pages in her lap. The map detailing Australian airlines' domestic routes was indecipherable now, ruined beyond any hope of use. She closed her eyes and prayed that Bundaberg was somewhere in the center of the outback, where water came no deeper than occasional puddles left by even more occasional rains.

The plane landed with no fuss and only a slight barking of the tires. While everyone else milled and descended the staircase that had been wheeled into place, Mandy breathed shakily and sat in her seat, telling herself that her ordeal was finally over. This was it. It was all done, finished, and she hadn't disgraced herself. Tomorrow—whichever day that might be, for she had lost track of time somewhere in the endless midnight over the ocean—tomorrow she would feel proud of her accomplishment. Right now all she wanted to do was to crawl into bed and sleep for a week.

"Miss Blythe, are you well?"

Mandy lifted her head and smiled wearily at the anxious attendant. "Jet lag," she said. "My stomach is somewhere over Hawaii and my brain is still in California. The rest of me isn't worth a bent penny."

The woman smiled. "Let me get your rucksack. The pink striped one, right?"

"Yes. Thank you."

Slowly Mandy stood up, feeling as though she were using a body that was on temporary loan rather than the one she had lived in for nearly twenty-eight years. The sunlight pouring in the airplane's open door was so bright that she pulled sunglasses from her purse. The lenses were utterly black, contrasting starkly with the pallor of her skin, but the glasses reduced the sun's tropic glare to a bearable level.

Mandy closed her hand over the rail of the rolling metal staircase, only to yank her fingers back. The rail was uncomfortably hot, and the air was so steamy that it was an effort to breathe. Very slowly she went down the stairs, sensing the attendant hovering helpfully behind. Finally her feet touched the apron. The solid feel of the earth was like a benediction to Mandy. She had never liked flying even before the accident; afterward, airplanes had become something she endured only because she wanted to be able to look herself in the mirror and not see a complete coward staring back out—just a partial coward.

With a sigh Mandy started toward the terminal, not even seeing the man who stood impatiently to one side, watching her. Sutter's eyes had narrowed into unwelcoming slits of green when he recognized Mandy slowly descending from the airplane. The rum he had drunk had loosened the muscles in his neck but hadn't otherwise improved his disposition. The last thing he needed right now was three weeks of one-liners from Anthea's smart-mouthed assistant—even if she did have the most elegant, sexy back he had ever seen or touched.

Sutter didn't need Mandy, but he was stuck with her. There was no help for it. She was there and he was there and Anthea was wisely beyond reach. Swearing beneath his breath, Sutter covered the few yards separating him from Mandy.

"Get your tail in gear," Sutter said in a clipped voice, grabbing her arm just above the elbow. "We've got to weigh you in. Where's your luggage?"

Mandy stared at Sutter, too thick-witted to do more than hear his words. Barely. Understanding or answering him was beyond her.

"Here you go, mate," the stewardess said, handing over Mandy's backpack. "She must be an experienced flier. She didn't bring anything more than this."

Sutter took the backpack, grimaced at the color, grunted his thanks to the stewardess and resumed hustling Mandy toward the small terminal. Before her body could adjust to the cool impact of the air conditioning, Sutter had lifted her onto the scale's low platform, shoved her purse and back-pack into her arms and let go of her.

"Sutter?"

He ignored Mandy, looking only at Ray.

"No worries, mate. I've got diving gear that weighs more than your Sheila."

"She's not mine," Sutter snarled.

Mandy flinched.

Ray looked over Mandy's trim, womanly length. Even Mandy's dense sunglasses couldn't dim the impact of Ray's smile as he helped her down from the scale. Despite her exhaustion Mandy smiled in return; Anthea had been right about Australian men. Compared to Sutter, they were marvelous.

But then, so was a rabid gorilla.

"There's a good 'un," Ray said soothingly, steadying her. "Tough flight?"

"Yes," Mandy said, her voice cracking from dryness and relief that her torment had ended.

"No worries, luv," Ray said, giving her arm a reassuring squeeze as he removed the backpack. "Earl will have us out to Lady before you can say vegemite. Just don't try eating the stuff. Bloody awful. I've got to stow your gear now, but if you need anything on Lady, ask for Ray."

Rather mournfully Mandy watched as the handsome, energetic young man vanished through a back door in the terminal. She hadn't understood much of what he had said, but his smile had been like the local air conditioning—nearly overwhelming yet basically wonderful. She turned her attention back to Sutter. His mouth made as thin a line as his glittering jade eyes.

"Look, you have no idea how sorry I am," she said wearily, pushing the sunglasses up on her forehead so that she could rub her aching eyes. "Believe me, this wasn't my idea." She tried to smile placatingly at Sutter, but her lips kept curving down rather than up.

Sutter's glance was more comprehensive and less approving than Ray's had been. All that kept Sutter from venting his anger and frustration over his ruined vacation was the certainty that Mandy was on the ragged edge of exhaustion. There wasn't a bit of sauciness left in her. Obviously Anthea had been right; Mandy needed a vacation as much as he did. Equally obviously, she hadn't been prepared for this one. The conservative suit, nylons and heels she was wearing fairly screamed of Anthea's old-fashioned office.

"How much warning did you get?" Sutter asked reluctantly, feeling unwilling compassion stir for the wilted waif standing in front of him, silently pleading with him not to be angry.

"Warning?" Mandy made a choked sound and shook her head.

"She means well," Sutter said, taking Mandy's arm again and hustling her toward the door through which they had just entered the terminal. "C'mon, kid. They're waiting for us. You can flake out on the way over."

Mandy barely had time to pull her sunglasses into place before she stepped into Bundaberg's natural outdoor sauna. It took a moment for her to realize that Sutter was taking her toward the landing strip, not the parking lot. She slowed. His grip on her arm tightened.

"Is the car around at the side?" she asked.

"What car?"

"The one that…oh, no. *No.*"

Behind her sunglasses, Mandy's eyes widened in horror. Ahead of them was a plane that looked like an overgrown white dragonfly. The tiny twin engines were revving, making conversation impossible as Sutter dragged her closer to the open passenger door. She tried to speak but was too exhausted and too frightened to make her tongue work. Her legs weren't working very well, either, but Sutter didn't seem to notice. He simply swept her along, ignoring her futile attempts to stop. When it came time to scramble into the plane, she balked. She couldn't do it. She simply couldn't.

"N-no," she stammered. "I d-don't like small planes."

"If you think this is small, wait until you see the runway at the other end. Come on, get in," Sutter said impatiently, wanting to get out of the sun. "We've waited an hour for you already."

Mandy tried to think, to explain, but all she could do was stare in horror at the little plane that seated eight, including the pilot. Suddenly she felt herself being boosted aboard. She tried to fight, but it was like her worst nightmares; her muscles turned to sand, every movement was in slow motion except the world around her and it was hurtling forward so fast that nothing could stop it or the lethal crash that waited for her. With the last bit of her willpower Mandy turned to Sutter, forcing herself to speak.

"S-Sutter, p-please! I'm t-terrified of f-flying!"

"Cute, real cute," Sutter said curtly, stuffing Mandy through the fuselage door with more muscle than ceremony. "You're so terrified that you flew halfway around the world on one plane and then flew up the length of the Australian continent on another, right? So knock off the bad comedy and get your butt in the damn seat."

He boosted himself in right behind Mandy, sat her firmly in her seat just behind the pilot and flopped down in the seat next to her. The sound of the engines changed in pitch to a mechanical scream. Mandy only wished she could scream, as well, but her mouth was too dry, her throat too constricted.

"S-Sutter…"

He hadn't heard her aching whisper. She grabbed his wrist, trying to make him understand.

"Listen, honey," he snarled, jerking free. "I haven't slept in three days, I haven't bathed in a week and the last thing I ate was a lizard charred in a camp fire. I'm sure as hell in no mood for any more of your silly jokes. Give it a rest!"

Mandy tried to speak again but her mouth was too dry, the engines had become too loud, and the earth itself was hurtling away beneath her. Within minutes the plane turned and headed out over the sea. She closed her eyes and prayed that she would die in the crash rather than be trapped alive in the fuselage, sinking, drowning, no one to hear her screams but a dead man who had never loved her.

Chapter 4

To Mandy the sound and smell and feel of the plane were part of a nightmare revisited. There were vibrations shaking her, too much noise for a scream to be heard and no voice left with which to scream, no strength, nothing but the empty sky above and the uncaring sea below.

Nightmare and memory became one and the same, hammering at her, shaking her, until all she could do was endure as the devastating past rose up and overwhelmed her....

Mandy wheeled her bike off the early-afternoon ferry to Catalina Island. She stepped onto the left pedal and swung her leg easily over the seat, feeling happy and healthy and very much alive. Early summer clouds swelled silently overhead, pushed up from the Mexican tropics by a southerly wind. The unusual humidity didn't bother Mandy. Nothing could bother her today. Humming softly, smiling at people she passed, Mandy began pedaling toward the campground that was halfway up the island, closer to the tiny airstrip than to the small resort town of Avalon.

She pedaled faster than usual, eager to give Andrew the good news. Her husband had been unusually moody lately. His research hadn't been going well. At least, that was what he had blamed his bleak silences and sudden outbursts on in the past. Once she had thought Andrew's dark mood had to do more with the fact that his forty-second birthday had come and gone—placing him securely within that dread territory called middle age—with no baby in sight despite nine months of trying. But when she had mentioned his age and lack of a child as a possible source of his temper, he had stormed out of the house, leaving her to wait up until 3:00 a.m., when he had come in smelling of alcohol and smoke from nameless bars.

That had been the first time he had come home in the early hours of the morning, but not the last. It had happened more and more frequently during the past nine months. Andrew's forty-third birthday—and their fourth wedding anniversary—was tonight. That was why Mandy had begged, wheedled and bullied the doctor to get an early answer from the lab so that she could surprise her husband by arriving early on the island that lay only twenty-six miles off the coast of California.

Mandy and Andrew had honeymooned on Catalina, diving along its steep, rocky sides, seeing ocean life that was far more varied and abundant than the marine life to be found off mainland Southern California's heavily populated and often heavily polluted shores. The honeymoon had been one of the happiest times of Mandy's life, despite the fact that the pleasures of marital sex hadn't lived up to their advance billing. The ocean had more than compensated for the awkwardness she felt during her husband's swift, turbulent lovemaking.

The novelty of her sexual inexperience had quickly worn off for both herself and her husband, leaving little to take its place but her efforts to understand what had gone wrong.

The ocean's novelty had never worn off for Mandy. The siren call of the green-shadowed depths sank more deeply into her soul with each dive.

At least we have that in common, Mandy thought.

The insight startled her. She and Andrew had a lot more in common than diving, didn't they? He had been her faculty adviser while she got her Ph.D. in oceanography. He had encouraged her, respected her work, tried to seduce her repeatedly and unsuccessfully and had ultimately married her on his fortieth birthday. His second marriage. Her first. The fact that there had been no children from the first marriage had reassured Mandy at first; Andrew's demanding schedule left little enough time for a wife, much less for children.

But Andrew wanted children. Desperately. Mandy hadn't been ready for immediate motherhood. She had wanted time to adjust to juggling marriage and her burgeoning career as an ocean resource specialist for the state of California. Yet before her marriage was more than a few months old, fights had begun over when to have children, fights that left Mandy angry and crying and confused. In all the time before their marriage, she and Andrew had talked of their joint careers, of exploring the oceans of the earth together, of teaching and dissertations and the color of the sea fifteen fathoms down on a sunny day.

Never once had Andrew mentioned wanting children at all, much less immediately after marriage. Just as Mandy had naively assumed that sex would be wonderful after marriage, she had assumed that Andrew shared her desire that she establish herself in her field before she took a leave of absence to have children. She had been wrong. Andrew had wanted her to throw away her pills the day they were married. The fact that she had just been given an important grant to study the dietary habits of the Pacific sea otter had meant nothing to Andrew. The fact that her work might ultimately be used to determine whether or not that endangered species survived had also left him unmoved. He had wanted her pregnant, period. Everything else came second.

Mandy had thrown her pills away the day her work on the otters was complete. She had assumed that her marriage would improve immediately. And it had, until her period came.

After her third period had come, she had gone in to see her doctor, received a thorough checkup and been told to come back in nine months if she hadn't conceived. Nine months later she had returned. After an exhaustive series of tests it had been determined that her fertility was all that it should be and then some. She was told to send her husband in for tests.

Andrew had flatly refused.

It doesn't matter now, Mandy told herself, pedaling fiercely. *I'm almost two months pregnant and everything is all right. I can tell Andrew and see him smile at me again. He'll be a good father—God knows he really wants children, which is more than you can say for a lot of men.*

The thought of their future baby made Mandy smile and then laugh. She couldn't wait to feel the baby move, to give birth and to hold the baby in her arms, to teach her child to swim and to read and to ride a bike, to share with her child the beauty and mystery of the shimmering sea. She couldn't wait to tell Andrew, either, to see his delighted smile, to know that she had finally given him something he desperately wanted.

Anticipation made Mandy impatient with the miles between herself and her husband. She wished that she had been able to call him, but that hadn't been possible. She wished that she had flown over with him in their little plane a few days ago, but if she had, she wouldn't have been able to get the lab report back until next week, and she had wanted the report in time for it to be a birthday and anniversary present in one. Besides, she really didn't enjoy flying, especially in a small plane, which was another thing she and Andrew argued about. He took her unease as a slap at his abilities as a pilot, and nothing she had been able to say had convinced him otherwise.

That's all in the past, Mandy told herself firmly. *Now that I'm pregnant, he won't be so touchy about his age, his abilities, his career. Everything. We'll be able to laugh together again.*

Mandy's thoughts veered back to the coming baby. Mentally she began making lists of things to do, things to put on hold for a year, people to tell, papers to be rushed before she was too big to do the research. She was still making lists when she wheeled into the campsite where Andrew had been for three days. No one was in sight. She bit her lip, then sighed. He was probably out diving with one of the locals.

Deflated, Mandy parked her bike beneath a big bush at the back of the campsite and headed for the tent. The first thing she noticed was the compressed-air tanks propped against a nearby boulder. The second thing she noticed was the components of two wet suits strewn across the ground between the tanks and the tent, as though whoever had worn the suits had been in a terrible rush to get out of their neoprene prisons. The third thing she noticed was an oddly shaped scrap of fuchsia cloth dangling from a guy rope near the tent's entrance. Puzzled, she pulled back the tent flap and stepped in.

It took a moment for Mandy's eyes to adjust from full sun to the tent's dim interior light. Her ears had no such problem. She heard the feminine voice with awful clarity.

"Oh…more…harder…harder…!"

Mandy barely recognized Andrew as his hips slammed rhythmically into the girl who was squirming frantically beneath him, both of them panting, her nails raking down his naked back as her body bucked and then went rigid. Mandy's horrified cry was lost beneath the noise of her husband's climax and that of his partner. The difference in the light level inside the tent registered on the girl, however. After a few more cries, she opened her eyes lazily.

"Oops," she said.

"Huh?" he said.

"When did you say your wife was coming over?"

"Tomorrow."

"I think she decided to come early."

"She never comes," Andrew said, laughing. "That's why I like getting off with you. You like it the same way I do, hot and fast."

"Hon, I'm not fooling. We've got company."

Andrew followed the girl's glance, shifting onto his elbows in response to his partner's pushes. He squinted into the light streaming through the open tent flap.

"Mandy?" he asked.

Her only answer was a choked sound of rage and hurt and disbelief.

With a muttered obscenity, Andrew rolled off the girl. "What the hell are you doing here today?"

Mandy could hardly believe what she was hearing. "I think a better question would be what *she* is doing here."

"What she's doing here is fornicating, and she's doing it a hell of a lot better than you ever do," he retorted, peeling off a condom and dumping it in an ashtray.

The words slid past Mandy's anger, slicing into her until she couldn't speak for the pain.

"Hey, hon," the girl said, stretching, "I think I'll give this whole scene a pass, know what I mean? Righteous wives just aren't my thing."

The girl grabbed a scrap of fuchsia cloth from the foot of the sleeping bag. The cloth turned out to be a bikini bottom, which she wriggled into before brushing past Mandy on the way out. The tent shivered as the girl snapped the other scrap of fuchsia cloth off the rope.

"Thanks for the use of the diving gear," the girl called from outside the tent. "Catch ya later."

Mandy looked down at her husband, who was pulling on a pair of wet swimming trunks. She wasn't able to say anything or even think of anything to say; all she could do was try to cope with the anger, humiliation and disbelief that were shaking her.

This can't be happening.

But it was.

"Mandy, Mandy, Mandy," Andrew sighed, running his hand through his thinning hair. "Well, you were bound to find out sooner or later. The miracle is that it wasn't sooner."

"Find out?"

The dry rasp of Mandy's words surprised her. That couldn't be her voice. That couldn't be her husband, the father of her child, still slick from another woman's body. She made a low sound of pain and wrapped her arms around herself.

"You're so damned naive," Andrew said, exasperated and almost sad at the same time. "It used to fascinate me how anyone as brilliant as you could be so dense about men and sex. I kept fantasizing how great it would be to initiate you, to know I was getting something no other man had ever had. And then I thought what bright kids we'd have together. So I married you and took you to bed and—" he shrugged "—well, it wasn't great and it didn't get any better. I didn't have the patience to teach you how to please me and you didn't have any interest in learning." He sighed. "So I found my sex elsewhere. That shocks you now, but you'll get used to it. And I'm careful, Mandy. I learned my lesson with my first wife. I don't bring anything home but memories, and they're not contagious."

Mandy didn't realize that she was shaking her head in automatic denial until Andrew cursed and came angrily to his feet.

"Grow up, Mandy! Stop looking at me like I've just drowned your favorite kitten. I don't know of one man who doesn't step out on his wife—and I know of damn few wives who don't return the favor! But they live together in relative harmony and raise kids anyway, because nothing human is perfect and they're grown-up enough to know it!"

For a long time Mandy looked at her husband, then asked raggedly, "What about love?"

"What about it?"

Mandy closed her eyes. "Then why did you marry me?"

"I was nearly forty and I panicked. Like every other fool since Adam, I thought an injection of young tail would make me young, too. But I couldn't get in your pants without a ring. Then I decided, what the hell, why not? I wanted kids. I wanted them a lot. I didn't want to grow old alone and die knowing that nothing of me lived on."

Silence stretched, then stretched more, until Andrew asked tiredly, "Any more questions?"

Mandy shook her head.

"You sure?"

She nodded, but she felt as though she had been torn in half and was watching herself from a distance—talking, breathing, all the normal gestures and signs of life. But nothing felt real. The tent wasn't real. She wasn't real. The moment wasn't real.

"Great," Andrew said, looking relieved. "Let's go diving. It's not too late to bag something for dinner."

As though at a distance Mandy heard herself say, "I'll eat on the ferry."

Her husband looked at his diving watch. "No, you won't. You can't pedal back in time to catch the last ferry. Come on, Mandy," he coaxed. "Suit up. The only thing we're good at together is diving. You'll feel better once you're down there." He smiled ruefully. "You know, if you'd taken to sex with a tenth of the instinct and skill you show for diving..." He sighed. "Well, you didn't, and I need a lot of sex and that's the way it is."

"No."

"No what?"

"If you think I'm going to crawl into my wet suit—the wet suit that your little sand bunny just peeled off—you are crazy."

Mandy's words were as quiet, flat and blank as her eyes.

She still had the eerie feeling of being divided in two—half of her screaming soundlessly in pain and anger, the other half watching with unnatural calm.

"Fine," Andrew said curtly. "So we'll have hamburger."

"Like hell."

He rubbed his forehead in sudden pain. "Mandy, I've got a real splitter. Could we put this on hold?"

"You can put it where the sun don't shine," she shot back. "I'm going home right now if I have to swim."

"If I break camp and take the gear, there will be too much weight in the plane."

"Who said anything about breaking camp?"

"Mandy—"

"If we hurry," she interrupted, her voice brittle, "in a few hours you can be back here grunting and sweating on top of little miss loose thighs."

"Why don't you stay and watch? Maybe you'd learn something about how to make a man feel like a man!"

Mandy spun around and left the tent, heading for the airplane.

It wasn't that easy, of course. Andrew couldn't believe that his young wife wouldn't change her mind once she had cooled off. Mandy endured the arguments and pleas and insults because there was no other choice, no place to go, nothing she could do but wait for Andrew to give in or for tomorrow's early ferry to leave the island, whichever came first.

It was Andrew who finally gave in, sometime in the lost hours before dawn. Grim-faced, unnaturally pale, he strapped himself into the little plane. The tiny strip was unmanned and not set up for night takeoffs, but Andrew had flown in and out of Catalina so many times that he didn't even hesitate. The small plane leaped into the air, climbed, executed a crisp turn and headed for the mainland.

For once Mandy wasn't nervous about being in the little plane. She was more afraid of what her husband's next cutting justifications for adultery might be than she was afraid of the plane itself. A swath of city lights glittered on the mainland horizon, a beacon of life and color beyond the blank darkness of the sea. Next to her Andrew piloted the plane in silence, his hands too tight on the controls. Several times she thought he was going to speak, but beyond kneading his neck and left shoulder from time to time, he concentrated exclusively on flying.

Gradually Mandy became aware that Andrew's breathing had changed. Simultaneously she realized that the altitude of the plane had changed, as well. Instead of flying level, they were descending. The plane had lost so much altitude that the mainland's glittering lights were barely a tiny thread across the darkness. It was as though Andrew were going for a landing, yet there were no lights below, no airport, nothing but the black sea.

"Andrew? What are you doing?" She turned and saw him. "Oh, God! Andrew!"

His face was bathed in sweat and his mouth was flattened in a grim line of pain. He was flying one-handed. Before her horrified eyes he groaned and went limp. Instants later the plane ripped off the top of one wave and bounced onto the peak of another and then another, skimming the surface of the sea like a flat rock thrown by skillful hand.

But unlike a rock, the plane could float. For a time. Long enough for a dazed, battered Mandy to realize what had happened. Long enough for her to claw off her harness and her husband's. Long enough for her to pull futilely at his slack body, wrenching with all her strength and calling incoherent prayers, trying and trying to pull him out the buckled passenger door, kicking at the door with her feet and screaming and yanking at Andrew's dead weight.

Suddenly cold water surged upward, engulfing the white wreckage, pulling the fuselage down and down, taking her and her immovable burden with it....

Sutter lifted his attention from the fascinating patterns of indigo and glittering silver reflections that gave the sea around the Great Barrier Reef so much visual variety. Each difference in color represented a change in the depth of the sea, a change caused by the presence of the tiny animals that were in the process of further enlarging the greatest mass of material ever assembled by any life-form anywhere on the face of the earth. From orbital distance, even the most dense metropolitan sprawls of humanity didn't register on the human eye; the Barrier Reef did. More than twelve hundred miles long and sixty stories from bottom to wave-combed top, the reef formed a 100,000-square-mile fringe to Australia's northeastern edge.

And just off the nose of the plane, only a few minutes away, lay tiny Lady Elliot Island, a scuba diver's paradise. Elation surged within Sutter, making him smile. He had wanted to go to Lady Elliot since the first time he had heard of the island twenty years before. Now it was finally within reach, the southernmost coral island of the immense Great Barrier Reef complex, an island that was no more than a tiny mote decorated with white breakers, lime green lagoons and an ocean so clear that he could count more shades of blue than he had words to describe.

The plane banked, shutting off Sutter's view of Lady Elliot Island. Eagerly he leaned to his left, over Mandy's lap, peering out her window. The plane straightened, shifting his weight unexpectedly. He bumped into Mandy.

"Excuse me," he said loudly over the engine noise, "I..."

Sutter's words trailed off as he realized that Mandy hadn't noticed him. She was rigid in her seat, her hands clenched together, her face gleaming with sweat. It occurred to him that he couldn't remember her moving at all during the flight. She hadn't even crossed and recrossed her ankles or shifted her purse or rummaged inside it for a comb or a piece of gum. It was as though she were a statue.

"Mandy?"

There was no answer. Sutter touched Mandy's hands.

The chill of her skin shocked him; the plane was too small to be air-conditioned, which meant that the interior temperature was well into the eighties. There was no reason for her to be so cold.

If Mandy felt Sutter's touch she didn't show it. Nor did she appear to notice the plane's descent. She was unnaturally still, as white as the coral beaches and landing strip below, her skin icy to the touch.

Abruptly Sutter understood that Mandy hadn't been joking at the Bundaberg airport; she really was terrified. Even as he reached out automatically to comfort her, he overrode the impulse, forcing his hands back to his sides. So far she had somehow managed to control her terror. Anything he did might snap that fragile restraint and send her into a bout of hysterical screaming. The pilot didn't need that kind of distraction at the moment—there was a hard crosswind blowing and the coral landing strip was little more than a white line gnawed through the sturdy she-oaks that had colonized the island.

The pilot crabbed in, compensated for the relatively calm air between the she-oaks and dropped down onto the crushed coral runway, dumping speed as fast as he could. Sutter's eyes widened when he saw why the pilot was in such a hurry to stop—a colony of terns was nesting on the far half of the strip.

The pilot knew precisely what he was doing. He stopped short of the birds with room to spare. He shut down the engine, popped open the side window for ventilation and stretched. The passenger sitting next to him hopped out, followed by the pilot himself. In order for the four people seated behind Sutter to exit, he had to get out first, for until his seat was folded down, there would be no way for anyone in back to scramble out of the plane. He looked over at Mandy. She hadn't moved.

Sutter got out quickly, helped the remaining passengers out and then climbed back in. Mandy neither moved nor acknowledged her surroundings in any way.

''Mandy, it's all right. We've landed.''

Sutter's voice was low, soothing. She didn't seem to hear him. Slowly he removed her black, oversized sunglasses. Her eyes were wide, unfocused, dilated, and what he had thought was sweat was actually a slow rain of tears. Gently he stroked her white, cold cheek.

''Mandy, you can come back now. It's all over. You're safe.''

He repeated the words many times, touching her very carefully, telling her that she was safe. After a few moments she shuddered once, violently, like a swimmer struggling up from the black depths to the surface of the sea. Slowly her eyes focused on Sutter.

''That's it, golden eyes. Look around. You're safe,'' he murmured, smoothing the back of his fingers down her cold cheek once again. ''Ready to get out now?''

Mandy fumbled at the fastening of her seat belt, but her hands were shaking too hard to accomplish anything. Sutter took care of the buckle with a swift motion, then eased her from the seat, taking most of her weight when her legs proved to be as uncertain as her hands had been.

''Lean against the frame while I get out, okay?''

Before Mandy managed to nod, Sutter had slipped out and was turning to lift her onto the blindingly white coral runway. Carefully he set her on her feet.

''Can you walk?'' he asked.

He watched her lips form the word *yes*, but before she could speak she crumpled. He caught her, lifted her into his arms and began to walk toward a small building that was all but hidden by she-oak trees.

Ray, who had been unloading the plane's small baggage compartment, saw Mandy faint. He sprinted forward.

''What happened?'' he demanded.

''Jet lag,'' Sutter said laconically. ''Which tent is ours?''

''This way. Need a hand?''

The idea of turning Mandy's limp form over to anyone else was frankly distasteful. Sutter shook his head in curt refusal. Then, realizing how rude the gesture had been, Sutter added in his best Australian accent, "No worries, mate. She's not that big."

Ray hesitated, smiled slightly and led Sutter at a brisk pace along a crushed coral pathway. As he walked, Sutter shifted Mandy until her head was supported by his chest. He kept her tucked in close, dividing his attention between the path and her white face. The slow, even movement of her breast against his left hand told him that she was breathing well, despite her pallor. He hurried between tents and a few spartan cabins, barely noting the dive gear propped everywhere. There were curious glances from a few well-bronzed, husky young men lounging in front of one tent, cans of Fosters Lager firmly in hand. A wave-off from Ray told the men that things were under control.

"In you go," Ray said, pulling aside a ragged tent flap.

Two single mattresses rested on the tent floor, one to each side. The clean white sheets, neatly folded white blankets and oversize white towels looked rather incongruous against the worn canvas.

"Usually there are double bunks," Ray explained hastily, "but they're all taken. This tent wasn't rented because it was a spare that needed mending. Wind can blow bloody hard here. We got the worst rips repaired, but—"

"It's fine," Sutter interrupted, laying Mandy on one of the mattresses and propping her feet instead of her head on the pillow. "I'm still surprised you fit us in on such short notice. Anthea must have moved heaven and earth."

Ray grinned. "Don't know about heaven, but there was a hell of a to-do here until we found a place to put you." He knelt beside Sutter and looked at Mandy's pale, delicate face. "You sure she's all right?"

Sutter held his fingers against the pulse in Mandy's throat. The flow of blood was steady, even and reassuring. There was nothing to suggest that anything more than exhaustion and fear was at work on her body. Color began coming back into her face even as he watched.

"She's coming around right now."

"Water is in the thermos by your bed. I'll go out and tell the blokes what's what—unless you need me?"

Sutter shook his head, never lifting his intent green gaze from Mandy as he stroked her smooth cheek. Long, dense black eyelashes fluttered. She murmured and turned toward the source of the slow, gentle caresses that were warming her cheek. Her lips brushed the back of his knuckles and her breath sighed warmly across the sensitive skin between his fingers.

Desire coiled suddenly, heavily, in Sutter. He told himself it was only that Mandy had aroused his protective instincts—and then the memory of her elegant, naked back and the satin gleam of her skin beneath the stage's spotlight came to him. A hot shaft of desire pulsed through him, pushing his shorts into a new shape. It was a response that had occurred more than once when he had looked at Mandy.

I need this like I need the bends. Damn Anthea! How did she know that Mandy turns me on? Did I somehow give it away during the few days I was in the office? I spoke less than twenty words to Mandy, and all of them were strictly business.

There was no answer to Sutter's silent question except the hard thrust of desire lying heavily between his legs, tightening his body until he ached.

Too bad Mandy isn't like whatsherfanny, the glamour girl Anthea shipped off to New York. But Mandy isn't the type for fast affairs and faster goodbyes, and that's all I want from a woman. So stand down, John Thomas. There's nothing doing with this woman.

Mandy nuzzled against Sutter's hand. He yanked it back as though she had bitten him. Even so, the sensory impact of her lips burned on his skin, making a mockery of his attempts to control his unruly sex. Sudden anger rushed through Sutter, anger at himself for not understanding that Mandy truly had been afraid, anger at Anthea for meddling by throwing matches and gasoline together on a remote coral island, anger at his pulsing body for demanding something it wasn't going to get and pure masculine rage at Mandy that she could arouse him simply by being alive.

Three weeks. In a tent. Listening to her breathe. God, I'll go crazy.

But first I'll throttle my damned meddling aunt!

Mandy made a low sound as she swam up from the depths of her nightmare. Her eyes opened, focused, and her breath came in sharply. Sutter's green eyes were very close to hers, watching her with something that looked like anger.

"What...?" Mandy asked, wondering what she had done wrong now.

"You fainted," Sutter said in a clipped voice. "How do you feel?"

Slowly Mandy looked around. She was in a tent and a wind was gusting, alternately belling out the canvas sides and collapsing them again. The screened flap of the tent's front opening was in shreds that fluttered with each movement of the air. Beneath the wind came the sound of distant surf. The unmistakable smell of the sea was rich in the humid air.

"We didn't crash," Mandy said.

"You seem surprised."

She looked at him blankly. "Crashes happen."

"Not very damned often or people wouldn't fly." Sutter came to his feet in a powerful, impatient movement, not wanting to stay any closer to Mandy than he absolutely had to. "Feel like sitting up?"

Slowly Mandy brought herself into a sitting position. Sutter clenched his hands into fists to keep from reaching for her. He wanted to help her, sure, but not half as much as he wanted to feel her in his arms again. The knowledge only fed his anger. He should have let the handsome, solicitous Ray haul Mandy to the tent and nurse her to consciousness.

Sutter's instant, savage rejection of that idea did nothing

to take the sharp edge off his temper. The rational part of his mind calmly pointed out that jet lag, fatigue and lack of sleep were taking their toll of him as surely as they had of Mandy. The irrational part of his mind told the other part to get stuffed—his long-awaited vacation had been ruined and he was in no mood to be gracious about it.

"Dizzy?" he asked curtly.

Mandy shook her head. All she felt was utterly drained.

"Good. Why don't you get in your suit while I get Ray to walk you down to the lagoon. You can take a ride in the reef boat or go for a lazy swim in some of the most beautiful water in the world. You'll feel much better and—"

"No," Mandy said, shuddering. "The only thing that scares me more than small planes is the ocean."

"Then the reef boat—"

"No. I can't take anything smaller than the *Queen Mary*."

Sutter's last hope of a decent vacation evaporated, and with it went his temper.

"Let me get this straight," he said coolly. "I've spent a lifetime trying to get to the Great Barrier Reef, and my sainted aunt has fixed it so that I'll be locked up in a tent for three weeks with an amateur comedian who's afraid of her own shadow!"

"I'm not so hot on the idea myself," Mandy retorted, feeling strength return on a rush of anger. "I'd rather spend the time in a cage with a hungry tiger than trapped here with you!"

"I sense an area of agreement emerging," he said sardonically. "If you get your butt in gear, we can stuff some tranquilizers down your throat and get you back to the airfield before Earl takes off for the run back to the mainland. We'll give you some for the road, too. With luck, you'll be safe in your little burrow at home before the last of the pills wear off."

"Never," Mandy said, her voice climbing. "I will never get on that little white plane again!"

"Fine. I'll charter a boat."

"No. It won't be big enough."

"Then I'll blindfold you so you won't know the difference," he shot back. "Or are you afraid of the dark, too?"

"Go to hell, Sutter."

"You're the one who would like it there—it's dry and there's not a pair of wings in sight!"

Chapter 5

"How's the little Sheila doing?" Ray asked, his blue eyes vivid with health and good humor.

Sutter grunted. The quarter-mile walk from the tent to the "dive shop"—little more than a small shed—had taken some of the edge off Sutter's temper, but not enough. He looked longingly through the dark green fringe of narrow she-oak leaves, trying to catch a glimpse of the fantastic coral reef he had come so far and waited so long to see. Though invisible from where he stood, the presence of the sea was palpable in the brine-laden air, the distant murmur of breakers, the crushed coral lying white and pure beneath his feet.

"Any chance of a dive today?" Sutter asked wistfully.

"Sorry, mate. It's blowing too hard to take out the dive boat. The only other way to get out is to walk out through the lagoon to the reef at low tide and dive off the far side. But it will be dark by the next low tide."

Even as Sutter swore, he knew it was just as well that he

didn't go diving. He was too tired and too edgy to dive. "What about tomorrow?"

"S.S.D.D." Ray saw Sutter's lack of comprehension and smiled. "Same manure, different day."

Sutter's mouth kicked up at one corner.

"If it's windy," Ray continued, "most of the blokes are going to walk the reef tomorrow morning and dive off the wall. You're welcome to come along. The Sheila, too, if she's up to it. Walking the reef both ways in diving gear takes it out of you."

"I doubt that Mandy will feel like taking on the sea," Sutter said sardonically.

"She did look a bit like old beer," Ray said. "But we'd better go over her diving gear as well as yours just the same. That way when the fancy takes her, she'll be ready to go."

The next hour of checking equipment to see how it had survived the baggage handlers on two continents went a long way toward smoothing Sutter's ragged temper. Not for the first time in his life, Sutter wondered if diving weren't all that had kept him sane in a brutally crazy world. It was months since he had gone diving in anything but Brazil's opaque jungle rivers. As a form of release, that kind of river diving served its purpose, but only barely. He hungered to feel the cool, clean sea sweep around him in shades of blue, buoyant salt water taking the weight of the world from him and giving him the incomparable gift of flight.

By the end of the hour Sutter had relaxed completely, and Ray had accepted Sutter as a member of the informal fraternity of scuba divers. Sutter's ease and expertise with the gear, his critical attention to detail and his wry stories of the drawbacks of diving in unknown jungle rivers all had combined to make the young diver watch Sutter with growing interest and admiration.

"Looks like your Sheila bought herself all new gear to meet the Lady," Ray said, setting the last of the equipment aside and looking at it with mild envy. "Only the best, too."

Sutter grunted. He was certain Anthea had bought the expensive wet suit, tanks, mask, fins and all the rest. He also had no doubt that everything would fit Mandy perfectly. Anthea left no detail overlooked when she committed herself to a project.

Suddenly the sound of children's laughter burst into the dive shed's masculine silence. Sutter's head snapped up in surprise.

"That's the Townehome lot," Ray said. "Family comes here every year. The girl was nearly born here, but we got Linda to the mainland in time."

"They sound a little young for diving."

"Ted and Linda swap off the nanny duties. One dives, the other wades." Ray glanced at his dive watch. "Time for tucker. Do you know where you eat?"

"No, but with only a few buildings on the whole island, the cafeteria can't be hard to find."

"It's just back of the office, which is just below the bird sanctuary and facing the lagoon."

Sutter smiled. "Got it."

He stood, stretched and walked back down the coral pathway, past the handful of small, frankly plain cabins and wind-battered tents. There were two bathhouses, one per sex, although the men on the island probably outnumbered the women four to one. Lady Elliot was not for the casual tourist; the accommodations were spartan, the island utterly isolated, and if you didn't like diving, there was little else to do other than walk laps of the tiny island. Even walking slowly, he doubted that it would take Mandy more than an hour or two for a complete circuit. She was going to be one very bored tourist before the three weeks were up—maybe even bored enough that a boat or plane ride to the mainland would be welcome.

As Sutter approached the tent that had been hastily set up within a she-oak grove and at a distance from the other tents, his long stride slowed to a crawl. He wasn't looking forward to the next few minutes. Mandy had been as much a victim of Anthea's good intentions as he had. He owed Mandy an apology and he knew it. He just didn't know how to phrase it.

"Mandy?" Sutter said quietly, not wanting to startle her by walking in unannounced.

No answer came.

Concerned, Sutter pushed aside the ragged flap and looked in. Mandy lay on her side, deeply asleep, her hands tucked beneath her chin and her knees slightly bent. Her dark hair was fanned across the pillow like a silky forerunner of night. Her suit jacket had been discarded, her blouse was half-pulled out from her waistband, and her skirt had crept half-way up her wonderfully sleek thighs. One of her shoes was still on. The other teetered on the edge of slipping off her toes.

Silently Sutter knelt next to the mattress and eased off Mandy's shoes. Beneath the thin nylon her foot was warm. He held her instep in his palm for a moment longer than necessary before he gently released her. She didn't stir. He considered waking her for dinner, then discarded the idea. The darkness beneath her eyes told him that sleep was more necessary to her than food. But would she sleep, or would she be haunted by nightmares, residue of her earlier terror?

Sutter thought of lying down with Mandy and holding her against the nightmares he suspected would come. Maybe that would serve as an apology…his hard body pressed against her trembling one, his arms holding her, his mouth kissing away even the memory of her fear.

A hissed curse sizzled through the silence. Sutter came to his feet in a single motion and turned away from Mandy. Without looking back, he left the tent. As he strode down the path to get dinner, he cursed himself every step of the way. Miraculously he didn't get lost, but that owed more to the handful of people straggling toward the cafeteria than to any innate cleverness on his part.

The dining area was as spartan as the dive shop. There was a linoleum floor that was clean and old, perhaps twelve plastic-topped tables arranged at random, metal folding chairs, no curtains for the open windows. Dinner was served buffet-style and cooked by the college-age kids who vied for the privilege of spending time on Lady Elliot Island. Sutter lined up, accepted a lot of everything available and found an empty chair. It wasn't difficult. There looked to be no more than twenty guests camped at Lady Elliot's rustic resort.

The food itself was just what Sutter had expected—hearty, high calorie and plentiful. Perfect fare for divers who burned off thousands of calories every day simply keeping their bodies warm; for beneath the sun-heated surface of tropical waters lay the cool blue depths, where seventy degrees was considered quite warm, yet seventy was nearly thirty degrees below body temperature. Even in wet suits, diving used calories as fast as they could be replaced. As a group, scuba divers tended to be muscular and very hard, for all fat had long since been burned off.

By the time Sutter was halfway through dinner, Ray and two other divers had joined him. They told Sutter that beer and wine were available from the "bar," which boasted one of the two refrigerators on the island. Adding a can of Fosters beer to the menu perked it up considerably, Sutter discovered.

After dinner the men adjourned to the bar, which was about the size of a small bus. The decor consisted of six stools, a handful of tiny tables and the much-prized refrigerator, which cooled everything from beer to medicines to film. The spartan amenities were more than compensated for by the lively conversation and Australian beer, but an hour after the abrupt sunset, people began yawning and wandering off to their beds. Sunrise came early, and with it came the possibility of diving. That was what had lured everyone to the remote island—diving, not sleeping or fancy dining or hard drinking. On Lady Elliot Island the sea was the center of all conversations and actions; and as with all demanding mistresses, the sea required that the men who enjoyed her favors be strong, alert and skilled.

It was full dark with a lid of tropical clouds when Sutter walked back to the tent. Heat lightning danced on the western horizon, but Sutter knew there would be no rain. Not yet. There would be a period of buildup before the clouds were released from their turmoil, days of waiting and seething and growing toward the glorious storm.

Wind rushed through the she-oaks, stirring their long, soft, needlelike leaves. The sound of breakers was very distant, almost lost beneath the wind, telling Sutter that the tide was at full ebb.

There was no light shining inside the tent.

"Mandy?"

Sutter's low query brought no answer. He hadn't really expected it to. He ducked into the tent, moved very quietly to the empty mattress and began patting along the side closest to the tent, searching for the "electric torch" Ray had assured him was there. The other tents all included a post with electrical outlets, but not Sutter's tent; it had been hastily erected in answer to hard pressure from the folks who owned Lady Elliot Island—the Australian government.

Sutter put his hand over the flashlight lens and turned it on. Red-toned light bloomed in the tent. He opened his fingers just a crack, allowing enough light to escape so that he could see the details of the tent's interior. Mandy hadn't moved. Her face was flushed; her breathing was regular and deep.

Even though Sutter suspected that he could have banged scuba tanks next to Mandy's ear without getting a response, he was careful to make as little noise as possible. As he played the light around the tent, he saw that someone had set Mandy's glitzy pink backpack just inside the doorway, alongside his own battered khaki model.

Suddenly the thought of getting out of his clothes became incredibly appealing to Sutter. He kicked off his canvas jungle boots, unbuttoned his short-sleeved bush shirt and stuffed it into the backpack pocket he reserved for dirty clothes. The khaki shorts followed, leaving him wearing nothing more than the narrow cotton jockstrap that was all he tolerated in tropical climates. He started to pull out a pair of cotton briefs and fresh khaki shorts, then stopped himself. If he had been alone he would have slept bare. He would wear the jockstrap for the sake of civilized sensibilities, but he'd be damned if he would wear shorts over it. Even now, in darkness with the wind blowing, the temperature in the tent was too close to eighty to bother with modesty. Surely a woman of Mandy's age and looks wouldn't faint at the sight of a man wearing a jockstrap.

The thought of fainting and clothes made Sutter glance over at Mandy again. She was wearing full office regalia, including suffocating nylon panty hose. After a few moments of wrestling with his conscience—and even Sutter couldn't have said which side of the question his conscience advocated—he stuffed the flashlight into a pillowcase. A soft glow filled the tent as the cloth muted the light's white glare. He knelt next to Mandy's mattress and began undressing her.

The skirt's zipper sounded loud in the tent's breathless silence. Mandy didn't stir even when Sutter eased one strong hand beneath her hips and lifted her so that the skirt and half-slip could slide freely off her body. Forcing himself to look away from the allure of her long, nylon-clad legs, Sutter went to work on the stubborn buttons on her navy-pinstriped blouse. When he finally lifted her upper body to peel away the cloth, she murmured protestingly.

He barely heard. In the muted light her skin gleamed tantalizingly through the openings in the bra's dark lace. Tiny drops of sweat glowed in the shadowed valley between her breasts. Sutter wanted nothing more than to lower his head and lick up each mesmerizing bit of moisture. He wanted that so fiercely that his lips almost brushed her skin before he prevented himself.

A throttled groan escaped Sutter. Fists clenched on his thighs, he fought to control the wild desire that was stabbing through him like heat lightning, telling of turbulence and need...but no release, no healing storm filled with passionate rain. Mandy was a woman for marriage. He was a man who had no belief in that particular institution.

Damn Anthea!

Sutter stared down at the sleeping Mandy. He knew he should remove her panty hose. Wearing that kind of suffocating underwear in tropic heat and humidity was asking for the most uncomfortable kind of rash. Yet he was reluctant to remove any more of Mandy's clothing. It wasn't concern for her modesty that slowed him down, for she was wearing bikini briefs of the same dark lace as her bra; but Sutter wasn't sure he trusted himself to touch Mandy again, even for her own good.

The realization shocked him. He was known for his self-control, for the steel will that drove him past the point where other men gave up and gave in. Nor had his own sexuality ever held him hostage, not even when he was a teenager angry at the world for giving him a mother who was a coward and a father who cared only for hard liquor and fast cars.

Sutter closed his eyes. Surely he could remove a sleeping woman's nylons without falling on her like a starving dog on a bone. Couldn't he? With an impatient curse, he opened his eyes, hooked his long fingers over the waistband of Mandy's panty hose and peeled them from her in a single continuous motion. When he was finished, he threw the filmy nylon aside as though it had burned him.

Because it had. The heat of her body was held in each gossamer strand. Moving swiftly, jaw set in a rigid line, Sutter lifted Mandy enough to allow him to pull down the top sheet of the bed. He eased her into the covers, lifted the sheet up to her waist and yanked back his hands.

A veil of hair had fallen across Mandy's cheek. Without stopping to think, Sutter reached out and smoothed the hair back from her face. With a sigh, Mandy turned toward the caress, her hands reaching. Sutter froze, then let out a long breath when she tucked one hand beneath her chin and let the other open limply on the sheet. He saw that her fingernails were very short.

Bitten off to the quick, I suppose. Damned little rabbit.

The partially sympathetic, mostly exasperated thought made Sutter's mouth turn down. Then he realized that her nails were broken off, not chewed, and his mouth became a grim line. Gently he picked up the hand that lay motionless on the sheet. A dark line of blood on two of the fingernails gave silent testimony to the force with which she had clenched her hands on her purse during the flight to the island. She had bent and broken off her nails below the quick, making them bleed.

She had been terrified, but she hadn't been without courage. The realization shook him. After his mother, Sutter expected very little from women in the way of fortitude. Yet everything he had seen of Mandy hinted that she fought to master her fears rather than to have them master her. And she fought with an intensity that transcended pain.

"Golden eyes," Sutter whispered as he very gently kissed Mandy's fingertips one by one. "I'm so sorry. If I had only known...."

There was no answer. Sutter hadn't expected one. His fingers had a fine trembling as he gently replaced Mandy's hand on the cool sheet. The back of his hand accidentally brushed the resilience of her breasts as he withdrew. The feminine softness made his gut wrench with desire.

An instant later Sutter was across the tent and stretched out full-length on top of his own mattress, carefully thinking of nothing at all, most particularly not of the silken allure of Mandy's breasts. Normally he would have been asleep as soon as his head met the pillow, but not tonight. He lay awake, restless, but it wasn't merely hunger that kept sleep at bay. The disturbance Sutter felt went beyond simple desire. He had undressed women before, but never had one been so defenseless. He couldn't forget how he had ignored her protests and stuffed her into the little plane, and how she had sat in a state of sustained terror throughout the flight. Yet she hadn't given in to fear. That kind of self-control was totally unexpected, especially for a woman like Mandy, who seemed to see life as a series of one-line jokes delivered on any and every subject that occurred to her.

How could the same woman who crooked her finger at me with a saucy, sexy smile in front of hundreds of people be in a state of stark terror over a half-hour flight in a small plane?

Sutter rolled over and looked at Mandy sleeping within arm's reach on the other side of the tent. In the cloth-filtered illumination of the flashlight, her body was all golden curves and black velvet shadows. The sight was so disturbing that he reached to turn off the flashlight. Before he touched the pillowcase his fingers hesitated and finally withdrew. If a nightmare awakened Mandy, she would need the comfort of light to orient herself.

With strong, impatient hands Sutter pushed his pillow into a more comfortable shape. As he lifted his fingers from the cloth he realized that they retained the faintest scent of Mandy's perfume. He rolled over abruptly, turning his back on the golden woman who slept in velvet shadows. For a long time he lay without moving, listening to the silky rush of air through the she-oak needles. Finally he fell into a deep sleep permeated by scented, elusive dreams.

Wind gently rocked the tent, making the enclosure expand and shrink as though breathing. Sun poured in a thick triangle of brilliant yellow light through the half-open front flap. Mandy stirred, stretched and smiled before she was fully awake. The soft sounds of wind and sea were a lullaby she hadn't heard for two years, soothing and renewing at the same time. Her stomach growled, disturbing her contentment. An instant later memories came—a long flight in a big plane, a shorter flight in a smaller plane and a timeless period of hell trapped in a tiny plane suspended over an endless sea.

Mandy sat upright, her heart pounding. The prosaic canvas ceiling assured her that she was no longer flying. Floor, walls, sheets, mattress. A tent. But where? Vaguely she remembered the auctioneer saying something about Sutter's Australian vacation not being a tour of luxury resorts.

You will be sleeping in a tent.

Well, that explained it. She had finally arrived at her destination, whatever and wherever that might be. Now, was she supposed to cook and eat the tent as well as sleep in it? A single look at the faded canvas floor checked that particular flight of fancy. Perhaps the mattress....

As Mandy looked down to measure the mattress's potential edibility, she realized that she was wearing almost nothing. She couldn't remember undressing the previous night. In fact, now that she thought about it, she couldn't remember the previous night at all. Frowning, she tried to calculate how many hours she might have lost. The angle of the sunlight streaming into the tent suggested either midmorning or midafternoon. She looked at her wristwatch before she remembered it was set for California, not Australia. She had no idea how many time zones she had crossed. She did know that she had crossed the international date line, which meant she had flown into tomorrow. Or was it yesterday?

Sighing, Mandy decided that it didn't matter. She was on vacation, so she must be having a hell of a good time, if only she could remember it.

Think.

The last thing she remembered was gratefully getting off the plane at a place called Bundaberg, whose location in the greater Australian geographic scheme of things was still a mystery to her. She knew the town was close to the ocean, because the little plane had turned immediately on takeoff and had been out over the water very quickly.

Sudden sweat bathed Mandy's body as memories returned. A little white plane waiting. Sutter's eyes green and narrow and furious, totally indifferent to her terror. His shocking strength as he boosted her into the plane and strapped her down with the seat belt. A rush of ground, a sickening leap into air, pure cold terror exploding. Waiting to crash. Praying to die in the crash this time. Waiting. Praying. And then a low, comforting voice, an encouraging touch, Sutter's strong hands lifting her out of terror. Safe. Finally safe, gentle strength and blessed darkness descending.

Comforting voice? Encouraging touch? Gentle strength? Sutter? Lord, I must have been hallucinating!

And then the rest of the memories came. She had embarrassed herself in front of Sutter, revealing her weaknesses and carefully hidden fear of small planes, the sea, boats. Humiliation swept through Mandy in a red tide that went from her toenails to her scalp. Had she really told Sutter to go to hell? And had he really said that she was the one who would be comfortable there?

It's dry and there's not a pair of wings in sight.

Oh, yes. It definitely had happened.

Mandy put her flaming face in her hands. She wanted to crawl beneath the sheet and hide forever. It was bad enough to know that she was a coward; to have others know it was unbearable. And to have Sutter know it was unspeakable.

Her stomach growled again, insistently, informing her that embarrassment was no reason to starve to death. People never died of humiliation—they just wished they had. Lack of food, however, could definitely be lethal.

Too bad starving takes so long, Mandy thought wryly. *No matter how much my stomach growls, I'll still be alive and kicking wretchedly when Sutter comes back here to sleep.*

The thought of Sutter sleeping within reach of her mattress made Mandy's stomach do an odd little flip. How would she manage it in the small tent? How would she be able to fall asleep listening to him breathe? How would she undress without bumping into him?

As a matter of fact, how had she managed to undress last night?

No matter how hard Mandy tried, she couldn't remember anything after an angry, disgusted Sutter had left her and strode off to who knows where. She had fallen asleep within moments, and she had been fully clothed at the time. She was sure of it. She couldn't remember awakening to undress herself, either. No matter how hard she tried, she couldn't remember awakening at all except for this morning.

If it was morning.

Mandy went over every instant that she remembered since being manhandled into the tiny plane. Gradually she was forced to acknowledge that Sutter must have undressed her after she had fallen asleep. The evidence of it was everywhere. Skirt and blouse set aside haphazardly, panty hose in a tangle on the floor, shoes kicked down to the end of the mattress. She wasn't the most tidy creature on earth, but she wasn't in the habit of shedding clothes at random and leaving them where they dropped.

With a sinking feeling Mandy looked down at the two bands of blue lace that were all that stood between her and complete nakedness. Staunchly she told herself there was no reason to be embarrassed; women all over the world went swimming in public with suits that covered less flesh than her underwear. Besides, it wasn't as though Sutter would have taken any pleasure in undressing her. His contempt for her couldn't have been clearer.

Locked up in a tent for three weeks with an amateur comedian who's afraid of her own shadow. And then, even worse, *With luck, you'll be safe in your little burrow at home before the last of the pills wear off.*

Her mouth turned down in a wry curve as she acknowledged the aptness of Sutter's description; she was a silly little rabbit afraid of its own shadow. It had been two years since the accident, yet all she could do was take shallow baths and fly on 747s. Well, not quite all. The second plane she had flown on had been about a quarter the size of the big jumbo jets, and she hadn't disgraced herself on that one. She hadn't panicked or screamed or wept or thrown up, and she had been fully capable of walking off the plane under her own power at the end of the flight.

When you got right down to it, she hadn't disgraced herself on the little plane, either; at least, not right away. She

had shut down rather than come apart in hysterics, and if the
effort of keeping herself together had exhausted her so much
that she had fainted at Sutter's feet at the end of the flight,
well, that could be endured. The bottom line was that she
had flown in a small plane.

And she had survived it.

Mandy's breath came out in a long sigh. Despite all the
fears and humiliations she had endured since she had left
California on her totally unexpected vacation, she felt more
at peace with herself than she had since the instant she had
walked into a tent halfway around the world and had seen
her husband topping off a sand bunny.

Smiling wryly, Mandy reached for the garish backpack,
hoping Anthea had managed to pack some cool clothing for
her most recent project. The first handful Mandy pulled out
was promising—underwear of an extraordinary silky lace.
Black, deep rose, cream, the underwear was as thin as a
whisper and twice as soft. The second handful yielded two
pairs of khaki shorts and several pairs of thick cotton socks.
The third handful looked more like a pile of colored string
than anything to wear. After a few moments, Mandy sorted
everything into three bikini bottoms and six bikini tops. That
answered the question of what she was expected to wear with
the khaki shorts.

Further rummaging yielded several plain white blouses, a
slinky sarong skirt and wrap top that would serve for covering up at the beach or for dressing up anywhere else, a
pair of slip-on beach thongs and a pair of delicate leather
sandals. Then there were various cosmetics, a hairbrush,
toothbrush, comb, soap, heavy-duty sunscreen, feminine
items and a small box of...

"Ohmygod."

For a moment of stark disbelief, Mandy stared at the trade
name and happy couple that covered one side of the box.
She opened it quickly, still unable to believe that the contents
were as advertised. As small, neatly wrapped packets fell
into her palm, she laughed helplessly. Anthea hadn't been

joking when she had urged an affair with an Australian, and
she had included just the thing to make sure Mandy would
have an affair to remember rather than one to regret.

Almost afraid to continue, Mandy went back to emptying
out the backpack. Nothing else unexpected turned up until
the very bottom. There was an envelope with her name written across it in Anthea's clear, distinctive handwriting. Inside
was six hundred dollars Australian, plus a note.

Mandy,
I sent your scuba gear ahead so you wouldn't have to
worry about it. If something is missing or doesn't fit,
buy a replacement with the enclosed. Otherwise, spend
it all on something that makes you smile.

Diving gear?

For an instant Mandy was utterly motionless, torn in opposite directions, helpless. Part of her ached to know again
the beauty and freedom of diving in the blue infinity of the
sea. And part of her froze in terror at the thought. With hands
that weren't quite steady, she began repacking the backpack,
putting the damning little box in first. She could just imagine
what Sutter would think of her if he saw it.

Mandy dressed quickly, stuffed a few of the Australian
bills in the pocket of her khaki shorts, grabbed the backpack
and a frayed white towel that had been folded neatly at the
end of her mattress and headed out of the tent. No matter
how rudimentary the accommodations, she was certain they
included some kind of bathroom.

Fifty yards away there was a scattering of tents. A hundred
yards distant were several small cottages. Two larger buildings were somewhat closer. Mandy headed for them. A few
minutes later she was enjoying a freshwater shower, soaping
the residue of her trip from hair and skin, loving every instant of it. Feeling as though she had been reborn, she dried
off, combed her hair, stepped into her new clothes and set

off to find something that would end the rumbling complaints of her stomach.

Her luck held. The first building she tried contained the small bar. Ray was sitting there, flirting with the sunstreaked blonde who was handing him a beer.

"G'day, luv," Ray said, smiling when he saw Mandy. "Looks like a day's sleep was just the thing for you."

"A day?"

"Near as the same. The afternoon flight just left."

"Well, that explains my stomach. It's sure my throat has been cut."

Ray grinned. "We'll be serving in twenty minutes. I'll stand you a beer until then."

"Thanks, but I'd better not. I'm empty all the way to the soles of my feet."

Ray's blue glance moved from Mandy's sleek wet hair, past the well-filled black bikini top to the low-riding and very brief khaki shorts, down to the narrow feet clad in the plastic beach thongs that were practically part of the Australian national uniform.

"Empty? If all the Sheilas were empty like you, I'd die a young and very happy man."

Mandy smiled just enough to show Ray that she appreciated the compliment but not enough to encourage him to continue with more of the same. It was a smile she had honed to perfection on her way through school, when she had worked sixty hours a week to pay for her education. No time had been left for flirtations or socializing. That was why she had been so naive and so ripe for the attentions of one of the most famous men in her chosen field of oceanography.

Before Mandy could open her mouth to ask where the dining room was, the sound of a man's voice came clearly through the wall. It was Sutter's voice, deep and clipped and cold. He was talking about her, and he was mad as hell.

Chapter 6

"All in all, this is some vacation you planned for me," Sutter continued savagely, hoping that the radio phone was up to the task of carrying every nuance of his voice. He wanted Anthea to be in no doubt as to the extent of his anger at her manipulations. "I don't know about you, dearest aunt, but being stuck in a tent for three weeks with a basket case for a bunk mate isn't my idea of fun and relaxation!"

Angrily Mandy strode through the open door to the tiny combination office and gift shop. An instant later she was standing as though nailed to the floor, staring, unable to help herself. Sutter was wearing only a swimsuit, a black swath of cloth barely wider than her hand. The male strength that had startled her when she had been swept into the plane was very obvious now beneath the expanse of Sutter's smooth, tanned skin. Wide, well-muscled shoulders tapered to narrow, equally muscular hips. Long, powerful, covered with dark bronze hair, his legs were braced in a fighting stance, every muscle defined as he stood with one hand on his hip and listened impatiently to his aunt's explanations.

"You have no idea how reassured I am," Sutter said in a sarcastic tone. "If she's so bloody damned efficient around the office, why didn't you keep her there!"

There was another pause before Sutter burst once more into clipped, furious speech.

"Give it a rest, Anthea. I know precisely what you had in mind when you shanghaied Mandy for this trip. Just forget it. When I need your dubious expertise in finding a sex partner, you'll be the first to know. Until then, stay the hell out of my private life." Sutter's tone was icy, flat, utterly without softness. "As for Mandy, if she's so hard up for a man, find her a nice pencil pusher whose idea of a hot time is watching wallpaper fade."

That galvanized Mandy. Without stopping to think, she snatched the phone from Sutter's hand.

"Anthea?" Mandy asked, her voice tight.

"Oh, dear, I'm so sorry you had a rough flight. If I had known, I would never have—"

"I understand," Mandy said, talking right over Anthea's unwanted apologies. "Don't worry about a thing. I'm firmly on the ground without a plane in sight. Everything's just hunky-dory."

"Good. Er, I understand that you don't care for water sports, either?" Anthea asked delicately.

"I'll survive. I'm sure there are other things I can do here besides going diving," Mandy added, ignoring Sutter's sardonic smile.

"I hope you hadn't planned on Sutter helping you, er, amuse yourself," Anthea said hesitantly. "That is, I'm sure he would be glad to help you learn how to dive, but—"

"No problem," Mandy interrupted, not wanting to hear another word. "If I want to dive, I know just how to go about doing it."

Sutter's smile flattened angrily. "If you think I'm going to teach—"

"Just shut up," Mandy interrupted, her eyes blazing, her voice vibrating with anger. "You've had your turn. Now it's mine. No, not you, Anthea. Sutter is talking in my other ear.''

"Tell him to go away."

''Anthea says for you to go away,'' Mandy said, giving Sutter a killing look.

Sutter crossed his arms over his chest and stayed put. Mandy shrugged and went back to her conversation with Anthea.

''Don't worry, Anthea. I'm not counting on Sutter for one damn thing.''

There was a long pause at the other end of the line before Anthea plunged ahead.

''When I said you needed a lover, I hadn't really considered Sutter. He's rather...too...too...''

''Much?'' Mandy offered laconically.

''Well, not for the type of woman he's been with since his divorce. They must do fine with him, because they stand in line hoping for another chance. But you're a little too...too...''

''Ugly? Poor?''

''Heavens no! Sutter doesn't care about money and you're a striking woman, as every man who has ever been through the office has pointed out. It's just that Sutter doesn't really like women very well. His mother was a fragile little thing and his former wife was little better. You're too...well, inexperienced. You would walk starry-eyed into an affair with Sutter and walk out crying. You're much too nice, my dear. Sometimes my nephew can be very...er, that is...''

''Cold? Arrogant? Overbearing? Altogether insufferable?'' Mandy offered, looking Sutter right in the eye.

Anthea sighed. ''Oh dear, he *has* been difficult for you, hasn't he?''

''Yes,'' Mandy said, remembering how Sutter had casually forced her into the plane and strapped her in. Then she remembered how gentle he had been getting her off the plane. ''No.'' But had that really happened, or had she just dreamed it? ''Oh, hell, I don't know.'' Mandy sighed and shifted her weight. "Anthea, there's one thing I do know. If I ever decide to have an affair with a man, he'll have to feel something a lot warmer than contempt for me. My former husband gave me all of that any woman should have to take."

Sutter's eyes narrowed as he looked at the pale, determined set of Mandy's mouth. He wondered how her husband had burned her, and why, and how deeply, and if it had anything to do with her fear of water, of flying, of everything except staying locked within the safe walls of Anthea's office. Or perhaps it was those very same fears that had driven her husband away.

"Anthea," Mandy said soothingly, "everything is all right. Don't fret about a thing. I'm here, I've slept nearly a day and I'm so hungry I could eat a coral reef. In short, I'm fully recovered from my travels."

"But what about getting back home? Sutter said you were afraid of…er, that is, he mentioned that you didn't like boats, either."

"I'll charter a submarine," Mandy said wryly, forcing herself not to think about how in God's name she was going to get off the island. Three weeks was a long time. She'd spend every minute of her days and nights nerving herself up for the inevitable ride home. "Don't worry, Anthea. Really. It's my problem, not yours."

"Is there anything I can do to help?"

"No, but thanks for the thought."

"All right, dear. And do keep your eyes open for the right kind of man. Australia is reputed to be full of handsome knights in khaki armor. I want you to come back with a smile full of wonderful memories."

Mandy opened her mouth to say that she had no intention of cornering the first handsome Australian male she saw and asking him to try on the latest colors in American condoms. Then she remembered that sounds carried very clearly through the thin-walled building. She took a deep breath and controlled her too-agile tongue.

"Thank you, Anthea. Was there anything more that you wanted to say to Sutter?"

"Nothing he'll believe, I'm afraid. The poor boy is convinced that I'm meddling in his private affairs. But I ask you, is it my fault Sutter chose such a remote place to vacation that separate accommodations simply weren't to be had on such short notice? I couldn't very well demand that someone else's vacation be cut short or canceled just to accommodate Sutter, could I?"

The plaintive tone of Anthea's voice came through quite clearly. Mandy looked at the "poor boy" in question and decided that it was a clear case of mistaken identity. Sutter was neither poor nor a boy.

"No, you couldn't," Mandy sympathized. "I'm sure that point will occur to the 'poor boy' about the time hell freezes solid. He's nothing if not bullheaded."

Anthea laughed. "I can't argue with that. Say goodbye to my nephew for me. And don't worry. If you stay out of his way, I'm sure he'll take care of the rest. Good hunting, dear."

As Mandy replaced the receiver in its niche she turned to face Sutter. "Just in case you didn't catch the drift of what I told your aunt, I'll repeat it. I don't have designs on your vacation time, your masculine body or your vaunted expertise in the sack."

One of Sutter's bronze eyebrows climbed upward in arch query. "'Vaunted expertise'? Don't tell me my sainted aunt has descended to pandering."

"It wouldn't have done any good. I require more from a man than a fast wrestling match."

"How about a slow wrestling match?"

Sutter's knowing smile made Mandy wish she had kept her mouth shut on the subject of sex. "How about going to—"

"Dinner," Sutter interrupted smoothly. "If food doesn't take the edge off that sharp tongue of yours, you'll never find yourself an Australian lover. Honey catches more flies than vinegar.''

"Really? And what makes you think I'm after flies?"

For a moment Sutter looked startled, then he smiled unwillingly. "Feeling feisty, are we?"

"Feeling condescending, are we?" she retorted. "Look, Sutter—"

"Damon," he interrupted coolly. "Since we're sleeping together, I figure you should at least know my first name. Don't you agree?" He looked past her stunned expression toward Ray, who had just walked into the office. "Hello, Ray. Chow time already?"

When Mandy realized that Ray had heard Sutter's outrageous remark, she blushed furiously. Sutter had deliberately made it sound as though she were the type of woman whose thighs were so loose they rattled when she walked.

"Demon," she said. "I'll remember that."

"Don't push it, honey. Sleeping together doesn't mean a thing these days."

"It doesn't mean a thing these *nights*, either."

"Disappointed?" Sutter retorted.

Seething, Mandy turned toward Ray. "What's the failure rate of your dive equipment along the reef?"

"No worries, luv. We haven't had an accident in years."

"What a pity. I was so looking forward to Sutter's last dive."

Mandy brushed past a startled Ray and followed the food smells to the other side of the building. She was early, but one of the girls loaded up a plate and handed it through the serving window to her. Meat, bread, pasta, canned vegetables and fruits, coffee and canned milk. It all tasted heavenly. Mandy cleaned her plate within minutes, unable to remember when she had had such a vital appetite.

Before any of the other diners arrived, Mandy was gone. She hurried back to the office, pausing at the doorway long enough to listen for Sutter's voice. She heard only silence and decided that he must have gone somewhere with Ray.

The bar, probably. It was part of the same building, just a thin partition away, as were the cafeteria and kitchen.

"G'day," said the girl behind the small counter.

"Hi," Mandy said. "Is this the gift shop, too?"

"Gift shop, radiophone, clinic, office. Everything but eating and diving. Did you want something?"

What Mandy really wanted was to know precisely where she was on the globe, but she could hardly ask the girl. The sound and smell of the sea, plus the pure, crushed coral pathways had told Mandy that she was somewhere within the coral belt of the South Pacific. But where?

"Er, do you have any pamphlets that can tell me more about this place?" Mandy asked innocently.

"This is the lot," the girl said, pulling out a faded ditto sheet and giving it to Mandy. "The postcards will tell you a bit, but the best thing is one of those books."

Mandy looked up from the sheet, which was entitled "Lady Elliot Island, Paradise Preserved." Her glance fell on a short shelf full of books at eye level behind the counter. "Yes, please."

"Which one?"

"All of them."

"Right."

Three of the books were of the oversize, four-color, glossy variety. Two others were definitely scholarly. The books covered the Pacific Ocean in general and the Great Barrier Reef in particular. One of them dealt exclusively with Lady Elliot Island. Another had detailed photos and information about the myriad species of coral and varieties of reef ecology. A single quick perusal of the stack told Mandy that she wasn't going to lack for reading material.

"I'll take them all." She reached into her pocket and pulled out a handful of crumpled bills. "Blast. Not enough," Mandy muttered as she counted. "I'll have to go back to the tent."

"No worries," the girl said, writing out a receipt for the cash. "Bring the rest by anytime we're open."

Mandy looked startled. The girl laughed.

"It's not like you're going anywhere, right?"

"Er, right." Mandy hesitated. "You don't happen to have a lantern of some kind, do you?"

"Did your lamp go out?"

"There wasn't one in the tent. Just a flashlight."

"Oh, right. You must be the Yank that Ray was in such a stew about. Finally awake, are you?"

"So far so good."

The girl laughed. "Hang on, luv. I've got a battery lantern in the back I can lend you." She vanished out a side door and returned within a few minutes. "Just bring it in every morning to recharge."

Mandy gathered up her books and the lantern and headed back for the tent, intent upon finding out the dimensions of her self-imposed coral prison. She read as late as she dared that night, then casually draped one of the extra—and wholly unnecessary—blankets over the books, concealing them from Sutter. The thought of what he would say if he found her cowering in the tent and reading about the reef when she could be out diving on it was enough to make her flush with shame.

Hastily she pulled out the sheer, lacy black nightgown and matching bikini briefs that had been part of Anthea's generosity. The wind had dropped steadily since sunset. Now the air was almost completely still. Warm, humid, smelling of salt and sun-bleached coral, the night closed around her like another layer of black silk. She didn't need the sheet for warmth, but she didn't kick it aside. The thought of Sutter seeing her in the provocative, hip-length black nightgown made her stomach do another of those odd little flips that were so disconcerting to her when she was around Sutter.

Mandy yanked the sheet up to her chin, closed her eyes and forced herself to think about something other than the vision Sutter had made standing in the office wearing nothing but a diver's brief swimsuit. She had expected to have trouble sleeping, but she didn't. The distant sound of the surf breaking on the reef unraveled her.

By the time Sutter came to the tent Mandy was deeply asleep, the sheet had been kicked aside, and she was lying in a pose of graceful abandon that made Sutter's whole body clench around a fierce shaft of desire. A long time later he fell asleep cursing women in general and his meddling aunt in particular.

For the next three days Mandy and Sutter managed to avoid each other. They spoke not at all. If one of them was eating at the cafeteria, the other was not. If one was awake, the other was asleep. If one was diving, the other was reading...and growing ever more restless.

Reading about the miraculous, intricate reef complex that lay within her reach made Mandy yearn to dive once more. In graduate school she had specialized in the ecology of coral reefs, working long hours with laboratory and computer simulations of reef conditions. But before now she had never had the opportunity to dive along a coral reef, to physically experience the gemlike beauty that stared up at her from the pages of the glossy books.

And now she was too cowardly to take advantage of the opportunity that lay within her grasp.

If I don't get my tail out of this tent I'll never be able to look myself in the mirror again. It should be about low tide, so I won't drown walking along the beach or even wading a little bit in the lagoon.

The bracing self-lecture brought Mandy to her feet. It also helped her to know that anyone who was going to dive had already gone long before and was now drifting down the reef's outer wall. In short, Sutter wouldn't be able to witness her fear. She slathered herself with sunscreen, rolled the bottle into the all-purpose towel that had come with the tent and went outside, determination in every line of her body.

There was just enough breeze that morning to ruffle the she-oaks' intricate, fine-leaved foliage and to give texture to the surface of the sea. As she had every day, Mandy went to the beach edge of the small grove, dropped her towel in the shade and stood staring out over the water that both tantalized and frightened her.

As always, the lagoon was exquisite. In its most shallow parts there was no color to the water, simply a polished, transparent surface that transformed sunshine into shimmering ripples of silver light. Farther out in the lagoon the water took on an aquamarine glow while still retaining its utter transparency. Here and there tiny pockets of deeper water shaded into pale emerald. Beyond the boundary of the lagoon the reef complex fell away into sapphire depths so pure they had to be experienced to be believed.

As Mandy looked out to the unbridled sea beyond the reef, she realized that her heart was pounding as though she had been running. She dragged her glance away from the open ocean's dangerous beauty and concentrated on the small white beach in front of her. As always, the composition of the ground came as a surprise. Though she understood intellectually that coral islands were different from the normal variety, Lady Elliot's lack of dirt or ordinary rocks was still new, still arresting. It was the same for the sparse vegetation. The island had no languid palms dipping down to white sand lagoons, or glorious bursts of jungle flowers, or fern-covered canyons filled with mist and silence. There was a flat island surface made up of the sun-bleached remains of billions of tiny corals, a few salt-tolerant plants and the small, dark green casuarina trees, which the Australians called she-oaks. The beach was the same composition as the land. The coarse sand wasn't ground-up rock at all but the wave-pummeled remains of once-living corals, corals that had been torn by storm and tide from the Great Barrier Reef itself.

Concentrating only on what was directly beneath her feet, Mandy edged closer to the water. Because the camp was on the lagoon side of the island, there were no waves breaking along the shore to threaten her. The full force of the Pacific combers hit the outer wall of the reef at the far side of the lagoon, perhaps a quarter-mile distant from the beach. The

meeting of upthrust reef and sea was marked by a wide ribbon of flashing white water. The lagoon itself was serene,
its crystalline presence untroubled by anything but the random stirring of the breeze.

At low tide the entire lagoon was reassuringly shallow. In
fact, it was so shallow and so transparent that the water itself
was nearly invisible. All across the lagoon to the outer reef
beyond, blunt coral formations rose just above the surface
of the water. Because the coral organisms couldn't live in
air, the surface of the reef rose no more than a few inches
beyond the reach of the low tide. Varieties of coral grew in
profusion, looking like dark, many-hued shadows beneath
the sheen of pure water.

The corals' incredible variations in shape fascinated
Mandy. She edged closer, trying to get close enough to identify some of the many different species of coral. It was almost impossible to do from a distance; the corals often grew
together, branching and intertwining until the original, distinctive shape was lost. Those corals closest to the beach
were the most distorted, often dead, for constant exposure to
sun with each change of tide killed the delicate organisms
that built the reef.

Mandy shaded her eyes against the brilliant reflections and
watched wistfully while several people walked and waded
across the barely submerged inner reef toward the far boundary of the lagoon, where white water foamed and swirled
over the outer reef. The people wore brief swimsuits and
sneakers and carried stout reef sticks for testing the footing
before trusting their weight to the sometimes-deceptive coral
formations.

*I could do that. The water is ankle-deep in most places
and barely above the knees in the rest. I could go out there
and see at least a few of the extraordinary corals I've only
known from books. And it's day, not night; warm, not cold.
Surely I can do it.*

Can't I?

Taking a deep breath, Mandy edged closer to the water.

HOW TO GET YOUR
2 FREE BOOKS AND FREE GIFT!

1. Peel off the MIRA sticker on the front cover. Place it in the space provided at right. This automatically entitles you to receive two free books and an exciting surprise gift.

2. Send back this card and you'll get 2 "The Best of the Best™" novels. These books have a combined cover price of $11.98 or more in the U.S. and $13.98 or more in Canada, but they are yours to keep absolutely FREE!

3. There's <u>no</u> catch. You're under <u>no</u> obligation to buy anything. We charge nothing – ZERO – for your first shipment. And you don't have to make any minimum number of purchases – not even one!

4. We call this line "The Best of the Best" because each month you'll receive the best books by some of today's most popular authors. These authors show up time and time again on all the major bestseller lists and their books sell out as soon as they hit the stores. You'll like the convenience of getting them delivered to your home at our special discount prices . . . and you'll love your *Heart to Heart* subscriber newsletter featuring author news, horoscopes, recipes, book reviews and much more!

5. We hope that after receiving your free books you'll want to remain a subscriber. But the choice is yours – to continue or cancel, anytime at all! So why not take us up on our invitation, with no risk of any kind. You'll be glad you did!

6. And remember...we'll send you a surprise gift ABSOLUTELY FREE just for giving "The Best of the Best" a try.

SPECIAL FREE GIFT!

We'll send you a fabulous surprise gift, absolutely FREE, simply for accepting our no-risk offer!

Visit us online at
www.mirabooks.com

® and TM are trademarks of Harlequin Enterprises Limited.

The Best of the Best™ — Here's How it Works:

Accepting your 2 free books and gift places you under no obligation to buy anything. You may keep the books and gift and return the shipping statement marked "cancel." If you do not cancel, about a month later we will send you 4 additional novels and bill you just $4.49 each in the U.S., or $4.99 each in Canada, plus 25¢ shipping & handling per book and applicable taxes if any.* That's the complete price and — compared to cover prices of $5.99 or more each in the U.S. and $6.99 or more each in Canada — it's quite a bargain! You may cancel at any time, but if you choose to continue, every month we'll send you 4 more books, which you may either purchase at the discount price or return to us and cancel your subscription.

*Terms and prices subject to change without notice. Sales tax applicable in N.Y. Canadian residents will be charged applicable provincial taxes and GST.

If offer card is missing write to: The Best of the Best, 3010 Walden Ave., P.O. Box 1867, Buffalo, NY 14240-1867

BUSINESS REPLY MAIL
FIRST-CLASS MAIL   PERMIT NO. 717-003   BUFFALO, NY

POSTAGE WILL BE PAID BY ADDRESSEE

THE BEST OF THE BEST
3010 WALDEN AVE
PO BOX 1867
BUFFALO NY 14240-9952

NO POSTAGE
NECESSARY
IF MAILED
IN THE
UNITED STATES

There was no point at which she could say that land stopped and the coral formations began. The island was itself coral from top to bottom. The interior of all reefs plus the dry areas above the waves were all composed of dead coral. The rest, the exterior of the reef that was washed by the ocean, was alive, billions of tiny plants and animals growing and breathing, building and rebuilding, reproducing and dying, leaving their microscopic skeletons behind; and in the process, creating the most massive structure ever built on earth by any living creature. Man's biggest cities paled in comparison to the vast, interlocking complexity of the Great Barrier Reef.

And a small fragment of that wondrous creation lay right at Mandy's feet.

At first she wasn't able to force herself to surrender more than her toes to the lagoon. The water itself was so warm that it barely registered on her senses. The thongs she wore protected the soles of her feet but tended to come off at the least excuse. If she was really going reef walking, she should be wearing sturdy sneakers. As it was, if she went into water that was more than ankle-deep, she would quickly find herself barefoot. That would be foolish. For all its beauty, coral was hardly defenseless. A few varieties were poisonous. Most of them could cut or abrade unwary, unprotected feet.

Moving slowly, Mandy paralleled the narrow margin where lagoon met beach, never getting in over the top of her feet, ignoring the too-rapid beating of her heart. She looked only at the area just around her toes, where the water was more shallow than the baths she had forced herself to endure in the past months.

As she concentrated on identifying the larger bits and pieces of coral debris scattered about, her heartbeat settled into more normal rhythms. For minutes at a time she forgot she was within reach of the deadly sea, closer than she had been at any time since her husband had died and she had finally drowned, only to wake up in agony in the bottom of a small, wave-tossed boat that smelled of dead fish.

"G'day. Are you the Yank that slept longer than Rip van Winkle?"

Mandy's head snapped up. Standing in front of her was a boy of about eight and his younger sister, who looked perhaps five. Both of the children were wiry, fit, tanned all over. Their swimsuits were the barest concession to modesty.

"Er, yes, I guess I am. My name is Mandy."

"I'm Clint and this runty little Sheila is my sister Di. Mum's diving. Pop's over in the shade asleep."

Di stuck out her tongue and took a poke at her brother's ribs. He fended her off with the ease of long practice. Mandy looked beyond the children, toward the fragile shade of the she-oaks fringing the beach. She caught a glimpse of a scarlet towel and a muscular body wearing little more than a deep tan. Like the children, the man had a thick mop of sun-and-salt-cured chestnut hair. Unlike the children, he was content to laze away the hours until the divers returned.

Mandy looked from the sleeping man to the lagoon. Though shallow, it was still deep enough in places for small children to get into big trouble, especially as the tide had turned and was slowly reclaiming the beach.

"Do you swim?" she asked.

Clint looked at Mandy as though she had just climbed out of a flying saucer.

"Too right we do! What do you think we are, Dubbos?"

Mandy suppressed a smile and decided that, for now, discretion would be the superior part of her valor; she wouldn't ask what a Dubbo was.

"Right," she said in her best Australian accent, making it sound like "roight." She smiled at Clint. "That was my silly question for the day. Your turn."

Long, flaxen eyelashes descended in a blink. Suddenly Clint smiled in comprehension. "Fair dinkum! You're not a blind Freddy after all. Want to feed the fish?"

"I don't know. Do I?"

Clint blinked again, then shook his head and smiled widely at the same time. "Let's get the bread."

Wondering what she had gotten herself into, Mandy followed Clint and the silent Di to the dining room. The door was closed, but the crusts and heels of bread leftover from breakfast had been put in a bowl outside the door. Clint grabbed the lot and distributed it almost evenly among the three of them. As soon as he turned his back to lead the way to the Fish Pond, Mandy slipped Di a few extra crusts and was rewarded with a shy, thousand-watt smile.

Despite its name, the Fish Pond wasn't a pond. It was simply a thirty-by-twenty-foot gap in the coral formations that otherwise carpeted the lagoon. At low tide the pool was only a few feet deep, which meant that the coral formations around the edge acted as a natural cage, confining whatever fish hadn't escaped before the tide fell. Visitors to Lady Elliot Island had gradually tamed the resident fish, feeding them crumbs, teaching the quick, wary little beggars to eat from a person's outstretched fingers.

Clint and Di waded out until they were waist-deep. Holding the bread aloft in one hand, feeding crumbs with the other, the children were soon the focus of a rippling, twisting blur of small fish. Mandy inched forward until the water came to midcalf. As she came down on a hidden bulb of coral, she lost one sandal and her balance at the same time. She nearly panicked. Pieces of bread went flying in all directions as her arms windmilled. Only the delighted laughter of the children as they fed fish kept Mandy from screaming her fear of falling in the water. Trembling, she backed up a few steps, leaving her rainbow-hued sandal behind.

Don't be ridiculous! she raged at herself as she stood on dry ground once more. *Even if you had fallen facedown you couldn't have drowned unless you were too stupid to brace your arms and keep your head above water. For God's sake, it wasn't even up to your knees! Now get back down there and pick up your sandal before you cut your foot.*

Mandy looked at the cheerful sandal lying in ten inches of water. She thought of bending down, putting her hand into the water, picking up the sandal and returning triumphantly to dry land.

Breath locked in her throat as her heart tried to hammer free of her body.

I can't.

Coward!

All right! I'm a coward! So what else is new?

Clenching her hands together, Mandy watched the tanned, laughing children stand waist-deep in the transparent lagoon while fish swirled around them like wind-driven silver leaves. Her dropped, forgotten crusts of bread absorbed water and then settled soddenly to the bottom of the lagoon only a few inches from the beach. Her body motionless, her fingers interlocked to keep them from trembling, Mandy stood, seeing nothing but the dark sea of her nightmares, hearing nothing but her own silent screams of terror.

Behind Mandy voices called back and forth from the direction of the dive shed. Carrying air tanks and wet suits, divers strode toward their tents, laughing and describing the wonders of the reef beyond as they walked. Mandy didn't hear. She was wrapped too tightly within her waking nightmare.

Sutter saw Mandy from a distance as he carried his equipment to the tent. He stopped suddenly, caught by something in her stance. As he watched, he realized that she was unnaturally still, the way she had been on the flight to the island, too terrified to move. No matter how carefully he looked, he could see no reason for her fear, yet there could be no doubt that she was afraid.

With a muttered curse Sutter turned off the path and headed toward the lagoon, which was only a few yards away. When he was within reach of Mandy he stopped. A single look at her deathly pallor and her white-knuckled grip on herself told him that she was once again in the grip of intense fear. But of what? There wasn't a plane in sight. All he could see was the Townehome kids feeding the lagoon fish.

Sutter spotted the bright colors of what looked like a rainbow beach thong dropped in the shallow water. He looked at Mandy's feet and realized that she was missing one sandal. Just when he was about to chew her out for risking an infection from a coral cut, Clint turned around and spotted Mandy.

"Don't you Yanks know anything?" Clint asked in a disgusted tone of voice. "You wasted your bread. You have to come out where the fish can swim up to you."

Dimly Mandy heard Clint's words and knew she must respond, must somehow shake off the paralyzing grip of her fear if only for a few moments.

"My mistake," she said in a strained voice.

Di turned and held out a crust of bread. "Here you go," she said softly. "I'll share."

Mandy suppressed a shudder at the thought of wading out into that clean, treacherous water once more. "That's okay, sugar. You go ahead and feed the fish. I'll watch and see how it's done."

"Nothing to it," Clint said, grabbing his sister's crust. "You rip off a piece, hold it underwater and the fish come swarming. Even a sleepy Yank like you can do it."

A little desperately, Mandy smiled. "I'll take your word for it."

From up the beach and behind Mandy, a woman's voice called out to the children.

"Now hear this! Now hear this! All 'roos fall in for tucker!"

Instantly Clint and Di splashed to shore, leaving a turmoil of disappointed fish behind. As Clint passed Mandy, he spotted her bare foot.

"Better get shod," he called over his shoulder. "Some of this coral is wicked."

"Took the words right out of my mouth," Sutter said.

Mandy flinched when she heard Sutter's voice behind her. Rather bitterly she wondered what else could go wrong that morning. Perhaps if she ignored Sutter he would go away.

"Mandy?"

And then again, maybe he wouldn't.

"Mandy," Sutter asked calmly, "what's your thong doing in the water instead of on your foot?"

"I—I was playing a silly game." She turned away from him and headed up the beach. "But I'm tired of playing it now."

"Mandy."

She froze.

"Don't you know better than to walk barefoot around here?"

"Yes!" she said savagely. "I know better!"

Before Sutter could say anything more, Mandy spun around and glared at the missing thong. It was less than five feet from shore, under no more than ten inches of water. She could either go and get the damn thing or she could spend the rest of her life hating herself for revealing to Sutter just what a blazing coward she really was—Sutter, a man who had been beaten, shot, stabbed, jailed and yet had never once flinched from doing what he believed had to be done.

In a rush Mandy took four steps into the lagoon, grabbed blindly and connected with the thong. She ripped it from the lagoon and raced back to the beach, where she stared at the dripping thong in delighted disbelief.

"I did it! Did you see that, Sutter? I waded out and picked up my sandal!"

Triumph radiated from Mandy, putting color back into her cheeks, taking fear away.

"Yes, I saw," he said softly.

Belatedly Mandy realized how she must have sounded to a man who had just returned from diving in the open sea. She bit her lip as she shoved her foot into the thong.

"It was just—just a silly game," she said.

Silently Sutter watched as Mandy ran up the beach and disappeared into the she-oaks. He didn't know what had been going on a moment before, but he was certain of one thing.

To Mandy, it hadn't been a silly game.

Chapter 7

"Is that the lot?"

Mandy smiled as she glanced from Clint's wide grin to shy little Di's hand held out trustingly to her.

"That's the lot," Mandy said, taking Di's hand and surrendering the bread crusts to Clint's eager grasp.

"You're sure you don't mind?" Ted asked.

"Not at all. After we feed the fish, we're going to walk around to the south end of the island and see if any turtles have come in to lay eggs."

"And then we're going to finish our coral castle," Clint added. "It's going to be bigger than you, Pop."

"Fair dinkum?" Ted said, ruffling his son's hair with a broad, blunt hand.

"Then it will be low tide and Mandy will show us how the starfish eat and what the sea squirts do and if there are any eggs floating around and…" Di's voice dwindled as she ran out of breath.

"Sounds like you have an exciting day planned," Ted said absently as he looked over his shoulder. "Gotta fly. The other blokes are waiting for me. Clint, you remember what I said about those fancy cone shells?"

"No worries. Mandy knows all about the ones that sting and the ones that don't."

Ted gave Mandy a quick, concerned look. "A lot of blokes are fooled or get careless. It doesn't matter so much for an adult, but for a joey…"

"I understand," Mandy said. "I've told the children not to touch any of the textile cone shells that have washed up until I've handled them first. If we go reef walking out far enough that there's a chance of seeing a live one, I know the difference between the siphon and the proboscis, and I'm well aware of the dangers of that particular mollusk's paralytic poison."

There was still a certain hesitation on Ted's part. Mandy knew why; she had told the Townehome parents she would be glad to watch the children as long as it was clearly understood that she was a nonswimmer. It was difficult for Ted to understand how someone who didn't swim at all could comprehend the ocean's many dangers.

"I spent years in school studying the ecology of coral reefs," Mandy said crisply, answering the unasked question. "If you have an hour to spare, I'll give you a list of every reef predator and whether that predator represents a danger to man, and if so, how the danger can be avoided or countered medically."

Ted couldn't conceal his surprise. "Coral reef ecology, eh? Then why don't you swim?"

"I choose not to," Mandy said in an even voice. "If that worries you, then perhaps you would feel better sleeping beneath the she-oaks while Clint and Di build their coral castle."

The father's grin told Mandy where Clint had gotten his casual masculine charm.

"Told me what's what, didn't she?" Ted said to his son.

"She's a mean 'un," Clint agreed, grinning.

When Ted turned back to Mandy, he was still smiling.

"I'm not worried. A Sheila who can keep this lot under control can take care of the odd stonefish or poisonous snail."

Ted trotted off toward the other divers. Even from the corner of her eye, Mandy could see that Sutter had joined the adults—six days on the island had given his hair a pale, metallic sheen that was unmistakable, as was his rangy, well-muscled body. To her surprise, she had managed an unbroken exchange of civilities with him since she had made a fool of herself crowing over her sandal. She had expected Sutter to be caustic on the subject, but he had said nothing to her about it, then or later. He had simply appeared at dinner with a full plate in his hand and had sat down beside her.

Once Mandy had gotten accustomed to the frissons that chased through her every time Sutter was close, the two of them had passed an amicable half hour topping each other's Anthea stories. Sutter had offered to buy Mandy a beer after dinner. She had started to say how much she hated beer but hadn't wanted to end the unexpected truce. She had been shocked and delighted to discover that Australian beer was far superior to its American counterpart. In fact, she had a hard time believing that the two liquids shared anything in common but alcohol and a generic name.

"Your bloke's waving at you," Clint said.

Mandy didn't bother telling Clint again that Sutter wasn't her bloke and she wasn't his Sheila. She simply waved back at Sutter, then watched with unexpected yearning as the divers turned away and vanished into the she-oaks. The group was going to the opposite side of the tiny island, where the dive boat awaited them. It was a superb day for diving. The sea was calm, the air hot, the sun a burning brilliance overhead; and beneath the surface of the water it would be cool, silky, swirling with graceful fish and living corals sweeping up from the floor of the sea.

Suddenly Mandy wished she could see it all for herself, could feel the sea surrounding her, caressing her, freeing her from gravity until she came as close to unfettered flight as a human being could.

I can do it. I know I can. All I have to do is want it more than I fear it.

There was no answer for that bittersweet truth, not even in the deepest reaches of Mandy's silence. Quietly she followed the children to the Fish Pond, wading in as they did, feeling triumph as the water climbed above her ankles, her calves, her knees, partway up her thighs, then a few more inches, just a few more. She stopped when the water lapped at midthigh and forced herself to stand and endure the knowledge that she was partially within the sea's grasp once more.

The lagoon was warm, transparent and tasted far more salty on her fingertips than the Pacific Ocean off the coast of California. The air and water were so warm, so motionless, that when she closed her eyes, it was difficult to believe she was in the sea at all.

Fish swarmed just beneath the surface of the lagoon, bumping against Mandy's legs in their rush to get close to the crumbs, tasting her skin with tiny tickling touches. She broke off bits of bread crust, gingerly immersed her hand in the water and watched as the racing, flashing scraps of life vacuumed up every offering. Firmly she ignored her accelerated heartbeat and breathing, hoping that fear would pass as soon as her mind accepted that her body wasn't in danger. Finally, common sense won out over brutal memories. Her heartbeat slowly returned to normal and her hands became steady once more. Only then did she allow herself to retreat just a bit closer to shore, and then only for a few moments.

Meanwhile, Clint, who had wheedled a mask and snorkel from Ray, was lying facedown in the water with his feet pointing toward the outer reef. Sculling idly with his hands, he watched the fish dart about. He became so absorbed in watching that he drifted farther and farther out into the lagoon. Because the tide was partially up, the Fish Pond wasn't completely bounded by coral formations. He could float right out over the wall of coral and into the rest of the shallow lagoon, where coral formations grew in an uninterrupted carpet and the water at that moment was very shallow.

Mandy glanced up from the greedy fish nibbling on her fingers and realized that Clint had drifted too far away. He was already out of the pond, floating in water that was barely eighteen inches deep. If he tried to kick his legs to propel himself back into deeper water, he would flail against coral rather than water.

"Stay here, Di," Mandy said.

Gingerly, ignoring the sudden race of her heart, Mandy waded deeper into the Fish Pond. From experience gained in the past few days, she knew where the most shallow parts were and where the bottom dipped down without warning. She made use of every high spot and skirted the low ones. It was barely twenty feet to the other side of the pond, but she felt as though it were miles. When she looked up she saw that Clint had discovered his difficulty. He was trying to scull forward with his hands but was succeeding only in pushing himself farther out over the corals lining the shallow lagoon.

"Just float," Mandy called. "I'll pull you in."

Clint's hands stopped churning. Mandy looked at the six feet of water separating her from the coral wall that marked the outer limit of the Fish Pond. She feared the water was at least waist-deep, perhaps more. On the other hand, Clint wasn't really in danger of more than a skinned knee if he kept his head and didn't thrash around too much.

I'm a great one to talk about someone keeping his head. I expect a child to do something I can't do myself!

Mandy bit her lip. Hard. Then she waded forward, welcoming the pain in her lip because it distracted her from the fear racing through her body, shortening her breath, making her body feel too brittle to move.

The warm water slid higher up Mandy's legs and then higher still, despite the fact that she had resorted to balancing precariously on knobs of coral thrusting up from the bottom of the pond. Midthigh, then an inch more, then another inch. If she lost her balance and fell now, there would be no way to prevent her face from going under the surface, and she was trembling so much that a fall seemed inevitable.

Finally Mandy was able to reach out and grasp one of Clint's hands. Slowly, carefully, she towed him beyond the shallow area and into the deeper pool. With a cheerful wave of thanks he jackknifed his body and dove to the bottom for a closer inspection of the resident wildlife. Mandy just barely managed to stifle a scream as warm, very salty water splashed over her, compliments of Clint's windmilling feet. After that, it was several minutes before she could control her trembling enough so that she was able to retreat to the beach end of the pond.

It was with a great sense of relief that Mandy watched the final bread crusts shredded by busy little fingers and fed to even busier little fish. For her, the ordeal of the Fish Pond was over until lunch, after which more bread crusts would appear in the bowl outside the cafeteria. For now, however, Mandy was free to lure the Townehome kids up onto dry land.

"Candy bar for whoever spots the first turtle," Mandy called.

Instantly Clint's head popped out of the water. He and Di hit the beach running.

"Well, come on, don't be such a slow lot," Mandy teased as the children stormed past her.

Shouting and laughing, the Townehomes raced along the beach until they were even with the office. Then they slowed to a walk and lowered their voices to a whisper. Ever since Mandy had explained to them how important it was not to disturb the nesting terns, the children had all but tiptoed past the segment of beach that touched the birds' breeding colonies. Even so, sooty terns screamed and wheeled overhead constantly, not so much disturbed as simply being their normal, noisy, agitated selves. A few huge black frigate birds took flight, looking like shadows from a prehistoric time when birds were reptiles wearing more scales than feathers.

Farther up the beach, small gulls unique to the Great Barrier Reef perched in gray-and-white profusion on the wreckage of a ship whose captain had misjudged the depth of water over Lady Elliot's barrier reef. The shipwreck had occurred many years before. Now little more than the hull remained—curving timbers bleached by salt and sun and washed clean by sheets of tropical rain. Beyond the wreckage the lagoon ended. No coral formations rose to the surface of the sea, which meant that the island itself took the brunt of the ocean's ceaseless, sweeping waves. The beach became more narrow, steeper and of a white so pure it was almost blinding.

Clint and Di zigzagged through the coarse sand, picking up chunks of coral that had been ripped free by storm and wave and finally washed onto shore. A few of the pieces retained their original colors, rich scarlet or deep chestnut or, rarely, jet black. With time they faded to pale pink or antique gold or slate gray. In the end, all debris would be bleached to a dazzling absence of color, ground smaller by the waves and finally reduced to shimmering white sand.

Mandy walked slowly behind the children, forcing herself to look out over the restless, gleaming surface of the sea. The water looked less intensely blue than it had earlier and there were many subtle variations on the color gray. The change in color reflected the change in the sky itself. A sheer veil of clouds had covered the sun. The humidity, always high, had soared. If a wind didn't come up, the atmosphere would become oppressive. Clouds were piling up over the mainland in immense billows that even now were reaching toward the island. Tonight, chain lightning would coruscate through the vast, creamy towers in dazzling display.

A disappointed call from Di returned Mandy's attention to the beach. There were no odd, broad marks in the sand, as though a single caterpillar tread had gone from the sea to the warm sand above high tide line. The track of a green turtle was unmistakable—and unmistakably absent. None of the ancient reptiles had appeared mysteriously from the vast sea in order to haul themselves up the beach and lay their eggs in the warm sand. Nor could Clint or Di spot one of the big animals swimming through the sparkling clarity of the water. No dark bodies appeared against the flashing white of breaking waves. In the end even Clint gave up and joined Mandy and Di in building the coral castle to new heights.

As they worked, Mandy answered the children's endless questions about the creatures that had once inhabited the intricate coral skeletons and about the creatures that had no true skeleton at all. She described the difference between sponges and sea hares, snails and corals, fish and man, and she explained how the reef had been built of the same kinds of coral that they were using to build their own castle. With time, the reef corals became compressed by the weight of all the coral that had been built on above. As the reef bottom was slowly squeezed, it reacted with dissolved chemicals in the sea, transforming the millions upon millions of skeletons into a rock known as limestone. It was that fossilized reef structure that made up Lady Elliot Island.

"You mean like that shelf of rock on the other end of the island?" Clint asked.

"That's right. Limestone is all around us. If you dig down in the sand here you'll hit limestone very quickly."

"You mean that rock was once like this?" he persisted, holding up a handful of staghorn coral. "With patterns where the animals once were and tiny little holes and pretty branches and everything?"

Mandy nodded.

"Fair dinkum!" the boy said in astonishment.

Clint spent the time until lunch enthusiastically comparing every variety of coral he found with a slab of limestone that had been battered free from its island mooring during a storm and left high along the margin of the beach. No matter how carefully he looked, he found few traces of the limestone's previous life as a portion of the living reef.

"How did you learn all that?" he finally demanded of Mandy.

"School."

Clint muttered something Mandy wisely chose not to hear. Then he sighed.

"School, eh?"

"That's right," she said cheerfully.

"I want to go to a Yank school. All they teach in mine is the alphabet and little words and one plus one and smearing nasty colors on butcher paper."

Mandy hid her smile by turning toward the castle, which had grown until it was nearly as high as the Fish Pond was deep at low tide. The castle resembled an explosion in a pasta factory more than a stately building, but the children insisted that all things built upon a beach were castles, and this mess was no exception.

"I had to go through the gloppy painting," Mandy said. "Once you learn how to read—"

"I know how," Clint interrupted impatiently. "I've known since kindergarten."

"Then all you have to do is get your parents to take you to a library. You'll find books there about anything you can think of, and books are very good teachers, because they're so patient. Anytime you want to learn, there they are, waiting, just stuffed full of things to share with you."

Frowning, Clint looked from the coral in his hand to the limestone slab. "Wish there was a library here."

Mandy smiled. "Tell you what. After lunch, I'll bring some of my books down to the beach and we can look at them together."

Mollified, the young boy went to scavenging hunks of coral for the growing, teetering castle. After lunch Mandy surprised the kids with two brightly wrapped candy bars. As delighted as they were with the candy, they were even more fascinated by the glossy, full-color pictures in the books Mandy brought from her tent. To Mandy's surprise, Di was able to read almost as many of the words as her brother could. Mandy was kept very busy trying to translate Latin taxonomy into plain English—and repeating explanations as to why the names hadn't been in English in the first place.

For once neither child looked longingly toward the tents each time a scattering of adult voices indicated that the dive boat had shuttled in one group of tired divers and had taken off with a fresh batch. Even Clint, who was normally in a fever to go snorkeling with one of his parents, ignored everything but the books and the various chunks of coral he kept retrieving in the hope he would be able to stump Mandy.

Sutter, who had been standing motionless in the shade of the she-oaks since he had come in on an early dive boat, was watching with growing amazement as Mandy identified variety after variety of coral or shell from a piece of bleached remains.

"Bet you can't guess this 'un!" Clint said triumphantly, waving a broken hunk of something beneath Mandy's nose.

She took the object from Clint and looked at it critically. "Mollusk, not coral," she muttered.

"I know that," Di said instantly. "There's no place for the little animals to poke out and feed."

"What else do you see?" Mandy asked.

"One side is real smooth."

Mandy made an encouraging noise.

"And the lines here bend off in a…a…spiral? Is that the word?"

"That's exactly right, Di. Good for you."

"You mean good *on* you," Clint said.

"I do?"

"You want to learn to talk like a 'Straiyan, right?"

"Roight," Mandy said carefully.

"Good on you!" Clint and Di said together, laughing.

Smiling, motionless, Sutter enjoyed the easy give-and-take between Mandy and the kids as she taught them Latin taxonomy and they taught her Australian pronunciation, idioms and slang. The more he listened, the more he realized how little he knew about Mandy beyond the fact that she was intelligent, had an irrational fear of small planes and water, a quick tongue, surprising self-discipline for someone who was so timid...and a body that brought every masculine nerve in him sizzling to life.

It had also become obvious to Sutter that Mandy had a knowledge of coral that went beyond that of the books she had open around her on the overlapping beach towels. She didn't have to look up the corals and shells that were brought to her; she identified them on sight, talked about their place within the larger reef community, and only then did she turn to the index of one of the books to find on which page the creatures were pictured in their living state.

The chunk of shell Clint had just brought proved to be difficult. Di protested that there wasn't enough of the shell for Mandy to identify.

"It's bigger than some of the pieces of coral she named," Clint retorted.

"That's because coral animals are smaller than whatever made that silly bit of junk," Di said indignantly, standing up for her new friend. "An ant's an ant but you can't tell 'roo from goanna if the piece is only ant-sized!"

"Your sister has a point," Sutter said before Clint could argue.

Mandy's head snapped around. "What are you doing here? Is everything all right?" she demanded.

"Yes. Why?"

"You're back early," she said simply.

"I told the Townehomes I'd take Clint snorkeling so they could spend more time diving together. It's their last day here." Sutter paused, then looked into Mandy's golden-brown eyes. "Want to come snorkeling with us?"

"She doesn't swim," Clint said in disgust.

"Really? Then maybe I should stay here and make sure she doesn't get too close to the water," Sutter said calmly. "She could get hurt."

"She *can* swim," Di said in an earnest voice, defending Mandy once again. "She just *doesn't*."

One of Sutter's sun-bleached eyebrows climbed upward in silent query, but all he said was "I see." He stepped forward and sat cross-legged next to Mandy. "Since you won't go to the reef, I brought a bit of it to you."

Mandy looked down at Sutter's long-fingered, tanned hand. In the center of his palm was a perfectly formed, milk-white shell. It gleamed like the finest bone china against his skin. She made a sound of surprise and pleasure as she picked up the shell.

"A Malward's cowrie! Do you have any idea how rare they are?" she asked. "Did you find it while you were diving out on the reef?"

"Yes and yes," Sutter said, smiling at Mandy's pleasure and the reverent way she was handling the shell.

For an electric instant he wondered what it would be like to feel her slender fingers touching his body with half that much pleasure and sensitivity. Ruthlessly he shunted the sensual thought aside. Sitting as he was, wearing only a brief swimsuit, he had no choice but to keep his mind on shells rather than sex. He had no business wanting Mandy. She wasn't the kind of cool, free-living sex partner he preferred. He couldn't even honestly say that he liked her; he had spent a lifetime *dis*liking the kind of woman who couldn't cope with even the luxurious reality of life in one of the most stable, wealthy countries on earth. His mother had been a prime example of a woman too weak to survive without constant pampering. His former wife had been another. It appeared that Mandy, with her host of irrational fears, was yet another.

Now all he had to do was convince his body of what his mind knew to be the truth: Mandy was not for D. M. Sutter.

"Is the shell worth pots of money?" Clint asked eagerly.

With an effort, Sutter gathered his restless thoughts and focused on Clint.

"Maybe one pot, to a collector," Sutter said. "But this

shell isn't going to be sold. I'm not even going to keep it for myself or give it to Mandy, much as I'd like to. Lady Elliot Island is a preserve, which means that all land and sea life is protected.''

"But the shell isn't alive," Clint objected.

"It once was part of a living animal. Have you ever been to a curio shop or any place that sold shells?" Sutter continued quickly, seeing Clint's bottled objections in the boy's frowning expression.

Both children nodded.

"Did you ever think how those shells came to be in the shop?" Sutter asked.

"Someone picked them up on the beach," Di said immediately.

"How many perfect shells do you find on the beach?" Sutter asked. "And I mean perfect. No chips, no cracks, no faded colors, no missing chunks."

"Oh," the little girl said, understanding. "They only sell perfect shells, right? So where do they come from?"

"Divers find the living animal. The snail is killed and the perfect shell remains. Those are the shells you find in stores and collections."

Clint frowned. "But your shell was empty when you found it, right?"

"Yes."

"Then what's hurt if you keep it?"

"What's to keep someone from catching live cowries, killing them and then saying they found the shells on the beach?" Sutter countered. "That's why no one is allowed to take anything from Lady Elliot Island except pictures. We aren't even allowed to catch fish for dinner out on the reef."

Clint sighed and looked regretfully at the glistening cowrie shell. "Still, it seems a blood—er," he corrected hastily, "a terrible shame to throw such a pretty shell away."

Sutter smiled. "We'll keep it in the tent for two more weeks, then we'll give it back to the sea."

"Two weeks? You'll be here that long?" Di asked, turning to Mandy.

"Yes."

"We go home tomorrow," the girl said glumly. Then she sighed. "But at least I get the window seat this time, so I'll be able to see the island and the reefs and the cane fields and all."

"How nice," **Mandy** said in a faint voice, barely repressing a shudder. She had managed to keep the plane out of her mind very well so far, probably because she was much closer to another fearful object—the sea. Blankly she handed the cowrie back to Sutter and stared at the broken piece of shell Clint had brought to her. "Triton," she said.

"What?" Di asked.

"This is probably part of a triton shell. Like this one," Mandy said, picking up a shell that had been brought to her earlier.

The shell was long, fluted, wider than her hand. The shell's graceful lines were still intact, though the delicate interior colors had long since faded. There was a definite resemblance between both the vague pattern on Clint's piece of shell and the intact shell held by Mandy. Clint and Di promptly jumped to their feet and went off in search of another bit of debris for Mandy to identify.

"May I?" Sutter asked, reaching for the big shell balanced on Mandy's palm. He held the opening to his ear and murmured, "Still there."

"What is? The sea?"

He gave a rumble of agreement that was as low pitched as the voice of the distant breakers.

"You know it's just the sound of your own blood moving," Mandy said.

Smiling slightly, Sutter shook his head. "It's the sea. Listen."

With one hand he held the triton's flared opening against Mandy's ear. With the other he held her cheek, gently pinioning her between the shell and his own palm. Her eyes widened as she felt his fingers easing into her hair, seeking and finding the living warmth of her scalp. The sudden race of her heart was magnified by the shell held so gently, so immovably against her ear. Like distant storm surf, the sound beat rhythmically through her.

"Hear it?" Sutter murmured, watching the acceleration of Mandy's heart in the pulse beating beneath her neck.

"Yes," she said, her voice strained. She gasped when his thumb lightly caressed her lower lip.

"You cut yourself. How?" he asked.

"I—I bit it. In the Fish Pond."

"Does being in the water frighten you that badly?"

"Yes," Mandy said, closing her eyes, not wanting to see the contempt she was certain would be in Sutter's eyes when he heard her admission.

"Are you afraid of all water or just the sea?"

"All of it," she said harshly. "Even my damned bath!"

"Then why did you go into the pond?"

Sutter's voice was puzzled rather than rough or condemning, and his touch was reassuring, subtly caressing. Mandy opened her eyes. There was no contempt in his expression, simply an intense concentration that was almost tangible.

"I'm trying to get over it," Mandy said, her voice low. "I had worked up to my knees and even a few inches beyond, then Clint drifted out of the pond and over the coral knobs and I had to go get him or really hate myself for the coward I am so I just bit my lip and did it."

The rush of words took Sutter a moment to sort out. He remembered Mandy's puzzling elation at having retrieved her sandal from ankle-deep water. He looked from Mandy's golden eyes to the transparent glitter of the Fish Pond amid the dark brown carpet of coral that covered nearly all the lagoon. To him, there was absolutely nothing worth fearing there.

Yet there was no doubt Mandy's fear was real. There was also no doubt she had fought against it, forcing herself to go to Clint's aid. For a few moments Sutter tried to imagine how being in the small pool had felt to her, how much bigger fear had made the pool, how much deeper, her heart hammering, her teeth digging into her until blood flowed.

"Clint wasn't in any real danger, was he?" Sutter asked softly.

"No. Almost none of the coral is alive. Unless he panicked, the worst he would have done is skin his knees."

"But you went after him anyway."

Mandy took in a deep breath and let it out. "Yes."

Eyes as green and fathomless as gems watched her. "Why?"

"Because I have to live with myself," she said succinctly. "There was no more danger to me in the pond than if I had been walking across an empty road. My mind knew it. My body...didn't. How would you feel about yourself if you could have saved a child a bloodied knee just by walking across an empty road, but you were too big a coward to do it?"

There was silence and more intense scrutiny from Sutter's clear green eyes as he tried to understand Mandy. His mother had had many irrational fears but had never made any attempt to confront them. After his father had died in a drunken race through the Alps, his mother had retreated first to the country house, then to a single wing of the house, then to her room, to her bed, until all that was left was Valium. She had crawled into the pills, going away for weeks at a time. One day she hadn't come back.

His former wife had been afraid in a different way. She had been afraid of being alone. That fear had ruled her life and nearly ruined his. He had tried to adjust to always being in the center of a party or an outing. She had never tried to adjust to being with silence. Finally he had taken one trip too many for OCC and had come back to find that his wife was in Mexico, obtaining the fastest divorce available. She had remarried before she came back to the U.S. and had become a hostess known for the number and variety of her parties—and sycophants. Like his mother, his former wife had succumbed to fear rather than trying to overcome it.

But Mandy was fighting. If what had happened on the plane was any example, she was fighting with the kind of guts and sheer determination that he couldn't help but respond to. He, too, had known debilitating fear. He, too, had had to reach down deep in himself to go on despite fear, because there were things that simply had to be done no matter what the obstacles.

"You're tired of being afraid," Sutter said finally, softly.

Golden eyes widened in surprise as Mandy realized that what Sutter had said was the exact truth. She was very tired of being imprisoned within her own fears, cut off from the elemental mystery and beauty of the sea, cut off from the career she had loved, cut off from...herself.

"Yes," she whispered. "I am very, very tired of being afraid."

"And you risked wading across that pond for a child when you wouldn't risk it on your own behalf."

"Children are given to us to protect," Mandy said simply, "not to pay the price of our failures."

Sutter felt an instant of emotion so strong that it was nearly painful. Never had anyone put into words so clearly the reason he kept working for a better future despite the odds against success. He looked at Mandy as though she were a rare, perfect shell he had found unexpectedly, a gift from the sea.

Then he realized that it was sorrow as much as fear that haunted Mandy's golden eyes. He didn't know what had caused her sadness; he only knew that he wanted to ease it, to cherish her, telling her wordlessly that he would help her if he could, if she would allow him.

Sutter bent down to Mandy slowly, watching her eyes widen, feeling the warmth of her breath sigh over his mouth. The tip of his tongue slowly caressed the cut on her lip, drawing a small sound of surprise and pleasure from her. He very much wanted to deepen the kiss, to slide his hungry tongue into the heat and softness he knew waited within her mouth, but he heard the sound of the Townehome kids running back up the beach. He allowed himself one more light, gliding touch on her cut lip before he slowly released her.

"Thought you said he wasn't your bloke," Clint said slyly, watching Mandy's blush with great interest.

"Old American custom," Sutter said, hoping the child wouldn't understand the meaning of his suddenly husky voice. "It's called kissing a small hurt to make it better. Mandy cut her lip."

"Whatever you say, mate," Clint retorted dryly. He flopped down next to Mandy and opened his empty hands. "Couldn't find a ruddy thing."

Di stood nearby, her expression disconsolate.

"Di? Is something wrong, honey?" Mandy asked, wondering what had made the little girl so unhappy.

"Will you see us off tomorrow?" Di blurted out.

The last thing Mandy wanted to do was to get anywhere near the ghastly little plane that made twice-daily trips to the island. In fact, she usually made it a point to be in her tent when the plane appeared or disappeared. But Di was watching her so hopefully, her eyes clouded with the unhappiness of having to leave her new friend.

"Of course I'll see you off," Mandy said, forcing a smile.

"We both will," amended Sutter.

"Won't you be diving?" Mandy asked.

"Doubt it. Wind is forecast. I've been meaning to try my hand at a reef walk anyway. Will you give me a guided tour?"

Mandy started to refuse, hesitated, then said, "I'll do as much as I can."

Sutter brushed her cut lip with the pad of his thumb and lowered his hands, releasing her. "That's all anyone can ask, isn't it?"

Chapter 8

Sutter's understanding and his kiss haunted Mandy for the rest of the day. She hadn't suspected that he was capable of such aching tenderness. The thought of being held and caressed and made love to with even a fraction of that gentle masculine care sent odd sensations glittering through the secret places of her body. She found herself watching every motion Sutter made, every breath he took, the sheen of light on his spun-gold hair and the satin allure of his skin stretched over hard muscle; and most of all she was caught by the obvious strength of his male body and the careful restraint of that strength while he played with the two children.

After dinner a strange restlessness claimed Mandy. She told herself it was the rising wind and the falling barometer, but she knew it was as simple and complex as Sutter's green eyes watching her watch him. When the divers adjourned to the bar for beer and tall tales, Mandy slipped outside, driven by a need to walk far and fast...for if she stayed, she wouldn't be able to keep herself from running her fingertip along Sutter's full lower lip, returning the caress he had given to her earlier that day.

Mandy walked to the end of the tiny island. Along one fifty-yard stretch of beach, the limestone understructure of the island pushed through the veneer of sand. Not even the hardy she-oaks grew there. A stone shelf sloped down to the lagoon. When the tide was out, there were pockets of sand here and there, long, pale ribbons filling troughs that currents had worn into the limestone. Mandy had discovered the previous day that the sand made a cushion to sit on and the water-smoothed, sun-warmed, slanting limestone shelf provided a comfortable backrest. But tonight the tide had already passed its lowest ebb and was well launched into its return. Soon the comfortable portions of the limestone shelf would be covered by water lapping over rock still warm from the sun.

Besides, Mandy was too restless to sit still. She walked on until she rounded the end of the island and headed back up the far side where waves beat in sunset-tinged ranks against Lady Elliot Island, the first obstacle the ocean had known in thousands upon thousands of watery miles. The wind blew steadily, making the eighty degrees of heat and equal percentage of humidity feel silky rather than suffocating, giving the brilliant carmine sky a cool polish.

Very swiftly light vanished into the velvet darkness of tropic night. Mandy made a complete circuit of the island, walking by the few small resort buildings without pausing. She needed no more illumination for her walk than that offered by the cloud-veiled moon and white coral sands. She encountered no one on her second circuit of the island; though the island was barely a mile long and a half mile wide, there were too few people around for there to be any danger of tripping over each other after dark.

The tent was deserted by the time Mandy had finally walked off the worst of her restlessness. She fell asleep quickly, only to dream of being caressed by a tender warmth that was both Sutter and the sea.

When dawn came, Mandy awoke in a rush. Just enough light filled the tent for her to see that Sutter was asleep on his back, one arm flung over his head, the other trailing onto the gritty canvas floor. The sheet had been kicked aside by his long, powerful legs. His nearly nude body looked like a pagan sculpture, overwhelmingly male, each masculine line heightened by shadow and caressed by ruby light. The aura of barely leashed potency was emphasized by the stark white of the minimal jockstrap that stretched to contain him. Dark gold hair grew thickly across his chest, narrowed into a line down the center of his body and then fanned outward again, curling out from beneath the cloth pouch.

Sensations streaked through Mandy like hot rain as she watched Sutter. When she could bear it no more she rolled over and faced the tent wall, which glowed redly with the caress of the rising sun. Yet it was the image of Sutter's relaxed, beautifully male body that she saw. Certain she wouldn't sleep, she began to count the random places where light leaked through the canvas weave.

When Mandy awoke again she was alone in the tent. Though Sutter's mattress was empty, she couldn't look over there without seeing him as she had at dawn, fully aroused, fully male. Hands shaky, arms oddly weak, she changed into her island uniform—bikini and sandals. She grabbed her towel and knapsack and went to the shower. Half an hour later she emerged much cleaner and as restive as the tropic wind.

No sooner had she eaten breakfast than she heard the savage mechanical cry of the white plane swooping down for a landing. Memories surged up violently, threatening to immobilize her. She replaced them with the image of Sutter at dawn. After a few minutes she was able to climb down the cafeteria steps and walk toward the runway she had avoided since her first day on Lady Elliot Island. By the time she walked past the dive shed toward the runway, the plane had turned off the crushed coral strip and was taxiing toward the shed. Engine noise hammered rhythmically through the thick air.

Mandy slowed as memories rose like a cold, midnight sea, threatening to overwhelm her. Suddenly she felt a man's hand close around one of hers, lacing their fingers together securely.

"Ready?" Sutter asked.

Mandy's fingers tightened within his. She let out her breath slowly and nodded. Sutter squeezed her hand in return. Unconsciously she waited for him to gently prod her closer to the source of her fear. Nothing happened. Startled, she looked up into Sutter's calm green eyes. He smiled encouragingly but made no move forward. She realized that she would have to take the lead, confronting the plane by her own choice and in her own way. Sutter would neither force nor persuade her; he was simply there if she needed him. Her throat ached with sudden emotion.

"You understand," she whispered.

"What it is to fight fear?"

She nodded.

Sutter's lips curved in something that was too sad to pass for a smile. "Does that surprise you?"

"Yes."

"Everyone is afraid of something, golden eyes. The only difference is that some people fight and others go under without a struggle."

"What fear do you fight?"

"I'm afraid of being chained and beaten again," he said matter-of-factly, "of being helpless."

Mandy's breath came in with a harsh sound. She lifted Sutter's hand and smoothed it against her cheek, then pressed a kiss into his hard palm.

"Hey," he said, tilting her face up to his. "I didn't mean for you to feel sorry for me. Being beaten like that taught me fear. Up to a point, fear is a very healthy thing. It has saved my life more than once. I just have to make sure that fear doesn't *rule* my life."

Mandy couldn't speak. She simply watched Sutter with wide amber eyes, aching for all that he had suffered, not knowing why his past pain should matter so deeply to her, but knowing that it did.

"Damon," she whispered, "I..."

The sound of high, childish laughter drew closer as the Townehome kids raced each other to the plane. Slowly Mandy released Sutter's hand but was unable to keep herself from skimming one more kiss across his fingers before she turned toward Di and Clint and held out her arms. Instants later she was buried in exuberant hugs. Both children began talking at once, issuing explicit instructions for the continued construction of the coral castle. Finally the parents boosted their offspring into the plane, shaking hands all around and thanking Mandy for the extra dive time her baby-sitting had permitted.

Suddenly the engine of the plane ripped up the scale of sound as the pilot pulled back on the throttle. Instinctively Mandy reached for Sutter's hand. An instant later his fingers were interlaced with hers. He said nothing despite the painful tightness of her grip. The plane taxied down to the end of the runway, then accelerated hard up the crushed coral strip. The little aircraft leaped into the sky well short of the half of the runway that had been preempted by nesting terns. When the plane circled, gained altitude and vanished in the direction of the mainland, Mandy let out a long breath of relief.

"Have you always been afraid of flying?" Sutter asked casually as they turned away from the strip.

"I've never liked small planes," Mandy said in a flat tone.

Sutter sensed that Mandy's answer was only half the truth, and probably the less important half at that. He said nothing, however. He didn't blame her for not wanting to talk about her fear; he hadn't talked about his brutal experience in a South American jail since he had been debriefed at the American embassy after he had been freed. Even Anthea had been rather curtly told to satisfy her curiosity through the embassy report. In truth, Sutter was rather surprised that he had brought it up to Mandy. She hardly had the experience to comprehend what it meant to be beaten until you were held upright only by the same chains that had rendered you utterly helpless in the first place.

Yet Mandy had not only understood, she hadn't pitied him. She had been appalled that he had had to endure such an experience, but she hadn't made the mistake of trying to mother him as several of the women at the embassy had. Mandy had given him compassion, not pity. Empathy, not sympathy. She had offered no easy words because she had known there was nothing she could say to alleviate the brutality of his experience. There was no magic motherly act that would make it all better. He hadn't been a boy when he had been chained and beaten. He had been a man and he had suffered as a man, and no amount of mothering could change that. Mandy knew that and respected it.

"Thank you," Sutter said quietly.

Startled, Mandy looked up, only to be held captive by his clear green eyes.

"Some of the women at the embassy tried to mother me after I was freed," Sutter explained. "They meant well, I suppose, but they had the effect of reducing everything to the level of skinned knees on the rugby field. I was 'poor Damon' and 'dearie this' and 'sweetums that' until I blew up and told the women if they wanted to mother something so damned bad, there were thousands of orphans out in the streets who would benefit from it a hell of a lot more than I would." Sutter smiled ruefully. "I'm afraid I really put a high gloss on my reputation as an evil-tempered S.O.B. It was worth it, though. The women finally figured out that I wasn't a boy to be cuddled and petted and coaxed into giving mummy a tearful smile."

Mandy's own answering smile was almost sad. "Don't be too hard on them, Sutter. They were just trying to make a place for you in their world, a nice place where nothing happens that can't be cured by a mother's kiss and a red lollipop.''

Sutter grunted. ''I'm not a boy and I don't want to be one.''

''A lot of men don't feel that way.''

''Good. There are a lot of would-be mothers out there waiting to take the poor little dears to their maternal bosoms,'' Sutter retorted. ''Why the hell women like that don't just have kids of their own…'' He shrugged.

''Oh, sometimes they do. It's usually a disaster. The 'boy' they're married to has to grow up and share mummy with a squalling, helpless stranger who has first call on mummy's time and attention. How many boys do you know who like sharing the limelight?''

Sutter's teeth flashed in a sardonic smile. ''Yeah, I suppose you're right.'' His smile gentled as he looked down at Mandy. ''I'm glad you save your motherly instincts for kids like the Townehomes. You performed a small miracle with them, by the way. Both parents told me that Clint is a real handful.''

''No disagreement here,'' Mandy said wryly. ''He's also very, very bright. So is Di. When you get their attention, it's like being the focus of searchlights. Do the Townehomes know that both kids have taught themselves to read?''

''I made sure to pass on that tidbit, along with your suggestion about turning Clint loose in a library.''

''Thanks. I was never with either parent long enough to find the right moment for telling them. For you, that was no problem.''

''Are you hinting that I'm blunt?''

Mandy had only meant that Sutter had spent more time with the older Townehomes than she had. On the other hand, it was true that Sutter could be breathtakingly outspoken at times.

''How do you define blunt?'' she asked blandly. ''Is a baseball bat blunt? Is a torpedo blunt? Is a fifty-megaton—''

''That did it,'' Sutter interrupted, his threatening tone belied by the humorous line of his mouth. He grabbed Mandy's bare shoulders and shook her very gently. "I always knew your smart mouth would get you into trouble someday. Well, golden eyes, this is the day."

"I'm terrified. I take it all back. Sutter, you're the very soul of subtlety," Mandy said dramatically, putting a hand over her heart to show her earnestness.

"Convince me," he murmured, flexing his fingers, enjoying the sleek feminine resilience of her flesh.

"No one," she said instantly, "and I mean no one, has ever curled his eyebrow, lip and index finger at me with such incredible arroga—er, deftness as you did at the auction. Finesse, even. Yes, finesse. It was a stellar display of fine coordination," she said, struggling not to smile.

"My lip, too?"

"Your lip most definitely!" she shot back.

Sutter laughed and wondered why he had been avoiding Mandy for the past week. The answer came in an unwelcome avalanche of common sense.

Because she feels too damn good between my hands, that's why! Because she isn't into casual love affairs and I don't want anything more, that's why! Because awake or asleep I dream about what it would be like to slide into her and watch those beautiful golden eyes get smoky with passion. Because right now I want to cherish her in a very special way, with my words and my hands and my mouth, with my body, all of it, so deep that neither one of us will ever be the same again, always joined no matter how far apart....

Very carefully Sutter lifted his hands from Mandy's smooth, too-tempting body.

"Accusing me of having lip is like the pot calling the kettle black," Sutter said, his voice husky with laughter and something much deeper, much hotter. "You've got enough lip for both of us."

When Mandy glanced into the green blaze of Sutter's eyes, her smile slipped. For an instant the look in his eyes went through her veins like chain lightning through night, a burst of sizzling brightness and many-tongued fire. She took a short, sharp breath and retreated behind her facade of humor once more.

"Are you calling me a duck?" Mandy asked.

"A duck?"

"As in having enough lip for two birds."

"Do birds have lips?"

"Only if ducks are birds. Then there's plenty of lip to go around."

"I think I'm going to cry foul."

"Roight," she said instantly, "but you have to cry real tears or it doesn't count."

Laughing, shaking his head, Sutter conceded defeat. "I begin to understand how you handled Clint. I, however, have a tactic that wasn't available to him. Brute strength." Sutter's arms snaked out and gently pinned Mandy against his body. He brushed his lips over her forehead before he hugged her. "You're good people, Mandy," he said against her ear. "It will be a long time before I forgive myself for chaining you into that damned airplane seat."

Mandy's smile vanished as she remembered what Sutter had said about his own past, his own worst fear—to be chained, helpless.

"It was a seat belt, not a chain," she pointed out.

"There's no difference when you're too terrified to open the buckle. I'm sorry, Mandy. I should have known you weren't joking. I should have seen your fear."

"Why? Do you come across my brand of cowardice often?"

"You're not a coward, honey."

"Don't," she said abruptly, twisting away from Sutter. "I may be afraid of my own shadow, as you pointed out a few days ago, but I'm not a child. I don't like being chucked under the chin and told fairy tales any better than you did at the embassy."

For an instant Sutter was tempted to grab Mandy and

show her just how little he considered her a child. He wanted to kiss her until she melted and ran over him in a hot rain of passion that wouldn't end until neither of them had enough strength left to lick their lips. Sweet, sizzling oblivion, to fall asleep with her taste in his mouth and her body slick and hot around him, caressing him even as he drove more deeply into her one last time.

Sutter expelled a sharp breath, wrenched his thoughts into another track and said evenly, "I'm glad you don't want to be a child, because I sure as hell don't want to be your daddy. Now that we've got that settled, let's get some reef shoes. I promised Clint I'd find something you couldn't name if it took me the two weeks we've got left."

Giving Mandy no time to answer or argue, Sutter turned away. She hesitated only momentarily before following him. The reef shoes were kept in ragged rows on the cafeteria steps, right next to the bowl that held crusts for feeding the fish. Sutter and Mandy sorted through the wet, scarred, sandy shoes, looking for a pair that fitted well enough for them to tolerate for a few hours, using thick cotton socks as a cushion. Sutter finally found shoes that were long enough for his feet. The shoes Mandy found were long enough but too wide. While Mandy rummaged hopefully for a better fit, Sutter trotted back to the tent through the blustery wind, retrieved an extra pair of socks and presented them to Mandy with a flourish.

By the time Mandy and Sutter got to the beach, seven other people had scattered over the reef, which was being unveiled by the dropping tide. Sutter declared Mandy the guide, letting her choose the way out through the coral maze. Most people gravitated toward the tiny pools and narrow cracks where water and reef life concentrated. Mandy avoided the areas where water gleamed among the blunt coral shapes, choosing to teeter and balance on uneven coral knobs rather than wade in the crystalline water and sandy patches that occurred in the shallowest parts of the lagoon.

The reef sticks Mandy and Sutter carried made her balancing act possible. Five feet long, two inches in diameter, the sturdy reef sticks probed for weak patches of coral and braced people for whom two legs just weren't enough for the demands of reef walking. Even with the stick, a timely hand from Sutter saved Mandy more than once, and vice versa. Slowly, randomly, they zigzagged over the coral floor of the draining lagoon.

Whenever Sutter spotted a new shape of coral, he required Mandy to name the creature that had created it. Every time she replied quickly, effortlessly, unintentionally revealing to him how utterly familiar she was with the denizens of the reef. Yet at the same time, her small sounds of delight and surprise at seeing the living animals told him that experiencing the reef was very new to her. The paradox baffled Sutter, but he was reluctant to question her. He didn't want to replace her wonder and delight with hesitation and withdrawal.

"Oh, look!" Mandy said, her voice ringing with excitement. "I've heard about this and seen pictures, but it's unbelievably beautiful in its natural habitat."

Mandy crouched down, bracing herself with one hand on the reef stick and dipping into a small coral pool with the other. Carefully she pried up a starfish. The animal was a sapphire blue so brilliant it looked unreal.

"What's that?" Sutter asked.

"Starfish," Mandy said absently, turning over the animal to appreciate the alien beauty of myriad tiny, slender "feet" rippling like grass in a slow wind.

"Really?" he said dryly. "You're sure? Maybe you should count the arms again."

"Five."

"What's its name?"

Mandy gave Sutter a sideways, impish smile. "I know just enough of the Latin name to fake you out the way I've been doing for the last hour."

"Aha! Thought so. I didn't think there was such a thing as a *Roseate vucuumupi*."

Mandy snickered.

"But you can redeem yourself by telling me why the beast is so blue," Sutter offered generously. "And if you say it's blue because it's unhappy I'll make you walk back barefoot."

"Would I say such a rank untruth? Never! This little beastie is happy because it isn't seasick."

The words were spoken with such casual certainty that it took a moment for their meaning to sink in.

"It isn't seasick," Sutter repeated carefully, trying not to smile.

"Roight. If it were seasick, it would be—"

"Green," Sutter interrupted, groaning.

"Good on you," Mandy said, laughing, her eyes brilliant with enjoyment.

Sutter's warm, salty fingertips brushed over her cheek. He whispered her name once, then again, knowing that he had never seen a woman quite so beautiful to him as Mandy was at that moment.

"I'd like to bottle you and take you out when I'm in some place so poor and remote that sunlight has to be piped in," Sutter said softly. "At the end of the day I'd pour you into my hands and bathe my senses in you until finally I'd fall asleep smiling, dreaming of all the colors of your laughter."

Mandy blinked back sudden, stinging tears as she thought of how often Sutter must have been tired and hungry and alone at the end of the day.

"I'd like that," she said huskily. "I'd like to give you warmth when you're cold, laughter when you're alone."

With an odd, almost sad smile, Sutter caressed Mandy's cheek again and then turned away abruptly, not trusting himself to touch her anymore.

The humid wind gusted over Sutter, lifting his hair, making him restless. Mandy's golden eyes watched him, wondering what he was thinking, what she had done to make him turn away so abruptly, why he affected her so deeply.

He had always affected her, from the first day she had

walked into Anthea's office and seen Sutter's intense green eyes and go-to-hell smile staring at her from a picture frame. In the background had been empty grassland and a low tree where a leopard lay asleep in kingly ease. Sutter had been photographing the big cat when another photographer had called out. Sutter had turned, seen the camera, smiled challengingly...and the result had been the arresting snapshot that had been enlarged and framed for Anthea's office.

The picture had haunted Mandy. Every time she heard of another one of Sutter's close escapes, another diplomatic coup, another reluctant government talked into allotting more money for education and less for ostentation, her admiration had increased.

And with each of Sutter's adventures, Mandy had become more uneasy at being around him on the few occasions when he came into the office. She had been certain that a man of such proven courage would have nothing but contempt for her cowardice. So she had kept him at bay in the same way that she had kept the rest of the world from coming close enough to hurt her again; she had turned aside every potentially serious moment with a quip and a flashing smile.

But she couldn't smile when she was in the grip of her private terror. Sutter had seen her terrified, yet ultimately he had come to respect rather than to sneer at the depth of her fear. He was too much a man to fatten his own sense of self-worth by being contemptuous of people less strong than he was. Instead of lecturing her on her fear or self-righteously dragging her into the water—for her own good, of course— he had simply accepted her as she had come to him.

Quite imperfect.

Yet despite her imperfections he had wanted to bathe his senses in her, to dream of all the colors of her laughter. She wanted that, too. She wanted to know she could bring him ease when the rest of the world brought him only pain. She wanted that with an intensity that shook her.

My God. I'm falling in love with him.

"Hey, careful!" Sutter said, catching Mandy as she stumbled without warning on the coral. "You okay?"

Mandy looked at the green eyes so close to hers and trembled. "I—I was thinking of something else."

"You're shaking. Are you sure you're all right?"

She nodded. "I just scared myself, I guess. You know me. Afraid of my own shadow."

Strong fingers closed more tightly around Mandy's arms in silent rebuke. "But that's just it," he said flatly. "The better I get to know you, the more I realize you aren't a coward. If you were, you wouldn't fight your fear with the last breath in your body." His hands gentled on her arms. "Come on. The tide has turned. We'd better head back."

Mandy looked toward the outer reef. Her eyes widened. Instead of standing dark and rugged above the surface of the sea, the reef had once again succumbed to the ocean's irresistible embrace. By the time Sutter and Mandy had crossed half the lagoon toward the beach, she was wading through the low, sandy points by choice, because it was so much faster and safer than balancing on the slippery, water-smoothed corals. The presence of water didn't disturb her in the way that it had just a few days before. She was even able to stop in a long, narrow slit where water came to mid-thigh and enjoy the astonishing beauty of a piece of frilled sea life unfurled to its maximum scarlet glory, looking for all the world like a spiral chrysanthemum as it filtered the returning seawater for food.

"Wonder what a fish would make of that," Sutter said.

"It would never bite twice on one. I think that's a stinging variety of tubeworm."

"Ugly name for such a pretty thing."

"You know how it is in the ocean," Mandy said. "The more brightly colored the object, the better the chance that it's no good to eat."

"Mother Nature's little joke on man."

"More like Mother Nature's way of saying 'Look but don't touch.'"

Sutter gave Mandy a sideways look, wondering if Mother Nature knew she had utterly failed to warn off predators in Mandy's case—golden eyes and black hair, skin tanned to a honey brown by the tropic sun, laughter and grace and the promise of sensual heat in every move she made. He was having one hell of a time looking and not touching. As he followed her back to shore he admired her elegant back, her long legs and the inverted heart shape of her bottom, and he found himself hoping she would lose her footing and give him an excuse to grab her and run his hands over her just once. Then he wondered how he would make himself let go of her.

Damn Anthea anyway....

Yet even as Sutter mentally cursed Anthea, he was watching Mandy, remembering her laughter, and his curse lacked its usual force. Even so, he knew he would be a fool if he succumbed to the womanly temptation of her. The fact that he had come to like Mandy and to respect her attempts to control her fear rather than be controlled by it was simply one more reason for not succumbing to raw desire and seducing her. She wasn't a woman for casual sex. She felt too much, too deeply. He would hate himself if he took advantage of that.

But unless he stayed away from her, he didn't know how he'd manage to keep himself from reaching out and taking all that golden sensuality and secret fire for himself, and to hell with his civilized scruples.

"Blackjack," Mandy said, turning over the ace and lining it up next to the king of spades she had just been dealt.

Ray and Tommy groaned.

"That's three in a row," Ray grumbled, pushing four pennies toward Mandy. "If I weren't dealing, I'd wonder...."

"Isn't it time for you to feed the fish?" Tommy asked, tossing his two cards at Ray while looking at Mandy.

"Nope. Tide's too high."

Tommy muttered, "Bet it isn't more than four feet deep

in the pond." He took the cards from Ray. "I'll deal for a while. Sally, you want in on this round?"

"Sure."

Sally, who had been tending bar, looked at the other customers. Two of them were elderly teachers from France, who could make a single beer last for an hour between them. The other five were divers who, like Ray and Tommy, were very restless after three days of enforced time on land. The men had tried to get out diving that afternoon by walking out over the reef at low tide, but the surf had been too violent. The divers had returned grumbling and had been drinking beer and playing cards and listening to the wind ever since. An hour ago the wind had died as suddenly as it had come up, but it was too close to sunset to do the divers any good.

"What about you lot?" Tommy asked, looking toward the other disappointed divers. "You want to help me take this Sheila to the laundry?"

"Sounds like that's as close to water as we're going to get today," said one of the men. The others muttered agreement.

Moments later the tables had been pushed together, beers had been ordered all around, pennies were thrown into the pot and cards were dealt.

"Where's the big Yank?" Sally asked.

"Sutter?" Mandy asked, peeking at her hole card.

"He's the biggest Yank on the island," Tommy said. "Bloody good diver, too. Never makes a careless move."

"He's going over his scuba gear," Mandy said, hoping that she was keeping her disappointment out of her voice. She had no right to expect Sutter to entertain her. Her presence on his vacation had been unexpected, to say the least. All in all, he had been a very good sport about it. He had gone reef walking with her several times, fed the tiny fish, made circuits of the island looking for turtle tracks, eaten meals with her and had always tactfully withdrawn from the tent at night until she had fallen asleep. What more could she ask?

A little less tact, she admitted to herself ruefully.

"Hit me," Mandy said.

"Don't tempt me, luv," Tommy said, giving her a flashing smile and the card she had requested.

Mandy smiled in return, remembering Anthea's advice about finding an Australian lover. With a cross between amusement and exasperation she looked over her cards at the expanse of bare, muscular male chests and sexy grins surrounding her. She had yet to see an Australian male who wasn't tall, well built, tanned, easygoing and good-looking. She had no doubt that Ray or Tommy or one of the tourist divers would be more than happy to accommodate her with a sandy fling, especially when the wind was blowing too hard for the dive boat to get out. Sally and the other girls who worked on the island certainly never lacked male attention.

So why didn't Mandy take Anthea's advice and snaffle one of these engaging Australian males?

Because they aren't Sutter, she admitted to herself.

"I'm good," Mandy said absently, frowning at her own thoughts.

Tommy's smile changed indefinably. His blue glance shifted from the cards in his hands as he made a leisurely, thorough appraisal of the womanly flesh that filled out the black bikini top Mandy wore.

"I'll just bet you are, luv," he said, winking at her.

Mandy blinked, then laughed, shaking her head. Even if she never so much as kissed one of these Australian males, they were good for her ego.

"Hit me," Ray said.

Indolently Tommy flicked him a card.

"Again."

Another card fell.

"Busted," Ray said in disgust, turning his other card face-up. The three cards totaled twenty-two.

Tommy went around the tables until no one remained but himself. He turned over a ten to match his nine.

"Pay twenty."

"That's me," Mandy said promptly, showing a jack and a queen.

"You keep that up and I'm going to feed you to the fishes," Ray said in disgust.

"I'd poison them."

"A sweet little Sheila like you?" Ray said. "Not a prayer, luv. Not a single prayer."

On the next deal Mandy got a blackjack. It was the same on the following deal. When she turned over a blackjack for the third time in a row, everyone threw in the cards in disgust.

"That's it," Ray proclaimed loudly. "To the fishes with her!"

Laughing, Mandy tried to divide her modest mound of pennies among the losers so that the game could continue. The divers were having none of it.

"The door, Sally," Ray said, reaching for Mandy with a gleam in his eyes.

"Right," Sally said, grinning.

Suddenly Mandy found herself out of her chair and hanging upside down over Ray's shoulder. She didn't believe what was happening until the door slammed shut behind the laughing, rowdy divers who were urging Ray on. A few feet beneath her nose the coral path sped by.

"Beer!" Mandy called out, thinking fast. "Drinks are on me, guys, but only if I stay dry!"

The other divers didn't bite on the offer. They had been drinking beer most of the afternoon. Dunking Mandy promised more diversion than one more round of brew.

The upside-down world went by Mandy with dizzying speed. Most men would have had the wind taken out of their sails just by carrying her halfway to the Fish Pond, but not Ray. His diving career had given him both strength and endurance. He wasn't even breathing hard.

Damn these muscle-bound Aussie men! Mandy thought as she struggled to free herself.

It was futile. Short of biting, she could make no dent in Ray's strength. She wasn't ready to resort to her teeth before she had tried reasoning with the men.

"Ray? Ray, put me down," Mandy pleaded, shouting over the raucous encouragement of the other divers. "I promise I won't play cards anymore."

"Too late, luv," he said cheerfully. "I warned you."

The path gave way to the beach. Blue water flashed beneath the heat-misted tropical sky.

"Ray! Please! I don't like water!" Mandy shouted, her voice high. "Please! Listen to me! This isn't funny anymore! I—I'm afraid of water! Don't drop me in! Please!"

Shouts of laughter and pure disbelief greeted Mandy's frantic cries.

"Sure you are, luv," Ray said, laughing. "That's why you spent a pot of money to come to this little bit of nothing in the middle of the biggest ocean on God's earth. Afraid of water? That's rich, luv, really rich. All right, you lot. Make way for the fish food. Give us a hand, Tommy, there's a good lad."

Suddenly the world flipped over and Mandy found herself even more helpless than she had been before, unable even to bite or claw or kick, her feet held securely in Ray's grasp and her wrists in Tommy's while the rest of the divers called outrageous suggestions as to the best way of launching the fish feast.

"One," chanted the divers as Ray and Tommy swung Mandy between them, her hips skimming the surface of the water. "Two."

Suddenly Mandy screamed and twisted frantically in the grip of the two divers. It was no use. She was utterly helpless to free herself. With that realization came both terror and despair. She screamed again, a single raw sound that was Sutter's name.

"Three!"

There was a giddy time of flight and then the Fish Pond splashed up and over Mandy just as she was taking another breath to scream again. Instantly she choked and panicked. She thrashed around futilely, unable even to get to her feet in the shallow water. She opened her mouth again but there was only water surrounding her, engulfing her, drowning her.

Chapter 9

Suddenly Mandy was pulled free of the water and held in a man's powerful arms. She knew it was Sutter who had rescued her even before she heard his deep, icy voice flaying Ray and Tommy in measured phrases of contempt. Knowing that she was safe, she wrapped her arms around Sutter and hung on while he walked to shore. Her body convulsed with sobs and coughs as she cleared her lungs of the lagoon's salty water.

"I heard her pleading with you all the way over at the dive shed," Sutter continued, his green eyes narrowed as he watched understanding dawn on the divers. "How in God's name could you do it? Are you as deaf as you are cruel?"

"Bloody hell," Ray said softly, looking from Mandy's shaking body to Sutter's barely contained rage. "She meant it, didn't she? She's really afraid of water!"

"Your mental acuity leaves me breathless," Sutter said, anger vibrating in every word.

"How was I to know? Bloody hell, mate, people who are afraid of water don't come *here*. It makes no sense! When

I found out I had no stomach for heights, you can bet your arse I never went rock climbing in the Snowy Mountains again!''

Ray had a point and Sutter knew it, but he was far too angry at the moment to be reasonable. His arms closed protectively around Mandy when she sagged against him, her body shuddering with the strength of her sobs as she tried to speak. He couldn't understand what she was trying to say. He bent until his ear was next to her mouth. She was repeating two words over and over again, the syllables broken by sobs: *The baby, the baby.*

''It's all right, golden eyes,'' Sutter murmured soothingly, stroking her gently. ''You're safe.'' He continued holding and caressing her, speaking reassurances over and over again until he sensed that she finally had heard him. ''That's it. Hold tight to me. You're safe, darling. You're safe.'' He smoothed his cheek over the wet, tangled hair, kissed her salty cheek and held her even closer, wishing he could understand what she was trying to say. Maybe then he would be able to ease the terrible sobs shaking her.

''Mandy,'' Ray said softly, his voice as troubled as his blue eyes. He touched her shoulder. ''I'm sorry.''

The words were repeated many times as the other divers apologized.

Mandy didn't hear anything but her own wild grief.

''Mandy…?'' Ray asked.

''Give it a rest,'' Sutter said, pinning the young diver with a hard green glance, then moving on to look at the others. ''All of you. Clear out.''

Sutter had faced down armed men with a similar look. The divers wasted no time in finding somewhere else to be. Neither did Sutter. There were people all over that part of the beach—reef walkers chased to shore by the rising tide, swimmers who enjoyed a lazy paddle in the Fish Pond as it deepened with the tide, and other people who simply liked to stretch out on the sand and dream while the sun descended into a sea stained purple by the end of day.

With long strides Sutter walked down the beach, away from the office and cabins and other people. He ignored the tent set apart from others. It would be stifling in there. There was no wind stirring now, nothing to ease the intense, sultry heat of the tropics. Clouds had formed in the absence of the wind, holding the hot air close to the earth. Light flickered oddly within the clouds, heat lightning made almost visible by the descending sun.

As he walked, Sutter felt the shudders that took Mandy's body without warning, heard her tearing breaths, felt the scalding touch of her tears against his chest. With every step he took he raged at himself for not reaching the Fish Pond a few seconds sooner—and for having left her alone in the first place. He should have guessed what kind of horseplay a bunch of young, bored divers would find appealing. He should have stayed in the bar and kept the lid on things.

But it was his own self-control he had been worried about, not that of the divers. It had been driving him slowly wild to sit next to Mandy, to feel the occasional brush of her bare leg against his when she shifted position, to sense her smooth feminine warmth so close to him that all he would have had to do was to move his hand a few inches and it would have lain in the soft, shadowed darkness between her thighs.

He had taken it as long as he could, and then he had fled to the dive shed to check equipment that didn't need checking.

The sand beneath Sutter's feet changed to a pea gravel made of tiny hunks of coral. A hundred feet farther down the beach the gravel gave way to a limestone slope striped with random small troughs of sand. The sand cushions were barely inches above the incoming tide, but that would be enough for now. There was no one else at this end of the island. Mandy could hold on to him and cry in privacy, working out the last residue of her fear.

Sutter lowered himself until he was sitting with his back braced against the smooth limestone. Gently he arranged Mandy across his lap. In silence he held her against his chest, smoothing her hair and her back with slow sweeps of his hand. After a long time she was quiet, with only random trembling to mark the aftermath of her panic. She took in a deep, shaky breath and then simply leaned against Sutter, absorbing his undemanding presence. Slowly her breath evened out.

"I'm sorry," Sutter murmured, brushing Mandy's forehead comfortingly with his lips. "I should have known they would make the same mistake with you that I made. Not believing until it was too late."

Wearily Mandy shook her head. "My fault," she whispered. "I should have told everyone that I was afraid of planes and boats and water on the first day." Her mouth turned down in self-contempt. "Like you said—afraid of my own damned shadow."

"Don't," Sutter said, putting his fingers gently across her mouth. "I was tired, jet-lagged and wrong from the first word I said about you."

Mandy simply shook her head and tried to sit up, but Sutter's arms were too tight. When she persisted, he turned her shoulder blades to his chest, opened his legs and settled her on the sand between his thighs.

"Use me for a backrest," he offered. "I may not be much smarter than limestone but I'm a hell of a lot more comfortable."

At first Mandy resisted the temptation of Sutter's offer. She sat awkwardly upright, feeling chilled despite the heat trapped in the sand and air and ocean around her. But after a few minutes the lure of Sutter's living warmth was too great to deny. Mandy sighed raggedly and leaned back. Big, gentle hands stroked down her arms, silently reassuring her, warming her.

In silence Sutter and Mandy watched the sun complete the last of its fiery arc before being consumed by the restless, incandescent sea. When the molten rays of light vanished into a surreal gloaming, Sutter began talking about sunset on the African veld, about projects that had worked and those that had not, about the animals and the men and the laughing, black-eyed children whose future well-being depended on the generosity of tyrants.

Mandy listened in a dreamy, suspended silence, feeling Sutter's deep voice vibrate subtly through her body, seeping into her soul. Only gradually did she become aware of the water that had risen slowly, flowing across the reef, flooding the lagoon, the ocean licking softly at her outstretched feet. There was no coolness, no hint of chill in the water, simply a tidal exhalation of warmth lapping slowly closer.

Distantly Mandy knew that she should move, retreat up the beach, get away from the devouring sea…but she was held suspended in the warm and gentle moment, Sutter's hands smoothing her arms, his breath feathering against her cheek. She didn't want the time of peace to end. If that meant enduring the sea's blind caress, then she would do so as long as she could. The water was barely three inches deep, no threat to her.

And Sutter was so close, his living warmth radiating into her body, sinking into her very soul.

Sighing, Mandy shifted her weight slightly, a matter more of relaxing utterly against Sutter's chest than of any real movement on her part. He felt the subtle increase of her weight against him and closed his eyes for an instant in reflexive response to the emotion twisting through him. Mandy's wordless declaration of trust in the face of the rising tide moved him as nothing else could have. Gently he brushed his cheek against her hair. The strands were damp, scented with the sea, infused with the warmth of her body.

Overhead, the sky was half glittering stars, half towering clouds, where chain lightning silently danced through velvet darkness. The moon was a distant, tilted smile, as though approving the sequined shimmer of lightning so far below. The surface of the sea reflected darkness and light, becoming both, breathing warmth into the air and the land alike.

Mandy smiled back at the moon as she drifted within the timeless moment of peace, suspended between the warmth of the sea and Sutter alike, feeling as though she were in a different reality, a world where Sutter's words were intangible caresses, phrases murmuring through her flesh and bones, whispering deeply to her soul. She murmured in return, sound without meaning, soft echoes of her serenity.

Sutter heard and understood Mandy's wordless message. With subtle movements of his body, he gathered her closer against himself. Closing his eyes, he held her, wishing that he had the power to turn back the rising tide so that Mandy could always stay as she was, relaxed in his arms, allowing him to ease the icy terror of past helplessness with the healing warmth of present companionship.

But no man could hold back the hushed silver glide of the sea. When it lapped almost over Mandy's calves, she brought her feet in close to her hips, raising her knees and most of her legs above the water. Reluctantly Sutter shifted position, as well. He didn't want Mandy to get up, for then the time of peace and intimacy would end. He wasn't ready for that. There had been nothing in his experience quite like these languid moments when he had been suspended with Mandy between warm limestone and the swelling tide.

Finally the rising water dissolved Mandy's peace.

"Sutter, have you ever heard the phrase, 'caught between a demon and the deep blue sea'?"

He laughed softly. "Getting too wet? Try this."

Sutter lifted Mandy, turning her until she straddled his lap facing him. In that position the sea claimed her only from the knees down.

"Better?" he asked.

Mandy was so close to Sutter that she could see the flash and gleam of distant lightning reflected in his eyes. His smile was like his hands, like his body, like his words, warmly reassuring, demanding nothing of her.

"I was wrong," she whispered. "You're not a devil at all."

"Does that mean we can stay out here for a while?"

She nodded.

"Good. I don't want to leave. Not yet. Not until we have to."

When Mandy realized that Sutter was enjoying the gentle intimacy as much as she was, a fragile shimmer of warmth unfurled deep within her. She lowered herself very slowly against Sutter's chest, feeling her breath unravel as his living heat touched her from her forehead to her thighs. Sensations shivered through her body at random, sweetness dancing like distant, silver lightning over her nerves.

Sutter smoothed his hand down Mandy's back in a gesture that was meant to be soothing and reassuring but somehow fell short of its intended goal...or far surpassed it. With a sigh, Mandy tucked her cheek against his shoulder and turned her face into his neck. For an instant he thought he felt the lightest brush of her lips against his throat.

Suddenly he became aware of far more than the relaxed trust of Mandy's body lying against his. He felt the soft weight of her breasts behind the bikini top's scant confinement. The cloth was damp and vaguely cool, her skin satin and warm. Every time he took a breath his skin brushed hers, sending heat through him, heat gathering from the pit of his stomach to his thighs, heat changing him with each quickening heartbeat.

For a few moments Sutter fought the urgent surge of his body; then he succumbed with a mental shrug. He could get as hard as the limestone shelf and it wouldn't make any difference. He wasn't a boy to lose control of himself at the first rush of desire, and Mandy wasn't an inexperienced girl to be embarrassed by a man's aroused body. Besides, they were hardly in a position to do anything more than savor the unexpected rewards of peace and companionship. Peace, not passion, because at any moment someone might come walking up the beach. It wasn't particularly likely, but it was still possible.

The thought didn't prevent Sutter from enjoying the sweet weight of Mandy lying along his chest. Nor did it make him turn away from the warmth of her lips against his neck.

Instead, he closed his eyes the better to savor the sensation of a gliding, butterfly kiss breathed onto his skin. Slowly, inevitably, he turned toward her, intending to do no more than brush his lips across her cheek as he had done before.

Somehow it was Mandy's lips Sutter touched, not her cheek. There was an instant of brushing contact, then another, then another and yet another until finally his mouth was rocking very gently over hers. By the time he fully realized what he was doing, it was too late.

Mandy sighed, sending a wave of sweetness and warmth over Sutter's lips. She returned his kiss so delicately that he held his breath at the unexpected beauty of the caress. Never had he guessed there could be such exquisite, piercing pleasure in a chaste kiss.

Nor had Mandy. With a tiny sound that could barely be heard above Sutter's own heartbeat, she nestled once more against his neck, warming his throat with her breath. Slowly his hand came up to her face. Fingertips traced her forehead and the line of her cheek, the curve of her chin and the warmth of her lips. She shivered delicately, feeling as though she were being licked by tender fire. Turning her face into his hand, she returned the pleasure he was giving to her. The warm caress she breathed into his palm became another kind of kiss as he tilted her face up to his. Their lips met again, rocked softly again, separated for the space of a breath, then met once more, clinging gently, repeatedly.

Mandy's hands crept up Sutter's chest until she could hold his face between her palms. The holding was as gentle as the kiss, as soft as the glide of his hands down her back. She felt suspended once more, only this time she was being gilded with sensual pleasure, quivering with the beauty of it. Never had she imagined that a man could be so exquisitely restrained with his caresses.

The touch of Mandy's hands and lips on Sutter's face sent pleasure shimmering through his flesh, through his bones, through his mind. Part of him was astonished that such a simple caress could so ravish his senses, and part of him cared only that the heated, oddly fragile touching not stop. Suspended amid passion and tenderness and sweet surprise, he held himself very still, focusing himself entirely in the moment, wanting that moment never to end.

When Mandy's gentle mouth finally lifted, Sutter let out a long breath and captured her hands. Holding them cupped before his face, he turned his head slowly from side to side, causing her hands to slide caressingly over his face while he kissed her palms and fingertips and the softness of her inner wrists. Her breath caught as she remembered what he had said while they were walking on the reef...*I'd take you out and bathe my senses in you.*

That was what Mandy would like to do, as well, to bathe in Sutter's warmth and masculine textures, savoring each instant, immersing herself in him.

When Sutter lifted his head from Mandy's cupped hands, moonlight washed over his face, giving his eyes a haunting intensity. He looked at her as though he had never seen her before and was afraid he might never see her again. He memorized her with his eyes and his sensitive fingertips tracing every bit of her face. Her eyelids fluttered down as pleasure radiated through her body, bringing warmth in its wake. The instant before his lips touched her cheek she felt the heat of his breath. Very slowly she turned her head from side to side, offering herself to his mouth as he caressed her. With a low, husky sound he accepted her gift, brushing kisses over her face until only her lips remained untouched, aching.

"Damon," Mandy whispered, not even knowing that she spoke. "Please...."

By slow degrees Sutter's fingers worked into Mandy's hair. He flexed his hands very slightly, but she was so sensitized to his every movement that she tilted her head back, giving herself to his hands as he had silently requested. His mouth feathered the hollow of her throat with heat, and the tiny probings of his tongue called a broken sigh from her. Lips that were both gentle and firm traced the tendons in her neck. The curving line of her jaw knew his touch next, soft kisses and the heat of his tongue tasting her lightly. She trembled between his hands, wanting to speak, trying to tell him that he was unraveling her so slowly, so completely...but she had no words, only the soft unfurling of warmth deep within, pleasure radiating through her body.

When the tip of Sutter's tongue outlined Mandy's lips, she moaned very softly. The sound sent a shiver through him. He lifted his head and looked at her lips glistening from his caress. The sight sent another ripple of emotion through his powerful body. By increments he lowered his head once more until he could taste the curve of her smile. She breathed his name again, parting her lips, sending a rush of warmth over him. The tender penetration of his tongue drew a low sound from her throat. She caressed his tongue with her own, tasting him, trembling.

It was the same for Sutter, his senses spinning slowly, revolving around the woman who came to him so softly, so completely. When he finally raised his head again, he couldn't bear to be without Mandy's taste on his tongue for more than an instant before he bent to her once more. Her lips opened for him willingly, letting him dip repeatedly into her mouth, probing her softness while she caressed him in turn.

When Sutter's mouth lifted again, Mandy made a husky sound of protest that became a sigh of pleasure as he caught her lower lip between his teeth and taught her how exquisitely gentle a love bite could be. She murmured his name wonderingly, feeling as though she were being held captive by a loving fire, and the world had begun to spin slowly around captor and captive alike.

Sutter's big hands tightened in Mandy's hair when he heard the throaty cry that was his name. Her head tilted back even more, offering the smooth curve of her throat to his mouth. Slowly one of his hands slid from Mandy's hair. The remaining hand tightened, holding her arched and aching for the feel of his mouth once again. As he bent to kiss the pulse beating in her throat, his fingertips stroked her spine from nape to hips, untying the two strands of cloth that interrupted the elegant length of her back.

Mandy felt only the caresses, the sliding warmth of Sutter's fingers, the shivers of sensation chasing down her spine; and she moved always toward his touch, his warmth, his taste. Feeling her instant, uninhibited response to his lightest touch made Sutter almost dizzy with unaccustomed emotion. Holding Mandy in his arms was like spinning slowly through soft flames, tongues of heat licking everywhere over his big body, teaching him how sensitive every bit of his skin could be.

His hand moved again, this time tracing the delicate curves of her ear, touching the pulse beating at the base of her throat, gliding down the center line of her body to her navel, circling the sensitive dimple until she shivered. Breath held, Mandy waited for the next caress, the next touch that would teach her that her body was made of silken heat and dizzying sensations. When the touch didn't come, she opened her eyes.

Sutter was motionless but for the heavy beat of blood at his temple. His eyes were half-closed, glittering, and he was looking at the creamy flesh he had uncovered. Mandy knew an instant of surprise that she was no longer wearing her bikini top, but that didn't matter nearly so much as the pleasure Sutter clearly took from looking at her bare breasts.

"Mandy?" he asked softly.

"Yes," she whispered, sliding her fingers deeply into Sutter's thick hair, caressing him even as he bent to her.

As he had once done with Mandy's cupped hands, Sutter turned his face slowly from side to side, caressing her breasts, being caressed by them in turn. His tongue traced the lower curve of both breasts, touching her with fire. She closed her eyes and went very still, living entirely in the instant, knowing only the gliding heat of his tongue outlining her. Lips kissed each warm curve as he nuzzled against her softness, yet somehow he avoided the dark crowns that awaited him, drawn tight with anticipation and need.

Mandy's fingers worked through Sutter's hair, caressing and silently pleading at the same time. When his breath washed over one nipple she made a soft sound at the back of her throat. When his tongue licked a velvet crown, her breath came out in a sighing rush. A small, hoarse groan was pulled from him as he felt her change even more with each stroke of his tongue, her nipple drawing tighter and tighter until he could not hold back from suckling her in the same primal rhythm that was pulsing through his aroused body. Her fragmented whimpers of pleasure sank into him, urging him to feed deeply on her softness, making the world spin more quickly around them with each tiny cry.

Slowly Sutter pulled Mandy up his body until she was kneeling astride him, her back arched, her hands gripping his shoulders, her head tilted back as his mouth drew rippling sounds of surprise and pleasure from her. Sutter heard and shuddered in response, never lifting his head, drawing her ever more deeply into his mouth, wanting to become a part of her and at the same time to consume her as gently, as completely as the sea was consuming the lagoon.

As though at a distance Mandy heard soft, glittering cries of pleasure. Dimly she realized that she had made them, was making them even now, but the realization had no meaning to her. Nothing had meaning but the exquisitely restrained strength of the man who was caressing her, making pleasure tremble and burst sweetly, secretly inside her, sensations she had never before known, never dreamed, never imagined. His hands stroked languidly down her back, caressed her waist, sent expanding rings of pleasure from her navel, smoothed over her hips and slid down her thighs. When his hands returned, they eased up her inner thighs until he brushed against the feminine mound between her legs, rocking gently against the narrow triangle of cloth that was infused with more than the heat and dampness of the sea.

Knowing he should stop, unable to deny himself just one gliding caress, Sutter eased his finger beneath the cloth, heard and savored the ragged intake of Mandy's breath.

Slowly he touched her, his fingertip as delicate as his tongue had been, and he felt the quivering of her response all the way to the soles of his feet. He eased more deeply into her, savoring her fire and softness and the heat of the satin flesh that clung to him, wanting him.

"Oh, love," Sutter groaned, retreating slowly from Mandy, feeling her soft flesh tighten around him, trying to hold him within her. "We've got to stop," he said, but even as he spoke he was sliding into her once more, probing tenderly, trembling as her response washed over him. "At first I thought I could just hold you, and then I thought I could just kiss you, and then I told myself that I could look at your breasts, no more, just that. But you're so beautiful," he said hoarsely, "so responsive. Your nipples tightened with a look, and when my tongue touched you..."

Sutter closed his eyes, unable to bear the exquisite torture of her breasts so close to his lips, so sweet. He shouldn't touch her anymore. He knew he shouldn't.

And he knew he must.

"Just once more," he said, his voice hoarse.

Mandy murmured dreamy pleasure while Sutter's lips and tongue caressed first one breast, then the other, then the first yet again. Each sultry, changing pressure of his mouth sent streamers of fire licking through her. It was the same for him. When his palm rubbed lightly over the cloth between her legs, he remembered how it had felt to be held within her incredible satin heat.

"Just once..." he whispered, slipping a long finger beneath the triangle of cloth, caressing her even as he slid within.

Mandy's body arched as sweet lightning shimmered through her. With a strange, rippling sigh she began to move in slow motion, rocking against Sutter's hand, wanting only to know more of the caress that was making her melt in rhythmic waves of pleasure.

Sutter felt both the tightness of Mandy and the sleek ease with which she accepted his touch. He whispered her name as he redoubled the caress, stretching her gently, feeling the immediate heat of her response. Instinctively he tried to deepen the touch, wanting to feel her pleasure all around him, to taste it, to bathe his senses in her and then to slide deeply into her, bringing her ecstasy.

But he had to stop.

"Mandy," he said huskily, trying to withdraw his touch once more.

It wasn't possible. She felt too good, wanted his caresses too much. And her hand was over his, holding him inside her deepest warmth. He kissed the smooth skin of her belly, then probed her navel with his tongue as he probed her feminine secrets with his hand.

"Help me to stop," Sutter said in a hoarse voice, turning his cheek against the warm, resilient flesh below Mandy's navel.

Her answer came in the smooth glide of her hips, a motion that caught him deeply within her once more.

"Mandy, we..."

Her fingers slid down Sutter's body and beneath the warm surface of the sea until she cupped the hard, aching flesh between his legs. Whatever he had been going to say was lost in a husky cry of pleasure when she caressed him with slow sweeps of her hand.

"Love, you're killing me," he said raggedly, unable to keep his hips from moving in counterpoint to her hand.

Mandy's only answer was a sweet, broken cry of pleasure as his thumb found and teased the hard bud in the midst of her softness. The sound made Sutter smile despite the urgent ache of his flesh. He moved his thumb again, felt her tighten around his fingers and wanted to laugh with the deep sensual heat of her response. Then suddenly her hand was inside his swimming trunks, naked skin moving over naked skin, and their mutual cries of discovery and pleasure sent shudders through his powerful body.

With the last of his self-control, Sutter prevented himself from pulling on the strings that fastened the maddening triangle of cloth in place between Mandy's legs. He told himself he could pleasure her and know the bittersweet heat of partial release. Slowly he turned his head and caught first one of her nipples and then the other in his mouth, gently sucking on the hard, velvet flesh, feeling his whole body clench with her instant response.

Without thinking, Sutter moved his hand to the strings that were fastened precisely in the crease where thigh met body. The feel of cloth instead of hot, soft skin warned him of what he was doing. Abruptly Sutter knew he couldn't trust himself anymore. He turned his mouth aside from Mandy's too-tempting body, but when he would have withdrawn his touch from her soft heat, her own hand prevented him.

"Mandy, no," Sutter whispered, kissing the small hand that was holding him within her. He felt her other hand caress him one last time, withdraw, and he bit back his helpless sound of protest. Then he saw Mandy's fingers catch the end of a bikini string and pull slowly, unraveling the bow, and he groaned. "Mandy, we can't."

"Why?"

"I came to the island to dive, not to have an affair," Sutter said huskily. "I have no way to protect you from an unwanted pregnancy."

Mandy looked into Sutter's eyes and felt a shaft of pure pleasure arrow through her at the thought of conceiving and bearing his child. Two years ago the sea had taken more from her than she had to give…and tonight, with the warm tide lapping higher and higher between her thighs, the sea could return it all to her again.

"I'm sorry, golden eyes. I never should have let it go this far," Sutter said. "I thought I could just pleasure you, but I don't trust myself anymore. Not with you. You're… different. With you it's…too good."

Even as he spoke, Sutter's hand moved slowly between Mandy's legs, caressingly, because feeling her response to his touch was a pleasure more intense than he had believed possible. She smiled and moved with him. The bikini strings separated beneath her hand. She reached across herself to tug on the other bow.

"Mandy. Don't. If you take off that bit of cloth… Haven't you been listening to me? I can't protect you!"

She tried to tell Sutter that there could be no such thing as an unwanted pregnancy with his child, but no words came through the waves of sensation that had begun rippling through her at the thought of holding Sutter deeply within her body, feeling him shudder and cry out as he poured his seed into her. Finally she bent down and kissed his mouth very gently, stopping his protests.

"I don't need protecting," she murmured against his lips.

Sutter felt the warm triangle of bikini cloth give way, allowing him the absolute freedom of Mandy's body. With aching slowness he caressed her taut hips and the sultry heat between her legs. Kneeling, she swayed with his touch, wholly lost.

"Are you sure?" he asked huskily, nuzzling the soft, dark tangle of hair that lay revealed at the apex of her thighs.

"Yes," she whispered. "Oh, yes."

The last words came from Mandy's lips in a broken cry as Sutter's hot tongue sought and found her in a caress that was utterly unexpected. Her eyes closed and lightning splintered delicately through her body, setting off tiny, satin contractions deep inside.

Slowly Sutter increased the pressure of his fingers within her, smiling at the sleek heat of her, wanting to feel all of that heat closing around him in the rhythms of ecstasy, wanting to catch her most sensitive flesh very gently between his teeth, holding her captive for an exquisite kind of loving. Yet even as he moved to follow his desire, Mandy sank bonelessly back onto his legs, too weak to support herself any longer and hungry to caress his masculine flesh once more.

Her hands slid from his shoulders down his back to his lean waist and then to his hips. Slender fingers eased inside the strip of black cloth that was all Sutter wore. Gently she freed him, smiling to see the instant, hard rise of his erect flesh above the water's reach.

Seeing Mandy's smile, Sutter felt as though he had been dipped in loving fire. His fingers sank luxuriantly into the creamy flesh of Mandy's hips, urging her closer. Then his hands slid forward, caressing and pressing against her silky inner thighs, separating them until she was poised just above his rigid flesh, her feminine heat utterly open to him. He held her that way for long, shivering moments, brushing her with the same fiery flesh that ached to be within her. When he could stand no more of the sensual teasing, he gently began to part the soft, hot folds between her thighs.

Mandy moaned as she felt Sutter coming to her. She convulsed delicately around him while he moved slowly into her, so slowly, taking her by sensuous increments, savoring the sweet, repeated shivering of her climax at the satin penetration, hearing her breath catch again and again at the ecstasy pulsing through her.

Her response dragged a deep groan from Sutter. He wanted to drive hard and deep into her, but once he sheathed himself fully in her, he knew it would be impossible for him to hold back his own climax. He didn't want it to end so soon, before he had even begun to plumb the depths of her response, or his own. He had never taken a woman like this before, never before felt so perfectly the shimmering pulses of feminine release, never felt himself so full and hard, so much a man, pressing into sultry heat and shivering ecstasy, sliding deeper and deeper and then deeper still, until finally he was fully sheathed and time stopped and his flesh pulsed with hers, he was joined to her, giving himself to her again and again until he thought he would die of the endless release he had found within her.

Chapter 10

For a long time Mandy was aware of nothing but a silky lassitude claiming her in the aftermath of a pleasure so intense that she still trembled with almost every breath. Gradually small elements of reality condensed around her once more. She realized she was naked and Sutter was naked and their bodies were still joined beneath the silver glinting of the sea...a sea that was even now lapping gently higher up her bare hips. She knew the slowly deepening water should bother her, but she felt too supremely cherished at the moment to be frightened. With a contented sigh she closed her eyes.

Sutter felt the stirring of Mandy's body over his and guessed that she must be uneasy about the increasing depth of the water lapping at the limestone ledge. For an instant his arms tightened around her, holding her in place. He didn't want the moment of intimacy to end. It was too new, too unexpected. He felt renewed, reborn, everything utterly right...except for the tide, licking higher with each instant.

He didn't want the boneless relaxation of Mandy's body to change into tight fear.

Reluctantly Sutter loosened his embrace. Even if Mandy wasn't afraid of the water at the moment, there was another problem. No matter how warm the sea seemed in the heat of mutual passion, he knew the water was slowly but surely sapping their body heat. Gently he ran one hand down Mandy's lovely back and nuzzled against her face, which was tucked against his chest.

"Wake up, golden eyes."

Mandy murmured and kissed the corner of Sutter's mouth. He smiled and brushed his lips over hers. From the distance came the sound of laughter, a door closing and someone calling across the velvet darkness. A moment later an answer came, sound without meaning.

"Time to get up, you lovely, lazy wench," Sutter whispered, caressing the warm curve of Mandy's hip.

"After you," she said, kissing his neck.

He laughed softly. "That's not how it works, darling. You're on top. You have to get up first."

"Oh." Then, "Sutter?"

"Mmm?"

"You haven't encountered my bikini lately, by any chance?"

There was silence followed by tiny splashing sounds. After a few moments Sutter's hand appeared above the water. Odds and ends of clothing hung limply from between his fingers, shedding thin streamers of water.

"This what you're missing?" he asked.

Mandy looked, looked again and said, "Actually, I think it's what *you're* missing."

Sutter examined the fistful of cloth in the moonlight. "I think you're right. Wait a sec." He fished around in the water for a few more moments before emerging triumphantly with other pieces of cloth. "Got it."

Reluctantly Mandy began to separate herself from Sutter in order to get dressed. Before she could do more than register her intention with a slight shift in her weight, she felt his arms close snugly around her, holding her around him while he sat fully upright. He tied the neck strings of her bikini top in place, then began to pull the tiny triangles of cloth into place over her nipples. The temptation of her breasts was too great to entirely ignore. He nuzzled the cloth aside and kissed her slowly, tasting the sea on her skin, licking salt from her nipples. Finally, very reluctantly, he eased the two triangles into place.

"These things should be outlawed," Sutter said huskily, looking at Mandy's tight, erect nipples pressing against the bits of cloth as he tied the strings behind her back.

"That would upset a lot of babies."

"What?" Then Sutter laughed softly, understanding. "Not these," he murmured, bending his head to bite her nipples lovingly. "The two little scraps of cloth. Makes a man want to run his tongue around the edges and then slide it underneath to sample the goodies."

Mandy laughed but couldn't conceal the shiver that went through her at the thought of Sutter's tongue gliding beneath the bikini top to caress her nipples. He felt her telltale trembling and knew an instant, hot response that surprised him. He had just taken her, he was still inside her, he shouldn't want her so urgently; and he knew it would be all he could do to withdraw from her body long enough to drag her to the tent before he buried himself deeply in her once more.

"You're a witch," Sutter said thickly, closing his eyes in an involuntary reaction to the vital hardening of his body. His hands closed around Mandy's waist, lifting her from him as slowly as he had entered her, then allowing her to slide back down, then lifting her slowly again. "If you sit in my lap for another instant I'm going to…ah, love, help me," he groaned, "you feel too damned good."

Only the sound of voices coming closer up the beach permitted Mandy to move the final fraction of an inch that separated her completely from Sutter. Even so, she had to bite back a tiny cry as his hardening flesh caressed her in the act of leaving her. Blindly she took her bikini bottom from his hand and untangled the strings by feel alone. Her fingers were trembling so that by the time she worked over the second hip tie Sutter had already pulled his suit into place and stood up next to her. The realization that his swimsuit was fighting a losing battle to cover his burgeoning masculinity did nothing to calm Mandy.

Still kneeling, Mandy looked up and saw Sutter watching the small triangle fastened at the apex of her legs. She knew suddenly that he wanted to slide his tongue beneath the edges of the cloth until he found the secret, responsive flesh beneath. The thought of such intimacy sent a rush of fire through her that made her weak.

"Damon," she said, her voice shaking.

"Don't say my name like that," he whispered.

"Like what?"

"Like you're reading my mind…and loving it."

"But I am…loving it."

"God," he groaned, "I'm going to be lucky to get you back to the tent!"

Mandy looked at Sutter's powerful body heightened by shadows, silvered by water and the moon and so very male it made anticipation tingle through her.

"We'd better not meet anyone on the way," she said in a throaty voice.

Sutter followed Mandy's glance to his swimsuit. The contest had definitely been lost. Before he could rearrange himself in a semblance of modesty, Mandy was there. Gently, almost possessively, she eased his erect flesh back within the confines of the wet cloth. When he was covered to her satisfaction, she trailed a fingertip lightly along his hard length.

"There. All done," she murmured.

Torn between humor and raw desire, Sutter lifted Mandy to her feet.

"What you need is a cold shower," he said thickly, biting her neck just hard enough to leave tiny marks.

"Is that what you call it?" she whispered, boldly moving

her hips against him, savoring the hard thrust of his arousal. "I thought that was called a—"

Sutter kissed her hard and deep, shutting off the teasing words. Finally he lifted his head. "You have a saucy mouth, woman."

Mandy's smile slipped. "Isn't that—is that all right?"

For a moment Sutter thought she was still teasing him. Then he saw her stillness and realized that she was uncertain of his response. He caught her face between his hands, tilting it up to his lips.

"I love your saucy mouth," Sutter said, biting Mandy's lips gently. "I love feeling your hands on me, and I love your smile when you see what you do to me. You're the sweetest, sauciest, sexiest woman I've ever had the privilege of touching. And that's just what I want to do right now. Touch you. All over. Everywhere. I feel like a boy with his first woman. Everything I do with you is new and I want to do everything at once and yet I want to do it all slowly, perfectly, because I'm afraid nothing will ever be this good again."

Tears magnified Mandy's eyes for a moment. Smiling, blinking, she clung to Sutter. "Yes," she whispered. "That's how it is for me, too."

For several long, electric moments they simply held each other in warm silence. Then Sutter moved his hips against Mandy once, very slowly, caressing her with his hard, aroused flesh.

"And for your information," he murmured, "that's called a—"

"Sutter!" Mandy said threateningly, covering his mouth with her hand.

His tongue probed between her fingers, tickling and teasing her until she couldn't bear it and lifted her hand so that she could kiss him. The taste and heat and textures of her mouth tempted him into a long, intimate exploration that did nothing to improve the fit of his swimsuit. After too long a time, he lifted his head.

"Rooster," he murmured lovingly against her lips.

For an instant there was silence, then Mandy's silvery laughter surrounded Sutter like another, richer color of moonlight. His smile became a wicked grin and then he was laughing, too, enjoying the combination of passion and humor that was uniquely Mandy, the intelligence that made her as unpredictable and fascinating as the chain lightning pulsing across the far horizon.

Smiling, Sutter took Mandy's hand and walked out of the warm lagoon. After a few steps she lagged behind noticeably. He turned questioningly and realized that her feet were bare. Instants later he lifted her into his arms.

"You should have said something," Sutter whispered, brushing his mouth over Mandy's hair.

"It's not far enough to the tent to matter," she said.

"You've never had a coral cut, have you?"

Mandy shook her head.

"Come to think of it," Sutter said, smiling to himself in anticipation, "I'd better check you over completely. You might have picked up some scrapes in the Fish Pond."

Mandy's body stiffened at the memory of being helpless and then being tossed into the very sea she feared so much.

"I didn't thank you for pulling me out," she said, turning her face into the strong, warm neck that was so close to her lips. "Thank you, D. M. Sutter. That's one more rescue to your credit."

"You would have found your feet without me," Sutter said, kissing her forehead.

Mandy's arms tightened around his neck but she said nothing. She wanted to believe she wouldn't have been too frightened to stand up and save herself from drowning in shallow water, but she wasn't sure. When she had felt the ocean close over her face she had panicked in a way that she hadn't even during the horrible flight to the island.

Win some, lose some, she told herself.

The thought didn't cheer Mandy. Sutter had been quite

right about her emotions. She was very tired of her prison of fears.

"Trees ahead. Hide your face," Sutter warned softly.

Mandy buried her face in Sutter's neck and felt his shoulder muscles bunch as he bent and turned sideways, avoiding the graceful she-oak branches in the grove that surrounded their tent. A flap of canvas trailed over her back as Sutter ducked into the tent and carefully set her on her feet before he released her. It was much darker inside the tent than it had been on the beach.

Soft illumination bloomed suddenly, revealing Sutter bent over the flashlight. He wrapped the cloth one more time around the lens, muting the illumination to a golden glow that suffused everything it touched with riches. After he braced the flashlight in a corner, he shook out his beach towel, threw it over his bed and turned to Mandy.

"Lie down, darling. I want to check your feet."

"My feet?" she asked skeptically, giving him an amused, sideways kind of look.

Sutter smiled in a way that made Mandy's knees weak. "Of course. What else?"

Mandy blushed, feeling suddenly shy. It had been one thing to make love with Sutter in the silver and shadow of a moonlit lagoon. It was quite another to see him in the clear, golden illumination that filled the tent. The thought of her boldness in the lagoon was embarrassing to her now. She was more than happy to sink down on the mattress and turn her flushed face away from the too-revealing light.

Sutter noticed Mandy's sudden shyness but said nothing. As soon as she settled, he picked up her right foot matter-of-factly, brushed off a few particles of shell and crushed coral, touched every bit of suddenly sensitive skin and pronounced her whole. Mandy felt his long, strong, fingers pick up her other foot, hesitate and then probe gently.

"Hurt?" he asked.

"No."

Sutter made an approving sound and resumed checking

her. Mandy's curiosity overcame her embarrassment. Lying on her back, propped half-upright on her elbows, she looked down the length of her body at her foot held in Sutter's large, strong hands. While she watched, he brushed every bit of her foot carefully, almost caressingly. She thought she saw a smile just beneath his calm expression as his finger rubbed tenderly between her toes, removing each particle of shell or coral no matter how small.

"Sutter?"

"Mmm?"

"I thought that a cut from living coral was the only kind you had to worry about."

Absently Sutter nodded, only half-listening, caught up in tracing the high arch of Mandy's foot with his index finger.

She didn't really notice what Sutter had said or not said. She was too fascinated by the picture he made sitting nearly naked at her feet, touching her as though she were made of spun crystal and dreams. In the muted light his eyes were a green so intense it was nearly black. His hair was molten gold, catching and holding the light with every motion of his head. Dense, long eyelashes cast feathery shadows across his tanned skin. His wide, high cheekbones and blunt, masculine jawline fully suited the strong tendons in his neck and the muscular width of his shoulders. The damp, curling hair on his chest was a rich amber color. The dusky, wedge-shaped pelt emphasized the smoothness of Sutter's skin and the supple male strength that was so much a part of him.

"Sutter?"

Mandy's voice was husky, barely a breath in the silence as she watched him with eyes that were as warm and clear as the golden light. There was no shyness in her now, only a very female appreciation of the man who was cherishing her with his hands.

"Mmm?"

"There isn't any living coral on the beach, and probably none between the tide lines, as well."

"Probably," he agreed.

Mandy's breath caught as Sutter kissed the most sensitive area of her arch with unerring accuracy. Involuntarily her toes curled. Sutter smiled and touched her arch with the tip of his tongue, drawing a small sound from her lips.

"Sutter?"

"Mmm," he said, biting Mandy's sensitive skin very carefully, feeling her foot flex in helpless response, "I'm beginning to think the foot fetishists have a point."

Smiling, feeling laughter and desire shimmering through her body, Mandy watched light and shadow flow over Sutter as he caressed her foot.

"Of course," he murmured, circling her slender ankle with one hand, "ankle fetishists aren't all crazy, either."

Strong teeth closed just above Mandy's heel, making her gasp at the unexpected sensations rushing up her leg. Sutter kissed the tiny indentations his teeth had left, caressed her with his tongue and fingertips and moved farther up her leg.

"Have you ever heard of a calf fetishist?" Sutter asked, kneading the resilient muscle in question with his strong hands.

"No," admitted Mandy, sighing with pleasure, "but don't let that stop you."

He smiled and bent lower, rubbing his cheek against her calf. Involuntarily she closed her eyes, caught by the sensuous feel of his cheek's sandpaper masculinity against her soft skin. When the tip of his tongue found and traced the sensitive nerve that went down her shin, she drew in her breath with a soft, rushing sound. When he retraced the passage with his teeth, she felt as though she were coming unraveled.

"Knees…" Sutter began in a husky voice.

"Are ticklish!" Mandy gasped.

"Sensitive," he amended, caressing her with a touch firm enough not to tickle. "Very sensitive," he added, "especially here."

A soft, ragged sound was Mandy's only answer. Until that moment she hadn't guessed that the back of her knee had so many nerve endings, and that they were connected to so many interesting places on her body.

"But," Sutter continued in his deep voice, "I've never known of a knee fetishist, have you?"

Mandy tried to answer, felt the sultry heat of Sutter's tongue behind her other knee and flexed her leg in sensual response.

"Probably no man is really into knees," Sutter said, running the back of his fingers over the soft flesh he had just kissed, "because by the time a man gets up to a woman's knees, he's so close to some truly beguiling territory that he can't help skimping the knees and going on to higher things. Such as…"

Mandy half closed her eyes and shivered visibly as Sutter trailed his fingertips up her inner thighs. Her quickening breaths were a soft, almost secret sound in the tent's intimate silence. Hearing the sensual catches and quivers in her breathing with each of his caresses made Sutter want to shout in masculine triumph and at the same time to cherish Mandy with utmost tenderness. Watching his touch take her from blushing shyness to uninhibited lover aroused him fiercely. Slowly he bent his head and kissed the warm skin his fingertips had been stroking.

Mandy's eyelids closed as she simultaneously felt the heat of Sutter's mouth on the inside of one thigh and the silky brush of his hair against the other. He rubbed his cheek over the inside of each thigh, letting her feel the soft, exciting rasp of beard stubble, then soothed her with his tongue, teased with his teeth, feasted on her warmth while her soft cries lapped around him like the rising, moon-drawn sea.

After a time Sutter's teeth closed on Mandy not quite gently and his mouth sucked hard on her tender flesh for an instant; yet the cry that was torn from her lips came from a lightning stroke of pleasure rather than from pain. He turned his head and gave another measured, fierce caress to her other thigh, smiling as he heard her pleasure and felt it in the heat of her skin. He smoothed his hands repeatedly over her slender, rounded thighs from inner knee to the sea-damp warmth of the bikini between her legs and back again.

"Yes," Sutter murmured, looking at the long, shapely legs and the alluring shadow between, stroking Mandy's thighs with a subtle pressure that spread them farther apart. "It's easy to understand why a man would become a thigh fetishist. Especially with you. You have such lovely legs, darling. But they're only the beginning...."

With a sense of spinning anticipation, Mandy waited to feel Sutter's gentle hands caressing the softness that ached for his touch. When she felt nothing more between her legs than the tropic warmth of the air in the tent, she opened her eyes slowly. Sutter was watching her, sharing her anticipation, smiling in a way that made sensual lightning shimmer in the pit of her stomach.

"Sutter?" she whispered.

"Read my mind, golden eyes," he said huskily, bending down to her.

Sutter's tongue probed teasingly beneath the tie on one hip, then traced the edge of the damp cloth across the top of the triangle that lay between her legs. At the same time his hands caressed her legs, holding her captive as though he were afraid that her shyness would suddenly return.

Shyness was the last thing in Mandy's mind. After the first glittering instant she was lost. Every hot, wet glide of his tongue over her skin, the hard edges of his teeth biting through cloth, his breath mingling with her own warmth, everything about the moment combined to hold her in delicious captivity, enthralled by a slow, heated sensuality that dissolved her bones, leaving her wholly at the mercy of the man who so clearly was enjoying her.

With a final, loving rake of his teeth over cloth, Sutter became impatient with even the bikini's minimal restrictions. Long fingers unfastened both bows and slowly peeled the damp cloth away from her, leaving nothing between Mandy and himself but the hot rush of his breath as he bent down to her once more. The first touch of his tongue surprised a ragged cry from Mandy's lips, a cry that soon fragmented into whimpers as he pursued the sweet secrets he had uncovered, his big hands holding her for his slow, sultry explorations. When he lovingly teased the sensitive nub he had aroused, her back arched helplessly. Heat flushed through her suddenly, almost frighteningly.

"Damon."

His answer was the exquisite restraint of his teeth holding Mandy captive for the kind of loving he had never given and she had never imagined. She shivered repeatedly, echoing the lightning strokes of pleasure stabbing through her, each stroke hotter and brighter, driving her higher, heat and pleasure so intense she would have screamed if Sutter's elemental male sensuality hadn't taken from her even the ability to breathe. Something burst deep inside her, dragging a hoarse cry from her throat in the instant before ecstasy convulsed her, waves of molten pleasure sleeting through her with each of his hot, consuming caresses until she could take no more.

Reluctantly Sutter lifted his head slightly, releasing Mandy's violently sensitive flesh. He whispered soft, loving words as he brushed his cheek against the musky triangle of her hair, trembling even as she did in the aftermath of her sensual storm, whispering her name, holding her hips between his strong hands, nuzzling her incredibly delicate flesh, giving her slow, gentle caresses until he felt tension rising in her again.

Smiling, shuddering with the leashed wildness of his own body, Sutter bent to Mandy once more, stroking her, loving her with a gentle intensity that drew sweet shivers from her. With each of his sultry caresses her breathing and heartbeat quickened, sending heat streaming out from the pit of her stomach once more, giving her skin the sheen and taste of passion. His hands flexed until his fingertips sank into her thighs, holding her utterly captive. He felt her fingers thrusting into his hair, her nails flexing against his scalp as she shivered within his loving grasp.

The thought of thrusting himself into the center of Mandy's gathering storm dragged a thick groan from Sutter. He was on fire for her, hard and thick to the point of agony, needing her until it was tearing him apart; but he didn't want to take her just yet. The consuming sensuality he had discovered within her and himself was too new, too hot, too elemental for him to bring to an end. There had been no woman for him like Mandy, and he sensed at some deep level of his mind that there never would be one like her for him again. Whatever he didn't know or do or feel or be with her right now might never happen for him at all.

Mandy moaned as she felt the shivering forerunners of intense consummation surge through her again and again, drawn by Sutter's exquisite caresses. She called his name in a broken sigh and was answered by the hot perfection of his mouth and the sweet power of his hands holding her helpless. A wave of pleasure ripped through her, followed by another and then another, matching the primal masculine sensuality of the lover who was bringing her closer and closer to the kind of passionate discovery she wasn't sure she could survive.

"Stop," Mandy cried finally, her voice hoarse, low, shattered. "It's too much…I can't bear any more!"

"Not even this?" Sutter murmured, caressing the velvet bud of her passion.

Her answer was a tiny, ecstatic convulsion that stripped away his restraint. With a thick cry he knelt between her legs and fitted himself to her, feeling the hot, slick perfection of her cling to him as he sank deeply into her. He held himself utterly still, every muscle in his body rigid with restraint as he absorbed the wild shivering of her body, heard the breathless cries of her ecstasy, drank the sensations of her climax into himself, feeding on her satin fire.

And then, when the last of her cries faded, he began to move within her.

Mandy's eyes opened, dazed, golden. Disbelief and searing pleasure exploded through her violently sensitized body.

The sweet friction of Sutter within her brought with it a ravishing heat that grew greater with every motion of the man who filled her so completely, so perfectly.

Sutter's eyes were a blaze of green, watching her as he moved, his body advancing and retreating in ancient, always new rhythms. Looking at him, utterly lost to him, she moaned and convulsed softly around him with each measured penetration, each slow withdrawal, each motion a new revelation as her body learned that rapture had no beginning and no end, existing beyond place, beyond time. She was in the fiery, luminous center of ecstasy and it was in her very core, and there was nothing left of reality but the man whose body had become part of her own.

"Damon?" she gasped, frightened.

"Love me, Mandy," he said hoarsely, bending down to join their mouths as deeply as he had joined their bodies. *"Love me."*

Mandy tasted herself and the sea and Sutter all at once, felt him driving into her even as her hips strained upward to claim him, to hold him fiercely inside her, all of him. He arched into her again and again, each time harder, deeper, and he felt the sweet violence take her, racking her with pleasure at each powerful stroke of his body until she wept and called out his name with every broken breath. Suddenly she gave a raw cry and went rigid, transfixed by unbearable pleasure. Her satin convulsions ripped the world away from Sutter. He knew nothing but the hot, intense pulses of completion pouring endlessly from him until he could bear no more…and then he tasted her tears and his own while chain lightning pulsed between their joined bodies once again, a rapture so fierce he had no choice but to give himself to it and to the woman who had become part of him in the free-fall through fiery oblivion.

Chapter 11

Morning had filled the tent with a soundless tide of light, illuminating every shadowed corner. Sutter looked across the tent at Mandy's relaxed, sleeping body concealed by the sheet he had pulled over her a few minutes before to prevent himself from stroking her into wakefulness and passion once again. With a silent, searing curse he looked away from her and pulled on his clammy swimsuit. He had been awake for half an hour, cursing Anthea's meddling and his own baffling lack of self-control, wishing that he could change what he had done, knowing that he couldn't, wondering how he would prevent himself from making the same mistake all over again as long as Mandy was within reach.

Sutter knew that no decent man would have taken advantage of a frightened woman who had turned to him for help, and that knowledge sent self-contempt twisting within him. But nothing was as painful as the visceral certainty that he would do it all again if he were offered the least excuse. In the bleak light of day he knew he would have killed or died to be inside her once again. She was a sweet, honeyed fire and he was a man who had discovered yesterday that he had lived his life in darkness and bitter cold.

He didn't know how long he would feel as he did about Mandy; he only knew that while he felt this way he must have her. Yet she wasn't the type of woman who slept with a man casually. He had known that before he touched her, yet he had seduced her anyway. Being the kind of woman she was, she would have to call what had happened between them last night "love," and then he would feel an even more ruthless predator than he already did.

Mandy stirred, seeking the powerful body of the man who had held her through the long night, coming to her for the last time just before dawn set the sky ablaze. Her moving hand met only emptiness. There was no one next to her on the single mattress.

"Love?" she asked sleepily. "Where are you?"

Sutter closed his eyes against the pain of the first word she spoke.

"Mandy," he said, "we've got to talk."

She woke up instantly. Sutter's voice was too low, too tight, almost harsh. It belonged to a different man than the one who had taught her the torrid, consuming, unspeakably beautiful ecstasy a man and a woman could share with each other. There was no teasing lilt in Sutter's tone that morning, no husky hunger, no hoarse delight, nothing but...anger?

Mandy's eyes focused on Sutter. His mouth was tight, flat, and his eyes were opaque. He looked even more angry than he sounded.

"Do you always wake up in a good mood," she asked, "or is this a special effort on my behalf?"

Sutter shot Mandy a sideways glance out of bleak green eyes as he kicked into his sandals.

"Will coffee improve your mood?" she continued.

"Mandy—" he began grimly, wanting to get it over with.

"I thought so," she interrupted, sighing. "Waking up vicious is genetic, you know."

"Like stupidity?" he retorted. "Like doing my part and

then some when it comes to paving the road to hell with good intentions?''

Mandy closed her eyes, knowing she wasn't going to like what would happen next, and knowing that didn't matter; it would happen, willy-nilly, whether her eyes were closed or wide open. Her long lashes lifted as she rolled onto her side to confront Sutter, the man she had stupidly fallen in love with.

The man who clearly wasn't thrilled to have become her lover.

''I can't vouch for my intentions,'' Mandy said neutrally, ''but when it comes to sheer stupidity, I can hold up my end of any paving operation.''

As Sutter looked into Mandy's luminous golden eyes he felt a shaft of regret and something much stronger, much deeper, raw need twisting through his guts. The realization that he wanted her again both baffled and angered him. He shouldn't want a woman at all. Not after last night. He had barely been able to drag himself out of bed a few minutes ago. Yet when he looked at Mandy's slender, bare shoulders and the black bikini bottom thrown carelessly onto the floor of the tent, he felt passion's white-hot claws raking his loins into readiness, torrents of blood pouring through him, hardening him in a single wild rush.

''I came to Lady Elliot Island to go scuba diving, not to seduce a frightened innocent,'' Sutter said harshly, as much to himself as to Mandy.

''Congratulations. You've achieved the first and avoided the second.''

''Mandy—''

''So relax,'' she continued, ignoring Sutter's attempt to speak. ''Divorcées are hardly classified among the world's innocents, and the fact that my husband died before I could divorce him is a mere technicality.''

Sutter's head snapped up. He hadn't known that Mandy's husband was dead. He wanted to say something, to ask questions, to find out more about the woman who destroyed his steel self-control with such baffling ease. But she was talking quickly, not allowing him to speak, as though she were afraid of what he would say.

"As for diving, have at it," Mandy continued. "I don't expect you to drop everything and build shell castles on the beach with me just because we're lovers. I can amuse myself quite nicely during the day. I've been doing it for years."

"So have I. At night, as well as during the day."

Mandy flinched, telling Sutter of her vulnerability. He swore explosively, knowing he was making a hash of what should have been a simple, adult explanation of what had happened last night and why it couldn't happen again.

"Look, Mandy, I'm sorry about last night. I only meant to calm you down and give you a little comfort after Ray scared you, but once I started touching you…" Sutter made an oddly helpless gesture with one big hand. "It's my fault. I lost control, I took advantage of you, and I feel guilty as hell about it. It never should have happened. It won't happen again."

Mandy's mouth drew into a thin line as she understood what Sutter was saying: he had made love to her out of pity not desire, and now he regretted it.

"Save your guilt for one of your many worthy causes," she said in a voice that was too calm. "We aren't the first adults in creation to have a one-night stand and we won't be the last."

"That wasn't a one-night stand and you know it!"

"You're so right," she retorted. "We did it every way *but* standing."

Even as Mandy spoke she was swamped beneath a flood of sensual memories—Sutter's eyes a passionate green blaze, his hands and mouth and body touching her exquisitely, drawing from her depths an untamed sensuality she had never imagined to be part of her, showing her an ecstasy whose sweet aftershocks still echoed through her memories.

With memories came the realization that no matter why Sutter had made love to her, he had given far more than he had taken. He deserved better from her than the cutting edge of her dismay that he had found less to enjoy than she had.

After a moment Mandy found the strength to turn back toward Sutter. Her barb had indeed gone into its target; the bleak lines on Sutter's face were deeper and his mouth had flattened as though he were in pain. He hissed a curse between his clenched teeth when he met her eyes.

"Sorry," Mandy said, keeping her voice neutral as she lay back and closed her eyes. "I guess I'm not at my best in the morning, either. In any case, there's not a damn thing for you to feel guilty about. Before last night I often wondered what all the hoopla between the sexes was about. Now I know. So accept my profound gratitude, forget your guilt and go diving with a squeaky-clean conscience."

For a long moment Sutter stared at Mandy, silently willing her to explain what she meant; but she neither spoke nor opened her eyes. She looked tired, fragile, far too tightly strung. Guilt coiled coldly in his stomach. He should never have touched her. She had needed reassurance last night, not sex.

We did it every way but standing.

Sutter winced as Mandy's words echoed painfully in his mind. "Please don't think less of yourself," he said, his voice gentling. "What happened was my fault, not yours. You were too frightened to act rationally. I wasn't."

"Hold it. Let me get this straight," Mandy said, trying to curb her tongue and her rising anger at the same time. She doubted that she was being successful. The knowledge that her night of love had been Sutter's night of pity was simply too bitter to wholly conceal or absorb. "Are you saying that last night I was in the same category as one of the children you're saving the world for?"

"If you had been a child, last night never would have gone beyond comfort," Sutter said keeping his voice calm with an effort.

"Comfort," Mandy repeated bleakly. "Ah, Sutter, what

a diplomat you've become. The word you're too polite to say is pity.''

"That's not what I meant and you know it," he retorted, feeling his uncertain grip on his temper slipping away.

"Wrong. It was precisely what you meant."

Sutter closed his eyes, unable to watch Mandy's unhappiness any longer, knowing that his own lack of control had caused it. "What I meant was simply that I knew you weren't a woman for casual affairs but I took you anyway. My fault, not yours. I knew what I was doing. You didn't."

Mandy flinched again. "Sorry my technique wasn't up to yours."

"Damn it!" exploded Sutter. "Stop taking my words and twisting them! All I'm trying to say is that I don't think any less of you for what happened last night and you shouldn't think any less of yourself, either!"

"Save your pity for the children of the world. They need it. All I need is a few hours of sleep."

"Mandy—"

She interrupted without hesitation. "You'd better hurry, Sutter, or you'll miss the dive boat."

"Mandy, listen to me. It wasn't your—"

"No! You listen to me, D. M. Sutter," she said, slicing across his words as she came up on one elbow to confront him, ignoring the sheet that slid off her bare breasts. "I don't want your pity. I had one hell of a good time last night. I'm sorry you didn't, but when it comes to sex, one out of two ain't bad. It's sure better than my husband and I ever managed!"

"What the hell are you talking about?"

"Read my lips. You have nothing to feel guilty about. Not…one…thing."

"Oh, sure," Sutter agreed caustically, his fists clenched on his lean hips. "I carry a hysterical woman off into the night and seduce her repeatedly, but I have nothing to feel guilty about the next morning when she wants to talk about love and I know there's not a damn thing to talk about but white-hot sex!''

A moment of quivering silence was followed by another and then another.

Finally Mandy spoke very softly. ''There's a whole ocean waiting out there for you, Sutter. Go soak your white-hot rooster in it.''

It was several hours before Mandy got out of bed. Sutter hadn't returned. Nor had she expected him to. She pulled on a white bikini and left the tent. Someone had found her sandals and placed them neatly next to the path. She kicked into them and went to the shower.

By the time she emerged she felt more in control of herself. At least she wasn't blushing every time she saw the faint bruises on her thighs and remembered how she had gotten the loving marks. Now if she could just stop her breath from unraveling and her bones from going soft every time images from last night surfaced in her memory, she might be able to get through today. As for tonight...

One thing at a time. Right now it's food. Then it's the Fish Pond. Then it's...

One thing at a time.

Mandy kept lecturing herself because it was preferable to having her mind revolve around what had happened the previous night. Every time she thought of what it had been like to be Sutter's lover she would stumble or drop something or stand as still as a coral lump in the lagoon. The only thing that saved her from embarrassing herself was the fact that nearly everyone else was out diving on the reef, trying to beat the storm that was surely brewing within the towering clouds.

With a determined set to her mouth, Mandy walked up to the Fish Pond. Crusts of bread stuck out every which way from her clenched fingers. The fish, which had been on short rations since the Townehome kids had left, came to meet her in a glittering wave. Deliberately she walked into the water

up to her knees before she knelt down and thrust her fists
beneath the surface of the warm lagoon.

"All right, you little beggars. Come and get it."

Mandy's voice was strained almost to breaking and her
heart was hammering much too hard, shaking her, adrenaline
pouring through her in a tidal wave of irrational fright. The
warm, crystalline water just barely reached her hips. She
knew that all she had to do was stand up and the water would
only reach to her knees once more. She was as safe as though
she were standing on the beach.

And that was where she desperately wanted to be.

But first you feed the fish, Mandy told herself, clenching
her teeth until her jaw ached. *What are you afraid of, anyway? You were in deeper than this with Sutter last night and
you barely noticed. Hell, you were in way over your head
with Sutter and fear was the last thing that crossed your tiny
little mind.*

Little fish darted and feinted, but few came to eat from
Mandy's hands. She might have fooled herself about the
depth of the water by kneeling, but the fish knew that the
lagoon where Mandy waited was far too shallow to protect
them from feathered predators. When Mandy finally admitted to herself what was holding back the fish, she came to
her feet and walked forward until the water slid up her thighs
to her hips and then beyond, not stopping until she was
waist-deep in the lagoon's liquid embrace.

For the first few minutes her hands were so tightly
clenched that no bread oozed out between her fingers. Fish
swept around her in flashing clouds, secure in the deeper
water and driven wild by the scent of withheld food. When
her initial burst of fear finally ebbed, Mandy drew a slow,
ragged breath and forced her fingers to relax. She was rewarded by a swirling, nibbling mass of reef fish skimming
over her fingers. Within moments her hands were empty of
all but the tactile memory of tiny mouths vacuuming her
palms.

Watching intently, Mandy stood motionless while the

clouds of fish thinned into individual bodies shining in shades of silver and unexpected jeweled flashes of color. As the fish sorted themselves into species and went about their usual business in the Fish Pond's small world, Mandy realized that, while she might not be able to go out and over the edge of the reef, she could see at least some of its life-forms in a natural habitat.

Eagerly Mandy watched the various fish. She knew from past study that none of their motions was random; each movement was in some way related to fish survival, whether it be eating, hiding, courting or defending a particular patch of coral as their very own. The skimming of wind over the surface of the lagoon hampered her observations by ruffling the water's surface, making it opaque to a land dweller's eyes. With a sudden stab of yearning Mandy remembered what it had been like to swim beneath the sea, her vision enhanced by a watertight mask. She had been in ocean water from Alaska to Scammon Lagoon in Mexico, but never had she gone diving in anything as clear as the sea surrounding Lady Elliot Island. If she had been wearing a mask, the water would have inhibited her sight barely more than air.

Brilliant observation, Dr. Samantha Blythe-Cameron, she congratulated herself, underlining her sarcasm by using the name she had signed on her academic papers, *but just how do you propose getting your face into the drink long enough to enjoy all that rare marine visibility?*

Suddenly Mandy had an idea of how she might see beneath the surface without getting wet. She was still congratulating herself on the idea's brilliance when she returned from the cafeteria carrying two colorless water glasses. At first she simply waded in thigh-deep and poked the bottom of the glasses into the lagoon. Instantly a clear circle of vision appeared in the wind-ruffled water. All she had to do was stand around until something interesting swam into the narrow circle of focus formed by the bottom of the glass.

The fish weren't feeling cooperative. Gingerly Mandy inched around the shallow end of the Fish Pond, holding the glasses partially submerged, trying to look through the clear circles without bending down or getting her face any closer to the lagoon's liquid surface. She caught just enough tantalizing glimpses of marine life to keep her trying to see more. As the tide dropped she waded out farther, until finally she was waist-deep once more, utterly enthralled by her small windows into the warm world of the lagoon.

Finally voices seeped into Mandy's awareness, the calls and laughter of the first wave of divers returning from the outer reef. She knew Sutter wouldn't be with them. He would still be out in the shimmering blue world of the sea…weightless, soaring, watched by fish that were living jewels.

Mandy would have given her soul to be with him, free and unafraid, no longer the object of unwanted masculine pity.

Slowly she turned and waded ashore, reluctant to end her contact with even the brief flashes she had seen of the life beneath the warm sea. But she hadn't eaten breakfast, and unless she wanted to face Sutter over lunch she had to eat with the divers who had just returned. So she traded her two wet glasses for a dry one at the cafeteria, ate hurriedly and then went to the dive shed before her courage deserted her.

Ray was there refilling tanks with Tommy's help. Both men looked up at the same instant.

"G'day, luv," Ray said. "Are you…is everything all right?"

"Fine," Mandy said quickly.

"I'm sorry as bloody—" began Tommy.

"It wasn't your fault," she said, cutting across Tommy's unwanted apology. "I should have told everyone right away that I have a problem with water. I was just too ashamed."

"No reason to be," Ray said matter-of-factly. "Some people just don't like water or heights or dark nights. Hold it steady, Tommy, or we'll be squirting air all over the bleeding island."

Mandy watched until the two men finished with the tank before she said, "Ray?"

He looked up.

"Is there an extra snorkeling mask around?" she asked.

"Sure thing, luv, but why don't you just take your own?"

Mandy blinked. "Mine?"

"It's got your name on it, just like those two tanks, that wet suit, the fins, all that lot," he said, pointing toward a corner of the dive shed. "Came to Lady on your ticket."

"Oh." Mandy looked at the new, beautifully made diving gear, mentally added up the cost and wondered how she would ever repay Anthea. "Well, in that case, I'll take the mask."

Ray handed it to her with a curious sidelong look but said nothing.

"Thanks," she muttered.

Before either man could ask what a woman who was terrified of water was going to do with a diving mask, Mandy had turned and quickly walked away, her fingers tightly wrapped around the familiar shape and texture of a diving mask with snorkel attached. She made a brief detour at the bread bowl just outside the cafeteria, but she didn't hang around to listen to the divers talk about angelfish and sharks and anemones as big as soccer balls. She wouldn't be seeing anything that spectacular where she was going.

But she would put her face in the water if it was the last thing she did on earth.

"Thanks, Ray," Sutter said, shrugging off the weight of the scuba tank and passing it over to the other diver. "Sure you have time?"

"No worries, mate. I'm here to keep the paying blokes happy," Ray said, grinning as he took the tank and set it up to be refilled for an afternoon dive. "Besides, it's a pat on the back."

"What is?"

"Letting me take care of your equipment."

Sutter paused, then grinned in return. He usually didn't trust other people enough to let them take care of all those little items on which his own life could depend during a dive. But Ray had proven to be as meticulous as Sutter himself.

"And here I thought I was just getting lazy in my old age," Sutter said.

"Not you, mate. You're like one of those deep-water sharks. No frills, no noise, no racing about, just muscle and confidence." Ray hesitated. "Your Sheila was in just a bit ago. Wanted her mask. You taking her snorkeling?"

Sutter's eyes narrowed. He had spent most of the time since waking trying to keep Mandy out of his mind. He hadn't been successful. "Did she say I was?"

"No."

"Did she take her fins?"

Ray shook his head.

The breeze freshened suddenly, rippling through the low vegetation surrounding the dive shed and landing field.

"Squall line coming through," Ray said, breathing in, tasting the difference in the air as he scanned the changes in the sky. "Be raining soon."

"Wind?"

"Too right," Ray said, sighing. "Maybe we can walk out on the reef again and dive off the wall. Depends on the swell."

"Her mask, huh? Anything else?" Sutter asked, unable to keep his mind off Mandy.

"Just a smile and a white bikini."

Involuntarily Sutter's expression changed as he thought of Mandy's sweet body and of how little of that sweetness would be covered by a bikini.

Ray saw Sutter's annoyance and smiled. "No worries, mate. There's more cover in her bikini than in most around here."

Sutter grunted and walked off toward the cafeteria. He had hoped a morning of particularly demanding diving would defuse the sexual tension that had had him in its grip since his first look at Mandy after dawn. Diving, however, hadn't done the job. Although his body definitely knew that it had spent a physical morning—and an even more physical night—there was no decline in his baffling, prowling sexuality.

A swift look down the beach told Sutter that Mandy was wading in the Fish Pond, apparently oblivious to the comings and goings of the people on the beach. She was wearing the big mask pushed up on her forehead in the manner of a diver who had just come from the water, yet it was obvious that her hair and upper body were dry.

Sutter stood and watched for a few moments, screened by the she-oaks that grew up to the edge of the beach. Mandy was doing nothing but standing up to her hips in the lagoon, stirring her hands through the warm water, stroking it as though it were a lover. The thought of having her fingers stroking him in the same way sent sudden, white-hot desire spearing through Sutter, a need so fierce that it almost drove him to his knees. He closed his eyes against the sight of Mandy's long, graceful back, her golden-brown skin curving in to a slender waist and her high breasts filling the bikini top as they had once filled his hands.

But closing his eyes didn't banish Mandy from Sutter's mind. Memories of the night before condensed, Mandy's body glistening with moonlight and sensual heat, her hips sinuous, graceful, moving in slow, sexy rhythms until tiny cries rippled from her lips, cries that matched the rippling heat deep within her body.

Abruptly Sutter turned away from the beach, determined to put Mandy out of his mind. After a shower, a huge lunch and a desultory beer, he turned down an offer of cards. He was too restless to put up with penny-ante poker. A single look at the combers booming over the reef even at low tide told him that diving was out of the question. He turned his back on the beach leading to the Fish Pond, choosing instead the path that went in the opposite direction, skirting the noisy bird colony.

In the hot, sultry afternoon, the sky was a turmoil of wind-shredded clouds. The sea seethed and churned in shades of stormy gray.

Before Sutter was halfway around the island, rain began to fall. The drops were as warm as the air, as hot as his body. They gathered in his hair and ran down his cheeks like tears. He barely noticed. He simply walked on until he rounded the far end of the island to complete his circuit, striding along the section where waves were held at bay by the inner reef. A few hundred yards farther up the beach brought him to the sloping limestone shelf where he had first comforted, then wanted and finally seduced Mandy. He stood and looked at the small ribbons of sand caught in limestone troughs and fought not to remember how it had been to push into Mandy's tight satin depths, to feel her clench in pleasure around him.

With a wild curse Sutter turned away from the rain-washed stone and strode up the beach. There was no one around to distract or disturb him. The weather had driven everyone into tents or cabins or to the card games and conversations in the tiny bar. Sutter walked on, oblivious to the wind and sheets of rain, until he suddenly realized that he wasn't alone on the beach. Mandy had stayed in the Fish Pond, sitting so still that he hadn't noticed her until he was within ten yards.

Without stopping to think, Sutter faded back into the she-oaks that fringed the beach. Motionless he watched while Mandy stared at the water that was barely up to her rib cage even though she was sitting down. The diving mask had been pulled into place and the attached snorkel was held between her lips as though she were going to push off and float facedown in the rain-swept lagoon. But she didn't move.

At first Sutter couldn't figure out what Mandy was doing. She would bend forward a fraction of an inch at a time, then jerk back and sit utterly still for several minutes. Then she would begin leaning forward again, slowly, slowly, slowly, only to jerk upright once more and sit motionless for a time.

After watching the sequence several times Sutter suddenly understood that Mandy was trying to force herself to put her face in the water. Chills roughened his skin at the realization. He had known that Mandy was afraid of water. He had heard the panic in her scream, seen it in her face, felt it in her thrashing body when he had pulled her from the Fish Pond; but he hadn't truly understood just how great her fear was until this moment. She approached the surface of the lagoon as though it were molten metal that would burn her to the bone…or a prison where she would be chained, beaten, tortured. The certainty of her own destruction was written in every trembling line of her body.

Yet Mandy leaned closer to the water's surface anyway, closer and then closer still—visibly, physically torn between the opposite demands of her fear and her determination to overcome that fear.

Why? Why is she so afraid? Why is she so determined? And where in God's name does someone who is afraid of so many things get the courage to confront fear?

There were no answers to Sutter's silent, almost anguished questions. There was nothing but rain pouring down in warm sheets, Mandy bending closer, closer, closer to the water while minutes sped by and he held his breath and prayed that this time she would make it…this time…this time, *please, God, let it be this time, let her torment end!*

Mandy jerked back from the water.

Sutter's breath hissed out through gritted teeth. His hands ached from being clenched into hard fists. His whole body was drawn with a tension almost equal to Mandy's as she tilted her head toward the rain-churned sea and began to lean forward once more.

Sutter was halfway to Mandy before he realized what he intended to do: he was going to drag her out of the water, ending her torment.

She's not in any danger and you know it. So why inter-fere? What's wrong with you? he asked himself savagely.

The answer was as simple as it was baffling.

I can't bear to watch her pain.

So don't watch.

I can't bear that, either.

In the end Sutter remained where he was, fighting the nearly overwhelming need to end Mandy's self-imposed ordeal. Yet, as much as he wanted it to end, he couldn't help admiring the sheer grit Mandy displayed each time she forced herself to begin all over again.

Suddenly Mandy bent at the waist and fairly rushed the water, sending it splashing over her face and hair. Instantly she yanked herself upright again. Sutter felt waves of triumph and relief so great they made him light-headed. Finally it was over. She had done it. Now she could get up and get out of the water she so clearly hated and feared. Now he wouldn't have to watch, feeling savage and helpless because there was nothing he could do to affect the outcome of Mandy's ordeal, nothing he could do to take away pain or to give her strength or comfort. He was helpless. But no longer. It was over. Now he could take a deep breath and…

Slowly, Mandy began to bend toward the water once more.

"Mandy," Sutter whispered, appalled, wanting to hold her, to cherish her, to restrain her, to do anything but stand helplessly on the beach watching her. "Don't, love. Don't."

Sutter was speaking far too softly for Mandy to hear him above the rain. Not that it made any difference. He knew she would have ignored him just as he had once ignored all the well-meant advice never to go back into the primitive country whose government had chained and then beaten him, teaching him the meaning of helplessness and fear. But he had gone back because he couldn't give in to fear and still respect himself.

It was the same choice Mandy faced, and his heart turned over for what she was going through.

Slowly Sutter withdrew to the cover of the she-oaks once more. From there he watched Mandy try to push back her dripping hair from her face but her hands were shaking too hard. She flipped her head, slinging her hair away from her face. Ten minutes and three tries later, she was able to bring her face into contact once again with the water's warm surface. And once again, she jerked back.

Sutter waited and prayed. When Mandy began bending slowly forward once more, it took all his self-discipline not to walk into the lagoon and drag her back to land. He lost track of time while he stood and watched, hands clenched, guts knotted, his face grim, sharing her ordeal in the only way that he could. When she finally held her face in the water for three seconds before she jerked upright again, Sutter wondered if she felt half the elation he did.

Without warning Mandy stood up and pushed back her mask with the easy motion of someone who had used diving gear countless times. Sutter remembered that it had been the same when she had flipped back her wet hair—the gesture spoke of long familiarity with water. But that didn't make sense. Someone who was as terrified of water as Mandy was wouldn't be a swimmer, much less a diver.

Mandy stepped out of the lagoon and removed her mask with a single quick movement of her hand. Again, the ease and economy of the motion betrayed expertise with diving gear. Most novices grappled with the awkward mask-and-snorkel combination, tangling their fingers and their hair, grimacing and struggling to master the stubborn equipment without ripping out every hair on their head.

Where did Mandy learn to use the equipment?

And then Sutter realized that wasn't the important question.

What taught her to fear the water she once must have loved?

There was no answer in the falling rain, none in the warm lagoon, none in the drenched she-oaks screening Sutter from the beach. Yet Sutter knew he must have an answer. He needed it with an urgency that transcended the driving sexual heat Mandy called from his body.

Determination in every hard line of his body, Sutter left the she-oaks and went to find Mandy. Behind him, delicate foliage shivered quietly, caressed by the warm rain.

Chapter 12

"G'day, luv. Dry off while I get you a beer," Ray said, tossing a towel toward Mandy.

"Thanks."

Mandy caught the towel one-handed and blotted up the worst of the rain. The small bar area was steamy, filled to overflowing with divers who, being unable to dive, were doing the next best thing—talking about diving. When she looked up from drying herself Tommy caught her eye, hooked his foot under Ray's empty chair and dragged it closer to the ragged circle surrounding his table.

"Here you go, luv," Tommy said.

"What about Ray?"

"Ray who?"

After a brief hesitation Mandy smiled and took the chair. She was too wrung out from her hours in the Fish Pond to refuse the chance to sit on something dry. Ray didn't object to the loss of his chair. He simply snagged a stool from behind the bar, grabbed a beer so cold that the can sweated icy drops, and put the stool next to Mandy.

"Wrap your throat around this," he said, handing her the beer.

With a sigh she took a swallow of the mellow, lively beer and smoothed the cold can over her forehead and cheeks. The diving mask she had slung over her wrist banged against the table when she took another drink. Ray removed the mask and set it on the bar.

"Go on, Tommy," Ray said, opening his own beer, "tell us about the hammerhead as big as a house trailer that followed you last summer."

Tommy finished the shark story, which had been interrupted by Mandy's entrance. She listened, smiling in appreciation and gentle disbelief, and drank the incredibly refreshing beer. Very quickly the contents of the can disappeared. Ray held up his hand. The girl who was tending bar leaned over the counter and slapped another Fosters into Ray's palm. He opened the can and substituted it for the empty one in Mandy's hand. She gave him a startled look, received a beguiling smile and decided that one more delicious Australian beer wouldn't hurt.

Sipping at the heady, frothy brew, Mandy listened while each diver in turn around the table volunteered a story about the biggest chunk of marine life he had ever encountered. For one man it had been a manta ray as big as the bar. For another it had been a sixteen-foot shark. By the time it was Mandy's turn, her second beer was fizzing softly through her blood and a third was in her hand. She spoke without stopping to think, wanting only to share a special moment in diving with the people who would most appreciate it—other divers.

"I once swam with the gray whales in Scammon Lagoon, on the west coast of Baja California," Mandy said softly, remembering the eerie, enchanted experience. "The visibility was thirty, maybe forty feet. Whales would just kind of condense out of the sea at the edge of your vision, blue on blue, huge shadows moving with the kind of massive grace that made you think of God."

"Grays? Aren't they the ones that migrate from Alaska to Mexico and back each year?" Tommy asked.

Mandy nodded.

"Tell us about it, luv," Ray said as other divers added their encouragement. "None of us blokes have ever been close to a whale."

She took another swallow of beer, then continued talking, encouraged by the enthusiasm of the men and relaxed by the two beers she had drunk.

"One female was especially curious," Mandy said. "She condensed out of the blue and came toward me, and just kept getting bigger, swimming straight for me, and I thought she would never end. She was so big I couldn't see all of her at once in the murky water. She had to have been more than thirty-five feet long, which meant that at least thirty-five tons of curiosity and intelligence and power were cruising to a stop less than a foot away from me. I hung there like a fly on a blue wall, my heart hammering. It was exhilaration, not fear. Grays are as gentle as they are huge."

Slowly Mandy rubbed the cold beer can over her cheek as she continued to talk. "She looked at me out of one black eye, then turned her whole body to put her other eye on me. Each time she moved it was like I was caught in a wave, water rushing everywhere, displaced by that huge body. I was so close I could make out the smallest detail of the barnacles that clustered on her skin. I held out my hand very slowly to see what she would do." Mandy laughed with delight, remembering. "She turned and presented her nose for a good rubbing!"

"Fair dinkum!" Ray said, shaking his head in wonder, laughing.

"It's true," Mandy said, smiling around another sip of beer. "I found out later she was one of the whales that followed scientists and tourists everywhere in the lagoon. She'd surface by boats and let people touch her or even scrub her with soft brushes. Guess the barnacles made her skin itch, and she had figured out real fast that the tiny and otherwise useless humans littering the lagoon made excellent ladies' maids.''

Another shout of laughter went up, followed by a spate of questions about diving off the west coast of the Northern Hemisphere, a place as alien and exotic to the Australians as the Great Barrier Reef was to Mandy.

''Well, I know you're proud of the taste of your Morton Bay bugs,'' Mandy said ''but have you ever eaten fresh California abalone? It's like eating the most delicately flavored crab crossed with a truly succulent Maine lobster. And like anything tasty, abalone aren't very easy to get to. Today you have to go down so far that the water is black and the chill eats into your wet suit long before your air is gone, and you have to carry a crowbar to pry the animals loose from the rocks. But it's worth it. If you don't believe me, ask a sea otter.''

''You've seen them?'' Tommy asked eagerly. ''I'd give my right arm to dive with otters.''

''They'd take you up on it,'' Mandy said dryly. ''They're every bit as mischievous as they look, and they can outswim silver salmon from a standing start. Otters love to play, to hunt, to eat, and they are among the most tender mothers I've ever seen in the animal world.''

The men murmured and leaned closer eagerly, encouraging Mandy to continue.

''When the babies aren't old enough to hunt with the adults,'' Mandy said, ''the mothers take the cubs to the surface of the kelp forest, wrap them carefully in the fronds and then dive deep into the forest in search of dinner, confident that their cubs will stay safely cradled.'' Mandy paused for a moment, remembering, and then added softly, ''The months I spent diving with the otters were extraordinary. Otters are so vividly alive. Sometimes, in my dreams, I'm back with the otters, playing hide-and-seek through amber kelp forests eight stories tall....''

Ray and Tommy exchanged sidelong glances, each silently urging the other to ask the question that burned between them. But it wasn't the Australians who spoke first. It was Sutter.

"Why did you give up diving?"

The reality of the present returned to Mandy like a blow. Color and laughter went out of her between one breath and the next. Slowly she set her beer can on the table and pushed back her chair. Without looking at anyone she turned and went to the door.

"Mandy," Sutter said as she passed.

His voice was hard, urgent, as was his hand on her arm. She opened the door without looking at him and stood watching the silver veils of rain.

"There was an accident," Mandy said finally, her voice lifeless. "People died."

Sutter waited, but she said no more. So he asked another question, one whose answer he suspected he already knew. "Was your husband one of them?"

"Yes. And I was another, Sutter. I died, too."

Mandy slipped from his grasp and stepped out into the rain, shutting the door behind her. She walked quickly to the tent, only to realize while she was drying herself that she couldn't bear to be within the sultry confines of the canvas. With a low sound of distress she rushed back out into the rain, still carrying the towel.

The first surge of her restlessness took her to the tiny airstrip. She crossed it and went into the she-oaks beyond, passing a tiny lighthouse before turning toward the beach, where huge combers boiled up onto crushed coral that was as white as the sea foam being torn from the waves. Standing beneath the rain-tossed casuarina trees, she watched the ocean and thought about the extraordinary seascape that lay so close at hand, yet had never been farther away. Desperately she wished she had come to the Great Barrier Reef before she had learned to fear the sea.

But she hadn't, and it was too late now to do anything but clench her teeth and hate the coward she had become.

"What are you thinking about?"

Sutter's voice wasn't unexpected to Mandy. She had known he would follow her. That knowledge had driven her from the confines of the tent.

"Cowardice," Mandy said flatly. "Mine."

"You listen to me!" Sutter said savagely, cutting Mandy off and spinning her toward him so quickly that she lost her grip on the towel. "I know what a coward is, lady. A coward is a woman like my mother, who couldn't take a less-than-perfect life so she took Valium instead, until finally she took enough and died, leaving a bitter, confused son behind. A coward is a woman like my ex-wife, who couldn't face her own emptiness, so she filled every instant of every day with parties and sycophants."

Sutter's hands gentled suddenly, stroking Mandy's arms. "You're not a coward, Mandy. I know that as surely as I know you're alive. I stood and watched you this afternoon. You were fighting, not running. You were trying, not denying that anything was wrong. Again and again you fought to bring your face down to the lagoon and—"

"Lost," Mandy hissed across Sutter's words. "Over and over and over again. Because I'm a coward."

"No! You won, Mandy! I saw it! It tore me apart to watch, but I saw every instant of it. You forced your face into the water three times. That's victory, not failure, Mandy. Victory!"

"Three times in as many hours, for maybe five seconds total," Mandy said bitterly. "That's not victory, that's a bloody rout!"

"But—"

"But nothing," she interrupted, her voice tight, her eyes almost wild. "Three-quarters of the world is water, and I'm cut off from it because of my own cowardice! For you, diving is a hobby. For me it was everything. All that I had wanted since childhood, all that I'd studied and worked for, a career that I loved, *all that is gone because I'm a coward.*"

"Mandy," Sutter whispered helplessly, stroking her

cheeks where tears and rain mingled. "What happened, golden eyes?"

Mandy shuddered suddenly but couldn't prevent the words from spilling out of her, the past welling up like a dark current, drowning her but for Sutter's strong, warm hands holding her afloat in the present.

"Andrew was an oceanographer," Mandy said. "I was first his student and then his wife. Marriage wasn't all that I'd hoped it would be, but then, what is? I was a virgin. Andrew was used to experienced women who were quick off the mark." Mandy laughed abruptly. "In bed we were a bad match. We should have made up for it professionally, because our strengths in oceanography were complementary. But Andrew wanted children, not a co-researcher, and he wanted the children the same way he wanted sex—instantly. He had turned forty, you see, and I was his second wife. There were no children from the first marriage. He told me he didn't want to grow old and die knowing that nothing of himself lived on."

Slowly Mandy shook her head, not realizing that she did it. "As soon as I could wrap up my research on sea otter habitats, I went off the pill. It took a long time to conceive. Too long. Andrew got more and more depressed, more angry, more difficult. When I finally got pregnant I was thrilled. It was our anniversary and Andrew's forty-third birthday. I took the ferry out to Catalina, where Andrew was camping and diving. He didn't expect me that early. I was going to surprise him."

Mandy felt Sutter's hands tightening on her arms again and smiled crookedly. "Yeah, you guessed it. He was having sex with some neoprene bunny when I walked into the tent. When he finished explaining how it was all my fault because I was such a lump in bed, we went to the airport. Did I mention that he was a pilot and owned a small plane?"

"No," Sutter said softly.

"Well, he was. I'd never liked flying. It was something I tolerated because it was the most efficient way to get from point A to point B. And that's what I wanted that night. Efficiency. We took off. It was dark. It felt like it had always been dark. Somewhere over the ocean, something went wrong. Heart attack. Stroke. No one knows because his body was never found.''

The pupils in Sutter's eyes expanded suddenly. "Mandy?" he whispered, his voice raw.

"Oh, yes," she said, shuddering. "I was with him. All the way. The plane went in and floated but not long enough. I dragged at Andrew and dragged at him and kicked out the window but he was too big and the ocean was too cold and it was pouring in the window and we went down and down and down and my lungs ached and burned and burst and I breathed icy water and I...I drowned," she said, her voice broken.

Sutter's arms closed around Mandy in a crushing hug as he tried to convince her and himself that she was alive. The thought of what she had been through was agonizing. The realization that he had forced her to relive her terror during the flight to the island was a knife of regret turning in his guts.

And then he remembered her incoherent words after he had pulled her from the Fish Pond's shallow waters: *The baby, the baby.*

"Oh, God, Mandy," Sutter said, his voice raw. "No...."

But she was still talking, still telling him things that were too painful to bear. Yet they had happened. They must be borne.

"I woke up at dawn in the bottom of a tiny boat that bounced all over the sea. I was dead but it still hurt. It still hurt! It was...hell. I was sure of it." Mandy took a deep, tearing breath. "Somehow the fisherman got me to the hospital before cold finished what the sea had begun. But.." her voice faltered and then went on, a sound as ragged as her breathing "it was too late for the baby. I could have lived with failing Andrew, but not my child. The child I was going to teach to dive and to laugh and to love...my child died before it even had a chance to live. I should have died, too." She shuddered. "Sometimes...sometimes I think I did."

Sutter whispered Mandy's name again and again, gathering her even closer, holding on to her with fierce strength, as though he were afraid the sea was going to sweep up and claim the woman who had evaded drowning two years ago.

"You're alive," Sutter said in a low, intense voice. "Do you hear me, Mandy? You're alive, more alive than any woman I've ever known!"

"Am I?" she whispered, pulling back until she could look at him with shadowed golden eyes.

"Yes."

"I felt alive last night, with you. Alive as I never have been. But in the morning you...walked away."

Sutter closed his eyes against the pain in Mandy's voice. "You're not a woman for affairs. You would want more. You sure as hell deserve more, and I know it, just as I know I'm not the man to give it to you. I learn from my mistakes, Mandy. And that's what marriage was for me. A mistake. But I wanted you so damned bad I stopped thinking!"

"Two years ago you would have been right about me and affairs," Mandy said. "But not now, Sutter. Not now. Like you, I've learned. Now I want what I had last night. I want to be alive, to feel you inside me, to be so close to you I can't tell where I end and you begin. That's all I'm asking. I don't expect pretty words or deathless promises or anything but you, body to body, breath to breath, heat against heat, hard against soft. Come inside me, Sutter," she whispered, running her hands over his bare, rain-wet chest. "Please."

"Mandy," Sutter whispered, shuddering with the onslaught of desire, a cataract of heat pouring through him, gathering between his legs, making him so full and rigid that he groaned. "No."

But Mandy wasn't listening to anything except the pounding of storm surf and the rain and her own blood matching the hammering of Sutter's heart beneath her hand.

"Don't worry, Sutter," she continued, words tumbling out in a torrent, pushed by her own tearing need to make Sutter understand. "I won't expect you to change your diving schedule or your meals or anything else about your vacation. I just want a little of your time when you aren't diving, that's all. I don't expect to be your lover back home. I don't expect you to acknowledge me in any way. It ends when we leave the island. No fuss, no muss, no tears or recriminations. Just a vacation affair between two consenting adults."

Mandy took a broken breath and looked into the blazing green of Sutter's eyes and the warm rain washing over his body. She wanted to be like that rain, bathing him in heat. She stood on tiptoe and whispered against his mouth, kissing and biting and tasting him between words.

"Teach me what you want, how to please you, how to make you feel as though you've been dropped into the hot center of life," Mandy said while her hands slid down Sutter's lean body and inside his swimsuit, pushing it down and away in a single twisting stroke, freeing him for her touch. The size and heat of him transformed her, suffusing her with an answering readiness, preparing her for the presence within her body of the very male flesh that pulsed so urgently between her hands. "I know I'm not much as a lover," she continued, "but I'll do any—".

Sutter's tongue thrust between Mandy's teeth, cutting off her words as he ravished her mouth, pinning her in his arms, pressing their aroused bodies together while silver rain poured over their hot skin. She made a shivering sound of desire and sucked on his tongue, pulling him even deeper into her mouth, not even realizing what she did, knowing only that she must have more of him or die.

He ate her mouth hungrily while his splayed fingers slid down her wet stomach to push inside her bikini, spearing through the musky dampness of her hair, probing until he found her slick readiness bathing him more hotly than any rain. His other hand raked down her back, tearing away her bikini in two powerful jerks even as he kicked aside his own suit. With a thick, hungry sound he sank his fingers into her thighs, spreading them and at the same time lifting her, plunging into her until he could go no deeper for he was completely, tightly sheathed in her wild heat.

The sudden thrust and hard pressure of Sutter within Mandy ripped reality away. Arms wrapped around his powerful neck, body quivering, Mandy hung on to Sutter, knowing only him, feeling only his potency filling her and ecstasy convulsing her. Her body clenched and stroked and clenched around him again, pulling him in even more deeply, her consummation streaming over him in a torrid rain until he stood transfixed, pouring himself into her in return, his breath coming out in an extended, broken cry.

For long moments Mandy and Sutter held on to each other, oblivious to the weather, the waves, to everything but the shivering aftermath of intense pleasure. Slowly their breathing returned to normal. Even more slowly Sutter lifted Mandy, separating himself from her, allowing her legs to slide down his until she stood on her own feet once more. After the steamy heat of her body, the air felt cold on his still-aroused flesh.

"Are you all right?" Sutter asked, his voice uneven as he hugged her.

She made a sound of contentment against his chest.

"I didn't hurt you?" he pressed.

"What?" she asked, looking up at him with puzzled golden eyes.

"I was very...aroused."

Mandy smiled. "Yes. I liked that, Sutter. I liked it very much."

She ran her fingertips down the center line of his body until she found the blunt, partially aroused flesh nested in a dense thicket of amber hair. She heard Sutter's breathing change as she traced the growing length of him before she went on to cup the twin weights suspended just below. With curiosity and gentle care she stroked the different, very male textures.

"Do you like that?" she murmured.

Sutter heard the catch in Mandy's voice, saw the sensual shiver that claimed her and felt his blood rushing heavily once more.

"'Like' isn't the word for what I feel right now," Sutter said huskily, putting his hands over Mandy's, guiding her in the ways of pleasuring him.

She was a very fast learner. Sutter's breath caught in his throat as he stifled a groan. He knew he should stop her, walk her back to the tent, get out of the open so that there would be no chance of someone stumbling across them. But the beach was utterly deserted and the casuarina grove partially shielded them and the rain was falling in sensuous silver veils. He decided that next time he would take her to the cloistered shelter of the canvas walls and lie between her legs for a long, deep loving. But not this time. This time he wanted to lie in the open with her, licking the hot rain from her body in a loving as wild and free as the storm sweeping over the island.

Mandy closed her eyes, caressing Sutter as she absently tasted the rain on her lips with the tip of her tongue.

"Let me," he said huskily.

"What?"

Sutter's answer was the warm, velvet rasp of his tongue over Mandy's lips. She shivered and held his responsive flesh in her hands, caressing him, loving him. He was smooth and hard and flushed with heat, his skin stretched as tight as a satin drum, slick with passion and rain.

"Love?" he asked.

"Mmm?" she murmured, eyes closed, lips parted.

"What happened to that towel you had?"

"I think I'm standing on it."

Sutter's lips curved in amusement despite the heavy beat of desire in his blood. He reached down and slowly, gently caught Mandy's erect nipples between his fingers, rolling the tight buds, tugging at them. Her breath broke and her knees sagged.

"You have the same effect on me," he said, caressing her breasts with rain-wet hands before he released her. "This time I want to lie between your legs, Mandy. I want...*you*."

She sank to her knees and fumbled with the drenched towel, spreading it over the crushed coral and fallen she-oak leaves. Her task wasn't made any easier when Sutter distracted her by kneeling behind her. He rubbed his long fingers down her spine to the shadow cleft of her bottom and then lower still. She gasped when she felt him spear sweetly into her warmth. Heat rippled out from the pit of her stomach with a force that made her dizzy.

"Sutter?" she whispered, unable to speak aloud.

Mandy looked over her shoulder at Sutter just as his tanned, powerful thigh eased between her legs, pressing them apart, rubbing rain-slick skin over her bottom, unraveling her with the unexpected intimacy. The pressure increased, pushing her thighs apart until she swayed on her knees.

"What do you want me to do?" she asked raggedly.

Sutter bent and gently bit the nape of her neck and whispered, "Rain on me, Mandy."

His left arm came around her just beneath her breasts, holding her shoulder blades against his chest while his leg opened her thighs to the ravishment of his palm sliding over her swollen, heat-flushed flesh, retreating and sliding and retreating until she swayed with his caresses. His long fingers teased the velvet bud of her passion, making her tremble with need. His teeth closed deliberately on the nape of her neck at the same instant that his finger penetrated the slick, hungry core of her. He felt the tiny convulsions deep within her, the hot rain of her pleasure over him.

"I love touching you," Sutter said hoarsely, biting Mandy again, caressing her even more deeply. Feeling her steamy, shivering reaction, he groaned and closed his hand possessively on her hot flesh.

"Sutter," she moaned. "Stop. I want to hold you...."

"I can't stop," he admitted, rubbing his hand slowly between her thighs. "You're so damned responsive you make me lose control."

Mandy made a broken sound that could have been laughter or passion or both. "But I'm not," she said, then moaned at the sweet, involuntary shuddering of her body as he caressed her again.

"Tell me all about it," Sutter said huskily, sucking drops of rain from Mandy's spine with hard pressures of his mouth, sending wild bursts of pleasure through her. He laughed thickly, sucking hard on her soft skin, thrusting deeply, feeling himself drenched with her passion. "Yes," he murmured, "*Yes*. Tell me how unresponsive you are while you come apart in my hands."

Mandy tried to speak, but Sutter's fingers had captured one of her erect nipples and he was tugging at it with the same slow, sensuous rhythms of his hand moving between her legs. The twin assault was too much. She swayed like a slender casuarina caught in a storm, letting the warm rain wash through her to her lover. Sutter closed his eyes and caressed Mandy gently until the storm passed and she could speak once more. Then he turned her and lowered her to the towel, where he kissed her flushed lips with a sensual thoroughness that soon had her shivering again.

"Do you want me?" he asked.

"Yes," she whispered, "oh, yes."

"How?" he murmured, spreading her legs apart, stroking her hot, delicate skin. "Gentle? Fast? Slow? How do you want me, Mandy? *Tell me*."

"Deep," she whispered. "So deep it never ends."

"Oh, love," Sutter said, shuddering in a vise of need, "that's how I want it, too."

Mandy's eyes opened when she felt her legs pulled first around Sutter's waist, then up over his shoulders until her hips were lifted clear of the towel.

"Tell me if I hurt you," Sutter said, his voice husky with need. "You're so sweet, so tight, and you make me so hard...."

She started to answer, to tell him that she wanted him, all of him, but her voice unraveled into a husky moan as he pushed slowly into her. She saw his face become oddly flattened, his eyes slitted, his lips thinned with the force of his passion and the self-control that held him in check. Slowly he gave her more of his weight, more of his power, more of the potent flesh that was filling her until she was sure she could hold no more...and then he taught her how little she had known about her capacity to receive and his to give. The pressure was fierce, burning and so delicious she trembled helplessly and rocked against him, wanting more. He gave it to her with a smooth thrust of his hips, embedding himself completely in her, hearing her shattered cry. He shuddered and held himself savagely still.

"Mandy?" he asked hoarsely. "Mandy?"

Her eyes opened. Her pupils were so dilated that only a tiny rim of molten gold remained. She could feel Sutter from the back of her knees to the small of her back and she wanted only to measure him again and again and again until she died of it, but she could think of no way to tell him what she so desperately needed. Her slender hands pulled his head down until her lips were against his ear. As her teeth closed on him, she whispered a hot, dark command that ripped away his control.

Sutter's powerful body flexed and he began driving into Mandy, plumbing every last bit of her softness as she cried out in wild pleasure and urgent demand. Her hands raked down to his buttocks, clenched, then instinctively gentled as she followed the cleft and discovered the exciting male flesh below, twin spheres drawn tight with excruciating need. At the first soft caress of her palm Sutter threw back his head and bared his teeth in an agony of pleasure. Her hand moved again, shaping him, loving him, making him explode. She felt it happening for him, the tiny convulsions and the long, shattering release, the secret dance of life in her cupped hand; and then heat burst from the pit of her stomach, burning through her, stripping away the world, leaving her impaled on ecstasy even as she was sheltered within her lover's arms.

Chapter 13

The island days took on a new pattern for Mandy and Sutter. Each morning they awoke as they had slept, body to body, warmth to warmth, breath to breath. While Sutter dove out in the open sea, Mandy went to the Fish Pond. Each time she went she was able to endure having her face in the water for a few minutes longer and then a few minutes beyond that, until finally she was able to enter the water at high tide and float on her back or patrol the pond with a languid breaststroke that kept her face clear of the water.

When Sutter returned from his dives, they would eat and she would listen to his descriptions of the Great Barrier Reef. He would see the yearning in Mandy and feel it in himself; he would have given his soul to share the exotic beauty of the sea with her. But the reef was not his to give. All he could bring to her was his touch, his smile, his body locked deeply within hers as they explored together the sensual sea they had discovered in one another.

Both Sutter and Mandy tried not to count the days remaining to them on the island. Both failed. The morning before they were due to fly out, Sutter left Mandy in the Fish Pond and called his aunt instead of going off to the dive boat.

"Anthea?"

"Sutter! I had almost abandoned hope of ever hearing from you again. Is everything all right?"

"Everything's fine, except my vacation is too short."

"A common problem."

"I have an uncommon solution. You're going to give us two more weeks."

"Us?"

"Mandy needs more time, too."

There was a long pause from Anthea's end, followed by a sigh.

"Damon? Is there something I should know?"

"Two years ago Mandy and her husband crashed at sea in a small plane. He died. She was sucked down with the plane and damn near drowned, and she lost the baby she was carrying."

"Dear God," Anthea said in an appalled voice.

"Since then Mandy's been terrified of small planes and any water deeper than a sidewalk puddle. But she doesn't want to be afraid anymore. She got to Lady Elliot Island on sheer guts, and now she's at the point where she can put her face in the water and even swim around the lagoon a little. If she had more time, she'd be able to dive along the Great Barrier Reef. I'm sure of it. I want her to have that chance."

"Damon, my dearest boy, that's an enormous amount to ask of Mandy. Learning to dive would be hard enough, but learning to dive when you're terrified of water—and for excellent reason!—is too much to ask of anyone."

"Learning won't be a problem for Mandy. She's been scuba diving from Alaska to Mexico. She has a Ph.D. in marine biology, with a specialty in the ecology of coral reefs. Before the accident the ocean was her life. I want her to have that life again."

There was another long pause.

"Is that what Mandy wants?" Anthea asked finally.

"If you heard her talk about the ocean, you wouldn't have to ask," Sutter said, smiling almost sadly. "Anthea, remember that paper on fish farms and coral atolls that OCC commissioned a few years back?"

"But of course. I still use it as a model of the type of work we should be commissioning."

"Mandy was a major contributor to that paper. Even if she never dives again, she's wasted in her present job. OCC needs someone who understands the ocean more than you need a girl Friday. I'd have given my eyeteeth to have Mandy along last year when I was trying to convince that little tin tyrant that his people needed an intact reef to attract edible fish more than he needed crushed coral to build roads for people who had no cars! I can think of a hundred times I could have used Mandy's advice in the last year. She's a hell of a lot more than a good-looking woman with a sassy mouth. She's intelligent and gutsy and—"

"Your lover," Anthea interrupted calmly.

"That, my dear aunt, is none of your business."

She sighed. "Two more weeks?"

"Yes."

"You'll have to fly straight to Darwin afterward. That man Peters doesn't get along with the aborigines as well as you did. Apparently he can't stomach the local delicacies. Without the support of the adults, we can do little for the children."

Sutter grimaced at the thought of more baffling conversations, warm beer and charred lizard. On the other hand, there had been a few times in his life when he would have been glad to drink boiled beer and eat lizard, charcoal and all.

"We'll be into the monsoon season in a few weeks," Sutter pointed out. "It will be hell to get into the bush, much less to get out."

"Then perhaps you could fly over for a few days now,

patch things together and then have your two weeks' extra vacation.''

"Not a chance. There's no such thing as 'a few days' when you're dealing with a culture that has no concept of European time," Sutter retorted. He smothered a curse. "Two more weeks for both of us on the island. Then I'll eat goanna until I get things straightened out. Deal?"

"Deal."

"Good. You can use those two weeks to write out a job description for a resident OCC oceanographer."

"Damon..."

"Yes?"

"Have you changed your mind about marriage?"

Sutter held the receiver until his hand ached. When he spoke it was in a clipped voice that invited no confidences. "To quote my dear aunt, 'a discreet, mutually satisfying affair is far superior to the lackluster social convenience known as marriage.'"

When Anthea spoke, there was an indefinable sadness in her voice. "I meant that only for myself, not as blanket advice for my nephew."

"What's sauce for the goose, et cetera."

"Is that how Mandy feels?"

Sutter's temper slipped. "Do you think I'd be her lover otherwise?"

"That would depend on how badly you wanted her, wouldn't it? Or, perhaps, on how badly she wanted *you*."

"Thanks for the vote of confidence in my personal integrity," Sutter snarled.

"Damon, I didn't mean—"

"The hell you didn't."

Sutter broke the connection and spun toward the door in the same savage motion, startling the girl who was racking postcards. A few moments later the phone rang. Sutter was gone. The girl listened and then noted in the resort log that the couple in the unnumbered tent were extending their vacation for two more weeks.

* * *

The days became a sensual kaleidoscope for Mandy, a colorful wheel whirling faster and faster around her. Sutter made love to her with his smoky green glances and his long-fingered hands, with his powerful body and his hot, insatiable mouth; and she loved him in the same way, sweetly devouring him, taking and giving and sharing until the world splintered into colors and fell away, leaving only ecstasy behind.

One day Sutter came back from diving to find Mandy snorkeling within the lagoon's clear water. He watched for fifteen minutes, and then he had waded out and lifted Mandy into his arms, exulting in her success, giving her a deep kiss that had left both of them trembling with something more than triumph. On the first calm day after that, Sutter went with Mandy into the unbridled sea on the opposite side of the island, where waves swept in from a distant horizon. He led her to a place called the Garden, a favorite local snorkeling ground. There, beyond the creaming waves, she swam by his side, their bodies propelled by lazy movements of their flippers, their fingers interlaced, their masked faces turned down toward the extraordinary alien beauty of the coral growths.

For a week Sutter went scuba diving in the morning and snorkeling with Mandy in the afternoon. And then Mandy turned up at the dive boat in the morning with the other divers, her scuba gear in hand and her heart in her mouth. Sutter gave her a smile and a kiss that made her feel as though she could breathe underwater and to hell with air tanks and mouthpieces.

"Are you sure, love?" Sutter asked softly. "You don't have to."

"I want to. I'm scared, but I want to."

"What about being in the dive boat? It's hardly the *Queen Mary*."

Mandy hesitated, then smiled tremulously. "I won't know until I try."

Ray turned away from instructing a newcomer and saw

Mandy standing next to Sutter, her tanks leaning against his. Sutter's fingers slid between Mandy's in a gesture of approval and sensual possession. He looked up from Mandy's red lips and saw Ray's smile.

"The boat will be a little crowded," Sutter said casually. "Mandy and I will wait until you drop off the first group."

"No worries, mate. Tommy is going to take this lot over to the Garden for a bit."

Tommy suppressed a look of surprise. One of the other divers started to say something, caught an elbow in the ribs and shut up instantly. Mandy's steady success in overcoming her terror of water was a source of very real pride to all of the divers. If Ray wanted to take Mandy and Sutter to the outer reef alone, then the rest of the divers could amuse themselves until the boat returned.

"Bloody good idea," one of the divers said. "I've been wanting a go at the Garden but the tide has never been right."

There was a ragged chorus of agreement as the men abandoned their scuba tanks and drifted down the beach to a point opposite the Garden.

"Right, here we go," Ray said to Mandy.

He took Mandy's tanks, waded out and hefted them into the dive boat, which was moored by a line leading from the bow to a sturdy little she-oak. Sutter scooped up Mandy, waded out and placed her carefully in the bobbing craft. He waited several moments.

"Okay?" he murmured.

Mandy let out a long breath. "Yes. It's...fine. Not like I thought it would be. Not nearly as bad as the plane was."

Sutter wondered which plane she meant, the one that had nearly killed her or the one that had flown her to Lady Elliot Island. He didn't ask because he didn't want anything to upset the balance of Mandy's control.

"If you change your mind," Sutter said, "don't fight it. Tell me right away. Promise?"

Mandy nodded.

Sutter signaled for Ray to bring in the bow line. After both men had hoisted themselves aboard with an easy strength Mandy envied, Ray set off for the diving grounds on the outer reef, which was on the opposite side of the island. Gradually Mandy relaxed. Before the accident she had spent many long, contented days in small boats, as opposed to only a few hellish hours after the crash. Most of her memories of small boats, unlike those associated with small planes, were good.

After a time Mandy let out a long breath and turned to Sutter with a smile, letting herself enjoy the gentle motion of the boat on the blue swells. Sutter smiled down at Mandy in return, watching her with affection and pride and the sensual hunger that was so much a part of him when he was close to her.

The boat turned, bringing the sun behind Sutter's profile. Mandy realized that sunlight and seawater had bleached his hair until it was incandescent shades of flax and gold, pale wheat and tropical sunshine. Dense, amber eyelashes shaded the green intensity of his eyes. The aggressive Scandinavian planes of his face showed cleanly beneath his taut, tanned skin. His male power and vitality were heightened by the black wet suit that was molded to his body. She watched him and wondered if she were pregnant, and which parent the baby would resemble.

Would our child be like you, beautiful enough to break my heart? Would our baby have your intense green eyes and burning gold hair, your incisive mind and your glorious passion for life? Am I carrying that child even now? God, I hope so! Believing that will give me the courage to let you go with a smile and a final, silent cry of love.

The boat came to a stop, shaking Mandy out of her private speculations. She realized she had been staring at Sutter for a long time. He wasn't disturbed by that, for he had been staring at her with equal absorption. She wondered what he had been thinking or if he had guessed her own thoughts.

"Over you go," Ray said to Sutter.

Sutter shrugged his tanks into place, checked the air feed and positioned his mask before he sat on the gunwale with his back to the water. If he had been diving with Americans he would have given the traditional thumbs-up before he went over backward into the sea. But he was diving in Australia, where that particular hand signal was an insult.

"Mandy? Want me to lift you over?" Ray asked.

She hesitated, then said, "Thanks. The first few times it would be easier if I didn't go in with a splash."

"No worries, luv. I never complain about the chance to get my hands on a good-looking Sheila. Put those long legs over the stern and your bum on the gunwale. I'll support you until you're ready to go in."

With Ray's help, Mandy maneuvered herself into position despite the cumbersome scuba gear strapped to her back. Ray braced her in place.

"Tell me when you're ready. No hurry, luv. I'm having a good time. You smell much better than the last diver I helped over the edge."

Mandy laughed. "Eau de wet suit, the new fashion sensation down under."

Despite her laughter, Mandy's hands grasping the gunwale showed white on the knuckles. There was a whole lot of ocean out there, blue on blue, fathom on fathom, swallowing the world.

Suddenly Sutter surfaced in the center of Mandy's vision. Even darkened by the sea, his hair still looked like a piece of the sun. He tongued out his mouthpiece, caught the stern with one hand and hung before her in the clear water, smiling up at her.

"The denizens of the Fish Pond must have passed the word about free lunches," Sutter said easily. "The finned hordes are waiting for their goddess to descend with manna."

"And me without a crust of bread to my name," Mandy said.

"They'll understand. That's the thing about friends, Mandy. They understand."

She looked into his green eyes, eyes so vivid that no mask could conceal them. Suddenly she understood what Sutter was saying: he wouldn't think less of her if she decided not to dive after all. Tears burned behind her eyelids. She took a deep breath, checked the airflow through the mouthpiece and nodded to Ray. He eased her over the stern and into the sea next to Sutter, not releasing her until she had a firm grasp on the boat's gunwale.

"Thanks, luv," Ray said when she was in the water.

Mandy looked up, startled.

"For trusting me not to pitch you in," he said simply.

Scuba gear prevented Mandy from speaking, so she squeezed Ray's hand, silently telling him that she had long since forgiven him for tossing her into the Fish Pond. Then she turned to Sutter and held out her hand. Strong, slick, wet fingers intertwined with hers. She released the stern and began sinking into the blue depths of the sea.

After the first burst of adrenaline passed, Mandy was able to regulate her breathing. It was still too fast, too shallow, but it no longer threatened to run through her supply of oxygen four times faster than normal. She looked at Sutter and gave him the thumbs-up signal, which he returned. Then he turned her around slowly until her back was to him.

One hundred feet away an immense, ragged wall rose from the sapphire depths to culminate just beneath the surface of the sea in a fantastic crown of multihued life. As enormous as the wall appeared, it was just one tiny fragment of a coral complex that went north for thousands upon thousands of square miles: the Great Barrier Reef.

Slowly Mandy swam toward the reef, drawn to its enormous, living presence as inevitably as a river is drawn by gravity to the sea. Sutter swam at Mandy's side, monitoring the bursts of bubbles she expelled, literally counting her breaths. With growing elation he realized that the longer she stayed in the water, the more her breathing slowed; her fear was diminishing, not increasing. Her breathing was still too fast, but no worse than his had been the first time he had found himself face-to-face with Lady Elliot Island's contribution to the immensity of the Great Barrier Reef.

Mandy didn't stop swimming until she was little more than an arm's length away from the reef. Six feet below the surface, bathed in warmth and light and nutrients, the section of reef that she could see was a fantastic garden of fixed animals and mobile plants, of individual lives so small she could barely make out their delicate shapes and of communal skeletons so overwhelming in numbers that man couldn't comprehend them. At each succeeding downward level of the reef there were more shapes and sizes and colors of coral, more varieties of life than seemed possible, a dazzling fecundity that shamed the land by comparison.

At the upper levels, staghorn coral grew in interlocking splendor, arms reaching into the warm sea to make a chaotic, living garden where tiny fish thrived, scattered among the prongs of coral like broken necklaces of citrine and emerald, amethyst and sapphire and gold. A soft coral grew in deeply sinuous array, its fleshy-appearing folds turned and refolded upon itself with muscular grace. Coral as intricate and as delicate as Irish lace shawls grew from a section of wall in stark contrast to the dense convolutions of maroon brain coral.

Starfish whose countless arms were as delicate as feathers and as flexible as whips clung to the living outer surface of the reef, adding bursts of magenta and white and red to the multihued coral display. Sponges whose shapes went from the ridiculous to the unbelievable grew from hollows and irregularities in the reef wall. An enormous shoal of tiny white fish wound across the face of the reef in a wild river. The fry of oceangoing fish hung against the reef like clouds against a rugged mountain.

Crevices and grottoes were everywhere, and each had its own inhabitants. At first they were only shapes hanging in the darkness. Then Sutter would flash a hand-held diving light, bringing the dark hollows and their dwellers into sharp focus. Sometimes the residents were vivid coral ''trout'' or muscular cod sporting freckles of electric blue, and sometimes there were banner fish whose long fins were breathtakingly graceful as they wove in fragile sine curves through the sea. Corals in the shape of enormous, deeply folded fans descended the face of the reef like gigantic footholds leading down and down and down to the levels where sunlight and warmth slowly were absorbed into the serene lapis depths of the Pacific Ocean.

Everywhere there was life. Mobile or motionless, camouflaged or shouting with colors, hunter or hunted, succulent or spined, wearing its skeleton on the outside or the inside or doing without altogether, graceful or grotesque, aggressive or shy, beautiful, ugly, haunting, overwhelming— Mandy barely had time to comprehend even the smallest fragment of the reef's stunning profusion of life before Sutter tapped her shoulder and pointed to his watch and then up to the surface. She was startled to find that nearly all of her dive time was gone. She was even more startled to discover just how far she had been drawn down the ragged face of the outer reef. The surface was far, far above, little more than a silver banner unfurled against the darkly luminous blue that surrounded her.

Slowly, reluctantly, Mandy followed Sutter back to the world of dry land and warmth, gravity and white sunlight.

In the days that followed, Mandy and Sutter spent every possible minute diving together, sharing the incredible beauty and infinite variety of the sea. After the first few dives fear stopped clutching at Mandy's heart and plucking unexpectedly at her nerves. Once more she was a part of the ocean, swimming easily in the clear water, cradled and at peace within the mother of all life. Mandy put away all thought of time, all fears, all knowledge of a life beyond the coral seclusion of Lady Elliot Island. It was the same for Sutter, no thoughts of what was to come, no bleak shadows of the past, nothing but the glorious reef by day…and by night a sensual beauty that grew until he could no longer measure it, he could only immerse himself in it as he did the sea, asking no questions, knowing no time, simply living within the endless, incandescent perfection of his lover.

The peace endured until the last day on Lady Elliot, then Mandy and Sutter emerged from the cradle of the sea and knew that their time together was almost gone. In silence they sat close while the dive boat was hurried back to shore by the wind, which was companion to the squall line that had pulled tangled skeins of cloud across the sky. At the dive shed, Sutter gently shooed Mandy off for a predinner shower while he supervised the packing of their equipment.

But later, when Sutter went to the tent, Mandy was no-where around. Inside the tent there was only twilight dimness and the pearlescent, almost secret gleam of the white cowrie shell Mandy had placed at the head of their bed. Kneeling, feeling claws of sadness sinking and twisting through him, Sutter ran a fingertip over the shimmering beauty of the rare, flawless shell that would have to be left behind.

Sutter closed his eyes for a moment and his hand became a fist. Then he came to his feet in a rush and went in search of Mandy, needing her in a way he neither understood nor questioned. There was no one in the bathhouse. There was no one on the beach. The tide was higher than he had ever seen it, the wind was swirling over the crystal water, and tattered veils of warm rain were sweeping the surface of the lagoon.

Suddenly the breath rushed from Sutter's lungs as he saw a familiar, slender shape cruising facedown through the rain-washed, crystalline waters. He watched Mandy patrol the Fish Pond and then go out into the rest of the lagoon, pro-pelling herself with very small, controlled flipper motions, her arms relaxed at her sides. When she headed back for the Fish Pond again, Sutter was chest-deep in the warm water, waiting for her. She swam up to him, reversed neatly and stood in water that came to her neck.

"It was too beautiful to give up just to eat dinner," Mandy said, sliding her mask onto her wrist, bobbing a bit in the chin-deep water, out of her depth but not frightened at all. "No weight, nothing dragging, just floating and the warm water everywhere, a whole world opening up around me."

Sutter smiled at Mandy, wanting her until he ached, wishing he had the words to tell her how much he enjoyed her renewed love of the sea. The setting sun sent a single, slanting shaft of light through the clouds, turning the beads of salt water on Mandy's mouth into pure gold. Sutter saw, and remembered a time when her lips had been silvered by rain and he had licked them until she moaned.

"I haven't thanked you," Mandy said, touching Sutter with sea-wet fingertips. "You've given me so much...."

"No," he said softly, kissing her fingertips. "It's you who have given so much to me. You're beautiful, Mandy. So elegant and determined." He smiled as his fingers gently caressed her cheek. "No matter what happens, no matter where I go or what I do, I'll never forget your courage." His big hands closed gently around her ribs, keeping her from drifting in the chin-deep water. "Give me a hug before you float away forever," he whispered.

Sutter's hands slid down Mandy's back to her thighs, lifting her slowly, anchoring her legs around his hips. The thin strip of cloth running between her legs didn't prevent her from feeling the hard, quintessentially masculine bulge pushing against Sutter's bathing suit. Her breath shortened as she realized that only two thin strips of cloth prevented her from taking Sutter into her body once more, here, now, the heady warmth of the lagoon enfolding them, concealing their joined bodies beneath water turned incandescent orange by the dying sun.

The erotic thought changed Mandy, sending softness and heat flowing through her even as she dismissed the idea as impossible. It was too light. Too public. Someone might walk down the beach at any moment.

But that didn't mean that she couldn't enjoy a small taste

of the sensual pleasures Sutter brought to her. She could rub her hands down his chest through the thick mat of hair that concealed his nipples. She could kiss his neck and taste the lagoon and wish that the salt had come from elemental passion rather than the eternal sea.

As Mandy shifted slightly to reach the pulse beating in Sutter's neck, the cloth between her legs rubbed over the swollen ridge of male flesh. She made a ragged sound and wished fiercely that it was dark and they were naked in the sea and he was pushing into her with the hard, hot flesh she loved to arouse and hold within her body.

"Sutter," she said raggedly, leaning back to look up into his face, her body caressing him once more.

Blazing green eyes looked into her heavy-lidded ones. "I know. Oh Lord, Mandy, I know what you're thinking because that's what I'm thinking, too!"

She arched her back, rubbing lightly against him as she brushed her lips over his mouth, whispering, "Tell me."

"You're thinking there's no one around, and even if there was, the water is up to my collarbone and the surface is scuffed by the wind and covered with burning colors," Sutter said in a low voice, shifting his grip until his left forearm took the sweet weight of Mandy's hips and his right hand was free. "Who would know if I untied just one bow on your hip and you took me out of my suit and guided me to that sweet, hot place between your thighs and let me…" He groaned as his finger slipped beneath the triangle of her bikini bottom. She was soft, hot, welcoming. "Let me," he said hoarsely, stroking her just once. "Who would know, Mandy?" he asked, undoing one of the two ties that held the bikini bottom in place. "We'll be quiet and outwardly casual, just two people enjoying a sunset and talking and hugging up to their necks in water."

"Damon," Mandy whispered, feeling the warm lagoon caressing her most delicate flesh as he pulled the bikini bottom aside. "*Damon.*"

"Take me, Mandy," he said in a low voice, running his

fingertips over the softness he had uncovered, feeling her utterly open to his touch, wanting to join with her while the sky and sea turned to fire around them. "Take me," he whispered, "if you want me." His fingertips deciphered the message of her satin heat and shivering response as he probed her soft, feminine secrets. "Ah, you do want me," he murmured, caressing her with his hand and his voice. "Take me, love."

"Damon…we…can't."

"It will be our secret," Sutter whispered, watching Mandy through half-closed eyes, feeling her softness opening for him, yearning, wanting. "I'll be very slow, very quiet. Someone could walk by on the beach and be no wiser. I promise you, love."

The beach was deserted, the liquid warmth of the sea surrounded Mandy, and between her legs her lover's fingers slid and teased, parted and caressed her. She didn't know if she had enough self-control to act outwardly casual while Sutter was inside her, but when his hands moved to her hips, supporting her and at the same time leaving her bereft of all but the sea's lapping caress, she knew she was going to find out.

Mandy brought her hands down Sutter's muscular torso, all the way down, sliding her fingers inside the black strip of cloth that was all he wore. His breath hissed out as he felt her hands caressing him with small, secret motions. He tilted his head forward and brushed her lips with his own in a caress that would have looked quite casual from the beach.

"It's a good thing no one is within fifty yards of us," Sutter said in a low, raspy voice. "Your smile would give our game away for sure."

Mandy's only answer was a husky sound of pleasure and discovery as she stroked the potent male flesh she had uncovered. She looked up at Sutter, her eyes vivid with a combination of sensual mischief and frank passion. "You know," she murmured, her breath tight, rapid, "you bring a new meaning to some old phrases."

Sutter smiled despite the hunger racking him with each

knowing, teasing movement of her fingers. "Like skin diver?" he suggested, flexing his fingers into her naked hips.

"That's one of them," she agreed, squeezing him with loving deliberation. "Then there's 'stand up and be counted.' Or take 'standing ovation,' that's another one. Or take 'a stand-up guy.' Or take—"

"Me, love," he interrupted, groaning. *"All of me."*

The husky command sent desire glittering through Mandy, scattering her thoughts, focusing her on the naked thrust of Sutter's arousal and the moist heat of her own response. Watching his face, wanting him wildly, she tugged his suit down just enough to give her the freedom of his body. His hands shifted as he moved her slightly, holding her just in front of the blunt, hungry flesh she had freed. Smiling, he watched her eyes as he felt himself brought closer and closer to her satin sheath, touching, teasing, nuzzling for heart-stopping seconds until he penetrated her with a slow, smooth pressure, watching her eyes take on a haze of pure sensuality as he filled her.

Mandy's breath unraveled in a soft, exciting thread of sound that went no farther than Sutter. She discovered that she could control her outward movements but not the secret, rhythmic shivering deep inside her. Her slick, intimate stroking pulled a throttled groan from Sutter. He smiled rather ferally at her and bit her lips in a wild caress that made them as red as the sun sliding deeply into the sea.

"Much as I'd love to do the same to your breasts," he said in a low voice, "it would be…"

"Indiscreet?" she offered.

"Very. It would be even worse if I…moved."

With heavy-lidded eyes, Mandy watched Sutter's taut expression. "What if I move instead?" she murmured.

"Same problem. Why don't we just count backward from one thousand in Sanskrit and look at the sunset until it's so dark that…" Sutter's breath was sucked in suddenly as he felt Mandy's torso tighten and then relax, stroking him as surely as if she had visibly moved. "Love," he said through clenched teeth, sucking in another whistling breath as she stroked him secretly once more, "this isn't fair to you. Taking you…like this…is too…hot. No more movements…like that…or I'll lose control."

Sutter barely restrained a wild shudder as he felt Mandy's body tugging invisibly at his. She saw his response, felt it in the steel of the muscles bunched beneath her hands, tasted it in the suddenly salty moisture above his upper lip. She flexed her legs, pressing herself over him, pushing him even more deeply into her body. Then she clenched the muscles of her torso once more, stroking him, loving him in secret.

"Like this?" she murmured.

Sutter's nearly closed eyelids quivered as he focused on the incredibly erotic feel of his lover's satin depths caressing him, and at the same time he fought not to lose his control. "Yes, love…like that…like…that…." He groaned very softly and clenched his teeth. "Mandy," he whispered, opening his eyes, looking into hers, "love…" wanting to watch her, "yes…" wanting her to watch him while he gave himself to her, *"yes…"* with countless deep, ecstatic pulses, *"just…like…this."*

Mandy whispered Sutter's name as she watched his face and loved him with hidden movements of her body. Without warning, waves of pleasure shimmered wildly up from her core, stealing her breath, her body, her soul, giving them to the man who was secretly joined with her, pouring all of himself into her caressing, welcoming heat. For a time neither he nor she could move, or even breathe, for they were too deeply embedded in each other and in the rapture weaving them together with hot, invisible lightning.

Finally Sutter reclaimed himself by tiny increments, a breath, two breaths, the ability to think, to hear, to speak.

"Mandy," he murmured, brushing his lips across her forehead, her eyelids, her lips. "I've never known anything… like this…like you."

She smiled up at Sutter, the last of the glorious sunset reflected in her eyes, wanting to tell him of her love and knowing that she must not. He hadn't come to her for that. Just a vacation affair between consenting adults. She had promised him that because it was all he wanted, all he would accept. So she kissed him softly and substituted a lover's words for the vastly greater truth that was consuming her.

"I love…being…with you," Mandy whispered, kissing the line of Sutter's jaw and the corners of his smile, holding him within her. "I love having you in my body, in my arms, in my mind. I love…"

The last words were breathed into Sutter's mouth as Mandy kissed him. Then they held each other in silence until the sunset was little more than a thin carmine flush across the horizon. Finally they separated slowly, reluctantly, rearranged their bathing suits and walked hand in hand back to the tent, where Sutter once more licked the sea from Mandy's body, loving her, dying within her and being reborn again when she lay between his thighs, tasting herself and the sea on him, loving him.

Those were the memories Mandy held tightly in her mind when the little white plane taxied up to the dive shed the following morning. She scrambled in without help and strapped herself into her seat in the same way, knowing that Sutter would break every bone in his hands rather than confine her again in a place she feared. When he sat next to her she took his big hand and held it between both of hers. This time she forced herself to look out over the island and the maze of interlocking coral structures that surrounded it and carpeted the floor of the azure sea.

Memories of Sutter's voice husky with passion and warm with praise helped Mandy when the plane began its steep descent to Bundaberg's small airport. Memories of being cherished, desired, consumed; memories of laughter and triumph, passion and release, sleeping and waking and diving through beauty that knew no end; those memories gave Mandy strength when Sutter helped her to the apron, touched her temple, her cheek, her lips…and then turned away without a word.

Mandy stood motionless, watching Sutter, desperately hoping for a word, a wave, a look, anything to tell her that he cared just a little for her beyond the self-imposed boundary of their passionate affair.

There was neither a word, nor a wave, nor a look; simply another small plane waiting, two men rushing forward to shake Sutter's hand and pull him aboard, and the rising whine of engines revving as the plane started to turn toward the runway.

Don't look back. Don't look. Don't.

But in the end Sutter could not prevent himself. When the plane paused at the end of the runway he turned back, looked…and saw only empty tarmac and lightning dancing against towering, slate-bottomed clouds.

Chapter 14

The couple in the picture were tanned and healthy. Salt water beaded like diamonds on their skin, their fingers were interlaced, their mouths smiling, and all around them was a blinding-white coral beach, turquoise water and scuba gear glistening from recent immersion in the sea. The big photograph was an unexpected gift from Ray, who had wanted to commemorate Mandy's victory over her fears.

And now she couldn't look at the photograph without wanting to laugh and to cry with bittersweet pleasure. It was the same for the lab report telling her that another life was growing in her body…sweet triumph and only a few salty tears. What the sea had once taken from her, Sutter had returned. She had what she wanted. She could dive, she was using her scientific knowledge toward making a better world for the next generation, and she was carrying a piece of that future within her own womb. All she lacked was the man who haunted her every dream, her every silence, even the breaths she took.

"Mandy, did Jessi give you that study on coral reefs and

petroleum seeps?'' Steve asked. ''Yo, Mandy. Anybody home?''

With an effort Mandy focused on Steve rather than on the lost past or the unreachable future.

''Er, coral reefs, seeps, study…let's see.'' Trying to keep her mind on the task and off a man with blazing green eyes and hair the color of the sun, Mandy sorted through the mounds of scientific papers that Anthea had heaped on the desk. ''Reefs from old cars…oil pollution…natural tar on beaches…edible reef fish of the…ah, here it is.''

Steve took the bound sheets, read the concise summary Mandy had attached and smiled. ''Don't know why you spent the past year hiding your light under a cabbage leaf, kid.''

''I think you mean under a basket. Kids are what you find under cabbage leaves.''

''Knew there was a reason I hated gardening. Thanks,'' he said, waving the study as he walked away.

With ambivalent feelings, Mandy turned back to the remaining papers. She knew busywork when it was piled under her nose. OCC might need a marine expert from time to time, but at the moment there was no special niche waiting to be filled. It was catch as catch can—a summary of a scientific study here, a word of advice there, a flat thumbs-down on a shortsighted scheme to turn inedible reef life into fertilizer for the export market.

Yes, there was work of a sort at OCC for Mandy, but her future lay elsewhere. No one knew that fact better than she did. She had to be gone before her pregnancy showed. Anthea would know instantly that Sutter was the father. What Anthea knew, Sutter would learn just as soon as he emerged from the Stone Age amenities of the Australian bush in monsoon season. With the first phone call Sutter made, he would know that his neat vacation affair had suddenly leaped the agreed-upon boundaries.

He would be furious, and justifiably so.

Mandy refused to let that happen. Sutter had given her too

much. She wouldn't go back on her promise and hold him responsible for a child he had never wanted. He had told her he couldn't protect her and she had told him that was all right. She had meant it. The pregnancy was her choice, her responsibility, her joy. She didn't want Sutter to feel guilt or anger, treachery or betrayal. Each of them had achieved his separate desire. *Just a vacation affair between consenting adults.*

And now the vacation was over.

Even if Mandy weren't pregnant, she wouldn't have hung around OCC like the Ghost of Vacation Past. She had heard enough gossip during her time at OCC to know that when Sutter was finished with a woman, he was finished. Mandy had promised him there would be no fuss, no muss, no tears, no loose ends. The only way she could keep that promise was to be gone when he returned. She simply couldn't face having him walk into the office and nod civilly to her as he would to any OCC employee, nor could she stand seeing him and not touching him.

Mandy could endure a great many things, but not that. Not that.

The only thing holding her at OCC right now was the hope that Sutter had missed her as much as she missed him, that he would call from Australia and tell her that he couldn't sleep for wanting her, couldn't watch a sunset without remembering her, couldn't taste the sea without tasting her, couldn't breathe without remembering how it had felt to be completely joined to her....

He haunted her.

With fingers that trembled very slightly, Mandy reached for another report. She read quickly, making notes, trying not to think about anything beyond the words printed on the page in front of her. She was successful to the point that the phone had to ring four times before it got her attention. As she picked up the receiver she automatically glanced at the clock. After six. Vaguely she remembered saying goodbye to Steve and the others as they left for the day.

"Our Children's Children," Mandy said into the phone, the words automatic, her voice sounding odd from lack of use in the past few hours.

There was a background of static and voices and a loudspeaker saying something Mandy couldn't understand. The caller cursed and spoke loudly.

"Sutter here. Give me Anthea."

For a moment Mandy thought she was drowning. She was dizzy, couldn't breathe; her whole body felt weak. Without a word she punched in the hold button and rang Anthea's office.

"Yes?"

"Sutter. Line one," Mandy said, fighting to control her voice.

"Wonderful! How is he? Is he coming home? Did he get the job done?"

"He didn't say."

There was a pause while Anthea absorbed Mandy's colorless voice. "Thank you, dear. Don't leave yet, if you don't mind. He might…"

But Mandy had already hung up. She stared at her desk without seeing it. There were two possible explanations. One was that Sutter hadn't recognized her voice. The other was that he had but hadn't wanted to talk with her. Neither explanation was comforting.

There was a lot of noise on his end. Maybe that's why he didn't recognize my voice. He must have been exhausted and hungry and harried and it was noisy and there's no reason he should have recognized my voice, he's never said more than twenty words to me on the phone. But Anthea will tell him I'm here and then he'll…

Mandy didn't realize what she was doing until she had the knob of Anthea's office door in her hand. She opened the door soundlessly but made no move to go farther into the room. Anthea's back was to her.

"Dear boy, my heart goes out to you. I can't imagine eating lizard once, much less for three weeks. And leeches...!'' Pause. "Well, of course, I understand that the leeches were eating you rather than vice versa." Pause. "Two days? Wonderful. I'll have Man—er, someone—pick you up." Pause. "Don't be foolish. You sound terrible. It only makes sense for someone to pick you up at the airport. When will your plane land?" Pause. "You are in an exceptionally vile mood, Sutter. Perhaps it's just as well that no one meet you." Pause. "Is there anything you need taken care of on this end? Any messages for me to pass on?" Pause. "I see. Well, then, I'll talk to you in two days. Try to spend the whole time sleeping."

Mandy's mind was too numb to get her body moving in time to evade discovery. She was still standing in the doorway when Anthea turned around to hang up the phone. The older woman gave Mandy a compassionate glance.

"I'm sorry, dear. I've never known Sutter to be like that except for the time after we got him out of jail in that wretched country. He wouldn't let anyone near him. He hated being helpless."

"Yes. He told me."

Anthea's eyebrows climbed. "Did he? How odd. He's never spoken to anyone about that."

"He was trying to make me feel less a coward for being afraid of the water, that's all," Mandy said, turning away.

"Mandy? Are you all right, dear?"

She stopped and faced Anthea once more. "Don't worry about me," Mandy said in a strained voice. "I'm a survivor."

"Mandy," Anthea said hesitantly, "do you understand that Sutter doesn't mean to be cruel? He just...doesn't trust women. Give him time. He'll learn that you're different, that he can trust you."

Unconsciously Mandy's hands moved to cover her womb, where life grew, a secret that couldn't be kept. "No," she said, her voice low. "He'll think that I'm no different." She saw the distress in Anthea's face and added softly, "Don't be unhappy for me. Sutter gave me far more than he took.

I have no regrets. Not one." She turned away again. "Better hurry. You're scheduled for cocktails in half an hour. With downtown traffic the way it is, you haven't a moment to spare. I'll lock up behind you."

Long, long after Anthea left, Mandy sat and worked, skimming and summarizing scientific papers until nothing of importance remained on her desk. Finally she pulled out a clean sheet of office letterhead and picked up a pen, only to discover that there was too little to say. Or too much. Finally she wrote two words, clipped the sheet to the photo and left them on Anthea's desk.

After that, there was nothing for Mandy to do but go to the apartment and pack. With luck she would be far away before Sutter's plane even landed.

Sutter leaned over the sink at the airline terminal and splashed cold water on his face. The water was refreshing, but it wasn't eight hours of sleep. It was all he had, however, so he splashed more water over his hair and skin, trying to chase away the fatigue of the past few weeks. He hadn't slept but a few hours a night; and when he had slept, he had dreamed of holding a graceful, golden-eyed mermaid in his hands, bathing himself in her beauty, and then she was receding from him, swimming faster and faster until she vanished and he was left exhausted and alone in a cold midnight sea.

He looked in the mirror and grimaced. Bronze stubble and black circles, his hair wet and roughly finger combed, his mouth set in a flat, angry line. He had spent a lot of time like that in the past few weeks. Angry. He wasn't sure why, but he suspected that he had committed some irretrievably stupid act. His problem was that he couldn't decide whether the stupidity resided in ending his affair with Mandy or in not wanting it to end.

With an impatient curse Sutter picked up his baggage and hunted down a cab. He knew he should go home, sleep for a day, shower, eat, sleep; and then maybe, just maybe, he might feel whole again instead of only half-aware, half-awake, half-alive, the other half missing, lost and alone in a midnight sea.

The cab dropped Sutter off in front of OCC's offices. He took the elevator up, pushed open the office door impatiently and strode into the lobby. A new girl was at the receptionist's desk. She started to ask Sutter if she could help him but he brushed by before she could say two words. There was another strange woman sitting at Mandy's desk. Sutter didn't even hesitate. He went to Anthea's office, opened the door and slammed it shut behind him.

"Where is she," he said flatly, a demand rather than a question.

"Welcome home, Sutter," Anthea said, eyeing him rather warily. "You look like death warmed over."

"Where is she."

"Who?"

"You know damn good and well who I mean," Sutter snarled. "Where is Mandy!"

"I don't know."

"Is she sick?"

"I don't know."

"Why isn't she at work?"

"I—"

"Don't know," he interrupted savagely, finishing Anthea's sentence for her. "What *do* you know, dearest aunt?"

"Many things, dearest boy," Anthea purred. "Is there any particular area of inquiry you wished to pursue?"

"Don't push me, Anthea. I'm not in the mood for it."

Anthea's eyebrows climbed, but she said only, "When I arrived at work yesterday morning, there was a note on my desk and this." She handed over the note and the photo.

The note said, simply, *Thank you.* The photo made Sutter's breath hiss out as though at a blow. He had never seen a woman so incandescent...or a man so damned pleased with life.

"Go on," Sutter said tightly, struggling to contain his

anger at himself and life and the woman who had promised a neat, no-strings affair.

But she had lied. She haunted him.

"That was all," Anthea said. "It covered the ground adequately, don't you think? As they say, a picture is worth a thousand words."

Sutter knew his aunt was baiting him again, but it no longer mattered. Nothing mattered but getting his hands on Mandy and teaching her...

What? What did he want her to know? How could he teach her what he didn't know himself?

"There wasn't anything else, no message for me?" Sutter asked.

"Were you expecting one?"

"She didn't even give notice? She just left? Of all the ungrateful—"

"Yes," Anthea agreed, cutting across Sutter's anger. "It certainly was ungrateful of the wretch to leave before you were through with her. What is this younger generation coming to when a girl doesn't wait around for her lover to break off the affair? So impatient to get on with life. No time for all the amenities. No sense of proportion at all. And after all you promised her, too."

"I didn't promise Mandy a damned thing," Sutter retorted.

"When a man declares his love to a woman, there is an implicit—"

"I didn't say a damn thing about love to her, either!" he interrupted curtly.

"In that case, dear boy, what on earth are you complaining about? You enjoyed her, you walked away from her, and now she's gone."

Sutter closed his eyes on a wave of fury so great that it could barely be contained. He swore in an icy monotone until there were no words left, only ice.

"Where did she go?"

Anthea flinched at the clipped words and savage green

eyes of her nephew. "There's no point in being angry with her," Anthea pointed out. "She was only doing what any—"

"Where did she go?"

Anthea gauged the sound of her nephew's voice accurately and gave up all attempts to bait or reason with him. "I don't know where Mandy is."

"Where are you sending her paycheck?"

"I'm not. Damon, believe me, I don't know where she is!"

"Call her apartment."

"I did. The phone has been disconnected. The apartment is empty."

Sutter shook his head in denial even as he felt the chill of truth condensing around him. "The post office."

"She left no forwarding address." Anthea hesitated, then said softly, "She made a very clean break, Damon. She even pulled her job application from the file. We have no previous addresses for her, no names of family members, nothing. It's as though she never walked through the door of Our Children's Children."

"My God. How she must have hated me."

"She loved you," Anthea said in a flat voice. "She loved you, and you didn't even speak to her when you called from Australia. Why?"

"I could barely hear myself think. I didn't know it was Mandy until it was too late. And what should I have said?" Sutter asked harshly. "That I can't sleep for wanting her? That I can't smell the sea without remembering what it was like to fall asleep with her in my arms? That I can't look at a woman without seeing Mandy, tasting Mandy, needing her until I think dying would be easier than living without her? What could I have said to her, Anthea? There are no words to describe the hell I've been going through!"

"Try 'I love you.'"

The words were like a knife gliding between Sutter's ribs

into his heart, twisting. He turned away, saying nothing, for the only words that mattered had already been spoken.

Mandy was gone.

November rainstorms swept down over Northern California, carrying the chill of the distant Aleutians in each slashing gray drop. The tidal flats around Monterey Bay were deserted except for disgruntled sea gulls and a lone figure walking along the rocky shore, pausing from time to time to pick up a bit of sea life stranded by the falling water. The wind gusted suddenly, roughing up the sea and rushing over the land in a long, sighing moan.

Mandy shivered and turned up the collar of the red-and-black-checked lumberjacket she had bought at a garage sale. The coat was too large, but its thick wool defeated the wind and the big scarlet checks always looked cheerful against the winter land. When worn with a sweater, scarf and waterproof fisherman's boots, the coat kept her warm on her long daily walks around the bay.

But it was time to get back to the little beach cottage she was caretaking in lieu of paying rent. Soon it would be dark. She didn't want to take a chance of stumbling or falling on hidden rocks. She wanted nothing to happen that might jeopardize the baby growing within her. Not that she had any reason to worry—her doctor had assured her that everything about the pregnancy was normal.

Groping in her pocket for her key, head bent against the wind, Mandy had no warning that someone was on her front step until she ran right into a solid wall of flesh.

"What—?" she gasped, looking up. "*Sutter!* What are you doing here?"

"Freezing my butt off waiting for you."

"How did you find me?"

"In the telephone book, under Dr. S. Blythe-Cameron, the same name on the OCC paper you wrote."

He took the key from Mandy's fingers, opened the door and pushed her in ahead of him. The door thumped shut with the help of his solid heel. After the chill outside, the room felt almost tropical. A single glance took in the huge, colorful throw pillows scattered about, the lush plants and the open futon that was doing double duty as Mandy's bed.

"Sutter, what—"

"Later," he interrupted, catching Mandy's face between his cool hands. "First I want some answers of my own."

Mandy felt the heat of Sutter's breath, the sudden thrust of his tongue between her lips, tasted him, and the world came apart around her. Her breath jerked out in a shattered moan as her arms circled his neck. She didn't know if he was real or a waking dream; she only knew that she had to taste him, had to feel his power and warmth, had to feel fully alive with him once more.

Sutter had been expecting Mandy to fight or flee or freeze, anything but the wild answering hunger of her mouth mating with his. He lifted her off her feet, wanting to know all of her sweet weight pressed against his body. But even that wasn't enough. He had to feel her hair, her skin, taste her warmth, her passion; yet everywhere his hands moved they found only cloth and more cloth.

"My God, you're wrapped up with more layers than a Chinese puzzle box," he muttered.

Impatiently he unwound the wool scarf from Mandy's head, kissing and biting her lips lightly every few seconds, finally spearing his fingers into the warm, silky mass of her hair, groaning with pleasure at the remembered silk and scent of her. He caught her lips once more, rubbed his fingers against her scalp and slid his tongue into her mouth, tasting her with a slow, rhythmic intimacy that unraveled her.

Mandy's hands stroked continuously over Sutter's chest, probing through his heavy jacket for the heat and feel of his body. More by accident than intent her fingers found the cold metal tongue of the jacket zipper. She pulled it down and thrust her hands inside, feeling his vital heat and the power of his flexed muscles. Her nails raked down his spine to his hips, making him shudder heavily. Without lifting his mouth from hers, he undid the buttons of her heavy jacket, only to be confronted by the much smaller buttons of her cardigan. He pulled it free of her waistband and eased his big hands beneath her sweater.

The feel of Sutter's cool fingers caressing her skin made Mandy gasp with pleasure. When his thumbs skimmed repeatedly over the tips of her breasts, her gasp became a moan and liquid heat spread through her body. Her hands slid up his back from his hips, rubbed down his chest to his waist and then lower, seeking and finding the ridge of hard flesh that burgeoned beneath his jeans. Suddenly the world spun and Mandy found herself flat on her back on the futon with Sutter's big body moving against her in an agony of need. With a thick, broken sound, he rolled aside and fought for self-control.

"I'm sorry," Sutter said hoarsely. "I was just going to kiss you, to see if it was half as good as I remembered." He put his forearm over his eyes and shuddered. "It was twice as good. Three times. Four." Suddenly he rolled over onto his side and said angrily to her, "There aren't enough numbers, enough words. You're a fire in my body, in my mind, in my soul. *And you left me.*"

Mandy touched Sutter's beloved face with fingertips that shook. "That was what you wanted," she whispered. "You wouldn't touch me after that first time until I promised no strings, no tears, just a vacation affair. The only way I could keep my promise was not to see you again. So I...left."

"I've changed my mind. I want you, Mandy."

Her beautiful, sad smile sliced through Sutter's passion and anger to the fear that lay beneath. He knew before she could speak the words forming on her lips that she was slipping away from him, receding like the golden mermaid of his anguished dreams.

"No," he snarled. His hand went between Mandy's legs, anchoring her in place. "Damn it, you want me as much as I want you. Don't try to deny it, Mandy. I can feel the heat of you!"

She closed her eyes for a moment, unable to face the fear that had haunted her since she had discovered she was pregnant. She wanted to remember Sutter with desire in his eyes, not disgust for the woman who hadn't kept her promise. But she had learned that running from fear simply wouldn't work. She had tried to run from this moment, but it had come to her just the same. Slowly she opened her eyes and looked at the man she loved.

"Yes," Mandy said tightly, "I want you. If it matters, I'll want you until the day I die."

"If it matters?" Sutter said. "Of course it matters! What the hell are you talking about?"

"I'm pregnant."

Sutter went completely still. "What?"

"*Enceinte,*" Mandy hissed, angry at having to explain the obvious, "as in 'expecting a blessed event,' 'with child,' 'eating for two.' Ah, the light dawns."

Even the narrowing of Sutter's eyes couldn't wholly conceal the savage blaze of his emotions. "You told me—"

"I told you there could be no such thing as an *unwanted* pregnancy for me," Mandy said, cutting across Sutter's words, wanting to get it over with so she could crawl away and lick her wounds in peace. "That was the exact truth. I want this child!"

"You're carrying my child," he said in an odd voice.

Mandy started to demand that Sutter tell her whether he had any doubts about the paternity when she felt the warmth of his big hand sliding caressingly over her womb, and the ability to speak deserted her.

"*My child,*" he breathed.

Biting her lip, unable to hold back the tears spilling down her cheeks, Mandy watched as reverence replaced anger in Sutter's face.

"Is everything…normal?" he asked hesitantly. "Are you all right? Is the baby?"

"Everything is fine," Mandy said. "The doctor told me I couldn't be healthier."

Without a word Sutter turned and began pulling off and discarding Mandy's boots and socks. Then his hands went to the waistband of her jeans and stopped suddenly, as though he had just realized what he was doing.

"May I?" he asked huskily. "I want to see...."

She nodded.

Very gently Sutter slid Mandy's jeans and underwear from her legs. The skin of her abdomen was warm, still tanned from her island days, and taut with the first swelling of her pregnancy. She trembled and bit back a cry at the sweet touch of his hand over her womb.

"I'm sorry," Sutter said instantly, retreating. "I didn't mean to hurt you."

"You didn't," Mandy said, taking his hand and pulling it back to her body. "It's just that I've...I've dreamed of you touching me like that...wanting the baby as much as I do."

Sutter closed his eyes and fought for self-control. It was impossible. Her words had moved him beyond bearing.

"Mandy," he whispered, bending down and kissing the warm skin he had uncovered.

Sutter tried to say more but his throat had closed, leaving him no voice, nothing but the tears that brushed over Mandy's skin as he turned his head from side to side, bathing his senses in her, cherishing her, absorbing her presence, feeling her hands softly stroking his hair even as his face caressed her. For a long time there was only silence and the sound of their ragged breathing.

Suddenly Mandy twisted beneath Sutter. His arms tightened around her waist, not wanting to end the healing embrace.

"Mandy?"

"There have been other changes, too," she murmured, twisting again, throwing aside the last of her clothes. "Don't you want to see them, too?"

Sutter's breath wedged in his throat when he looked up and saw that Mandy was nude, a smile trembling on her lips, her golden eyes radiant with tears and happiness. Without looking away from her, he began stripping off his own clothes, not stopping until there was nothing between their bodies. Only then did he bend down to her, giving in to the wild, oddly tender hunger that was ravishing him.

Mandy's breasts were taut and golden, their centers darker than Sutter remembered, fuller, and they tightened into velvet crowns at the first brush of his tongue. He barely restrained a thick sound of need, but his caresses were as gentle and reverent as his hand over her womb. Very slowly he sat up and looked at her, missing nothing of her beauty.

"I understand now why some cultures worshiped the female figure," Sutter said huskily, stroking Mandy lightly from her temples to the soles of her feet, lingering over each subtle sign of her pregnancy, cherishing her very femininity. "They were really worshiping life." His hand spread over Mandy's womb as he bent to kiss the same breasts that would someday nourish his child.

"Half of that life is your gift, not mine," Mandy said, biting back a low moan of pleasure as Sutter's tongue moved over her.

"My mind knows that," Sutter murmured, kissing her breasts, tasting them, making her shiver, "but my emotions are a hell of a lot more primitive. I see life welling up in you, Mandy. I've always seen it in you, life that's hot and sweet and wild and clean, and I want to bathe in that sacred upwelling, taking some of your life into me even as I give myself to it."

Mandy whispered Sutter's name against his lips as her hands found and cradled his hungry masculine flesh. His shuddering reaction made her feel as though she were holding lightning pooled within her cupped hands. Answering fire streaked through her when Sutter's large hand moved down between her legs to caress her. His husky sound of pleasure as he cherished her was echoed by her unraveling words.

"Is there anything else I should know before we're married?'' Sutter asked, smiling down at Mandy as he smoothed his palm over her, caressing her with her own sultry heat.

"The baby is growing so fast..."

Pleasure radiated hotly through Mandy, taking away her words. Sutter watched, smiling, caressing her, calling more torrid rain from her gathering storm.

"Yes?" he murmured encouragingly.

"The doctor is...talking about...twins," she said, moving against Sutter's hand, seeking a deeper joining.

"Twins," Sutter said, sucking in his breath, then laughing with delight. "Twins. My God." Still smiling, he knelt between Mandy's legs to kiss the swelling mound that might contain not one of his babies but two. "Any other miracles that you've been saving for a rainy day?" he murmured.

"Just that I love you."

Sutter's whole body froze in the instant before his breath came out with a husky, ragged sound.

"I love you, Mandy. I must have loved you since I carried you off that damned plane. That's why I couldn't get enough of you no matter how many times we made love." As he spoke he kissed her womb, her breasts, the pulse beating beneath her throat, her trembling lips, smoothing his words into her skin as he slowly joined his body to hers. "You're my life and I didn't know it until you walked away. But I know now. I'm going to spend my life loving you."

Mandy tried to tell him that she loved him in the same way, but he was moving within her, stealing her thoughts, her breath, her words. With a cry she gave herself to him and took him in the same instant, moving with him, chain lightning weaving between their bodies, ecstasy calling a passionate rain from the depths of their love until they could bear no more and slept deeply in each other's arms.

Within six months a son and then a daughter were born from Mandy's body into Sutter's gentle hands. Later, as he put each babe to suckle against her breast, she smiled and wept and whispered her love to the man who had returned to her twice what the sea had once taken.

When the babies were full of milk and love and sleep, Sutter put them in their bedside cribs before sliding into bed with the woman he loved. Even as he gathered her into his arms, she came to him, holding him. They slept as they would always live, body to body, breath to breath, love to love...complete.

*   *   *   *   *

POPCORN AND KISSES

Kasey Michaels

* * *

To Eleanor Durkin...
    I can scarcely bid you good-bye,
    even in a letter.
    I always made an awkward bow.
    God bless you!
                    (John Keats, 1820)

To me you shall always be forever young.

Dear Reader,

Talk about having a fun book to write!

I grew up going to drive-in movies with my parents, my friends...and as I grew older, there may have been one or two evenings spent at the drive-in on a Saturday night with a "special" friend, if you catch my meaning.

Drive-in movies are disappearing from much of the country, but there are still plenty around, including one owned by a dear friend of mine (please see the author's note at the back of the book).

When I got the idea for *Popcorn and Kisses,* my friend gave me free access to the business, so if I didn't exactly learn the business inside and out, I did get to see the projectors, hang out in the ticket booth and taste-test all the homemade goodies in the snack bar.

Popcorn and Kisses is a romance about two people who love the movies, but aren't quite so sure that either knows the best way to run the *business* of showing those movies to the public.

I think you'll have fun watching them sort it all out. You might want to pop some popcorn before you turn the page!

Enjoy

Chapter 1

The old-fashioned clock face projected onto the wide, curved screen showed the seconds slowly ticking away. The clock was surrounded on all sides by a host of cartoon popcorn boxes, hot dogs, candy bars and soda cups. Each character was equipped with stick-figure legs and arms and all were merrily dancing to the beat of a familiar-sounding syncopated tune.

As the single hand on the clock reached twelve, the large number six that had been displayed in the center of the dial disappeared and was replaced by an equally large number five. The music was momentarily muted as a voice announced: "Five minutes, folks! Just five minutes till show time. There's still time to visit our snack bar before our feature presentation of the evening. Five minutes to show time."

The clock hand had already begun another circuit before the music came up again, but the sprightly red-and-white-striped popcorn chorus girls in their high spiked heels, the cane-carrying, top-hat-clad hot dogs, the brightly wrapped candies and the foam-topped fizzing soda cups never missed a beat.

The crowd at the snack bar was smaller now, as most of the patrons at Wheeler's Drive-In Theater had already stocked up on the goodies they believed necessary to get them through the second feature without fear of starvation, and the usual long lines that extended outside the rest room doors had already disappeared. Parents hustled their pajama-clad youngsters back to their cars before the lights inside the snack bar were dimmed and they had to make their way along the gravel paths in the dark.

"Three minutes, folks! Three minutes till show time. There's still time to visit our snack bar. Three minutes till show time," the faceless voice droned out, and a few harassed mothers were forced to physically remove their balky toddlers from the playground located directly beneath the movie screen, promising that the movie they were about to see was much more fun than the swings, the sliding board or the old-fashioned foot-powered merry-go-round.

There was one section of the drive-in that seemed to escape the hustle and bustle of the between-shows intermission, and that was the area that made up the shadowy last three rows of the outdoor theater. Here there were no station wagons loaded with sleeping bags and jugs of homemade lemonade. No lawn chairs were set up outside the cars, which tended to be mostly older sports cars, pickup trucks or supercompacts.

There were speakers in the back rows, two on each of the metal poles that lined the built-up parking ramps between the small roadways, but many of them were never turned up or hung on an open side window so that the movie could be heard as well as seen. No matter what story lines were being projected, from lighthearted comedies to action-adventure thrillers, for the patrons in the secluded back rows the subject was always the same—romance.

It was springtime, and just one more night in the seemingly endless string of nights when Wheeler's Drive-In attracted moviegoers with its double features, cartoon specials and homey atmosphere amid the softly rolling hills just outside of Allentown, Pennsylvania.

At last the ticking clock disappeared, and the feature presentation, a parental-guidance-suggested spy spoof, appeared on the screen. The lights on the snack bar roof went out, and soon the only sounds to be heard other than the actors' voices were the occasional outbursts from cranky children fighting for equal space in the back seat, and a few inadvertent horn honkings as the moviegoers struggled to balance their popcorn and get comfortable at the same time.

The door to the dark projection booth opened and closed. "A pretty full house for our first Thursday night of the season, considering that it looked like rain earlier, don't you think, George?" the feminine voice asked above the whir of the projector.

George Blakeman, head—and only—projectionist at Wheeler's for more than forty-five years, only grunted, busy with the job at hand, loading the second reel onto the forty-year-old number-two projector that he had dubbed Veronica Lake. Number one had been christened with the name Gloria Swanson and would run out of film right after the scene in the Turkish bath that was already on-screen.

"Can you believe they actually get paid to write this junk?" he asked, shaking his balding head in disgust. "This guy's walking around in all that steam with nothing on but a towel, and when the bad guys show up he calmly reaches behind his back and pulls out a damn *machine gun* to blow them all away. I didn't see any bulges under that towel. Now where do you suppose he had that gun—taped to his rosy butt?"

Sharon Wheeler smiled at her friend's criticism of one of the previous winter's top-grossing movies—for Wheeler's was a second run theater—and pulled herself up to sit atop the large, scarred wooden worktable, her sneakers lazily swinging back and forth a good distance above the floor. "What else could he do, George? Snap them silly with a rolled-up Turkish towel? Besides, if he'd done that they'd have lost their PG rating. Just be glad we could get the film before it came out on home videotape. We need a couple more crowds like this one to make back what we lost on those three rainy nights last weekend.''

George watched through the small square paneless window of the concrete-block projection booth for the flashing white circle to appear in the corner of the screen, a cue that would alert him to switch on the second projector. Seeing the quick flash, he hit the button, waited for a second signal, then shut off the first projector so he could load the third reel.

"How's the cash box doing, Shari?" he asked, still not looking at his young boss, whom he had known since she was born. "Is the snack bar holding its own?"

Sharon's pert, freckle-dusted nose crinkled a bit as she added and subtracted some figures in her head. "The steak sandwiches sold out already, but since the price of the meat went up, I'd say we won't pick up anything extra there. I think I can up our price a quarter, but I can't make it too high or we'll scare the customers away. The ice cream went well, too, probably because it's been so darn hot outside."

As if to prove her point about the heat, Sharon undid the last two buttons on her blouse, then tied the two sides together under her breasts, baring her midriff. Her tanned legs, highly visible beneath the cutoff denim shorts, continued to swing back and forth, trying in vain to create some small breeze in the airless projection room. "We've got to get the air conditioner in here fixed tomorrow, before the weekend. It can't be good for the film to be in so much heat."

"It's not exactly great for the projectionist either, Shari," George pointed out gruffly, wiping his shiny forehead with a big red printed handkerchief. "Maybe the new owner will spring for a new air conditioner. This one's nearly as old as I am."

Sharon ran her hands through both sides of her shoulder-length honey-blond hair, tucking the heavy strands back behind her ears. "Dreaming again, George?" she asked, lightly hopping down from her perch. "Wheeler's has had two owners since Popsie died, and neither of them spent so much as a cent on the place. We may be the oldest operating drive-in theater in America, but to our esteemed owners we were only a tax write-off to balance out the companies' indoor theaters downtown and in the malls. What makes you think this St. Clair Theater Corporation is going to be any different?"

George carefully replaced the rewound reel in its case, slid the case into its proper slot in the numbered reel storage bin located under the worktable, then shrugged his shoulders hopefully. "The St. Clair bunch picked us up for next to nothing when it bought the indoor theaters from Hardesty Features. The way I figure it, it's not like it would break them to throw a little of the green stuff in our general direction. Right?"

Sharon started for the door, knowing she had to get back to the snack bar to supervise the six high school girls she had hired as summer help, but she turned back for a moment to seek some more assurance from her old friend. "You don't think they'll decide to turn Wheeler's into an X-rated theater, do you, George? I mean, companies are doing a lot of that sort of thing in some areas—although I don't think St. Clair's has any of them."

"It's anybody's guess, Shari," he answered, wishing he could say something to allay her fears. "But, hey, if they do, you won't have to worry your pretty head anymore about replacing the playground equipment. The whole place will be one big playground—and no kids allowed. It's a good thing the cows in Old Lady Harrison's field next door don't know how to use binoculars. Right?"

Sharon shook her head and turned away. "Thanks, George, for those stirring, truly inspiring words. You've been a big help. If I'm ever stuck at the bottom of a well I know I can count on you to toss me down a bucket of water."

"Hey," he called after her as she opened the door, "don't go away mad. I was just making a joke. St. Clair doesn't have any X-rated theaters, Shari, I checked. Just stop worrying that pretty head of yours until somebody from the company shows up to inspect the place. After all, there's nothing you can do about it anyway. Right?"

Relenting, Sharon's mouth formed a small smile as she nodded her agreement. "Like you say, George, we'll just have to wait and see. I guess it's just that I love this place so much—" As she heard the tremor come into her voice she shook her head as if to banish her darker thoughts. "Oh, well. I've got to get back to work. And tomorrow is Friday— we should get an even bigger crowd. I'll send one of the girls in soon with your usual, okay?"

George licked his lips with exaggerated fervor at the mention of his nightly snack of two hot dogs barely visible beneath mounds of ketchup, mustard and Sharon's secret sauce. "Send them in when our hero turns his motorbike into a rocket launcher and wipes out enemy headquarters. That'll give me plenty of time to eat before the next reel change. Oh, yeah, and I wouldn't say no to a couple of those nachos—just hold the jalapeño peppers. Right?"

"You got it," Sharon promised. Then she added thoughtfully, "You know, George, after watching *Spy in the Eye* seven times in three days, X-rated films don't sound so bad."

Sharon sighed before slipping out the door.

Zachary St. Clair had spent the better part of his Friday driving around Allentown and some of its nearby suburbs, cursorily examining the St. Clair Theater Corporation's latest acquisitions. So far, he was satisfied. The two shopping mall theaters, each comprised of six screen houses, were fairly new, strategically located and economically sound investments.

The three downtown theaters, two in Allentown and one in nearby Bethlehem, were older, and Zachary had already jotted down some notes concerning the feasibility of converting at least two of them into multiscreen houses.

But as pleased as he was with his findings, he was weary, having driven to Southeastern Pennsylvania from New York City that morning, and was beginning to regret his decision to inspect the last theater, Wheeler's—a drive-in of all things—before calling it a day and returning to his hotel.

He had already been on the road an hour, driving in circles as the daylight turned to dusk, trying to locate the rural theater that was advertised as being just fifteen minutes from center-city Allentown, and his never placid temper was beginning to surface with a vengeance. It had become a challenge, finding the theater, and now he was determined to ferret it out no matter how long it took.

This was the third time he had passed the same country inn, he was sure of it, and he decided the moment had come to throw in the towel and ask for directions. Pulling into the parking lot that fronted on the rural highway, he was just about to swing the car around when he saw the sign out of the corner of his eye.

"Wheeler's Drive-In Theater, Oldest Operating Drive-In in America" was spelled out in faded paint on the weather-beaten wooden sign that was lit by one small spotlight. Spying out a narrow-topped road just to the right of the inn, Zachary steered his sports car in that direction, cursing succinctly under his breath at the stupidity of placing a sign thirty feet back from the edge of the highway.

As he rounded a slight turn his headlights picked up the huge vintage black-backed outdoor screen that perched atop a heavy cross-beamed wooden base. "I feel like I've just entered the Twilight Zone," he muttered under his breath as he stopped the car beside a small wooden shed that served as the ticket office.

"Hi there! Neat car," the gangly, red-haired youth said cheerfully after blowing a shiny pink bubble, drawing it into his widely opened mouth and biting down so the bubble burst with a large pop. Then, maneuvering the huge wad of gum to one side so that his cheek had to stretch around it, the boy continued, "You're just in time for the cartoon if you hurry. We've got Woody Woodpecker this week. You alone? No kids in the back?" He leaned out of the shed and peered into the empty back seat. "We give lollipops, you know."

"Bully for you. One, please," Zachary said shortly, then looked down at his hand, amazed to see change from the five dollar bill he had passed over to the boy.

"Come to see *Spy in the Eye*, huh? Saw it three times myself. Great picture! All alone, huh? You know the first feature is a Disney?" The boy looked warily at Zachary, as if wondering just what was wrong with the guy that he'd come to a drive-in on his own.

Zachary didn't answer. He just pocketed his change, pushed the button that raised the darkly tinted side window to shut off any further conversation and stepped on the gas.

"Hey, mister—shut off your headlights! Only parking lights from this point. Can't you read the sign?" the boy yelled after the departing car before turning to greet a station wagon holding two adults and a small army of pajama-clad children.

Zachary chose a spot about six rows back from the screen and pulled in, hearing the bottom of his sports car scrape against the loose gravel as it moved over the rounded hump that angled the front of the car higher than the rear, giving a better view of the screen.

He lowered his window to reach for the speaker, only to find that he had parked too far away for the cord to reach inside the car. "I needed this," he growled softly, restarting the engine to pull back and move closer. The undercarriage scraped again, bringing a short, satisfying curse to his lips. It took two backups, and five more scrapes, to finally pull the car in at the correct angle, but once the speaker was hooked over the open window Zachary discovered that the sound didn't work.

"I should have known," he said ruefully, replacing the

useless box on its stand, for he really hadn't come to see the movie anyway. Turning front, he looked toward the screen and saw dancing beams of light chasing one another around the white surface. "What the hell?" he mused, looking around at the other cars until he understood that several of the patrons had spotlights attached to their cars and were passing the time playing tag with one another on the blank screen.

He decided to take a closer look around before the movie started, and opened his door—just to hear it slam against the speaker post, dislodging the speaker, which then bounced against the fiberglass car door before falling to the ground. "Damn!" This wasn't getting any better.

Pulling the door shut, he angled his six-foot-four-inch frame around the floor-mounted gearshift and twisted himself onto the other bucket seat before nearly falling out of the passenger door as his left leg went into a cramp.

Limping slightly, and madder than he'd been since the day his golf cart had lost its brakes and landed him waist-deep in a water hazard on the third hole three years earlier, Zachary made for the front of the theater to inspect the screen up close.

He stopped dead, though, as he passed the first row, unable to believe what he was seeing. There, at the base of the screen, and enclosed by a sorry, sagging wooden fence, was the poorest excuse for a playground in the history of the world.

Ancient metal play equipment, all painted an uninspired slate-gray, was scattered willy-nilly over a large patch of weeds mixed with even larger patches of packed-down dirt. Two park benches placed together at one end of the playground were all the seating provided for the many mothers who were watching their children as they climbed and swung and whirled round and round on a huge flat metal circle, hanging on to the contraption's projecting metal arms for dear life as they screamed in glee.

"The liability insurance for this death trap has to be

enough to choke a horse,'' he muttered under his breath before lifting his head to peer intently at the screen, checking on its condition. After only a moment, he shook his head, mouthed a short, unlovely word and turned on his heel, having seen enough—more than enough.

Car horns began to blow as the night grew darker and, in the customers' opinion, it was show time. The discordant sounds followed Zachary as he picked his way carefully back across the humps that made up the parking ramps and the pothole-pitted gravel paths separating them.

He headed straight to the low, white cement-block building that housed the snack bar and projection booth. The aroma of hot buttered popcorn, a smell he was used to, mingled incongruously with those of hot dogs, onions, frying steak and, of all things, sauerkraut.

As he stepped through one of the opened doorways into the brightly lit snack bar he nearly collided with a chubby, pajama-dressed, giggling toddler clutching an overflowing box of popcorn, who was running full tilt for the door, her older brother in hot pursuit, yelling, ''You hafta *share*! Mom said so! *I'm telling!*''

Once completely inside, Zachary stood with his back against the wall and watched as seven young women raced back and forth across the open area behind the counters, which spanned the width of the room facing each of the two doorways, taking and filling huge orders without benefit of written bills or adding machines.

The smallest woman, a petite pony-tailed blonde, was dressed in an oversize red T-shirt, which had Wheeler's printed in large white letters on the back, and a pair of very short white shorts. She seemed to move up and down the length of the counter with the speed of light, filling orders and making change from a wide, three-pocket canvas belt she wore loosely tied around her waist, and never missing a beat—all accomplished while smiling at all the customers and winking at all the children.

Zachary shook his head yet again. He wasn't against hiring teenagers—all the St. Clair theaters hired teenagers—and the young women seemed pleasant and efficient enough, but how could the manager let them get away with dressing like that? Where were their uniforms, their aprons, their caps? Sloppy, slipshod management, he concluded. Damned sloppy.

Walking around to the front of the building, he located the door to the projection room and turned the handle. Locked. Well, he thought ruefully, that's something. At least the projectionist must have something on the ball. He raised his hand and rapped sharply on the door.

"Bathrooms on the other side," a male voice bellowed. "Can't you people read?"

"I'd like to speak with you for a moment," Zachary called loudly through the door, for the cartoon had begun and the snack bar speaker was located just above his head.

"I gave at the office," the voice yelled back. "Get lost!"

"I said open this door!" Zachary bellowed, almost glad to have an excuse to yell.

"Take a hike!"

"Now listen, buster—"

Zachary never finished the sentence. He was instead distracted by the sound of a high-pitched female scream, and he ran toward the snack bar to see who was getting killed and by whom. Rounding the corner he abruptly stopped in his tracks, having come face-to-face with, of all things, a large, brown-eyed cow.

"What the bloody hell—" he exploded, stepping back a pace.

"Moo-o-o-o," the cow responded, starting to move toward him, the heavy metal bell hanging from around her neck clang-clanging as the animal rocked her large brown and white head from side to side, her massive jaw working as she chewed her cud.

"Help me! Help me! That wild bull is trying to trample me!" pleaded a woman clad in a pink cabbage-rose-flowered cotton robe, fuzzy blue slippers and two dozen purple plastic hair rollers, as she convulsively grabbed Zachary by the arm.

Zachary might have been a city boy, but he knew damn well that the gentle-eyed bovine in front of him was no bull. "Calm down, lady," he snapped unsympathetically. "It's just an ordinary, everyday cow. Go back to your car, it's perfectly safe."

"No it isn't," she contradicted shrilly, still hanging on to Zachary's arm, her hot dog squashed in her fist, dripping catsup. "There's a whole herd of them stampeding through here." She disengaged one arm to point in the direction of the eighth row. "Look at all of them! Oh, my poor babies. They're all alone in the car. I only wanted a hot dog. What will I do?"

Suddenly the blonde from the snack bar appeared around the corner, a yardstick clasped in her right hand, a big red apple in her left. "I thought as much. Here we go again," she sighed, eyeing up the cow. "Hello there, Gertrude. So, how's tricks?"

When the cow only continued to chew, the young woman turned to the lady and smiled. "Go inside the snack bar, ma'am, and one of the girls will escort you safely back to your car," she said calmly, giving the woman a gentle push toward the corner. "There's nothing to worry about, I promise. You just make sure the girl gives you a free car pass you may use any time this season." Then, looking at the unappetizing lump squished tightly in the woman's right hand, she grimaced slightly and added, "And tell her to throw in another hot dog for you while she's at it, okay?"

"A free pass? For our whole car?" the woman repeated, lifting up her head so sharply that the curlers in her hair seemed to be reacting like finely tuned antennae. "Oh, aren't you nice! But—but, what about the cows? Where did they come from?"

"The fence must have broken down between the theater and Mrs. Harrison's pasture again, and her cows decided to try out our snack bar. You go on along now and I'll—um—

I'll try to make like a shepherd and get the flock out of here.'' She lifted her hands to show the yardstick and apple as if to display just how she would go about rounding up the strays. "Come on, Gertrude, my dear, it's time you and your lady friends called it an evening," she said, patting the cow affectionately on her wide forehead as if to prove how totally harmless the animal was.

The lady reluctantly released Zachary's arm without bothering to thank him, and sprinted for the safety of the snack bar. The blonde, he noticed after inspecting his sleeve for creases, had already set off in the other direction, yardstick raised above her head as she held the apple out behind her like bait. Gertrude followed along behind her like a well-behaved house pet.

One hand to his mouth, Zachary watched as the young woman skillfully rounded up the dozen or so animals and paraded them down the path toward the far end of the theater lot while a loud woodpecker laugh echoed from the many speakers. As the strange procession passed by, patrons blew their horns or blinked their headlights on and off, and the girl alternately waved an imaginary hat in the air and executed exaggerated low bows in acknowledgment of their strange applause.

"I...own...this," Zachary said out loud slowly, unable to believe anything that had happened from the moment he had left the highway. "I actually *own* this nightmare."

Within a few minutes the blonde was back, minus the apple and the cows. She walked right up to him, smiling broadly, and placing her hands on her hips said, "A three-piece suit. Wild! You know, for a moment there I didn't know what seemed more out of place, Old Lady Harrison's herd or that suit. Anyway, thanks so much for letting that absurd woman latch on to you like that. My name's Sharon, by the way. If you'll wait here a moment I'll see if I can dig up a couple of free passes for you for your trouble."

She had already started to move away when Zachary fairly spit, "I don't want one of your free passes—or, for that matter, any of your free hot dogs—after all, it's not as if anyone in their right mind would be so foolish as to come here twice.''

Walking back to him, still smiling, she offered, ''All right. No passes for the man in his right mind. But how about a Wheeler special steak sandwich before you ride off into the sunset? You'll love it. Grilled paper-thin sliced steak served on a steamed roll and topped with cooked onions, sauce, pickles and hot peppers—pure ambrosia! It's the least I can do.''

''You can skip the sales pitch, miss. Let's go inside. I want to see your manager,'' Zachary informed her, his voice hard.

Sharon's smile finally faded, and she winced slightly as she looked up into his grim face. ''It's Sharon, remember? Oh, dear, you're not going to make a mountain out of this little molehill, are you, sir? After all, if you think about it for a while, the whole thing was really rather funny.''

''You'll notice that I'm not laughing.''

Wrinkling up her nose, Sharon answered dully, ''Yeah. Actually, I'd already noticed that, sir. Very well, follow me. I guess it might be better to go inside.'' Once again she turned and headed for the snack bar. ''It *is* a lot cooler out here, you know. Don't you think—''

''*Damn it!* Woman, would you please move!''

''Whoops! Sorry about that, sir,'' she ended lamely, turning to look up at the man, who had collided with her as she had stopped without warning to take one last stab at placating him. ''We'll go inside, right?''

Zachary was busy rubbing his chin, the part of his anatomy that had so lately met up with the top of Sharon's head. ''You're very astute,'' he bit out angrily.

''I'm really sorry, sir,'' she said hurriedly. ''It's just that I thought, well, it's such a lovely night, and it would be much more pleasant if we could—''

''I want to see your manager. Now!''

As if trying to put a bright face on it, Sharon spread her

arms wide and grinned. "Your wish is my command, sir. One manager, at your service." Shifting the yardstick to her left hand, she held out her right hand and said, "Sharon Wheeler, manager of Wheeler's Drive-In, oldest operating outdoor theater in America. And you're—"

Zachary stared at the small hand for a long moment before taking it in his large one which nearly swallowed it as he gave it a firm shake, then held on. "Zachary St. Clair, owner of St. Clair Theater Corporation—and your boss," he replied, his dark eyes narrowing into dangerous slits.

"And I'm dead," Sharon whispered under her breath, closing her eyes.

"Not yet, Miss Wheeler," Zachary, overhearing, replied tersely. "But I'm beginning to believe it could be arranged."

Chapter 2

He's rather good-looking—for a fire-breathing monster, that is, Sharon thought as she reluctantly preceded Zachary St. Clair into the snack bar. But then, she thought as a small smile tugged at the corners of her mouth, Beelzebub had also supposedly been rather handsome, if one overlooked the horns and tail!

The lights inside the snack bar were dimmed, the girls inside the enclosure scurrying here and there, replenishing the supply of hot dogs on the carousel griller, loading freshly popped corn into the standby holding compartment and re-stocking the candy shelves; but it was neither dark enough nor hectic enough to keep the teenagers' attention from zooming in on Zachary St. Clair.

"Wow, Sheila, would you get a load of *that*!"

Sharon stopped, closed her eyes and sighed, convinced she could already hear the townspeople building the gallows outside her jail cell. Either that, or it's the sound of someone hammering yet another nail into my coffin, she mused, wondering if things could possibly get worse before they began to get better.

"Worse," she decided aloud, suddenly realizing that, in order to get to her office, Zachary St. Clair would first have to bend his ridiculously tall frame so that he could fit under the cut-out section in the snack bar counter. Oh, yes, she agreed with herself silently, I could lead him back outside and into the office via the projection room. But that would mean introducing him to George, and I think the poor man has had enough for one night!

Turning to face her new employer, Sharon attempted to dazzle him with another of her wide smiles, fingered an imaginary cigar beside her mouth, chirped, "Walk this way, please," in her best Groucho Marx impersonation, and then quickly bent almost in half to scurry underneath the counter.

She didn't stop until she had threaded her way through the milling employees and past the small, open door marked Private. The room she entered was slightly smaller than minuscule, containing a child-size wooden school desk and single chair, an oversize refrigerator, a green metal table laden with tools and several speakers in varying stages of disrepair, and a half dozen industrial-size boxes of soda cups, napkins and other snack bar supplies. There was no window, little light and no more room to run.

Bracing the seat of her shorts against the back of the chair, she carefully folded her arms beneath her breasts, awaiting the verbal drubbing she was sure St. Clair was about to deliver. She didn't have long to wait.

"You call this rabbit hutch an office?" he began in his smooth, educated voice.

"Actually, Mr. St. Clair, I call this office a rabbit hutch," Sharon returned almost calmly, inwardly amazing herself at her own daring. "But then, at a time like this I imagine we really shouldn't be splitting *hares*, should we?"

St. Clair looked at her steadily for a long, heart-stopping moment, during which Sharon could feel the last of her bravado cravenly folding its tent and slipping silently away, then he said, "If you could possibly bring yourself to attempt it, I have somehow retained a slim hope that this discussion can be conducted at something at least approaching an adult level."

Sharon shrugged yet again. "Sorry, Mr. St. Clair," she apologized in a sincere voice. "I'm listening. Fire away." Grimacing at what she had just said, she then shook her head and muttered softly, "Bad choice of words, Wheeler."

But St. Clair ignored her, busy with figuring out just how he could maneuver himself into a position that would allow him to close the door, locking out the intrusive sounds from the snack bar. After several unsuccessful attempts, the last of which left him standing wedged between the edge of the door and the handle to the refrigerator, he applied to Sharon for assistance.

"I'm sorry, sir," she replied, spreading her hands helplessly. "To tell you the truth, I don't remember anyone ever shutting the door before. There's never been any need."

His green eyes narrowed, St. Clair scanned the room, obviously in search of something. "No need? Then you keep the box office receipts in a safe in the projection room?"

Sharon stepped away from the chair back and belligerently thrust out her chin. "We have never found it necessary to hide the money away from our employees. Wheeler employees are honest, Mr. St. Clair. Besides, money is never kept here overnight. I use the night drop at the branch bank down the street."

That was good, that was very good, she cheered herself silently. Keep it up, Sharon, and keep your fingers crossed that he doesn't ask to see the safe anyway.

"I'd still like to see the safe, Miss Wheeler, if you don't mind," St. Clair pushed on relentlessly.

Like a dog worrying a bone, Sharon concluded, beginning to really dislike the man standing in front of her. "Don't you think you've seen enough for one evening, Mr. St. Clair?" she asked hopefully. "I'd be more than willing to meet you out here tomorrow morning—or whatever time you choose—to inspect the theater. I mean after all, what with Gertrude, and that silly woman, and all—''

"The safe, Miss Wheeler," he repeated, reaching up to loosen his tie and undo the top button of his white silk shirt as the heat in the small office began to take its toll.

Sharon lifted a hand to rub at the back of her slim neck. "All right, sir," she said, capitulating. "But never say I didn't warn you. The money is behind you, in the lettuce keeper. Rather apt, right? Bottom shelf, behind the chopped onions."

St. Clair turned his head slowly to stare incredulously at the white enamel door behind him, then just as slowly looked back to stare at Sharon. "You keep the box office receipts in the *refrigerator*?" he ground out angrily.

Already mentally scanning the help wanted ads, Sharon leaned back against the chair once more, spread her arms wide and grinned. "Doesn't everybody?"

Zachary sat alone in a dark corner of the nearly deserted hotel cocktail lounge, his long, lean legs wrapped around the bar stool as he slowly sipped his Scotch on the rocks.

Raising his lips from the rim of the glass, he peered desultorily into the marble-veined mirror behind the back bar, unsurprised to see the deep lines that weariness had cut into his face on either side of his mouth, then shifted his gaze back to watch the amber liquid as he swirled it around in the glass in front of him.

He was tired, so damnably tired. He had a solid year of deal making, merger producing, hostile takeover maneuvering and buy-outs behind him, the culmination of more than eight years of careful planning and old-fashioned hard work. The St. Clair Theater Corporation, begun by his father thirty years earlier with the purchase of a single indoor theater in upstate New York, had finally lived up to all expectations— thanks to the financial brilliance of Lucien St. Clair's whiz-kid son, Zachary, "the college boy."

The St. Clair Theater Corporation now owned 127 theaters

in the thriving market on the Eastern seaboard, boasting 863 screens. The theaters, or houses, as they were called, were almost all automated multiscreen facilities, equipped with the most up-to-date xenon projectors, and operated under what Zachary believed to be the most modern management program in the industry.

Automation—that was the ticket to sound management. The bottom line in theater management was profit, just as it was in any other business, and projection automation, though costly to install, meant a large reduction in staff—and in the payment of salaries.

Taking another sip of his Scotch, Zachary remembered how his school-of-hard-knocks father had refused to consider the installation of automated projectors and manager-projectionists when the proposal had first been presented to him, causing their first real argument since the younger St. Clair had officially joined the company Lucien had named with him in mind.

But Lucien had at last agreed to a compromise, Zachary recalled now with a slight smile, agreeing to allow his college-educated son to automate a small regional five-theater chain the company had purchased in Delaware as a sort of test. "He wanted me to fall flat on my face," Zachary softly told the half inch of Scotch still remaining in the bottom of his glass, "but eight years and several million dollars later, I think I can safely say Dad's seen the light."

Thoughts of his self-made father, now retired and living in Florida with Zachary's shopping-mall-mad mother, brought him rudely back to reality—a reality that took the form of Wheeler's Drive-In.

"Dad would love that run-down old place," he ruminated, shaking his head. "Folksy, he'd call it." He lifted a long, pale hand and ran his fingers through one side of his coal black hair. "God, I'm tired. So tired, I'm talking out loud to myself in a public place. What's the matter with me anyway?"

Temporary burnout. That's what it is, he decided silently,

looking once more into the mirror, this time inspecting his reflection with a critical eye. *I've been under a lot of pressure lately, wanting to wrap up this final deal before the end of the fiscal quarter,* he thought. *Look at my face. It's already May and I'm still so pale I look like the underbelly of a fish. I don't remember the last time I had a golf club in my hands, let alone the time for a game.*

"All work and no play make Zachary a dull boy," he paraphrased prosaically, saluting his reflection with the glass before downing the last of his drink.

"What did you say, Mister?" asked the hotel bartender, who had been making a great business out of wiping down the long mahogany bar in hopes his last customer would take the hint and hit the road. "You want another drink?"

Standing up and reaching into his pocket to deposit a large tip on the top of the bar, Zachary replied, "No, thank you anyway. I believe I'll call it a night." He began to walk slowly toward the door that led into the lobby, then stopped and turned back to ask, "You know of any good golf courses around here? I'll need to rent clubs."

"Golf courses? Of *course* I do!" the bartender quipped, unknowingly reminding Zachary of an infuriating small blonde who seemed to be equally fond of puns. "Let's see. You got your Allentown Municipal, your Twin Lakes, your Willow Brook—that's a small course—your Wedgewood. Then there's your private courses, if you know anyone who can get you on. Those would be your country clubs. You've got your Lehigh Country Club, your Brookside—"

Zachary held up his hand to stem the dizzying flow of words. "Thank you very much, I believe I get the picture. I think I might know somebody who can arrange a round at one of the private clubs," he said, remembering the local lawyer with whom he had worked concerning the purchase of the theaters. Surely the guy owed him something for not warning him about Wheeler's.

A few minutes later, lying fully dressed atop the king-size bed in his room, his arms loosely folded behind his head,

Zachary could feel the tension slowly leaving his body. He'd spend the weekend playing a few rounds of golf, getting a little time in the sun to clear out the cobwebs, and then on Monday he'd call Sharon Wheeler and take her up on that offer to inspect the theater.

It was the least he could do, considering the way she had nearly begged him for the chance to make up for his poor first impression of the place. After all, he wasn't heartless. He'd give her every chance to convince him that holding on to Wheeler's Drive-In was in the best interest of his company.

And *then* he would order the place to close, tossing that obnoxious young female out on her pert little nose!

"Move it, George, please! We have two measly days in which to turn this place into a tight ship."

George Blakeman, sitting at his ease atop the cool metal lid of the ice cream freezer in the snack bar, sniffed rudely. "Tight ship? Big deal. Everybody thought the *Titanic* was a tight ship, and look what happened to it. Right? Calm down, Shari. You'd need a miracle to turn this place into the kind of theater that St. Clair wants to see, and I'm all out of loaves and fishes."

"George! That's blasphemous!" Sharon exclaimed, shocked into stopping what she was doing, which looked, as George had told her earlier, as if she was running around wildly in three directions at once—while accomplishing nothing.

Reaching up a finger to idly scratch the side of his long, bulbous nose, which had been broken more than once in his checkered lifetime, the projectionist returned calmly, "Maybe. But since the place they'll send me to can't be any hotter than that projection room in there, I don't see as how I'll even notice."

Sharon tilted her blond head to one side and narrowed her eyelids to look searchingly at her old friend. "You've been working at Wheeler's since before I was born, George. Don't you care about the place? Not even a little bit?''

The man shrugged diffidently. ''I've been working here on borrowed time ever since your grandfather died, Shari, honey, and you know it. Either one of our two previous owners would have tossed me out on my ear long ago if only they'd taken the time to come see the place. Right? It just hasn't been the same, and the road keeps calling. You can't keep covering for me forever. Besides, I'm pushing seventy now and, truth to tell, when summer comes and we start opening every night instead of just weekends I don't think I'm going to be able to hack it at all anymore. Sorry.''

Sharon stuck her hands on her hips and took one step toward him. ''So that's it? Just like that? You're giving up? I'm disappointed in you, George, really I am. After all, you were Popsie's right-hand man. He took you in when nobody else would touch you with—oh, never mind, forget I said that. Just remember what Popsie did for you. Is this how you pay him back?''

''That was all a long time ago, honey,'' George argued, his thin face showing every year of his age. ''There's been a lot of water under the bridge since then. Your grandfather's been gone a long time, and things just aren't the way they used to be. Besides, I paid your Popsie back for hiring me. Right? I never ran out on the job while he was alive, and you know it.''

Putting her fingers to her throbbing temples, Sharon dropped her head forward slightly, guilt washing over her at the plaintive sound in George's normally gruff, raspy voice. ''Of course you have, George. I'm so sorry. Please forgive me. It's just—'' she spread her arms wide as if to take in the whole of the theater ''—it's just that I love this old place so much. Oh, George, he's going to shut us down. I just know it. I hate that Mr. Three-piece-suit St. Clair!''

George gave a weak smile. ''I can hardly wait to meet this fella, if he's everything you say he is. A real 1980s businessman, with calculator ink in his veins, you said. But

I'll bet you're only putting me on about that pointed tail. Right?''

Sharon laughed, George's banter succeeding in breaking her mood. ''Don't forget the horns, George,'' she reminded him, motioning for the man to shift himself to one side so that she could open one of the smaller lids on the freezer and get them each an ice cream sandwich, George's favorite confection.

''What's this? I know what you're doing, you sneaky child. You're trying to bribe me with ice cream. Right? It won't change the facts, but I won't say no to the bribe,'' George quipped, snatching one of the sandwiches from her hand.

''Wretch,'' Sharon sniffed huffily, barely hiding her amusement.

''Oh, yeah? Well, sticks and stones, and all that,'' George retorted happily, just to show he had forgiven her for her earlier outburst.

''So,'' she said after removing the paper wrapper and taking her first satisfying bite of ice cream, ''you think I'm beating a dead horse, don't you, trying to hang on to this place? Come on, George, sock it to me.''

The projectionist waited until he had finished his ice cream, which only took him four big bites, before obliging. ''The day of the drive-in theater in this part of the country is just about over, Shari, like I've told you a thousand times before. What with the multiscreen houses and the malls, there's just no need for them anymore. Like me, they've outlived their usefulness.''

''But, George,'' Sharon interrupted, ''people *like* to watch movies outdoors. It's great for families, kids—''

''In *Texas* it's good,'' George broke in, pointing a finger at her. ''In *New Mexico* it's good. In *California* it's good. They can keep their theaters open year round. In *Pennsylvania* it's ridiculous. We can only stay open from April until September or October. In the warmer parts of the country they're even building a couple of new houses, five-screen outdoor theaters, with modern sound systems. But then, I've heard it told that it doesn't snow much in Southern California. No, the only way Wheeler's has any chance of staying alive is as a mom-and-pop operation. Right? No chain is going to cotton to a house that can only open in the summer. It's just not good business economically. You understand?''

''Now you sound like St. Clair,'' Sharon grumbled, wrinkling up her nose. ''Before he stomped out of here last night he was mouthing words like 'green sheets' and 'bottom lines.' Do you know his corporation actually bought this place without even *looking* at it! Where has the romance of the theater gone, the thrill of ownership? To him it's nothing but a business. Doesn't anyone have any respect for the past, for the institutions that helped to make this country great?''

''Drive-in movies made this country great? They may have added a bit to the population explosion, maybe, but *made this country great*? Aren't you stretching things just a tad?''

Sharon pouted, totally frustrated. ''Don't split hairs with me, George, you know what I mean. I—I just can't seem to put it into words.'' Seeing that George was about to offer her the comfort of his arms—a move that would surely reduce her to juvenile sobs—she stuck out her chin and said, ''Go home, George. You're right. There's nothing we can do in this short time to change anything. Especially after Gertrude's appearance. Mr. St. Clair is just going to have to take us or leave us the way we are—and before you say it, no, you can't have odds on what he'll choose to do! I'll see you tonight about six.''

The projectionist looked at his young employer and friend carefully for a moment. Then, seeming to come to a decision, he mumbled, ''Right,'' eased himself down from his perch and headed for the door. ''See you at six.''

It was only after she heard the sound of George's ancient Plymouth starting up and pulling away that Sharon allowed her tense body to relax, slumping against the snack bar counter in an attitude of total defeat.

"How could I have said those things to George?" she berated herself aloud, shaking her head in self-disgust. "It isn't as if I don't know the full story, for heaven's sake!" She then closed her eyes, remembering the long-ago conversation during which her grandfather had told her the story of George Blakeman.

Back in the early 1940s, in the days before nonflammable acetate film, the projectionist's job was considered to be both the most romantic and the most dangerous in the movie theater business. Working in their underwear in the extreme heat of the high, airless booths, the projectionists, who always worked in pairs, were constantly exposed to the possibility that the film could become jammed in the projectors, causing the nitrate film to ignite. Once burning, the fire would quickly spread upward to the reel house, the metal box holding the feeding reel of film, and an explosion would result within the space of a few moments.

George's projector at the downtown theater where he worked had been involved in just such an incident. Sharon could almost hear Popsie's voice as he recounted the drama of the incident. "It all happened so quickly, Poppet. One minute George and his assistant were laughing about one of the girls in the snack bar who had a crush on George, and the next moment the film in George's projector jammed, concentrating all the white-hot light from the carbon lamp on a single frame of film. George tried to shut down the lamp house but it was already too late. Bang, the fire shot right up into the film house. Then all hell broke loose."

Sharon shivered as she pictured the scene. There were no windows in such a projection room, only four holes cut into the walls abutting the theater proper, two to let the film be shown, and two for the projectionists to look through. As the fire grew, the special lead safety fuse holding the chain that in turn held the steel plates that sat just above each of the four small openings melted in the heat, and the plates dropped into position, closing the holes with loud bangs like cell doors slamming. The room was submerged in total darkness.

Both projectionists knew they now had only a few moments to get out of the booth before the burning film inside the metal reel house caused it to explode. They had to grope for the door to the hallway in the dark, get through it as quickly as possible and then try to contain the explosion by shutting the door behind them.

George made it out.

His friend didn't. The man's burns had put him in the hospital for more than a year, and George held himself responsible.

"George was one of the best in the business," Sharon remembered Popsie telling her as she, her ten-year-old skinny, tanned bare legs kicking back and forth as she perched on the workbench in the drive-in projection booth, hung on her grandfather's every word. "But he was never the same after that day, poor fella. He drinks sometimes, you understand, just to stop the memories, but mostly he just goes off on his own, to sulk. He's still one hell of a projectionist. He'll never let you down, Poppet, I can guarantee it."

"And he never did, Popsie," Sharon murmured aloud now, slowly wiping away a tear. "But I think I'm finally asking too much of the poor old dear. It's clear that George just doesn't have it in him to fight St. Clair. Besides, even if the theater could by some miracle get a second life, St. Clair is bound to want to replace George's faithful Gloria and Veronica with two of those new xenon projectors. The poor guy just couldn't take that, it would break his heart. I couldn't ask it of him. It's over. It's all over."

Closing her eyes against the realization that there was nothing she could do to halt the closing of Wheeler's, Sharon picked up the damp towel she had been using to bring a high sheen to the chrome butter dispenser, tossed it carelessly onto one slim shoulder and walked out of the snack bar into the bright Saturday morning sunlight.

Chapter 3

It had been a full house Saturday night, thanks to pleasant weather and the popularity of *Spy in the Eye* with the largely teenage crowd, and Sharon was feeling a bit more confident about the theater, the future and life in general that Sunday morning on her drive to the Lehigh Country Club and her weekly game with her friend Hugh Kingsley, who considered her his permanent guest partner on the golf course.

Tonight would mark the final showing of the adventure film, but Sharon wasn't too worried about the success of next weekend's offering, a parental-guidance-suggested adventure film and, by some stroke of luck she didn't care to look into too deeply, a first-run Disney movie as their feature presentation. Unless the weather refused to cooperate, Wheeler's should realize another very profitable weekend run. Yes, Sharon was happy, and she was looking forward to the golf match ahead of her.

She arrived at the country club just after ten, once the worst of the crush of golfers had teed off and, after donning her golf shoes in the parking lot because she loved the sound the metal spikes made while crunching across the graveled lot, made her way to the pro shop to meet Hugh.

Her clubs and bag, both gifts from her grandfather, were already securely strapped to the back of one of the white motorized golf carts, for Hugh had long ago convinced her of the foolishness of refusing his offer to store her clubs in the locker room at his expense. After all, he had reasoned, it was cheaper for him to do that than to pay off the seven million dollars in bets he owed her in their five-year-old-and-still-running gin rummy competition.

Rounding the corner of the white-painted brick pro shop at a brisk pace, Sharon smiled and waved gaily as she saw Hugh Kingsley turn away from the two men he was speaking with and motion her to join him under the wooden canopy. Her smile faded, however, when she realized just who was standing in the shadows beside Hugh on the bricked patio.

"Zachary St. Clair," she fairly hissed, nearly tripping over her own feet as she stumbled to a halt, a flush of confusion mixed with anger flooding into her cheeks. "Maybe somebody's put a curse on me, and I just don't know it yet. Please, please *don't* let him be playing along with Hugh and me. *Please!*"

Zachary and his lawyer companion, Fred Staples, had spent an enjoyable afternoon on the course Saturday, followed by a quick dip in the club pool and a leisurely dinner in the main dining room. So congenial was their day that Fred, a bachelor himself, had asked Zachary to join him for a repeat of their activities again today. The young lawyer didn't have a regular foursome on Sundays, so he was free to make the invitation, and he had asked the golf pro to arrange a foursome for him.

What Zachary didn't know, information that most probably would have had him hastily declining Fred's generous offer, was that the pro had managed to pair them up with Hugh Kingsley, a local hotel owner, and his female partner.

A woman golfer, Zachary was thinking as the blond-haired

woman approached. *Just what I need. I can only hope she and this Kingsley fellow are engaged or something, or I could end up spending the day trying to fend off her obvious advances as she asks me to help her with her swing.*

If Zachary had voiced this thought aloud his companions would have thought him egotistical in the extreme, but then neither Hugh nor Fred had witnessed the many close calls Zachary's extreme good looks and favorable fortune had caused on the links, in dark hallways and on secluded beaches between Florida and Maine.

Now, looking once more at the woman, who had for some reason or another stopped some distance away from the small group, Zachary slowly reassessed his first reaction.

She presented quite an attractive picture, dressed as she was in a thin, sleeveless, scoop-necked cotton blouse that had a row of tiny buttons running neck to waist between attractively rounded breasts and a knee-length grass-green culotte that cinched tightly at her small waist and revealed straight, tanned legs that ended in low green socks and white golf shoes. Her shoulder-length honey-blond hair, he noticed, was held away from her face by a white terry visor that shadowed her features, allowing the sun to highlight only her finely sculpted chin line and full, pouting mouth.

Strange, Zachary thought, wrinkling his brow slightly, *but that mouth almost looks familiar. But that's impossible, isn't it?* "Oh, no!" he whispered hoarsely after a moment, leaning forward slightly to stare at the woman, who had at last moved to join them. "It couldn't be!"

"Zachary," Hugh was saying congenially, "I'd like you to meet my golfing partner, good friend and ruthless opponent, Sharon Wheeler. Sharon, please allow me—"

"It is!" Zachary mumbled almost under his breath, Hugh's voice fading into the background as Sharon gingerly held out her hand. Taking it automatically, Zachary was struck, as he had been on Friday evening, by the smallness, the seeming fragility of Sharon Wheeler's hand.

"Mr. St. Clair and I have already met, Hugh. It would

seem that he's my new boss,'' Zachary heard her say, and he mentally shook himself into speech.

"Too true, Miss Wheeler," he then heard himself reply. "But if you'll allow me to use a movie title to express my feelings about our business relationship, please, *Never on Sunday*. It's entirely too nice today to be talking shop, don't you think?"

I think I'd like to do to you what the hero of Spy in the Eye *did to Dr. Death—but then there's never a handy pit of molten lava around when a girl needs one,* Sharon thought privately, deciding that the only thing worse than a frowning, obnoxious St. Clair was a smiling, obnoxious St. Clair.

Aloud, however, with her hand still tingling from its encounter with his, she only said, "I bow to the wisdom of my employer." Then, turning to his companion, she immediately launched into a long discussion with Fred about the court case he had won that week, a victory that had earned him quite a bit of good local press.

Ten minutes later the foursome, having hit their tee shots down the first fairway, were barreling after their balls in two motorized carts—and Sharon Wheeler had not so much as looked in Zachary's direction.

By the time the foursome got to the third hole, Zachary had become grudgingly appreciative of Sharon's form on the tee, her controlled swing with a chipping wedge and her accuracy with a putter. She was a good golfer, better than Hugh, her partner.

By the time they had completed the sixth hole, his appreciation had become less that of a competitor and more that of a man for a woman.

After all, he would have to be blind not to notice the fine line of Sharon's slim body as she leaned over to mark her ball on the putting green.

He would have to be an eunuch not to notice the way the soft white material of her blouse tautened across her firm, high breasts as she held the driver above her head and watched the progress of her ball after completing her follow-through off the tee.

And he would have to be deaf not to enjoy her sharp, witty banter with the other two men who made up the four-some; two men whose easy relationship with Sharon—even whose very presence on the golf course—Zachary was rapidly beginning to resent with a passion that shocked him to his core.

Perhaps this was why, after teeing off on the seventh hole, Zachary found it hard to maintain a solemn expression when Hugh suggested that, since both their balls had hit to the right side of the fairway, Sharon and Zachary share a golf cart as they all rode to their second shots.

"But my clubs are on your cart, Hugh," Sharon protested as she bent down to retrieve her tee and secure it between the laces of one of her golf shoes.

"No problem, Sharon," Hugh said, reaching into her bag and drawing out the three iron. "Here, take this with you. Unless you think it's going to take you two shots to reach the green. I'll be waiting there with your putter."

"Sure you will, Hugh," Sharon shot back, snatching the club from his hand. "Would that be before or after you dig your own ball out of the sand trap?"

"Ouch!" the hotel owner said, wincing comically at the verbal slap. "I forgot you were with me that day." Turning to Zachary, he explained, "Sharon has just been so kind as to bring up something I'd rather forget. A few weeks ago I was buried so deep in that trap off to the left of the green that by the time I got done swiping at the blasted ball I thought I could see glimpses of Hong Kong."

"Then that wasn't a fortune cookie you had stuck in your mouth when you finally climbed up onto the green?" Sharon asked, smiling at her partner. "All right, Mr. St. Clair," she then said, sighing a little, "I'm ready. It's a little tricky getting down to the fairway from this hill. Do you want me to drive?"

"I think I can handle it, *Miss* Wheeler," Zachary told her.

Sharon's words had reminded him of his accident three years earlier. He should have known better than to let his guard down, no matter how easy Sharon Wheeler was on the eyes. When it came to hitting his sore spots, she seemed to have some inner radar that told her just where to probe. "If you'll notice," he told her from between clenched teeth as he walked to the driver's side of the cart, "after playing the course without incident yesterday I've been allowed to navigate without training wheels today."

Sharon laughed aloud at his joke, but Zachary was sure she had done it only for Fred's and Hugh's benefit. He was close enough to see that her smile hadn't quite reached her eyes.

Her beautiful, cornflower-blue eyes.

Sharon turned straight ahead immediately after waving the two men to her left on their way, but the slight breeze that lifted her hair from her nape sent a faint hint of perfume wafting in Zachary's direction.

Her flowery scent that, against his will, teased and tantalized him.

"There's another path to this side of the tee, Mr. St. Clair," she informed him woodenly. "Once you pull forward slightly you'll be able to see it."

"Thank you, *Sharon*," he answered smoothly, stepping sharply on the accelerator and causing the cart to start off with a small lurching movement.

The woman was beginning to drive him out of his mind! The sooner he got this hole over with the better, he reasoned, then wondered why he was disappointed to see that no ball-trapping woods lay to the right of the seventh hole. "You don't mind if I call you Sharon, at least for the rest of the day, do you? I certainly don't mind if you call me Zachary. After all, it seems silly to be so formal when we're all out here trying to enjoy ourselves."

"Meaning you're not really enjoying yourself, *Zachary*?" she asked him, still keeping her gaze glued to the macadam cart path in front of them. "I seem to recall that you have a somewhat limited sense of humor. Perhaps you're disappointed that we aren't playing for money?''

"Meaning?" Zachary asked, his green eyes narrowed.

"Meaning, *Zachary*, that you only seem to be interested in ventures that can be measured by a balance sheet—a bottom line."

"I said I didn't wish to discuss business today," Zachary shot back tersely, drawing alongside Sharon's ball and stopping the cart. "There's your ball. You honestly believe you'll reach the green from here? But, as you play this course a lot, I guess you know what you're doing."

"Sure, that figures," she said, seemingly addressing the club in her hand. "I strike a nerve and he immediately changes the subject—or runs away, like he did Friday night."

Zachary grabbed Sharon's arm just above the elbow, interrupting her descent from the cart, her one foot already on the grass as she swiveled her head sharply to look at him. "On the contrary. I was just trying to be polite after you said something singularly ridiculous, comparing my work to a game of golf."

"I did not! I admit that it might have sounded that way, but I merely said that—"

"The St. Clair Theater Corporation isn't just a small hobby of mine, Miss Wheeler. Or a game to be enjoyed," he persevered, cutting her off. "I have stockholders to answer to, and sharks in the water ready to try to take over if the business should show signs of stumbling in any way. Please forgive me if I fail to find any *humor* in that."

Looking pointedly at his hand, which was still wrapped around her arm, then up into his eyes, Sharon said passionately, "Well, all right, but that's no excuse for calling my theater a disaster zone and then stomping off like some spoiled child without even giving me a chance to show you the place. There's been no money put into improvements in nearly ten years. Of course there are problems, but they're only physical. You refused to see any of the charm of the place.''

"Charm?" Zachary sneered. "Oh, yes, I remember now. You must be talking about the bucolic scene I witnessed, with Mrs. Harrison's cows grazing so elegantly between the rows of parked cars. How could I not have been struck with the beauty, the serenity of the scene?''

"Don't be sarcastic," Sharon ordered, finally succeeding in pulling her arm free.

"No, no. Please, Miss Wheeler, allow me to defend myself. You're accusing me of being humorless, and a man devoid of an appreciation of—what was it—oh, yes, *the charm of the place*! Is that what you call keeping the box office receipts in a lettuce bowl? Because if it is, I must tell you that I'd find the practice extremely charming—if my mother did it! For a business to do it is just plain stupid!''

"Hey! Are you going to hit, Shari, or just sit there hoping a stiff wind comes along and blows the ball onto the green?''

"She's almost ready, Fred," Zachary called back across the fairway to the two men waiting in the other cart. "She was worried about the three iron not being enough club for the shot.''

"Liar," Sharon muttered, rounding the cart to approach the ball. "Very glib, but still a liar. And, oh, so careful to put the blame on somebody else.''

"Just hit the ball, Miss Wheeler," Zachary told her. "Pretend you see my face painted on it and you may just overshoot the green.''

Her feet spread about a foot apart, her hands already positioned in an interlocking grip, Sharon raised her head to look at her companion, her big blue eyes sparkling with anticipation. "With pleasure, *Mr.* St. Clair!''

Okay, Wheeler, Sharon told herself as she climbed back into the cart alongside Hugh and allowed herself to be driven to the eighth tee. *So you had a par and Mr. High-and-Mighty St. Clair took a bogie. Do you feel better now? No, you don't,* she answered her own mental question, shaking her head. *I believe that's what they call winning the battle only to lose the war.*

She might have shown him up back there, putting that chip shot within two feet of the cup, but she sure as heck lost the war of words out there on the fairway—kissing goodbye any lingering chance to keep Wheeler's open. What a way to get the boss on your side—by insulting him!

Turning to look at Hugh, she said aloud, "Hugh, have you got any jobs open at that hotel of yours for an unemployed theater manager? I think I just talked myself out of a job back there with St. Clair."

"You, Shari?" Hugh asked, a puzzled expression on his face. "I don't believe it."

"Believe it, Hugh. Every time I come within ten feet of that man I either insult him or—come to think of it, at least I've been consistent. I just seem to insult him. Anyway, the man doesn't like me."

"Don't be ridiculous. Everybody likes you, Shari, even my mother," Hugh assured her, smiling. *"Especially* my mother. She keeps after me to get married and settle down. You, my dear, are her number-one candidate. I keep telling her that I can't marry someone who beats me so mercilessly in golf, at cards, even on the tennis court; but she won't listen. I think she's hoping you'll keep me humble. Sorry, but it's the only job I've got open at the moment. Interested?"

Sharon reached across the small space separating them in the cart and kissed her friend on the cheek. "Thanks, Hugh, but I think I'll pass—you nut! Doesn't your mother understand that we're just good friends?"

"That's us, Shari," the handsome young hotel owner returned, smiling. "Just good friends. Now come here, friend, and give me a real kiss. I just took a double bogey and I need some cheering up. Besides, you're much more fun in a golf cart than old Fred."

"Nut!" Sharon scolded happily, then leaned sideways to allow herself to be kissed.

Zachary had his worst round of golf in his recent memory, but he refused to acknowledge that his troubles had all begun on the seventh hole, then doubled after he saw Sharon and Hugh doing their lovers' routine on the way to the eighth tee.

What did he care what Sharon Wheeler and Hugh Kingsley did, even if it was mighty poor golf etiquette? They should have just steered the cart off into the bushes and rejoined him and Fred on the back nine after they'd gotten all that juvenile need for a public display of passion out of their systems, because he sure didn't need to be treated to another such scene. You'd think they'd been parted for years, not just for the length of one hole, the way they had fallen all over each other in the cart.

Hugh Kingsley could just count himself lucky that he'd kept his paws off Sharon for the remainder of the round!

Get a hold on yourself, boy! Zachary ordered, giving himself a mental kick at the violence of his thoughts as he nursed his third ice-cold diet soda in the clubhouse, waiting for the rest of the foursome to join him after their showers. *It's none of my business if, at this very moment, Hugh is dragging my manager across the parking lot by her hair, taking her back to his blasted hotel for a night of sin and decadence. I couldn't care less, dammit.* Zachary was still too tense, still overreacting to things that normally wouldn't bother him. *Just be careful,* he warned himself. He still had the rest of this day and the next morning to get through before he could get back to New York and away from that ridiculous woman.

That woman.

Sharon Wheeler. How that small blonde had gotten under his skin! He couldn't understand it.

Okay, so she has a beautiful face and body, he conceded. So did every female he dated, and he had dated quite a few.

Yes, she played one tremendous game of golf. So did Jan

Stephenson, another blonde, yet he had never felt any urge to drag the beautiful, calendar-posing golf professional off into the bushes and kiss *her* until she was senseless.

So what was it about Sharon that so attracted him to her, infuriated him while not repelling him in the slightest?

Funny, he thought, shaking his head, *but she reminds me a bit of my father.* How he loved the theaters, much more than he ever loved the business. Zachary remembered the many times he and his father had gone head to head, as the younger man tried to pull the older—kicking and screaming all the way—into the modern world of theater ownership.

Zachary loved the arguments, the mind games, the confrontations he had faced, first with his father, and then with the men with whom he sought to do business—men who initially refused to take him seriously, who found it hard to believe that "daddy's little boy" actually knew the difference between a projection booth and a tollbooth, let alone anything they themselves didn't know.

But in the past few years the sheer size and power of the St. Clair Theater Corporation had done most of his fighting for him, and the thrill of the chase had somehow disappeared. Today, and for at least three years, he had been going through the motions, but feeling none of the satisfaction of ownership. He was ready for a challenge, primed for a good old-fashioned toe-to-toe fight. He had been accumulating "screens," not purchasing "theaters."

He took a quick drink from his glass, suddenly feeling guilty.

Maybe that's why she's gotten to me—the way she argues with me, stands up straight and all but dares me to prove that I care about something more than just the black ink in a ledger book. "That's ridiculous," he mumbled aloud then, putting down his halfful glass with a small thump as he realized that he was beginning to feel slightly queasy from all that carbonation. "What do I care about Sharon Wheeler's opinion of me?"

It's good I don't care, he told himself, chuckling a bit

under his breath, *because I can just bet my bottom dollar I'm not number one on her Christmas list this year.*

Absently utilizing the bottom of his glass to make a design of round wet circles on the shiny wood tabletop, Zachary tried very hard to understand just why Sharon's dislike of him intrigued him so much.

Looking up from his small decorating project long enough to see a well-built redhead looking across the room at him speculatively, he found the answer to his question. Sharon Wheeler was an exception—a woman who didn't throw herself at him, or use her beauty to manipulate him, or try to charm him into seeing things her way.

No, she didn't use any of the female tactics he had been used to facing ever since he'd reached his middle teens and his physical appearance and his father's income had both risen to "handsome" heights. And, Zachary acknowledged, it wasn't as if she hadn't the ammunition for such an assault either, because she was one very beautiful lady.

Ah, but she doesn't like you, Zachary St. Clair, he pointed out to himself, *she doesn't like you one little bit.*

He was back to square one, understanding more of the questions, perhaps, but still not coming up with any workable answers.

"So," Hugh Kingsley said heartily, interrupting Zachary's private thoughts by coming up to the table and seating himself in one of the large captain's chairs, "I guess you'll be heading back to New York tomorrow, you lucky devil. What I wouldn't give for a few days in the Big Apple."

His teeth are too white, Zachary thought idly as he returned Hugh's smile. *His teeth are too white and his face is too tan. He's probably never worked a full day in his life.* "Actually, Hugh," he heard himself saying, "this weekend has proved to be too short. What I really need is a good, long vacation, and Allentown is as good a place as any. I can take my time inspecting my latest acquisitions firsthand instead of sending in my usual team and relax a bit at the same time."

"Really," Hugh answered, the flat tone of his voice doing wonders for Zachary's mood.

"Yes," he went on as he rose to his feet to hold out a chair for Sharon, who, along with Fred Staples, was just joining them, "I think the personal touch is just what my new theaters need."

Hugh Kingsley's very white teeth disappeared behind his tightly shut lips for a moment before he smiled once more and said, rather hollowly, "The personal touch. How nice."

"Yes," Zachary agreed, motioning to the waiter, "yes, indeed. Suddenly I find myself ravenously hungry. Anyone else? My treat."

Chapter 4

The moment Sharon pulled her car onto the theater grounds early Sunday evening she knew something was wrong. Sam, who was usually at his post at the ticket booth, setting up the cash box and hanging up a new reel of tickets over the nail hammered into the wall, was nowhere in sight. Neither was Denny, Sam's assistant.

"They're probably up at the snack bar getting themselves some sodas," she assured herself aloud, trying hard to quell the nervous fluttering that had suddenly invaded her midsection.

She guided her car past the first four rows of speakers, then turned into the fifth row, heading for the small parking area behind the snack bar that couldn't be used for patrons because the roof of the building interfered with the view of the screen.

George's Plymouth was already there and she breathed a quick sigh of relief until she realized that the old car was sitting at an awkward angle, looking as if it had not been parked, but abandoned.

"Dammit, George!" she exclaimed, pounding one small fist against the steering wheel. "Not now! Of all the times in the world, why did you have to pick *now*?"

She was out of her compact car almost before the engine died, running for the snack bar. After scuttling under the cutout in the Formica bar, she skidded around the center island holding the steamer table and soda dispensers, to arrive, breathless, at the doorway to the projection booth.

"Where is he?"

Sam, his balding head bent close to check Veronica's lamp house, answered without turning around. "He's in your office. Denny's pouring some coffee down him now. He'll be fine by show time. Denny and I have the house trailer ready on Gloria and the first reel's all threaded up here on Veronica, so you've got plenty of time."

"Thanks, Sam," Sharon said fervently, knowing that Denny and Sam were doing all they could to help cover for George. "Now if only you guys could find a way to take tickets *and* run the projectors, we'd be home free."

"That's the trick, isn't it, Shari? We know how to thread them up, Denny and me, but neither of us can run them worth a darn. Just get George another gallon of coffee, and we'll make it yet."

"Either that, or I'll wave the open can of jalapeño peppers under his nose," Sharon called back over her shoulder as she crossed the snack bar on her way to the office.

Denny, a half-empty cup in one hand and a steaming glass pot of coffee in the other, stepped back from the projectionist, who sat slumped over the small desk, as Sharon edged her way sideways into the small room. "We found him hanging over Gloria in the booth, mumbling something about the good old days. He's really tied one on, Shari. Poor guy."

"That you, Shari?" George croaked, lifting his head from its resting place on his crossed arms. "I'll be fine in a minute, honest I will. I was just drinking a few toasts to Gloria and Veronica, sort of a goodbye party, you know. I guess things got a little out of hand. Right?"

Sharon's heart was nearly breaking to see her old friend and mentor in such a sorry state. He usually just takes himself off to sit in a dark theater all day, Sharon thought, deciding that he must be very upset. She closed her eyes in mingled sorrow and frustration, wondering which emotion, pity or anger, would win the battle raging inside her.

"Oh, George, you poor darling! *He* did this to you, didn't he?"

Even as she was cradling the now sobbing George against her slim shoulder she didn't realize that both emotions had found an outlet; pity directed at George, her old friend, and anger directed at Zachary St. Clair, the bogeyman who was about to take away George's last reason for living....

George gave it his best shot, but although his mind seemed steady enough, his legs refused to cooperate, and in the end Sam and Denny had to man the projectors, with George propped up in one cool, dark corner of the booth, directing their movements.

Sharon took over duty in the ticket booth, hoping against hope that the Sunday night crowd would not descend on the theater all at once, giving her time to pass each car through the gate without allowing the line to back up onto the highway.

She was doing fine for a while, counting noses inside each car and then dispensing tickets and lollipops accordingly, greeting many of Wheeler's regulars, who always made it a point to arrive early in order to have plenty of time for either the playground or stock-up visits to the snack bar.

It was only as dusk began to fall that the line of cars suddenly became too much for one person to handle and Sharon began to wish for another pair of hands to help her.

"Where's the redheaded kid with the mouthful of bubble gum? He should be here to help you."

Sharon, in the midst of making change from a twenty dollar bill, answered the question without turning around. "Sean's studying for finals. I gave him the night off to— *What are you doing here?*"

"And a good evening to you, too, Miss Wheeler," Zachary said, putting one sneaker-clad foot onto the cement floor of the small, double-doored ticket booth, then following it with the rest of his tall, lean body. "I was beginning to get bored back at the hotel and thought I'd come out here to Wheeler's and look around a bit—hoping against hope that Gertrude won't get the itch to travel again so soon, of course. Need some help?"

Just what I don't need! Sharon thought anxiously, remembering George back in the projection booth. After hurrying through one more transaction, she took the time to look anxiously at her employer and adversary, frantically trying to figure out some way to convince him she didn't need his help.

He's beginning to get a tan, she found herself thinking rather irrationally. *It looks good with his green eyes. Maybe it's the green shirt and white slacks that set off the tan so well. His hair looks nice, too, so dark, and more casual with that small bit in the front falling down over his forehead like that, and the hair at his neck is still a bit damp and curling, like he just stepped out of the shower.*

I think I can actually smell the cleanness of him. The hair on his forearms is already bleached almost blond from the sun, and his hands look almost beautiful. He doesn't look anything like a stuffed shirt tonight; he looks more like he did this afternoon on the golf course, not that I really noticed, with him being so totally obnoxious and all. Now he's smiling at me, actually acting human. I wonder why he's—

"Hey, lady, get a move on! I've been holding out my hand so long with this money I'm gettin' a cramp already. What's the matter with you? Don't tell me you're sold out."

"Wha—what?" Sharon asked absently, still staring at Zachary's cheek-creasing smile and wondering how she could have been so blind to his masculine attractions.

"The gentleman would like to pay for his tickets, Sharon," Zachary supplied helpfully, putting out a hand to gently move her unprotesting body out of the way while he ripped four tickets off the large roll and swiftly completed the transaction, even remembering to place two lollipops in the outstretched little hands hanging over the back seat.

"Thank you, Mr.—er—thanks, Zachary," Sharon stumbled at last, shaking her head in the hope that the action would serve to bring her back to her senses before she made an utter fool of herself. "You did that very well."

"Thank *you*, Sharon," she heard him reply as he motioned through the front window of the booth for the second car in line to pull to the other side of the booth. "I used to spend my summers helping my father in our indoor theaters in New York. Of course I can't remember ever thinking that a can of insect repellent would come in handy. The mosquitoes always this bad? Three, madam? Here you go. Please be sure to visit our snack bar, and I hope you enjoy the show."

"Your next customer's in a van. Tell him to park at one of the yellow speaker poles—they're higher," Sharon heard herself saying as she snapped back to attention and began waiting on people driving up to her side of the booth. He's being nice, she told herself in disbelief. He's being *extremely* nice. *Why?*

The phone in the booth rang then, and Sharon jumped to answer it, listening for a minute while she waited on another customer, then telling the caller the first show would start when it got dark, in about half an hour.

"Why don't you get an answering machine?" Zachary asked her after she had hung up. "We have them in all our theaters. It would save you a lot of time."

Sharon shook her head. "We do use a machine during the day, but it wouldn't work for the evenings. People are always calling to ask for directions to the theater and things like that."

Zachary was silent for a moment, as if he were considering her answer. "I wish I had thought of that," he said at last, smiling at her. "I drove around forever on Friday looking for this place. It never occurred to me to call for directions. I figured I'd just get one of those damned machines.''

''You mean like the kind you just got done saying we should have?'' Sharon quipped. ''You forget, Zachary. Wheeler's believes in the personal, human touch.''

''Don't forget the homey touch, little one,'' he said easily, reaching up to pull four more tickets off the roll. ''Your ticket dispensing 'machine,' in fact, this entire booth, could only be called 'rustic.'''

Instantly Sharon bristled. ''It serves its purpose,'' she returned coldly, turning her back to him. So much for thinking the man was softening a bit, she rued silently, already wondering how she was going to get rid of him once this rush was over.

''My daughter wants to hand you the money for our tickets,'' she heard a man saying, and she turned in time to see Zachary holding out his hand to the opened car window. ''Give the nice man the money, Jennifer.''

''No!'' Jennifer declared, her long pigtails slapping about her shoulders as she shook her head.

''Jennifer!'' her father yelled from behind the steering wheel, which was on the other side of the car, away from the ticket booth. ''Give the nice man the money!''

''No! Don't want to,'' Jennifer answered, clutching the ten dollar bill tightly to her pajama-clad chest.

Okay, Mr. I-can-do-anything St. Clair, Sharon challenged silently, trying hard to hide her amusement. Let's see you try to charm your way out of this one.

''I'll trade you a lollipop for the money, sweetheart,'' Zachary bargained in an encouraging voice.

''Don't like lollipops,'' Jennifer pouted.

''If you give me the money, I'll give you these pretty tickets,'' Zachary promised, holding out the bribe enticingly.

''Tickets are dumb,'' little Jennifer told him, eyeing him carefully.

''*Jennifer Marie Simpson*, you listen to me!'' Jennifer's

father, clearly angry now, ordered, trying without success to catch hold of his daughter from the front seat.

"I'll give you a kiss if you give me the money," Zachary promised softly, leaning down to rest his elbows on the car door. Sharon stood openmouthed, watching Zachary St. Clair winking at a four-year-old child.

"Right here?" Jennifer asked, pointing to one chubby cheek.

"Right there."

"And Stephanie, too?" the child bargained, holding up a battered, well-loved doll.

Something happened to Sharon in the few moments it took for Zachary to bend down and bestow his favors on Stephanie and Jennifer, something she didn't really desire to investigate too closely. But when he straightened once more and turned to her, a smile of delighted satisfaction lighting his newly tanned face, she knew she didn't have to examine her reaction.

Against all her better judgment, weighed up along with her innate distrust of big businessmen in general, Sharon knew she was beginning to like Zachary St. Clair.

Even worse, she was beginning to look at him the way a woman looks at a man.

Suddenly, in the barely waning heat of early evening, Sharon shivered.

The last car straggled through the gates about fifteen minutes after the movie had already begun and Sharon finally closed the lid on the cash box and reached up to remove the roll of tickets from the nail. Zachary, who had also reached up for the tickets, purposely allowed their hands to meet, watching for Sharon's reaction to their slight physical collision.

He wasn't disappointed. Sharon's hand sprang away from the contact with lightning quickness and her cheeks immediately flushed an extremely becoming pale pink beneath her golden tan. He rather liked the expression of maidenly confusion that crept into her lovely, clear blue eyes before she lowered her lids to hide her reaction.

Slowly, as Sharon stood quite still in front of the low shelf under the front window of the booth, Zachary took the cash box she was holding and returned it to its spot on the shelf. Just as slowly, he took her by the shoulders and turned her to face him in the nearly total darkness inside the small wooden shed.

"Just how close are you and Hugh Kingsley?" he asked quietly, putting one finger under her chin so that he could look into her eyes while she answered.

"Hugh?" she questioned, blinking, her T-shirt-covered breasts rising and falling rapidly in innocent enticement as she seemed to be having trouble gaining her breath. "We— we're friends. Just good friends."

"You have any other 'good friends?' Any—boyfriends?"

"Just—just George, the projectionist. He's almost seventy, though. And Sam. And Denny. They work here."

"And how old are they—Sam and Denny?" Zachary prodded, allowing his hands to slowly slide off Sharon's shoulders and down her bare arms to her elbows, the action meant to ease her body closer against him.

"I—I don't know. They're just—older. Married. Denny even met his wife here, fifteen years ago. Why?"

Zachary could feel an actual knot painfully tightening his insides as he watched Sharon wet her lips with the tip of her tongue, showing him her nervousness. "Because I don't like poaching on another man's territory, Sharon. Because I don't want to lose my head over you if you're involved with some other man. Because," he ended seriously, realizing he too was a bit breathless, "I'm going to kiss you, Sharon Wheeler. Right now."

Her lips were warm, as if kissed by the sun, and the taste of her mouth was sweet, like silken honey licked straight from the honeycomb. The well-conditioned muscles of her slim lower back served to fashion an enticing little hollow against her spine, and he could feel his fingers tingling as they lightly stroked the area, feeling her, learning her, drawing her softness against his own firm muscles.

He could again smell the flowery scent he had noticed earlier that day, and he lifted his mouth away from hers to bury his face in her unbound hair, savoring its texture. "Honey," he whispered against her ear. "Your scent, your skin, your hair, your mouth—you're as sweet, as delicious, as honey. I can't believe it."

Then his lips trailed a row of kisses back across her cheek to find her mouth once more and he felt his control begin to slip as her arms, which had remained tight to her sides, slowly reached up behind him to clasp him firmly around the neck, as if actively seeking his kiss.

"Hey, in there! Are we too late to see the show? Hey! What are you two doing in there? Making out? Fan-*tastic*! This is better than the movie!"

Zachary's mind did a quick battle with his body as his common sense told him that Sharon, now leaning weakly against him, was in no condition to handle the car full of teenage boys now parked beside the booth, its engine rumbling loudly as the driver continuously revved the motor.

Reluctantly shifting Sharon's unresisting form so that she could lean against the low shelf, he quickly opened the cash box and took care of the customers, then coughed as the car pulled away, leaving a large blue cloud of dirty exhaust fumes in its wake.

When he turned around once more, Sharon was gone.

Oh, my Lord, I can't believe I did that! I can't believe I actually did that! I let Zachary St. Clair kiss me. Worse—I kissed him back! Sharon silently beat herself over the head with self-disgust as she slammed her sneakered feet into the loose gravel on her way back across the theater lot to the snack bar.

"No, Mr. St. Clair," she gibed aloud in a singsong voice, "I don't have any boyfriends, Mr. St. Clair; George is seventy years old, Mr. St. Clair; Denny met his wife here, Mr.

St. Clair; *three bags full, Mr. St. Clair!* Oh, God, what an idiot you are, Sharon Wheeler! What a complete and total idiot!''

Reaching the front end of the building, the half housing the projection booth, Sharon slammed through the entrance to see Sam and Denny working together to make a reel change, while George, yet another cup of black coffee in his hands, supervised from his place in the corner.

''That damned door is supposed to be locked at all times, and you know it,'' she shot out testily, never slowing her pace as she walked behind the two large floor-mounted projectors and headed for the snack bar. ''And for God's sake don't goof up in here. The boss is on the grounds.''

''St. Clair? Here?'' George said, quickly gulping down some more of the hot coffee. ''What do we do now, Shari?''

Halting for a moment in the doorway, Sharon put her hands on her hips and looked slowly around the room, seeing the reel holding the film for the house trailer and previews as well as the first reel of the film now in progress lying on their sides on the workbench, still not rewound and put back in their cases. ''We get it in gear—fast. *That's* what we do. I'll be right back.''

The first person Sharon saw when she entered the snack bar was Sheila, the teenager who had been working at Wheeler's for the past two years. Knowing she could count on the girl to take control of the intermission crowd that would begin descending on the snack bar in less than an hour, she quietly called her aside and delivered several quick, broad orders.

''It's Sunday night and the crowd won't be overwhelming,'' she told the girl, putting her arm around her and walking with her to a corner of the snack bar. ''We can't save them until Friday, so push the hot dogs and turkey barbecue. If it looks like they aren't moving, offer a free soda with each sandwich, okay?''

''Yeah, sure Sharon, but—''

Sharon didn't let the girl finish. ''The popcorn supply

looks good, but I think you ought to get Marianne to restock the candy shelves. In about fifteen minutes have Gail start pouring out sodas and lining them up on top of the ice cream freezer. The girls all have got to take their share of the load. Push them if you have to. You're in charge, Sheila, and I'm counting on you.''

"But where are you going to be?" Sheila asked as Sharon began to walk away. "You're always here for intermission."

"I'm going to help in the projection booth. George isn't feeling well and Denny has to help patrol the grounds as ramp boy because Sean has the night off. Don't call me if it isn't an emergency, okay?"

Sheila tilted her head to one side, looking puzzled: "I didn't know you could work the projectors, Shari. You never have before."

Sharon allowed herself a small smile. "I'm still a card-carrying projectionist, even if I haven't run Gloria or Veronica for a long time. But I may be a little rusty, so just hope the film doesn't break in the middle of one of the chase scenes."

Then, just as Sheila was about to inform the rest of the crew that she was in charge for the evening, Sharon added, almost as an afterthought, "Oh, yes. Sheila—I'm not to be disturbed, understand? I mean, if someone were to come in here asking for me, just tell him, er, I mean, just tell them that…" Her voice trailed off. She saw the teenager's eyes widen as Sheila's attention was taken by someone standing on the other side of the Formica counter.

"You forgot the box office receipts and the tickets," she heard Zachary say in his deep, rather husky voice.

You may run, Wheeler, she told herself, trying not to wince, but you can't hide. Taking a long, steadying breath, Sharon dug deeply into the reserves of the little bit of composure she had left, mustered up a painfully false smile, and wheeled around to face the man who had so lately held her in his arms.

Zachary was standing no more than four feet in front of

her, the two of them separated only by the narrow width of
the counter. He held the cash box lightly in his hands, the
roll of tickets balanced on the lid.

"Oh, dear," she trilled in a rather strained voice that she
barely recognized, "I did, didn't I? How silly of me." Then,
holding out her hands, and offering a silent prayer that he
wouldn't see how they were trembling, she took possession
of the box and tickets, said, "Thanks a million—bye, now,
I really must fly," and skipped off to the safety of her office
before Zachary could say another word.

She stopped just inside the door, resting her suddenly
warm body against the cool doors of the refrigerator, knowing that she had merely delayed the inevitable. She could
issue orders to Sheila that she not be disturbed until—she
sniffed aloud at the thought—until old Mrs. Harrison's cows
came home. It wouldn't matter. The teenager would be like
putty in Zachary's hands. All females were. Little Jennifer
was. *She* was. Getting himself past man-crazy Sheila Bizinski would be a piece of cake to a man like Zachary.

"Hi, again," she heard Zachary say from somewhere
above her left ear, and she opened her tightly shut eyes to
see him standing in the doorway, one bare forearm resting
against the doorjamb as he leaned his body into the room.
"Playing hide-and-seek, are we? Strange, you didn't strike
me as the type to play games."

Oh, how this man's enjoying himself, Sharon seethed, her
cornflower-blue eyes turning as coldly cobalt as midnight
snow. Stepping away from the refrigerator, she opened the
door and reached behind the large bag of chopped onions
for the plastic lettuce crisper, daring—just daring—him to
say a single sarcastic word as she transferred the box office
receipts to the container and placed it back inside.

Still without uttering a word, she sat down at the small
desk to begin counting out the change from the cash box,
scribbling the totals on a torn piece of scratch paper someone
had used to play several games of tick-tack-toe, all the time
fighting the fact of Zachary's presence with every fiber of

resistance in her body. Finally, the small job done, she could no longer ignore the fact that the man simply refused to take the hint and *go away*.

Turning around slightly in the chair, she went on the offensive. "You want to double-check my addition?" she challenged. "We don't add up the lettuce crisper until the snack bar closes, but you might want to make sure I didn't miscount the change."

"Now why would I think a thing like that, Sharon?" he countered. The look of guileless innocence on his face made her want to throw something at him—maybe a nice, solid roll of quarters.

"You weren't supposed to come here again until tomorrow morning," she went on, knowing that somehow, some way, she had to get rid of the man. "You don't play fair."

"Then we are playing games?" Zachary asked, cocking one well-defined dark eyebrow at her.

"We aren't. You are. You come barreling in here Friday night like some sort of Attila the Hun on a rampage, treat me as if I remind you of a nagging toothache you once had earlier today when we were on the golf course, and then show up here tonight like some knight riding to the rescue, acting as if your only goal in life was to spend eternity working in a broken-down drive-in that you know darn well you're going to close tomorrow. And that's not even mentioning what you did down at the ticket booth."

"Oh, come on, Sharon," Zachary prompted, with what Sharon considered a rakish leer on his handsome face, "don't quit on me now. By all means, let's mention it. After all, I thought we were getting along famously."

Suddenly Sharon forgot her embarrassment, forgot the temporary insanity that had her believing that she was—wild as it seemed now—*falling for* the arrogant man standing in front of her, forgot that she had planned to beg, plead and to do everything else she could to save Wheeler's from extinction. She merely reacted.

She slapped her hands sharply against her bare thighs,

exposed beneath her red cotton shorts, and then hopped to her feet, saying, "That's it. End of discussion. I have a theater to run, at least for one more night. Mr. St. Clair, I believe you know your way out. Excuse me, please," she apologized abruptly, edging past him quickly with her breath held before jogging across the width of the snack bar toward the safety of the projection booth, then closing the door behind her.

"Denny, you can go outside now and keep an eye on the customers. I'll take over here," she said, taking up her position alongside Gloria Swanson. "Sean's flashlight is on the center island in the snack bar. Don't forget to check the fences; Sean caught three kids trying to sneak in the other night."

Denny and Sam exchanged looks at Sharon's obvious nervousness before the younger man shrugged his shoulders and quietly took his leave. "You'll need to replace Gloria's positive carbon after one more reel, Shari," was all he said as he turned the knob to open the door.

"Oh, Denny, don't go that way. Go out and around the other—"

But Sharon was too late with her warning. The moment the door opened Zachary St. Clair stepped inside the dark booth, his right hand outstretched, calmly asking Sharon to introduce him to the two men. George, now snoring softly, remained out of sight in the corner.

"Good grief!" Zachary exclaimed with a short laugh as the introductions were completed. "I haven't seen projectors like these since I was a kid. Quite the museum pieces, aren't they?"

Sharon bristled yet again, wondering just how the man so instinctively knew where to place his needles. "Gloria Swanson and Veronica Lake aren't spring chickens anymore, but they hold their own," she told him defiantly, reaching out a hand to touch Gloria as if her action could protect the old machine from attack. "Popsie—that is my grandfather, had them installed when this theater was built. They're terrific projectors—they just don't make equipment like this anymore.''

''I'll say they don't,'' Zachary replied, moving forward to inspect Veronica, first from one side, then the other. The projector, which stood about five feet high and half as wide, was made up of three separate parts, a lamp house, a projection head and a sound head, all mounted on a strong metal base that was bolted into the floor. He reached out one hand to touch the side of the projector. ''My report said Wheeler's was a carbon house, but I never imagined—''

''Keep your miserable hands off my Veronica!'' George ordered, his voice slightly slurred as he lurched to his feet and took a step in Zachary's direction, one clenched fist in the air. ''What do you know about anything, huh? You with your newfangled automated 'platter' houses. I know why you're here. Shari told me. You're only interested in putting hardworking men out of their jobs—just so you can make more and more money. Right, Shari?''

''Here now, hold on, old boy,'' Sharon heard Zachary warn as she watched him reach out to steady George before the man could topple to the floor. Her heart hit her toes as she saw the owner of the St. Clair Theater Corporation wrinkle up his fine, aristocratic nose and exclaim, ''Why, you're drunk!''

''Got that in one, smart boy. Darn right I am!'' George declared proudly before he slumped, rag doll-like in Zachary's arms.

Everything after that moment would later seem rather hazy for Sharon, as she somehow heard the soft ringing of the warning bell that said a reel change was coming up in one minute. Calling to Sam to keep his eyes open, she ran around the projector to stand beside Gloria, watching the screen intently out the small window, waiting for the cue dot in the corner, which would signal the first change.

When she saw the dot she told Sam to start up Veronica, then counted slowly to ten before the second cue dot appeared and she cut Gloria off. She had fifteen minutes to strip Gloria down, change the lens size for the intermission reel, insert a new carbon in the lamp house and thread up the projector head. Somehow, some way, in that short span of time, she told herself as her hands moved automatically at her tasks, she had to find a way to explain George's actions.

But when she turned around to face the music both Zachary and the projectionist were nowhere in sight.

"Where—where did they go?" she asked Sam, fear coloring her voice. "Are they in my office?"

"Mr. St. Clair said he'd make sure George got home all right," Sam told her as he turned up the projection booth speaker to check on the sound. "I gave him George's house key and directions to the place. Didn't you hear him say goodbye? Mr. St. Clair said he'd meet you here tomorrow morning at eleven. Nice guy, huh, considering George wanted to punch his lights out."

Sharon, one hand to her mouth, sank back against the cool concrete wall and shut her eyes.

Chapter 5

Zachary took his time as he drove the sports car along the narrow back-country roads that led from George Blakeman's small house to Wheeler's Drive-In, rerunning the events of the previous evening in his head. He'd had quite a night, all in all, first with Sharon in the ticket booth, and then later, before falling asleep in George's small living room, going through the man's many scrapbooks that traced back through the years to the late 1930s.

While reading the newspaper clippings, Zachary had learned all about George's close brush with tragedy in a downtown Philadelphia theater, and seen the yellowed pay stub of the projectionist's first paycheck from Wheeler's Drive-In, signed by Sharon's grandfather. It wasn't hard to put two and two together, and it certainly went a long way toward explaining George's problem—and his violent reaction to the possibility that the drive-in that had become his refuge would finally be shut down.

From thoughts of George, Zachary's mind turned to the many pictures of Al Wheeler that appeared in the scrapbooks and the realization that his own father had begun his first indoor theater on just such a hope and a prayer as Al. Sharon would like Dad; he's a lot like her grandfather was, he thought again as he drove along, a rueful smile on his lips. What an operator old Al Wheeler must have been, he decided, remembering the newspaper clipping that told the story of how the drive-in had begun.

Wheeler, so the story went, had seen an outdoor movie theater during a visit to Atlantic City, New Jersey in 1933. Inspired, he then returned to Pennsylvania, hung up a big sheet of white cloth between two tall trees, set up a single loudspeaker in the middle of an old cornfield and begun showing films to the local residents.

"And the rest is history," Zachary said aloud in admiration of the man's daring. "When his only son sold the business after the old man's death, Sharon must have been devastated, if all those pictures showing her working alongside her grandfather as she was growing up meant anything. The drive-in's last two owners haven't helped my case any, either, considering the way they both let the place go to seed. She and George have every right to hate my guts."

And that bothered Zachary, it bothered him more than he liked to admit, even to himself. He liked George, what little he had gotten to know of the man through his scrapbooks after he had helped the projectionist to bed. Earlier that morning, over breakfast, Zachary had realized that George also reminded him of his father, while the man's reminiscences had given him a glimpse of what the theater business must have been like when his father had opened his very first small theater.

Oh, yes, his father had told him stories of the good old days, the days when the projectionists were in their heyday—the heartthrobs of every vaudeville girl—but Zachary hadn't really worked around a theater since the year before he left for college, and the memories had faded under the pressures of building a comfortable business into a multi-million-dollar corporation.

Zachary had even spent a summer running a projector like Veronica, although the dubious "romance" of working with the dangerous, highly flammable nitrate film had passed with the changeover to acetate film just before he was born. During that summer he had struck up a friendship with gruff Charlie Barrows, one of his father's first employees, and the two of them had helped pass the hours on their lengthy ten-hour shifts by trying to best each other on little-known movie trivia.

"Frontiersman Jim Bowie was portrayed by Alan Ladd in *The Iron Mistress*, Sterling Hayden in *The Last Command*, Jeff Morrow in *The First Texan*, and—oh, yes—by Richard Widmark in *The Alamo*," Zachary recited aloud now as he turned onto the main highway and headed for the drive-in. "Damn, but I lost a lot of money to Charlie that summer. But I learned. Boy, how I learned."

A shadow of sadness descended on Zachary then, removing the reminiscent smile from his face as he realized that he had absolutely no idea what had ever happened to Charlie Barrows since that long-ago summer, or if the man was still alive.

Even the theater they had worked in together had changed. It was an automated "platter" house now, with a single manager-projectionist responsible for the three screens that had been carved out of the old single screen building. Silently, he acknowledged that Charlie would never have been able to make the transition to the automated projectors, that a man like Charlie wouldn't even have bothered to try.

"It's not my fault, dammit!" Zachary protested out loud as he turned sharply onto the gravel path that led to the drive-in. "We've progressed to the point where I can run an eight-screen house with two projectionists, not sixteen. It's cost-effective, it's rational, it's the wave of the future."

Driving through the opened gates and onto the lot, Zachary took the time to look at himself in the narrow rearview mirror. "Then why do you feel like such a rat, St. Clair? Why do you feel like apologizing to George, and Charlie—

even your dad? And why do you feel like you owe Sharon
Wheeler the biggest apology of them all? Answer me that,
St. Clair, answer me that!''

Still feeling rather bemused, Sharon was just in the process of hanging up the phone after talking with the thoroughly delighted though slightly hung-over George Blakeman when she heard Zachary's car pull up behind the snack
bar.

Instantly, her heart began to pound almost painfully in her
chest. She dug nervously into her purse, hunting for her mirror, just to make sure she still looked passably human after
spending a nearly sleepless night, worrying about what she
could possibly say to explain away the happenings of the
previous night.

But now it wasn't necessary, at least according to George.
She heard herself giving out with a quick, nervous giggle as
she tried to take it all in. *Wheeler's was going to stay open!*
George had just gotten through telling her that Zachary had
told him so just that morning while he—the president of the
St. Clair Theater Corporation—had served up bacon and
eggs to the man who had so lately insulted him before trying
to punch him in the nose!

Not only that, George had told her, but Zachary had given
the projectionist the week off, telling him to get some rest,
while he, Zachary, would take over his duties at the drive-
in.

''And he's going to order repairs, Shari. Can you believe
that!'' the projectionist had fairly yelled into the phone. She
had heard the sounds of the old man's grateful tears in his
raspy voice. ''He said that Wheeler's Drive-In is a part of
history and it's up to us to keep that history alive. What a
guy! Right?''

''Yes, George. Right,'' Sharon said now pensively as she
rose to go greet her employer. ''What a guy. My only question now is—can I really believe his motives are so straight-

forward? Or am I flattering myself? Am I simply reading too much into one stolen kiss in the moonlight?''

Oh, Lord, no one man has the right to look that good, especially a man dressed in one of George's faded plaid shirts, Sharon thought as she rounded the side of the snack bar a few moments later to see Zachary, his lean length propped casually against the left front fender of the low slung sports car.

"Hi, there," he said cordially, turning his head in her direction as she slowly approached the car. "I was just standing out here for a moment, admiring the view. There certainly is a lot of countryside out here, isn't there?"

"There usually is, in the country," Sharon responded, cursing herself for being flippant. It was just that she was so nervous! "But we do have several houses behind us that were built some years after the drive-in opened. Popsie always said it was the free speakers that made the people decide to build here."

Zachary turned around to look at the row of ranch homes that all had backyards facing the theater. "Free speakers?" he said, his tone incredulous. "For—let me see—seven houses? With this place barely holding its own? You've got to be kidding."

Nice job, Wheeler, Sharon told herself. *Open mouth, insert foot. Now how do I make Mr. Bottom Line understand?* "Popsie always considered it to be a cheap insurance policy, Mr. St. Clair. In return for the speakers, our neighbors keep a pretty close watch on the place, alerting us to vandalism, or people trying to sneak in under the fence. Don't forget, no one is here all winter long. It's simply one hand washing the other—just like in any business."

"You're right, of course," Zachary agreed to her amazement, smiling at her as he began walking slowly toward the snack bar, "although I wonder just how that little piece of information is going to look in the annual report. You tell me—do we list the cost under insurance, or public relations?"

Sharon lowered her head for a moment in relief, then followed him, saying quickly, "I talked to George this morning and he told me you plan to keep the drive-in open. He also told me how nice you were to him. I—I want to thank you, for—everything."

Zachary stopped just short of the snack bar door, turning around to take hold of her at the shoulders. She looked up into his smiling green eyes as he said, his voice gentle, "Now, that didn't hurt so much, did it, Shari? And you're welcome—*for everything*."

She swallowed hard as her attention was taken by the sensuous long line of Zachary's mouth as it hovered so close to hers, and she wondered yet again if Zachary was beginning to take more than a businessman's impersonal interest in Wheeler's. More than that, she found herself wondering why she hoped his interest was on more of a personal level.

Easy, Wheeler, she quickly told herself, you're not thinking straight again. Determined to bring the discussion back to reality, she rushed on, "I—um—I think I also need to apologize to you. I haven't treated you very well since you got here."

"No, you haven't, have you?" Zachary remarked, his thumbs beginning to lightly massage her shoulders as he gave her a quick glimpse of the long slashing dimples that appeared in his lean, tanned cheeks whenever he smiled. "But—being the heck of a nice guy that I am—I have to tell you that I'm more than willing to let you try to make it up to me."

Sharon, startled by what he might have been implying, quickly stepped back two paces, looking hopefully to the right and left of her as if for assistance before speaking again. "Yes—er—yes, well, I'm sure we'll be able to maintain a reasonably civilized working relationship for the short time you'll be here. George already warned me that—um— that is, George said you told him to take the week off and you'd stand in for him. That wasn't really necessary. The drive-in is closed until Friday, you know, so all that has to be done for the week are a few routine jobs.''

She stopped speaking momentarily, trying to get her breath, then continued. "Like policing the grounds, cleaning the snack bar area, packing up *Spy in the Eye* and its co-feature to send back to the distributor, and previewing the weekend films when they come in Friday morning; that sort of thing. I really think—"

"Sounds like fun, Shari," Zachary interrupted her just as she thought she was losing her mind, babbling on and on as if she had actually been flustered beyond coherence by his last, fairly suggestive statement. After all, she was almost twenty-five years old, and it wasn't as if she had never been propositioned before—*if* that was what had just happened.

"Good grief—er, that is, good, *good*!" she amended hastily. "I just thought you ought to know what you're letting yourself in for, that's all," she then ended fatalistically, nodding her head rapidly as if glad that everything was settled.

"Just tell me what to do first. I'm so unused to taking a vacation that a working vacation might be just what the doctor ordered."

Sharon looked at Zachary for a long moment, then spread her arms wide and shrugged, figuring she might as well go along with him. "In that case, I'll bow to your wishes, Mr. St. Clair. You'll find the plastic bags and shovels in a corner of the storage shed next to the front gate. George usually starts in the last row and works his way forward. I've already got *Spy in the Eye* packed up and ready to go, so the cleanup detail is next on his list of chores."

Zachary looked around the sprawling three-hundred car theater grounds, which were littered with discarded paper cups, crumpled hot dog wrappers, popcorn buckets and small bits of food that were providing a meal for several dozen birds, which were at the moment picking their way through the debris. "You're kidding, right? I mean, you don't really expect me to play *janitor*?"

"Why not?" Sharon asked, her tongue firmly in her

cheek, taking a small slice of satisfaction out of knowing that the tables had been turned just a little. "After all, I'm management—after a fashion. You couldn't actually believe *I* would assign myself such a menial, disgusting job. Besides," she added, already walking away, "then I wouldn't have time for my very favorite job of all—cleaning the bathrooms."

"Over my dead body!" she heard Zachary shout, and turned back to see him standing right behind her, his handsome face revealing the fact that he was absolutely furious. "There's no way in bloody hell I'll see you cleaning bathrooms."

Sharon could feel herself bristling at his arrogance. "Is that right? Well, then, what do you suggest? I hire a cleaning service? You already said Wheeler's is barely breaking even. How do you think we've lasted this long, if I hadn't found some way to cut a few of the costs? Grow up, St. Clair. This isn't some plush and mahogany boardroom, this is the real world. And in the real world people have to clean bathrooms."

She stood very still as she waited for his reaction. They were back to square one, she thought sadly, knowing that only moments ago he had been ready to take her in his arms. *Now,* she told herself ruefully, *all he wants is to shake me silly. I get the feeling this is going to be the shortest working relationship in history.*

After silently deciding that she had somehow destroyed something she really wasn't sure had even existed, Sharon could not hide her astonishment when Zachary at last announced evenly, "Very well then, boss, clean bathrooms if you want. But *I'll* take care of the men's bathroom, if it's all the same to you. In return, we can split up the garbage detail. Deal?"

Sharon looked warily at his outstretched hand, wondering if she could possibly have heard him correctly. Then slowly, hesitantly, she held out her own right hand. "Deal."

As soon as she felt his warm hand clasp hers, she knew

she was lost. It took only the slightest tug on his part to pull
her completely into his arms, and the bargain, begun in anger, was sealed with a most satisfying kiss.

If you were smart, Zachary lectured himself as he made
his way up aisle seven, a halfful plastic bag in one hand, a
shovel in the other, *you'd get back in your car and drive
away from this place as fast as you can. You haven't done
anything this stupid to get to first base with a woman since
the third grade, when you hung upside down from the monkey bars to get Maryjo Handley's attention.*

"My arm was in a cast for six weeks," he said out loud,
putting down the bag in order to wield the shovel on a small
mountain of garbage that seemed to be attracting more than
its share of flying insects in the early-afternoon sunshine. "It
sure was a lot easier cleaning up the aisles in Dad's theaters.
At least I didn't have to worry about getting stung."

Just as if the thought had conjured up the deed, Zachary
suddenly felt a sharp, stinging sensation on the back of his
neck. He dropped the shovel and began slapping furiously
at his face and upper body, as if to ward off any further
attack, then began walking in carefully controlled haste toward the sports car parked behind the snack bar. "Sharon!"
he called out as he walked. "I've been stung. I might need
some help."

Sharon, who had been working her way along the third
row of parking ramps, looked up in time to see Zachary
opening the passenger door of his car and climbing inside.
"Hey!" she called as she stripped off the thin latex gloves
she always wore when working around the grounds and
started in the direction of the car. "I couldn't quite hear what
you said, but if it has anything to do with taking a coffee
break, I'm all for it. Gosh, but it's hot."

"I'm not resting, Sharon," Zachary told her as she
reached the open car door. "I've been stung."

Ah, poor baby, Sharon thought, raising one bare forearm
to push an errant lock of honey-blond hair back away from

her forehead. Aloud, she taunted, "Oh, ye of the faint heart! Don't tell me you're going to give up just because of a little bee sting? There's always a lot of bees around here—they're attracted to the soda and bits of candy, all the sweet stuff."

"That's me, all right," Zachary said, surprising her by his apparent breathlessness. "Sweet stuff. Dammit. Why can't I get this blasted thing open?"

Sharon stood up very straight for a moment as the shock brought on by her realization of just what might be happening finally hit her. Quickly dropping to her knees beside the open car door, she looked inside to see Zachary struggling to open a small black case. Beads of perspiration stood out on his forehead and upper lip.

"Here," she ordered, reaching out her hand, "give me that. You sit still, okay?"

Zachary let go of the case without protest, then reached up to rub at the front of his throat. "I—I'm allergic."

"Yes, I may not be an Einstein, but I think I've figured that out," Sharon told him as she opened the case and looked at the small syringe that lay inside. "Are you having trouble breathing?"

"A little. I think my throat is getting tight, but—but sometimes just the thought of what could happen is enough to give—symptoms. Damn, I'm getting dizzy. Better hurry. Before I start seeing double."

Sharon could feel the burning-cold heat of panic racing through her veins. Zachary looked awful, his exposed skin beginning to take on a mottled appearance and purplish blotches marring the smooth skin of his throat. She lifted the syringe holding its premeasured dose of medication from the case and gingerly held it out to him. "Here, take it," she ordered, fighting her lifelong fear of needles. "You'd better hurry—you don't look so good."

Zachary was literally gasping for breath now. She watched him open his eyes and stare at the needle as if he was having trouble focusing on it. "Sick to my stomach. Can't see. Can't do it."

"You have to do it!" Sharon fairly screamed. "I don't know what to do. Don't you have to have the shot as soon as possible?"

"Twenty—twenty minutes," Zachary gasped. "Hospital."

The nearest hospital was more than twenty minutes away, and more than five minutes had passed since Zachary had been stung. Sharon pressed her fist to her mouth, more frightened than she had ever been in her life. "This is no time to be playing Miss Faint Heart," she then told herself bracingly, purposely looking straight at the syringe. "Zachary, listen to me. You'll have to give yourself the shot. Now tell me how I can help!"

"Alcohol wipe," he told her, shakily pointing toward the case and the small, white flat packet still lying inside. "Rub it on the side of my arm, the fleshiest part."

Get hold of yourself, Wheeler, she instructed herself silently as she completed the task.

"Tell me what to do next," Sharon said as she quickly rubbed the alcohol-saturated swab roughly against his arm.

Zachary raised his head and blinked twice, looking at the syringe she now held in her right hand. "The needle," he croaked. "Uncover the needle."

Stupid! Sharon berated herself, carefully wiping her left hand on her shorts before pulling off the small plastic cover and exposing the short, wickedly thin needle. "Oh, my God," she breathed, swallowing hard as a wave of nausea rolled over her.

"Now hand it to me," Zachary was telling her. "And turn your head. I don't want you fainting on me."

Sharon gingerly handed him the syringe, then followed his advice and turned her head. After all, it wouldn't look good for the patient to recover while the nurse faded away at his feet.

"Do you want some more water?" Sharon asked ten minutes later, taking the empty paper cup from Zachary, who was still sitting in the front seat of the sports car. He looked so much better now—she could see that by both his color and the fact that his hands had finally stopped shaking—but she couldn't help but wish he'd agree to go to the hospital for a checkup.

"I'm fine, Sharon," Zachary assured her, turning slightly in the car seat as if he was about to get up. "I told you, the adrenaline works very quickly. Another couple of minutes and you'd never know I was stung. I'll follow up the shot with antihistamine pills later if I feel the need, but the worst is over. I have to admit, though, that I wasn't feeling too thrilled a few minutes ago. It's been a long time between stings, and I didn't think I'd react so violently."

Still squatting on the ground beside the open car door, Sharon slowly crumpled the cup and placed it carefully on the ground. "So you're just fine?" she said evenly. "Good. Very good. Because now I have another question for you."

She took a deep breath and then fairly shouted, *"Why didn't you tell me you're allergic to bee stings, you ridiculous man!* Dammit, Zachary, you scared me half to death! I never would have allowed you to do the stupid job if you had told me what could happen."

Zachary sank back again against the soft leather seat. "You care, Sharon. How nice. It almost makes the whole thing worth it."

"Of course I care! Don't go reading anything into that, Zachary St. Clair. I'd care just as much if it happened to anybody—George, Denny, Sam—*anybody*! Besides, even if it wasn't really terrific for you to be lying there, sweating and shaking all over the place, it sure as heck didn't make my day, either. I thought I might have to go jabbing that needle into you."

"I guess we can just thank heaven for little favors, Shari," he soothed, stroking her cheek with his right hand. "As it is, with luck, I may even play the violin again some day."

Sharon's eyelids narrowed as she glared at the man who

had so recently scared her half to death. "That's it, make a joke of the whole thing!"

Sharon didn't know what else she could have said if he had given her the chance, because suddenly she felt her body being pulled unceremoniously across his in the front seat. She looked up to see Zachary's face just inches above her own and all her fear, all her indignation, melted under his hot, green gaze.

"All I want to do is thank you for possibly saving my life, Sharon Wheeler. Why don't you be a good girl, and just accept my thanks gracefully?"

"You—you're welcome," Sharon heard herself squeak as the intimacy of their position turned her bones to water. He was going to kiss her, she just knew it. He had kissed her before—twice—but she instinctively knew that this time it would be different. This kiss wasn't going to either be stolen, like his first kiss Friday night, or playful, like the one they had shared just an hour earlier.

Oh, no. Zachary was demanding her full cooperation in this kiss, she could see it in his eyes, and her recent, fairly intimate acquaintance with his lean attractive body fueled her imagination with possibilities she could not—did not want to—ignore.

"But I didn't really thank you yet, Shari," she heard him saying as she concentrated on the enticing movements of his mouth as he spoke. "Still, it's nice to know I'm 'welcome.'"

Oh, Lord, this man does things to me that couldn't possibly be legal, Sharon thought, struggling to keep her composure as she realized that somehow, without her explicit instructions, her arms had wound themselves betrayingly around his neck. "That—that's not what I meant. I can understand what you're thinking—at least I think so—but I didn't really mean that you're—well, maybe I did—but not *really* welcome—"

The whole time she had been speaking, rambling actually, Sharon had been acutely aware of Zachary's hands, which were molding and shaping themselves to the contours of her back, and his legs, which formed such a warm, suggestive cradle for her body. "You—you're just feeling grateful, that's all," she told him, trying to reason away the almost hungry look she saw in his green eyes. "You're just not yourself yet. I really think you ought to go back to your hotel and—"

He didn't let her get any further. She had been faintly disappointed that he had even let her get as far as she had. But finally, unable to stifle the satisfied sigh that escaped her slightly parted lips, she felt the gentle firmness of his mouth against hers.

The loudest on-screen kiss took place between Jack Palance and Shelley Winters in *I Died a Thousand Times*, Sharon thought, unbidden. The longest screen kiss took place between—oh, Lord, who cares!

She forced herself to remain motionless for a few moments, to savor the warmth and texture of Zachary's mouth as he moved his lips slowly against hers, then retreated, then suckled first her top, and then her full lower lip, his moist tongue lightly tracing a sanity-destroying circle on her soft, inner flesh.

But when she thought he was really drawing away from her, Sharon moved forward slightly, reluctant to end the embrace. His reaction to her switch to the initiative, which wasn't long in coming, sent her spiraling helplessly into a mindless whirl of ecstasy. She was crushed tightly against his body, her mouth feeding from his, her hands exploring new territories he opened to her, her heartbeats racing in time with his.

Sharon didn't know where it would end, didn't care where it would end—didn't want it to end. Her entire universe had narrowed; to this car, this man, this glorious feeling.

She wasn't kissing the St. Clair Theater Corporation, or her profit-conscious boss, or even the rescuer who had so lately given Wheeler's Drive-In a new lease on life.

She was kissing the man of the laughing green eyes, the

man who flirted with pigtailed little girls, the man who fed George Blakeman bacon and eggs, the man who had argued with her, infuriated her, intrigued her and occupied her every thought since he had first appeared in her life.

And she would go on kissing him, holding him, loving him, until this spectacular scene had reached its culmination, until the credits had all run by, even after the screen had gone blank and the world had faded away.

Chapter 6

"Sharon. Shari, honey," Zachary whispered into her ear as he pressed her head against his chest. "Someone's coming."

No! They wouldn't dare! Sharon clutched her arms even tighter about Zachary's waist as she fought to bring herself back to reality. But then she heard it too, the soft crunching sound of rubber tires moving along the gravel path toward the snack bar. She felt like a teenager caught in the back seat of a parked car, as she rapidly pulled herself out of his arms, tucking her T-shirt back down into the waistband of her shorts as she spied the delivery truck heading directly for the space next to the sports car.

She looked at Zachary, on whose lap she still rested, her bare legs hanging outside the opened car door, and realized that he was just as upset by their unexpected visitor as she was. "Just—just like in the movies," she heard herself saying. "The timely interruption. That's how they keep their PG ratings. Though I don't ever remember the interruption taking the form of the propane gas man. I didn't know Gary was coming today."

She tried to extricate herself from her compromising position, earning Zachary's rather painfully uttered "Take it easy, Shari, I'm not a well man at the moment," for her troubles.

Then, still pushing at her disheveled hair, and with a becoming flush of pink still riding high on her cheeks, she walked rapidly over to the edge of the grass parking area to greet Gary, the deliveryman, noticing out of the corner of her eye that Zachary was also out of the car and heading for the snack bar.

Fifteen minutes later, just enough time for Gary to complete his delivery and leave—and more than enough time for Sharon to realize exactly what had almost happened in the front seat of Zachary's sports car—she walked into the coolness of the snack bar to see her boss sitting in *her* office, inspecting the account book.

"He's gone," she said nervously, leaning against the doorjamb. "Would you like some ice cream? We've got plenty."

If she had been nervous before, she was doubly apprehensive once Zachary turned around to face her, for he had that forbidding, closed look on his face that he had worn the night Gertrude had invaded the drive-in. "Sharon, you said you weren't expecting that deliveryman. How would he have gotten in here if you weren't here? Don't you lock the gates?"

Instantly Sharon was on the defensive. She should have known better than to think that scene in the car had really changed anything—that any of Zachary's recent actions had changed anything. Scratch a businessman like Zachary and you'll find a profit and loss statement under his skin. "Of course I lock the gates!" she was stung into answering. "What do you think I am—stupid?"

"Then I repeat my question. How would Gary have been able to make his delivery if you weren't here?"

Sharon looked down at the toe of her sneaker as she absently kicked at a loose corner of the linoleum. "He—he has a key," she told him reluctantly, waiting for the explosion that she knew wouldn't be long in coming. "So do the dairyman, the restaurant supply man, the meter man and the butcher. Popsie always said it was easier to do that than to always be running out here in the middle of the week to let them—"

"I don't give a flying fig what your Popsie said!" Zachary shouted at her, slamming the accounts book shut and rising to his feet to stare down at her. "Don't you read *Reel People*, or any of the trade magazines? There are pirates out there stealing movie prints left, right and center, then selling them for videos, or overseas."

"Now just a minute. Just a darn minute! If you're insinuating that—"

"We're responsible for the films we're showing, and you—you give every Tom, Dick and *Gary* a damn *key* to the place! Woman, do you have any head for business at all—or are you only concerned with keeping in a good supply of sauerkraut for your damned hot dogs?"

So much for worrying about telling him you're not that kind of girl, Wheeler, she told herself, feeling herself beginning to shake with fury. Romance seems to be the last thing on his mind. Well, if it's a fight he wants, I'm sure not going to disappoint him!

Sharon shoved out her firm chin and jabbed a finger repeatedly into Zachary's chest as she answered his accusations, her belligerence lending a warning note of sharpness to her voice. "I am fully aware of the warnings issued by the Motion Picture Association, Mr. St. Clair, as are all Wheeler employees. That projection room is locked at both entrances every moment it's unoccupied, and the films are all kept under separate lock and key to boot. I couldn't care less about your poor opinion of our snack bar, but I would like to go on record as saying I do resent very much your insinuation that Wheeler's has anything to do with the print piracy going on in the industry. How dare you make such an accusation!"

"I dare, *Miss Wheeler*," Zachary growled at her, pushing her accusing finger away as he took another short step in her direction, "because this theater, for my sins, is now a part of the St. Clair Theater Corporation. It is Wheeler's Drive-In no longer. And I am going to haul this place—kicking and screaming all the way, I'm sure—into the present, *with or without your help.*

"And that, if you are still unclear as to what I have in mind, means that in the future there is going to be a person on duty here at all times—not just when it won't interfere with your friendly little golf dates."

"How dare you—"

Zachary went on as if she hadn't spoken. "That means that the only keys to the gates will be in the hands of authorized personnel; period. It means that—that sauerkraut will no longer be on the menu, dammit. Now get on the phone and find somebody to come out here and clean this place up! You're the manager—for the moment. I suggest you start acting like one." He then reached out his hand and gestured toward her T-shirt and shorts. "And for God's sake, don't you own a skirt?"

Sharon abruptly closed her mouth, as she belatedly realized that it had dropped open the moment Zachary had begun his tirade. Then she hurried after his departing back. "Just where do you think you're going?" she called to him as he slammed his way out the snack bar door. "You shouldn't be driving yet, you idiot!"

"Why not?" Zachary hurled at her over his shoulder. "You have more surprises in store for me? Perhaps you want to tell me that you also gave gate keys to the entire Vienna Boys' Choir? Please, I don't think I could take any more today."

"Very funny," Sharon told him in a tone that said she didn't think he had been funny at all. "It's just that it hasn't been that long since you were stung. It might not be safe. The last thing I need is to have your untimely death on my hands. I doubt there would be a jury in the world who would believe I hadn't killed you!''

Zachary stopped, then turned around for only a moment, looking her up and down in a way that had her involuntarily taking one step backward. ''It's a damn sight safer than staying here with you,'' she heard him say before he was off again, his angry strides taking him rapidly out of sight. ''I'll be back tomorrow at noon to check on your progress. Be here.''

''You're the Scotch guy. I remember,'' the hotel bartender said jovially that evening as he approached the end of the bar where Zachary sat staring blankly into the mirror above the back bar. ''You ever get in that game of golf?''

Zachary looked across the width of the bar at the man, who was placing a short glass containing an inch and a half of amber liquid in front of him. ''Yes, yes I did. Thank you, er—''

''Stosh,'' the bartender supplied eagerly. ''Stanley Wojewodzki, actually, but everybody calls me Stosh. It's easier. You?''

It's Mudd—with two Ds, Zachary almost said, then realized Stosh didn't deserve his sarcasm. ''Zachary,'' he told the man. ''Are you from around here, Stosh, or did you come to Allentown to work in the hotel?''

''Me?'' Stosh answered, whipping out a damp cloth to wipe at the already shiny surface of the bar. ''Nah, I'm a local—lived here all my life. No big cities like Philly or New York for me. Allentown's got it all, you know. You've got your shopping malls, your good schools, your nice housing—''

''Do you go to the movies, Stosh?'' Zachary heard himself asking, wondering why he was interested.

Stosh nodded his head vigorously. ''Oh, sure. Me and the wife go every Saturday night like clockwork. Wouldn't miss it. This is a big movie town.''

''Indoor theaters, of course,'' Zachary prodded, nodding

his head in agreement, already knowing that the theater market in the district that included eastern Pennsylvania, southern New Jersey, and Delaware was one of the most profitable in the country. After all, why else had he invested in the area?

"Oh, sure, but only in the wintertime, when Wheeler's Drive-In isn't open. I've heard a rumor that the old place has been sold again and the new owner might shut it down. That would be a darn shame. The wife is sort of partial to Wheeler's, and the kids like it. It's okay by me, too, because it's cheap. And the food! Hey, you've got your steak sandwiches, your hot dogs, your nachos, your—"

"Yes, yes," Zachary cut in before Stosh could recite the entire menu, "I've heard Wheeler's is a nice place. It would be a shame to see it closed down."

He watched as the bartender smiled reminiscently. "Me and the wife—we met there, you know. 'Course, that was three kids ago. Now we even watch the movie," he said, winking, "if you know what I mean!"

Had the entire population of Allentown met and married thanks to Wheeler's Drive-In? First Sharon had told him about Denny, the employee who worked in the ticket booth, and now Stosh was telling him the same thing about himself. *Maybe that's what's behind my moment of madness this afternoon with Sharon,* Zachary told himself, looking for any excuse with which he could comfort himself. *There must be something in the air out there.*

"Hey, I guess you didn't want Scotch tonight, huh?" Stosh suggested, interrupting Zachary's thoughts. "You haven't touched your drink. You can have something else, you know. We've got your beer, your wine, your—"

Zachary hastily lifted his glass and took a drink, the fiery liquid stinging the back of his throat and sending a reviving jolt of liquid warmth through his body. "The Scotch is fine, Stosh. I guess I'm just tired. I think I'll make it an early evening." He finished off the drink, stood up and reached a hand into his pants pocket. "What's the damage?"

The bartender held out his hands and smiled. "Hey, keep your money in your pocket. You're a visitor to our fair city. This one's on me."

Zachary thanked the man, then made sure to leave a sizable tip at the other end of the bar before making for the lobby and the elevator that would take him to his room on the fourth floor of the downtown hotel. But the smile Stosh's antics had put on his face faded as Zachary unlocked the door to his room and faced the dark emptiness that waited on the other side.

After stripping off the suit he had donned earlier and climbing into the running shorts that were the closest thing to pajamas he would wear, even while traveling around the country to visit his business holdings, Zachary stretched himself out full length on the king-size bed, his arms at his sides, as he stared up at the ceiling.

Lifting his right hand after a moment, he began absently rubbing at the site where he had injected the adrenaline. "It's good I could use the needle myself," he said aloud in the empty room. "As it is, I'll probably be black and blue for a week."

If that were the only place I've been bruised, I might still have been able to walk away from this town with no regrets, he thought, abruptly rising from the bed to walk over to the window and look down on the street below.

But, no. Sharon Wheeler had left her mark all over him, whether he wanted to acknowledge that fact or not. She and George had already sent him on one guilt trip by showing him that he'd somehow lost sight of the theaters and the people who work in them. They may have done him a favor in the long run, he thought, because a good businessman has to remember where he's been, if he is to keep some perspective on the future.

But Zachary knew he could not convince himself that it was only a few good memories of the past—of his years spent listening to his father's reminiscences, of his summer spent working with Charlie Barrows in that glorious old Art

Deco theater in Buffalo—that had somehow resulted in his decision to keep Wheeler's open. His motives were much more involved, much more closely connected with his awareness of Sharon Wheeler as a desirable female, than he would like to admit.

What had begun that first night as an infuriating awareness of her strange effect on him had mushroomed that Sunday at the golf course when he found himself ready to punch poor unsuspecting Hugh Kingsley in the mouth for daring to kiss Sharon in his presence.

Lifting his arms to push his fingers wearily through his dark hair before sliding his hands down the back of his neck to begin massaging his aching shoulders, Zachary felt the sharp sting of guilt yet again as he silently acknowledged that he had deliberately set out to seduce one Miss Sharon Wheeler, using his power of life and death over Wheeler's as a shortcut through her defenses.

"You are despicable, and conniving, and everything else Sharon called you," he berated himself aloud, turning away from the window. "You were tired, burned out and looking for a change when you got to town. You took one look at Sharon Wheeler, were attracted to the girl and then deliberately used charm and personality to take what you wanted from her without a thought to the damage you might be doing to an innocent young woman.

"Then, this afternoon, when you realized you were getting in over your head, actually beginning to feel something more than mere physical desire for her, you took the first opportunity you could to lash out at her, wield your almighty power over her head. You're a real gem, St. Clair, you really are."

Dropping heavily onto the bed, Zachary put his head in his hands as he let the full weight of what he had done sink in for the first time. "So far today I've committed myself to keeping Wheeler's open, and I've succeeded in making the first woman I've ever been in danger of seriously caring for hate the sight of me. Now I've got less than a week to turn

Wheeler's into a money-making proposition I can defend to the stockholders and—most importantly—to win Sharon Wheeler.''

His head popped up suddenly as a thought hit him—as something very near to divine inspiration sent a flash of new strength coursing through his weary body. ''Of course!'' he exclaimed in elation, leaping to his feet in order to pace rapidly up and down the room. ''It's perfect, absolutely perfect! Why didn't I think of this before!''

He fairly ran to the nightstand to pick up the phone. As he dialed the long distance number he laughed aloud, raising his eyes to the ceiling as he said, ''If this works, all I'll have to do is find some way to make Sharon want me as much as I want her. And, by God, I do *want* her!''

Sharon walked around to the rear of the snack bar and dumped the bucket of soapy water onto a small patch of weeds that had sprung up through some gaps in the gravel pathway. It had taken her all morning, but the snack bar was spotless, from the projection room floor to the mirrors in the restrooms.

She had not given a second thought to Zachary's angry demand that she hire someone to clean the theater. She wanted to—had to—do it herself. It had been a labor of love.

Returning the bucket to its place in the small shed that stood next to the ticket booth, she then began walking slowly back toward the snack bar for what would be her final visit, mentally calculating how long it would take her to write out her resignation and be off the premises.

She had been able to keep her thoughts at bay throughout the time she had been cleaning and sorting and scrubbing, but now there was nothing else left to be done, nothing left to delay the inevitable.

It was time to say goodbye.

Just the thought of what she had to do brought helpless tears to her eyes, and she stopped in the middle of the third row and looked around at the open-air theater one last time.

There was not a single bit of debris left anywhere on the grounds; she had stayed until dusk the night before, policing the area as if she were readying the place for inspection by some commanding officer.

But that wasn't what she was looking at now.

Now she was looking at memories.

Like the time Popsie had spent an entire summer afternoon convincing the five-year-old Sharon that the sliding board located in the small playground at the foot of the movie screen was great fun. "And then he had had to spend the rest of the day trying to convince me to *stop* sliding down the silly thing," she reminisced aloud, smiling a little in spite of her sad mood.

Looking back toward the wooden shed that served as the ticket booth, Sharon remembered the night a huge camper had pulled onto the grounds and the top of the vehicle had slammed into the roof of the booth, turning the entire structure nearly sideways on its cement base. What a night that had been, with the patron screaming about the damage to his camper and Popsie having a fit because the camper was blocking the entrance and he was losing business.

In the end, she recalled, Sharon's grandfather had gone from car to car, enlisting the aid of every high school football player he could find, and the ticket booth had been shoved back into place. "It's still just the least bit crooked," she said now, tilting her head to one side as she looked fondly at the wooden shelter.

"And then there was Errol Flynn," Sharon said, her voice breaking slightly as she remembered her grandfather's old German shepherd, Popsie's constant companion. Errol had been part pet, part watchdog, and he could always be found lying on the grass in front of the box office until the last car of the night had pulled through the gates. Many people had stopped to admire the handsome animal on their way into the theater, but one incident in particular stood out in her mind.

She laughed aloud as she remembered the night she had

been helping her grandfather in the booth as an older woman had driven up, stopping her car for a full minute to admire Errol before finally driving up to purchase her ticket.

"What a beautiful dog!" the old lady had gushed, and Sharon could not help but notice that the woman's admiration for Errol seemed to extend to her grandfather, who had always been a handsome man. "Whose is it?"

"Mine," Sharon had heard her grandfather growl, clearly not in the mood for any romantic dalliance.

"Oh, aren't you lucky?" the lady had pushed on, even though Sharon's grandfather had already handed her both her change and her ticket. "Does he always lie there?"

"Yep," Popsie had answered shortly, already looking through the front window of the booth as the line of cars got longer.

"Really? How lovely," the woman had gushed girlishly. "Whatever does he do there?"

"He's keeping a count on the cars for me," Popsie had gritted, throwing his giggling granddaughter a broad wink.

Sharon wiped at the tears now on her cheeks as she recalled the delighted expression that had come over the woman's face at her grandfather's ridiculous explanation.

"Really!" she had heard the woman exclaim delightedly, looking back toward Errol, who had just then been in the middle of a huge doggie yawn. "Isn't that wonderful!" the silly woman had exclaimed, much impressed with Errol's canine abilities, before at last driving away, leaving Sharon and her grandfather holding on to each other, dissolved in laughter.

"Oh, Popsie, how I loved those times," Sharon said into the silence of the vacant theater lot. "Leaving this place is going to be like having to say goodbye to you all over again. But I have to go. I would only be fighting a losing battle if I stayed. Nothing will really ever be the same anymore, not with the St. Clair Theater Corporation turning the place into one of its nondescript clones. I don't think I could bear to watch that, be a part of it. I just don't think I can fight anymore.''

Suddenly Sharon heard the sound of an approaching car on the gravel pathway, and for a moment she thought that she had left her departure too late. Seeing Zachary St. Clair again would deplete the last of her reserves, and she'd end up making a complete fool of herself. "He'd misunderstand completely—think I'm leaving because of him. Because he kissed me. Because I kissed him back. Because he hates me. And that's not true,'' she told the speaker poles that stood along the aisles like sentries at attention. "It's the farthest thing from the truth I ever heard.''

That's good, now tell us another one. The dark-faced speaker boxes seemed to mock her, and Sharon turned to run for the snack bar away from her three hundred silent accusers, away from the approaching car bringing Zachary St. Clair back into her life just long enough to remind her of exactly how empty that life would be without him.

"Hey, Shari! Where's the fire?''

She stopped running, relief flooding through her as she recognized the voice of her old friend. "Hugh!" she cried out, turning to see the hotel owner's midnight-blue Chrysler convertible pulling up beside her. "What in the world are you doing all the way out here? Don't tell me your mother sent you.''

"Cheeky female,'' Hugh Kingsley chided, waving Sharon away from the door so that he could open it. "I never should have told you about Mother's little fantasy. You're getting a swelled head. Maybe that's why you forgot our lunch date today at the club. You were just exercising your power over me. Well, here I am, come begging. Are you happy now?''

Sharon clapped a hand to her mouth in dismay. "Oh, Hugh, I'm so sorry! I was going to meet you, wasn't I? I completely forgot.''

Hugh shook his head in mock dejection. "You could have said you were busy, Shari. That I could stand. But to *forget* me? I'm wounded to the quick. But I guess I wouldn't be honest if I said I was surprised. I checked the register at the hotel this morning, and Casanova is still in residence.''

"Casanova?"

"Zachary St. Clair. Our handsome captain of industry *is* making a move on you, isn't he? I'd be jealous, but from the way he was looking at you on Sunday, I'd say his intentions are honest.''

"Oh, Hugh!" Sharon wailed, then hurled herself into her friend's comforting arms, to cry as she had not cried since she had lost Popsie six years earlier.

Chapter 7

Zachary woke very early that morning, eager to rush over to Sharon's house as soon as possible to share his good news with her, but he was being frustrated at every turn.

Her phone number and address were not listed in the telephone directory, and repeated calls to George Blakeman's house went unanswered. Zachary chafed at the knowledge, but there was nothing for him to do but wait until closer to noon, and then meet her at Wheeler's as planned.

As he lay back against the propped-up pillows on the bed in the midst of his elation at his brilliance, he slowly began to feel a few niggling doubts creeping unbidden into his mind.

He could dazzle Sharon with his news only if—and it was a big if—she planned on obeying the order he had flung at her so nastily yesterday afternoon. "How could you have been such an idiot as to yell at her that way yesterday? Some genius you are, St. Clair!" he berated himself aloud. He wouldn't be the least bit surprised if he arrived at the drive-in to find that she was nowhere to be found. Even worse, he knew he couldn't blame her!

"And you don't have the slightest idea where to find her if she doesn't show up at the theater! She could live on the moon for all you know. You've been so busy planning Sharon's future, you haven't taken the time to learn anything at all about her. Talk about your chauvinists, St. Clair. You really take the prize!" he continued as he rose from the bed and headed for the bathroom.

Zachary's elation at having satisfactorily resolved the problem of Wheeler's Drive-In might have temporarily banished thoughts of his latest argument with Sharon from his mind last night, but this morning's enforced cooling-off period before he could meet with her was rapidly chilling his good mood even more effectively than the cold shower he stood under for ten minutes, trying to marshal his thoughts.

Once dressed and down in the dining room, Zachary pushed his sausage and eggs aimlessly around his plate as he waited for the long morning to end, all his actions of the previous day playing again in his mind, like a bad movie he had been forced to sit through twice.

Not that he regretted their interlude in the front seat of the car, for he didn't. As a matter of fact, he found himself feeling almost grateful to the bee that had sacrificed its little life in the name of romance.

It was his asinine performance— "Yes, St. Clair, asinine," he told himself bitterly fifteen minutes before noon as he finally rounded the corner to drive through the open theater gates—after Gary, the gas man, had left that were giving him second thoughts about how Sharon would take the news he had for her today.

He'd have to handle his explanation very carefully, explain it all in great detail so that she understood that what he was doing was for the best—the only possible solution that was fair to everybody involved. He owed it to his stockholders, he owed it to Sharon and George and the rest of the Wheeler employees.

Mostly, he thought guiltily, *I owe it to myself—because, if I don't handle this exactly right, I just might not escape this place today in one piece.*

Smiling a little as he turned the sports car down the pathway behind the snack bar, his green eyes narrowed a little as he spotted the dark blue convertible parked beside Sharon's compact station wagon.

"Probably just some girlfriend who stopped in for a visit," he consoled himself, eyeing the expensive-looking automobile warily as he climbed out of his own car. "Control yourself, man," he warned under his breath. "You're beginning to act like you've posted no-trespassing signs on the woman."

But no matter what Zachary told himself, no matter whether or not he viewed himself as being a civilized man, nothing could keep his hands from bunching into fists at his sides when he saw the customized license plate as he walked behind the convertible.

"'KING-1,'" he growled. "Hugh Kingsley! Damn it! How dare she allow her boyfriend to visit her at work? She knew I wanted to talk to her today—*demanded* to meet with her today. Does she think she needs reinforcements—that I'm some kind of monster?"

Zachary's well-intentioned, carefully rehearsed-under-a-cold-shower speech went winging off into oblivion as he strode purposefully around the snack bar to the side door, which stood open in the warm noon air. He stepped inside the doorway, his eyes taking a moment to adjust to the dim light inside before he saw the touching scene that was being played out in front of him.

Sharon, clad once more in T-shirt and shorts, was sitting propped atop the snack bar counter, her bare legs dangling a good two feet above the floor, her honey-blond hair hanging in a molten mass on either side of her woebegone little face as Hugh Kingsley, dressed with a casual elegance that suited his lean frame, hovered over her solicitously, unfolded handkerchief at the ready.

"Now doesn't this make a pretty picture," Zachary fairly snarled as he advanced farther into the room. "Wait! Don't tell me. Let me guess. Cinderella's got a bit of smut in her eye, and Prince Charming has volunteered to get it out for her. Well, don't look now, but the wicked stepmother—or in this case, boss—has just shown up to throw a monkey wrench into the happily-ever-after plot. Too bad, isn't it, Kingsley, and just when you looked like you were getting someplace. Or am I wrong, and I've come in on the last reel, too late to see the love scene?"

"I said, I don't wish to discuss it!" Sharon picked up the five rolls of wrapped bathroom tissue one by one, quickly jamming three of them into the crook of her left arm before barreling out of the office and past Zachary, threatening him with the two rolls of tissue she brandished in front of his face like a weapon as she went.

"All right, all right," Zachary compromised, trotting after her as she slipped neatly under the cut-out section of the Formica bar and lightly skipped outside. "We won't discuss it."

"You're being redundant, St. Clair. I've already said that," Sharon shot at him, breaking into a run.

Vaulting over the bar rather than struggling to bend his tall frame under it, Zachary picked up some ground on her retreating form, but she was still three paces ahead of him as she rounded the corner of the snack bar and headed for the women's rest room. "We won't discuss it," he called after her yet again. "Heaven knows I'd just as soon forget the whole thing ever happened. But, please, Shari, at least be fair enough to let me apologize for what I said."

"Oh, sure. How like a man! Now you want to shift all the responsibility to *my* shoulders, just because I won't let you soothe your conscience with a quick apology. You do all the damage with that overdeveloped imagination of yours, and then a simple 'I'm sorry' is supposed to fix everything?

Well, you can just forget it! I don't know how I'll ever be able to face Hugh again.''

"In that case, I withdraw my apology," Zachary called after her. "In fact, now I'm *glad* I did it!"

After Hugh—still smiling like some demented Cheshire cat—had left her to fend for herself against a wildly raving Zachary, the only salvation she could think of was to head for the sanctuary of the women's bathroom. Sharon pulled open the main door to the rest room and went inside, believing the sign saying Women would be enough to keep Zachary away. Picking up the tissue paper first in her office was only an afterthought.

She was just opening the white wooden door to the first stall when the main door crashed against the wall behind her, and she whirled around to see Zachary stepping inside. "I don't believe it! Get out of here, you idiot. Can't you read?"

Sharon watched him look around blindly for a moment, taking in the light yellow-painted concrete block walls, the small sink and the row of five white wooden doors that made up the long, narrow room. "The door, St. Clair!" she shouted, exasperated. "Look what it says on the door!"

Zachary turned and looked at the stenciled printing, then turned back to look at Sharon, who had already disappeared behind the door of the first stall. "When are you going to be through in there?" she heard him ask, and she took comfort in his obvious discomfort.

Having installed the new tissue in the chrome holder, Sharon pushed the door open once more, then peeked around it to glare at Zachary. "September!" she replied with a quick dismissive jerk of her head. "Now, go away!"

Letting the first door slam back into place, she then threw back the door to the second stall, entered and heard it slam shut behind her with a satisfying bang. At least he has some gentlemanly good manners left, she soothed herself as she slammed the second roll of tissue paper home before kicking the second door open in order to proceed to the third stall.

But the door stayed open; it didn't swing shut again to soothe her soul with yet another satisfying bang. Jerking her head around as she still held the three rolls of tissue paper close to her body, she saw Zachary's face leering down at her from over the top of the door.

"You had me there for a minute, Shari," she heard him say. "But as we're not open for business, I doubt that it matters that I'm in here."

"It matters to me!" Sharon told him, pulling open the door to the third stall and letting it crash shut behind her. "Can't you take a hint, St. Clair?" she called to him from inside the stall. "I don't want to talk to you. I don't want to look at you. I don't even want to be on the same *planet* with you. And just as soon as I'm finished with this one last job I'm leaving—so that I never, ever have to look at you or listen to you again! Have I made myself perfectly clear?"

"As crystal, Sharon. Tell me, what planet are you aiming for?" she heard Zachary ask, his gibe causing her to growl in exasperation as she ruthlessly jammed the tissue into the holder.

"Ha, ha, very funny. You're a real laugh riot, St. Clair; you ought to be in the movies," Sharon said as her temper got the best of her. "You know very well what I mean. I'm just leaving!"

She waited until she heard the door to the second stall close, then threw open the door to the third stall with all the force she could muster, gaining a large measure of satisfaction from the clunking sound the wood made when it came sharply into contact with Zachary's knees. She didn't make the mistake of standing around in the narrow aisleway to admire her handiwork, but bolted for the fourth stall as fast as she could.

"You know you don't mean that, Shari. Now stop slamming doors and listen to me!" Zachary called after her.

Sharon clapped her hands over her ears and began loudly humming 'The Battle Hymn of the Republic,' trying to block out the sound of his voice.

"You can't leave," Zachary continued to shout. "You love this place. Look, Shari, I've already apologized for getting the wrong impression when I walked in on you and Hugh. I don't know what got into me."

That did it! Sharon had asked him to leave her alone, spelled it out to him in words of one syllable, and still he persisted. Now, she decided with a sharp intake of breath, he was going to get a piece of her mind!

Sharon shot the door open as hard as she could, holding the solid piece of wood ajar to stand as a barrier between Zachary and herself in the narrow aisle. Looking up at him as he hung his head over the top of the door, she sneered, "Nothing 'got into' you, Zachary. You were just being your usual, obnoxious self. Flying off the handle seems to be a hobby of yours. As a matter of fact, the only predictable thing about you is your very *unpredictability*. Is that how you keep your employees on their toes? By being nice one minute and then biting off their heads the next? Well, no thanks. You can just take your kisses and your tantrums somewhere else. *I quit!*"

Her explosion of wrath over, Sharon quickly disappeared behind the last door, but she didn't bother trying to install the one remaining roll of tissue. Her hands were shaking so badly she knew it would be impossible. Instead, she just stood leaning against the side wall a moment, trying to catch her breath as tears pricked behind her tightly shut eyelids.

This wasn't quite the way she had envisioned saying her final goodbye to Wheeler's—playing hide-and-seek in the women's bathroom with an irate soon-to-be ex-boss. She should have just stormed out with Hugh, and then sent someone else to pick up her car later, but her so-called friend had deserted her before she could gather her thoughts enough to do more than hop down from the countertop and make a mad dash for her office.

Now, after counting to ten several times, Sharon leaned her head back against the wall and raised her gaze to the whitewashed ceiling, sniffling self-pityingly a time or two at the curious hand fate had dealt her. "So this is the way the career ends," she mused aloud, "not with a bang but a whimper. The manager of Wheeler's has just resigned in the women's bathroom. As resignations go, Sharon, old girl, I think this one lacks something for glamour."

"Are you ready to talk now? Or are you only going to talk to yourself?"

Zachary's questions jolted Sharon back to reality. "I'll never be ready to talk to you!" she shouted back at him. "Not if I live another million years. I've quit. Resigned. Handed in my notice. I don't have to do anything I don't want to anymore. Now stand back, or this door is going to smack you right in the nose."

She counted to three, then slapped her hands against the door as hard as she could, hoping he hadn't heeded her warning.

The door didn't budge. She pushed at it again, leaning all of her weight into the movement. Nothing. The door remained firmly shut, Sharon on one side, Zachary on the other.

"Let me out of here! You're not playing fair," she ordered, banging her fists against the door. "Locking a woman in a bathroom! Who do you think you are? One of the Marx Brothers? Grow up, St. Clair."

She ground her teeth in impotent fury as she heard the amusement in Zachary's voice as he answered. "The Marx Brothers? Oh, I don't know about that. The way I've been chasing you, I think I feel more like Mack Sennet doing one of his Keystone Kops chase scenes. Besides, shame on you, Miss Wheeler. I don't believe I heard you say 'please.'"

Sharon repeatedly slapped her hands furiously against her thighs as she looked around the small booth, considering and then rejecting the ignominious solution of crawling out of the booth underneath the door. "All right," she said at last, forcing an air of politeness into her voice. "Zachary, *please* let me out of here."

Zachary smiled as he heard Sharon's voice and her obvious attempt to control her anger. "No," he replied cheerfully, still standing at his ease, his arms crossed at the elbows, his back leaning comfortably against the stall door. "I don't think so. I'm beginning to think this is the only way I'll be able to make you listen to me. Now, Sharon, are you ready to listen to me?"

"*Arrgh!*"

Zachary smiled yet again. "I'll take that as a yes. All right, Sharon, here goes. First of all, please accept my apology one more time for reading anything sinister into that little scene with Hugh. I realize now that you were upset and he was merely comforting you. The fact that *I* was the reason you were crying is just one more thing I need to apologize for. I know I wasn't very nice to you yesterday."

"Nice? You were awful!" Sharon's voice was rather thick, as if she were crying yet again. "But you didn't hurt me. I always cry when I get angry, not that it matters anymore. I can take a hint. You don't think I'm a good manager, so just as soon as you let me out of here you'll have my resignation. Unless you want to slip a pen under the door— I can write it on the tissue paper."

Zachary turned his head to look at the door, as if he could see through it to where Sharon stood, probably making a face at him. "Getting a little flippant for a person who's gotten herself locked in a bathroom, aren't you?" he teased. "I hate to disappoint you, Sharon, but I *can't* accept your resignation. *Now*, will you listen to me?"

"What do you mean you can't accept my resignation?" she asked, again pushing on the door. "You mean you *won't* accept it, don't you? Well, I don't care. And you can't fire me. I've already quit you."

"You're right there, I can't fire you. I'm not your boss. Oh, I did buy the place from the corporation, but that was only so I could give it away to somebody else last night," Zachary informed her evenly, then waited for her reaction.

"Give it away?" Sharon squeaked. "But you promised! Who owns us now?"

"Another St. Clair. My father, actually," he told her, feeling just as pleased as he had the night before when the idea had first occurred to him. "As of this morning my father, Lucien St. Clair, owns one hundred percent of Wheeler's Drive-In. You'll love him, and he'll be crazy about the place, just as it is. There's no more St. Clair Theater Corporation to bother you anymore, Shari. My lawyers are already drawing up the necessary papers to transfer ownership."

At last, his little speech over, although there was still so much he had left unsaid, Zachary moved away from the door, allowing Sharon to exit her temporary prison.

Within seconds he was rewarded with the appearance of her head as she peeked around the corner of the stall, a thoroughly bemused expression on her beautiful face. Her cornflower-blue eyes were glistening with unshed tears as she looked up at him, her dusky pink lips moving as she tried to say something.

"Still going to quit, Shari?" he couldn't resist asking as, slowly, hesitantly, she moved completely into the narrow aisle that ran in front of the stalls. "My dad's retired to Florida, so you can't really just leave the place to run itself, can you? I'm still going to advance the money for all the necessary repairs. I mean, Gertrude's nice and all that, but I don't think we should go on encouraging her to wander. Come on, honey, what do you say? Will you stay now?"

"What do I say?" Sharon told him slowly, her voice husky with passion, "I'll tell you what I say. I say that you are…the most hateful…thoroughly despicable…underhanded…*conniving* man who has ever lived!"

Zachary stepped back against the wall, involuntarily clutching the roll of bathroom tissue Sharon jabbed sharply into his midsection as she swept past him at top speed and ran out into the sunlight.

"Women!" he shouted into the empty room, his angry condemnation echoing back at him from the concrete block walls as he ran after Sharon. But she had already reached her car and was in the process of backing out of the parking area. "Sharon!" he yelled over the sound of the engine, banging his hands against the hood of the station wagon, "Wait!"

She either didn't hear him or refused to acknowledge him, and a moment later the only sounds left in the parking area were the fiercely soft whisperings of Zachary St. Clair as he cursed himself for being the biggest fool of all time.

The crickets are sure in full voice tonight, Sharon thought idly as she sat slumped in her cotton nightgown on one side of the old wooden porch swing, absently pushing it back and forth with the force of the foot she had propped against the nearby porch railing.

I can almost hear a couple of them furiously rubbing their little legs together, chirping out the message far and wide to all their friends, she mused, saying aloud: "Sharon Wheeler's made a fool of herself; Sharon Wheeler's made a fool of herself."

It was past midnight, fully twelve hours since Zachary had stormed into the snack bar to set off the bizarre chain of events that had sent Sharon scurrying for the shelter of her bedroom, where she had hidden herself away until an hour ago, like some wanted criminal on the lam from the law.

Hunger had finally prodded her out of her seclusion, and she had just finished downing half a cold chicken, a heaping mound of day-old potato salad and a gargantuan slice of homemade double chocolate layer cake. "I feel sick," she told the chorus of insects, although she knew that her recent meal had little to do with the queasy feeling in her stomach.

"Oh, Popsie, what do I do now?" she wailed aloud, rising from the swing to stand at the railing, looking out over the large front yard that surrounded the isolated century-old farmhouse her grandfather had left to her directly, circumventing her father's decision to sell everything that wasn't nailed down just as soon as Al Wheeler's will was read so that he and his young second wife could move to California.

"The drive-in has been sold again, Popsie," Sharon said,

turning back toward the swing and talking as if her grandfather was once again sitting in his favorite spot, his unlit
pipe stuck firmly between his gleaming, store-bought teeth.
"It's privately owned again, but the new owner lives in Florida. I'm supposed to stay on as manager, but I don't know
if I can. You see, there's something about the whole thing
that I don't think I can live with."

Sharon closed her eyes, and then rubbed one hand against
her mouth, trying to find some way to tell her grandfather
about Zachary St. Clair. How could she tell her grandfather,
even his spirit, that she believed Zachary had only sold
Wheeler's in some perverted act of charity?

"I get the idea he's just cast himself in the role of Daddy
Warbucks," she said, feeling like some storm-tossed orphan
who'd just been handed a lollipop.

That was the only explanation she could think of for Zachary to have done what he had. It certainly wasn't a good
move for him to have made economically, and Zachary had
already proved to her that he was first and foremost a businessman. Well, if he wanted to play philanthropist, *she*
wasn't going to stay around to applaud.

That was the reason she had stormed out of the drive-in,
barely able to see past the red-hot fury that burned in her
eyes, that pulsated throughout her entire disillusioned body.

She hadn't believed she had been flattering herself with
what she had thought earlier, what she was still thinking.
Zachary had made it all too clear that he found her attractive,
even desirable. After all, his kisses haven't been exactly pla-
tonic!

*Heaven only knows, I was so dazzled by his unexpected
gentleness, so intrigued by his many moods, so wildly attracted to him physically, that he could have had me for the
taking,* she thought now, feeling her cheeks grow hot with
shame as she remembered their rather torrid interlude the
day before in the front seat of his sports car.

"Talk about your infatuations. Lord, was I naïve. I actually thought he cared for me. Well, so much for foolish

dreams. I should have known better. Anyone would think I actually believe that stuff Hollywood is always putting on the screen.

"Now, just when I think he's beginning to care for me, he signs me up for the part of Orphan Annie. Well, Zachary St. Clair has another thought coming. Sharon Wheeler is nobody's charity case!" she declared feelingly, lifting her chin proudly.

She was silent for a few moments, waiting for the rush of satisfaction that she should have been feeling at this pronouncement of her overwhelming integrity, but it didn't come.

"Well, anyway," she tried to defend herself, fidgeting a bit as she began to feel uncomfortable in her cloak of righteousness, "I have the satisfaction of knowing that I was right to tell him how despicable I think he is. After all, did he think I just came down in the last rain, as Popsie used to say, to fall for some story that he was acting out of concern for his stockholders? If he wants to ease his conscience, he can find another place to toss his money."

He could have been trying to be your friend, her inner self told her, offering one solution.

"Hah! That would be the day," she answered, scoffing at such foolishness. "I can see us now, exchanging friendly Christmas cards every year. 'All the best of the season; let's do lunch.' Not on your life! Zachary doesn't know the meaning of the word friend. Maybe I was wrong about the charity; maybe he's trying to *buy* me!"

All right, her inner voice countered, still trying to reason with her, *forget the friendship bit. But how do you explain away involving his own father in the deal? Do you really think Lucien St. Clair would allow himself to be a party to any hanky-panky going on between his son and his theater manager?*

"He's Zachary's father, isn't he?" Sharon pointed out meanly. "He probably taught his son everything he knows. Like father, like son, they always say."

Oh, you're something else, aren't you, Sharon Wheeler, her conscience interrupted. *What's the matter? Is your nose out of joint because he didn't drop to his knees and declare his undying love for you? Because he didn't tell you that he was giving the drive-in away so that he could remove any obstacles that could stand between you and his love for you? I suppose you wanted a formal proposal of marriage, too— just because he kissed you? My gracious, I can almost hear a violin playing in the background. You don't want much, do you, Sharon Joan Wheeler? Only the whole world, all neatly tied up in a pretty package, and with a big red ribbon on top.*

Sharon clapped her hands over her ears, trying hard to drown out her silent accuser. She turned back to look warily at the swing, convinced that somehow her Popsie had to be there—talking to her in that way he'd always had of cutting through all her nonsense and getting straight to the heart of things.

"All right, all right!" she cried, surrendering at last to the truth. "I don't hate Zachary for giving his father the drive-in. I know he never wanted the theater in the first place— hated the very fact that it was a part of his so-modern theater circuit—but I can't shake the feeling that he also did it out of some misdirected expression of charity. But even if I don't know exactly *why* he did it, I'm being an ungrateful idiot to even *care* why he did it. I should be doing hand-stands that he *did* do it! I must be crazy, looking a gift horse in the mouth. With the owner in Florida, and Zachary's promise to make the repairs, it's almost like I have Wheeler's back as my very own. I should be the happiest woman in the world!"

So, what's the problem? the nagging voice asked.

Sharon sat down on the swing once more, tucking her legs up under her chin and wrapping her arms around her knees. Her voice cracked a bit as she rested her chin on her knees and whispered, "Oh, Popsie, you know what's wrong. I've only known the man for less than a week, but I know what's wrong with me. It's knowing that he did it only because he feels sorry for me, not because he loves me. It's knowing that if Zachary doesn't love me, nothing—not even having the drive-in back—will ever be able to make me feel happy ever again.''

Chapter 8

It had been two days since Sharon had stormed out of the women's bathroom at Wheeler's Drive-In and driven out of Zachary's life. Two days, six hours and seventeen minutes, he corrected mentally, peering at his watch as he sat at the far end of the bar in his hotel, slowly nursing a second, unsatisfying Scotch.

Stanley Wojewodzki stood halfway down the length of the bar, drying shot glasses with a towel, having tried without success to draw Zachary into a conversation concerning the total inability of the Philadelphia Phillies to come up with a good left-handed pitcher to replace Steve Carleton.

Zachary felt rather guilty at his own impoliteness, but he couldn't find it within himself to concentrate on anything more morally uplifting than his intention to get himself completely and numbly drunk in the shortest possible time. As he had never been much of a drinker, he was still sober—and developing a healthy dislike for Scotch.

You really blew it this time, St. Clair, a small inner voice needled him as he threw back the last of his drink with a grimace of distaste and held out his glass to signal Stosh for a refill. Obviously his brain was still functioning, and he needed another dose of liquid amnesia.

I thought you were supposed to be the silver-tongued wheeler-dealer, the great negotiator, the man who could sell ice to the Eskimos. Some salesman. Not only wouldn't Sharon buy what you were selling—you couldn't even give it away.

His timing was off, that's all, he argued silently, putting another twenty dollar bill on the bar. He should have waited until Sharon had cooled down after his stupid reaction to seeing Hugh Kingsley hovering over her like some fairy godmother about to wave a wand and make it all better. But he was afraid she'd run away before he could explain what he'd done, and he wouldn't be able to find her.

Sure, you were only thinking of her. What a guy. Isn't there a Nobel prize for people as pure of heart as you? In a pig's eye, you were thinking of her. What you were doing, St. Clair, was showing off for the lady. You were so full of your own brilliance that you couldn't wait to share it with her, dazzle her a bit. Nice play, Shakespeare. What do you have in mind for an encore?

Zachary squirmed a bit on the bar stool, unable to answer his own question. He knew where to find her. He'd known since speaking with George Blakeman yesterday, after it became obvious to him that Sharon wasn't about to show up at Wheeler's. And no matter how much soul-searching he did, no matter how hard he had tried to rationalize it away, he knew there was only one reason he hadn't driven out to Sharon's country home to plead his case.

He was afraid.

All right! Now you're talking. Let's brainstorm this for a minute, run this concept up the old flagpole and see if anybody salutes! The great Zachary is afraid. Why?

God, Zachary thought, wincing, even his subconscious was beginning to sound like the corporate ridiculousness he'd been living with for so long—for too long, if he could still be considered any judge in the matter.

Hey, don't blame me, his inner self protested. *Where do you think I got this stuff—some mail order catalog? Now stop stonewalling and start giving with some answers. Why are you so afraid of a small blonde only half your weight?*

Because he cared about her! he admitted. Because she was hurting, and he was to blame—even if he didn't know how. He, with his grand schemes and his funny little games. Even when he tried to help her, he hurt her, and the last thing he wanted to do now was hurt her again. *I don't know what to do, which way to jump. I've never felt so stupid or so useless in my life.*

"Zachary? What in blue blazes are you doing in here? I asked at the desk and some handsome-looking fella with real white teeth said I'd find you here. You know him? Since when do you start drinking before dinner?"

Zachary's spine stiffened and he lifted his head slowly to look into the mirror behind the back bar. "Hello, Dad," he said at last, wondering wildly just when the Fates would think he'd had enough and back off for a while. "I already ate. We dine early in Pennsylvania. What brings you up here? Did Mother throw you out?"

Lucien St. Clair chuckled softly and then lowered his long frame onto the next bar stool. "Your mother's off to the Bahamas with some friends from the club. Something to do with good prices on jewelry, I believe. So, what's this about giving me a theater as a present? Your mother isn't exactly known for keeping telephone messages straight, you know, especially when she's on the scent of a bargain. Why on earth would you want to give me a theater? The corporation owns hundreds."

Shaking his head ruefully, Zachary summoned up a weak smile. "Not like this one, Dad. Not like this one. Wheeler's Drive-In just happens to be the oldest operating drive-in movie in America. And don't be too thrilled. It's going to cost us a bundle just to get the place back on its feet."

"A drive-in? You've got to be kidding! Where is it? Texas? How many screens?"

Zachary lowered his head once more, rubbing the side of his neck as he muttered, "Five miles from here. One screen. A carbon house with two ancient projectors. Gloria Swanson and Veronica Lake. And, oh, yes—sauerkraut."

Lucien reached over and removed the glass that was sitting in front of his son, carefully smelling the liquid inside. "Nope, it's just Scotch. I thought maybe you were drinking something weird. Now, you want to run that one by me again, son? I can't believe I heard you right the first time."

"How may I serve you, sir?" Stosh asked, walking up to the end of the bar. "Hey! You two related? You sure do look alike. You drink Scotch, too? Maybe you're a beer man. We got your domestic, your imported, your light, your—"

"Stosh!" Zachary said, smiling in a way that caused his father to look at him closely. "You're just the man I need. I have to go up to my room and make a phone call. Maybe you can fill my father in about Wheeler's Drive-In. He's the new owner."

"You bought Wheeler's?" the bartender asked, a wide grin splitting his chubby face. "How about that! Well, you came to the right place if you want to hear all about Wheeler's. Me and the wife met there, you know. I told your son all about it the other night. Let's see, where do I start? Well, first, you got your double features, of course, and your cartoons. You also got your snack bar, now that's really something—"

"Zachary," Lucien called weakly after his son, who was already halfway out of the bar. "You wouldn't leave me here like this, would you?"

"I'll be right back, Dad," he said, not turning around or else his father would see the amused look on his face. "Stosh will entertain you while I'm gone."

The older St. Clair watched his son leave, then turned back to listen to the bartender, a painfully polite expression on his face.

* * *

"That was Zachary on the phone, Shari," George Blakeman said, easing himself into his favorite chair in the living room of his small house. "He wanted to know if I'd heard from you. He said he called your house but there was no answer. He sounded upset."

Sharon hopped up from the comfortable, worn couch she was lying on and looked quickly around the room, as if seeking the nearest exit. "You didn't tell him I was here, did you, George? You know I don't want to see him again—ever."

"Relax, I didn't tell him. But you're going to have to see him sometime, aren't you? After all, you're working for his father now. Right?"

Sharon flopped back down onto the couch, resting her elbows on her knees. "I don't think so, George. That's really what I came here to talk about, although I guess I've been too busy bending your ear about my miserable love life to get around to the subject. I haven't agreed to manage the place yet, and I'm not sure I want to."

"How can you *not* agree when you know that if you don't you'll have lost any chance you ever had of keeping a Wheeler as part of the place? You love that drive-in. You lasted through two other owners. Right? Do you think Al would want you to abandon it now—just to soothe your injured pride?"

Sharon sank back against the soft cushions, sighing. "You aren't playing fair. Popsie wouldn't want me to accept charity, just so I could stay a part of Wheeler's."

George got up from his chair and walked to the television set, turning down the sound. Zachary's phone call had interrupted the rerun they had been watching, and he no longer knew which of the actors with day-old beards were the cops and which were the bad guys. "Shari, I think you've been watching too many movies. He was just making an honest gesture of friendship, hunting for a way to keep the place open and still keep his stockholders happy. I think he likes the drive-in in spite of himself. The guy couldn't have been nicer to me, and after I'd taken a swing at him, too. You ought to talk to him, give him a chance to explain. Right?''

"You men!" Sharon exclaimed incredulously. "When you get right down to it, you all stick together. People don't buy businesses just to give them away, for heaven's sake. Not without a good reason, anyway. Charity's fine, huh? Sure, let's toss poor Shari a bone!''

"Maybe he had a good reason for being nice to you," George suggested. "From what you told me tonight at the dinner table, the two of you were getting pretty chummy there for a while. Right?''

Sharon made a face at her old friend. "Forget I ever brought up the idea. It was just a few kisses, George, not a scene from *A Man and a Woman*. But if his 'friendly gesture' wasn't charity, why hasn't he come to see me to explain? It's been two days.''

George laughed, shaking his head. "Are you the same Sharon Wheeler who almost ran out of here a minute ago because you thought I might have told Zachary that you were here? No wonder the man sounded so upset. If you've been acting as hot and cold around him he'll be lucky if he knows which way to jump. Right?''

Sharon's mind went unbidden to her actions of the previous few days, her belligerence that had turned to passion, then anger. And she had accused Zachary of being mercurial! She should be ashamed of herself. "I don't care to think about my experiences with Mr. St. Clair, if you please," she informed George firmly, tilting her chin in defiance.

"All right. Then think about this a moment, Shari. You have to come to some sort of a decision soon. We've had a break, since we're only open three nights this week, but the film's due in tomorrow morning, and somebody has to get the show made up for tomorrow night. Right? And don't ask me to do it. I'm on vacation.''

Sharon bit on the side of her thumb as she considered what to do next. She'd hidden out in her house, working on a project connected with her part-time job until George had called that afternoon, wanting to know why Zachary St. Clair was looking for her, and she'd spent the hours since then alternately crying out her troubles to her old friend and finding excuses for not going back to her empty, silent house.

She was so confused. Didn't she have enough to think about, trying to convince herself that Zachary meant nothing, even less than nothing, to her? Did she have to worry about Wheeler's, too? After all, it wasn't like it was really hers. Oh, she might have continued to think of it as hers, even after the theater had been sold and then sold again, but somehow the atmosphere had changed once Zachary had come on the scene.

She was beginning to see his point about Wheeler's. The drive-in wasn't exactly a money-maker, not in the sense that the multiscreen houses in the area were. It had been fine for her grandfather, who had an independent income to fall back on, but nobody was ever going to get rich running a theater that could only remain open from late May until October. Even she, Sharon, had to take on extra jobs to make ends meet. An owner like Zachary's father, retired and self-sufficient, was the perfect answer, much as she hated to admit it.

As if he could read her mind, George said now, "Al knew the drive-in couldn't stand on its own, Shari. If you think about it, we make most of our money at the snack bar. Right?"

"I guess so," Sharon mumbled, listening to these damning words in spite of herself.

"That's why he didn't leave it to you in his will," her old friend pushed on. "I think he was hoping you'd see it as a chance to strike out on your own once he was gone, build a life for yourself separate from Wheeler's. Lord only knew Al wasn't counting on his son to hold on to it. Jim never liked the place. Right?"

Sharon reached into the pocket of her shorts for a tissue, which she then blotted against the tears on her cheeks. "You waited six years to tell me all this, George? And I guess you only stayed on because of me. Now I really feel awful. I thought I was a businesswoman, but I've only been a little girl playing house. Only instead of playing with dolls and having tea parties, I've been showing movies and pushing popcorn. Oh, George, I feel like such a fool!''

The old man turned his head away, seemingly to avoid looking directly at Sharon. ''Yeah, well, there's no fool like an old fool, because I went right on playing the game with you, even though I knew better. Up until a few minutes ago I was still so caught up in the game I was trying to get you to accept St. Clair's offer and pretending your grandfather would have wanted you to stay. But no more. It's time we all stopped playing make-believe.''

''So what do I do now? I've already talked you into hiding me here tonight, but I can't keep avoiding Zachary forever.''

''Yes. It looks like you've got a decision to make. Right?''

Sharon's mind immediately conjured up a picture of Zachary and she sniffed a time or two, then slipped the tissue back into her pocket. But she knew George wasn't thinking about her supposed love life. ''You mean about Wheeler's, don't you? But there's really no decision to make. Zachary's father owns it; it's up to him to say who runs the place for him. Maybe he'll even want to manage it himself.''

''That's what the place needs, all right. Another old man trying to recreate the past,'' George slid in quietly. ''And who do you think is going to run Gloria and Veronica? None of those young puppies who work in the platter houses know the first thing about real projectors. Right?''

''Wouldn't you—''

''Not in a million years. I learned my lesson Sunday night. I can't take the pressure anymore. If you go, I go.''

Sharon sat up very straight. ''Well *somebody* has to run the projectors tomorrow. The ads are already on the paper for this weekend's show. Maybe Zachary—oh, who do I think I'm kidding—Zachary St. Clair wouldn't know a projector head from Mr. Potato Head. He's a businessman, not a projectionist. What will he do?''

George walked over and turned up the sound on the television. "I don't know. And why do you care what he does? You don't even like the guy. Right? Or do you still have some more decisions to make?"

"No, George," she said firmly. "My decisions are all made. I'm going to leave Wheeler's *and* the St. Clairs to fend for themselves. From now on, they can just count me out!"

Friday morning came and made liars of them all.

George was up and out early, leaving a note on the kitchen table telling Sharon he was taking his car to the garage to have the tires rotated.

Sharon didn't eat the breakfast George had left warming in the oven for her, using the back of his note to scribble a message thanking him for his hospitality and saying that she had just remembered she had promised to feed a vacationing friend's cat.

Lucien had left a note at the hotel desk, telling Zachary he had chipped a tooth at breakfast and had gone off to see a local dentist.

Zachary, who had no one else left to lie to, got into his sports car after reading his father's message and lied to himself, thinking he was merely going for a mind-clearing ride in the country.

And at twenty minutes past nine that Friday morning, the first meeting of the unofficial Liar's Club was called to order in the snack bar of Wheeler's Drive-In.

"Stosh!" Zachary said as he walked into the snack bar. "What are you doing here?"

The bartender, smiling as he stood just behind the Formica bar, clad in red-and-white-striped Bermuda shorts and a bright red cotton knit shirt, replied happily, "It's my day off, and Lucien asked me to drive him out here and sort of show him around the place. I've never seen it from this side before. Look at this. You got your hot butter holder, your steamer table, your popcorn popper. Did you ever see such a big can of jalapeño peppers?''

''Where's my dad now?'' Zachary could hear voices coming from the projection booth, and he was wondering who was in there with his father. ''How did you get through the gate?''

Stosh explained that they had been having a bit of a problem there, standing outside the gate trying to figure out what to do next, but then this old guy in a battered Plymouth had driven up and let them in with his key. Lucien and the old guy had been walking around the grounds, but now they were inside, looking at some funny-looking machines in the other room.

An old guy in a battered Plymouth? ''George? George is here? I don't know how I missed seeing his car,'' Zachary commented as he bent down to work his way under the counter. ''Is there a pretty blonde with him?''

''Now, would I be in here looking at a popcorn machine if there was a pretty blonde around?'' Stosh asked, throwing Zachary a broad wink. ''Oh, ho. Don't look now, but I think one just walked in.''

Zachary swiveled around quickly, in time to see Sharon standing just inside the door, looking like one of the Christians about to say hello to the lions. ''Sharon!'' he called, just as she seemed ready to bolt. ''Thank God you're here. I have to talk to you.''

''I came to make up tonight's film, if it's arrived,'' she told him, her head high as she walked toward the Formica bar. ''I see George is already here, so I'll assume that all I'll have to do is prepare the beef barbecue for the weekend and check on our kitchen supplies.''

Zachary backed up a few paces as she joined him inside the enclosed snack bar serving area, not wanting to make her feel as if he was crowding her. ''I don't know if George is working or not. My father just came in unexpectedly from Florida to inspect the place. I believe they're together now, in the projection booth. I'd like you to meet my dad, if you want to.''

Sharon answered without really looking at him. "If I'm going to be working for the gentleman," she said, repositioning a salt shaker one-half inch closer to the napkin holder, "I imagine I should take the time to meet him. Your presence, however, I believe to be entirely superfluous. Now, if you'll excuse me?"

Zachary automatically stepped to one side to let Sharon pass by, wondering what it was about the look in her big blue eyes that made him feel as if he had been guilty of kicking a helpless puppy. "I'll go with you anyway," he called after her. "Sometimes my father takes a bit of explaining."

As soon as he rounded the corner and entered the projection room, Zachary knew he had been right. His father hadn't been in town a full day and already he was up to his old tricks.

"And I tell you it was Joan Crawford," he heard his father arguing with George, who was standing beside the worktable examining a reel of film and looking like a man about to commit mayhem.

"Bette Davis, and I've got five dollars here that says I'm right," George declared, digging in his pocket for the money. "Ah, here's Sharon, the girl I was telling you about, Lucien. She'll know. She has all that stuff tucked up in her pretty little head."

"What's the problem, George?" Sharon asked just as Zachary came up behind her, silently making a face at his father that literally begged the older man to be good. "Are you two having a disagreement?"

"Lucien here says it was Joan Crawford who made a cameo appearance in *Scent of Mystery*, and we all know it was Bette Davis. Right? Tell him, Shari."

"Well, George," Sharon began hesitantly, "to tell you the truth, I don't really think I know—"

"You're both wrong. It was Elizabeth Taylor," Zachary

said quickly, stepping around Sharon to approach his father. "How's the tooth, Dad? You don't look any the worse for wear."

"So I lied," Lucien retorted, unrepentant, motioning with his head toward Sharon. "Who's this? My manager? George said she was pretty, but now I know why you were trying to drown yourself in that bar. George told me all about it. You really made a botch of things. I must say I expected a little more finesse from you. What's the matter, son, losing your touch?"

"*Oh!* I was right all along. You're all alike!" Sharon yelled at the three men, turning to leave. "I don't know why I came here in the first place. I must have been out of my mind, feeling sorry for all of you. Well, you can just forget it. I'm leaving. Make your own damn barbecue!"

Sharon ran back into the snack bar, past the man in the awful Bermuda shorts, and out into the sunlight. She didn't make the mistake of heading for the women's bathroom again, but instead made for the ticket booth, thinking to lock herself inside until Zachary gave up and went away.

As she ran she tried to understand what had prompted her to say she wanted to meet her new boss. She had only come to the drive-in to help out temporarily, until someone could be brought in to take her place; she certainly had no intention of staying on as manager.

But when she had opened her mouth to tell Zachary that, something entirely different had come out, and now she had given him the impression that she had accepted the job. "No wonder they say blondes are dumb!" she muttered as she jogged along, knowing full well that Zachary was only one row behind her and coming up fast.

Changing direction, she headed for the playground, and hopped onto the merry-go-round, pushing with one foot to set the circular metal disk in motion. She was being ridiculous, juvenile, but all she wanted to do was spin round and round, as her jumbled thoughts were doing, hoping against hope that she would somehow be granted time to figure out what to do next.

She had spun around five or six times, not quite long enough to get dizzy, when suddenly she felt her upper body being surrounded by two strong masculine arms, and she had no choice but to allow herself to be lifted back onto solid ground.

Her eyes tightly closed, she leaned back weakly against Zachary, taking in the solidity of his body, the spicy scent of his after shave, the heat of his embrace, and she knew her sudden giddiness was not a result of either her flight from the projection booth or her short ride on the merry-go-round.

She was dizzy from his nearness, breathless with anticipation as to what he would do next. Would he kiss her? He was holding her in a way that told her she could run again if she chose, and this time, perhaps, he wouldn't follow. He was giving her a choice.

And the last thing she wanted at that moment was a choice. She wanted him to take charge, to demand that she surrender to his kiss, to his embrace, to his every desire. He had already stepped into her life and turned it upside down; why couldn't he continue to dictate to her? Then she could tell herself that she had nothing to do with the decision. That he had coerced her, dazzled her with gifts, seduced her with his commanding physical attraction.

But no, he just continued to hold her against him, his arms loosely draped around her waist, his cheek pressed against her hair. He didn't say anything, explain anything, ask anything—take anything. He just gave her time, all the time she didn't want to take, to make the next move.

She wanted to turn in his arms and be held the way a woman wants to be held, kissed the way a woman longs to be kissed. But would he think she was kissing him out of love for him—or because he had made some absurd humanitarian gesture and saved Wheeler's?

Why, oh why, had she made that stupid crack back at the snackbar? Why had she run away—again? Why hadn't she told him immediately that she didn't want to stay at Wheeler's as if both she and it were some sort of charity cases he had contributed to, told him that she loved him for himself, and then stood back to wait for his next move.

Because then there might not have been a next move, her inner voice pointed out prudently. *Because, if you'd told him you love him he might have turned on his heel and beaten a path back to New York so fast you'd have been blown down in the breeze. Because even if you might think he wants you, in today's world wanting a person and loving her are two very separate things.*

"Sharon? Have I knocked the wind out of you? You've been standing here for two minutes and you haven't either yelled at me, kicked me in the shins or tried to run away. Does this mean you're ready to talk?"

I love his voice, Sharon thought randomly, tilting her head slightly to one side as his husky tones, spoken so close beside her ear, sent a shiver down the side of her neck. "Talk?" she repeated, fumbling for something to say. "What do you want to talk about? Your father seems very like you, and he and George seem to be hitting it off nicely. Actually, they looked like two little boys set loose in a candy store, the way they were working together making up tonight's feature."

"Bully for good old George and good old Lucien," Zachary told her, slowly turning her around to face him. "I couldn't be happier for them. No, Shari. I don't want to talk about my father and George."

Sharon moistened her suddenly dry lips. "Then I guess you must be wondering about my, er, rather dramatic reaction the other day to your decision to give the drive-in to your father." She purposely looked down at her toes as she gave a forced laugh and said, "I imagine you must have figured out by now that I thought you had done it as a form of charity. Silly, aren't I?"

"Not so silly, Sharon. That same thought occurred to me as I stood there trying to catch my breath after you jammed that roll of bathroom tissue into my gut like a football,'' Zachary answered, running his hands up and down her bare upper arms. ''I wish you had given me a chance to explain instead of running off like that.''

''Well, it took me a little time, but I did realize that you hadn't meant anything like that. You didn't, did you?'' she asked, looking up at him a moment, then quickly averting her eyes when she saw the passionate expression in his.

''No, Sharon, it wasn't charity,'' she heard him answer, and breathed a sigh of relief. ''The drive-in was standing between us, and I wanted it out of the way. You see, no matter how good my intentions, the more I looked at Wheeler's, the more I knew it could never fit into the St. Clair Theater Corporation. It just isn't our sort of house. There's no way I could have justified the money it would take to update this place.''

''Update it? You mean put in platters. Replace Gloria and Veronica?''

''Don't bite my head off,'' he told her. ''I said I couldn't do it, didn't I? But if I'd shut it down, you'd never have spoken to me again. For some strange reason, that bothered me. It bothered me a lot.''

Sharon bit her lip to hide a smile. ''It did?''

''Yes, it did. But don't get a big head, lady, because I didn't buy it just so we could stop fighting over it.''

''No, you didn't, did you? You didn't even keep it for yourself,'' Sharon interrupted, seeing the faraway expression in Zachary's eyes. ''You gave it to your father.''

''In lieu of an apology, yes, I did,'' he told her, taking her hand and starting the walk back to the projection booth. ''Dad loves places like this, small one-owner theaters. After I'd finally gotten him to let me update and expand our operations, the heart seemed to go out of him, only I was too blind to see it. When the company went public a few years ago, Dad retired. I think he's been miserable, but too proud of me to complain. Wheeler's is perfect for him. He and

Mother can have their winters in Florida, and they can come up here in the summer and be theater operators again.''

You seem to have everything all tied up in a nice little bow, Sharon thought as they walked along. *But, if Lucien is going to run the place, where do I come in? Even more to the point—do I want to come in? Do I still want to be a part of Wheeler's? Last night I didn't think so. But now?*

"It sounds nice, Zachary," she said aloud, hoping he couldn't hear the unhappiness in her voice. Her emotions were swinging back and forth so rapidly that she couldn't figure out if she was happy for him, sad for herself or just plain confused. "Maybe Lucien will want George to stick around, as sort of an assistant projectionist?"

Zachary nodded. "I think so. And you can go back to pushing your hot dogs with sauerkraut. I saw the books, Shari, and I know the snack bar is where most of the profits come from. It seems like a good arrangement all round, and the stockholders can't say anything because I made them a ten percent profit on the sale. Now, are you still angry with me?"

"Angry with you?" Sharon repeated dully, feeling like a disillusioned child who had yearned for the moon only to learn that it was out of reach. Then she forced a lighter tone into her voice. "Of course I'm not. I'm flattered that you would think enough of me to handpick my next boss. I love this place, you know. I even love it enough to have finally given in and agreed to go on working for you if you hadn't sold it."

Zachary stopped walking and turned her around to face him once more. "But then I couldn't know that, could I, especially when we haven't been able to discuss the place without clawing at each other like cats. But I was still taking a chance, wasn't I? You might even have decided that you hated me enough to want nothing more to do with *any* St. Clair."

"And that bothered you." Sharon's heart began to beat a

little faster. "That I might not want to have anything to do with you—I mean, with a St. Clair."

Zachary drew her against his chest and lifted her chin with his finger. "Again, Shari, don't go getting power mad. After all, it might just be that I don't like to lose." His head began to slowly move down toward hers as she instinctively withdrew at his words. "But then again, I might have another reason entirely."

Sharon was lost, and she knew it. She surrendered to his kiss, trying wordlessly to communicate all that she felt with her mouth, her hands, her body. His response was immediate, and very rewarding.

But it wasn't the answer she was looking for, it was only another question.

Chapter 9

The remainder of the day went smoothly, Sharon and Zachary having privately assured themselves that if everything between them wasn't perfect, it was at least considerably better than it had been twenty-four hours earlier. For the time being, that had to be enough.

They spent the rest of the afternoon working side by side in the snack bar, with Sharon giving the orders and Zachary docilely carrying them out.

George and Lucien remained closeted together in the projection booth, checking the newly arrived release prints of that weekend's feature presentations by hand before placing each of the reels in its own separate numbered storage bin, while comparing notes on their combined almost-century-long careers in the theater business.

Stosh, who had passed the hours wandering back and forth between the snack bar and the projection booth, showed no signs of becoming bored, and Sharon finally set him to work popping popcorn, a job the bartender accepted as a high honor indeed.

The five met in the snack bar for a quick meal of Wheeler's special steak sandwiches before the rest of the crew showed up, and it was only after Sharon had set the teenage girls to work that Lucien and George made their little announcement.

They were going back to George's house to look at his old scrapbooks.

"But I thought you were going to run the movies?" Sharon asked in confusion, looking at her old friend.

"George explained that Zachary had given him the week off, Sharon," Lucien supplied as George abruptly developed an overwhelming interest in the ice cream sandwich he was eating. "It doesn't seem fair to cut his vacation short, does it, considering the fact that we have two other licensed projectionists on the grounds?"

Sharon looked around the small circle for a moment, her bewildered gaze finally focusing on Zachary, who was leaning against the counter next to the hot dog carousel, a devilish grin on his face. "Him?" she asked incredulously. "You've got to be joking."

Zachary straightened, looking assessingly at his father. The man had a smile that reminded him that Lucien never had much of a head for subtlety. Obviously George and Lucien had spent the afternoon talking about more than their glorious pasts. *Methinks I smell the scent of matchmaking in the air,* he thought in wry amusement, inclining his head to the man in acknowledgment of his intentions.

Then he looked over at Sharon, who was showing all the outward signs of panic. *There's another one who should never play poker,* his meaner self decided. *Hugh Kingsley must be one heck of a rotten gin rummy player if he can't read Sharon like a book. She'd rather face a horde of stampeding buffalo than work with me in that projection booth. I wonder why.*

"You're right, Dad," he said at last. "I did give George the week off. But it shouldn't take two people to run the projectors. I'll do it alone. That way Sharon can stay in here where she belongs—out of trouble.''

"Now just a darn minute!" Sharon exclaimed hotly, falling right into his trap just as Zachary knew she would. "George! Are you really going to let him in there alone with Veronica and Gloria?"

"Doesn't bother me any," George said, shrugging. "Lucien here says Zachary can do it. He's the boss, Shari. Right?"

"And what does that make me—chopped liver?" she countered, busily untying her apron and slamming it down on the counter. "I'm still the manager here if I remember correctly. Stay out here where I *belong*, will I? Well, we'll see about that! Come on, St. Clair, why don't you show me what you can do."

"Yes, boss," Zachary answered with dutiful subservience, stepping forward quickly to hold open the door to the projection booth and allow Sharon to enter ahead of him. He hesitated a moment, then looked back to see his father and George shaking hands as if congratulating each other. "You're quite a pair of connivers, you know that? Well, don't be surprised if your Machiavellian scheme backfires and the lady murders me before the cartoon is over."

"If she does, son, I wash my hands of you," Zachary heard Lucien say just before the sound of cabinet doors being slammed inside the projection booth commanded his attention and he stepped inside the room, closing the door behind him.

He saw Sharon over at the worktable, ruthlessly rooting through a cardboard box she had unearthed from somewhere in the room. "What are you looking for?" he asked, walking up behind her.

Sharon turned abruptly, nearly colliding with him, a small can in one hand, a paintbrush in the other. "You should know," she told him, ducking around him and moving to the center of the room. "After all, you were the one who said we'd always be fighting if we had to deal together in business. Getting the snack bar organized is one thing, but I don't think our relationship—if you want to call what we have a relationship—could stand actually working together in here for a full weekend without this.''

Zachary reached up a hand to scratch his head, realizing that she was holding an open can of yellow paint. "I call it a relationship, Shari," he said softly, comprehension slowly dawning on him. "But you're not really serious about this, are you? I mean, I can remember Charlie Barrows telling me about old-time projectionists doing this when they couldn't get along together, but I can't believe—"

"Believe it," Sharon told him, striding over to the front of the projection booth between the two projectors and then dropping to her knees. "I'm painting a line down the middle of the room. You stay on your side, and I'll stay on mine. It's the only way we're going to be able to make this thing work. Now, who do you want, Gloria or Veronica?"

Zachary leaned back against the worktable and watched as Sharon began painting a five-inch-wide yellow line on the floor down the middle of the booth. "The door to the snack bar is on Veronica's side. I'll take her," he said, deliberately trying to upset her.

"Figures," he heard her mutter, and then he lost interest in the topic and just enjoyed the spectacle of watching Sharon backing her way across the booth on her knees, the yellow line growing longer as she went.

"You do nice work," he said when she had finished. "You never told me what you do in the off-season. Perhaps you hire yourself out as a housepainter."

"Wrong. I teach martial arts at a girls' school, so they can learn to defend themselves against men with a perverted sense of humor," she said as she tapped the lid back on the can and returned it to the cabinet.

"No, you don't," Zachary responded, carefully stepping over the wet paint to his side of the room. "If you did you wouldn't have had to paint that line. You could have just...*tossed* me for which projector you wanted. Besides,

I'm being serious, Sharon. I realized the other day that I know very little about you. What *do* you do in the off-season? Remember, I saw your salary listed in the books. You must do something else besides managing the theater."

Zachary surprised himself with the depth of his interest, knowing that in the past he hadn't cared if the women he knew wrapped themselves in plastic sheeting and hung themselves in the closet between dates with him. Sharon intrigued him, and he wanted to know everything about her, although he was beginning to believe that he could spend the rest of his life with her and never know all of her.

"I work part-time for a small local company that specializes in preserving and restoring old buildings," she told him as she began threading up Gloria with that night's trailer. "Hugh owns part of it. We buy up old buildings, repair them so that they look the way they did when they were new and then sell them. I'm in charge of the research, dating the structures, then scouting out replacement materials to fit each building. You wouldn't believe how badly some of the places we buy have been remodeled—or remuddled, as we call it. The company's small, only about three years old, but someday I might be able to work there full-time, if I ever leave Wheeler's."

Hugh Kingsley again, Zachary thought, bristling. The guy seems to be everywhere, like a bad rash. "That sounds interesting," he said, watching her back as she worked. "Do you have a degree?"

He saw her spine stiffen. "You don't have to have a degree to have an interest, or an aptitude. I love what I'm doing, and I bring that love to my work. You ought to try it sometime. Maybe then you wouldn't go around the country, taking beautiful old theaters and turning them into plastic cutouts."

I knew we had differences, Zachary thought as Sharon opened the first reel bin and practically threw a loaded reel at him, telling him to start threading up the movie, *but I didn't know they went this deep..* "Those big old theaters were beautiful, I grant you," he said as he worked, "but they're not profitable any longer. It's either cut them up into multiscreen houses, like I'm going to do with the theaters I just bought here, or close them down entirely. That's progress, Sharon, something you seem to fight at every turn."

He stepped back from Victoria as Sharon came swiftly over to his side of the room and yelled at him, "Progress! Then you call what they did to the Michigan Theatre in Detroit *progress*! They turned that lovely old building into a parking garage, Zachary. All that gorgeous plaster carving, and those beautiful paintings on the walls and ceilings— stripped away and mutilated as if some hungry giant had reached in his ugly fist and ripped out its heart. Is that what you call *progress*, Zachary?"

Sharon's huge blue eyes were spitting hot sparks at him, and Zachary involuntarily recoiled from the flames. He felt a momentary twinge of guilt, because he had seen before and after pictures of the Michigan, and knew she was right. And although he hadn't sold any of the theaters he'd acquired knowing that they would either be razed or, like the Michigan and so many others, raped of their beauty, he was guilty of gutting many of the theaters so that they could be rebuilt as multiscreen houses.

"Now you're letting your heart rule your head. Not every old theater can be converted into a nightclub or a symphony hall, Sharon. Some of them just have to go. The day of the big downtown theater is past. Unless the house can be updated, it'll lose all its business to the shopping mall theaters. It's too bad, but you're looking at the whole thing from only one angle."

He watched as Sharon's eyes lost their luster, as if she was somehow closing in on herself. "No one could ever accuse you of that, could they, Zachary?" she said in a small voice. "Even here, with Wheeler's, you found a way to make the place turn a profit, even if it wasn't in cash. You bought your father a little bit of happiness and salved your conscience at the same time. Not only that, but you made sure you got a little fringe benefit just for yourself, in the person of one very grateful female manager. I really have to hand it to you, Zachary. You've got more angles than Paul Newman did in *The Sting*.''

''Here we go again! I thought we settled that. I told you—''

''Hey, Sharon?'' Both the occupants of the room turned to look at Sheila, who was standing just inside the door, her eyes wide. ''Um, sorry to interrupt. Sam says he thinks he's got a hot one in row six. Fire-engine-red compact. One patron. Sean's busy fixing a speaker pole in row two some yo-yo knocked over. You gonna check it out? Hey, what's that yellow stuff doing on the floor? You guys doing something weird? I smell paint.''

Zachary looked over at Sharon, who was standing with her hands on her hips, slowly shaking her head. ''What's she talking about? It sounds like some sort of code.''

Sharon looked at Gloria and Veronica, then back at Zachary. ''We're ready to roll here, Sheila, so we have time. Tell Sam that Mr. St. Clair and I will handle it.''

''Yeah, well, when you're done with that, maybe you'll get that Stosh fellow out of here,'' Sheila complained. ''He keeps eating all the popcorn.''

''Yes, Sheila. Thank you. I'll see to it,'' Sharon answered brusquely as the teenager looked at the yellow line on the floor once more and opened her mouth to ask another question, before thinking better of it and backing out of the room, slowly shaking her head.

Then, turning to Zachary, Sharon went on, ''We'll leave our discussion until later, if you don't mind. Right now I think we could both use some comic relief. Follow me.''

After carefully locking both doors to the projection booth, Sharon headed for the sixth row, past the teenagers sitting on the hoods of their cars, walking in between the lawn chairs set up by other patrons, and around the many spread blankets littered with small children in pajamas. Zachary spotted the small compact the same time she did, and he stopped beside her behind its rear bumper, copying her stony-faced, spread-legs, folded-arms stance.

"What are we doing?" he asked out of the corner of his mouth, trying hard to keep a stern look on his face. "I feel like a cigar store Indian standing here."

"Just shut up, and try to look menacing," she told him, pushing out her bottom lip and blowing at an errant lock of blond hair that had fallen down over her eyes. "Look. He's already beginning to squirm."

Zachary did as he was told, and immediately noticed that the young boy sitting behind the steering wheel was looking decidedly uncomfortable, darting several quick glances into his rearview mirror while fidgeting about in his seat as if someone had slipped a thumbtack underneath him when he wasn't looking.

Then something very strange happened. The small car began to rock up and down, and a dull, thumping noise drew Zachary's attention to the small trunk. "What in hell is—"

"Shh," Sharon cautioned softly. "Now the fun starts."

The thumping grew louder, the rocking more pronounced, but the driver of the little red compact only faced front and tried to look as if nothing out of the ordinary was going on.

He was fighting a losing battle. Finally, first looking at Sharon and Zachary in a way that had Zachary feeling almost sorry for the teen, the boy got out of the car and walked back to the trunk. The moment he turned the key in the lock the lid of the trunk flew open.

"Holy cats, Pete, what's the matter with you anyway?" the first boy out of the trunk asked, shaking his head. "Tony had his foot in my stomach the whole time. Do you have any idea how big his feet are?"

"Yeah, Pete," complained the second boy as he levered himself out of the trunk and onto the ground. "Why didn't you let us out?"

"Good evening, boys," Sharon then purred, walking up to the three boys. "I hate to be the bearer of bad news, but

I do believe you two gentlemen might owe me some money."

"Who's that?" one of the boys asked Pete, who was looking as if he just might become ill.

"Unfortunately for you, she happens to be the manager," Zachary supplied cheerfully, joining Sharon beside the trunk. The three boys looked up, all the way up to Zachary's face, which was nearly a full foot higher than theirs. He smiled down on them almost kindly, then said, "And me, I'm her hit man."

"I told you that you'd enjoy yourself," Sharon said, watching Zachary counting out the small mountain of change onto the worktable. "For a minute there I thought you were going to do a little *Dirty Harry*, and tell the kids to 'make your day.' I can remember Popsie doing the same thing to kids when I was little. Some things never change, and every summer teenagers try to sneak in here by hiding out in car trunks. Poor kids, with today's small cars it must be quite a squeeze."

Zachary finished counting and swept the coins off the worktable and into his hand. "We're still twenty cents short, Sharon," he told her, hefting the weight of the money, "but I think we can let it go, don't you? Lord, I thought I'd die when that kid in the trunk handed me thirty-five cents in pennies and two peppermint candies. When I used to usher at my dad's theaters we had to watch the fire exits. One kid would pay, then open the side door and let all his friends sneak in for free." He smiled and shook his head. "Funny how you forget those things, isn't it?"

Sharon looked at him, standing there holding the money out in front of him, his fascinating green eyes alight with memories. He looked so young, and so thoroughly pleased with himself. He looked, she thought as a small, sharp pain pierced her chest, so utterly lovable.

Watch it, Wheeler, her small voice warned, *you're falling right back into the same old trap. That theater he's talking*

about probably doesn't even exist anymore. He probably
turned it into just another chrome and plastic multiscreen
platter house, with no personality, no history, no beauty.
Now it's nothing more than another notch in his corporate
belt, another good investment. He doesn't have any finer
feelings. He just uses things for his own benefit. His thea-
ters…and you.

"Yeah, well," Sharon said now, nervously looking
around the small room. "It's getting dark. I've got the house
trailer and cartoon ready here on Gloria. I think it's time to
get the show on the road."

Zachary put the money back down on the worktable and
walked over to stand beside Veronica. Tipping an imaginary
hat to her, he quipped, "Ready when you are, C.B.," and
turned to look out the small window at the blank screen.
"Roll 'em."

Sharon ignored his antics, gave Gloria one last quick
check, and then started the projector. The blank screen immediately came to life, dotted with dancing popcorn boxes,
soda cups and well-dressed hot dogs. A merry tune accompanied their lively jig around the big clock face that showed
there to be six minutes still remaining until show time.

The cartoon and previews for the two films to be shown
at Wheeler's the next weekend followed, before a huge picture of an American flag waving in a stiff breeze appeared
on the screen, while a John Philip Sousa march played over
the speakers.

"You've got to be kidding. An American flag? I've been
good, you know. I didn't say anything about the tap-dancing
hotdogs. But this is really too much."

Sharon looked at Zachary strangely, not quite understanding his amusement. Popsie had always shown this film before the first movie. It was as much a part of Wheeler's as
she was. "What's wrong with it?" she asked, too surprised
to be angry. "We used to play the national anthem around
the Fourth of July, but the sound finally wore out."

"The national anthem?" Zachary repeated, and she could

hear the amazement in his voice. ''Good Lord, woman, what did the people do when they heard it? Hop out of their cars and stand at attention?''

Drawing herself up to her full height, Sharon replied haughtily. ''We're an American theater. That's the American flag. What do St. Clair's theaters run before the movie—a reminder not to throw litter in the aisles?''

''Litter's a problem,'' Zachary answered, a bit shame-faced, and Sharon felt a rush of satisfaction as her verbal dart hit home. ''Chewing gum's the worst. We're thinking of not selling it anymore in the snack bars.''

''Oh, please, stop,'' Sharon pleaded nastily. ''You're breaking my heart. Now look lively, it's almost time to start *Veronica*.''

She watched Zachary take his cue and then set *Veronica* in motion, silently admonishing herself to behave. She knew she was being mean, but she couldn't help but try to get a little of her own back for, after all, she had been listening to him tearing down Wheeler's, hadn't she? Now the score was just a bit more even.

As she broke down the house trailer reel and inserted the second reel of the movie that would pick up where *Veronica* left off, she tried her best not to watch what was going on over on Zachary's side of the yellow line. She had to admit to herself that he had been doing well so far, to her complete surprise, and if nothing unforeseen happened they might just get through this evening without a major catastrophe. She rather doubted it, but she hoped so.

Zachary seemed to be hoping the same thing, she decided an hour later as the final reel of the first movie was running down and the other five reels had been rewound and returned to their bins. As a matter of fact, he had been absolutely charming, bringing her a soda from the snack bar, and even helping her to pull out a stubborn carbon stick that had some-how gotten wedged too deeply into its holder.

But it wasn't until intermission that Sharon finally let her guard down completely, laughing uproariously as Zachary took over the microphone and read off the sales pitch George had written on a file card before he and Lucien had deserted them.

"Please don't forget to visit our snack bar," he read in a loud, booming voice, "where we feature freshly popped hot buttered popcorn. That's right, ladies and gentlemen, *real butter*! No artificial flavoring here at Wheeler's. And while you're at it, don't forget to check out our beef barbecue, steak sandwiches and hot dogs, as well as our wide variety of cold beverages, candy, ice cream and *delicious* nachos. My God, what a ridiculous spiel. There, how did I do?"

Sharon raced over to turn off the microphone. "That was wonderful, Zachary," she told him, giggling, "but if you don't mind a little friendly criticism, next time you might want to turn off the mike before you ask for a critique of your performance."

She watched as Zachary looked blankly down at the microphone, then at her, before his face split in an embarrassed grin. "Tell me I didn't really do that," he begged, leaning his forehead against hers.

Instantly their on-again, off-again rapport was back in full force, and Sharon gloried in the warm feeling his closeness evoked, closing her eyes and allowing herself to melt against his chest. "Shari?" she heard him say from somewhere just above her. "Do you think we'll ever stop fighting long enough to figure out what it is that's happening here? You do feel it, too, don't you?"

Slipping her arms around his waist and giving him a slight squeeze, she leaned back in his embrace and looked up into his eyes. "Oh, yes, Zachary, I feel it, too," she admitted huskily, aching for his kiss.

She watched entranced as his head slowly began to dip toward hers, and her mouth opened slightly as his lips hovered just inches above her own. Their differences faded away as she melted into a soft puddle of feelings, knowing that, on this level at least, they seemed to be of the same mind.

Impatient for his touch, she moved her head slightly forward, eager to taste him, hungering to love him, oblivious to the world around them.

Chapter 10

But the world came crashing in anyway.

"Hey, guys, would you believe it?" Sheila Bizinski called, pushing open the door from the snack bar. "This guy comes in here and says he wants me to come outside and watch the movie with him after intermission. He was kind of cute, so I took a peek outside a couple of minutes ago. Get this—he came here on a *bicycle*! Now I ask you, where does he think I'm supposed to sit—on the handlebars? Hey, guys?" she called again, stepping completely into the room. *"Whoops!"*

Sharon and Zachary sprang apart guiltily and immediately tried to look very busy, making totally unnecessary adjustments to Veronica's aperture plate. "Yes, Sheila," Sharon said inanely, not looking at the girl, "I know I forgot to speak to Stosh about eating the popcorn. I just have to finish setting up in here. Okay?"

"Sure—er—sure thing," she heard the teenager reply carefully. When she finally heard the soft closing of the door,

Sharon collapsed weakly against Veronica's metal frame, totally undone.

She felt Zachary's cool lips begin to trail a hot line of kisses down her exposed throat and shivered. "At the risk of starting another argument, my dear, I believe we had discussed keeping that door locked at all times," she heard him say as his lips hovered above her left ear.

Sharon sighed before flipping the switch that would start the first reel of the feature presentation, then turned around to pull Zachary's head down to hers. "I'll say this for you, St. Clair. When you're right, you're right."

It was dark in the projection booth, and the only sounds they heard were the whir of the film as it passed through the projector and the muted bangings going on behind the door to the snack bar as the workers began to close up for the night. Standing close together, their arms around each other, their lips straining in a kiss that went a long way toward healing the wounds they had inflicted upon each other all week, Sharon and Zachary found it easy to divorce themselves from their surroundings.

As she ran her fingers through the soft curling hairs at his nape, Sharon felt as if she had been caught up in a great love story, like the ones she had watched with Popsie on the late show. Like Deborah Kerr and Burt Lancaster in *From Here to Eternity*, Sharon could believe that she and Zachary were lovers, lying together on the shore as the waves of passion rolled over them. All of her being centered on him, her very heart beat for him, her soul cried out to his, and nothing and no one else mattered.

Zachary, too, appeared to be oblivious to anything but her, feeling him drawing her closer, ever closer into his embrace, as if he could somehow meld them together into a single whole. His lean, muscled body was hard, straining against hers, and the rough, uneven tenor of his breathing sent a dizzying sense of power through her.

This time it meant something real, something honest. This time there was no denying it, no rationalizing it away. She loved him. And he loved her. She knew it, sensed it, exulted in it.

Until, from somewhere in the distance, the discordant sound of several dozen honking horns rudely shattered the moment, and sent the two of them scrambling to one of the small windows to see what was wrong.

"There's no sound," she heard Zachary whisper hoarsely before he turned away from the window and began inspecting Veronica. "There's no damn sound!"

Sharon stayed at the window a moment more, watching the actor's lips moving and hearing nothing but the impatient car horns of her disgruntled patrons. Her mind went totally, frighteningly blank. *No sound, no sound,* she chanted silently. *What do I do if there's no sound? Dammit, George, how could you do this to me!*

Zachary had already removed the covering plate from the sound box beneath the projector head, and was looking inside at the maze of wires and tubes. "What the hell do we do now?" he asked, his voice steely cold. "I don't remember the first thing about the insides of this damned museum piece."

Running over to the cabinet over the worktable, Sharon reached inside and grabbed a handful of pamphlets, scanning them quickly until she came up with the repair manual for the sound head. She paged quickly to the index, then turned to the last page and the list of troubleshooting ideas printed there.

"Zachary," she called loudly over the sound of the horns, "are all the switches on?"

"Of course they are. The thing was working a minute ago. What are you doing? The natives are getting restless out there. Hurry it up before they charge the place."

"I'm reading you the list of possible problems."

"Does it say anything there about the damn thing being too old? Veronica here should be collecting old-age benefits, not showing movies."

"Shut up and listen," Sharon ordered, quickly scanning

the list in front of her. Were the speakers plugged in? What a stupid question! Of course they were plugged in. Who made up these lists, anyway—sadists? "Zachary, is a fuse or breaker blown either on the main circuit breaker or on the projection control panel?"

Zachary ran over to check the circuit breaker while Sharon opened the projector panel and scanned the interior.

"No luck here," Zachary told her before running back to Veronica. "How about the amplifier?"

Sharon checked the amplifier, sighed and picked up the pamphlet once more, while Zachary did the only other thing he could think of—he kicked Veronica right in her solid metal base.

"Ouch!" he yelled, holding his foot. "Dammit, Sharon, find something!"

"Here's a good one, Zachary!" she yelled at last. "Look inside the sound head. Is your exciter lamp burned out?"

There was a long silence, long enough for Sharon to look up from the page she was reading and see that Zachary was staring at her with a strange look in his eyes. She felt suddenly naked, as if he had inspected her from head to toe.

"It is now, Sharon," he said at last, his voice sounding defeated, and then he shut Veronica off, picked up the microphone and made an announcement. "Sorry, folks, but we've had a small mechanical problem. Please bear with us; the film will be starting up again shortly."

Still holding the open booklet in front of her, Sharon watched as Zachary removed a bulb from the sound head and replaced it with another he found underneath the worktable. Once the film was running again, she walked over to him and tentatively placed one hand on his arm.

"I'm sorry, Zachary," she said, feeling the tension in his body. "I guess I panicked. George is always here to help at times like these."

"You know, of course, that there wouldn't be times like these if Wheeler's had decent projectors?" Zachary pointed out. "Are you ready now to come out of the dark ages and admit that I'm right? How do you expect to keep customers coming back if they can't be sure of your service? Tomorrow morning I'm going to take you to one of my theaters. Then maybe you'll understand what I'm talking about. That is,'' he ended, moving past her to stand beside Gloria and watch for his cue to change reels, ''if you think you're up to facing a little reality.''

Sharon stepped back against the wall and watched Zachary work, his quick, efficient movements made even crisper by his obvious anger. She closed her eyes, wondering how everything that had been so lovely just a few minutes before could have turned to ashes so quickly.

Then, closing her eyes against the tears that threatened to fall, she remembered that Burt and Deborah hadn't had a happy ending, either.

Sharon tried her very best to dislike everything she saw late that Sunday morning at one of the St. Clair Theater Corporation's multiplex theaters Zachary took her to in a nearby town, and for a while it worked.

''Imitation butter flavor. It figures!'' she scorned, after taking a bite of the popcorn Zachary offered her as they stood in the huge modern foyer of the shopping mall theater. ''At Wheeler's we use real butter—and lots of it. And look at those prices! You do know that's highway robbery, don't you, Mr. St. Clair?''

''Indoor theaters have captive audiences, Sharon,'' Zachary told her as they walked through the foyer toward the stairs. ''Operators can charge pretty much what they like. Of course, this carpeting could never survive if our menus were as varied as yours. Just popcorn, drinks and candy here, no barbecue.''

As they rounded the corner and began walking down the wide hallway, she saw that there was even a second, smaller snack bar at the other end of the theater. ''Just how big is this place? I've never been here.''

''Nine screens,'' Zachary told her as he took hold of her

elbow and guided her up the carpeted stairway to the second level. "We built this place when the mall went up, about five years ago. Each theater holds between 150 and 600 patrons, although we don't always have every theater open."

"That's a lot of popcorn," Sharon said in a small voice as she allowed herself to be led down a narrow hallway toward a plain tan-colored door.

Opening the door ahead of her, Zachary ushered her through to another hallway, lined with more than one hundred huge plastic bags containing popped popcorn. "No, Shari," he said, waving his arm toward the bags, "*that's* a lot of popcorn. We pop it up here in a special room, then take it downstairs as it's needed. I'd say this supply should last us about three days, two if it's busy."

"That's almost obscene," Sharon said, turning away. She'd give her eyeteeth for a new popcorn machine, but he'd never know that. But then, she thought meanly, he's never had hot coconut oil splash onto his arms as he ladled it out of the top of Wheeler's antique popper.

"Here's the projection complex, Sharon," she heard Zachary say, pride evident in his voice. "I think it's time you saw these platters you seem to think are destroying the industry."

Sharon held back a moment as Zachary used a key to open another door, then slowly walked inside, ready to hate everything she was about to see.

The first thing that struck her was the color—or the absence of color. Everything was tan—the floor, the walls, the ceiling, the projectors, even those strange three-tiered metal platters that looked like oversized pizza pans that had been stacked to look like five-foot-high avant-garde Christmas trees.

Her second reaction was to be amazed at the sheer size of the projection area. It couldn't really be called a room. It was more like a very wide hallway that ran from one end of the theater complex to the other, with projectors and tiers of pizza pans scattered together along the floor at irregular intervals.

"I feel like I'm in a submarine," she said, taking a single step forward and then stepping back again, almost afraid to move in this space-age environment. "And it's so quiet. Almost eerie."

"There are seven projectors running right now," she heard Zachary say as he nodded to the young man who walked by on his way to one of the projectors at the other end of the room. "If we didn't keep the speakers turned down in here the noise would drive the projectionist crazy."

"The projectionist? As in *one* projectionist?" Sharon asked, spreading her arms. "For all this?"

As if her question was all he was waiting for, Zachary immediately launched into a description of the ins and outs of platter houses, explaining how seven reel films were spliced into one huge reel, then laid on a platter that fed directly into the projector.

"The second platter holds the film after it comes through the projector, winding it from the outside in, so there's never a need to rewind. Once the film is done, the projectionist just threads up again and he's ready to roll. With a hit film— like *Star Wars*, for example—the film can even be run along the wall, threading through three projectors or more at once, so that the film can be shown in three theaters at the same time."

That's it? It's that simple? A well trained child could operate these machines, Sharon thought, trying hard not to look impressed. "That's very interesting," she said dully. "I'm surprised you even need a projectionist."

"There's still plenty around here for a trained projectionist to do, Sharon," Zachary answered. "The platters simply eliminate the busywork and free him up for the more important jobs."

"How perfectly wonderful. Can we go now?"

But Zachary was just getting started. To Sharon, he looked like a child showing off his classroom on parents' night. He didn't look at all like a bloodless businessman. Could it be that Zachary actually felt something deeper for the theater business than the bottom line on the annual report?

Sharon watched as he went over to one of the glassed-in windows and looked through it to the screen inside one of the theaters. "Come here, Shari. I want you to see this."

She was beginning to feel petty, beginning to question her earlier doubts about Zachary and his motives. Dragging her feet all the way, Sharon joined him at the window, allowing herself to be only slightly mollified as she felt his arm go around her shoulders, drawing her closer to him. "This movie is almost over. Now watch what happens."

The sweating, muscle-bound warrior on the screen shook his oversize machine gun at the sky, then froze into fierce immobility as the words The End rolled up from the bottom of the screen. Just as the credits disappeared, the houselights began to glow brighter, intermission music began to play, a soft light went on behind the blank screen, and the projector turned itself off. No human hands ever touched a switch.

"Magnificent, isn't it?" Zachary whispered into her ear as they backed away to make room for the projectionist, who butted his cigarette into an ashtray and then joined them beside the projector. "Now all Harry here has to do is thread up again and the entire sequence will reverse itself, lowering the houselights, stopping the music and so on. The previews and any other short films we might be showing are already spliced onto the reel, ready to go. *That*, my dear, is automation; and *that* is why Harry can run so many screens by himself."

Sharon was impressed. She would have had to be a fool not to understand how automation had improved the quality of the theater business. But that didn't mean she had to like it. "Nine theaters, one projectionist. Three, I imagine, since Harry isn't a machine and can't work twenty-four hours a day, seven days a week. Very cost-efficient. In the old days, with two projectionists to a film, it would have taken eighteen men to run nine films. Your so-called progress has put a lot of people out of work, Zachary, people like George, who lived for their jobs. *That's* what automation means to me.''

Zachary grabbed her by the arm and walked her quickly down to one end of the room, away from Harry, who had begun looking at her strangely. "What are you trying to do, Sharon, incite a riot? I didn't invent automation, for crying out loud. We're trying to compete with cable television, videocassette recorders, all sorts of competition movie theaters didn't have years ago when they were the only game in town. We had to give better service, provide state-of-the-art sound systems, offer a larger variety of films or lose our audience.

"Nobody planned to put projectionists out of work. It was just a by-product of the progress we made. You know it, so why don't you take that chip off your shoulder you've been wearing ever since we came in here, and admit it?"

Sharon pursed her lips and stared at the blank wall opposite her, trying hard to ignore the truth that Zachary had pointed out to her, but it was a losing battle and she finally had to acknowledge it. "I guess Veronica and Gloria have outlived their usefulness," she said at last, trying hard to laugh. "Old projectors never die, right, Zachary? Their carbons just start drifting."

Her head jerked up as Zachary grabbed her arm and began pulling her over to the nearest projector. "No!" he fairly shouted in his excitement. "That's why I brought you here— to show you how, with a few simple changes, the old girls can go right on showing movies for the next twenty years. Look, Shari," he said, pointing to the lamp house on the projector, "that's a xenon bulb in there. We can replace the carbons with bulbs like that and, presto, Veronica and Gloria get a new lease on life. Instead of changing carbons every two reels George can change a bulb once a year."

Sharon leaned down to get a look at the bright light through the small, shielded opening. "Really?" she asked, biting her lip. "How do we do that?"

"There's a company in the Midwest that specializes in rebuilding old projectors. I called them Wednesday, and they say it can be done after this season is over." Zachary was speaking quickly now, and Sharon realized that he was nervous, worrying about her reaction to his news.

"And the platters?" She eyed him warily from her bent-over position as she asked the question. With a platter, only one projector would be needed.

"I see no reason to send George or my father into shock, do you? I think Veronica and Gloria are a great team, and I wouldn't want to break them up. Besides, if we don't keep them busy changing reels, George and Dad might start chasing the girls in the snack bar."

She straightened, turning away from the lamp house, and looked up into Zachary's beautiful green eyes. "You're a very nice man, do you know that?" she told him softly, not bothering to hide the love in her own eyes. "You had this whole thing planned, didn't you? I don't know how you stand me. I've been awful, haven't I?"

Zachary pulled her back behind the shutdown projector, out of sight of Harry. "Lady, you've been the toughest sell I've ever had," he said on a sigh as he drew her against his chest.

After lunching at a roadside café, Sharon and Zachary arrived back in Allentown just after three o'clock, then headed for one of the downtown theaters that had just become part of the St. Clair Theater Corporation.

Sharon had asked Zachary to explain the reason behind the visit, but he had been remarkably closemouthed about it. She might have continued to push him for an explanation, but she had all she could do to contain her happiness at their new closeness, and the thought never occurred to her.

Sharon stood admiring the stucco facade of the exterior of the Regency Royale Theater, which she already knew had been built in 1925, while she waited for Zachary to unlock the door. She remembered that the theater area had been executed in the French style, complete with carved imitation-marble columns and gilt opera boxes lining the side walls. The large balcony swept out partway over the floor seats in a graceful swirl, and she could remember the times she had visited the Regency with her grandfather, the two of them paying more attention to the ornate paintings on the vaulted ceiling above their heads than on the movie being projected on the screen.

What she didn't remember, she realized as she walked inside with Zachary, was how absolutely vast the foyer of the theater was, the entire area banded on three sides by carved mahogany double staircases with a view of the separate balcony lobby and massive crystal chandeliers marching along the three-story-high ceiling. To the left of the lobby, with its leaded-glass door padlocked shut, was the old-fashioned soda fountain she and Popsie would visit after the show, to feed her grandfather's sweet tooth on cold fudge sundaes with chocolate ice cream.

Wordlessly, she followed Zachary through the doors into the main theater, and they stood halfway down the center aisle, surrounded by silence. The huge chamber was cloaked in shadows even in the daylight, and when she spoke, it was in a whisper, almost overcome with sadness. "What do you plan to do with it? Please don't tell me you're going to tear all this beauty out and put in red, white and blue plastic arches."

"Actually," Zachary responded, looking very much like Little Jack Horner about to pull out a plum, "I thought I might be able to talk you into helping me with it. I'd like to make it into a three-screen house, but I can't see any way to do it and still keep the character of the place."

Sharon felt an immediate thrill rush through her body, her mind's eye already seeing the foyer as one small intimate theater. As for dividing the main theater into two separate rooms, well, it wouldn't be too difficult, if she could use the balcony someway to—

She quickly applied mental brakes to her enthusiasm. *Here*

we go again, she thought sadly, looking at Zachary, who was smiling at her in a way that made her feel as if all that was needed was a fat, juicy carrot dangling from his hand to make the picture complete.

"You want *me* to help you? Why?" she asked, eyeing him carefully. "Doesn't your corporation have architects—whole departments—to handle things like this? Why would you need me?"

She watched as he shook his head, a strange smile on his face. "You still don't get it, do you, Sharon? I guess I can't blame you, because it took me a while to figure it out myself. I *don't* really need you to help me with the theaters, but I think the theaters need you to watch out for them. You love these old places. So did I, at least until I let business get in the way of my memories, of my real priorities. You've rekindled that love, and I'll always be grateful to you for that. But now, with all that I've learned, I find that there's something still missing in my life. That something, Sharon, is you."

Sharon closed her eyes, hardly daring to believe what she was hearing. "Do—do you mean—"

"I mean, my darling Shari," he said softly, raising her chin with one finger so that she was forced to look directly into his eyes, "that I love you—very, very much. I don't know how it happened, or when it happened, but somewhere between meeting Gertrude and chasing you in and out of bathrooms, I have fallen madly, passionately and *eternally* in love with you."

Sharon swallowed hard on the lump in her throat. "Oh," she said, struggling to marshal her scattered thoughts. "So now you want me to work for you?"

"No, darling," he told her, drawing her gently into the circle of his arms, "now I want you to work *with* me, *beside* me. I want you to keep my eyes open to all of the beauty and the history that mean so much to you." He lowered his head toward hers, his green eyes sparkling in the dim light. "But most of all, I want you to love me, marry me and bear my children—all that hokey stuff they used to make such beautiful movies about. Am I asking too much, Sharon? I know this is all happening very fast, that I'm rushing you, but, please, don't tell me I'm asking too much.''

Sharon couldn't trust her voice, so she let her actions speak for her. Raising one hand to encircle his neck, she drew him down to her, parting her lips for his kiss.

And in the middle of the center aisle of the old Regency Royale Theater, just like in the movies, the hero won the heroine for his own, as the screen slowly faded to black.

The summer sun was just going down when the low-slung sports car pulled through the gates and drove up to stop beside the slightly crooked box office.

''Two please,'' the driver said, holding out a ten dollar bill, knowing there would be change. ''Hold the lollipops, at least for another few months.''

''What?'' Sam said, hanging up the phone after telling the caller that the movie would start in half an hour. ''Hey, Denny, look who's here! It's Shari and Zachary. Shari, does George know you're coming? He's just been saying that it's been a long time between visits.''

''Yes, it has, hasn't it? We haven't been back to Allentown since the reopening of the Regency Royale in March,'' Sharon answered, smoothing the skirt of her cotton sundress over her still-flat stomach, ''but I think he'll forgive us when we let him in on our little secret.''

Denny leaned across Sam to say, ''If you're talking about making Lucien a grandfather, Sharon, George already knows. I didn't know it was supposed to be a secret. You should have seen your father last Saturday night after you called, Zachary. He was handing out free candy bars to every customer who came into the snack bar. I told the wife, but she wasn't surprised. She said she knew you two would do just fine, seeing as how you met at Wheeler's, like we did. Now get going, you guys are holding up the line. We've got Disney tonight.''

Zachary pulled the sports car ahead to the fifth row, then turned into a spot next to a vacant speaker pole. "Come on, 'wife,'" he teased, opening the car door on his side. "You've been driving me crazy asking for popcorn with *real* hot butter, so let's see if we can beat the crowd at the snack bar. Then we can check in with Dad and George in the projection room before the movie starts."

"Don't forget Gloria and Veronica, darling," Sharon reminded him. "George said they look just gorgeous with their new face-lifts." Taking Zachary's hand after he opened the door on the passenger side, Sharon stood up outside the car and looked around the theater grounds.

The bright yellow sun was hanging just above the tree line on the horizon, and a boldly striped hot-air balloon was lazily drifting by over the top of the white movie screen. All around families were settling themselves on blankets or car hoods, munching popcorn and warning their children to be careful to watch for cars as they ran to ride the brand new merry-go-round on the playground.

Zachary slid his arm around Sharon's shoulders as they walked along the gravel pathway toward the snack bar. She pressed her blond head against the side of his chest, snuggling into his familiar embrace as the two of them silently shared the heartwarming feeling of coming home.

For it was springtime, and just one more night in the seemingly endless string of nights at Wheeler's—America's oldest operating drive-in.

Epilogue

Years passed, as they always do. Summers came, and summers went.

George finally retired, which only meant that he no longer drew a paycheck, because he could still be found most nights sitting in the projection booth, telling stories about the good old days.

Lucien St. Clair came to Allentown for three months every summer, indulging himself in his favorite toy, running the projectors, spinning tales with George and sneaking candy bars to all the children. No, he rarely did turn a profit on the drive-in, but that didn't matter. Not to Lucien.

Sharon and Zachary made it a point to visit every summer, and had this year, so Sharon was rather surprised when Zachary insisted on a second visit, this time in November, on their sixth wedding anniversary.

Piling five-year-old Adam and three-year-old Elizabeth into the back seat of a rental car, Zachary drove his family out to Wheeler's at dusk, Sharon still asking him questions as to what was going on, and Zachary still just smiling and saying "You'll see."

Zachary pulled onto the macadam road leading into the theater, stopping at the ticket booth just as Denny stepped out of it, looking both rather spiffy and definitely uncomfortable in his rented tuxedo. "Evening, folks, and welcome to Wheeler's Drive-In. You'll just have time to visit our snack bar before the movie begins. Lollipops for the kiddies?"

"Denny!" Sharon exclaimed, leaning across Zachary to get a better look at him. "What on earth? What are you doing here? The drive-in's closed for the season. And why are you all dressed up like that?"

"Didn't tell her, huh?" Denny asked Zachary. "I knew you could keep it secret. Bet Sam five bucks you could. Got a special spot all set up for you. Sixth row, just to the left of the snack bar. See you later, Shari."

"Zachary St. Clair, *speak* to me," Sharon ordered, turning around in her seat to look at Denny again as they drove away. "What is going on here? Adam? Do *you* know what's going on here?"

The blond-haired boy shook his head. "Daddy promised me anything I wanted in the snack bar if I didn't say," he told her, then grinned. "So I'm not going to say. Right, Daddy?"

As Elizabeth was napping in her car seat, Sharon knew she was out of luck—nobody was going to tell her anything.

"Well," she said, sitting forward once more, her hands crossed over the slight swell of her belly, as she was once again pregnant, "I guess I'll just have to wait, won't I? But I must say that bribing our son isn't playing fair."

Zachary's grin almost got him in *big* trouble. "That a girl, Shari. Nice to see you so graceful in defeat."

Sharon made a face at him, then sat up straight, to look at the parking space in the sixth row. It wasn't difficult to spot, as there were about a dozen helium balloons tied to the speaker post, bobbing in the breeze.

Zachary pulled into the spot, remarking that it certainly was nice not to have the undercarriage of the car scrape on the macadam, the way it had done before his father had redone the entire drive-in. "Come on, Sharon," he said, opening the door. "You take Adam and I'll grab Elizabeth. Dad's waiting for them in the snack bar."

"Dad? Your dad's here? He shouldn't be here."

"Oh really? He does own the place, remember." Zachary held out his arms to Elizabeth, who had awakened once the car had stopped. "Come on, pumpkin. Mommy and Daddy want to be alone."

"Yes, we do," Sharon agreed sweetly, taking Adam's hand and walking toward the snack bar. "That way there won't be any witnesses when I wring your daddy's neck until the truth pops out of his mouth."

Adam laughed. "You wouldn't do that, Mommy. Daddy says this is a happy surprise."

"I *hate* surprises," Sharon gritted out from between clenched teeth as both children spied their grandfather and went running toward him. "And you know that, Zachary."

"You'll like this one," he assured her, waving to his father, then turning Sharon back toward the car. "Come on. The main attraction is about to begin. You know how George always likes to start on time."

"George is here, too? Is the whole world here?"

"No, that's about it," Zachary told her, holding open the door she could slide back into the passenger seat. He went around to the driver's door, got in, and positioned the speaker over the top of the window. "Ready?" he asked, motioning for Sharon to move closer. "Now you know why I insisted on a bench seat. This is *not* going to be a bucket seat night."

There was a knock on the side window, and Zachary rolled it down. "Hi, Denny. Didn't we just see you?"

"Yeah, you did. But I'm ticket taker and waiter tonight, or so Lucien told me. Here," he said, handing in a large box of fragrant popcorn. "Just the way you like it, Shari. Double butter. And drinks," he added, handing Zachary two tall cups of soda. "Okay, that's it. Please don't forget to visit our snack bar at intermission."

When Denny didn't leave, but still stood there, bent over, his smiling face still poking into the car, Zachary hit the button that raised the glass. "Say good-night, Denny."

"Oh, yeah. Good night, Zachary. Sharon. Guess we'll see you later when—

The window closed on Denny's smiling face.

Sharon looked at Zachary for a moment, then smiled. "Hot-buttered popcorn, soda. This is nice. But you forgot to pick up one of the in-car portable heaters your dad is so proud of, darling."

"We won't need one," Zachary told her, drawing her close against his shoulder. "Now, just sit back and relax, and then you can tell me if you like my anniversary present."

"This is my anniversary present? A trip to the drive-in?" Sharon thought about that for a moment, then kissed her husband's cheek, offered him some popcorn. "What's the main attraction?"

"You mean besides you?" he asked, allowing Sharon to hand-feed him. "Oh, that's good. Well, since we probably won't watch much of it anyway, I'll tell you. It's *Spy in the Eye*. Remember that one?"

"It's the movie that was playing here the night we met. The night Mrs. Harrison's Gertrude and all her friends decided to crash the gate. Oh, Zachary, that's so romantic. But why aren't we going to watch it?"

"I could say that we'd be too busy necking, and steaming up the windows, but you're in much too delicate a condition for that."

"True," Sharon said, slipping her hand onto Zachary's chest. "But we could give it the old college try?"

He laughed, shook his head. "Can't. We've got two kids who need to be back in the hotel and in bed by nine, remember?"

"Kids? We have kids?" Sharon teased, her eyes wide as she stared at him. "When did that happen?"

"I can't help you out if you don't remember when, but I sure do hope you remember *how*," Zachary said, then turned up the speaker as the screen in front of them turned bright white. "Here we go, Sharon. We might not stick around for much of *Spy in the Eye,* but I think you'll like this one."

Sharon turned her attention to the large screen as classical music came over the speaker, wondering what would come next, then sighed, laid her head on her husband's shoulder, and said, "Oh, Zachary…"

She watched as a white limousine pulled to a stop outside a large stone church, then smiled as George got out of the rear seat, then turned to help her out of the car.

Six years ago. Her wedding day.

"Oh, Zachary, I don't believe this. Our wedding video? It looks so different up there, on the big screen."

"And you're as beautiful as any movie star," Zachary said. "More beautiful."

Sharon watched a younger version of herself smile at the camera and, while trying to keep her headpiece on straight in the rather stiff breeze, walk up the steps to the church.

"I was definitely thinner," she said, resting a hand on her expanding waistline. "That said, please pass the popcorn. And this is the best present I've ever had. Leave it to you to know that I'd rather have real butter-topped popcorn and a drive-in movie than just about anything else in the world."

"I love you, Sharon St. Clair," Zachary said as she snuggled against his shoulder.

"I know," she told him as he lowered his head toward her. "And I love you. Now let's watch the movie, because I always liked the ones best that have happy endings…."

Author's Note

Shankweiler's Drive-In, located in Orefield, just outside Allentown, Pennsylvania, is America's genuine oldest operating drive-in theater, and Wheeler's Drive-In is modeled after it. Owner Susan Geissinger and her projectionist husband, Paul, were both extremely helpful, lending their knowledge and expertise to the creation of this book. In return for their graciousness, this author would like you to know two things. First, Shankweiler's is today what Wheeler's became after the St. Clairs arrived on the scene, a beautifully kept, smooth-running operation that remains a favorite summertime theater. And secondly, they serve their popcorn with real butter!

* * * * *

MONTANA
Bred

From the bestselling series

MONTANA MAVERICKS

Wed in Whitehorn

Two more tales that capture living and loving
beneath the Big Sky.

JUST PRETENDING by Myrna Mackenzie

FBI Agent David Hannon's plans for a quiet vacation
were overturned by a murder investigation—and by
officer Gretchen Neal!

STORMING WHITEHORN by Christine Scott

Native American Storm Hunter's return to Whitehorn
sent tremors through the town—and shock waves of
desire through Jasmine Kincaid Monroe....

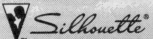

Silhouette®
Where love comes alive™

Every day is

A Mother's Day

in this heartwarming anthology
celebrating motherhood and romance!

Featuring the classic story "Nobody's Child" by Emilie Richards
He had come to a child's rescue, and now Officer Farrell Riley was
suddenly sharing parenthood with beautiful Gemma Hancock.
But would their ready-made family last forever?

Plus two brand-new romances:

"Baby on the Way" by Marie Ferrarella
Single and pregnant, Madeline Reed found the perfect husband in the
handsome cop who helped bring her infant son into the world. But did his
dutiful role in the surprise delivery make J. T. Walker a daddy?

"A Daddy for Her Daughters" by Elizabeth Bevarly
When confronted with spirited Naomi Carmichael and her brood of girls,
bachelor Sloan Sullivan realized he had a lot to learn about women!
Especially if he hoped to win this sexy single mom's heart....

Available this April from Silhouette Books!

Where love comes alive™

INTIMATE MOMENTS™

presents:

Romancing the Crown

*With the help of their powerful allies,
the royal family of Montebello is
determined to find their missing heir.
But the search for the beloved prince
is not without danger—or passion!*

Available in May 2002:
VIRGIN SEDUCTION
by Kathleen Creighton (IM #1148)

Cade Gallagher went to the royal palace of
Tamir for a wedding—and came home with
a bride of his own. The rugged oilman thought he'd married to
gain a business merger, but his innocent bride made him long
to claim his wife in every way....

*This exciting series continues throughout
the year with these fabulous titles:*

January	(IM #1124)	THE MAN WHO WOULD BE KING by Linda Turner
February	(IM #1130)	THE PRINCESS AND THE MERCENARY by Marilyn Pappano
March	(IM #1136)	THE DISENCHANTED DUKE by Marie Ferrarella
April	(IM #1142)	SECRET-AGENT SHEIK by Linda Winstead Jones
May	(IM #1148)	VIRGIN SEDUCTION by Kathleen Creighton
June	(IM #1154)	ROYAL SPY by Valerie Parv
July	(IM #1160)	HER LORD PROTECTOR by Eileen Wilks
August	(IM #1166)	SECRETS OF A PREGNANT PRINCESS by Carla Cassidy
September	(IM #1172)	A ROYAL MURDER by Lyn Stone
October	(IM #1178)	SARAH'S KNIGHT by Mary McBride
November	(IM #1184)	UNDER THE KING'S COMMAND by Ingrid Weaver
December	(IM #1190)	THE PRINCE'S WEDDING by Justine Davis

*Available only from Silhouette Intimate Moments
at your favorite retail outlet.*

Silhouette®
Where love comes alive™

Visit Silhouette at www.eHarlequin.com

SIMRC5

Silhouette Desire

presents

DYNASTIES: THE CONNELLYS

A brand-new miniseries about the Connellys of Chicago,
a wealthy, powerful American family tied by blood to the
royal family of the island kingdom of Altaria.
They're wealthy, powerful and rocked by
scandal, betrayal...and passion!

Look for a whole year of glamorous and
utterly romantic tales in 2002:

January: TALL, DARK & ROYAL by Leanne Banks

February: MATERNALLY YOURS by Kathie DeNosky

March: THE SHEIKH TAKES A BRIDE by Caroline Cross

April: THE SEAL'S SURRENDER by Maureen Child

May: PLAIN JANE & DOCTOR DAD by Kate Little

June: AND THE WINNER GETS...MARRIED! by Metsy Hingle

July: THE ROYAL & THE RUNAWAY BRIDE by Kathryn Jensen

August: HIS E-MAIL ORDER WIFE by Kristi Gold

September: THE SECRET BABY BOND by Cindy Gerard

October: CINDERELLA'S CONVENIENT HUSBAND
by Katherine Garbera

November: EXPECTING...AND IN DANGER by Eileen Wilks

December: CHEROKEE MARRIAGE DARE
by Sheri WhiteFeather

Silhouette®

Where love comes alive™